Praise for the Fabulous Novels of Judith Michael . . .

A RULING PASSION

"A novel of love, lust, passion, greed. . . . *A RULING PASSION* has something for everyone . . . a delight."

—*United Press International*

"Judith Michael scores again . . . a suspenseful, passionate story that takes you behind the scenes into a world of wealth and power. . . ."

—*Tulsa World*

"When Judith Michael writes, readers read. . . . Their blending of plot and characters is ingenius and readers line up for a chance to experience every nuance of their juicy plots. . . ."

—*Ocala Star Banner*

"A WINNER EVERY TIME . . . A BOOK BY JUDITH MICHAEL IS HARD TO PUT DOWN."

—[illegible]*o Sun-Times*

A LIT[illegible]CTION
A DOUBLEDAY BOOK CLUB MAIN SELECTION

INHERITANCE

"THE WRITING IS IMPECCABLE . . . FOR THE PERFECT RAINY-DAY READ, LOOK NO FURTHER."

—*The New York Times Book Review*

"Put aside reality and indulge . . . the writing is professional and seductive . . . *INHERITANCE* is a tale of redemption, class envy, and, in the best American tradition, upward social mobility and eventual financial success."

—*Chicago Tribune*

"Full of fascinating characters and plot twists. . . . The characters are so rich and the story so compelling . . . you will be ensured hours of reading pleasure."

—*Inland Empire* magazine

"Fascinating. . . . *INHERITANCE* is sure to please."

—*South Bend Tribune*

PRIVATE AFFAIRS

"A GRIPPING NOVEL. . . . I liked it enough to read it well into the wee hours . . . entertaining and easy to read."

—Providence *Sunday Journal*

"A story of romance and ambition. . . . *PRIVATE AFFAIRS* offers large doses of entertainment."

—*Chattanooga Times*

"*PRIVATE AFFAIRS* is charmed lives, repressed passion, and fantasies come true. . . ."

—*ALA Booklist*

"Judith Michael has struck again . . . a ride through the fast lane, where greed is the passion that rules all else. . . . *PRIVATE AFFAIRS* has plenty to please the fans."

—*Richmond Times-Dispatch*

Books are available at special discounts for bulk purchases for sales promotions, premiums, fund-raising or educational use. Special books, or book excerpts, can also be created to fit specific needs.

For details write the office of the Vice President of Special Markets, Pocket Books, 1230 Avenue of the Americas, New York, New York 10020.

Books by Judith Michael

Deceptions
Possessions
Private Affairs
Inheritance
A Ruling Passion
Sleeping Beauty
Pot of Gold
A Tangled Web

Published by POCKET BOOKS

For orders other than by individual consumers, Pocket Books grants a discount on the purchase of **10 or more** copies of single titles for special markets or premium use. For further details, please write to the Vice President of Special Markets, Pocket Books, 1230 Avenue of the Americas, 9th Floor, New York, NY 10020-1586.

For information on how individual consumers can place orders, please write to Mail Order Department, Simon & Schuster Inc., 200 Old Tappan Road, Old Tappan, NJ 07675.

JUDITH MICHAEL

SLEEPING BEAUTY

POCKET BOOKS

New York   London   Toronto   Sydney   Tokyo   Singapore

This book is a work of fiction. Names, characters, places and incidents are products of the author's imagination or are used fictitiously. Any resemblance to actual events or locales or persons, living or dead, is entirely coincidental.

POCKET BOOKS, a division of Simon & Schuster Inc.
1230 Avenue of the Americas, New York, NY 10020

Copyright © 1990 by JM Productions Ltd.

ISBN: 0-671-89959-7

First Pocket Books printing July 1992

10 9 8 7 6

POCKET and colophon are registered trademarks of Simon & Schuster Inc.

Cover art by Brian Bailey

Printed in the U.S.A.

For Ronald Barnard
in friendship and love

chapter 1

Anne stepped from the limousine and stood beside it, gazing at the massive, carved doors of the chapel, willing herself to go inside. The driver drummed his fingers on the steering wheel, and she knew he was wondering what she was waiting for after an hour of sitting impatiently in the backseat while he fought the expressway traffic to get from the airport to Lake Forest by ten o'clock. She was late, but still she stood there, staring at the cold, Gothic stones of the chapel, grayer and colder beneath dark clouds that hung over the town. Chauffeurs in other limousines parked along the length of the block looked up from their newspapers to watch her. All right, I'm going, she snapped at them silently, and walked to the front steps. They seemed to stretch ahead of her, rising to the heavy double doors with large brass rings for handles. I have to do this, she thought; I want to do this. For Ethan.

She pulled on one of the brass rings and the door opened noiselessly. She walked into the anteroom and an usher opened an inner door and stood aside for her. The chapel was full; all the seats were taken and people stood along the side aisles and at the back. A large man with a briefcase made room for Anne and she slipped in beside him. Someone was speaking, but she barely heard him. She stood still and looked at the backs of the Chathams, all the generations of Chathams, rows and rows of Chathams and

1

their friends and business associates and even a few of their enemies, and beyond all of them, at the front of the chapel, the coffin of Ethan Chatham, dead at the age of ninety-one.

The room rustled and swayed like a wheat field under a prairie wind as people bent left and right to whisper to their neighbors and listen to speakers reminisce about Ethan. They all knew each other; many of them had grown up together, and gone to private schools together, and now they were bankers, executives of multinational companies, owners of industries, commodities brokers, and presidents of insurance companies. They were the warp and woof of Chicago society, and Ethan Chatham had been one of them, and they had tolerated his eccentricities, even his running off to the mountains of Colorado, because, after all, he had made so very much money.

Quietly, Anne moved to the side aisle and made her way unobtrusively toward the front, to look at all the faces. Most of them were strange to her. But in the two front rows was the Chatham family, and as she looked at each profile, each one was so familiar she named them all in an instant. It was astonishing to her. But why would they change? she thought. I was the one who ran away. They stayed where they were; comfortable, smug, the same. For so many years.

"He was a great builder," said Harrison Ervin, president of Chicago's largest bank, "a creator of houses—of whole towns, in fact—that won him awards and brought prestige to all of us. And then he went west, as restless men always have done in America's history, and discovered Tamarack, in the mountains of Colorado, and made it a world-famous resort. He was a man who knew what he wanted and knew how to achieve it. That was his greatness."

Charles Chatham stopped listening. It wasn't greatness, he thought, for his father to turn his back on his family and spend the last twenty-some years of his life concentrating on a private paradise he'd built from the ruins of a little mountain ghost town. Turned his back on Chatham Development, too, the company he'd built; behaved as if it could rot in hell, and Charles—trying to run the company, trying

2

to run the family—could rot, too, for all his father gave a damn. That wasn't greatness; that was obsession.

"I visited him in Tamarack," Ervin went on. "He was building there, too, always building, molding the town into the shape of his dream. Sometimes he was impatient with how slowly things went, or frustrated because he knew he wouldn't live to finish it. But he never got discouraged or angry; he wasn't the type to let anger corrode his energy."

Marian Jax shifted in her seat. Ethan had been angry at her when she insisted on marrying Fred. More than angry; her gentle father had been furious. Because he wasn't at all gentle when he thought his children were being stupid; he roared at truly volcanic levels. He'd roared at Marian for not listening to him, for going ahead with her wedding to Fred Jax, who, he kept telling her, was sly and conniving and far more interested in Marian's money than in Marian. She folded her hands neatly in her lap with a brief glance at Fred, sitting smooth-faced beside her. And of course her father had been absolutely right.

"He was a good friend," said Ervin. "He'll be missed for so many things. His wisdom, his—"

I miss him already, thought Nina Chatham Grant. I needed him, probably more than most daughters need their fathers. He listened to me and never scolded when I got another divorce. He believed in love and faithfulness—he never remarried after Mother died; I don't think he even went out with anyone—but he was always sweet to me; he knew I wanted to be good, he knew I kept trying to be good. She shook her head sadly. I'm almost fifty-nine years old, and there's still so much I don't know about life. She looked sideways at her brother William, who met her eyes and put a comforting hand on her arm. Nina smiled at him through her tears. He wasn't as good as her father, but he was better than nothing. Everybody needs a family, she thought, just to listen and to be kind.

"—and most of all," Ervin said, "his affection for friends and family alike—"

Charles' granddaughter Robin, eight years old, saw

Charles' face tighten even more. "Don't be sad, Grandpa," she whispered. "It'll be all right." She scanned the crowd, looking for something with which to distract him. "Who's that pretty lady?" she asked suddenly. "Is she a relative?"

Charles followed her gaze, turning his head to look at the mourners standing along the side wall. He knew none of them, and he wondered again at all these strangers: how little he had known of his father's life.

"Isn't she beautiful?" Robin whispered. "She looks nice, too."

His gaze flickered over them again, and then he saw Anne, partly hidden behind someone else. He frowned, briefly puzzled. He peered at her, and then, suddenly, he was halfway out of his seat, poised as if to lunge toward the side of the chapel. He heard a rustling in the crowd behind him; from the corner of his eye he saw Harrison Ervin pause in his eulogy and look at him in surprise.

Confusion spread across Charles' face. He hesitated, knees bent, and then, slowly, sat down, staring straight ahead.

"So what is she?" Robin whispered impatiently. "A relative?"

Charles closed his eyes briefly, as if in pain. "Yes," he said.

"And he was a teacher," Ervin went on. "He taught us new ways of thinking about building; he shared with us his visions for our city; he taught us about ways to live."

He didn't teach me anything, Walter Holland thought. Only that it's a stupid, half-assed thing to marry into a family and a company at the same time. Shifting, he knocked against Rose's arm. The seats were too close in here; why did everybody have to be crammed against everybody else? It was like marrying into the Chathams: always hemmed in, pressured, squeezed, stomped on. Asking Rose to marry him had been like asking a whale to swallow him up. Like asking to disappear.

Rose Holland moved her arm from her husband's touch. There were too many Chathams here; she'd known it would annoy him. But what could she do? This was a funeral, not a cocktail party with a few handpicked guests. Walter knew that; he ought to behave himself. But he'd never managed to control his temper when he felt they were surrounding him as if he were the last survivor facing an army of occupation. It must be awful for him to go to work each day, she thought.

Down the row of seats she saw Uncle Charles shift restlessly, crossing and recrossing his legs, and she wondered if he was feeling sick or just had to go to the bathroom. He wasn't too uncomfortable to be interested in someone, she saw; he kept turning his head to look at the side aisle. She tried to follow his gaze, but she saw no one she recognized. A group of men casually dressed, probably from Tamarack, a few corporate types, a few women who looked like secretaries, a strikingly beautiful woman in a severe dark suit, standing partly behind one of the men. No one she knew. Rose shrugged and faced the front again, putting a cautionary hand on Gretchen, who was beginning to squirm. And why wouldn't she squirm? Funerals were no place for a three-year-old. But Charles had insisted they all come. As if to convince himself they were one big happy family.

Gail Calder, sitting on the other side of her daughter, Robin, saw her father and her cousin Rose turn to look up the side aisle. She looked, too. She studied the people standing along the wall; they stood two and three deep, and she tried to make out the faces in the dim light. She stared for a long moment. And then she whispered, "Anne?"

"I don't mean to sound too solemn about Ethan," said Ervin, gathering up his notes. "We had some rousing times together. But what I'll miss most is his affection, the way he cared about people—"

Others saw the family looking to the side aisle, and the swaying and rustling grew, with a rising hiss of whispers.

"Who're they looking at?"

"Got me."

"Who's that?"

"—and gave them his attention and his energy . . ." Ervin looked toward the side of the chapel, then, seeing nothing untoward, he looked sternly at his audience and raised his voice. "And his help. He was always my friend. To many of us, he was the best friend we ever had. He leaves an emptiness in our lives that no one can fill. That's what we're here to acknowledge as we say, for the last time, farewell."

There was a brief silence. Ervin picked up his notes and returned to his seat. The minister came to the podium to close the service. And the whispers grew louder.

"I don't know who she is. She look familiar to you?"

"You know, she does. Something about her . . . I've seen her; I'd bet on it."

"She looks a little like Gail. Wouldn't you say? But . . . sleeker. You know, like somebody took Gail and polished her up."

"Um, could be. She looks a lot harder, though."

"Right, but I bet she's a Chatham. Some branch of the family, anyway."

"Leo," said Gail to her husband, her hand clutching his arm. "I think Anne is here."

"Where?" Leo asked, turning. "Would she show up, do you think, after all these years?"

Neighbors from Lake Forest craned to look. "I'll be damned. You know who that could be? The older sister . . . what was her name? Anne."

"Whose older sister?"

"Gail's. But I don't know, she doesn't really *look* like Gail; there's just something . . . ."

"What happened to her?"

"She ran off, oh, fifteen, twenty years ago. Maybe more."

"Ran off?"

"Well, they said she went to boarding school, but she never came back, so . . . Anyway, that's what people were saying. She ran off."

"So she'd be Charles' daughter. Ethan's granddaughter."

"If it's really her."

"Why would she run off?"

"Who knows? You know what kids were like in the sixties . . . sex, drugs, bombs, revolution. Whatever."

"Friends," said the minister, "the family has asked me to

make a few announcements. Interment will be at Memorial Park Cemetery. The family will be at home . . ."

At the end of the front row, Dora Chatham put her hand on her father's arm. "Everybody's looking at that woman."

Vince, who had been reading, looked up. "What woman?"

Dora inclined her head and Vince turned. His eyes met Anne's. "For Christ's sake," he said softly. Anne was the one who looked away.

Gail stood and moved past Leo and their son, Ned, to the side aisle. She walked up it, her stride getting longer and more determined with each step. By the time she reached Anne, her hands were outstretched. "You are Anne, aren't you? I *feel* that you're Anne. Wouldn't a sister know—?"

Their hands met, and held. "Hello, Gail," Anne said softly.

Senator Vince Chatham watched them embrace. After a moment, he hung an arm over the back of his seat and beckoned to his nephew Keith Jax, seated just behind him. "That woman," he said when Keith leaned forward.

"The one everybody's looking at? You know her?"

"Get rid of her," Vince said. "Find out what she wants, give it to her if it isn't a problem, and then get rid of her. And see that she doesn't come back."

Chapter 2

Anne was thirteen when Vince began coming to her bedroom and opening the door without knocking. He was thirty, the handsomest man she knew, bright with charm, successful in business, her father's favorite brother. Her father's favorite.

She had always been in awe of him because of the way her father treated him: as if he were some kind of prince; as if he were the center of the family. She knew he wasn't; her grandfather Ethan ran the family and made all the rules, and Vince had to obey them just like everybody else. But still, when her father and Vince were together, her father seemed to shrink, and Vince, even though he was eleven years younger, and shorter than her father, seemed to grow taller and more handsome. Next to her father, who was always quiet, Vince was full of excitement with his travels and his business deals, and it was hard to remember that he was just one of the Chathams who lived in Lake Forest, north of Chicago, and worked in the family company, and besides, was the youngest of Ethan's five children.

They all lived within a few miles of each other, and whenever they were in town and didn't have an important engagement, they had to meet at Ethan's house for dinner, every Sunday and on birthdays and holidays. It was Ethan's rule, and everyone, even Vince, who hated rules, obeyed it. They would sit around the long table in the beautiful room Anne's mother had redecorated for Ethan shortly before she died, and one by one, they would tell about their week. Ethan always spoke first, and Anne loved listening to him as he reported with grave courtesy about Chatham Development Corporation—new houses, new shops, entire towns rising from the cornfields surrounding Chicago—and how that day they had planned the school site or laid out the shopping center or named the streets. Every Chatham town had streets named Vince, Charles, Anne, Marian, William, Gail, and on through the whole family. Ethan was too modest to name streets for himself, but his son Charles always did it for him, and then all the Chathams were there, enshrined on metal signs that swayed in the Midwest winds and pointed the way to the houses the Chathams had built.

When Ethan finished speaking, Charles spoke, and then Vince. Anne's attention would begin to waver because she thought business was dull. She preferred watching the faces around the table, imagining what they were thinking behind their smiles and chuckles and little frowns. They all seemed to be happy that they were eating together, but Anne knew you could never be sure; you had to dig a lot deeper than a smile or a frown to know what people were really like.

All the men worked together—Charles and Vince were vice presidents, William was finance director, and Marian's husband, Fred Jax, was sales manager—but each week they had different stories to tell, and Anne always wondered if they divided up the interesting news when they got together for drinks before dinner, so everyone would be impressed with how much they did each week. The women did the same: they had their own stories to tell. Vince's wife, Rita, told them what new words Dora, who was three, had said that week, and which swimming and calisthenics classes they had gone to. Nina talked about whatever small company she was investing in, and sometimes about getting married, or divorced. It seemed to Anne that Nina got confused about beginnings and endings; she always hoped for something good, or something better, whether she was starting a marriage or saying good-bye to one. Anne's sister, Gail, who was seven, talked about school or summer camp. Rose and Keith, who were two, just ate and made a mess with their food. Anne would have been silent if she could, but she was thirteen and had no excuse. She talked about her friends.

"Amy and I played word games by the pond."

"Amy?" asked Ethan. "Is that a new friend?"

"Sort of. She lives a couple of blocks from here."

"What's her last name?" Marian asked. "Do we know her family?"

"I think we should let Anne keep her friends to herself," Ethan said as Anne flushed. "Is that all?" he asked her. "You don't have anything else to tell us about your week?"

She shook her head, loving her grandfather but angry at him at the same time because he never spent as much time with her as she wanted. She loved him so much she wanted him all the time; he was the gentlest of all of them, and he seemed interested in her, and Anne hated it that so many people came between them. Of course he had his very important business and his very important friends; he had his own life. He was far too busy to spend time with Anne—and anyway, he probably wasn't that interested. Why would a sixty-five-year-old man want to hang around with a thirteen-year-old girl, even if she was his granddaughter?

It sounded sensible when she thought about it that way, but still, it made her angry. She seemed to be angry most of the time, at a lot of people. She didn't want to be; she just was. She hated people and she hated a lot of things that happened around her. She'd felt that way ever since her mother died. That was when she was seven, and Marian had come one night to take her and Gail to Ethan's house, where she was living. And then a little later she married Fred Jax and took Anne and Gail to a different house, and almost right away had Keith and then Rose. Starting with the time Marian took her from her own house, Anne never felt she belonged anywhere.

And that was when she started hating. It was something she couldn't stop, even though it made her feel different from everybody else, and always alone. It wasn't that her family didn't pay attention to her; they did. But it seemed to her it was mostly to criticize, and mostly about dirt: she didn't wash her hair or comb it, she didn't wash her face, she didn't clean under her nails, she tracked dirt into the house. All over the world people were starving or thrown in jail for talking about freedom, or sleeping in the streets because they didn't have a house, but *her* family worried about *dirt*. They criticized her for disappearing for hours into the woods near their house, too, but Anne knew they really didn't care what she did. They just wanted her to be quiet and nice and clean, and make them feel good about doing such a great job of bringing her up. Somehow Gail could do that, but Anne was too angry; she just couldn't do anything right.

"Could I be excused?" she asked.

"Not before dessert," her father said automatically.

"I don't want any."

"You're not going into the forest at night," said Aunt Marian.

"It's *sunshine,*" Anne said loudly. She stood beside her chair, rocking from one foot to the other, her body straining to dash off. They were all looking at her. "It's summer and it's only eight o'clock and the *sun* is *shining* and smart people go outside when it's warm and sunny, they don't sit around the dinner table getting soggy and fat from all that food just lying in their stomachs! That's like dying! Your life is just oozing away, puddling under the table in a pool of slime!"

"Oh, Anne, what kind of talk is that for the dinner table," Nina said reproachfully.

Ethan chuckled. "That's the picture I'll think of every time I sit over my coffee."

"Or you dry up," Anne went on, emboldened. "You sit around with lights on instead of being in the sunshine and smelling the flowers and the lake and you dehydrate and your skin peels off and floats away and after a while you're all skeletons, sitting around clicking your bones—"

"That is quite enough," Marian said firmly. "It's very clever, dear, but it's not appropriate and you know it. All we're doing is finishing dinner in a leisurely and civilized

11

manner, instead of gulping our food and then dashing off in all directions. We won't stop you if you insist on leaving the table, but you're not going to the forest. I've told you I don't want you there. It is not a wholesome place. You're not to go there at all. Ever."

"I'll be back," Anne said, and ran from the room.

She could feel them watching her through the tall French windows as she ran across the broad lawn, her figure silhouetted against the deep-blue expanse of Lake Michigan until she disappeared into the pine forest that covered the rest of Ethan's property. She kept running until she came to a clearing with a small pond bordered with grasses and daisies and wild hyssop that made the air smell of mint. Birds called to each other, but otherwise the silence was complete. Anne sat down, crossing her long, thin legs beneath the sundress she had worn for dinner. "Hi, Amy," she said. "Sorry I'm late. There was this big blowup at the table. I think Aunt Marian's going through menopause or something. You think thirty-three is too young? Maybe with her it doesn't matter; maybe she's just *innately* old."

She pulled a notebook and pencil from her pocket and began to write. "I'm making notes about the family; did I tell you? Someday I'm going to write a book about them. Of course nobody will believe it. I'm glad you're here, Amy; it makes everything better to have somebody to talk to."

She lay on her back, wriggling into the earth like a puppy making a nest in the pine needles. She chewed on a fingernail and gazed upward. The treetops swayed above her in the evening breeze, their narrow trunks tapering to small points far above; Anne had to squint to see them against the brightness of the sky. "Listen to that, Amy. The trees are creaking. Like in a horror movie. Doesn't it sound like a horror movie? Close your eyes and you can believe something really awful is about to happen."

She shivered and sat up. "Probably the spirit of Aunt Marian, slithering through the forest. Creeping respectability. We have to be on our guard, Amy." She wrote again in her notebook. "Creeping respectability. Only, with Aunt Marian, it gallops."

A little distance away, standing among the trees, Vince Chatham chuckled. "Marian in a nutshell," he said.

Anne sprang to her feet. The notebook fell in the dirt. "Uncle Vince?" she said uncertainly.

He walked forward. "I was walking and I heard your voice." He looked around. "Your friend must have made a quick getaway."

"What are you doing here?" she asked furiously. "You weren't out walking. You never take walks. You followed me."

He bent down to pick up her notebook. "Why won't anybody believe what you write about us?"

She flushed. "I wasn't talking to you."

"But you were talking *about* me; I'm part of your family." He walked to a grassy area near the edge of the clearing and sat on a fallen log that had been worn down to a natural seat. "I brought dessert for both of us. I'd be pleased if you'd join me."

Anne stood still. "Where is it?"

Vince reached behind him and brought a white box to his lap. "Chocolate éclairs. There is nothing in the world as good as chocolate éclairs. They're a perfect blend of pastry, custard, and icing, they slide down the throat with ease no matter how full you are, they're small enough to pack by the dozen for a picnic in the forest, and they're wonderfully messy to eat. Definitely my favorite."

"If you brought dessert, you weren't just out for a walk. You were following me."

Vince paused in opening the box. He smiled broadly. "People don't give you credit, Anne; you're the smartest of all of us. You're a remarkable young woman."

Liar, Anne thought. She knew she wasn't yet a woman; no one knew it more keenly than she, who so wanted to be grown-up. "You changed your shoes, too. You knew you'd be walking in the forest."

Still smiling, he said, "We'll have to watch our step around you, won't we?"

"Why did you follow me?"

He sighed. "To bring you dessert." He held out an éclair.

"We have a whole box of these." He glanced around the clearing. "It's a nice place for a picnic; as good as a private room. I like your choice."

Anne looked at him, at his brown eyes as bright as marbles, his golden hair waving back from his forehead, the thin lips that could break into such a wide smile, the cleft in his chin that seemed to divide his face, making it somehow more mysterious. He was so handsome and sophisticated—a thirty-year-old world traveler and businessman, a husband, a father—and she had always been in awe of him, but still, she had never liked him. He was so smooth and sure of himself she always felt even more grubby when he was around, and younger, almost a baby, and oddly, because after all he was her uncle, she was afraid of him. She thought that maybe no matter how deep she dug behind Vince's smiles and frowns, she still wouldn't know how he felt about things, and that seemed unnatural and ominous to her.

"I'm relying on you," Vince said solemnly, "to keep me from surrendering to greed and gluttony and having the entire contents of this box come to a masticated end in my stomach like a pool of slime."

An uncomfortable giggle broke from Anne. "You want me to eat them as a favor to you." She hesitated, reluctant to join him, as if that would make his invasion of her private place seem all right. But she had left the dinner table still hungry, and éclairs were her favorite dessert. "I guess I can do that," she said, her voice low, almost sullen. She sat cross-legged beside the log where he sat, and took the éclair he was holding out.

"What do you think?" he asked in a few minutes. He was taking two more from the box.

She nodded, her mouth full. She wasn't as angry as she had been, but she was still uncomfortable. This was her special, private place; it always had been. She hadn't known anyone else knew just where she went when she left the house. But now Vince was here and he'd somehow made the whole place feel different. It wasn't just hers anymore; it was theirs, and that bothered her.

The sun was low in the sky and the clearing was like a

shadowed cup that still held the warm fragrance of the summer day. Anne sat stiffly a few feet from Vince, staring at the dense bushes surrounding them that darkened in the deepening blue light of evening.

"Do you come here every day?" Vince asked. The éclairs were gone and he began to pick up pebbles and skip them across the pond. Anne watched the small round stones as they struck the surface and jumped two or three or four times, sending ripples to the shore. They were so buoyant, she thought; so light and free. Like Vince. She wished she were like that, instead of heavy and clumsy, the way she felt most of the time. But then, as she listened to the rhythmic *plunk, plunk* of the stones hitting the water, the sound seemed to swell until it was like a cannon, filling the clearing, filling the inside of her head until she thought she would explode.

"Stop it!" she cried.

He looked at her in surprise. "Stop what?"

"That damned noise! It's supposed to be quiet here! Stop throwing rocks in the water!"

He looked at the small pebble in his hand. A small smile touched his lips. "I'm sorry," he said softly. "I didn't know it would upset you." Dropping the pebble, he picked up a twig and drew diagrams in the dust at his feet. "Do you come here every day?" he asked again.

Anne nodded.

"To write your book about us?"

She shrugged.

"Now what does that mean?" he mused. "That the book isn't important? Or that you don't want to talk about it?"

"I don't want to talk about it."

"Do you want to talk about Amy?"

"She's none of your business!"

"But I'd like to know why you make up friends. Don't you have friends at school?"

She shrugged.

"What does *that* mean? That you don't want friends? Or you have friends but not enough of them? Or you don't want to talk about it."

"I don't want to—"

"Okay. What do you want to talk about?"

"Why you followed me."

He shook his head. "So stubborn, my little Anne. I liked the way you stood there, full of fire, and told them all to go to hell."

"I didn't! I wouldn't say anything like—"

"That was the message. I got it and so did they."

Anne stared at the ground. Her family would hate her if they thought that's what she meant. It wasn't ladylike and gentle; it wasn't what Marian wanted. But she couldn't stop herself; whenever she felt lonely or frightened or just generally miserable with nobody to talk to, the words burst out before she could stop them. And everybody would hate her; she knew it. She began to chew on her fingernail.

Vince watched her. Thirteen years old, already astonishingly beautiful, and totally ignorant of it. Or uninterested. Maybe she didn't like herself enough even to look in a mirror. He had never paid attention to her before: she was too young, too insignificant, too crude. His brother's daughter, being raised by his sister Marian after her mother died; a child who fit in nowhere. Even Charles seemed uncomfortable with her; he never acted like a doting father. But that evening, at dinner, Vince had seen Anne dominate the room, even if only for a moment, and he had been intrigued. He and Rita were fighting all the time these days; he was feeling bored and hemmed in by marriage, and here was Anne, a lovely distraction.

He leaned forward to see her profile. Her mouth was wide, the lower lip a little heavy, and when she was sullen, it dragged down her thin face. But in that brief moment when she had giggled, her features had been transformed, and even Vince, not often impressed by women, had drawn in his breath at the sudden illumination of her beauty. Her nose was small, slightly turned up at the tip, and she had high cheekbones that were a little too angular. Her eyes, hidden now beneath heavy lids, were a deep blue, flashing almost black when she was angry. She needed a scrub brush on her face and hands, and a comb through her tangled mass of black curls, and someone should have burned her shapeless sundress long ago and replaced it with cool linen or flared silk. Her elbows were sharp bones; Vince imagined long legs and hard knees beneath the limp folds of her dress. The image excited him. Sharp bones and soft skin, fiery eyes and a childish mouth, gangly limbs that no one had taught to move and cling and clasp . . .

"But it might not have been me at all," Anne said abruptly. She looked at him angrily. "If you got the message that I was telling them to go to hell, maybe it's because that was what you expected to hear. Or, maybe, the one you wanted to give them yourself."

There was a brief silence. Vince smiled. "Someday, little one, you're going to be a formidable opponent."

Anne looked at him gravely. "You think that's a compliment."

"Yes, and so do you. You like a fight: I saw you all primed for one tonight."

She shook her head. "I don't. I hate fights."

"You'll learn," he said. "Shall I teach you?"

"To like fights?"

"To win them. I'm said to be good at that."

"Who says so?"

"People who've watched me. People who've lost to me."

"I don't want to. I guess I'll learn other things."

"What would you like to learn?"

She shrugged. "It doesn't matter."

"Goddam it!" he snapped. Anne shrank from him. "I'm sorry," he said, lowering his voice, masking his annoyance. He expected women to answer him when he took the trouble to ask them about themselves. He leaned forward. "Of course it matters, Anne. I want to know you."

She sat back on her heels, farther away from him. "Why?"

An animal scurried through the brush somewhere behind Vince, startling him. His annoyance grew. He hated the unexpected. "I told you: I liked the way you were tonight, the fire in you. When I see something unusual, I want to know more about it."

"You never wanted to know anything about me before."

"But now I do. Anne, this is ridiculous. Why shouldn't we be friends?"

"You're my uncle," she said.

His eyebrows rose. "What does that have to do with our being friends?"

"I don't know," she said confusedly. "It's just . . . I don't know."

He smiled. "There's nothing to worry about, Anne; I promise you. But if there is—if I've missed something here—why don't you let me do the worrying? You don't have to; I'm sure I can handle it."

She jumped up and stood beside the pond, staring at its dark surface. "We're relatives," she said.

Vince nodded. "And relatives ought to be even closer than friends. Or don't you think so?"

Darting insects made little flecks and ripples on the surface of the pond. Anne concentrated on them. "I guess so."

"Well, I know so." Vince's voice was warm. "They should try to make each other happy. Aren't you happy to have me here? Isn't it better with someone real to talk to instead of an imaginary friend? Come on, Anne, isn't it better this way?"

Slowly, she nodded. It was better. It was nice having two voices in the clearing instead of just her own, talking to herself. Even a private, special place got lonely after a while. She didn't know why she felt so confused. She knew there was something wrong with this conversation, but somehow Vince made her feel that if she was uncomfortable, it was her fault; that she was being silly and saying the wrong things and messing up a nice time.

She glanced at him. He was smiling. He looked so handsome and so honest that Anne felt like crying, because she didn't understand anything. He stretched out his legs, crossing his ankles. "You said you'd like to learn other things. What things?"

Anne chewed on her fingernail. He really did care about her; he was interested in her. What was there to worry about? It wasn't that she was really worried, she told herself; it was just that she couldn't seem to figure out exactly what was happening, and that made her feel at a disadvantage. Standing on one foot and then the other, she said slowly, "I want to learn things that are hard and complicated and take lots of work."

He was surprised. "Why?"

"Because then I wouldn't have time to think about anything else." She looked past Vince to the forest. "It wouldn't matter where I live or how I feel or whether I have friends or not; I wouldn't care because I'd be too busy. And when I learned everything and got to be somebody, people would congratulate me and tell me how wonderful I am, and then I wouldn't be mad at them anymore."

"Mad at them," Vince echoed. "Why are you mad at people?"

She shrugged.

"Anne," Vince said softly. "Tell me. Tell me why you aren't happy."

"I am happy," Anne said defiantly.

"No, you're not. Tell me about it. We're friends, Anne; tell me."

She shrugged and started biting another fingernail. "I just don't like a lot of people, so I get mad at them. I don't want to be part of their silly groups; they scream and giggle and tell jokes about boys . . . it's all so dumb. Who wants to be part of all that?"

"And you think all that will be different when you learn hard, complicated things?"

"Sure it will. Because then I'll be important, and I'll find other important people and we'll all be friends because . . . because I'll be good to be with."

Vince rose and walked to her. He ran a finger lightly along her cheek. "You're already important, little Anne, and very good to be with. You're the best person to be with that I know."

The sun touched the horizon and slipped below it. The air was still warm, but the deep shadows made it seem cooler. Anne shivered.

Vince moved closer and took her face between his hands. "Sweet little Anne. People should love you." Anne stared at him. "And I will," he said, and moved still closer to kiss her. His mouth covered hers and his tongue thrust inside, pushing Anne's tongue back into her throat. It was terrifying, but Anne did not move or cry out; suddenly she was afraid of making him angry. He really cared about her. He loved her. He loved her enough to ask how she felt about things, and to listen when she answered. He loved her enough to kiss her. He said she was important. He said she was sweet.

She wished he wouldn't kiss her; she really just wanted to be held, the way she remembered her mother holding her, and her father, too, before her mother died. She shuddered and Vince put his arms around her, pulling her against him. It was as if he had read her mind. He held her so tightly it hurt, but she didn't care. She liked it when he held her. She liked hearing his warm, deep voice say she was good. She wanted him to say it again, but he wouldn't if he thought she was stupid and a baby, and she was sure that's what he would think if she flinched from his tongue deep in her mouth. She had to be careful or he'd leave and never pay attention to her again, and she'd come to the clearing and be all alone and know she'd be that way forever.

But what about Rita? Rita and Dora. Vince was kissing her, and he had a wife. And a daughter.

It's just a kiss. Her thoughts swirled like autumn leaves; they flew up and skittered along the surface of her mind, and she could not hold on to them. *It's just a kiss. It doesn't mean anything.*

Vince took his mouth from hers. He turned her sideways and with one hand clutching her buttocks and the other her shoulder, walked her to the grass at the side of the clearing and forced her to her knees.

"No! Uncle Vince—!" she cried, but he pushed her back until she lay beneath him.

"Vince!" she cried again. "I don't *want* to! Vince, please, please don't—!"

"You want to," he said harshly. Kneeling over her, he gripped her wrists in one hand and with quick fingers lifted the skirt of her sundress and pulled off her underpants. He kicked them aside.

"No, I don't! I don't! Vince, stop, please!"

He sat back on her squirming legs and undid his belt. "You loved it when I kissed you. I could feel it."

"I didn't! I just—"

"Don't lie to me!"

Confused, terrified, Anne stared up at him. He was flushed and breathing hard, and glaring at her. She squeezed her eyes shut so tightly they hurt. Was that true? Had she loved it when he kissed her? She did love it when his arms were around her; maybe she loved his kissing, too. She must have; she must have done something that made him think she liked it. He knew so much more than she did; he knew everything. She didn't know anything, except that she was afraid and she felt sick. She shook her head back and forth on the hard ground. "I don't know. Please, Vince, please let me go, I don't want to—"

"You want it. *I know what you want.*"

He tossed his pants aside. Still gripping her wrists he held her hands above her head and thrust his fingers between her tightly clasped thighs, forcing his knee between them, spreading them. "You'll love it. I'll teach you." He was tremendously excited. Her knees were knobby, exactly as he had imagined them; her thighs were thin and hard. She was skin and bones, taut muscles, closed and secret places. His to discover, his to take. He opened her thighs farther with his legs and shoved his fingers deep inside her, probing beneath the black, curly hair. "Don't fight me, Anne. I'm going to teach you how to love."

Through the roaring in her ears, Anne heard one word. *Love.* She gave a long moan that Vince took for passion. Without waiting, he rammed into her, gasping at her exquisite tightness. He did not hear her cry out; he did not see the tears that squeezed through her closed eyes. All he knew was that she was not fighting him; she was lying beneath him like a good girl, and she was the tightest he had ever known and he could not hold back; it would take practice to hold back with a girl like Anne. Eyes closed, he pounded into her and came with an explosion that made him drop like a stone on top of her, his face against her neck.

Anne opened her eyes and stared at the trees tapering above. The light was fading, but she could see them swaying in the evening breeze. They creaked as they swayed. *Doesn't it sound like a horror movie? Close your eyes and you can believe something really awful is about to happen.*

Chapter 3

*T*he next night he came to her room. She had been there all day, in her pajamas and seersucker robe, refusing food, refusing Marian when she stood outside the closed door, asking to come in and take Anne's temperature. "I'm all *right*," Anne said. "I just don't feel like doing anything. I'm *all right*. I just want to be by myself!"

"It's hard to deal with overly dramatic children," Marian murmured to herself. "But then, we're all overly dramatic at thirteen, aren't we?" she added wisely, and returned to her gardening.

Anne sat curled up on the flowered chintz cushion of her window seat. She was surrounded by bright flowers: in her wallpaper, on the canopy above her bed, on the skirt of her dressing table and the deep armchair in the corner of the room beside a round table with a flowered cloth that reached to the floor. Pictures of her mother, in silver frames, were everywhere. A picture of Marian and one of Charles were on the mantelpiece above the small marble fireplace across from the bed. Fresh roses were on the round table, put there by the maid every day. Everything was so bright and cheerful Anne couldn't stand it. She closed her eyes against it.

She burned between her legs, a throbbing, high-pitched pain. If someone asked her to paint it, it would be bright red, brighter even than the blood she'd found smeared on the

23

inside of her thighs when she undressed last night. Vince had walked almost all the way to the house with her, his arm around her shoulders to keep her from stumbling, while he talked about some trip Ethan was planning for him. "But that's a *long* way off," he said as they stopped near the side entrance. "I couldn't leave you now." He kissed Anne lightly on her forehead, then took her chin in his hand. "You won't talk about this to anybody. You understand that?" He was holding her chin too tightly; his thumbnail dug into her skin. "You do understand that?" She nodded. "That's my girl," he said, and let go of her chin. "Get inside, little one; I'll go around to the front. I'll see you tomorrow night."

The next day people came and went below her second-floor bedroom windows as if everything were perfectly normal. The gardeners gossiped in Spanish as they pruned bushes and mowed the lawn; the sweet smell of newly cut grass floated up to Anne's window. The mailman handed letters and magazines to one of the maids. Marian walked to the rose garden and put down her long wicker basket, pulled on flowered cotton gloves, adjusted her wide-brimmed straw hat, and carefully examined each flower before deciding which she would cut and place delicately in the basket. A nanny pushed Keith in his stroller, and Marian waved at them with her pruning shears as they went by.

There were no thoughts in Anne's head at all. She was empty. She had tried to confide in Amy, but she could not do it. No matter how hard she tried, Amy would not come to life, and somehow Anne knew that Amy was gone, and would never come back. She sat without moving as the hours passed, watching the life below. Fred came home and gave Marian a little peck on her cheek while she gazed off in the distance. A little later, she knocked on Anne's door. "May I come in?"

"No," said Anne. Her room was at the far end of the hall, behind a heavy door; she had to raise her voice to be heard.

"Well, of course, dear, if you'd rather I didn't." She, too, raised her voice. "It's time to go, Anne; Nina likes everybody to be on time. And we don't want to be late for your grandfather's birthday party, do we?"

24

"I'm not going," Anne replied, still staring outside.

"Of course we'll give you a few minutes to wash up, if you're worried about looking your best."

"I'm not going," Anne said again.

"Or to change your clothes. It's nice that we all look our best; it makes it more festive. And Grandpa does appreciate it."

Anne was silent.

"Well," Marian said. Her voice came calmly through the closed door; Marian never got upset. "Of course if you're not feeling well, you certainly shouldn't go out. I'll explain to everyone, and I'm sure Grandpa will be just as pleased with your birthday wishes tomorrow. I recommend that you stay in your room. I'll have dinner sent up. Soup. It's good for almost anything. Is there anything else you'd like?"

Somebody to talk to. She was crying.

"Anne?"

"No."

"Get to bed early, then. You'll feel much better in the morning."

The house was silent. The sun slanted across the empty yard, and the shadows of trees and fences lengthened until they lay like black bars as far as Anne could see. A little later the sun was gone, and everything was blue-gray, very still, waiting. And then the door opened and Vince was there.

"God, I've missed you." He pulled Anne up from the window seat. "Thought about you all day." He propelled her to the bed. "Dinner was endless; Ethan was in a mood to talk." He sat Anne on the edge of the bed. "Get yourself undressed, little girl; I won't do it for you. That's the first thing you have to learn."

Anne looked at him, unmoving, her eyes wide.

Vince let out a short, explosive breath. "Christ." He sat beside her and put his arms around her. "We need some preliminaries. Come on, little one, relax, there's nothing to worry about. Uncle Vince is going to take care of you. You need that; you need a lot of taking care of. Remember what I told you last night? Relatives should try to make each other happy. That's what we're going to do. You just be a good girl and we'll have lots of fun and be very happy. And you'll learn all about love."

He drew the word out until it was like a long sigh, and he smiled so sweetly that Anne swayed toward him, drawn to him, wanting to be held, wanting to be loved. Vince tightened his arms, and slowly, she let her rigid body rest against his warm, solid chest. He was not much taller than she was, in fact he was the shortest man in the family and she had always thought it bothered him, but maybe not: maybe nothing bothered Vince. He was so strong; he dominated everyone. His presence filled her room. Nobody was as strong as Vince, Anne thought. She snuggled against him and closed her eyes. She wanted to sleep there, safe and warm.

"Wake up," Vince said cheerfully. He held her chin and brought her face to his and kissed her, the way he had the night before, opening her mouth wide and pushing his tongue inside. But this time, while he kissed her, he was moving his hand up and down her body. He pulled up her cotton pajama top and rolled his palms over her small breasts; he slid his hand inside her pajama pants to grasp her buttocks and probe the raw, burning flesh between her legs. Anne cried out and he took his mouth from hers.

"Are you hurting there?"

She nodded, tears in her eyes.

"Well, don't give it a thought; we'll let it rest tonight. There's plenty of other things we can do. Take off your pajamas, I want to see you."

Her hands came up and wavered.

"Damn it, do what I tell you!"

It was the voice of authority. It was the voice of all the men in her family. It was the voice of Uncle Vince, and her father always said that Vince was the strongest of all of them. Anne stopped thinking. She took off her robe and unbuttoned her pajama top, letting it fall to the bed behind her, and then pulled off her pants. They lay in a pile at her feet. She sat absolutely still, looking at her bare thighs.

Vince took her chin again and made her look at him while he surveyed her. He brushed her tangled black hair from her forehead and ran a delicate finger from her forehead down the side of her face, down the long line of her neck, over the nipples on her tiny, hard breasts, and across her flat stomach. "Such a little girl," he said with his sweet smile. "My amazing little girl." He parted her legs and gazed at the swollen redness. "Poor little one, I'm too big for you. But we're going to change that; you'll be so proud of yourself when you see how open you'll be for me. God, we're going to have a hell of a time."

He crushed her thin body to him, then held her at arm's length. "I have too many clothes on."

Anne stared at him blankly.

"For Christ's sake," he said, "take off my clothes."

Her hands came up and fumbled with the buttons on his white shirt. "Now," he snapped. Quickly, she unbuttoned his shirt, and when he made no move to help, she pulled off one sleeve and then the other. She noticed fleetingly that his chest was as bare as hers and that he had no hair on his arms or the backs of his hands. The thought drifted through her mind that that was odd: her father's and grandfather's arms were covered with dark brown hair. But the thought was no more than a wispy thread and then it was gone. "Anne," Vince said, and she realized her hands were still. She undid his belt and put her fingers on his zipper. Her heart was pounding.

"Go on," he ordered, and closing her eyes, she pulled down the zipper. He raised himself slightly and she pulled off his pants and his underpants. The hardness of his cock whipped against her hand as it sprang free, and she jerked away as if from a hot poker. But Vince took her hand and pressed her fingers around it. "Hold it," he said. Anne had a moment of surprise at how soft it was. Underneath, it was rigid, but the skin was soft and she felt soft pulsations beneath her palm. It did not seem threatening at all. But then, accidentally, she glanced at it, and saw how enormous it was. She could see nothing else but that huge rod. Terror welled up in her, and she knew she was about to throw up. But she couldn't do that; he would never forgive her. She swallowed the terror and once again stopped thinking about anything. "Move your hand," Vince said. "This way. Not so tight, little girl; you're not strangling it, you're loving it. Like this." She began to relax. It wasn't so bad, moving her hand rhythmically along that soft skin; the firmness was comforting in her hand, and Vince liked it and she wanted to please him. If this was all he wanted, in exchange for his sweet smile and his love, it would be all right. She did it just the way he'd told her to, and was beginning to feel better when suddenly Vince put his hands on her shoulders and pushed her down, to kneel on the floor in front of him. "Keep your lips over your teeth," he said. "I don't want to feel them."

She did not know how long it lasted. After a while, Vince pulled her up to the bed, and told her what to do, and she did whatever he said. She hated it; she hated him and she hated herself. But Vince said it was love.

"My good girl," he crooned as they lay together much later on the tumbled bed. "Good little Anne, terrific little Anne. Such a good student. But you couldn't have a better teacher, could you? You don't know how lucky you are." He stood and pulled on his pants and shirt. "God, you get me more excited than any woman I've ever known." He slung his jacket over his shoulder, holding it with one finger. "I'll see you tomorrow night, sweetheart. Oh, a couple of things." He paused at the door. "Don't miss family dinner again; I want to look at you and think about you with everyone there. And from now on, when we make love, I want to hear you. I want to know how much you're liking it. I don't like dead silence. And one more thing, the most important. Listen to me. I expect you to remember what I told you last night, about keeping this our secret. I shouldn't have to repeat it; you're a smart girl and a quick learner; but I'll do it just this once. You won't talk about us to anybody, not even your imaginary friend. *Not anybody.* It's our special secret. Right?"

Anne lay still, watching him through heavy-lidded eyes.

"Anne," he said very softly, "I asked you a question."

She tried to nod, but her head felt too heavy to move.

"Anne." His voice changed to a low, rasping growl. Anne would not have recognized it if she had heard it coming from another room. "This is between us. Nobody is going to know about it. You understand me? Of course no one would believe you if you did say anything—they'd say you were crazy; they'd lock you up—but it won't come to that. You won't talk to them. I won't allow it. I don't want to have to hurt you, little girl, but I would; I'd hurt you or kill you if you disobey me. I'd hate to do it, but I would, in a minute, if I thought you were talking to anybody. You remember that. We have love now, and lots of fun. We're making each other happy; and we can keep it that way as long as you're good. And you will be good, won't you? *Answer me.*"

Anne made a sound in her throat.

"That's better. I wasn't really worried; you're a very smart girl. I'll remind you now and then, just in case, but I know I can count on you. I'm counting on you, Anne; don't let me down. Good night, little girl. Pleasant dreams."

Anne watched the door close. She could not move. Her lips and tongue were bruised and swollen, and there was a cloying, sweetish taste in her mouth. Her knees hurt, her neck was stiff, her fingers felt locked in the curve Vince had taught her to use on him. She took long, slow breaths and stared out the window at the delicate tree branch that brushed against the glass. *Maybe I'll die. They'll find me in the morning, dead, and they'll know it was because of what Vince did, and they'll punish him. Maybe they'll kill him.* She closed her eyes. *I wish they'd kill him.*

And then it was morning and she knew that somehow she had slept. She slid from the bed, feeling the cool morning breeze caress her warm skin, and when she took a shower, she touched herself gently. The swelling was down; the redness was almost gone. She brushed her teeth; her mouth hardly felt swollen, either. She stood in front of the pier glass in her bedroom and looked hard at her naked body. Nothing showed. You'd think something would have changed, but nothing had. A nice normal thirteen-year-old girl, she thought, and she saw her mouth harden. That's what Marian would say, because Marian liked things to be normal and under control. So did the whole family. So Vince would come at night, and she would do what he wanted, and no one would ever guess what was happening to her, because there would be nothing to see.

Unless I tell them, she thought. She stared at herself in the mirror. Marian doesn't like problems, but she doesn't like me to be unhappy, either. And Nina listens when I tell her things that happen at school. And my father would listen; he doesn't pay much attention to me, but he wouldn't want anybody to hurt me.

I don't want to have to hurt you, little girl, or do something worse, but I would; I'd kill you if you disobey me. I would, in a minute, if I thought you were talking to anybody.

How could he have talked like that when almost at the same time he was talking about love, and about how wonderful she was? She remembered the warm, solid feeling of his chest when she laid her head against it, and how strong his arms were when they held her close. She remembered the sweetness of his smile. He couldn't have meant what he said. People didn't talk about killing their relatives, or even hurting them. They only did that in books.

But he did say it. She couldn't pretend he hadn't because he'd been pretty specific. "And I'm not stupid enough to put it to a test," she said aloud. Her voice startled her in the silent room. "He probably only said it to see how I'd react," she told her reflection. "He wouldn't hurt me; he loves me. And that's the best thing, being loved."

She stripped the sheets from the bed. The maid would put clean ones on. I'll tell her I got my period, Anne thought. Or I won't tell her anything; why should I? Why should I tell anybody anything? They're not waiting for explanations; they don't care what I do. She threw the sheets down the laundry chute, pulled on a shirt and a pair of jeans, and went to breakfast.

She was supposed to go shopping for school clothes with Marian; that would take all day. And tomorrow she could ask the gardener to show her how to take care of orchids; he'd promised to do it whenever she wanted. She didn't really care about orchids, but she loved beautiful things and orchids were very beautiful, even the ones that looked evil and voracious. Anne thought they were probably interesting enough to fill most of tomorrow. And she'd buy some books when she and Marian were shopping; reading filled a lot of hours, too, and she liked getting lost in other people's stories. She had a lot of things to do with her days; in fact, she was going to be so busy she wouldn't have any time to go to the clearing in the forest. Amy wouldn't miss her. Amy was gone. I guess I've gotten too old for Amy, she thought.

She never went to the forest again.

Marian was delighted; she thought Anne was finally learning to be a lady. That week and the next, at Saks and Marshall Field's and The Pompeian Shop, they bought cashmere sweater sets and matching wool skirts, plaid wool dresses with little velvet collars, tweed slacks and coordinated Aran knit sweaters, and because Anne didn't argue about anything and Marian was beginning to be alarmed and wanted to make her smile, new blue jeans and oversize sweatshirts and a corduroy jacket lined with fleece.

"Thank you," Anne said gravely when the shopping was all finished. "These are very nice things."

Marian peered at her. "You're all right, aren't you, Anne? You look fine; it's just that you're so quiet. Is there anything else you need? Anything we forgot to buy?"

Anne shook her head.

"You're supposed to be happy, you know," Marian said. "Thirteen, almost fourteen: such a wonderful time for a young girl. Your whole life ahead of you, nothing to think about but having a good time, family, friends, love . . ." She sighed. "Of course you've seen that Fred and I aren't exactly romantic. You're such a smart girl; you don't miss very much, do you? It's not that we fight, you know; sometimes I wish we would. But there doesn't seem to be anything to fight about. Or talk about, for that matter. We just don't have anything to say to each other. Talking is more important than anything, you know: more important than sex, God knows. Oh, for goodness' sake, I shouldn't be talking about such things to you." She gave a little laugh. "You mustn't be burdened with any of this now; this is a time for you to be young and innocent. Innocence." She shook her head. "You don't know how lucky you are."

Someone else had said that.

Good little Anne, terrific little Anne. Such a good student. But you couldn't have a better teacher, could you? You don't know how lucky you are.

"How lucky am I?" Anne demanded of Marian. "Like being lucky at cards? Like being a lucky penny somebody can pick up? Or like somebody has the luck of the devil? Is that what I have—the luck of the devil?"

"Don't be difficult, dear," Marian said calmly. "We all know how clever you are."

They all said she was clever. They said it whenever one of them chastised her for being out too long, for slouching when she walked and slumping when she sat, for dressing sloppily, for not combing her hair, for swearing and using slang, for not washing her face and hands. "You're so clever, Anne," said her uncle William. "You're smart as a whip and you could be the prettiest girl for miles around, but first you've got to stop behaving like a hobo."

William was the second oldest of Ethan's five children, after Charles. He had never married, and he seemed to feel that was a serious error; that, by being single and childless, he'd let his family down and had to make up for it by being a model uncle to his nieces and nephews. For the most part that meant bringing them presents from his trips around the world, but he also was generous with advice. "You want to watch yourself for Gail's sake," he told Anne. "You have a seven-year-old sister, you want to act properly so she can follow your example. We all have to have someone to look up to."

"Do you look up to my father?" Anne asked.

"I've learned a lot from your father."

"And he looks up to Ethan?"

"You must call him Grandfather, Anne; it's more respectful. Well, now, does Charles look up to Ethan? I'm not sure. Sometimes Ethan seems to admire Vince more than anybody else. Odd, you know, since Vince is the youngest of us; doesn't quite fit my theory, does it?"

Anne saved those conversations to tell Vince when he

came to her room at night. By now he had a schedule. For the first few weeks it seemed he was always there, and she had felt smothered by him. School started, and she had to rush through her homework because he would show up right after dinner. But then that changed. When summer ended, his business trips began again, and sometimes he was away for a whole week. And on weekends Rita liked to go out. So Vince settled into a routine of coming to Anne's room twice a week, and he always told her in advance when the next time would be, so she would be ready for him.

Anne thought it must be like a marriage. She hated it, but she thought most people probably hated being married, because it was like a job, with things that had to be done and gotten over with. Wives would hate the sex and husbands would hate being answerable to somebody else, the way Vince said he hated it with Rita. Of course he wasn't answerable to Anne—she couldn't ask him to do anything at all—but still, when they were in her room at night and she was telling him stories between the times he wanted her on the bed or the floor or the chaise, it seemed to Anne they were just like a married couple. Her flowered bedroom was their whole world; they sat in it and lay in it and talked in it, and when he brought cookies or doughnuts or éclairs, they ate in it. It was just like a married couple's house, only smaller.

But she wondered about love. She was sure married people were in love; all the books said so. But she and Vince had no love. She knew now that he did not love her and hadn't loved her in the beginning. Whatever words he used, and he seemed to use that one a lot, love had nothing to do with what went on in her bedroom two nights a week.

Love was a joke; she knew that now. It was a word people used to disguise whatever it was they wanted. She would never love anyone. And she would never get married.

On her fourteenth birthday, Marian and Nina gave a party for her. She blew out all the candles on the cake, and everyone sang "Happy Birthday," even Rose, Marian's baby, who was only a year and a half old. Nina kissed her on both cheeks. "We all love you, dear," she said in her slightly breathless way. She was taller than Marian and her hair was dark brown where Marian's was almost blond, but the two sisters had the same pale skin, crinkly lines at the corners of blue-gray eyes, calm foreheads, and perfectly manicured nails. "I'm afraid we criticize you a great deal, and I for one apologize for that; it's just that we want you to be perfect. Marian and I agreed on that, you know, when you came to us after your poor mother died. We loved her so much and we felt we owed it to her to see that you grew up to be everything she would have wanted. And we feel sure you're doing that, my dear. You're going to be as beautiful as she was, and already you're far more clever. Of course she would never swear, and she was always so perfectly turned out . . . the most elegant, sophisticated . . . but perhaps, when she was your age . . . we can't be sure . . . well, I don't want to sound critical; that wouldn't do on your birthday. You're a dear girl, Anne, pure and good and no trouble to any of us. We couldn't ask any more of you. And I want to wish you a happy birthday, and many, many more."

Anne stared at her hands. She hated being the center of attention. She wished she could go to her room and be alone. But she wouldn't be alone. Vince had told her he would be there. To celebrate her birthday.

"Well, Anne." Her father raised his wineglass. "Fourteen, and such a grown-up girl. Your mother would have been very proud of you." He spoke to the whole table, looking from one face to the other, but Anne kept her eyes steadily on him. He was eleven years older than Vince, and not as flashily handsome, but he had a serious look and an upright bearing that she admired. His blond hair, never as bright as Vince's, had turned gray seven years earlier, when her mother died; his eyes, blue-gray like his sisters', were somber; but his eyebrows and small mustache were still blond and gave him a youthful, almost jaunty look. Anne liked it that he was dignified and strong and still young; he looked to her like a hero who could hold back hordes of enemies just by speaking sternly to them.

He had been only thirty-five when Anne's mother died, and everyone had expected him to marry again, but he had not. He had stayed alone in the big house that had once been filled with his family, three blocks in one direction from Marian and Fred's house where his daughters, Anne and Gail, now lived, and two blocks the other way from the house Vince and Rita had bought when Dora was born. Anne knew from Marian that he went out frequently, dividing his evenings between two women with such mathematical precision that neither could think she was more favored than the other. And she knew that he and William played racquetball on Mondays, tennis on Thursdays, and swam on Saturdays at their club. Once he had taken her to his office, showing her the surroundings of Chatham Development Corporation and letting her read his calendar, with its neatly ruled blocks of time. Charles Chatham led a careful life, controlling everything within his power, and sometimes, when he looked at Anne with puzzled eyes, she knew with a sinking feeling that he was wondering how someone so disordered could possibly be his daughter. Maybe that was why he didn't spend much time with her; he always seemed at a loss for words and nervous, as if he couldn't wait to go somewhere else, where he could know exactly how to behave.

"Your mother and I talked about the kind of children we wanted," Charles said in his birthday toast, his gaze coming to rest on Anne. "Of course first we wanted you to be healthy, but then, like all parents, we hoped for everything else: brains and talent and charm. And you have those. You're very different from your mother, but you have a spirit and drive that remind me of her, and you seem able to handle difficult situations on your own, without whining or running to others to get you out of them. That's very grown-up and it makes me proud. Happy birthday, sweetheart, and many more."

"Hear, hear," said William. "I couldn't say it better. You're a good girl, Anne, and we're all proud of you. Just don't grow up too fast; enjoy these years of childhood while you've got them, because they're gone before you know it and then you have to deal with the tough stuff: money and sex, that sort of thing."

"William," Nina said mildly, "I hardly think that's appropriate for a toast on Anne's fourteenth birthday."

"It's always appropriate to tell a child to stay a child."

Anne looked at William from beneath the tangle of black hair that came to her eyebrows. He always seemed most foolish, she thought, when he was being most kind.

"My turn," said Ethan. He leaned forward, smiling beneath his bushy mustache. "You're only at the beginning of the long road you'll travel, my dear Anne, but I know you will make the journey with strength and integrity and intelligence. I hope you make it with love, as well. And I hope, for as long as I'm here, you'll let me share it with you."

Anne blinked away tears. He said things she loved to hear, but it didn't mean anything. What she wanted was for him to say he'd spend a lot more time with her, go for more walks with her than he already did, even take her on some of his business trips—just her, no one else—so she could talk to him about everything she couldn't talk about at home. She wanted him to take care of her; she wanted him to protect her from Vince. But he couldn't do all that; he didn't even know she wanted it. Anyway, he was ancient: an old man of sixty-six; how much could he know about people her age? He was wonderful to her and once in a while he took her to Chicago for lunch and a trip to the Art Institute or the Field Museum or the Museum of Science and Industry, and he'd always say he wished they could do those things more often, but then he would be gone again, seeing his own friends, traveling on business, and Anne would know that she wasn't all that important to him after all.

She wasn't important to anybody, she thought. They all said they loved her, but they had their own busy lives and, anyway, none of the Chathams reached out to anybody else. They're a race of short-armed aliens, she thought with angry humor; they all came from a planet of people who never learned to cuddle so their arms atrophied and shrank to little stumps that can never, ever hug anybody.

"Happy birthday, sweetheart," said Vince, exactly as her father had done. He gave her a little mock salute and his sweetest smile. "As far as I can tell, you're growing up admirably, and I think that's the best thing you can do, even if William doesn't agree."

"Of course I agree," said William. "Anne is growing up beautifully; of course she is."

"And tired of hearing about it, I'm sure," said Marian. "It's time for presents, don't you think?"

Everyone watched as Anne opened the brightly wrapped packages and said thank-you and briefly held up the cashmere sweaters, records of rock and folk groups, books, and a necklace from Charles, before putting them away and stacking them neatly. She pushed back her chair, anxious to be gone. I probably look like a criminal making a quick getaway with the loot, she thought. But she didn't care. She just wanted to get out of there. "I'll put these away," she said, standing beside her chair. "Thanks again, it's all very nice."

"Don't you want more birthday cake?" Charles asked.

"I'm full." She gathered up the pile of gifts.

"But you haven't given us a birthday speech," said William. "We all talked and talked and the birthday girl didn't get a chance to say anything."

"I don't want to," Anne said. "I'm not good at speeches."

"'Thank you' was quite enough," Marian said. "We don't need speeches. But you might just want to stay with us instead of running off the way you always do."

Anne shook her head, feeling hemmed in. "I just want—"

"But you know, I told the children we might light the candles again," Nina said. "They like to watch you blow them out."

"Damn it, I did it once!" She was at the door. "That's enough!"

"Anne," Marian sighed, "I've asked you and asked you . . ."

"Sorry," Anne muttered, and slipped through the door. They were staring at her. It's my birthday, she thought angrily. I ought to be able to do anything I want on my own birthday. She ran up the stairs. If she was lucky, she'd have some time to herself before Vince came.

He was there in twenty minutes. "I brought you your present. We'll get to it later."

Anne had already taken off the silk dress Marian had asked her to wear for her party, and was wearing only her robe. She undressed Vince quickly and surely while he untied her sash, opened her robe, and ran his hands over her body. Her breasts were growing and he held them, pinching her nipples. "Fourteen," he murmured with a broad smile. "My favorite age. So lovable. So grown-up."

He lay on the bed and Anne bent over him, knowing exactly what he wanted. He never had to tell her anymore. Just by the way he sat or stood or lay down, or put his hands on her shoulders or waist to turn or push or lift her, she knew what to do, and how to do it in the way that pleased him most. He had trained her so well she didn't even have to think about it. In fact, most of the time her mind was on other things. Some of the time she thought about school. She didn't like it—she hated being told what to do—but she loved to read and she could forget everything else when she was absorbed in *Don Quixote* and *Moby Dick, Barchester Towers,* and *Leaves of Grass* and everything by Shakespeare. She could recite to herself whole passages from Walt Whitman while doing what Vince wanted her to do; it made her feel she was somebody else, not Anne Chatham doing what she hated.

She thought about other things, too: movies she saw on television, and a new book she'd bought that told how to name the birds that flew along the lake shore. She identified them when she was in her new secret place, hidden among boulders on the shore near Ethan's house, where she could curl up and read and write all day with no one discovering her, just as she had in the forest clearing. She especially liked to think about that while her body and mouth and hands went through their practiced motions with Vince; she would think about her own place, and how soon she would be back there, cool and clean and by herself.

Vince lifted her on top and she straddled him, bending

down so he could play with her breasts. He rolled the nipples between his fingers, waiting for them to pucker and grow hard. When they stayed soft and flat, he looked at Anne through narrowed eyes. "Feel something," he demanded. She met his eyes, her face impassive. He kneaded her breasts. "God damn it, feel something when I play with you!"

She never felt anything.

"Tell me how you feel," he said harshly.

"Good," Anne replied automatically. "You make me feel good."

"Tell me how much you love me," he said.

Anne bent lower until her lips were against his neck. She said something but it was muffled.

"I didn't hear that," said Vince. "I want to know how much you love me."

"More than anything," Anne said, repeating lines he had taught her long ago, and if Vince heard the thread of despair in her voice, he gave no sign of it. "More than anyone. You're so exciting . . ." She moved her hips as she spoke; by now she could do three or four things at once without even thinking, without even missing a beat.

"And you wanted me from the beginning," Vince said. "And made me want you. Go on."

"And I wanted you from the beginning. I made you want me, I led you on, I enticed you, I lured you."

And maybe it's true; otherwise, why would he be here? I'm not sure, because I don't know what leads a man on, but Vince knows. Maybe I wanted love so much that I enticed him into my bed. Then it wouldn't be his fault at all.

"Nice," Vince said, and pushed her upright so he could watch her as she moved above him. His eyes closed, his breathing grew faster and louder, his hips moved beneath her. Anne watched him as if he were a long way off, a stranger who had nothing to do with her, and then she looked past him, at a painting on her wall of a beautiful mother and her little girl on a flower-filled terrace golden with sunshine and love.

After a while, Vince lay still and did not reach for her

again, and Anne knew that was enough for tonight. She sat cross-legged on the bed beside him, gazing at the black square of her window and the tree branch that lay against it, faintly illuminated by the lamp beside her bed. There were small green leaves on the branch, new and glossy in the April breeze. When Vince had first come to her room, months earlier, the leaves were large and deep green. She had watched them turn red and then russet, and she had watched them fall. They had held on as if greatly afraid, until a gust of wind or a rainstorm had torn them off and sent them spinning to the ground, where the gardeners raked them up. The branch stayed dark and bare for months, except when snowstorms outlined each twig with a slender coat of white that sparkled in the next day's sun, a brief beauty that vanished when the snow melted, leaving the branch naked again, waiting for the spring.

Anne was getting to know all the seasons by heart just by looking through her window while she waited for Vince to leave.

Lying on her bed, eyes closed, he nodded toward his jacket, on her chaise. "Your birthday present, little girl. I didn't give you one at dinner; did you notice?"

"I thought maybe you'd decided you'd given me enough already."

His eyes flew open and he looked closely at her to see if she was being sarcastic. But Anne returned his look, her eyes wide and clear. It was a look he trusted. He smiled. "A woman never thinks she has enough, sweetheart. You'll learn that soon enough. Now open your present."

Anne found the small box and sat on the chaise as she lifted the lid. Nestled inside was a gold and enamel Raggedy Ann lapel pin. She looked at it for a long moment. "It's been a long time since I had a Raggedy Ann doll," she said at last. "You must have looked for it for a long time."

"It reminded me of you. Something about those big eyes, seeing everything." Vince propped himself up on another pillow. "What did you do today?"

Anne laid the pin on her dressing table and returned to sit

beside him on the bed. This was the time when she was supposed to entertain him with stories. "We had a history test, and part of it was to explain what history is. So I said it was like cooking. You take a whole bunch of things that are there for a long time with nothing happening, and then all of a sudden they get put together in a new way and you get a war. Or a gold rush. Or a revolution and a new constitution and a whole new country. If I ever saw a bunch of those things early enough, I'd like to add more heat and see what happens."

"What do you think would happen?" he asked, amused.

"Something really terrible that would destroy everything. It could blow up, like a pressure cooker, and everything gets splattered on the ceiling. Or it could be like a cake. When you add too much heat, it collapses."

Eyes closed, he smiled. "What else did you do?"

"Played softball. There's a new pitcher, a girl who just moved here, and she started by striking everybody out."

"Including you?"

"The first time. She's very tall and has a boy's haircut, and she's got incredible muscles, so I figured her father wanted a son and got her instead and he's bringing her up like a boy. So I thought she'd probably think like a boy, too, and after she struck us out once she'd feel superior to all of us, as if we're timid and *female,* and then she'd get careless. And she did. And I hit a home run."

Vince was watching her now. "What a pleasure to see that little mind of yours at work," he said softly. "And those big eyes that do see everything. Did your team win?"

"One to nothing. She concentrated more after I got my home run. She's really awfully good." She paused. "That's all that happened at school; the rest was infinitely dull, as usual. They're so slow you could take a nap and wake up and wash your face and change your clothes and have a snack and they'd still be working on the same algebra problem or reading the same paragraph they were on when you went to sleep. And then there was my party, and you know all about that."

"Everyone praising you to the skies."

"As long as I don't bother them," Anne said flatly. "That's what they like best about me."

Vince shrugged. "Well, why not? You don't need diapers anymore, you can hold your own fork, you can cross the street alone. They're giving you room and board and making sure you get an education. What more do you want from them?"

"I guess . . . nothing," Anne replied, her voice low.

He ran a finger along her arm. "You don't need them, little girl; you have me." He gave her arm a quick squeeze, and slid out of bed.

"Next Tuesday," he said when he was dressed. He took the enamel Raggedy Ann pin from its box and ran his thumb over it. "Wear it to dinner on Sunday." He opened the door and looked carefully down the long length of the hall, dimly lit by sconces between five other widely spaced bedroom doors receding into the shadows. He always left after midnight, when he knew the house would be sleeping, but still he stood there motionless, looking, listening, before taking a few long strides to the door that opened onto a stairway leading down to the side entrance of the house. Without looking back at Anne, he pulled the door quietly shut, and was gone.

Anne sat unmoving, cross-legged on her bed, letting the silence wash her clean. It was getting harder to shut her mind to what she was doing. A few months earlier, around Christmas, when the family's houses were warm and fragrant with holiday decorations and baking pies, she'd found herself having good feelings about Vince, brief flashes that shot through her without warning. It wasn't that he'd suddenly done anything special, it was just the season. Whenever she turned on the radio or television she heard the sweet sounds of Christmas carols; trees and streets and stores were strung with long rows of tiny white lights, like a fairyland; and it seemed that people smiled more and were nicer to each other. There was just a lot of love around. And Anne didn't want to be left out; she wanted to be happy, like everybody else.

So suddenly, in the midst of whatever she was doing, when she thought of Vince, she would remember something nice he'd said, and how sweet his smile was, and how, some of the time, he really acted like a friend. She hated what she had to do with him, but at least he paid attention to her. He still talked a lot about love, and she thought that was pretty stupid, because she knew it was just talk that made him feel good, for some reason or other, but he also asked her about herself and wanted to know about her life, and he was mostly the only one who did. Marian did, but she didn't listen as well as Vince; she always seemed to be thinking about something else. And Charles asked her about school and sports and even about whether girls and boys were dating at fourteen, but as soon as Anne mentioned problems or worries about school or dating, he'd get uncomfortable and find an excuse to leave the room. He just didn't know what to do with somebody's fears.

But Vince listened; Vince wanted to see her twice a week; Vince told her she had a good mind and a good body and he told her she was pretty. And a lot of the time, especially at Christmas, that made the other things they did together fade a little bit, like the horizon of the lake that blended into the sky on misty days and you could almost think it wasn't really there. So, for a couple of weeks in December, Anne had some nice thoughts about Vince, and she could feel she was really part of the season.

But six months after her fourteenth birthday, everything changed. It was a warm fall, warmer than anyone could remember, and everyone felt strange, as if the seasons had been turned inside out. In late October the trees flamed red and gold and bronze; beds of asters, salvia, chrysanthemums, and dahlias surrounded the homes of Lake Forest with white and yellow and a deep burgundy that reminded Anne of the wine they drank at Sunday dinners; and the sun blazed day after day from a sky streaked with thin clouds that made thin purple and jade shadows on the lake. Anne hurt from the beauty; she ached with wanting it in every part of her life. She wanted beautiful days and wonderful friends and exciting work that made her feel useful and triumphant. She wanted to feel good about herself. She wanted to be free of Vince.

That fall she had begun her second year in high school, and she found that she no longer knew how to talk to the girls in her classes. Suddenly it seemed they were all talking about dates and parties and petting; they giggled about how wet their underpants got when they were excited; they groaned about how gross the boys were when they started panting like puppies and trying to crawl all over them; they all said they were virgins, and after every weekend they tried to find out who wasn't anymore. Anne stayed away. This is how prostitutes feel, she thought: tired and bored and knowing too much. And old.

Her body was changing, but she could not take pleasure in it. Her breasts were becoming full and firm, her knees and elbows had lost their knobby look, and she seemed taller, with a slim waist and narrow hips. Vince said he missed her lean boniness, but still he liked staring at her nude body; he said it was due to him; he had made her a woman. She hated him when he said that.

She hated him most of the time that fall, and it reached a peak on Halloween. Rita and Marian had taken the young children out for trick or treat, and the house was quiet except when the doorbell rang. Anne heard it every few minutes when children came to their door, and she imagined groups of them in their costumes, waiting and giggling together until the maid came and handed out the packets of candy kept in a wicker basket in the front hall. I wish I was young again, Anne thought. I wish I could be a little kid and go trick-or-treating.

"This is our trick-or-treat night," Vince said with a grin when he came in. Anne looked puzzled. "You're turning tricks for me," he said. She had never heard that before. "And you have your bag of treats to keep me happy. To keep both of us happy." He sat on the edge of the bed and motioned to Anne to kneel in front of him. "Where else would I want to be on trick *and* treat night?"

Anne felt like screaming. She wanted to smash his smiling face. She thought of biting him until he cried and begged for mercy. But he wouldn't; he'd kill her. She clenched her fists as she knelt in front of him, and took him in her mouth and stroked his thighs. She was more afraid of him than she had been in months because he seemed invulnerable.

He was always very pleased with himself, but lately he had preened with new successes. He had been in charge of building a group of three office towers near O'Hare airport, and he had done it brilliantly. Everyone said so, even Ethan. And soon after the three buildings were completely rented, Ethan had announced he was putting Vince in charge of Tamarack, the little town he had been developing for twenty years without any formal plan. Now he would turn it over to Vince. When the announcement was made, it seemed that everyone in the family, even those who had been cool to Vince, admired and deferred to him, as if, Anne thought, he'd suddenly become the crown prince. And that made him especially terrifying because she felt weak and unimportant beside him. He was the prince of the family and she was just a commoner. And so was her father, she thought; or at least he was a lesser prince, if Vince was the one her grandfather preferred. So there was no one on her side who had any power in the family. Who would believe anything she said now if Vince didn't want them to believe it?

"Tamarack," Vince said on Halloween. He sat propped against the pillows on her bed, winding a strand of her hair about his finger as she lay beside him, staring out the window. "Do you know how far we're going to go with Tamarack?"

"It sounds like you're chewing when you say it," said Anne. "Like it's a candy bar and you're licking it and taking little bites. Like you're swallowing one tiny bit of Tamarack at a time."

Vince's eyes narrowed. He wound her hair more tightly, until she winced, and she knew she had gone too far; he didn't like it when she saw through him. "I asked if you know how big our plans are," he said softly. "And look at me when I'm talking to you."

She turned from the window and met his bright brown eyes. "I only know what Grandfather talks about at dinner on Sundays, and he hasn't said much lately. I thought he'd finished building there. Last summer, when we were there, it was all changed; I didn't know he wanted to do anything else."

"He wants to make it bigger. He wants it to be the best; bigger and more exclusive than Zermatt and Gstaad. He wants it to be the most famous resort in the world." When Anne was silent, he said, "And what do you make of that?"

She hesitated. Often in the past few months he had asked her what she thought, mostly about plans he was making for the company and for himself. She no longer had to entertain him with stories; now he wanted to talk about himself. He even talked about his quarrels with Rita. He asked Anne how she felt about all of it, as if he wanted her advice. But Anne never gave advice. She knew what he really wanted was to be listened to and agreed with. "I guess . . . if that's what he really wants. I didn't want him to change it at all. I loved it the way it used to be; it was such a funky little town. All those empty miner's cottages and falling-down buildings and unpaved streets . . . it was a nice little ghost town and the people in it kind of moved around in it without really touching it. I loved thinking it was so hidden away in the mountains it was eternal just the way it was."

"That was a long time ago," Vince said dismissively. "It hasn't been like that for ten years. It won't even stay the way it is now; in another year or two you won't recognize it. That's what I asked you about; you haven't answered me."

Once again, Anne hesitated. She didn't like to talk about Ethan to Vince; it seemed like a betrayal. "I don't know anything about famous resorts. I told you, I thought Grandpa had done what he wanted; I didn't know he wants to do more. In fact, I don't think he does. He's not interested in Zermatt or any other place. He just loves Tamarack. Why would he care whether it's bigger or smaller or more famous or anything than Zermatt?"

"He put me in charge of it," Vince said flatly.

"Well, but . . . just to run it, isn't that right? He didn't tell you to go change it all."

46

Vince frowned. "You don't know what you're talking about."

"Then why did you ask me?"

"I want to know what you think about him. Sometimes you see things that other people don't. What does he want there?"

"I think," Anne said after a moment, "he wants to make a paradise where everyone will be perfect and happy and no one will ever be sad or disappointed again."

Vince was amused. "He's not a dreamer, sweetheart; he's one of the shrewdest businessmen you'll ever meet. There's no room for paradise in the development business, and he knows it."

"That's why he's planning to get out of it."

Vince shook his head. "He's not going to Tamarack; I am. He'll come out now and then, the way he always has, but most of the time he'll stay right here."

"For now," Anne said stubbornly. "But I think he built Tamarack so someday he'll have a place to live that he likes better than here."

Abruptly, Vince got out of bed and began to dress. "That town is mine; I have plans for it. And he damn well knows it; I haven't kept them a secret. He doesn't want a paradise; he wants a town that will make money. That's what he wants from me: to see that he makes money on his investment."

Anne was silent.

"You think he has his own plans that he hasn't told anyone about. You think he already likes it so much he might not back what I want to do, that he might keep the money tight, keep me on a short leash."

Anne said nothing. She had not thought that far, but hearing Vince say it, she thought he was probably right.

"Next time you see him, ask him what he's got in mind. Not the pap he feeds the family, but what he's keeping to himself. If he's got his own private timetable, I have a right to know it."

"Ask him yourself," Anne said. "I'm not your corporate spy."

Vince paused in buckling his belt. "I didn't hear that," he said with a smile.

"I'd just rather you asked him," she said.

"And I'd rather not." He stuffed his wallet into his back pocket. "I'll see you next Wednesday. You can tell me then what he said."

"Wednesday? But last time you said it would be Tuesday. Because of your trip."

"I changed it. What difference does it make?"

"Well, it . . . I'm doing something on Wednesday."

Vince had unlocked the door; he stood there, his hand on the knob. "Doing something?"

"I decided to work on the school paper." Her voice came in a rush. "And there's an editorial meeting Wednesday at five; they're getting sandwiches, in case it lasts a long time."

He took his hand off the knob. "You didn't tell me about the paper."

"I didn't tell anybody."

"Why not?"

Because I need secrets that are just mine, and nobody else's. "I didn't think you'd be interested."

"I'm interested in everything you do, little girl. Are you the copyboy?"

Stung, she said, "I'm writing stories. I'm an investigative journalist."

"And what do you investigate?"

"Whatever they want me to. I like to interview people; I'm good at it. I like to figure out why people do things. Illegal things."

He looked closely at her, but she returned his look steadily, her eyes wide and direct.

"I want to see the next issue," he said. "All of them, in fact. I don't mind your doing it, but you're not to keep things from me. And I expect you to be here next Wednesday."

"Please, Vince." She felt powerless, sitting naked before him while he stood above her, dressed in his business suit, but she knew he would be angry if she pulled the sheet over her. "I can't miss this meeting."

"It's the only night I have free next week." He saw the tears in her eyes. "Is it so terrible to spend the evening with me?" he asked softly.

Anne dug her fingernails into her palms. "No, but—"

"Of course not. You love me. Tell me you love me, little one."

"I love you. But can't I go to this meeting?"

"Tell me again."

"I love you, Vince. But couldn't I, just this once—"

"No. Don't argue with me, sweetheart; I'm not about to change my plans just to accommodate you. Tell them to change their meeting; what else have they got to do?" Halfway through the door, he looked back. "Wednesday," he said, and closed the door behind him.

The scream Anne had held so long tore from her, low in her throat. Reaching out blindly, she picked up a graceful ceramic lady in a long gray gown, a valuable Lladro that Marian had bought her, and hurled it across the room. But even then, even in her anger and despair, she knew enough not to make too much noise, and she aimed it at the flowered draperies. It struck them and fell to the carpet, where one arm broke off with a sharp crack. And Anne began to sob.

She cried until she was so tired she could not cry anymore. Then, slowly, she went through the routine that always followed Vince's leaving. She stripped her bed and put on clean sheets, and she played some of her records: lilting folk songs that were light and happy. Then she took a hot bath, lying back, her eyes closed as she soaked in jasmine bubbles that rose to her chin. When she was dry and powdered, she put on smooth, freshly ironed pajamas. Finally, she slipped into her cool bed and read until two or three in the morning. By then she felt she had things under control, and she could go to sleep, and sleep soundly until her alarm went off at seven. She never remembered her dreams.

On Wednesday, she went to the newspaper meeting at five o'clock and left while it was still going on, to be ready for Vince. When Marian stopped her as she went upstairs, and asked about dinner, she said she was not hungry. "Growing girls are hungriest when they think they're not hungry at all," Marian said wisely. "Anne, dear, is there something you'd like to talk about? Do you need help with your schoolwork? Do you have—I know you're still a child, but young people seem to move so fast these days—do you have a boyfriend? You could invite him here after school if you like. Or your girlfriends; they're always welcome, you know. Come into the kitchen; we'll get you some dinner and you and I can talk."

Anne shook her head. "I don't have time."

"My dear, you have all evening. You can't have that much homework."

"I have a lot to do. Aunt Marian, could you send some food up? You're right; I'm really starved, but I've got to be in my room; I'm worried about doing everything I have to do."

Marian smiled and kissed her cheek. "It won't take long," she said, and went off to the kitchen. It was amazing, Anne thought, how often one could get one's way just by telling other people they were right. It didn't work with Vince; nothing worked with Vince. She always told him he was right; she always told him what he wanted to hear; but she never got her way with him. The weeks and the months passed, and despair and hatred were always inside her. They were like a tumor, Anne thought; a huge tumor swelling up like a balloon. That must be how people died, when the tumor got bigger and bigger and demolished everything until there was nothing left: no bones or blood, no lungs, no heart. I'm going to die, she thought. I'm going to die if I don't do something. And then it was April, and her fifteenth birthday.

Marian had bought her a new dress, as she always did, for the birthday party she and Nina always gave. And when everyone was there, they sat at the same places around the table they had taken on her birthday the year before. She blew out all the candles on the cake, and everyone sang "Happy Birthday." Nina kissed her on both cheeks. "We all love you, dear," she said. "I hope we haven't criticized you too much in the past year; if so, I for one apologize." She laughed a little sheepishly. "I say that every time you have a birthday, don't I? Well, but you know what we hope for you: that you're as perfect as you can be. We owe that to your poor mother." She held her glass up. "You're a dear girl, Anne, pure and good and no trouble to any of us. And I wish you a happy birthday, and many, many more."

Anne stared at her hands. She wanted to be in her room, alone. But she wouldn't be alone. Vince had told her he would be there. To celebrate her birthday.

"Well, Anne." Her father raised his wineglass. "Fifteen, and such a grown-up girl. Your mother would have been so proud. I can't tell you how I miss her, and how I wish she could share your growing up. She'd appreciate your spirit, and your wit, even though I see a tendency for you to be a little too sharp now and then. You must watch that; it can hurt your popularity. She'd admire your intelligence, too, and your charm. You're like her in many ways. And I admire your fortitude; you're not a whiner or a clinging vine. You're very grown-up and I'm proud of you. Happy birthday, Anne, and many more."

"Hear, hear," said William. "We're all proud of you. You're a real little woman. Just be sure you enjoy these years of childhood before they disappear. You don't want to rush into worrying about earning a living and dealing with the really tough stuff: money and sex, that sort of thing."

"William," Marian said mildly, "that's not appropriate on Anne's fifteenth birthday."

"It's always appropriate to tell a child to stay a child. And fifteen is still a child in my book."

"My turn," said Ethan. "Dear Anne, I don't know what goes on in your head in these years that you're growing up. I treasure our times together—I always wish we had more of them—but even when we spend an afternoon together, I confess I don't feel I know you nearly as well as I'd like. Well, maybe that's asking too much; I'm afraid your age often seems very strange to me—and I'll bet mine does to you. This year I promise I'll take more afternoons off and we'll scout out some new museums and shops and whatever else you'd like to see, and we'll talk about anything you like. If you want to, that is; I know how young people usually like to be with young people, not grandfathers. Well, you let me know. For now, I'll just tell you I admire you and I love you. and for the future I wish you inner strength and integrity. and intelligence and love."

"Happy birthday, sweetheart," said Vince. He gave her a mock salute and his sweetest smile. "I agree with William: you're quite a little woman."

Anne looked at all of them, and at the stack of presents waiting for her, and suddenly she felt that her whole life would be just like this: these people, these toasts, these gifts. Nothing would change; she would never escape. Even if she went away, she would always be a prisoner. Vince would find her, wherever she was, and he would open her bedroom door and call her *little girl* and make her do things she hated. Twice a week, forever, she would hurry home from whatever she was doing just so she would not make Vince angry by keeping him waiting. Twice a week, forever, she would take a hot bath and try to wash away all the . . .

"Grandpa," Anne said loudly in a fierce, despairing rush, "Vince comes to my room at night and . . . makes me . . . do . . . things."

There was a terrible silence at the table. "Oh no, oh no, oh no," moaned Marian.

"Vince?" said William incredulously.

"It can't be," Nina whispered. "It can't."

Charles was on his feet. "Vince, you bastard, what the hell did—"

"It's a lie," said Vince loudly. A vein pulsed at the side of his neck. "The little bitch. What the hell's wrong with her? We're all celebrating her—"

"Vince?" William repeated, more loudly.

"Christ," said Fred Jax, "what a stupid—"

"Be quiet!" roared Ethan. He leaned forward in his chair at the head of the table and stared at Anne, sitting two places away, hunched over, staring at her plate. "Is this true?"

Still looking down, she nodded. She was terrified. And then she began to cry.

"It's a damned lie," Vince said again. His voice rose as he turned to Ethan. "She's a liar! She always has been."

"Don't call her that!" Charles shouted.

"You can't trust her," Vince went on, "you know you can't. She's a wild kid, a delinquent—"

Gail, sitting beside Anne, started to cry, her voice a loud wail beside her sister's wrenching sobs.

"Oh, no," said Nina. "Look what you've done." She took Gail on her lap. "It's all right, sweetheart, don't worry; it'll be all right."

"Be quiet!" Ethan roared again at Vince. "If you can't, you'll have to leave."

"Leave? For Christ's sake, she's accusing me of rape!"

"He has to stay, Dad," said William. "He has to be able to defend himself. You can't shut him up."

"Anne, talk to us!" Charles cried.

"Defend himself?" quavered Marian. "How? What could he say? Unless . . ." She peered at Anne. "Are you very sure, Anne? It's such a terrible thing to accuse someone of, especially your uncle, who loves—" She bit off the word. "You might . . . do you think you might have dreamed it? Sometimes our dreams seem so real—"

Still crying, without looking up, Anne shook her head vehemently.

"Vince isn't that stupid," said Fred Jax ruminatively. "At least I never thought so. If it's true . . ." He looked at Vince speculatively, as if rethinking their relative power positions in the family and the company.

"I don't defend myself against lies," Vince rasped. "She's a child trying to get attention; she never grew up. Look at her: she never combs her hair, she's always dirty, she runs around in the forest like an animal, she stays cooped up in her room instead of being with the family like the rest of us, she swears like a truck driver, she talks back . . ." He raised his voice above the other voices clamoring against his. *"She's a goddam liar!* We all know it! How can you listen to her? She's uncontrollable, she's a—she's a—"

"She imagined it," Rita broke in when Vince faltered. Everyone stopped talking and looked at her in surprise. Rita almost never spoke at family dinners. "It's not hard to figure; she's just a kid and nobody likes her much . . . I guess nobody does 'cause she never goes to other girls' houses or brings them back here, does she? I mean, I never hear of her doing it. And Marian's always talking about how come she doesn't bring friends home after school. And I guess she doesn't date, either, does she? Seems like she's a real loner and she's probably been dying to have somebody give her the time of day, and she latches onto Vince, who's so handsome he's every girl's dream. She never looks at him, straight at him, you know? She runs off if he comes close and she won't look at him; it's like she's scared to death she'll blab something or her face will give her away. I guess maybe she finally tried to get him to say something nice to her and he probably just ignored her—he doesn't have the time of day for kids, you know, not even his own, usually— and it looks like she was mad or disappointed or whatever and wanted revenge."

Vince put his arm around Rita. Without looking at him, she shrugged it off.

Charles had walked around the table to stand behind Anne. "I don't want to hear it from Rita. I want to hear what Vince has to say."

"God damn it," Vince snapped. "There isn't a fucking thing to say!"

"Vince!" Marian cried with a look at Gail, who sat with her face buried against Nina's shoulder, and at the other children, who were looking wide-eyed from one speaker to another.

"Nina, take the children to the playroom," said Ethan. "Why didn't anyone think of that?"

Nina hesitated, reluctant to leave. But Ethan motioned toward the door with a sharp jerk of his head, and she went, holding Rose in her arms, herding Gail and Dora and Keith before her.

"I can't believe it," William muttered, over and over, shaking his head. "I can't believe it." He struck the table with his fist, rhythmically. "In our house . . . we're not the kind of people . . . I can't believe it . . . can't . . ."

"Nothing happened!" Vince exploded. He looked across

the table, at Charles, standing behind Anne. His eyes never moved down to Anne; it was as if he and Charles were alone. "Charles." His voice was soft and sweet. "Charles, you know me; no one else knows me as well as you do. You know I couldn't do anything like that. There's no way I could touch her. It would never occur to me! For God's sake, Charles, she's your daughter! And you're the dearest person in the world to me. Where would I be without you? You've helped me grow up, you've always been there when I needed you, you're my best friend. Do you really think I'd do anything to your daughter? My God, Charles, she's as sacred to me as you are!"

Charles looked down at the bent head of his daughter. "Anne, did you hear that?"

She sat without moving.

"Charles," Marian said. She stood, clasping and unclasping her hands, her mouth trembling. "I think we should wait. This is too hard for all of us. If we waited—"

"For what?" Charles demanded. He knelt beside Anne's chair. "Look at me, Anne. Now think carefully. This isn't a game. You've made a dreadful accusation that could do great harm to your uncle. Did you make it up? Or dream it? Be careful what you say, Anne, your uncle's future is at stake."

Anne felt herself shriveling up inside. Her father's face wavered through her tears. He was not smiling at her. He looked stern. She turned to Ethan. "Please," she whispered.

Ethan looked at her intently. "Tell us what happened, my dear."

There was another silence. "I can't," she whispered. She turned to Marian, who stood agitatedly at the end of the table.

"Tell us, dear," Marian said. "We'll listen to you. Tell us anything you want."

Anne stared at her. She was choking with her shame. No words would come. She shook her head.

"Well, then," Vince said smoothly. He walked around the table. Anne cringed as he came close. "I'm sorry you had to go through this, Charles. If I can help in any way . . . though I think I'd better be careful to stay away from Anne. I might touch her, you know, out of affection, and then everyone would think . . . Oh, Christ, Charles"—tears filled his eyes —"how could this happen to us?"

Anne glanced at her father as his eyes met Vince's tearful ones, and she saw what she had always seen there: admiration, a kind of helpless envy, and love for his favorite brother, his favorite person in all the world.

"Nothing happened to us," Charles said to Vince. He put his arm around Anne's shoulders. "Anne is a fine girl, and nothing happened to her. She's fifteen years old and growing into a woman as good and beautiful as her mother was. And nothing happened to her. Did it, Anne?"

"Why can't you tell us?" Ethan asked Anne. His voice was firm, not as gentle as it usually was when he spoke to her. "When I ask a question, I expect an answer, Anne. We don't make accusations in this family without explaining what we mean. I can't punish anyone or undo damage if I don't have facts. I expect you to tell me exactly what you meant, and then we'll know what to do next."

Anne squeezed her eyes shut so she would not have to see all the men staring at her: Ethan, Fred, Vince, Charles, William. Marian stood helplessly at the other end of the table; Rita had withdrawn into her usual silence. *It's all my fault. I led him on and enticed him and then I let him into my room and did everything he wanted and I did it over and over again all this time. I can't say that. I can't tell them . . . anything.*

Ethan was looking at her, puzzled, angry, helpless. Marian clasped her hands beneath her chin. "What can we do? Anne, I know you're having a difficult time, but you must talk to us so we know what to do."

You could believe me.

"Rita may be right, you know," Fred Jax said, still as if talking to himself. "I mean, girls do have these fantastic imaginations, and Vince comes on strong. Big smile, lots of teeth. You know."

"I'm sure Anne believes her story," said William. "She's not a malicious child; I'm sure she wouldn't willfully hurt anyone in our family. Something led her to say what she did, as shocking as it is; I just wish she would tell us whatever is in her mind. It's very hard on us, Anne; we're ready to help you, but you won't talk to us. Don't you trust us? We want to do what we can for you."

Anne slumped in her chair and was silent.

William sighed. "Well, what do we do now?" He looked around the table. "Is Anne going to tell the world about this? Or has she? Anne? Have you accused Vince to your teachers or your friends at school?"

"Anne," Charles said when she did not answer. He put his hand on her hair. She could not tell if it was a gesture of affection or of warning. "Have you told anyone else?"

Beneath his hand, she shook her head.

"Well, of course that's the way we'll keep it," Fred Jax said firmly. "None of us wants a scandal; it would hurt us all. The family and the company, too. We'll keep it quiet and work it out. Anne? We need to hear you say you understand that."

"Don't push her!" Marian said sharply. "We've got to give her some time. She'll talk to us later. I think"—she looked everywhere but at Vince—"I think she may be telling the truth."

"Oh, God, Marian, don't," Vince groaned; tears filled his eyes again. "You can't think that; you know I wouldn't . . . what the hell do you think I am?"

"I don't know," Marian said, shaking her head. "I don't know much of anything. But I know we've got to give Anne a chance to tell us what happened in her own way. She's frightened and you men are badgering her."

"Nothing happened!" Vince cried again. "She'll give you some fucking fairy tale!"

"Shut up, Vince, for Christ's sake," Fred muttered.

"But what do we do, if we don't know for sure?" asked William.

Nina came into the room. "I told the maids not to clear.

Did Anne say what happened?" She looked around the table. "Well, she must have said something!"

"Oh, Anne," Marian sighed. "You really must talk to us. Maybe we really can't wait until later. Please don't make it so hard for us! If you'd only talk to us! We can't just pretend this didn't happen, or promise not to tell anybody, because if it is the truth, we have to tell the . . ." Her voice wavered and she took a long breath. "We have to tell the police."

"That Vince raped his niece?" asked Fred. "That's what you'll—"

"You son of a bitch," lashed Vince. "I told you—"

"I believe you," said Fred. "I was asking my wife if that's what she wants to tell the police."

Marian looked at him for a long moment. "I would tell them the truth."

"Well, but we aren't agreed on that, are we?" he said. "I mean, until we are, I agree with William. I'd rather not turn your family into a circus for the newspaper reporters."

"It's for Anne's sake," Charles said. "She'd be hurt the most if this got out."

Fred nodded. "I agree with Charles. We have to think of Anne."

William snorted. "We're thinking of ourselves."

Ethan watched them. His face was heavy and brooding.

"Anne," said Marian suddenly. "Do you want to talk to me alone?"

It's too late.

"Anne, my dear, please help us," Marian begged.

You didn't help me.

"Anne, tell us what you want us to do," Ethan said urgently. "This is a terrible day for our family. We want to do what's right for everyone. Help us. If you won't talk to us about what happened, at least tell us what you want from us."

"I want you to love me!" Anne cried. She was sobbing and her nose was running and her voice did not sound like her own. She shoved her chair back.

"We're not finished here," said Charles.

"*I* am!" She scurried to the door, her voice trailing behind her in a wail. "I am. I am. I am."

In the darkness of her room, she sat cross-legged in the middle of the floor. Marian stood outside her locked door, calling her, and after her came Ethan and Nina and William. Then Gail came. Anne listened to her knocking on the door and finally let her in. She lit a small lamp on the desk so they could see each other.

Gail threw her arms around Anne. "I don't understand anything!"

"You shouldn't be here," Anne said. "You shouldn't even be hearing all this stuff; you're only nine. Go to bed."

"Tell me," Gail said. *"Tell me!* I love you!"

Anne shook her head. "I can't. Listen. Will you listen real carefully? Stay close to Marian. Really close. When anything happens that you don't like, tell Marian. She's okay, Gail; she'll help you, you just have to push her a little bit, otherwise she just kind of drifts around in her own world." Gail giggled. "No, seriously, are you listening? Stay close to her. Don't let anybody do anything to you that you don't like."

"Like what?"

"Just anything you don't like. Tell Marian if anybody tries. Okay?"

"Sure."

"Gail, I mean it. I'm serious."

Gail's eyes were wide in the dim light of the room. "Okay. I'll remember."

"Then go to bed." Anne held her close. "I haven't paid much attention to you. I'm sorry. You're really nice. Go on, now. Go to bed."

"I could stay here with you."

"I don't want you to. Go away, Gail, I don't want you here."

Gail's mouth drooped. "Well . . . I'll see you tomorrow."

Alone, Anne turned off the lamp and sat again in the middle of the room, in the darkness. When her window began to turn a faint gray, and then grew steadily brighter, she could see the roses all around her, in the wallpaper, in the draperies, on the bedspread. They looked wan and old, half-dead. Ugly, Anne thought. They're so ugly.

Just outside her window, a bird began to sing. Anne stood up. It's the day after my fifteenth birthday, she thought. And Vince is going to kill me.

She couldn't stay here and wait for him. She had to get away. It wouldn't do any good to tell anyone she was terrified of him because none of them believed her. For a minute she'd thought her grandfather did, and Marian did, maybe, but they didn't try to help her; they didn't get mad at Vince; they just looked miserable and not sure of anything. That made her feel more alone than anything Vince had ever done to her.

Standing near the window, Anne closed her eyes. "Mommy," she whispered, and tears stung her eyelids as the word fell softly in the silent room. "Mommy, please help me." But there was only silence, and the trill of the bird beyond the glass.

She opened her eyes and wiped them on her sleeve. She straightened her back, holding her head high. *I don't need them. I don't need anybody; I'm not a baby anymore. I can do everything alone. I won't ask anybody for anything, ever again. I don't need them. All I need is to be strong and not let anybody hurt me. Ever. And when I grow up, I'll be better than all of them. And I'll be very happy.*

She pulled her duffel bag from the closet shelf and stuffed clothes into it, whatever she could grab from her closet and bureau, without looking at them. She pulled off her party dress and picked up a pair of jeans. No, she thought, suddenly beginning to plan. Nobody pays attention to a teenager in blue jeans. She put on a tweed pantsuit and a white silk blouse with a bow at the neck. She emptied the birthday envelopes from William and Fred of the money they held and put it in her wallet and carefully put the wallet in her leather purse. Then she left the room.

She skirted the pile of presents Marian had placed outside her door during the night, and went to the side stairway and outside door that Vince had used for two years, and down the walk to the street. The sky grew brighter and she was followed by the songs of birds as she walked the mile into town and waited on the railroad platform for the Chicago train. Her eyes were dry. She was dry inside, all shriveled up, too tightly controlled even to feel fear for whatever lay ahead. She stood straight in the fragrant beauty of the April morning, and when the train arrived, she walked onto it, her duffel bag in her hand, and never looked back.

Chapter 4

Find her!" Ethan demanded. He glared at the detective sitting beside Charles. "Don't waste my time telling me how hard it is to find runaways; just do it!"

"All I said, Mr. Chatham, was that there's thousands of these kids, and they get to New York and San Francisco and places like that, and they kind of blend in, you know, and if somebody doesn't want to be found, they usually don't get found."

Ethan brushed his words away. "You haven't given him much to go on," he said to Charles. "Friends she had, people she trusted, give him some names!"

Charles shook his head. "I don't know anyone. Anne didn't talk about herself very much."

"Did you ask her very much?"

"She didn't like to be asked," Charles said defensively. "You know how she was. Is. Always going off by herself, talking back . . . I love her, but she made it damned hard; she was so different from Alice. I kept looking for Alice in her, I thought a girl had to be like her mother and I wanted to love her as much as I loved Alice, but she wasn't—isn't—anything like her. She could be, she's pretty enough, but every time Marian or I tried to get her to improve herself, she got worse. Marian is the one to talk to," he said to the detective. "She knows Anne better than anyone."

"Right," said the detective. "She knows the kid liked to

read; she bought books like mad and stacked them all over her room. She liked to hide out in the forest; she either had friends nobody ever saw or she made them up, nobody knows for sure; she wasn't crazy about school but she got pretty good grades; and she all of a sudden liked to go clothes shopping a couple of years ago. That's about it. Didn't anybody ever talk to this kid?"

"All of us had dinner together every Sunday night," said Charles, still defensive.

"I'm talking about *talking* to her." The detective picked up his briefcase and stood beside his chair. "Nobody knows nothing; that's what I got so far. I talked to her classmates at school and they liked her all right, she seemed to get along with everybody, but she wasn't close to any of them. They all called her a loner, a little strange, not comfortable with people, that sort of thing. Nothing you could put your finger on and say she was the type who'd run off. And nothing that can help me. If she had close friends, nobody knows it. If she had favorite teachers, nobody knows it. If she visited neighbors, nobody knows it. If she hung out at bars in Chicago, nobody knows it. If she was one of your rich North Shore kids who blow their allowance on pot and LSD, nobody knows it. If she ever wanted to take off for some city or other, nobody knows it. Nobody knows nothing." He glanced at his notebook. "Anne Chatham, fifteen years old, five feet four, one hundred five pounds at her last physical, which was a year ago, blue eyes, black hair, no distinguishing marks." He flipped through the pictures Marian had given him. "Pretty girl. Well, I'll be in touch. But I'm telling you, we've got a lot of these and the ones who show up do it on their own; they don't get found if they don't want to get found."

Ethan swiveled his chair and brooded at the lake beyond the wide, sloping lawn. Brown and gray waves churned beneath a steady rain and dissolved into the gray horizon. I hope Anne took her umbrella, he thought. But she did like the rain. Once I saw her dancing on the grass in her bare feet in a rain just like this one. That was a long time ago. I hadn't realized that; I haven't seen her dance for a long time. She hasn't done anything like that for years. "Tell Vince I want to talk to him," he said to Charles without turning.

"He's at the office."

"Call him."

"I tried to believe Anne," Charles said to his father's back. "But it's a terrible thing to think that someone in your family . . . It's too terrible to believe. And she wouldn't talk to us."

"Help us," Ethan muttered, staring at the lake. "That's what Marian said to her." He swung around and glared at Charles. "We asked *her* to help *us*. Who the devil was helping Anne? My God, my God, what did we do to that child? Failed her, betrayed her . . . How could we do that to her?" He lowered his head and wept.

What's wrong with this family that we don't go out of our way to protect each other?

They'd all let her down, but he was the worst. He was her grandfather, the head of the family. The worst, he thought, the worst, the worst. Because he should have been enraged. Anne's story demanded it. And if he had stood with her, enraged and insistent on resolving it, he could have swept everyone with him to a confrontation that would have brought out the truth.

Brought out the truth, he thought. But I know the truth. Why did I ignore it? As soon as that poor beleaguered child became difficult and uncooperative, I abandoned her. We all did. That's what this family does when there's trouble. We want things comfortable, clear-cut, manageable. And when they're not, we turn tail and run. Like a bunch of cockroaches scared by the light. We're no better than that.

He was still sitting there two hours later, when Vince and Charles walked in. "Not you, Charles," Ethan said. "Close the door behind you." He waited until Charles was gone. "How long did it go on?" he asked Vince.

"Jesus Christ, Dad, not again," Vince protested. He sat in a leather chair in the corner of the library. Behind him shelves of books reached to the ceiling, and illuminated globes of the world stood about the room on mahogany stands. He put his feet on a leather hassock, crossing the ankles. "We went through this a dozen times last night. I told you, I don't know what got into her. I haven't a clue why she picked me. She's got a lot of problems, you know. Rita was right about her being unpopular, and she didn't like school—"

"How do you know that?"

"I don't; how could I, for sure? But whenever somebody asked her about school at dinner she didn't seem excited, or even much interested. Did she? To you?"

"I don't know," Ethan replied, troubled because he had not noticed.

"My guess is, she was into drugs. I wouldn't say that to Charles, but that's what I think. God knows what kind of group she got in with at school—well, if God doesn't, Marian might—" He smiled briefly at his father; then his face became somber. "I've worried about her for some time, you know. I worry about all the young people today; they seem so lost. Too much drugs and alcohol and rebellion. But I worry about you, too, Dad. You can't blame yourself for Anne's craziness. She's enough of a grown-up to know she has a responsibility to her family, and if she walks out on us, we can't say it's our fault; we have to let her go. I'm not saying we shouldn't do our damndest to find her, and I'll help all I can, but if she's really gone, I think we should accept her decision and not get all worked up over it. I have a feeling she'll be fine. Underneath all that posturing and smart-aleck talk, she's a pretty strong girl."

There was a long silence in the library. Ethan listened to the echo of Vince's satisfied voice. In his memory, he saw Anne as a child, with gangly arms and legs and heavy black hair falling over her eyes, alone most of the time, trying to get attention in ways that often were rude and even wild. Once Ethan had watched her in the garden, talking to herself. A lonely, vulnerable little girl who never really felt at home in Marian's house.

For the first time, Ethan felt the pain of Anne's loneliness.

He saw again her desperate face at the dinner table as she said those terrible words, and then her crumpled figure, crushed and defeated by the wavering of her family.

"Are you feeling all right?" Vince asked. "Can I get you anything? Tea? It's about that time, isn't it? I'll ring."

"She was telling the truth," Ethan said.

Vince had been halfway out of his chair. He jerked upright. "You don't mean that." He stood with his weight on one foot, his hands in his pockets. "She was lying, Dad; I told you. I told you it wasn't true."

"I heard you. I believe Anne."

"You can't believe her! Dad, she was lying! Kids lie; everybody knows that. You wouldn't choose her over me; you're my father, for Christ's sake!"

His head thrust forward, his hands flat on his desk, Ethan contemplated Vince in silence.

Vince let out his breath. His body grew slack. He took one hand from his pocket and spun the globe beside him, gazing at it pensively. With his other hand he made a small gesture of helplessness. "I don't know how to convince you. I didn't have anything to do with her. Dad, you've got to believe me. She's a child! And I've got a wife and a child of my own; how could I do that to *them?* But how do I prove it if my own father doesn't believe me?"

Ethan was silent.

"In fact, I did try to be friends with her." Vince spun the globe again. "A few times I tried to talk to her, draw her out, but she wouldn't have anything to do with me. It hurt me, you know. It wasn't that she was so warm and outgoing with everyone else—we all know she wasn't; in fact, she was damned rude to us most of the time—but I made a special effort to be friendly, to let her know she had an uncle who cared about her. I did admire her, you know; she had so many fine qualities, really fine qualities. Admirable. But she wouldn't have anything to do with me. She must have had something against me even then—this was at least a couple of years ago—and whatever it was she stored it up for a long time; why else would she pull a stunt like this? Christ, why would she accuse me, when I'd tried the hardest of anyone to be her friend? I suppose she needed extra attention—poor kid, she really must have been miserable, with nobody liking her or wanting her around, and she must have known she brought it all on herself by being so unpleasant—but why pick on me? We haven't exchanged more than a couple dozen words in all these years. What did I do to her? What did I do to you, Dad, that you don't believe me? Here's a kid I barely knew, who was almost never around—she was off in that clearing in the forest or in her room—and out of the blue she makes up this damned crazy story, and when nobody believes her, she runs away, and then you don't believe me!" He sat on the edge of a chair near Ethan's desk, gripping his hands. "It's a nightmare."

"What clearing in the forest?" Ethan asked.

"What? Oh, some place she had; Marian told her not to go there, but she did. She always did what she wanted, no matter what anyone said. Maybe you don't know her as well as you think, Dad. As far as I could tell, she always did exactly what she wanted. Of course she's a remarkable girl and quite capable of taking care of herself, but she won't bend for anybody. Nobody ever forced her, you know; nobody could make her do a damned thing she didn't feel like doing."

Ethan scowled. How well had he known Anne? She was fifteen; he was sixty-seven. She was a schoolgirl, just beginning her life; he was closer to the end of his, already making plans to cut back as head of the company he had built and spend more time in his mountain paradise. How well could he know her? He admired her spirit and her strength, and enjoyed her sharp tongue, but how well did he understand her?

Vince went on, his voice picking up strength. "I haven't wanted to say this; I hoped I could avoid it—it's not the kind of thing you want to say about any young girl, much less one in your own family—but, knowing her as well as we do, why do we assume she's innocent at all, or has been for a long time? How do we know what she does, whom she meets, when she runs off after dinner, and on weekends? I'm not saying she's not a good girl—I'd never criticize her;

she's my niece and a lovable kid and I care deeply for her—but there are a lot of kids running around these days with nobody watching, and she probably got herself in too deep with some of them. I'd lay odds she got herself pregnant and panicked and looked for somebody to blame . . . and for some reason she picked me. I'm not saying that's exactly what happened, of course—how can we ever know, since she wouldn't talk to us even when we all begged her to?—but, with all the wild kids around these days, it's as good a guess as any. I'm just sorry—well, to tell you the truth, Dad, I'm damned mad—that she laid it on me. I did try to help her out, give her a few pointers, give her a little affection, and this is what I get. Damn it, I don't deserve this! I suppose she thought I'd let her get away with it; maybe she figured I was a patsy since I had a soft spot for her and she had a good time playing on people's sympathies—"

"That's enough!" Ethan was on his feet, his face dark, his breathing harsh, at last feeling the rage he should have felt for Anne the night before. "I saw her face! It wasn't easy for her, she wasn't having a good time, and *it was the truth!* You can spread your filth, but I understand her better than you think. You took advantage of her, you used her because she was young and weak. You like weak people; that's why you chose Charles of all of us to latch onto. You use people, Vince; you always have. Do you think I'm blind, that I don't see what you do? You use the family; you use the people in the company. You're shrewd and sharp and you get things done, and I'm ashamed to say I've ignored a lot of your little tricks because we benefited; the company benefited. That was my greed, I suppose; I let you go on making money for us. But to take advantage of Anne! To be so warped, so demented—so evil!—that you'd seduce that poor helpless child and then force her to . . . receive you . . . for . . . How long? *How long did you*— Good!" he roared as Vince sprang up and started for the door. "Get out of here! Out of my sight, out of my house, *out of my company!*"

Vince stopped short and swung around. His eyes were stunned. "What?"

"Out of my company! I don't want you in it. It's a family

company and I want you out of the family. You've disgraced us; I don't want to see your smarmy face again!" Ethan felt tears sting his eyes with the pain of what he was doing. "A man should look at his sons and know them, enjoy them, call them friends and partners. I don't recognize you anymore." His voice dropped. "I'm sick of you."

Vince watched his father's shoulders slump. "Dad." His voice was tight but very careful. "You don't mean that. Not any of it. You don't *know* she was telling the truth; for some reason you just feel it. You're entitled to your feelings, but so am I, don't you think? And I know I did nothing wrong. But I won't argue with you about it any more; in fact, I think we'd better not argue about anything. We have too much at stake. What about Tamarack, Dad? I thought it was your dream as much as mine; you can't take chances with it because of one girl. We still have a lot to do there; isn't that more important than any one person?" He waited, but Ethan was silent. "Dad, let's forget this whole mess. We'll forget everything we said today. We'll find Anne and bring her back and she'll be fine; we'll all help her, and we'll forget this ever happened."

Ethan looked at him from beneath heavy brows. "I told you to get out."

"But I know you didn't mean it." Vince smiled gently. "We're all tense from this whole thing, Dad, I understand that, I understand what you're going through. But it will pass. We have too much at stake—"

"I want you out of your office by tomorrow; I have other plans for it. And you'll be out of your office in Tamarack by the end of the week."

The smile faded from Vince's face. He stared across the width of the room at his father, who stood slump-shouldered behind his desk. "You'll regret this," Vince said at last. "I own shares in the company."

"And what would you do with them?" Ethan asked contemptuously. "Force a vote on your job? Who'd vote for you against me?"

Slowly, Vince nodded. "You'd win, but it wouldn't be a meeting you'd enjoy. I'd force it, though, if I had to."

Ethan waited; he knew more was coming.

"I'll need money. The easiest way would be to sell my shares."

"I'll buy them," Ethan said instantly. "Call the attorney; tell him to be here tomorrow."

Vince pulled open the door. Ethan felt a surge of pride in his son for his instant acceptance of the inevitable. He had seen him like this before, making decisions swiftly and decisively, without visible regret. We have that in common, Ethan thought; there are ways in which he is so clearly my son.

"You might wish me luck," said Vince, standing in the doorway.

Ethan's pride faded and tears again came to his eyes. He was thinking of Vince as a baby: the most beautiful of all his children, the quickest to walk and talk, the one with the brightest smile. The most clever, the most charming, the greediest. "Stay away from young girls," he said.

Vince walked out.

Fury propelled him. He walked the length of the living room and into the dining room and on through every room of the house in a swift, enraged tour. He had not lived there since he was eighteen, but he still thought of it as home, and now he was leaving it for good. No regrets, he thought. Except for Tamarack.

His rage over Tamarack consumed him. It was his; his father had given it to him. Ethan had been playing around with it for twenty years, developing it at his own pace. Now it was Vince's turn. He had his plans, his budgets, his schedules. Ethan had no idea of the scope of Vince's ideas: under his control, Tamarack was going to be transformed from a small, pleasant mountain resort to a town of highways, sprawling hotels, and exclusive shops, a glittering magnet for royalty and the world's wealthiest pleasure seekers, a town that would provide everything for those who could afford it. It would provide more, of course: it would be a cornucopia of riches for the Chatham Development Corporation, and in particular, for Vince Chatham.

That was Vince's plan. There were other plans the family had made, for a future reorganization of the company, with Charles moving up to president of Chatham Development in Chicago when Ethan retired, and Vince as vice president of Chatham Development and president of The Tamarack Company. That was settled; everyone had agreed to it; and everything Vince had done for the past two years had been in preparation for his move to Tamarack. He was going to make Tamarack the most spectacular project of the decade, and because of that, and because it would be so visible, it was also going to be the springboard—though no one knew this yet—for Vince Chatham to go into politics.

But all it took was half a minute, and a few whining sentences, for his father to snatch it away from him.

He left Ethan's house and automatically drove the half mile to Anne's house, as he had done twice a week for almost two years. He parked a block away, as he always did, and as always, went in through the side entrance, his stride strong and purposeful with anger. The anger was so intense he could not focus it. Bitch, he thought, as he took the stairs two at a time to the second floor. Fucking bitch. But as soon as he fastened on Anne as the center of his rage, his thoughts swung to his father. *Bastard. Kicked out like a goddam servant.* In the upstairs hall, he knocked against a small table and a lamp fell to the floor and shattered. He left it there. *Fired! His own son!* But his anger was already swinging to Charles—*mealymouth son of a bitch; none of this would have happened if he'd stood up for me and told them she was lying*—and then to Marian. *Another bitch. Taking her side. Two bitches: my fucking sister and that other one.*

He had reached Anne's room. He flung open the door and lunged in. It was unnaturally still. The bed was made, the books were neat on the shelves, the window was closed. The vase on the table that always held fresh roses was empty. Vince stood in the middle of the room, between the fireplace, where they had lain together on the soft rug, and the bed, where she had spread her legs for him whenever he wanted, and for the first time it struck him that she was truly gone. He'd been robbed of Tamarack and he'd been robbed of Anne. Both of them had been his, and both of them were gone.

His rage rose again, vast and incoherent, an overwhelming wave of blind fury. He attacked the window seat, her favorite place to curl up, flinging the fringed pillows to the floor and clawing at her stuffed animals, hurling them across the room. He tore down the draperies, then stumbled and cursed as he tried to extricate his feet from the soft folds almost to his knees. *Should have beaten the hell out of her. Should have killed her.* He'd threatened that, more than once, and she'd kept quiet for almost two years. And then destroyed it all. *Fucking bitch, I was too good to her. Too loving.*

He assaulted the bed, ripping off the flowered quilt, the pale pink blanket, the silken pillows, the sheets he'd stained, over and over and over, that bitch, that bitch to lead him on, then ruin him with his father, and then disappear, out of his reach, away from his cock—

"Vince!" Marian cried. "My God, Vince, stop!"

He froze, his back to her. His hands were filled with wadded sheets. The pink blanket trailed away from his fingers. A corner of a pillow was between his teeth. Slowly he let the sheets and blanket fall to the bed. He unclenched his teeth and the pillow dropped on top of them. He forced his heartbeat to slow down as he straightened and turned to face her.

"You don't have to screech at me, Marian," he said pleasantly. He gave her a sheepish smile. "I lost control; got completely carried away. I'm so sorry. I don't know what got into me, the whole awful week, I guess, and then I just had a row with Dad and walked out. I couldn't imagine working for him anymore, he's impossible, so damned uptight in his old age. So I walked out and there I was without a job, and I guess I just blamed everything on Anne—poor, sad little Anne, it's not her fault she messes up everything she touches, is it? I'll send someone over to take care of all this damage; don't you worry about it for a minute." He shook his head in disbelief. "I just can't imagine what got into me."

Marian looked confused. "You can be so sweet, Vince, why do you do all these things?"

"What things, my dear?" Vince asked gently.

"Everything. Having . . . sex . . . with Anne . . . Oh, God, Vince, how could you?"

"But my dear, I told you I didn't. I didn't touch her. She's a confused, wretched little girl who tells very big lies to get attention. I'm surprised you don't know that by now, Marian; you've spent a lot of years with her." He walked to her, noting the brief alarm that flickered in her eyes as he came close. He touched her shoulder lightly, and lightly kissed her cheek, as he edged past her through the doorway. "It's the worst thing in the world when a man can't count on his family."

"We were happy," Marian said mournfully. "We were so happy. And now Anne is gone and Father is miserable and Nina just cries and William won't talk to anyone and Fred is no help at all and I don't know what to do! Everything is so confusing and I blame you for that, Vince; whatever you did to Anne, you frightened her and upset the whole family, and I blame you for all of it."

He opened the doorway to the side stairway. "I know you do," he said coldly without looking back. "Maybe someday I'll be able to forgive you."

His step was jaunty as he left the house and walked to the car. That would shake her up; Marian couldn't bear it when people spoke coldly to her and left her without a smile and a kiss good-bye.

He whistled a march as he drove the short distance to his house. He had a lot to do, plans to make, options to sort out, people to call. He'd have to talk to Rita about some of it. He'd prefer to leave her out of it altogether, but she'd been in a foul mood since that damned dinner—in fact she hadn't spoken to him last night when they got home—and he'd never get her back to normal if he kept her in the dark now about his plans.

"Hi, sweetie," he said to Dora, swinging her to his shoulder. "How was your day? Don't I get a kiss?"

Dora giggled. "I can't kiss you from up here!"

"Well, then." Vince brought her down and held her against his chest, her face a few inches from his. For a fleeting moment he thought he saw in her eyes and the shape of her mouth a resemblance to Anne, but of course he knew there was none. Dora was only five; Anne was a woman. He let Dora give him a wet kiss, then put her down. "Where's your mother?"

"Upstairs. She's cleaning drawers. She's been doing it all day."

"Spring cleaning," Vince said, amused. A good wife, he thought. She's not speaking to her husband, for some reason or other, but she makes sure the house is in order. "You stay down here, Dora; I want to talk to her for a while. Watch television or something."

"Nothing's on."

"Then do something else. I don't want you bothering us."

Rita was in their dressing room. The mirrored closets on one wall and all the mirrored drawers on the other were open. Clothing was stacked on the floor and on the two velvet chairs in front of the mirrored wall at the back of the room. Rita's lush blond beauty was reflected dozens of times—an endless succession of Ritas—as she sorted, scrutinized, folded, and neatly piled their clothes. No, Vince saw. Not their clothes. Only hers.

He ignored them. "I want to talk to you. In the study."

"I'm busy." She was examining a button.

"You can do that later. Damn it, you can't refuse to talk to me forever. Things are happening; we have to make some decisions."

"I already did that." She picked up a blouse and folded it around a sheet of tissue paper. "I'll be out of here by tonight. Me and Dora."

Vince rocked back on his heels. "Out of here? What the hell is that supposed to mean?"

"It means I'm leaving you," she said.

She looked his way, briefly, her green eyes wandering over

his face, her full, glossy lips in a pout he still thought was sensual. Her hair was a mass of pale blond curls that reached almost to her waist, and her figure was rounded and full, with curves that a man could bury his face in and feel aroused and comforted by at the same time. Vince, who had always scoffed at what he called her tiny brain, and for two years obsessed with Anne, still could not keep away from his wife's soft nestling hollows. "I'm leaving," she said. "What else could it mean?"

"You're not going anywhere. Are you out of your mind? You've got a house and a child, you've got a husband, and you'll stay right here, where you belong." He smiled and took her hand. "You were upset last night, sweetheart; we all were. But you were magnificent; you stood up for me and said all the right things. I bought you a little something today; shall I get it? I was going to give it to you at dinner. I thought we'd go to Le Perroquet."

She pulled her hand away. "I don't want any presents and we aren't going to any fancy restaurants. You should watch your money, Vince; Dora and I are going to cost you a bundle. There's the apartment, and we have to buy—"

"What apartment?"

"The one I rented in Chicago. It's on Lake Shore Drive, very nice. But we have to buy new furniture; the stuff they've got there is unbelievable. And there's Dora's summer camp, and her tuition at the Latin School—"

"Bullshit. You're crazy. You're not going anywhere and you're sure as hell not taking Dora anywhere. She's mine and nobody takes her away from me."

Rita turned back to the piles of clothes. "My lawyer says you can talk to him about that."

Vince stared at her. "When did you go to a lawyer?"

"This morning."

"For what?"

"For a *divorce*. God, Vince, you're slow today. You always accuse me of being slow, but you take the cake. Could you hand me that suitcase? The one on the top shelf?"

Vince gave a bark of laughter. "Shall I pack it for you, too?"

"No, I can— Oh, you're being cute." She shrugged and pulled one of the velvet chairs to the closet, moving the clothes to the floor. "I'll get it myself."

Vince looked at the curve of her calf as she stood on the chair. He ran his hand down it, wanting her. "Come in the other room; we can settle everything there."

"No! Damn it, Vince, get the hell away from me."

He shoved his hand between her thighs and grabbed her crotch. "Get off that chair."

"I'll scream! And Dora'll call the police. I told her to, if she ever heard me scream. Call and tell them I'm being raped."

Vince jerked his hand away. "Why did you tell her that?"

"Because you raped Anne." She lowered the suitcase to the floor and dropped two smaller ones beside it. She looked down at him, her mouth tight, the pout gone. "And it went on, didn't it? On and on. I mean, she wasn't talking about one quick screw and then a good-bye. She said you made her do things. *Do! Things!* We know what she meant, don't we, Vince? All your favorite tricks, the ones you showed me how to do. Not a little screw one night when you had too much to drink, oh, no, oh, no, lots more than that. She was talking about lots of nights, and all your favorite stuff, wasn't she? You bastard, Vince, you rotten bastard. You think I'm staying around after that? You think I'd let my little girl stay in the same house with you after that? We're getting out of here; you're not fit to live with. I told your family those lies about that poor kid so you'd take care of me; you're gonna pay me for lying. You'll pay me for the rest of your life. You always think I'm so dumb; who's dumb now? Who's gonna pay for the rest of his life because he couldn't keep his prick out of a little kid who was scared to death of him and then he needed his *wife* to stick up for him with his family? Boy, are you dumb, Vince. Once upon a time I thought you were smart. But you're just about the dumbest bastard I ever knew. Get out of my way."

He backed away just as she jumped off the chair.

"So I'll be out of here tonight. And my lawyer'll call you and I guess we'll figure out some way for you to see Dora, 'cause there's no way I'm letting you be alone with her. I told my lawyer that. He said you probably won't make trouble about it; you don't want any publicity, he said. You think he's right?" Head cocked to one side, she scanned Vince's face. "I think he's right." She opened the large suitcase and began to fit neat piles of clothing inside. "Go away; I don't want to talk to you. I don't like you anymore, Vince. You're a real shit." She worked in silence. "Go away!" she cried, and slammed her palm against the floor. "I don't want you here!"

He moved. He had been moving all day, he thought. He walked down the stairs and out to the front yard. He had left his car in the driveway, and he opened the door and sat in the front seat, staring unseeing through the window. He had to think, he had to plan, he had to make decisions. But all he could think about was the women.

He was surrounded by harpies out to destroy him. Anne. Marian. Rita. And Dora, who would have called the police if her mother had screamed.

"Daddy!" Dora called from the back porch. "Where are you going? Can I come?"

Behind her, Rita swooped down and took her back into the house.

Vince started the car. Rita would get whatever he was forced to pay, not a penny more. And he'd see Dora whenever and wherever he wanted, and he'd find a way to get her away from her crazy mother. And he'd get Tamarack away from his father. He might take it away himself; he might find someone else to do it; but somehow, no matter how long it took, he'd do it. None of them would ever forget what they'd done to him.

He tried to whistle the march he had been whistling earlier, but no sound came. His throat was dry; his lips were dry. Angrily, he turned on the car radio, spinning the knob until he found some martial music, and turned up the volume until it filled the car. Then he backed out of the driveway.

He thought fleetingly of Anne as he passed her house, and remembered her awkward body and huge eyes that first time in the forest. Then he dismissed her. He wouldn't think of her again; she was already forgotten. She wasn't important. She'd take up with a bunch of other runaways and end up on the street. She'd be dead within a couple of years. Even if she didn't die, she'd never come back to the family; she wouldn't dare; none of them had believed her. They'd never see her again.

He left her house behind and kept driving. She wasn't important. She was already forgotten.

Chapter 5

Eleven of them shared a house on Page Street in the Haight Ashbury section of San Francisco, sleeping on cots, sagging couches, and mattresses on the floors. The house, like dozens in the neighborhood, had once been elegant, its three stories decorated with scalloped shingles and carved and painted wood that covered every inch of its towers, dormers, eaves, and window frames. At the turn of the century, it had housed a wealthy banker's family and had echoed with the laughter of children, the clip-clop of high-stepping horses, and balls that lasted until dawn. But by the time Anne arrived, it had been a boardinghouse for thirty years, its stucco flaking, its sweeping banisters scarred and splintered, its chandeliers in shreds.

"A sad decline," said Don Santelli, eyeing the house from the sidewalk. "But the toilets work, so do the lights, and the resident ghost is basically not too hostile."

"The ghost?" Anne asked.

"Adolphus Swain, banker. He built the place. We figured he's vexed by seeing hippies in his mansion, so he causes chunks of the ceiling to fall now and then, and the sinks to back up, and pieces of the floor to collapse under you when you're thinking of something else. Walk warily and very lightly is rule number one. Rule number two is don't look scared. You seem to have a problem with that one."

She darted a look at him. "Why?"

"You know why. What are you scared of? Somebody finding you? Or nobody finding you?"

"That's my business."

"Hey, I was being basically friendly." He put his arm around her. "Everybody goes through the exact same thing when they get here." Anne jerked away from him. "Sorry," he said. He took a long, exaggerated step backward. "I guess we ought to be properly introduced; then maybe we can be friendly. Don Santelli. I don't think I told you that when we met. Usually we don't pay attention to last names. I didn't get yours."

"Anne Garnett."

"Garnett. I like that. It's sort of a jewel, isn't it?"

"Sort of." It had been her mother's name before she married; now it was Anne's. Somewhere between Chicago and San Francisco, Anne Chatham had disappeared. She was Anne Garnett now, and she would be, for the rest of her life.

"So, now we know each other," Don said. "Are you hungry?"

She nodded.

"Let's see what we can find."

He was tall and thin, with black hair tied back in a long ponytail, jutting ears, a quick smile, and a scattering of pimples on his high forehead. He had lived in Haight Ashbury for two years, in one house and another, with one group of people and another. "Looking for a place where I felt good," he said as he took plastic cartons from the refrigerator and filled a plate with vegetables. "I may have found it; this is a decent bunch of people here. Bread," he muttered, and cut a thick slice from a sourdough loaf on the counter. "Juice." He filled a glass and put everything in front of Anne. "Eat up and relax. You've got nothing to do but be happy."

"I have to get a job. I can't do anything until I find some work."

"Bite your tongue, Anne; that's a dirty word around here. We came here to get away from all that. Work is for peons."

"But—"

"Now listen. What you do is, you collect food stamps every month. If you have to, you pick up odd jobs now and then, just enough for whatever you need. Rent is twenty-five bucks a month for each of us, food varies, maybe fifty a month, and you've got clothes, right? So what else do you need?"

Anne was staring at him. "But everybody works."

"Not here. You're talking about that awful place you escaped from. Here you do your own thing. Find out who you are and what's really important in life. You don't like the food?"

"Well, if you had some meat or something . . ."

"I don't eat that shit," he said amiably. "I'm strictly vegetarian. But we're easy around here; nobody cares what you do, as long as you don't try to convert anybody, and provide for yourself. But just today, we'll give you a break. Barbie has some tuna fish; she won't mind if I give you some, to help you feel at home. Just replace it sometime, okay?" He opened a can and shook the contents onto Anne's plate. "That okay?"

She nodded. "Thanks. If you don't work, do you go to school?"

"Nope, not interested. I'm a lousy student; I hate being told there's only one right way to do things, and I freeze on tests. My father offered me a hundred bucks for every A I got on my report card; I told him that was pretty shabby."

"Why?"

"Because it should have been eight or nine thousand for every A. Because I was working, right? And a hundred bucks an A was grossly below minimum wage when you figure class time and homework. I was totally disillusioned by my father doing this typical capitalistic thing, trying to screw me out of a decent living wage, and he and my mother didn't like my hair or my clothes or my friends or my smoking pot or I guess anything about me. And I didn't like the way they were always so careful with their life, planning everything before they made a move so they'd know the end of something before they even started it. I wanted romance and mystery and unexpected passion. So we had all these crises, lots of shouting, lots of tears, so I left and came out here. So now I play my guitar on street corners, talk to strangers and make them feel better about themselves. Life is a drag for most people, you know, but not me; I lie in the sun and take each day as it comes, and I never know what's going to happen tomorrow. That's the way life oughta be. Let's find you a place to sleep. It's probably best on the third floor; not so crowded. No bathrooms up there, but there's two on the second and one on the first, and everybody's easy about sharing."

He carried her suitcase and Anne followed to the second floor and then up a narrow, ladderlike staircase to the third. "Let's get you settled," he said, putting her suitcase on a bare mattress. He brought over an empty box. "Looks like your stuff will fit in here if this is all you have." He started to open the suitcase.

"Leave it alone!" Anne snapped.

He drew back. "Sorry. I thought you'd like some help."

"I don't like people touching my things."

"Hoo-ee," he said softly. "We share a lot around here. You might want to think about that." He turned to go. "No rush in getting settled; not a time clock in sight. Not any clocks, as a matter of fact. See you around."

Left alone, Anne sat on the mattress. It was in a corner of a large room with a carved ceiling and parquet floor that was gouged and dull with age. Once it had been a ballroom; now it held five mattresses, a few chairs, and cardboard boxes filled with clothes. Above Anne's mattress was a round window with square panes, and through it she saw similar houses across the street, and beyond them the treetops of the Panhandle, the long, narrow stretch of Golden Gate Park where she had sat for two days, telling herself that the park was so much like home that she'd get used to being there pretty soon.

She had told herself she wouldn't miss anyone, but she missed them all. Not Vince, never Vince, but all the rest of them, all the people who had filled her days since she was born, and who seemed to be getting brighter, bathed in a kind of mystical glow, the longer she was away from them. She had learned about Haight Ashbury in high school, where her classmates had talked about it with excitement and longing as the place of freedom and free love. They had vowed they'd go there the minute things got really bad at home, but none of them had. Anne was the only one who did, and those first two days, wandering around San Francisco, she hadn't felt free at all; she'd felt alone and piercingly lonely and sure she had done the wrong thing. And then she met Don Santelli playing his guitar in the Panhandle, and she went home with him because he told her she was welcome and could stay as long as she liked, and he didn't ask her anything about herself, and because she didn't know what else to do.

And then she was mean to him when he was trying to be nice. *We share a lot around here. You might want to think about that.* But she didn't want to share. She didn't want to get close to anyone. For the first time in two years, her body was hers again; she felt clean and pure and untouched. And she was going to stay that way. No one would ever degrade her as Vince had done. No one would get the chance.

But it wasn't only touching she found unbearable; it was hard to talk to people, too. She just wanted to be quiet; she wanted to be separate from everybody. But at the same time she didn't want to be alone. If they just kind of hang around but don't get too close, I'll be fine, she thought. If they get too close, I'll go somewhere else. She sat cross-legged on the mattress, looking out the round window. I don't have to do anything I don't want to do. Nobody can make me.

She didn't even have to work, it seemed. Little odd jobs, Don had said. Food stamps. Grandpa would be awfully disappointed, she thought. He'd say, *But wouldn't it be best if you at least tried to find a real job? You can always ask for help if you can't make it on your own, but wouldn't you feel better about yourself if you tried to use that good brain of yours?* And then he'd kiss me and tell me how smart I am.

She blinked back tears. "But I don't live there anymore," she said aloud. "I'm not part of them anymore. I'm part of

here. And I owe Barbie, whoever she is, a can of tuna fish."
She left her suitcase on the mattress and walked down the
steep stairway. The kitchen was empty when she passed it
on her way outside; the house was empty. No one cared
where she went. No one cared whether she went or not.
Marian would have asked where she was going. She always
wanted to protect me, Anne thought. But when it really
counted, she didn't.

She walked along the sidewalk, wondering where a grocery store was, but not wanting to ask. The street was alive
with people, groups of brightly dressed men and women
who parted for her as she approached, and came together
again as she passed. It made her feel very much alone, and
the tweed pantsuit and white blouse that she had worn when
she took the bus across the country made her feel out of
place. But everything around her was so exotic that she told
herself it was enough just to be the audience.

Nearby, young girls in gossamer scarves held hands in a
circle and danced; farther down the street men with pony-
tails and earrings, and women with long hair and headbands, sat cross-legged in doorways, smoking and gossiping.
Straight ahead, groups were coming from the park, or going
to it, and when Anne came closer, she saw what looked like
hundreds of people sitting and lying on the grass, lounging
against trees, reading or singing to mournful guitars.

It was spring in Haight Ashbury. From all parts of the
country new people came each day, lured by romantic tales
of freedom, peace, harmony, joy, and love. In the few square
blocks of that enclave bordered on two sides by Golden
Gate Park, they created a small world bright with the colors
of Indian saris, velvet and old lace rescued from forgotten
trunks, hand-painted T-shirts, sandals, and long strings of
beads. It was a world perfumed with incense and marijuana,
furnished with junk-shop furniture, and illuminated by
candles in wine bottles or bare bulbs dangling from high
ceilings. It was the world of the Jefferson Airplane, Ken
Kesey, the Grateful Dead, and Hippie Hill in Golden Gate
Park.

"Plenty of room," someone said to Anne as she stood

watching the crowd on the hill. He reached up to pull her down beside him. "You can squeeze in right here."

Anne shrank back. "I'm just looking."

"Plenty of room," he said, but as she scurried away, she saw he had already forgotten her.

Every day Anne walked through Haight Ashbury, watching and listening. After a month she recognized dozens of faces, and she was recognized by people who greeted her with a smile or a raised hand, palm out, that was like a salute among them. "I've waited two whole weeks to say hi," said a young man with a blond beard and long blond hair. "So, hi."

"Hi," Anne said briefly, and kept walking.

"I'm Sandy," he said, keeping step with her, "and I'm writing a song and it's dedicated to you. So I need to know your name."

He had moved close to her as they walked, and his shoulder and hand brushed hers. Anne moved away. "Pick somebody else."

"No, you're it. You are a very attractive girl. Could you slow down? You're walking too fast for me. Where are we going, anyway?"

Anne stopped, her eyes cold. "Go wherever you want; just stay away from me. I don't want you here. I was having a nice time and you're ruining it."

"Oh, come on. We're supposed to be together; that's what it's all about. I mean, look . . ." He pulled her to him and wrapped his long arms around her. "The whole thing is love, right?" She was struggling and he tightened his hold. "We could have fun; we could have a good time together—"

At that echo of the past, Anne screamed, shattering the quiet street. People whirled about and came running. "Why'd you have to do that?" he exploded. "You didn't have to act like I'm some rapist; I wanted to *love* you."

"Come on, let's run." A tall young woman grabbed Anne's hand, and before Anne had time to think, she was running across the street and along the sidewalk on the other side, toward the park, her hand held in a firm grip. People scattered to make way for them and they ran and ran, stretching their legs in long flying leaps, their hearts pounding, their sandals slapping against the sidewalk, their blouses wet with perspiration in the hot sunshine of the May afternoon.

"Oh, marvelous," gasped the young woman as they reached the park. She flung herself on the cool shaded grass beneath a tree, pulling Anne with her. "It was good, wasn't it? God, I love to run like that. Are you all right?"

"Yes," Anne said. Her face was flushed and bright with surprise. "I really am. I feel wonderful."

"Running always does that, and it doesn't matter whether you're running from or to. I'm Eleanor Van Nuys. Pleased to meet you."

"Anne Garnett. Thank you for rescuing me."

"Sandy would've let you go; he doesn't believe in force. But you're great to run with. We should do that once a day whether we need it or not. How long have you been here?"

"A month. What about you?"

"Oh, forever. A year. I came right after I finished high school. My family had my whole life strategically planned: I was going to graduate from college and get married right away to a somewhat older rich man who'd settle me down, have three kids—a girl, a boy, and I don't know what the third was supposed to be—and make a lovely home in the suburbs and a *très chic* roughing-it summer place in Maine. So what could I do but take off? I couldn't stand it every time they pushed me to do this or that to get ready for my future, and they grounded me when I went out with boys who weren't good for my image, whatever that means, and I just got to totally hate everything. Especially all the arguing."

"Arguing about what?" Anne asked. "What did you want?"

Eleanor shrugged. "Who knows? My own messy future instead of their tidy one, I guess." She was tall, with long, tangled red hair, a small mouth that was always in motion, talking or singing or whistling—"You cannot believe how my parents hated my whistling; it drove them absolutely bananas"—green eyes that narrowed to angry slits when she saw a wrong being done, and a fierce temper that could explode like a Roman candle, leaving her and everyone around her stunned and breathless. "I do have that problem; my temper. But I figure it ought to mellow out by the time I'm twenty-five. Most people ease up when they get old, don't you think? How old are you?"

"I'm nineteen, too," said Anne.

Eleanor tipped her head to the side and studied Anne's face. She reached out and brushed Anne's black hair away from her eyes. "More like seventeen, but you can be whatever you want, as far as I'm concerned. Where're you from?"

"The East Coast."

"Really? Me, too. Where?"

There was a pause. "I'm not really from the East Coast," Anne said slowly. "I guess I just don't want to talk about it."

"Okay with me. What would you like to talk about?"

"You."

"Really? I love to talk about me. Let's see, what else is there? I like to read, especially biographies, because I like knowing that people who turned out really great had as much trouble with their parents as I have. I try to sit through horror movies, but I just can't do it—"

"Why do you want to?"

"Oh, some guy told me it builds character to face your nightmares and walk out knowing that they didn't turn you into a blubbering idiot. He might be right, but I can't stand the tension. And then there's the other possibility: what if I end up blubbering?"

"Maybe you *should* blubber sometimes," Anne said, surprising herself. She had not volunteered an opinion or had a real conversation with anyone in all the time she had been in the Haight. "If you don't cry when things are scary, you probably don't care very much about anything or anybody, and then you're hardly even human."

"You're not talking about movies, are you? You're talking about real life. You really believe that? I'm usually afraid to cry. It's like, if I was really grown-up, I'd be able to cope with my emotions and incorporate them into my persona in productive ways."

Anne smiled. She felt the unfamiliar stretching of her muscles and knew it was her first smile in more than a month. "You read that somewhere."

Eleanor grinned. "I've got this neat psychology book; you can look at it sometime, if you want. It uses a bunch of fancy words, but it really has good stuff in it. Like what I just said; it means you're supposed to master your emotions instead of drowning in them. You're supposed to use them to solve your problems with the tools you've got, the personality you've got, instead of going to pieces over the things that happen."

"You can't always solve them," Anne said, her voice low.

"Well, then, you run away from them," Eleanor said cheerfully. "Like everybody around here did." There was a silence. "Anyway, I think the reason you're not supposed to collapse in horror movies is because you're supposed to know they're fake. My problem is I forget. I get mixed up about what's real and what isn't. I think of whole stories sometimes and I can't be sure whether they're about people I know or whether I just imagined them."

"You should write them down," Anne said. "Maybe you're a great writer and you don't even know it."

Eleanor tilted her head. "I might. That's not a bad idea. But don't tell anybody; they might think it's too much like work. Anyway, I gave up on horror movies because I don't think they're worth a damn in building my character. Another guy told me I should go rock-climbing to build my character. I think I might like that, but the opportunity never arose. Do you like them? Horror movies?"

"No. Or horror books either. I hate being scared. Who are all these guys who give you so much advice?"

"Just guys. Every guy I've ever known has given me advice. Do I look like I need it?"

Anne shook her head. "You look like you can take care of yourself."

"Well, sometimes. I like guys, though, and maybe I send signals without knowing it, asking for help. I'm not always sure about what to do next, you know. I kind of go in spurts, and sometimes I wonder how I got where I was and why I'm there and where I might end up next. How about you? Do you have guys telling you how to behave, trying to teach you to do things their way?"

Anne jumped to her feet. "I have to go."

"Where?" Eleanor looked up but did not move. "If you don't want to talk about something, just change the subject. I don't get insulted. Do you really have to go? 'Cause if you don't, we could talk some more. I'm having a great time. I thought maybe you were, too. I thought maybe we could be really good friends."

A small flame of gratitude flickered to life within Anne. For the first time since she had left home, the cold, hard dryness inside her began to soften. Slowly, she sat down, and very slowly she smiled, a wider smile than the first one. "I'd like that," she said.

From then on, Anne and Eleanor were together every day. They strolled the streets of Haight Ashbury and the park, they joined clusters of people who made room for them in their lazy conversations and songfests. It seemed to Anne that everyone was filled with love and kindness, and they tried to make everyone happy by reaching out to anyone who wandered by. They accepted differences in each other, and so they were casual about the snappishness Anne still could not always control, and the way she shrank from their touch. And they were just as casual when she began to relax as she grew accustomed to them and closer to Eleanor. All that summer Anne responded, without realizing she was doing it, to the undemanding warmth of people she barely knew: an atmosphere of easygoing affection that was like a salve on the wounds she had brought to the Haight.

And then it was autumn. The sun's rays were lower, casting a warm glow on the houses of the neighborhood, and the shadows of trees lay like long feathers across the festive streets. Anne had been there for six months. She was still the only one, it seemed, who was not always in physical contact with someone in that climate of touch and feel and love. But still, she belonged, and even though she never danced or sang with the others, she liked listening to their harmony and watching their sensual movements.

She went with them when they headed for streetcars to hand flowers to commuters. She stood in line with them to fill out forms for unemployment compensation and food stamps; she bought groceries and ate her meals with them; she traded her favorite books with them. Often she slept on the third floor of the house Don Santelli had taken her to, but frequently she stayed in Eleanor's house, or the two of them would stay in yet another house, on other mattresses or cots or couches, waking up to have breakfast with a different group and then going outside to spend the day with still others. In all those ways, she was part of the fluid life of the Haight without completely joining it, and she thought it was enough. She didn't need touching, and she certainly did not need love.

It was that September that Anne realized she could greet by name more than a hundred of her neighbors, and she met more every day and learned all about them. They made it easy, because they talked about themselves all the time. They never asked questions, saying they respected everyone's privacy; instead they told their life stories and their views of the universe to anyone who would listen. Anne liked to listen. She also remembered everything she was told, and the next day or the next week she would greet people by name and ask them about something important to them. She hadn't realized how much that meant to people, or how good she was at it, but she learned very quickly that it paid off in popularity. People liked her, they liked talking to her, and soon they sought her out so she could be their listener.

"You ought to charge," Eleanor said as she and Anne walked to the grocery store at the end of September and were stopped by people every few steps. "You could call yourself a psychiatrist. Nobody'd ask for a diploma; they'd just be totally grateful for somebody who listens and cares about them. And they'd pay you. They should, too."

Anne grinned. "They'd find other ears in a hurry if all of a sudden mine cost money."

"No, they'd want you," Eleanor insisted. "I could organize it for you, make appointments and send bills and collect your money and all those things."

Anne gave her a look of mock astonishment. "A respectable job. Your parents would freak out. Eleanor comes to her senses and gets a job. Almost as if she never left home."

"Home is nothing like here," Eleanor said emphatically. "Even if I did get a job." She walked in silence, her face suddenly brooding, and Anne knew she was thinking of home. They all did that now and then: they withdrew into some private place to remember, because some word or picture or stray thought had brought back their homes in that mystical glow that bathed Anne's family whenever she let herself think about them. Then they would remember all the problems of growing up that they hadn't been able to handle, and soon they'd rejoin the conversation and be part of the group once again.

"Anyway, it wouldn't be a real job if I did it for you," Eleanor said. "I wouldn't take pay; I'd do it to help you. That's what makes life good: friendship. Not money. Money fouls up everything." She pulled out her wallet to pay for the groceries, and they both broke into laughter. "Well, it's nice to have when you're hungry," Eleanor said, counting her change. "You're eating at my house tonight, don't forget."

"Oh, I can't. I promised Don I'd help him with his birthday dinner."

Eleanor sighed. "I told you I had somebody I wanted you to meet."

"And I told you I don't want to meet anyone." They left the grocery store carrying string bags bulging with food. They wore long, flowing sundresses and sandals and walked leisurely in the dappled light beneath plane trees that swayed gently in the afternoon breeze. "We keep going through this; why can't I be happy sleeping alone?"

"Because it's unnatural. I've got all these guys and you haven't even got one. I know you don't want to talk about it, but you've been here six months and it's time you tried something new. There's tons of neat guys around; more than enough for both of us. Why won't you at least try? This is an essential part of growing up. Go to a movie with us, have a pizza, sit around and smoke—"

"I don't smoke."

"I know and I love you anyway. But you do other things. How about bed? However old you really are, you must know all about it, and you must have fooled around a few times; everybody over twelve does, these days." She peered at Anne's face. "I know, I know, the subject is taboo. Okay, forget it. But would you do me a favor? Would you please come to me first when you feel like having a guy? So I can recommend somebody and make sure you're all right? Will you at least do that?"

"Yes," Anne said gravely. "Thank you."

Eleanor gazed at her. "Of course you could know a lot more than you're letting on."

"I could," Anne agreed, "but that would come out if I ever asked you for help."

Eleanor sighed. "It's totally impossible to get you to talk about something you don't want to talk about. You ought to be a scientist doing top-secret research."

"Instead of a psychiatrist?"

"Well, one or the other."

"I can't be either, if I don't go to college."

There was a silence. "I liked school," Eleanor said. "But I would have died before I told my parents that."

They reached Eleanor's house and sat on the front steps. Anne opened a bag of potato chips and held it between them. "I liked parts of it. I liked finding out how things work and why people do the crazy things they do."

"I liked math," Eleanor said. "I loved it when the numbers came out the way I wanted them to. It made me feel totally powerful."

"I liked learning about strikes and riots and wars and how they ended. We had mock trials in class, and I liked finding out who was at fault and making sure they got punished."

"I liked English Composition. I could make up stories and nobody called it lying."

They contemplated the street scene, waving to their friends. Anne sighed and took another handful of potato chips. "I don't know what I'm going to do."

It was easiest to do nothing. There were no timetables or schedules in Haight Ashbury; the days flowed into each other like long ocean swells, and when they were gone, they left no trace. Eating, sleeping, dancing, singing, even standing in line for food stamps, all happened when anyone wanted them to happen. Groups drifted together when they were in the mood; people ate when they were hungry and slept, day or night, when they felt like it; and the sense of free-floating time without urgency always was the same. And the seasons flowed into each other, just like the days, leaving no trace when they were gone. And then it was spring again, a year since Anne had arrived.

"A little dull around here," Eleanor said one day in April when a long spring rain had ended and the trees were shaking off drops of water beneath a cloudless sky. "How about going for a ride?"

"In what?" Anne asked.

"I borrowed a car from the friend I was with last night. I've been all over San Francisco in streetcars and buses and I'm tired of it. And you haven't done it at all; you always want to stay put. Come on. I'll even teach you to drive, if you want."

The car was an old Studebaker convertible that clanked and gurgled ominously, but Eleanor seemed unconcerned. She drove fast and intently, hunched over the wheel, reading street signs aloud, turning sharply when she made last-minute decisions to check out an interesting-looking street. "I think we're going to need some money to go over this thing," she said as she turned at the sign for the Oakland Bay Bridge. "Do you have any change?"

Anne gave her a handful of quarters. She was reveling in their speed. The wind blew her hair and made her feel she was flying. For an hour the city had spun past in a blur of pastel-colored houses and bright gardens, the gleam of cable cars' lacquered wood, and the kaleidoscope of the streets: women in flowered dresses, men and women in sober business suits, police in uniforms, nannies in white dresses, waiters in black trousers and long white aprons in outdoor cafés, children in jeans and sweatshirts. It was a life infinitely larger and more wondrously varied than Haight Ashbury, and Anne suddenly realized how good it was to be part of the whole world.

In Berkeley, Eleanor drove more slowly, past small shops and restaurants, and then she turned into the hills that rose above the town. "Let's go there," Anne said. "Maybe we can climb that tower." She pointed to a white campanile rising above the trees. As they came close to it, she gazed at the people they passed. "Where are we? It looks almost like the Haight."

"The university," Eleanor said. "Berkeley. You should have seen it last year; God, it was a great show. Speeches, marches, sit-ins . . . fantastic vibes. I never did know what it was all about; I'm not sure all of *them* did. They talked a lot about free speech, but it looked to me like the more they talked the more they had it. I don't know; I wasn't part of it, but it looked weird to me. All those kids who never left home until their mommies and daddies paid for it, and they're here because their mommies and daddies keep on paying for it, and then all of a sudden they're yelling that they want free speech. I figured I already had it in the Haight so I went home. I thought they were really stupid."

"Were you jealous?" Anne asked.

Eleanor shot her a glance. "Maybe." Her voice was subdued. "Probably. They're not stupid; they're a lot smarter than me. They get along with their parents and get their way paid to college."

They drove up the hill, past classroom buildings, past the campanile. "Do you want to see if we can climb it?" Eleanor asked.

"I'd just like to walk awhile. Could we?"

"Sure."

They walked in silence, and Anne looked at the students walking and bicycling and sprawling beneath trees. It didn't look like the Haight, she thought. These people had something to do. They wore backpacks or carried their books; they sat on benches reading books; they lounged on the steps of buildings with books piled beside them. Suddenly, sharply, she wanted to know what was in those books.

"Let's go in," she said, and walked toward one of the buildings.

"We can't; we don't belong."

Anne went inside and stood in the long corridor. She breathed deeply. "I remember that smell. It's a school smell." She opened a classroom door and walked to the front of the room and read aloud what was written on the blackboard. "'Fathers and daughters in the novels of Jane Austen.'" She read it again, silently, and wished she could be in this class.

Outside, she contemplated the students with their books. She had read Jane Austen, but alone, not with any help. Everyone around here knew more about Jane Austen than she did; they knew more about everything. They'll be able to do anything they want with their lives, she thought. And I'll be braiding flowers in the Haight.

The campanile was ringing. "Hey, what's the hurry?" Eleanor demanded as students rushed past them on their way to class.

Anne moved to the side. "They all have things to do." She felt left out.

"Everybody has things to do," Eleanor said.

"We don't."

"Sure we do. We eat and sleep and sit in the park and sing and give flowers to people to make them feel good . . ."

"It isn't enough!" Anne blurted out. She kicked a stone across the sidewalk. They were almost alone in the expanse of grass and trees, and she pictured the students taking their places in the classrooms, opening their books, learning things. "I don't mean *you're* not enough," she said to Eleanor. "You're wonderful. You're the best friend anybody could ever have. But it's like we're atrophying back there. We're like . . . specimens in a museum. Nobody gets any older in the Haight; nobody grows up. Don't you feel that? Don't you want to do other things? Like learn how to write, and maybe get published? Or do some more math and feel powerful? I don't feel powerful. Do you?"

"Well, I never was," Eleanor said. She watched Anne kick another stone, and she kicked one, too. They kicked stones as they walked. "I was always pretty weak, you know; I mean, basically I just went along. The only time I didn't was when I came out here, and I did that 'cause I was with a guy. I didn't tell you that, but it's true."

Anne looked at her quickly. "That doesn't mean anything. You're not weak at all. You just haven't figured out how to believe in yourself. I believe in you; I think you can do anything. I think lots of people live their whole lives and never find out all the things they could do with themselves, and then they get old and they look back and wonder what happened because not very *much* happened and now they're about to die. If I was old, I'd be really mad that I hadn't tried to do everything I could as fast as I could." She took a deep breath. "So I think we should come here."

Eleanor frowned. "What?"

"We'll come here, and we'll learn everything, and then we'll do something big and important so people will talk about us and wish they were us. Nobody'll ever do that if we stay in the Haight all our lives. Ellie, listen." She put her hand on Eleanor's arm. "We can do it. We'll live in the Haight, for a while anyway, 'cause it's cheap, but we'll come here every day. And we'll study together."

Eleanor shook her head. "I'm not smart enough." She walked on. "I told you."

Anne caught up to her. "That's not the problem. The problem is that you think your parents want you to be smart, so you say you won't do it. Listen, they didn't want you to be smart; they wanted you to be dumb."

Eleanor shot her a glance. "They wanted me to go to college."

"They wanted you to do what you were told, just do it, don't debate it. Isn't that right? Why would a smart person do that? A smart person wants to know what the alternatives are; she wants to try everything and find out what feels best for her. And what does a dumb person do? She stays home and follows somebody else's itinerary and never complains. Isn't that what your parents wanted?"

Eleanor stared at her. "They said they wanted me to be smart."

"They probably meant it, but what do *they* know?"

They burst out laughing. "You're good," Eleanor said. "Pretty convincing." They came to the car. "Maybe you ought to be a lawyer."

"Instead of a psychiatrist or a research scientist?"

"Well, whatever. You could probably do anything you decide to do."

"What I've decided," Anne said as they drove off, "is that I'm going back to school."

"School?" demanded Don Santelli the next night at dinner. "Why would you go to school when you've got all this?"

"Because," Anne said. It was her sixteenth birthday, and she was lingering over birthday cake with Don and Eleanor after everyone else had drifted off. The cake had eighteen candles. "I love it here and everybody's nice, but it's always the same. It doesn't go anywhere."

"Exactly why we're here," said Don. "If we wanted to go somewhere, we would have stayed wherever we came from."

They smiled. "It's like the park," Anne said. "I can see the beginning of it, and a little way in, but I can't see far enough to know what kind of place it is or what I might do inside it. That's my life. I haven't got any idea what it's going to be like in the middle and at the end. Once I thought it was going to be awful"—her voice wavered and she steadied it—"and it would go on that way forever and there was nothing I could do about it. But I did do something and I found all this, and it's wonderful, but I don't want it to go on forever, either."

"Forever sounds fine to me," Don said defensively. "This place is the best there is. It has people who make you feel good and a place to belong. What more do you want?"

When I grow up, I'll be better than all of them. And I'll be very happy.

The thought came and went swiftly, but for that brief moment, Anne saw again her flowered bedroom, her packed duffel bag, and the morning light as she walked to the railroad station. I will be better than all of them, she thought. I will be happy.

"I want to know things," she replied to Don. "I keep asking *why*. It's always in my head. *Why did this happen?* I have to understand things, or I don't feel right. I don't feel *whole*."

"Whole," Don echoed, shaking his head. "I don't get that."

"It's just that I can't stand it when there are loose ends dangling." Anne met his puzzled look. She cast about for something they could share. "And also, if I learn a lot, I'll be able to do things for people who need help."

"That's your problem? You want to do good deeds? Anne the Good." He shook his head. "You can't make people happy and solve the problems of the world by working at them; nobody pays attention. You stay with us, Annie; we're the example; we're the ones who'll change the world. People can see how loving and *sane* we are, and they'll want to live like us, and then there won't be any more unhappiness. Everybody will be happy."

"And asleep," Anne said with a smile.

He did not return her smile. "They'll still be plenty awake, and plenty alive. You didn't make fun of us when we took you in; you liked us a lot and you sure weren't in any hurry to leave."

"I still like you. And I'm not in a hurry to leave; I want to stay here. But I want to go to college, too."

"You told me you didn't finish high school."

"I didn't. But there's a GED test I can take, and if I pass it, I get my high school diploma, and then I take the SAT test and some Achievement tests, and if I pass them, they'll let me in and I'll be a freshman."

"God, you've *researched* this thing. And where's all this supposed to happen?"

"Berkeley," said Eleanor. "I guess I'm going to try to go, too."

Don reared back in his chair. "Listen, we're *happy* here. Why are you messing it up? Damn it, all those problems out there . . . we don't even have to think about them as long as we stay here where it's safe. I thought you felt the same way."

"I did, for a while." Impatience flared inside Anne; why couldn't he understand? He's afraid, she thought; he's where I was a year ago. But I don't ever want to be like that again. She met Don's defensive look. "It was really nice, thinking you'd always take care of me, but I just can't believe that anymore. *I* have to take care of me. But how do I do that? I don't know anything; I feel so dumb! I need to know things, millions of things, I have to pile them up like . . . like filling a storeroom. Like if there's a blizzard coming, you know you can take care of yourself if you've got everything you need in the storeroom. That's what I want, to be ready for bad things. That's why I'm going to school. I'll still be here, Don; we'll still be friends, but you can't talk me out of this. I have to do it."

Don stopped arguing. He never talked about it again, even after Anne passed all her tests and entered Berkeley that fall. He felt she had betrayed and belittled him and everyone else who lived in the Haight, by choosing a way of life their parents had wanted for them. She even had gotten a job, as if to show them how different she was: she was waiting on tables at breakfast and lunch in a restaurant near the campus. As far as Don was concerned, she had become someone else, and it didn't make any difference that she still lived in the Haight because she stayed on the third floor and no one saw her but Eleanor.

She still slept on her mattress, and her clothes were still folded neatly in boxes, but now she had a desk. She had found it in the basement, and cleaned and polished it, and she and some friends had carried it and an old piano stool to the third floor. She bought a lamp and notebooks and pencils at Woolworth's, placing them on the desk in precise order. Just looking at them made her feel like a student. And that was where she worked every night, until long after midnight, hunched over her books in a small circle of lamplight while the others who lived there straggled in, talked among themselves, played music, and finally went to sleep. Anne barely heard them. She heard only the words of the books she was reading.

"It's too much work," Eleanor said at Christmas, dropping the books she had brought home for vacation on Anne's desk. "Do I really want to do this much work? Does anybody? You like it, don't you? Every bit of it."

"Most of it," Anne said. She felt almost apologetic. "It's exciting, putting pieces together so things make sense. That's the best of all."

Eleanor shook her head: "I just can't get into it." She flipped open one of her books. "All I know is I'm working my ass off learning about algorithms and revolutionary wars, and who really gives a damn?"

Anne looked at her somberly. "Are you going to drop out?"

"God, Anne, it's eerie the way you see through people. As a matter of fact . . . well, I've been thinking about it."

"Couldn't you wait? Just finish this one year? It's only until May."

"What's the point?"

Anne looked at her books and the pads of paper filled with her neat handwriting. "I guess the point is different for everybody." She smiled at Eleanor. "Maybe I'm just afraid of being left alone on campus."

"You've made lots of friends there."

"I've made acquaintances."

"Well, you'll make plenty of friends. And then one day at the restaurant you'll wait on a handsome, successful businessman worth megabucks who'll carry you off in his carriage and take care of you forever and—" She stopped abruptly. Their eyes met. "I sound like my mother."

"I think you're getting ready to go home." Anne heard the wistfulness in her voice at the idea of home. "I'll miss you so much."

"Hey, I'm not disappearing, you know. I haven't even made up my mind for sure."

Anne studied her face. "You're going home for Christmas."

"I never told you that."

"No, it just seemed obvious."

"God, I hate being obvious. Well, but it's just a visit. I thought I'd surprise them. Christmas is such a big deal with them, you know. Not with me; I couldn't care less. But they're really into it and I wasn't there for the last two—I didn't even send a Christmas card—and it would mean a lot to them . . ."

Anne nodded seriously. "It's very nice of you to do that for them."

"That's what I thought. And I have a lot to think about, and maybe it's easier there than here. I mean, I don't know what I want. It seemed so simple when I came out here, but now it's all mixed up. I really love you, Anne, but you've changed, you know. It's like you don't need me very much anymore. And I feel pretty alone at Berkeley, like I'm in the wrong place. I don't know where the right place is; I guess that's what I have to figure out. Where I really want to be and what I really want to do."

"Then I think you ought to be home, with people who can help you decide."

"You really do? Honest to God? I don't want to run away from the Haight, you know; I ran away to come here, and it seems awfully childish to do it again in the other direction."

"You're not running away. You're going home to formulate a plan of action for the rest of your life."

Eleanor grinned. "What a great way to put it. *You're* great, Anne; you really are terrific. I was afraid to tell you, and now you've made me feel good."

"Why were you afraid to tell me?"

"I thought you'd be sad."

"I am. But I'm happy for you."

"I'll write, you know. And phone? We'll talk all the time."

"Where will you be?"

"I told you. Home."

"But I don't know where home is. You never told me."

"Oh. Well, neither did you."

"Lake Forest, north of Chicago."

"Saddle River. New Jersey."

"New Jersey," Anne echoed. "Such a long way." She hurt inside with the pain of parting and of knowing she would be alone again.

"I'll probably end up back here," Eleanor said. "I really love it. Just let me know where to find you, whatever you're doing." She picked up her books. "I'll keep these. You never know."

"When are you leaving?"

"Tomorrow. I, uh, they sent me a ticket. I thought, *I* sure can't afford it, and if that's what they really want, why not let them do it."

Anne nodded. "You'll have a wonderful time."

They hugged each other, and Eleanor went back to her house. Anne stood beside her desk. She looked around the large bare room with five mattresses. She peered through the round window above her own mattress, just as she had when she first arrived, and gazed at the houses across the street and the streams of people below. This neighborhood had been her refuge for nearly two years. But Eleanor was right: she was changing.

And even more drastically, Haight Ashbury was changing. At first Anne barely noticed it; she spent little time there, and when she did, she was always at her desk. But after a while, she could not miss the changes, or pretend they were unimportant. They were too big, and too harsh.

The changes had been slow at first, beginning with a few television and newspaper reporters. Then, suddenly, it seemed that people with notebooks and cameras were always on the streets and in the park, interviewing what they called "the flower children." Pictures of girls with long hair and headbands and men with tattoos and earrings were in *Time* and *Newsweek;* psychologists wrote heavy stories analyzing why young people became hippies; camera crews who had filmed the Summer of Love came back and tried to arrange other dramatic events for the nightly news and television specials on drugs and dropouts. Gray Line buses with sealed windows began bringing tourists to the Haight, inching through the traffic of gawkers and the hippies who walked alongside, holding up mirrors for drivers and passengers to see themselves. Some of the hippies still talked about love and joy, but no one listened; the simple years of the Haight were gone.

Don Santelli and his friends stayed inside, refusing to be interviewed or filmed. But the bright lights, the tantalizing lens of the camera, the gapers in the streets, and the idea of a national audience were too much for many of them to resist, and they began to create new kinds of theater meant to shock and get ever more attention. The quiet people left the Haight. Shopkeepers closed their stores and moved out as heroin replaced marijuana and drug dealers took over street corners. Litter swirled on the sidewalks where men and women had sung and danced and Anne and Eleanor had walked home from the grocery store.

It's not my place anymore, Anne thought, straightening up from the round window. It hasn't been for a long time; I just didn't pay attention. She almost never saw Don anymore; he avoided her. He was filled with anger, at Anne for being in school, at the reporters and invading tourists, at the drug dealers who had sent shopkeepers fleeing. His friends were leaving in the first wave of a mass exodus of hippies who were starting communes near Big Sur and Eureka and other rural areas. And Eleanor was leaving in the morning.

And so am I, Anne decided. If I have to begin again, I'll do it the way I did before, with no ties at all.

Friends in one of her classes had told her there was a room for rent in the house they shared near the campus. It wasn't the Haight, with its magical love and openness, but it wasn't solitariness, either. She would have a job, a place to live, people to talk to, and her books.

And my future, she thought. The last time, she had fled in terror of her life and in anguish over her aloneness in her own family. Now she was moving on because she had a place to go and a life to make. *And no one will ever make me afraid or helpless again.*

She turned away from the window and took her duffel bag from a shelf in the closet. It was time to go.

chapter 6

*V*ince had forgotten what she looked like. At first, when he left Lake Forest and moved to Denver, he saw her face everywhere, all his rage focused on her. But Denver was a long way from Lake Forest, and as the years passed and he became the city's most powerful developer, he barely thought of her. When he did, it was with a kind of automatic anger, the kind he felt toward Rita, another bitch who never missed a chance to make things hard for him. Occasionally an image came to him, almost always when he was in bed with someone, of bits and pieces of Anne Chatham: a slender hand pushing heavy black hair away from her eyes, bony knees, thin arms, small breasts, wide eyes looking at him without emotion, the hard core of her hatred that he had loved to smash.

He had not called it hatred then; he had not given it a name. Until the night she set out to destroy him. When he thought of it, he could call up, in an instant, his mounting fury at that dinner, and his cold vow, when she had vanished, to make his father pay for the sudden collapse of everything he had planned. He would destroy Chatham Development; he would see that Ethan lost Tamarack; he would make the family lose everything.

But that remembered anger always faded, as did the image of Anne. Vince never allowed himself to be weakened by the tug of memories or emotion or remorse.

Right now, he was far too busy to dwell on the past. He

was making his reputation. And he was making Denver his own.

He had moved there because of Ray Beloit, a fast-talking, high-stakes builder who thought of Denver as one big poker hand that he knew how to play. "Get your greedy ass out here," he told Vince on the telephone when Vince called him while cleaning out his office at Chatham Development. "There's still gold out here in the West, only now it's called climate and open space and lifestyle. This place is growing like crazy and you and me could build up a storm. Take my word for it. My word is as good as my wallet."

Vince had been in Denver often on his way to Tamarack; he knew its possibilities. The city beckoned newcomers, as it always had, by being the last oasis on the dusty plains before the mountains rose like battlements to the west. It had been growing slowly for years, but there were still thousands of empty acres scattered between its borders and the foothills. Downtown Denver was a tight cluster of skyscrapers standing like sentinels in the flat landscape, the tallest man-made structures between Omaha and Los Angeles. They stood shoulder to shoulder, rising from a sprawling mosaic of neighborhoods, and nearby, the gold-domed state capitol gazed serenely at the long, jagged line of the Rocky Mountains in the distance, clear as cutouts most days but occasionally blurred by a haze of yellow-brown smog that some experts were predicting was going to be the dark side of Denver's boom. Floating on the vast plain, Denver had an unfinished look compared to the granite and steel of Chicago, and as Vince walked its streets in his first weeks there, he was already envisioning the changes he would make. There were those thousands of acres on the outskirts filled only with sagebrush and wild grass; there were empty lots within the city limits; there were entire blocks of squat buildings begging to be replaced by skyscrapers. Vince walked through Denver and knew it was a city waiting to be conquered.

He had $25 million from the sale of his shares in Chatham Development—enough to set himself up as a prime developer and to live as well as he chose. He rented a duplex apartment in a luxury building, hired a New York decorator to furnish it, and used his connections from Lake Forest to move easily into Denver society. Less than a month after he arrived, he and Ray Beloit had opened an office and were planning their first purchase of land. That was when Charles called.

"I had to get your number from the operator," he said. "I thought we were going to keep in touch."

"I haven't had time. Has anything happened?"

"If you mean have we heard from Anne, we haven't. We fired the detective and we've got another one; hell, we've got two of them, from different agencies, but they don't seem any better than the first; they keep telling us not to expect too much. I don't know how much time they're really putting into it; nobody seems to care much about teenage runaways. It's like a tomb around here, Vince; you're lucky to be out of it. What are you doing with yourself? You hardly need to work with what you got for your shares . . ." There was a pause. "I wanted to go with you, you know."

Vince was silent.

"I thought we could start our own company somewhere else, away from all the pressure around here. We could have handled . . . what Anne said . . . whatever she meant by it—"

"You know what she meant. She accused me of raping her. And you stood there and let her do it; you didn't do a fucking thing for me."

"Christ, we went through this before you left; don't you ever let go? I'm caught in the middle here, Vince; I'm trying to understand both of you. How the hell could I do anything for you that night? You wanted me to call my daughter a liar; I couldn't do it."

"Why not? She is one."

"Don't call her that! Whatever she did, poor kid, dreamed it, or made it up for some crazy reason, whatever happened, a father has to be sympathetic. You'd be the same with Dora."

"Dora would never be that kind of girl."

"What kind of girl? Oh, for Christ's sake, look, I'm having

enough trouble; don't make it worse. I can't stand it that Anne's gone, that she ran away from us; I keep wanting to fix things between us. I was a pretty good father, you know; I always went to her school plays and spelling bees—she won every spelling bee, and I was damned proud of her—and I bought her whatever she wanted. I guess we weren't quite as close as we could've been; I've been thinking about it, and I guess we didn't really talk very much. And now I can't even talk to her about *that!* And if you can't understand that I'm feeling frustrated—and I miss her, too, you know—then the hell with it; we won't talk anymore. I won't call again; it's not worth it."

"We'll talk about something else," Vince said quickly, suddenly realizing that he did not want to lose this only connection with his family. "Is anything else going on?"

"No, it's quiet. Too quiet. We've all gone in different directions; we haven't had a Sunday dinner since she left. It's hard to believe. She was such a quiet little girl, half the time we didn't even know she was around, but now you can't go anywhere in the house without thinking about her. And then you're gone, too, Vince—both of you in the same week—it's like everything fell apart. That's what Dad said: everything fell apart. He's gone, too; he went to Tamarack last week and didn't say when he'd be back."

"To do what? What's he doing there?"

"I don't know; I suppose he's decided to start expanding it again. I thought he wanted to keep it small, but he doesn't confide in me; he never did. What are you doing in Denver?"

"I've started my own company. Did he take anybody with him?"

"You mean contractors or architects? Not that I know of. If he's really expanding, he'll probably use locals. Maybe some people from Denver. I guess you'll hear about it if he does. You started a company by yourself?"

"I've got a partner who's been around long enough to know the right people."

"God, I wish I could be there, part of what you're doing.

Starting in a new place, with nobody looking over your shoulder . . . Maybe I could do it next year."

"You figure it out," Vince said indifferently. "Let me know in advance."

"But we'll be talking. We have to keep in touch, Vince."

"Right."

"I mean it, Vince. I miss you. I always counted on you, you know, especially when we were starting something new; you see things clearer than I do, the whole project, start to finish, before we even get going. I can't do that; I can't imagine things I've never seen. It haunts me, you know; I can't get past it. Right now I'm worried about the Long Grove mall; we're supposed to start next month and I just can't get a feel for it. I need somebody to talk to; somebody who can help me envision the whole thing."

"Ask William."

"He's not you."

"Well, call me when you want to talk. You'll figure it out." Vince was bored. He wanted to stay in touch, but he would not play nursemaid. "I have a meeting; I'll call you in a week or two."

"Shall I say hello to anyone for you?"

"Anybody you want. Tell them I miss them."

It was an easy thing to say, the kind of empty phrase that could keep doors propped open even after the worst kind of family crisis.

"Smart fella," said Ray Beloit when Vince went into his office and told him why he was late for their meeting. "It's good to keep up with your family; family ties are thicker than water."

Beloit, ten years older than Vince, had been urging Vince to come to Denver since they'd met in Tamarack. He wanted a partner, a developer who could look at an aging building or a piece of empty land and see a shopping center or an office complex or an industrial park, and then forge ahead and make it happen. He wanted someone willing to risk money and time to turn a sleepy Western capital into a hot, modern city, and make a fortune doing it. "I like ambitious men in a hurry," he said. "I'm the same way. A genuine go-getter; a terrific, first-class A-one achiever."

Ray Beloit was his own greatest fan. He could not bear the tension of waiting for others to admire him, so he did it himself. Everyone in Colorado business and politics knew that Beloit would tell them frequently and glowingly about his achievements, and that they need only nod or murmur agreement for him to be satisfied. "A couple of highfliers; that's why we're a good team," he said, clapping Vince on the shoulder, and Vince, who hated to be clapped on the shoulder, forced himself not to jerk away. He needed Beloit.

He named their company Lake Forest Development, even though their office was west of Denver, facing the foothills, turning its back on Chicago and Lake Forest, just as Vince had, forever.

"Odd name," said Beloit, "but if you got your heart set on it, I'll go along; it's no skin off my nose. We'll make it big whatever it's called. You want to go to a movie with me and Lorraine tonight?"

"I have a date."

"Good. Good. I like a man who keeps busy. Like me. I don't let grass grow under rolling stones. Full steam ahead and watch for the whites of their eyes. She anybody special?"

"No."

"Well, take your time. Look around. You wade out of a divorce, you don't want to sink into hot water again." He clapped Vince on the shoulder. His hand was large and padded, like a bear's paw, and he resembled a bear, with his heavy face and small nose, his dense mustache, moist lips, powerful shoulders, and long arms. He walked with a forward lunge that made strangers think he was about to scoop them up, and those who thought they might have offended him scurried to put distance between them. Vince liked the faintly threatening aura that radiated from Beloit; even more, he liked his connections. Beloit knew everyone in and around Denver; he knew their secrets, their hungers, their alliances, their private wars. And that was the kind of knowledge a man needed to get where he was going as fast as Vince intended to go.

All through those early years, he flew to Chicago one weekend a month, to see Dora. He liked thinking of himself as a father, knowing he was shaping a pliable mind. That was why people had children in the first place, he thought; to have total power over another human being, to determine, without interference, the kind of person that creature would be. But as much as he enjoyed being a father, he also took pleasure in preventing Rita from having everything her way. As soon as the judge ordered her to allow him access to his daughter for two days a month, Vince was on a plane for Chicago, and after that he never missed a visit, except for rare occasions when he and Beloit had a crisis.

"I'd like her to come to me next time," he said to Rita one weekend when Dora was six. He had been in Denver for less than a year, but already he and Beloit had bought land and were developing plans for an office tower in Denver and a small shopping center in Colorado Springs. He sat in Rita's peach and silver living room on a bitterly cold Sunday evening in February, looking amiable and successful. "I'll take her to the mountains, teach her to ski; she'd love that."

"She stays in Chicago," Rita said.

Vince shook his head mournfully. "How much longer are you going to make me pay? I've been here every month since last May; I've given Dora all my attention and bought her whatever she wanted . . . haven't I been a good father?"

She shrugged.

"Rita, haven't I? Tell me! I want to be a good father, but this is all new to me and I'm not always sure what I should be doing. We don't have a normal home and family, and I'm trying to do the best I can. Rita, it's for Dora's sake, not mine! Tell me what I'm doing wrong!"

"Nothing," Rita said reluctantly. She glanced at his angelic face and saw tears glistening in his warm brown eyes.

"She's not as beautiful as her mother," he went on, almost wistfully, "but isn't she lovely? And smart as a whip, and a

111

wonderful athlete. Did she tell you we played hopscotch and she won?"

Rita smiled, drawn to his charm, as so many times before. Then she jumped to her feet and went to the far end of the room. She bit her lip. "She can't go to Colorado. I want her here, not in an apartment alone with you."

Vince stared at her. "You still think . . . Good God, Rita, you can't believe that! Whatever else you've ever believed—and that little bitch lied!—you can't believe that I'd do anything to my own daughter!"

Rita avoided his beseeching eyes. "I don't want her in Colorado."

A long sigh broke from Vince. "Maybe someday you'll relent. I thought it would be good for Dora to see where I live, and my office, and what I'm building. Of course we probably won't break ground for another year; maybe by then Dora will be able to . . ." He let the words trail away. Rita stared out the window at the lights of Lake Shore Drive. "If you'll just think about it," Vince said humbly, "I'd be very grateful." He stood and picked up his coat. "I thought I'd take her for pizza; I booked a later flight tonight. Is that all right with you?"

"Fine."

"I'll have her back in a couple of hours. I won't come up with her; I'll go on to the airport."

Rita nodded.

"And I'll see you next month."

She nodded again.

Vince watched her profile, a small smile on his lips. She'd come around. Women always came around with him. There was a moment there, when she'd leaned toward him . . . He knew it would happen again. He walked down the hallway to Dora's room. "How about some pizza?"

"Oh, yes!" She jumped up from the doll's house he had bought her that afternoon. It sat in a corner of the room with the dozens of stuffed animals, dolls, craft kits, building blocks, Lego sets, and games he had lavished on her since the divorce. She ran to him. "I love pizza. Uno's or Due's?"

"You choose. The pizza's the same in both of them."

"Uno's. It's dark and smoky and more like a place for grown-ups."

Vince chuckled. "You're a very grown-up young woman."

"I know," she said seriously. "I don't think childhood is a very big deal. Are we going?"

"Right now." He followed her to the coat closet near the front door, and when she handed him her coat, he held it for her. He watched as she wrapped a cashmere scarf at her neck and carefully buttoned the coat around it. He liked looking at her because it was almost like looking at himself. Her short blond hair curled in exactly the same way as his, her brown eyes were the same shape as his and could switch from warm to calculating almost as swiftly as his, her smile was as sweet. Her chin, like his, was a little too sharp, but in spite of it her face had an angelic beauty that was like his own.

Even more than her looks, Vince liked her precocious maturity. He had never liked babies or young children, and it was only by skipping much of her childhood that Dora got his attention.

"It's very cold outside," she said, pulling on a cashmere beret that matched her scarf. "I hope you're dressed properly."

"We'll be in a taxi," Vince said. "Shouldn't you say good-bye to your mother? She gets very upset if you forget."

"No, she doesn't. We've discussed it."

"Oh." He was disconcerted. "Well, that's good. She used to worry about that sort of thing all the time."

"Did she," said Dora coldly. She waited in silence at the elevator, and when it arrived, she walked ahead of Vince, nodding a greeting to the elevator man. She looked up at her father and smiled sweetly, unnerving him with her instant switch in emotions that was exactly like his. "I'm starved, Daddy. What a lovely idea you had, to take me to Uno's for pizza."

He always forgot Dora as soon as he was on the plane for Denver. That was where the real challenge was; that was where he had to make sure he controlled everything that happened, to take advantage of it all, to accumulate enough wealth and power to do anything he wanted. And especially —since it had not been hard to switch his plans from Illinois to Colorado—to go into politics.

It was the best time to be in Denver, at the beginning of what would become the biggest boom in its history. For a developer like Vince, who had learned his lessons in the minefields of Chicago and Cook County politics, and a contractor like Ray Beloit, whose contacts ranged from leaders of society to shadowy figures behind the scenes, Denver's boom was a long, heady binge.

"The right place, the right time, the right people," said Beloit to himself, his voice rich with satisfaction. He was standing at the back of an office, watching Vince handle a press conference on the opening of Chatham Place, the first project for Lake Forest Development, and Denver's first enclosed shopping mall. Vince was good, he thought happily; he was the best. He fielded questions with a smile that made you love him. Vince would go a long, long way.

"How come you didn't use a Denver architect?" asked an architecture critic for the *Denver Post*.

"I wanted to," Vince said easily. He perched casually on a corner of a table beside an easel with drawings and photographs of Chatham Place in its various stages. "And I intend to, as often as I can. This time it didn't work out."

"Why not?"

"I wanted the most daring, most controversial architect in the world. He happened to be in Japan, not Denver."

"Why? Why controversial?"

"To get your attention." Vince smiled at them, his face as open and honest as a child's. "I want to put Denver up there with New York and Chicago and Rome. I want to make Colorado famous for more than recreation. Why should Colorado rely on the mountains for grandeur? We can do better than that. You give me a few years and a chance to build the other projects we have on the drawing board and you'll see Colorado lead the world in transforming the landscape. Chatham Place is only a beginning."

"What did it cost?" asked a reporter.

"Eighty-five million dollars."

"And the return?"

"Respectable. Seventy-eight percent of the shops and all the restaurants are rented and open, the athletic club is open, we have ice-skating competitions scheduled on the ice rink for the next six months. We're confident we'll have one hundred percent occupancy before the end of the year."

"What's happened with your fight with Greenbriar Village?" another reporter asked. "Those people fought like crazy to keep you out of here. How'd you shut them up?"

"We didn't have to," Vince said gently. "They know we're as interested in this community as they are. You should ask them yourself. I'll give you the names of the top community leaders; I think you'll find we've become good neighbors."

"By burning down one of their houses?" the reporter asked.

The room was hushed. Vince gave the reporter a long look. "I assume you're talking about Oscar and Emmy Delaney's house."

"Right. There was a time when the Delaneys were always going to the newspapers or TV stations or city council meetings or marching in the streets, fighting your mall, them and their neighbors. Until their house burned down."

Vince nodded. "It was a terrible thing. We built them a new house, a bigger one, and furnished it and made a play yard for their kids. Losing their house was a tragedy, but we were able to help them, and make them part of the excitement of Chatham Place, and all it says about Colorado's future and American productivity and the good life. Oscar and Emmy head up the community council that handles relations between the mall and the neighborhood, and we consider them good friends of Chatham Place. So do they." He stood. "I'm going to turn this over to Ray Beloit; he has all the facts and figures at his fingertips. When you're finished, there's a buffet lunch in the restaurant. Thank you all for coming; I hope to see you here often. *I'll* be here; I may even learn to ice-skate. If you thought I was on thin ice just now, wait till you see me on the real stuff."

They laughed, admiring his daring. The official investigation of the Delaneys' fire had been inconclusive, but rumors persisted that it had been no accident. "Quite a guy," a reporter said as Vince left the room. "Remind me never to be on the other side of anything he wants."

Assholes, Vince thought scornfully as he left the building; they won't lay a finger on us. He knew then that he had guessed right: that the reporters, as much as any business-men in Denver, wanted to fatten the city through tourists, conventions, and shoppers drawn from all the Rocky Moun-tain states, and they would turn a blind eye to rumors if prosperity was on the line. We're all such cozy partners, Vince thought with a thin smile, but as he drove to his office that morning, he felt a deep contempt for the press that he would never lose.

His secretary rang as he reached his desk. "Mr. Charles Chatham is on the telephone; he said it was important."

Vince gave a grunt of annoyance. He picked up the telephone. "Yes," he said impatiently.

"I'm sorry to interrupt," Charles said, "but I've been thinking about your offer."

Vince frowned. "What offer?"

"For God's sake, Vince, vice president of your company! When I was there last week you said—"

"I remember. Well? When will you get here?"

"I won't. I can't do it, Vince, at least not yet. Dad needs me. There's nobody else to run the company while he's in Tamarack, and this morning he told me he's going to live there. Full time. He's leaving Chicago—"

"Why?" Vince demanded.

"He says he likes it better than Chicago. He's seventy, you know; I guess he's tired and wants to get away. He told me he's satisfied I can run the company."

Vince was silent.

"Well, he's right," Charles said. "I don't do business the way he does, or you either, but he trusts me and I can't walk out on him."

Still, Vince said nothing.

"I'll be fine," Charles said loudly. "We'll just be a little more low-key around here. I know you and Dad think I'm not aggressive enough, but that's the way I am, and if some things slip by me because I don't see them right away, we'll still be fine; we'll do fine. That's the way I am; I'm not a grabber."

Or a pusher or shover or manipulator, thought Vince. But he is in trouble. Vince had guessed that because Charles never talked about himself when he came to Denver. He tagged along with Vince to dinners and cocktail parties and benefits, and it seemed all he wanted was to hear about Vince.

But he's in trouble, Vince thought again. *If some things slip by me.* He wondered what opportunities had come to Chatham Development and then gone to other companies because Charles wasn't on top of things, and never had been.

But he'd known for a long time that Charles couldn't run that company the way it should be run; it took imagination and guts and he had neither. Ethan did; Vince did. Charles was a natural errand boy, the perfect front man. What I could have done with it, Vince thought, and for a moment, in spite of the brilliant beginning he was making in Denver, the past came back, with its losses and his rage. It was all supposed to have been his. The family company. Tamarack. Anne. His wife. His daughter. Everything he'd been sure of. There wouldn't have been any trouble if Anne hadn't babbled, if Ethan hadn't defended her, if Charles had stood up for Vince, if William had been squarely on Vince's side, if Marian hadn't waffled. He deserved their support—they *owed* it to him—because he was the smartest of all of them. But they'd collapsed, and Vince was on the outside.

"And William and Fred work with me," Charles went on. "We're a pretty good team. We don't have as many irons in the fire as when you were here, but we're on an even keel, and that's fine. Things don't stay the same, after all. Everything changes. Anne turned eighteen a couple of months ago, in April, and I don't even know what she looks like now. If she'd stayed at home, she'd be in college. How could someone just *vanish?*" he burst out. "If she's working, she's got a social security number; she'd have to pay income tax; if she went back to school, she'd be registered; if she has a bank account, she'd be on file. People leave a trail, whatever they do . . . how the hell could she just be gone? I've started reading ads, you know, the personals. You wouldn't believe how many people are looking for other people. Sometimes I think the whole world must be lost and there's just a few of us who know where we belong. God, I miss her, Vince. It's a terrible thing to lose a daughter. I've lost two daughters, really; Gail doesn't have much to do with me anymore; she blames me for her sister being gone. I suppose she's right."

"She'd rather you'd called me a rapist and a liar," Vince said coldly.

"She's only twelve, Vince; she doesn't understand all that. She just misses Anne." There was a pause. "We see Dora, you know; Rita brings her for dinner sometimes. She's a beautiful little girl; she reminds me of you. Maybe sometime when you visit her you could bring her for dinner."

"When Dad invites me, I'll come for dinner," Vince said. "Is he still pretending I don't exist?"

"He doesn't talk about you, if that's what you mean. He's like steel on that, Vince. He won't say your name; he won't even stay in the room if someone mentions you."

"Does anyone mention me?"

"Not very often."

"I have to go," Vince said abruptly. "I'm busy; we just opened a new shopping mall—"

"I read about it. Chatham Place. It reminded me of Dad naming streets after the family. It sounds tremendous. Maybe one of these days I'll just drop everything and move west. Dad's doing it; next time it'll be my turn."

Not fucking likely, Vince thought. You'll never break away, little man; you haven't got the gumption to do a fucking thing on your own, not even come out here and lean on me. "Anytime," he said to Charles. "There's an office waiting for you." He sat still for a minute after they hung up. The whole family, he thought; out of ammunition. Dad's too old and now he'll be gone. I could sink Chatham Development and make them lose Tamarack, and they couldn't do a damn thing to stop me. Then they'd understand that they kicked out the wrong man. He felt a brief regret that it would not be a tougher battle.

But that was for later. He'd take care of it as soon as he had time to give it some thought.

But they were still enough in his mind that the next week he sent Charles a clipping from a *Denver Post* special Sunday supplement on Denver that called Vince "Denver's new superstar." Beloit, purposely keeping behind the scenes, was not mentioned; it was Vince Chatham, president and founder of Lake Forest Development, with his charm and photogenic blond good looks, who was the center of the story. "Put it on Dad's desk," Vince wrote in a note to Charles clipped to the story. And through the next year, when Chatham Tower, a steel-and-glass office building with Denver's first shopping arcade, opened, and ground was broken for Chatham Center, a complex of office buildings, Vince sent clippings to Charles, telling him to put them on Ethan's desk or send them to him in Tamarack. All the stories said the same thing: Vince Chatham was riding high at the center of the city's business and social life; he was becoming a hero.

From then on, he and Beloit found easy construction financing at better terms than other developers were given. In a few years they had a staff of fifty, and were building office towers, industrial parks, and developments of office and residential towers, shops, movie theaters, and town houses in Colorado, Utah, and Arizona. And Vince, who had never been a joiner or a supporter of charities, joined the boards of directors of the United Denver Charitable Society and The Boys and Girls Clubs of Denver, and contributed money to every organization that came calling.

He went from triumph to triumph. The years slid into each other and he was always on the crest of the next wave. Everywhere he looked he saw the changed skylines of Colorado and neighboring states, the buildings that sprang up under the touch of his hand and grew tall or sprawled out, filling the land. He had made himself Denver's leading citizen, Denver's most sought-after bachelor, Denver's king of construction. It was put most precisely at a banquet honoring him as Denver's Man of the Year. "Vince Chatham," said the master of ceremonies, "is the perfect role model for all the youngsters of America."

"To the whiz kids," Beloit said, lifting his glass in a toast on their fifteenth anniversary. They were in Vince's office, looking out at the mountains past acres of buildings that had not been there when they arrived. Denver's sprawling metropolis reached out new fingers of growth each year, paving the land and bringing with it a shroud of yellow-brown smog that grew more dense with each mile of expressway that was built. "Fifteen great years," said Beloit, "and here we are with projects coming like a good woman, one after the other. Best fun I ever had." He drank and refilled his glass. "You want to go out with Lorraine and me tonight and celebrate?"

"I have plans for tonight."

"Well, that's true, you usually do. All these girls, Vince; where the hell do you find them? I didn't know Denver had that many. I didn't know anywhere had that many." He paused. "You thought about getting married again?"

Vince's eyebrows raised. "Why?"

"Oh, you might be happier. Settled down. You don't have to worry about who you're gonna sleep with every night."

"I don't worry about it."

"Well, maybe you don't now, but you never know."

"What's this about, Ray?" Vince asked after a moment.

Beloit shrugged. "Lorraine and I were wondering, is all. I mean, I know it's none of my business, but I've been thinking about it; I believe in mind over what matters. And what's important here is smooth sailing. We've built up a good head of steam; I like where we're going; but calm seas make a prosperous voyage—right?—and the calmest seas come from contented partners. I've got my family, my Lorraine, my little nest in the tree of life, but you're still running around like the playboy of the Western frontier. Don't frown at me, Vince, this is fatherly advice I'm giving you." He peered at the deepening frown on Vince's face. "Okay, you don't want fatherly advice; call it a partner's advice. All I'm saying is, I'm hoping you'll get tired of this life and settle down." He sighed. "And I also worry about all those playmates. I remember how confusing it is—a different name, different positions, different conversations every week or two or whatever—and one of these nights in bed you might whisper sweet business deals in one of those pearly ears—"

Vince stood, his face dark. "You son of a bitch, if you think I'd talk, especially to a woman—"

"It's possible," Beloit said, unfazed. "A woman is a tender trap and you're a sexy kid, Vince, and it's just possible that you might get carried away by a bundle of sweet charms. Sit down, sit down; we're not fighting; we're discussing. Sometimes things come up in business and you stew about them and you feel like talking at two in the morning. You've got a wife, it's okay. Not great, but okay. I don't talk to Lorraine, but if I did, I know she'd keep her cards close to her very nice chest. So what I'm saying is, you need a nest with a little bird making you happy; you need a companion whose bread is buttered on your side. It's safe and very comfortable." He drained his glass. "That's all. Not so hard to swallow, is it?"

Vince looked at him thoughtfully. "You're not entirely a fool, Ray."

"And you're not entirely a son of a bitch," Beloit said cheerfully. "By the way, Ludlow's going to bid on Cherry Creek Point."

"Is that definite?"

"I got it from one of his backers. He's been busting his ass over it and he's got a bigger team than us. Sounds to me like he figures he can empty his piggy bank to buy the land, maybe as high as thirty million, and make a pile on whatever he builds on it. You think he'll go that high?"

"We might be able to find out. Cal Zorick used to work for him."

"I forgot that. Your new assistant. And he probably still has drinking buddies over at Ludlow. He strikes me as a little greedy."

"Probably."

"You want me to call him?"

"It might not be a bad idea."

"I'll do it now. And you'll think about what I said? About nests and little birds and all?"

"I'll think about it."

He knew Beloit was right; it was something he had to take care of. In fact, Vince had known for some time that he could not continue unattached forever. If he did, his credibility and influence in the city would erode. Conservative Denver, dedicated to prairie values of stability and close-knit social and family groups, would not applaud or welcome him beyond a certain point, and after fifteen years of high visibility on the social scene, that point was not far off.

A year at the outside, he thought. By then, he'd be married: a model husband and citizen. And then he could move on. He was getting bored with being Denver's top developer; it was almost time for him to switch careers.

The next week, he went into Beloit's office. "Have you talked to Cal?"

"I talked to him. I told him everything he already knows. I told him Cherry Creek Point could be the biggest thing to hit Denver since Conestoga wagons if the city fathers sell the land to the right developer. I told him Ludlow's going to bid, and I wondered if he hadn't kept up his friendships over there. I told him the construction business is rich with rewards for the goose that lays the golden information. He's a bright lad, you know: he brought me Ludlow's bid this morning. Twenty-seven five for the seventy acres."

"Not bad. What did Cal say about it?"

"He wants to bid twenty-eight and do the job. He's crazy to do it."

"I'd like to shave that a little. Get everybody in here this afternoon; we'll work on it. By the way, what did you pay Cal?"

"Ten thousand. He did good."

Vince nodded. "Everybody here at three o'clock."

It was the kind of meeting he liked best, all the information at hand, his key people waiting for his decision, the opposition at a disadvantage. Their final bid, sealed and delivered to the city the following week, was for

$27,910,000. Two weeks later, the Cherry Creek property was theirs.

Because they had decided to use a fast-track method of construction, beginning to build even while they were still finishing drawings of many construction details, the ground breaking was that fall, five months after the land became theirs.

"Fastest time on record," Cal Zorick said, gazing at the sketches in Vince's office. "It's such a great project, Vince; it's, you know, visionary. Everything's on such a huge scale. The money, too; the cost of it. That part's hard to grasp."

Vince looked at him narrowly. "What is it that gives you trouble?"

"Oh, just thinking about what's involved. I don't mean what you paid for the land; that's pretty straightforward. But when it's all built. God, Vince, can't you almost hear the money dropping into all those little coin slots? The amusement park and putting green and tennis courts and the boathouse, and then all the rents, and then you get a percentage of the sales at the shops and restaurants, right? It's so awesome it's just hard to grasp. I mean, the rest of us just work on parts of these projects and make little salaries, but you see the whole thing, you've got this grasp of . . . everything. I really envy that."

Vince sat back. "Ten thousand dollars would satisfy anyone who thought he had a future in this business."

"But I'm not just anyone, Vince; if I was, Ray wouldn't have asked me to help you out. And then he said I did fine. I did, too, Vince; nobody at Ludlow even knew I was asking. I was very clever."

"You may have been, then. You're not now."

"Well, I don't know. See, what I'm getting at is I've been wanting to go out on my own and be a developer like you, and I could do it if I had a couple hundred thousand dollars. Not a lot to a big developer like you, but I'd be starting small, somewhere else; I was thinking maybe the Southwest. I thought you'd help me get started. It would be like an investment in me."

"Why would I do that?" Vince asked.

"Well, it'd be sort of benevolent. I mean, I helped you out when you needed it, even though what you wanted me to do was, uh, shady? Well, it was really illegal, right? And my conscience has been sort of bothering me. I wouldn't want to get you and Ray into any kind of shit; but if I can't get away and do my own thing, then I guess my conscience would get the better of me, and after a while I'd just have to, sort of, confess."

Vince stared at him until Cal's gaze slid away. "When were you thinking of moving to the Southwest?"

"Right away," Cal said eagerly. "In a couple of days. I move fast."

"So do I. We should be able to settle this tomorrow afternoon. Close the door on your way out."

"But—wait a minute—you mean you'll—"

"Tomorrow afternoon. Close the door behind you."

When he was gone, Vince went to Beloit's office. "Cal wants two hundred thousand to keep quiet. Will you take care of it, Ray? You're better at that sort of thing than I am."

"What did you tell him?"

"That we'd settle it tomorrow afternoon."

"That gives us tonight. Oh, wait a minute. I have one of these damn dinners. How about you going in my place?"

"Fine," Vince said instantly. And that night he was seated at Beloit's place at a round table in the grand ballroom of the Brown Palace Hotel with two hundred guests eating baked chicken and wild rice, the menu for every benefit in Denver that year. He and Beloit went to a number of these dinners every season; it was important that they be seen as community supporters, and it was crucial that they be able to hold quiet conversations with finance and government officials that often got far more accomplished than meetings in boardrooms and offices.

He scanned the ballroom, noting the men he had not reached during the cocktail hour, whom he would chat with after dinner. His survey paused two tables away as his eyes met those of a redhead with a wide smile who was looking directly at him. She left her table and came to him. "Maisie Farrell," she said, and held out her hand.

Vince stood and took it. She was wearing black, and against it her bare shoulders and arms were chalk white and her hair a flaming aureole. "I remember," he said. He dug deep into his infallible memory. "Are you still doing volunteer work with the symphony?"

"No. I've graduated to the museum."

"You *were* graduating, from the university, when we met—"

"Slept together."

"I remember that, too." Vince's smile was warm, though all he could remember for certain after five—or was it six?—years was that he had expected a college senior to be pliable and grateful, and instead she had been knowledge-able and ironic. "You were leaving for Europe the next week."

"The next month. We had time to see each other again. You didn't call."

Vince gazed at her unhurriedly. Her face was too long for beauty, her nose and chin a little too large, her forehead a little too low. But it was her smile that drew attention, and the unsparing scrutiny of her cool green eyes. Her biting remarks reminded Vince of Anne, though Maisie was older and more sophisticated, her aim more accurate. He was recalling more about her now. She was the only daughter of a wealthy oilman; a champion swimmer, skier, and tennis player who was known for her fondness for all-night parties. But it was her smile he remembered most: magnificent and open, so bright that, though it did not reach her eyes, most people thought she was fascinated by whatever they were saying. It was that impersonal smile that Vince had wanted most to crush. He had wanted her to smile just for him. "You made me nervous," he said. "I couldn't tell whether you were serious, and that was terrible for my ego. Men can't stand uncertainty, you know; they begin to doubt everything, even their own name, if they can't be sure of a woman."

Maisie laughed. "So you forgot your name, and mine, too. You're very good, Vince; I almost believe you. That's what I remember best about you: how good you are."

"I'll have to make sure you keep thinking it." He was still holding her hand, and he raised it to his lips. "I won't forget your name again."

"Or yours, I hope." Casually, she slipped her hand from his and stood, relaxed, studying him. His tuxedo was perfectly cut; his cuff links were gold; his blond hair was carefully combed to look just slightly uncombed. He was exactly her height, but he managed to give the impression that he was looking down at everyone else. "You're the talk of the town. I've heard people say you're changing Denver forever."

"They're right."

"And are you pleased? Do you feel triumphant and immortal with all those Chatham Towers and Chatham Places and Chatham Centers dominating the plains?"

"Of course. Would you like a Farrell Tower? I'll build you one."

"I've never wanted my name on a building. It seems such an odd desire. As if you have to convince everyone how big you are. I often wondered if men do that because they're worried about the size of their parts."

His face darkened. You fucking bitch, he thought; you're begging to be slapped down. He did not wonder why she would try to make him angry; Vince seldom concerned himself with motives, his own or those of others. He cleared his face and chuckled. "I hadn't heard that before. I'll have to give it serious thought. And examine myself in the mirror."

Her eyes saluted his swift recovery. "And what about all your buildings? Are they the children you'll leave behind?"

"Better than children. There's no question how they'll grow up."

"That must be far more comforting than taking chances with people. Do you visit them often? Do you stroke the stone and feel noble because you've created beauty and usefulness from it?"

"No." He was still angry, but also excited and keyed up. He wanted to wipe the mockery out of her voice and the superior glint from her green eyes; he wanted to make her proud body bend to his. "I'm not interested in touching stone or any other part of a building; I only care about seeing it take shape the way I want." He grinned like a little boy and noted the wariness in her eyes as his face became youthful and guileless. "The real fun is putting things together like a huge puzzle. Stone, mortar, steel; the crews who do the work; the money to pay for it; the people who rent the space when it's done . . . I make the pieces fit so no one can imagine them any other way. Other people can stroke the stone and marble and talk about beauty and functionalism; the game is putting the puzzle together in the best way. Are you married?"

"No."

"I'll take you home tonight."

"I'm with someone."

"Tomorrow, then. I'll be free at one."

"I won't be; I work."

"Oh, the museum. When do you get out?"

"Five o'clock."

"I'll be in front at five."

"I don't fit into other people's puzzles," she said. "Or other people's games."

"Then we'll make a new one, just for you." He took her hand again. "Thank you for coming over to say hello. It's the nicest thing you could have done. I'm looking forward to tomorrow. Five years is far too long."

"Six." She smiled the wide, automatic smile that told him nothing. "Tomorrow will be fine."

He was thinking about her when he awoke the next morning; he thought about her all that day. "You're not paying attention," Beloit said, sitting on the couch in his office just before noon.

"No, I was thinking. What were you saying?"

Beloit's look sharpened. "Who is she?"

There was a pause. Vince shrugged. "Someone I met last night."

"She have a name?"

"Maisie Farrell."

"Oh, very good. You really like her? And she likes you?

Very good, Vince; you couldn't do better. She's the perfect hostess, the perfect wife for you. Good in-laws, too; they're even richer than you. Half a billion, a billion, whatever. Rich in-laws are a prize beyond rubies. So are rich wives. She's on a dozen committees, she's a volunteer at the museum and the Women's League and God knows what else, she's so respectable she could be in the White House. Which brings me to another subject."

"What?" Vince was only half-listening while scanning the morning paper. "What subject?"

"Politics. You ever thought about politics, Vince?"

"No."

"When you say it that way it means you have."

"I may have. Wait a minute, I want to read this." In a moment he looked up. "Cal Zorick's car ran off the road in Clear Creek Canyon last night. They found his body a little after ten o'clock."

"No kidding. Cal? What a shame. He was a talented lad." Beloit pursed his lips, nodding slowly. "A real shame. He did some good work for us. Sounds like he wanted to go too fast and lost control. Too bad. Well, but what did you mean: you may have thought about politics? Either you have or you haven't. Which is it?"

Vince closed the newspaper. "What are you getting at, Ray?"

"Changes in the air. You have to sniff these things out, you know, and I keep my nose to the news. I'm spending a lot of time these days with fellas in the party, and they're looking around for somebody new. Good politics is always looking ahead, you know; it doesn't get stuck in the mud of the past, it gives the voters new choices, new everything. They want somebody new for the next election."

"For what?" Vince's voice was flat, almost bored.

"Senator. United—States—senator."

Vince was silent.

"It's only four years off, not a lot of time with what we'd have to do. But you're known, Vince, you've got nice visibility, and the big money around town likes you. That's a good start, and a start in time saves nine." He waited. "Well, think about it. Nothing to lose by thinking. I've got a list of people you'd have to meet right away, local groups you'd drop in on, talks you'd give to Elks, Rotary, the whole bit. And a list of places you'd give money. More than you've been giving; a hell of a lot more. There's no substitute for spreading the wealth, thick and rich, like icing on the cake, and the filling, too. I figure you're worth at least a hundred million—you don't have to comment on that; it's just my private guess—so you can be generous. Politicians perk up, their fingertips wiggle like a belly dancer, when somebody generous walks in the room. Even if they knew you before, they'll know you better when they see you writing six-figure checks."

Beloit examined his fingernails, then buffed them lightly on his sleeve. "Something else. Your old man's doing a lot of building in Tamarack. He's getting a lot of press—glitzy resort, playground of movie stars and CEOs and royalty . . . Definitely makes the Chatham name sparkle. You got anything to do with Tamarack?"

"Not yet. I keep track of it."

"Well, same difference: Chatham is Chatham whether it's you or your old man. One of you does a make-over job that brings new business to Denver; the other one turns a little old mining town into a highfalutin resort that brings big spenders to Colorado. And you get the credit; you're the one making speeches and running for the Senate." He heaved himself from the couch. "Oh, another thing. Maisie Farrell. She's good, she's tough, she's classy. She'd be a great campaigner. She'd be a great senator's wife. She's even . . ." He paused and strolled thoughtfully to the door. "Like I said before, she's even respectable enough to be in the White House. Talk to you later."

Vince sat at his desk for a long time after Beloit left. A powerful desire, at last unleashed, was building in him. Had he thought about politics? For Christ's sake, of course he had. Anyone who cared about power thought about politics. It had been almost too easy to become a power in Denver, and now he was tired of it. He wanted something new. Something bigger. And as the idea settled within him, he knew it was the perfect time. He was ready for politics. He was ready for the Senate.

She's even respectable enough to be in the White House. He was ready for all of it.

He saw Maisie every night for the next four months, wanting her in the same way he wanted the Senate seat. He had to marry her. Not because Beloit had told him he ought to be married; not even because she was a prime political asset. He had to marry her because he could not get her out of his mind; the first time that had happened in fifteen years, since he had owned Anne. And the more she consumed his thoughts, the more he was jealous of whatever she did without him. He was distracted with the fury of not knowing where she was at each hour of the day, what her plans were, what she was thinking when she was not with him.

He had not beaten the mockery out of her; he couldn't get close enough. But Maisie would marry him; he was sure of it. And she could help him get anything he wanted; Beloit was right about that. She was quick-witted and poised and she would have enough sense to control her mockery. She came from wealth; her connections were good and her credentials impeccable. She knew how to dress and how to handle herself with strangers. She was very young—twenty-eight to Vince's forty-seven—but she gave the impression of being older; she had a control few women of any age could match. She was worth a fortune in a political campaign, and she would be the perfect political wife.

Even if she was not all of that, he might still have married her. He wondered about that sometimes, but it was an idle thought. He had no interest in philosophical speculation, and except for her damned independence, Maisie was all he wanted.

"I might marry you, Vince," she said one night in January. They were sitting at a candlelit corner table at Chez Amis, and the flame flickered just enough to make Maisie's face seem to shift with sudden mood changes, and her green eyes to change from intimacy to coolness. She looked at

Vince with an amused smile. "You look like a racer, waiting for the starting gun. Relax, my dear; why are you always so impatient?"

"Why shouldn't I be? I told you once, I hate uncertainty."

"You don't mind it in business; you expect it. What really annoys you is not being sure whether you'll get your own way or not. Tell me about Dora."

He was startled. "Why?"

"Because whenever you talk about her, which isn't often, you're angry. What happened with her that you didn't get your own way?"

He signaled to the waiter to bring another bottle of wine. "I love Dora very much, and she loves me. She's a remarkable young woman."

"I'd like to meet her."

"You will."

"But why haven't I? After four months and all this talk of marriage, shouldn't I have met your daughter?"

"She'll visit one of these days, on one of her school breaks, and you'll meet her then."

"But she wasn't here at Christmas. And you said she didn't come when she was younger."

"Her mother didn't want her to. And this Christmas she wanted her in Chicago."

"She didn't want her to visit you. Why not?"

He shrugged. "She has warped ideas about fathers and daughters."

"Any father, or just you?"

"Damn it, what difference does it make? She got a new husband a couple of years after we were divorced, and she said she wanted Dora to have a real family, not hang out in a bachelor pad." He smiled wistfully. "How could I argue with that? I couldn't give her a family. And I saw her in Chicago twice a month. But from now on she'll be here whenever she wants; she's in college in California and she'll stop off in Denver all the time."

"That will be nice for you." Maisie was thoughtful. "So you don't need to marry me in order to be respectable enough for Dora."

"Dora has nothing to do with it. You do. I want you."

"But you've got me," she said seriously. "We go to dinner, we talk, we go to movies, we go to bed. What more would we have if we were married?"

He smiled broadly. "Not a thing, I guess. Let's forget it. Tell me what's happening at the museum."

Maisie laughed. "I do like to be with you, Vince. As for the museum, you know perfectly well what's happening. I found out today you funded the Sandor Tizio exhibit at the Berno Gallery and you bought two Tizios and gave them to the museum. You never told me any of that."

"I don't publicize it."

"Nonsense; you publicize most of your good works. Philanthropy is great for business. But when did you become the patron saint of young artists?"

"A few years ago. When I started collecting. What's so amusing?"

Maisie was laughing. "Saint Vincent. You really are so amusing, Vince. I like the easy way you accept sainthood; not even a feeble protest that you're only human, like the rest of us."

"What else do you like?" he asked tightly.

"Oh, lots of things. I like your ambition and the way you aren't afraid of work. I like the projects you and Ray are building; some of them are brilliant, and I imagine you'll go on to even bigger and more important ones, and I like to be close to people who leave their mark on the world. I like being in bed with you when you stop giving instructions and just enjoy it. I like the way you're helping young artists; God knows they need it. I like the way you've kept in touch with Dora; a lot of fathers give up. And you don't bore me." She paused. "That seems like a lot of things to like."

"And love?" Vince asked, and cursed himself because it sounded childish and pleading.

"Well, no," Maisie said. "But that goes two ways, doesn't it."

"Not true," he responded quickly. "I do love you."

"Oh, Vince, let's not lie; it's so dull and grubby. If we get married, you'll have to promise not to lie."

"Are we going to get married?" he asked.

She looked at him thoughtfully, and in the flickering light her smile seemed to grow and fade as if she changed toward him as the seconds went by. "I think we are," she said at last. "I think it will be interesting."

Quietly, Vince let out a long breath. Wait long enough, he thought, and everything you want comes your way.

By the time oil prices plunged and Denver began its long slide from the heights of its heady spree, the Chatham name was everywhere. Maisie no longer mocked it, for it gave Vince instant identification when he campaigned in the small towns of Colorado where the issue that roused the greatest passion was land use. He and Beloit had put together a campaign team that focused his speeches and brochures and position papers on the land. The message was always the same. Build. Use the land; that's what it's there for. It isn't there for a few backpackers or a lot of elk; it's there for the people of Colorado. It belongs to them. It's theirs to do with as they please.

The voters were loudly for or against the massive construction projects that radiated the name Chatham. Chatham Towers, Chatham Plaza shopping malls, Chatham Block office towers, the vast Chatham Place at Cherry Creek, Chatham industrial parks, Chatham hotels in Aspen, Vail, and Alta, and dozens of other buildings dominated the skylines and neighborhoods of eight Western states. Often daring in architecture and admired for their workmanship, Chatham projects were equally well known for the rough methods used to acquire land and get the designs approved over community opposition. No neighborhood was the same after Vince and Beloit were there, and the communities of Colorado and the Rocky Mountain states talked about them with a mixture of dread and eager anticipation.

"You love it," Maisie said as they rode in the limousine to Colorado Springs for a political dinner. She wore an emerald silk dress and a long sable coat, and her red hair was pinned back with emerald clips. "All this attention. People loving you or hating you; people never sure of what you'll do next, what you'll say, whom you'll attack, how soon you'll destroy their neighborhood."

Vince smiled sweetly. "Once you called those buildings brilliant."

"I said some of them were brilliant."

The limousine sped smoothly down the highway in the early darkness of November, taking them to a banquet hall where hundreds of people waited, having paid five hundred dollars apiece to eat and drink in Vince Chatham's vicinity one week before the election, and listen to him blast another target on his thunderous road to the Senate.

"I watched you mesmerize Ludlow last night," Vince said. "Is he going to give?"

"Twenty-five thousand. You didn't tell me you'd screwed him out of some land once."

"He doesn't know that; he's guessing. Twenty-five thousand? What the hell did you promise him?"

"He's not a fool, Vince; he knows you'll be the best thing that ever happened to contractors in this state; they're going to have a field day. But I did offer him a small private dinner at our home in Washington, with some very powerful people."

Vince grinned. "How many people have you invited to that small private dinner?"

"A few hundred. It doesn't matter; you'll have six glorious years to come through for your loyal contributors."

He gave her a long look. "You said 'our home in Washington.'"

"Of course. I couldn't very well say I wouldn't be there, could I? But I haven't changed my mind, Vince. I'm staying through the election; not a day after."

"You could. I'd forget the past year. We'd start—"

"*You'd* forget? Oh, my poor little Vince, you're the seediest kind of politician; you lie to yourself as much as to the rest of us. You've spent the last four years trying to make me into someone else, a sweet little appendage with no more will than a child. You don't want a grown woman, Vince; you'd be happiest with a thirteen-year-old girl who'd follow orders. And when you couldn't change me, you found someone else. Some*ones*. Plural. There've been three that I know of. Why would I tolerate that? I'm thirty-two; I'm attractive, smart, rich, and I know my way around. I like men, I think I like being married, but I want a partnership, not a stacked deck. Why would I stay married to a power-hungry son of a bitch who thinks he owns me and spends his spare time screwing fair maidens who're dumb enough to jump when he snaps his fingers? You don't even like them. You do it to degrade me."

Vince's face was rigid. "If I have other women, it's because my wife spends her time fucking men she picks up at the museum—"

"Oh, for God's sake, is that the best you can do? One little fling, Vince. Three months out of the past four years. I confess. I confessed at the time. I don't believe in being unfaithful, but he had a sense of humor and you have none and I couldn't resist. That was a year ago, Vince, and I've been such a good girl since then, but you're still talking about it. Could it be that a tiny molecule of guilt has crept into that vacuum where your ethical system ought to be, and you feel just uncomfortable enough that you have to blame me?" Her eyes met his cold ones. "No, not even a molecule." She shook her head. "It's such a shame. There was a time when I thought you had real possibilities."

"Is that why you married me? For my possibilities?"

"Let me see if I can remember. I married you because you could turn on your charm and be a wonderful companion for a whole evening, and I thought with my help you could learn to be wonderful for a week or a month, maybe even a year. I suppose I married you so I could share your stardom; it's fun to be at the center of power. What else? Oh, yes. You're very clever, Vince, and I always wanted to marry a clever man. I thought you might be smart, too, but I've decided you're not. You don't learn. I think that may be your fatal flaw. Oh, here we are." The limousine had come to a stop beneath a brightly lit canopy. "Smile, Vince; you've only got a week to go."

She said it again after dinner, when the television lights were turned on and the cameras were trained on the podium with its array of microphones. Looking deeply into Vince's eyes for the benefit of the photographers clustered below the main table, Maisie adjusted his bow tie with loving hands. "Smile, Vince. We've only got a week to go."

"Ladies and gentlemen," boomed the party chairman. "My job tonight is to introduce a speaker everybody knows. I looked around for something new to say about him— maybe he raises llamas, or he's a champion at barbecuing spareribs, or he buys his lovely wife pearls or cars or airplanes—but I decided to let him have his secrets, if he has any, because all we need to know about him is this: he believes in growth for Colorado and growth for America, and he knows what he's talking about because he's put Colorado on the map when it comes to growth. He's a *can-do* and *will-do* guy; his name stands for *big* and *biggest* and *get out of my way because I'm on a fast track,* and that's what we need more of these days when people say America is falling behind. His name stands for success, and that's exactly what *America* should stand for! We all know his name . . . ladies and gentlemen, Vince Chatham, the next United States senator from the state of Colorado!"

Four hundred people were on their feet, cheering. Vince took the few steps to the podium and erased Maisie from his thoughts.

"Good evening," he said when the room was quiet. His voice was low, as it always was when he began, but as he spoke, it grew in volume and intensity so that by the time he finished he was shouting. The speech, like all his speeches, was short, with short, rhythmic sentences and sketchy ideas that would come across on television with the speed of a variety show. "The chairman gave my speech so brilliantly I think I'd be better off keeping quiet." He waited for the ripple of laughter to die away. "But I would like to talk about a few ideas I have for now and the future. We're surrounded these days by naysayers. People who keep telling us what won't work. What can't be done. What isn't possible because it's too *expensive* or too *time-consuming* or too *risky* or too *uncertain*. These people mean well—though we can't always be sure of that, can we?—but are they the kind of people who built America? Are they the kind of people who won two world wars, and rescued Europe, and conquered space? Are they the kind of people to lead us back to greatness?" His voice rose. "I don't know about you, but let me tell you, *I am sick and tired of being told what I can't do!*"

The room exploded in applause. When at last Vince went on, he talked about Colorado and America, and growth. "Growth makes wealth!" he cried. He was coming to his conclusion and his voice was almost at full volume. "We can have steady growth and still protect every small business-man and every family farm. We can have large-scale growth and still preserve the land we love!"

"How?" murmured Maisie, but no one heard.

"We'll fill the empty acres of this vast country with houses for everyone. We'll fill them with splendid shopping centers so no one will be more than arm's length from abundance. We'll fill them with factories and schools and highways. We'll fill them with movie theaters and amusement parks and zoos to provide recreation for everyone. We'll fill the empty acres of this vast land with the good things of life because we know how to do it better than anyone in the world . . . *and because we've earned it!*"

Applause swept over him. He held up his hand. "Listen to this! Never forget it! And don't let anyone tell you other-wise! We gave freedom and democracy to the people of the world! We gave the principle of hard work to the people of the world! We gave the greatest industrial production and the most skilled management teams in the history of the world! We gave space exploration to the world! We gave the ethic of the family to the world: a strong, enduring, loving family that protects its young and helpless from the dangers around them! We made the world a better place for every-one, and now we deserve to build the best life for Americans that can be built! *We deserve it!* And that's what we're going to get, starting next week when I become your senator—"

Applause and cheers rose to the chandeliers.

"—and take that message to Washington—"

The roar drowned out his last words. No one cared. Vince was smiling, the sweet, humble smile of a public servant who was being loved. His brown eyes were bright as they swept the room, resting for just a second on his wife, who was applauding with a mockery only he could see.

His look moved on, skimming the excited eyes and cheering mouths and clapping hands of his voters, pausing at each television camera so it could send to the world his open smile and purposeful gaze. Everything was all right; everything was under control.

Maisie would stay with him; women like her never walked away from powerful men. Ethan and Charles and the others would be there when he needed them. Already they'd helped; they provided him with a visible family. His picture, surrounded by many of his loved ones, had been in *Time* and *Newsweek* and *People*. He was the ideal candidate, with the perfect wife, the perfect family, the perfect message.

And a week later, even before the polls closed, he was Senator Vince Chatham, on his way to Washington, and eventually, the rumors already said, the White House.

chapter 7

Anne was in her office when she read about Vince's election. It was early morning and she was alone in the thirtieth-floor labyrinth of lawyers' offices and secretaries' cubicles, drinking coffee and reading the *Los Angeles Times,* when, suddenly, Vince's face was before her, grinning in boyish triumph. With a cry, Anne dropped the paper. Coffee splashed on her desk as she clumsily put down her mug. She was trembling, and felt a coldness spread through her, a shame and helplessness that she had not felt for years. Stop it, she said silently, stop it, stop it, stop it; and gripped her hands together to force her body into stillness.

She swiveled her chair and stared unseeing through her large windows. It had been nineteen years since she had last seen that smile, and still it could cause her to tremble and draw her body together in defense. Bury it, she told herself —the same words she had repeated every day for the first year she was in Haight Ashbury. Bury it.

She tried to focus on the view that usually gave her such pleasure. Thirty floors below, the early-morning sun had turned the sprawling vista of Los Angeles to red and gold, with the mountains in the distance crisply outlined against a pale blue sky. The landscape was at its clearest and most beautiful in this hour before the smog built up; the towering palms, velvet lawns, and lush tropical flowers gave no hint that it was November and, in other parts of the country, the beginning of winter.

From the thirtieth floor, the city looked rich, orderly, and serene. It was a landscape that always gave Anne a feeling of comfort and safety, and in the midst of even her busiest days she frequently glanced at it as an antidote to the pinched meanness and splintered dreams that permeated her office as she dealt with clients in the midst of divorce.

Everything about the thirtieth floor gave her that feeling of safety and comfort, especially her office. It was large, with a wall of windows, and it seemed to wrap her in a protective embrace. The furnishings, like those of all the offices in the firm, were heavy walnut and leather, the lamps were brass, the carpet was dark green, the paintings on the walls were of English cathedrals and rural scenes. Anne liked the solid permanence of the room and had not added a single personal touch other than her framed diplomas from the University of California at Berkeley and Harvard Law School. But soon after she moved in, Eleanor came from New York for a visit, and said it needed something different.

"Maybe even a little eccentric," she said. The next week, a long, narrow mirror with an antique English frame was delivered to the office. "Hang it opposite your desk," Eleanor had written on the note that accompanied it, "so whenever you look up, you'll see the best lawyer in Los Angeles. And also my very best friend, whom I miss, damn it, because we don't see each other nearly enough."

Anne turned from the window and looked at herself in the mirror. Her dark blue eyes gazed back at her steadily, with no sign of distress. It was a look she had spent years perfecting. She was often admired for her beauty, but that was not as important to her as the image she presented to the world of a professional woman in perfect control of herself. Her black hair was sleekly coiled at the back of her long neck, her only makeup was a pale coral lipstick, small pearls were at her ears, and she wore superbly cut suits of wool and silk that made her look taller and more imposing. Her public image was smooth, guarded, and impeccable, and no one who met her doubted her reputation as a skillful, tough lawyer who had overcome her firm's prejudices to become a partner though she was just thirty-four and a woman.

She sat in her large, leather executive chair and gazed at the public image in her mirror. She had been polishing it for a long time, from the lonely, anxious years in Berkeley to the increasingly confident ones at Harvard when she discovered that the law was exactly what she wanted, and knew she would be good at it. She kept working on that image when she got to her first job in New York, and she still worked at it, even now when she was part of the most prestigious firm in Los Angeles and was already their top divorce lawyer, sought out by corporate executives and television and film celebrities who wanted her skill and discretion. She had lived with her image for so long that she had begun to believe she was indeed the person she saw in the mirror.

And then I fell apart over a photograph in a newspaper.

Beyond her door, the office was coming to life. Lawyers clerks, secretaries, and receptionists greeted each other, gossiped, told jokes, and discussed the day's activities as they walked to their desks or gathered in conference rooms. Anne heard snatches of conversations and bursts of laughter as the pace quickened. It was her favorite time of day, when she could anticipate everything that lay ahead: the high drama, the surprises, even the plodding details of the law. All of it was her world and it sustained her. It was only here that she felt truly at home, and alive.

It wasn't just a photograph. It was a reminder. A ghost. And now I have to start again, learning how to get rid of it.

She picked up the paper and forced herself to read the story.

A wealthy real estate developer who brought distinctive, often daring architecture and massive building projects to Colorado and the mountain states, Vince Chatham ran a well-financed campaign that avoided specifics and successfully fended off accusations of shady connections and questionable tactics in his rise to prominence. He won election to the Senate, his first political office, by a narrow but decisive margin.

It's just a story about a politician. It could be anybody. It has nothing to do with me.

It was quieter beyond her door; the office was at work. But still she sat, facing the mirror, as if waiting for something. After a moment, on impulse, she picked up her telephone and dialed Eleanor's number in New York.

The private secretary answered, and then Eleanor was there. "I was just going out; God, I'm glad you caught me; I haven't talked to you in ages. How come you're calling in the morning? Is anything wrong?"

"No, I just felt like talking. Where are you going?"

"Shopping and then a ladies' lunch, and then I'll pick up the kids and take them to New Jersey for the weekend to make their grandparents ecstatic. Are you sure nothing's wrong? You never just feel like talking; you're usually too busy."

"I guess I was thinking about when I was younger, and I thought of you. How's Sam?"

"Even busier than you, if that's possible. I don't see much more of him than I do of you, or anyway it seems that way, but maybe that's the formula for a good marriage. Or at least one that lasts. I think about being younger, too. I miss it; we had such a good time. Are you missing it?"

"No. I'm glad I'm through with it. I never felt in control of my life. I do miss going barefoot sometimes."

"You're one of the star lawyers out there; you could work barefoot all day long and nobody would say a word. You'd probably start a trend. Pretty soon the *Times* would be photographing upscale people going barefoot on Madison Avenue and the footwear industry would be writing letters to the editor, crying foul."

Anne laughed. "If I decide to try it, I'll let you know. Who's going to be at the ladies' lunch?"

"A bunch of very high-society types who wear Valentino for lunch and Ungaro for dinner. Or maybe it's the other way around. We're planning a benefit for the library. It's going to be a swell party; why don't you come for the weekend and go with Sam and me?"

"Not this time, Ellie. I'm too busy."

"I haven't told you which weekend."

"I'm busy on all of them."

"Listen, you called me, remember? I detect a need for a friendly ear. I could use one, too, in fact; we haven't sat up all night talking for years. Do I have to hire you to get you here for a visit?"

"What does that mean? You and Sam again?"

"Still. Yet. Always. It doesn't ever go away; we sort of simmer all the time and once in a while we boil over."

"But you haven't mentioned divorce for a long time."

"I think about it. But it's such a hassle—well, who knows that better than you? All our houses and cars, and two boats, and the antiques and the art . . . my God, we're in such a tangle of *things*. And I don't want to force the kids to go trotting back and forth all the time, but he'd have to see them, he's really good with them when he's around, which isn't often, but he talks about quality time and how do I know that's not enough? The kids like him a lot."

"So do you, I think."

"Most of the time. Sometimes I even love him. Other times I hate him. Maybe it goes with the territory. How can anyone like another person all the time? It doesn't make sense. So I guess we'll probably stay married. He's happy and I don't see what I'd gain by it—I mean, I'd most likely find somebody just like him and move to an apartment a few blocks away that looks exactly like the one I'm in now, and my kids would be in the same private school, and I'd be having lunch with the same ladies for the same good causes, and the only thing that would change would be the guy in my bed and they're all interchangeable, you know, after the first two or three months—so no, we probably won't get a divorce."

"I'm sorry," Anne said after a moment. "The last time we talked you sounded happier."

"I probably was. A lot of times I am. But last night I started thinking about the Haight—can you believe it, after all these years—and I was wishing I could just have one day, maybe even an *hour*, of the *hope* we had then. Remember? We really thought the world could be whatever we wanted it to be—beautiful and loving, with everybody sharing and being free and *caring* about each other. So I've been feeling melancholy and then you called and I dumped on you. Sorry about that. Anyway, I *am* happy. I fit in here a lot better than in the Haight; this is what I was brought up for. There's a lot that's good in my life and I know it; I just . . . oh, damn it, Anne, there's just so much that I *miss*. It doesn't matter how long ago it was, I still miss it." There was a silence. "Don't you? Even a little bit? I know, I know; you told me you don't think about the past. But doesn't it sneak up on you once in a while?"

"Yes. And I do miss parts of it. I miss the way you and I ran to the park and nobody could catch us. And I miss the way a bunch of us would sit on the steps singing and feeling together, like a family."

"I went back there about a month ago, right after I bought you your mirror. Don Santelli is still there; isn't that incredible? Poor guy, he's kind of lost; sort of an aging hippie. He told me he hates himself because he's just as bad as his parents, just as locked into a routine. It doesn't matter what the routine is—theirs was respectability and his is drugs and avoiding work—he always wanted to be free and spontaneous and he doesn't feel that way anymore. And he doesn't have any hope, either. He knows the future won't be any better. It was the most depressing thing I've done for a long time. So much for trying to go back. You were right, Anne; we had to get out. I didn't want to admit it, but it's true. But I still think about it. Tell me about you."

"I have a client coming—"

"Tell me about him."

"He's a screenwriter who has a wife and three children and a racing sailboat and he's just turned fifty and is terrified he's getting old. So he found a twenty-two-year-old model who makes him feel he can run the world—she asks his advice on everything, including her clothes and her hairdresser and what she should have to drink—and they've been in Aspen and Tamarack and Europe and now he wants to marry her."

"Why?"

"I asked him that. He says he needs stability and courage. I said he'd need those to get through the divorce; his wife wants to strip him of everything."

"She should; he's abandoned her—"

"Well, she's got a guy, it seems; a twenty-eight-year-old chef—one of the hottest ones in town. She doesn't want to get old, either. Staying young is everybody's obsession out here, and marriage doesn't have much to do with that."

"You hate it, don't you?" Eleanor asked.

"Marriage? No, I think it's fine for anybody who wants it and is willing to work at it. Ellie, I have to go; the screenwriter will be here any minute. When are you coming to LA again?"

They talked for another minute, then Anne put down the telephone, feeling better. They were as different as friends could be, but they had stayed in touch for eighteen years and still turned to each other when they needed what Eleanor called a friendly ear. Anne knew that Eleanor had many friends; she herself had no one else. Never again, after leaving Haight Ashbury, had she been able to let down her defenses and warm to another person. When she talked to Eleanor, she felt she loved her, and perhaps could love other people, too, someday. She wanted to believe that. And talking to Eleanor always helped. Once again she was in control of her feelings.

But who did the most talking? Anne thought with amusement. Who really needed comforting? She smiled. It usually happened that way; Anne listened; the friend or client talked. No one except Eleanor knew anything about her—and Eleanor didn't know much—because she never talked about herself. Once she had wanted to, but by now reticence had become so deeply ingrained in her, and was so much a part of her public image, that she never thought of confiding in anyone, and no one asked her to. For this morning, it was enough that Eleanor had been there when she called, that there had been someone at the other end of the wire. That was all she needed.

"Anne," said her secretary from the doorway, "they're waiting for you in the conference room."

"I'm ready," Anne said, and gathered up the files on her desk. The day had begun.

Ethan walked the streets of Tamarack every morning before breakfast, feeling the sun settle in his bones and ease the stiffness in his joints. He was almost alone at that hour; the shops had not opened, the joggers were at the other end of town, on the trail along the river, and almost everyone else, residents and tourists alike, still slept. Only the street cleaners were out, washing the dust from the cobblestone central mall and the commercial and residential streets surrounding it, so that, briefly, the town gleamed wet and shiny beneath the cloudless sky.

It was Ethan's favorite time. He walked down the middle of the streets, ignoring the modern buildings and huge new houses being built on all sides, imagining himself in the Tamarack he had first seen more than forty years before, when goats ambled along its dirt roads and Main Street was lined with tiny turn-of-the-century miner's cottages and a few frame storefronts. That was right after the Second World War. He'd been on a driving trip through Colorado and on a whim, drove over a spectacular pass to see what was on the other side.

He found a crumbling town in a narrow valley: a silent shadow of the past. Sixty years earlier, the valley had rung with the voices and laughter of eight thousand people served by saloons and churches, brothels and smithies, a school, a row of mercantile stores, a grand opera house, and a hotel with a lobby decorated in fringed velvet and brocades. But the real business of the town was silver. Miners dug tunnels beneath the mountains in vast honeycombed networks that reached down as many as twenty levels, into the core of the earth, and wound back and forth two or three horizontal miles. Smelters worked day and night, a train brought in supplies and took out the ore, and children went to work in the mines in their early teens.

Then, in the last decade of the century, Congress passed a law making gold America's official coin.

In that moment, silver became almost worthless. The owners of the mines shut them down; the miners moved out. The brothels and shops and the school closed. The churches were locked. Tamarack slept.

By the time Ethan drove over Wolf Creek Pass and into the town, not quite a hundred people were there, living in the sagging miner's cottages on Main Street. One gas station was open, a general store with a post office in the back, and the Lodestar, a restaurant with a counter and five tables and a scarred linoleum floor. A few rooms in the old hotel— those with windows and floors intact—were open. The opera house had burned and then been looted over the years by people passing through the valley until only the shell remained, with glints of gold leaf shining amid the blackened ruins like the nuggets that had lured the first miners over Wolf Creek Pass. Under the mountains, the mining tunnels were flooded or had collapsed into rubble. Dust swirled in the streets until winter came and the snow piled ten feet deep.

But what Ethan saw were the surroundings: lush green forests and alpine meadows, carpets of vivid flowers, the play of shadows at sunset that turned the ranges of hills gray and blue, violet and deep purple beneath a flaming sky, and the towering peaks of the San Juans, every ridge and crevice sharply outlined against the saturated-blue sky or shrouded in mist on a rainy day, their slopes brooding and mysterious. He saw the way the town nestled in the valley between the two long ridges of Tamarack Mountain and Star Mountain, the way rivers tumbled through long clefts of other valleys and met in the town. He breathed the dry, fragrant air and felt the headiness of the altitude; he listened to the silence and the birds, and he knew he had never seen a place as beautiful or as peaceful in his life.

That day, his first in Tamarack, he bought a house, one of a few three-story, ornamented Victorian mansions left behind by the mine owners and bankers when they returned to New York and Chicago. And then, as he went back again and again, and became convinced that this was the place where he wanted to live forever, he bought the hotel, the opera house, dozens of miner's cottages, empty lots in town, and then land around the town and entire ranches in the valley, and finally the abandoned mining claims on the north-facing slopes of Tamarack Mountain, because some friends had returned from skiing in Europe and told him they thought it was a sport that might catch on in America.

He created The Tamarack Company, a subsidiary of Chatham Development Corporation, with himself as president, and then he began to bring Tamarack back to life. He built an airport and a small ski area; he remodeled his house; he restored the hotel, built a row of stores on Main Street, converted the largest brothel into a bakery and restaurant, and built a movie theater.

And then, with the help of friends in Chicago, New York, and Los Angeles, he threw a huge, summer-long party, with a touring symphony orchestra that played in a meadow, a folk-music festival, and a series of lectures on books, movies, and politics by the greatest names in the world who were willing to come to Tamarack for a day, a week, a month. It was the party of the century, and no one wanted to miss it. Tamarack was launched.

From that summer, though Ethan tried to hold it back, it never slowed down.

In less than ten years the town had a new city council; a ski area; music, film, and jazz festivals held in an arts center on the edge of town; seminars open to the public with world leaders debating the great issues of the day; an art colony for painters, sculptors, jewelry makers, and writers; hiking, horseback, and bicycle trails; and five hundred full-time residents.

And then, "That's enough," Ethan said. It was the paradise he had dreamed of: a retreat for all those who, like himself, had to live most of the time in the bustle and dense air of large cities. He sat on the mall, four cobblestone streets in the center of town, and gazed with pleasure at the wild mountainsides visible from everywhere in town; he bicycled the length of the valley, past long rail fences bordering fields of hay and grazing horses, red barns, and snug farmhouses surrounded by vegetable and flower gardens; he became part of the easy flow of life in the town, its slow days and casual attire, and the spontaneous get-togethers at bars and impromptu barbecues where everyone mingled—plumbers, carpenters, waiters, bankers, musicians, politicians, heirs to great fortunes, and corporate executives—all together, indistinguishable in jeans and flannel shirts.

"It's enough," Ethan said. "Not one more house, not another store, not another concert or film or ski run. It's perfect as it is."

He knew that was impossible; nothing could stand still and live. But to keep it as close to perfection as he could, he made sure the mayor was always his handpicked choice, and he used his influence with the city council and county commissioners to control development in the town. Ethan had definite ideas about architecture, the height and depth of buildings, roofing materials, landscaping, even the color of the paint, and every structure had to be approved before it could be built. That way, he said, everything in the town would be harmonious. And it would stay small.

But Tamarack grew. It grew slowly until Ethan was almost seventy, when he finally handed the presidency of Chatham Development Corporation to Charles, and moved to his mountain paradise. But he was not retired—he could not imagine being retired—and because he was a developer who had to develop, he looked at Tamarack and found it ready to grow.

"Controlled growth," he told the city council. "This is what we're going to do. Expand the airport; we'll get bigger jets in here. Triple the ski runs and chair lifts on Tamarack Mountain; I've got an expert from Switzerland designing them. More trails for cross-country skiing and bicycling; they're being laid out by a fellow from New York. Permanent buildings for music, film, dance, and theater; an outdoor band-shell for popular concerts and the jazz festival; a small campus for the world-issues seminars. We'll need more lodges, more shops, and a parking garage. Those are all in the works. You just watch: Tamarack is going to become finer in every way. But underneath we won't change; we'll stay small and comfortable, not ostentatious, still a laid-back place where we all like each other and work and party together. We'll grow, but we'll grow the right way."

Growth is like a genie in a bottle; the only way to keep it under control is to keep the bottle tightly capped. Once the genie is free, it devours a room, a house, a neighborhood, a town. Ethan learned all about the genie. He was the one who let it out.

Within five years, the old Tamarack had vanished. It had been inundated by success. Because a strange and entirely unexpected thing had happened. As Ethan swung full speed into developing Tamarack, the small town in the narrow valley, not too easy to get to, not on a major highway or airline route, was discovered by the international set: the wealthy, restless, often bored modern nomads who spend their time and money in an endless search for something new.

And so the wealthy came, and royalty and ex-royalty, and with them, international film and television stars, and with them the tourists. And every part of Tamarack changed. And grew.

Ethan remembered those forty years as he walked down the middle of Tamarack's empty streets in the early morning. He was the one who had started it. And now he mourned the loss of that dusty little town where nothing much happened and no one came, and ranchers and herds of elk shared the unscarred land.

But look around, Ethan thought, quarreling with himself. The mountains haven't lost their beauty or their magic, and the town is more beautiful than ever. Everyone's prospering. Everyone's happy. I should be, too. I should be very satisfied. I'm ninety years old and most people would say I have everything. I should be a very happy man.

He turned to walk back. On Main Street, the bakery had opened and a group of bicyclists had stopped for breakfast. He sat near them on the terrace, listening to their plans for the day, envying the youth and assuredness in their voices, the strength in their jaws as they chewed, the casual way they took for granted their health, their muscles, the smooth road beneath their wheels. Ethan remembered when he had been like that, married to Alice, raising five children, building industrial plants for the government during the Second World War, then, in peacetime, turning to shopping malls and whole towns, making his company one of the largest and wealthiest in the country.

Everything he had done in those days had fed his ambition, his sexual energy, his appetite for work. The years had sped by in an exhilarating blur of success and prosperity, and he never could remember, later, the exact date an office building or factory or housing development had been built, or how old his children were when they did something that seemed noteworthy, or even the day when Alice first stumbled and fell, for what they thought was no reason at all.

He had become many times a millionaire in those glorious years, and he'd had a magnificent time doing it. He'd been like a god, straddling the world, carving forms from the wilderness, shaping people's lives by creating the homes where they lived, the buildings where they worked, the parks and playing fields where they relaxed.

But for all his power, he had not been able to stop the tumor from growing in his wife's brain and killing her; he had not been able to make his son Charles more aggressive and less afraid of the world; he could not transform Vince, his most beautiful and brilliant child, into a good man. And he had not kept his beloved granddaughter Anne from running away, nor could he bring her back now, more than twenty years later.

He gazed at the croissant and coffee the waitress had put before him. He wasn't hungry. Once, no matter what the time of day, he would have downed them voraciously, the buttery croissant, the strong black coffee, and demanded more. Now he looked at them without interest and wondered what had happened to all the appetites he had boasted of for such a long time.

"It won't bite back," said Leo Calder with a smile, pulling out the chair opposite Ethan. "I never saw anyone look at a croissant with more suspicion."

"I was waiting for it to look tempting," Ethan said. He sat back, glad to have company, glad it was Leo. "I thought I should eat—it's that time of day—but I don't feel like it."

"Then don't. Aren't you old enough to do what you want no matter what time of day it is?"

"Ninety," Ethan said thoughtfully. "I always wondered what it would feel like to be this old. I still don't know; I can't pin down how I feel. But my body's sure as hell slowed down a lot." He pushed his plate across the table. "You eat it. And talk to me. What's happening that I should know about?"

"It's quiet; I haven't got a single problem to report."

"Then you're not doing enough. You're coasting. Getting lazy and complacent and headed for disaster."

Leo laughed. "You've been telling me I was headed for disaster ever since I married Gail. Nine years of black predictions of what would happen if I didn't get off my ass and get busy. I've been busy. Have I ever let you down? Have you ever once been sorry you hired me to run The Tamarack Company?"

"No. But that's because I kept you on your toes."

They laughed together, and for a moment sat quietly in the sunlight. The bicyclists had left and other customers had taken their place; waitresses rushed back and forth across the crowded terrace. Beyond a low stone wall, vacationers strolled on the sidewalk: young couples pushing strollers, families studying maps of the town, men and women in khaki shorts and T-shirts, wearing backpacks, water bottles fastened to their belts. On both sides of the valley the mountains rose up, and the warm sun glided down their steep slopes and settled in the town like a benediction.

Ethan sighed with the beauty and serenity of the place. For all that it had changed, he still could sit outside a café on a sun-filled morning in late June, insulated from the turmoil of the rest of the world, and luxuriate in being alive in such a place, on such a day, with such a friend as Leo Calder.

He watched Leo ordering coffee and another croissant, liking him, liking his presence. He was short and compact, with straight dark hair, heavy dark brows, a determined chin, and a strength that belied his size. He had been a champion wrestler in college and now played tennis with a fearsome forehand, and skied with power if not with grace. His dark eyes compelled people to look straight at him, and it was almost impossible for anyone to sustain a lie when pinned down by that firm gaze. Leo was known as a man who could be trusted, and Ethan always felt better when he was around. He knew that The Tamarack Company, with its vast holdings in the town and the valley, had never been run as well as it had been from the day he named Leo its president. And it was all the sweeter to him that Leo was Gail's husband, and they were his family, here in Tamarack.

Charles had told Ethan that Vince had been furious that he made Leo president. It was amazing, Ethan thought, that after all these years Vince still would get angry because he had brought in an outsider—

"We heard from Vince last night," Leo said.

For a moment, confusion swept through Ethan. He felt dizzy. His thoughts and Leo's voice clanged in his head and he could not tell them apart. He clung to his chair to keep from toppling over.

"Ethan!" Leo was at his side. "What's wrong?"

"I don't know." Ethan squinted. The dizziness was almost gone. "A little shaky for a minute. Maybe the sun. It's very bright, isn't it?"

"I'll take you home."

"No, no, I like this. It's very nice, sitting with you, Leo; I like to do this. You don't have to get to the office yet?"

"Not for a little while."

"You were telling me something."

"About Vince. He called last night. He does that now and then, and then doesn't have much to say. He always wants to know about the company, but once I've told him everything's fine, we run out of things to talk about. Oh, he did ask if any of the family would be here for the Fourth of July. I told him they almost never come to Tamarack and this year didn't look to be any different. I asked him if he'd be up here."

Ethan scowled. "Why did you do that?"

"Because I thought you might want your family together again."

"You mean because I'm about to die."

"I didn't say that. Sometimes it's a good thing to make peace with the people who are part of you."

"Vince isn't part of me, Leo; he hasn't been for twenty years or more. Oh, I've thought about it; don't think I haven't. But what Vince did was cut out the heart of our family. He violated everything a family stands for. We're supposed to take care of children, give them sanctuary while they learn how to fight the battles of the world; that's the main thing we're here for. The rest of it—somebody to sleep with, somebody to eat with, somebody to talk to at the end of the day—that's all extraneous. The main thing is, we build a fortress to keep our kids from harm's way and give them a chance to grow confident and proud. That's sacred. And Vince destroyed it. He mocked it. I can't forget that. I can't forgive him. I don't know how much he cares now that he's such a busy, important senator, but it's not my concern whether he cares or not. He always did what he wanted in the past, you know, except when I told him to get out. That was a terrible time. I don't think any of us ever really got over—"

Ethan stopped. He rambled too much lately. He knew it, but he couldn't stop himself. The words just poured out, as if he had to keep talking, because as long as he talked, he was alive, and it didn't seem possible to him that anyone could die in midsentence.

"I didn't really think he'd come," Leo said, "and he

won't. He said he had to be in Denver that weekend, keeping his voters happy, and then he's going to Maine. He said Charles would be there with him." Leo paused. "He said that Charles always went to him when he was in trouble and needed help."

"What kind of trouble?"

"He didn't say."

Ethan shrugged. "Well, I don't want to know. If it's bad enough, I'll hear about it."

"Wasn't Charles supposed to be here for the Fourth?"

"He said something about it. I'd like it if the rest of them came; we could have a real family picnic. We used to have them on the beach, and then watch the fireworks over the lake. Not as spectacular as the show they put on here, on Tamarack Mountain, but it wasn't bad, all the flares reflected in the water, and boats all the way out, as far as you could see, with people sitting on them, looking up . . ."

"We'll have our picnic," Leo said. "There'll be the four of us, and you, and Keith. And Dora's in town."

"With her . . . whatever you call him."

"The man she lives with."

Ethan made a face. "I don't like it, you know. All these sample marriages, like those little bits of food that women in aprons hand out in grocery stores; you're supposed to nibble and then decide whether to buy. If people love each other, why can't they trust themselves enough to get married? I like *him*, though, Dora's . . . friend; I like him more every time I see him. But there has to be something wrong with him. If he were decent, he'd marry her. They've been together a long time. A year? Two years? More than two. They've been together two years at least. I'd like him more if he married her."

"Maybe she doesn't want to."

"I don't believe that for a minute. Women always want to; it's their nature. There's something wrong with him, that's all."

"But you don't mind if he comes to the picnic."

"No, no, of course he should come, as long as he and Dora

are . . . together. I told you: I like him. He's good to talk to. Like you. And Gail. Not Keith so much; he reminds me too much of his father. I don't mind it that Fred isn't coming; we won't miss him. I would like Marian, though, and Nina. Well, we'll still have our picnic; we'll be a family." He sat back with a long sigh. A family, a picnic, fireworks. He felt content. He had forgotten his dismay at not wanting breakfast, and his worry over the loss of all his appetites. He would probably recall them sometime later, but for now they were gone. So many things disappeared lately in just that way: one minute they filled his thoughts, and the next they had slipped away and all that was left was a vague tremor in his mind that told him something had been troubling him. Every time that happened, he was astonished, because the more distant past was so clear, so bright, his memories finely etched in such perfect detail: people's names, the plots of books, the scents of women, the touch of death when he kissed Alice good-bye.

But he wasn't going to weep over it; he had never been a whiner even when sorrow clung to him for years on end. He had his health; he had Leo and Gail and their two children, closer to him than anyone else in his family; he had Tamarack. He wasn't completely content, because he always wondered about Anne, and he worried about Charles, struggling to run Chatham Development, but as he sat in the sunlight, he thought he had come through pretty well. He had been like a god; he had left his mark on the world. Now he was grateful for every day he had left, and for his memories, unexpurgated by time. Only one of those memories caused him real pain, his memory of Anne, because he had been the one she'd turned to and counted on, and he had let her down.

And he still did not know why. He had never understood why he did what he did that night, at her birthday dinner. And it gnawed at him. After all these years, he could not think of Anne without guilt and pain.

"Dear Anne," he murmured, and because his eyes were closed, he did not see Leo turn in surprise. ". . . sorry, so sorry. I loved you and I failed you. I wish I could ask your forgiveness and hold you close and protect you. Of course you're a woman now, and you probably don't need my protection, but still, I wish I could make a place for you where you'd be safe and loved. I wish you'd come here, Anne, so I could tell you I love you and I'm sorry. I wish I could tell you that before I die."

The sunlight traced red veins through his closed eyelids; the heat made him feel he was melting into the earth. "Anne," he sighed. And then he was asleep.

Vince liked being a senator. He liked the beginning of the day when he walked into his reception room and was greeted with deference by his staff; he liked the end of the day when he paused on his way out to look through the noble windows at the smooth lawns and government buildings that were the hub of power, the center of the world. Senators who had been there for years tended to downplay their power and say they were just doing a job, working for the people of their states, but Vince never took any of that seriously. He knew that the Senate's reach extended to everyone in the world, from ignorant villagers to kings, presidents, and rock stars; and that the one hundred of them who were its members were the most envied people in the world.

Charles envied him. "My God, what a feeling, to be part of all this," he said on his first visit to Washington after Vince's election. "Like sitting at the center of the world." He was helping Vince hang paintings in his new apartment, and he stopped beside the window as he carried a large oil landscape across the room. The apartment was in a glittering new complex on the Potomac, its curved window walls overlooking the esplanade along the waterfront and the Watergate apartments and the Kennedy Center. In the other direction was the Key Bridge, spanning the river to Alexandria. Charles fixed his gaze on Roosevelt Island and the still water of the Potomac, turning bronze beneath the last rays of the sun. The center of the world, he thought with a sudden ache of melancholy. I'm sixty-two years old and I'll never be any closer to it than here, on the edge of Vince's life. But whose fault is that? When have I ever taken a risk? "You belong here, you know," he said, bringing the painting to Vince. "I wish I did, but I'd never get nominated, much less elected. I guess it's a good thing; somebody has to stay home and get out the vote."

"And raise money," said Vince, taking the painting from him. "You and William did a hell of a job."

Charles felt a rush of gratitude for Vince's praise. "I surprised myself. But I don't think I could do it for anyone else. It's too exposed, asking people for money; it's like asking them to perform a sex act in public."

Vince roared with laughter. "I won't ask you to do that. Just concentrate on money, Charles; you've got five years to get clear on the difference between it and sex before my next campaign."

Angered and embarrassed, Charles turned to the stack of paintings. "I don't understand why you chose the committees you did," he said.

"Because they're not popular." Vince joined Charles and took a painting from the stack. "Jasper Johns; we'll put it over the bed. A good place for it; all that nervous energy. It's not complicated, you know: I didn't want strong committees with strong chairmen; I wanted committees I could control. Nobody's passionate about Agriculture, Nutrition and Forestry; nobody's building a campaign around Environment and Public Works."

"For a reason," Charles said. "The voters aren't interested in them."

"Not yet. So the chairmen will be out playing golf and angling for other committees, and they'll be glad to let me do most of their work. I'll be the one to schedule hearings, and control the questioning of witnesses, and prepare the final report. And help write the legislation that comes from it. That's where the favors are, and the reputations."

"But agriculture and nutrition . . ."

"It could be sewers and warthogs; what the hell do I care:

But don't underestimate agriculture; there's a lot of ammunition there. The farmers are going to have their subsidies pulled out from under them in a few years, and the ones who come out heroes on that will be senators from the West who try to help, but get run over by senators from the East." He grinned. "You heard it here first."

"And public works?"

"Forget public works. It's the environment that's the sexy one. So far nobody knows how to use it without it backfiring somewhere, but one of these days we'll work it out; it's so fucked up it's a time bomb, and whoever figures out how to pitch it in a campaign can do just about anything he wants. Get elected to anything he wants."

"You didn't say it was fucked up in your campaign."

"And I won't, until I figure out how to handle it. The committee's a start. One of the wonders of life in Congress is that committee hearings replace thought and action. You don't have to have any beliefs at all. You just keep scheduling witnesses and asking sharp questions, and everyone thinks you're concerned and working hard at your job. You can go on a long time that way, and now and then get your thirty seconds on the evening news and a few paragraphs in the morning paper, and use some of the testimony in your campaigns. Your opponent hasn't been holding hearings, after all; he has to have real ideas, and since most candidates don't have any, you've got a nice head start. And if you're any good at all, you never lose it."

Charles was silent, repelled and fascinated and filled with envy. And when had he been any different with Vince? he thought. Younger and shorter, Vince had always dominated Charles, and the whole family. Of course Ethan had forced him out, but in the long run what good had that done? Chatham Development Corporation had gone downhill, Vince was far richer than before and a United States senator, and Ethan had left them all, for his damned mountain. Charles had less than ever: one of his daughters vanished, the other cool to him and living in Tamarack, his father gone, a company that was weaker because of him, his other brothers and sisters going their separate ways. All Charles had was a brother who had everything.

So he visited Washington as often as he could. The fascination was double: not only Vince, but the Senate as well, where Charles breathed the atmosphere of important men and felt himself as close to great events as he could hope to be. It was harder than ever to stay in Chicago; he wanted to be with Vince, who moved through Washington and its intricacies of power easily and assuredly, drawing attention wherever he went. And he took Charles with him: to parties where foreign leaders talked of events known to most of the world only through headlines, to small lunches where senators discussed the administration in scatological terms that would cause a scandal if they became public, to dinners with party leaders who talked of future elections, campaign strategy, polls, and above all, money. Charles tagged along, feeling younger than Vince, less experienced, an outsider in the heady whirl of politics, networking, policy-making, and women.

Vince always had women. He'd been bored with Maisie, he told an astonished Charles; he didn't know if he'd ever marry again. But meanwhile, Washington was full of single women, and unerringly, they found Vince.

In Chicago, Charles felt alone, sitting in his father's chair, trying to make money for his father's company, searching for ways to prove himself his father's worthy successor. It didn't matter that Ethan was gone; his presence hovered over everything; it all still seemed to belong to him. And Charles had no one to tell him what he longed to hear: that he was better and more dynamic than Ethan, more a master of Chatham Development than Ethan had ever been. Charles had no one to tell him anything. Over the years he had thought of marrying again, but somehow the image of his father, noble in widowed singleness, held him back. He saw little of William and Nina and Marian, mainly at family affairs on holidays. He always felt they were weighing his behavior against their father's, worried that he might destroy the company that enriched them all.

Instead, he went to Washington. He stayed in Vince's apartment and clung to Vince, and often Vince would find a woman for him and the four of them would go to dinner or to the theater. And each time, before he returned to Chicago, Charles would dream of selling Chatham Development and retiring.

Of course he couldn't do that; Ethan had entrusted him with the company. More than that, Ethan was still taking part in some of the company's ventures, and demanding financial statements and regular progress reports. And Charles was in the midst of an enormous project, the largest he had ever handled.

It was called Deerstream Village and he had begun designing it five years earlier, after an architectural critic said that Chatham Development could no longer be taken seriously; it had fallen from Ethan Chatham's brilliant and innovative leadership to the safety of small projects and timid designs. Stung, Charles had looked for a project massive and daring enough to bring praise from everyone. He chose as his site five hundred acres of cornfields northwest of Chicago with a small hamlet in their midst called Deerstream. The price had tripled since the federal government announced plans for construction of a highway linking Deerstream and Chicago, and other developers were hesitating, but Charles plunged in.

Fred Jax worked with him on Deerstream. Charles got along with Fred, though he knew others in the family didn't like him and hadn't, from the time Marian brought him home and Ethan disapproved of their marriage because of what he called Fred's cruel streak. Charles saw it, too, and did not admire it, but he could deal with it; occasionally it was useful.

Fred shared his vision for Deerstream, to make it the biggest of the western suburbs, with the largest enclosed shopping mall in the world, fronting on the new highway. It would take all the financial and manpower resources of Chatham Development, but it would be the greatest project Chicago had ever seen. It would give Charles a name even bigger than his father's. And then he would hand over the presidency to Fred Jax and walk away from the company with dignity.

Vince asked about Deerstream whenever Charles came to Washington. He showed more interest in it than in anything else Charles had done, as the land was surveyed, as plans were drawn and ground broken for the first mall, as blueprints were drawn and bids let for the first filing of single-family homes.

"And the highway?" he asked Charles on a warm night in September. They were taking a walk on the way back to his apartment from dinner at the Sequoia, ties loosened, jackets slung over one shoulder. A stranger might have taken them for relatives because of an elusive resemblance, though one was shorter by four inches, blond, and remarkably handsome, with an almost cocky stride, and the other, with gray hair and rounded shoulders, was handsome in a diminished way, because of an indecisive mouth and a scowl of worry between his eyes. "What about the highway?" Vince asked. "You were worried about it when we were in Maine in July."

Charles shrugged. "Still the same. Three years and they're still talking about where to put it. The bastards; it's not their worry, so they don't push it."

"But why would you worry? The funds have been appropriated."

"You know damn well why I'm worried. It isn't being built. You said, last time we talked, you'd look into it."

"I didn't get to it; I will, this week."

"You could put on some pressure, Vince; you know how much is riding on this. If we don't have a highway to the city, we've got nothing to sell. Who'd want to live in the middle of nowhere with no train and no road?"

Vince shot him a look. "Your holdings could absorb the loss; you haven't put everything into it."

"Damn near. We're not where we were a while back. You know what Dad did, and Leo, that son of a bitch, forcing Chatham Development to borrow that money—*seventy-five million dollars*, for Christ's sake—all of it for Tamarack, none for us. If anything happens to Deerstream, we've got nowhere to go. We can't borrow on our Tamarack holdings; they were our collateral when we borrowed the seventy-five million. We'd have to sell other properties."

Vince was silent. He knew all that; he made it his business to know everything about Chatham Development. But Charles had never before acknowledged the precipice they faced. He turned to walk along the C&O Canal, striding faster, hearing Charles behind him, scurrying to catch up. He tried to slow down for Charles, but something propelled him; an excitement that made him want to move, and exult.

More than twenty years before, Vince had vowed to make his family pay for forcing him out. Now the time had come. And Charles was making it easy for him by putting everything into Deerstream, betting the whole company on a highway that hadn't even been begun. He had weakened the company, put the family at risk, left them exposed. All Vince had to do was blow at them as he would a thistle in the desert, and they would go down. It would kill Ethan; it would destroy Charles. How could Charles live with the knowledge that he had undone in five years what Ethan had built up in a lifetime?

Vince smiled in the darkness. Wait long enough, he thought, and everything you want comes to pass.

"Mister," said a young voice, "gimme five dollars; I got a sick little baby in my family."

Charles stopped. "What?" he asked. He had been trying to keep up with Vince, and it took him a minute to realize what the boy was saying. He was small and very young—about ten, Charles thought—and he seemed to blend into the trees that bordered the path along the canal. Charles saw movement behind him and imagined other boys, waiting to pounce. Suddenly he was aware of how empty the path was.

"A sick little baby," the young boy said, his voice rising. "She needs medicine. Pills. Ten dollars."

"You just said five."

"She got sicker."

Charles saw the movement in the shadows and reached for his back pocket. The rule was never fight muggers. His life was worth more than ten dollars.

But before he could pull out his wallet, Vince stepped up and slammed his fist into the boy's face. The boy fell, his head tilted, his eyes closed.

"Vince, for Christ's sake—!" Charles cried, and dropped to his knees beside the boy as Vince turned to the shadows behind them.

Another young boy stood there. "Don't," he whimpered. He was standing on one foot and then the other, torn between helping his friend and fleeing. "We weren't gonna . . . we didn't hurt nobody!"

Charles jumped up and grabbed Vince's arm as he started for the boy. "Leave him alone, for God's sake, he's just a kid."

"A lot of them are kids. They have to be taught a lesson."

"You got lots of ten dollars!" the boy cried. "You wouldn't of even missed it!"

"Fucking little son of a bitch—" Vince pulled free of Charles and reached out a long arm to grab the boy.

"Leave him alone!" Charles shoved Vince aside and stood between him and the boy. "We're in enough trouble already; I think you've killed the other one."

Vince looked down at the boy on the path. He nudged him with his foot and the boy groaned. "It takes more than that to kill these punks," he said. "All right, let's go; his friend can take care of him. Fucking little bastards. They were ready to jump you, you know. Why the hell did you go for your wallet?"

"It wouldn't have been worth getting killed. Even if it was the whole wallet."

"Why were you so sure you'd be killed?" Vince was walking rapidly, his stride as long and confident as before. It was as if nothing had happened. They left the C&O path and were on K Street again, less than a block from his apartment.

Charles caught up to him. He was shaking, but it was not because of the two boys. It was because of Vince. *Why were you so sure you'd be killed?* There had been contempt in that question, and Charles could not bear Vince's contempt. But why *had* he been so sure? Why had it never occurred to him to attack? The kid was half his height, a third his weight, and probably terrified. Why hadn't Charles Chatham, righteous citizen, knowledgeable city dweller, and world traveler, smashed his fist into the kid's face, knocked him to kingdom come, the way his younger and shorter brother had?

He didn't know. He never knew why Vince always came across as the man of action and he himself as the timid follower. All his life he had been unable to break away from Vince's spell. And the most devastating evidence of that had come twenty-four years earlier, when he had wavered between his own daughter and Vince, and by his silence, had chosen Vince.

And he still did not know whether he had been right. He still could not believe that Vince would touch Anne. That would have meant there was evil within his brother that Charles could not fathom and had never seen. If he had, he would have leaped to his daughter's defense when she gave evidence that evil was in their midst. I would have, he told himself. Of course I would.

Vince walked around the circular fountain at the entrance to his building and waited for Charles. "I'll be in my study; I have some calls to make," he said as they rode the elevator to the twelfth floor. "Committee hearing at ten tomorrow morning, if you want to come."

"I'll let you know," Charles said. He nodded to the butler who opened the door. "I may go back tomorrow; I probably ought to stick close to the office for a while."

"Whatever you want. You can come and go; you know that. Help yourself to a drink. I'll see you at breakfast, unless you decide to take an early flight."

"Good night," Charles said. He poured a large whiskey and took it to the guest suite at the end of the hall. He pulled out his suitcase. For the first time, he was anxious to get away. It wasn't so much Vince that he wanted to escape; it was his own dependence. I'm sixty-seven, Charles thought —he seemed to think about his age more when he was with Vince than at any other time—what the hell is wrong with me? He knew he cut a ridiculous figure: a graying, sophisticated businessman who could not break away from the magnetism of his younger brother.

But I can't even break away from the success of my father, he added silently.

He sat on the edge of the bed. He would have to go to Tamarack and tell Ethan what was happening with Chatham Development. Too much was at stake. He had thought he might tell him a few months earlier, when Leo had asked him to come for the Fourth of July. Instead, he had gone to Maine with Vince. I'll tell him, he decided. Whatever happens, he has to know. Maybe we can pull it off, together. He won't mind if I ask for his help one more time.

There was a knock on the door and Vince walked in. "Leo called. Ethan's had a stroke; he's asking for you. You'd better book a flight."

Charles reached for the telephone. "How bad is he?"

"I don't know. They're flying him to Denver and Gail's with him in the plane. You might call me when you find out."

"You're not going?"

"I can't miss the hearing in the morning. I'll come later if you think I should."

They looked at each other. "He's ninety," Charles said. "We always knew he had to die."

"After a while it seemed he never would," Vince said neutrally, and left the room as Charles made his reservation for the earliest flight to Denver.

Ethan heard them come into his room, but he did not bother opening his eyes. He knew why they were gathering around his bed: his family had come to see him die. Well, that was fine; that was what they should do. He didn't really want to be alone right now because he was feeling a little frightened about what was coming. He thought it would be like sinking into sleep, and he certainly didn't mind that; he'd been tired most of the time since his stroke, whenever that was. It seemed a very long time ago. It had been in the fall, he remembered that, and Charles had flown from

Washington, where he'd been visiting Vince. They'd all expected him to die then, but he'd come through fine. Well, not so fine. He couldn't make people understand him, even though he knew exactly what he wanted to say; and he couldn't go anywhere, couldn't walk around Tamarack on a warm morning and sit in the café with a croissant and coffee that he wasn't hungry for. Lately he'd been thinking he ought to let go, just fall asleep and let everything go. But then he'd remember that he wouldn't wake up, ever, and he'd think, not yet, not for a while yet; I'm not ready to go that far.

He wanted to see Gail's children grow up; they were so bright and full of new ways of looking at the world, and they loved him. He wanted to help Charles; he didn't think there would ever be a time when Charles would not need help. He wanted to wait for Anne; he knew she would come back someday, maybe tomorrow, or even this evening, in time for dinner, and he had to be here to greet her. He wanted to watch over Tamarack, to try to head off its worst excesses as it continued to grow. He wanted to walk in the mountains and breathe the scent of pine trees after a rain, and the perfume of wild roses that were so fragile each one lived only a day, and the moist earth with succulent mushrooms growing at the bases of the spruce and Douglas fir.

But he knew none of that would happen. He was too tired, too old and too tired, and it was time to give up, to let go of the avid grasp he had had on life for ninety-one years.

". . . sell. I told you: we have no choice."

It was Charles' voice, low and urgent. Ethan could just make out the words. Sell what? he wondered. Maybe his house in Lake Forest; God knows why he kept it all these years. His wife dead, Gail here, Anne gone; no new wife to sweeten the dead air in those big formal rooms. Crazy that he kept it all these years. So now he's going to sell it. Probably get a good price; the market was good in the whole Chicago area.

"You can't." That was Leo. What did Leo care whether or not Charles sold his Lake Forest house? "It would kill Ethan."

"He won't know."

"He'd know. Anyway, it's mortgaged to the hilt; you wouldn't get enough to make it worth losing Tamarack."

Tamarack? Ethan opened his eyes. "Rack," he said. His voice was thready. "Rack and ruin." He struggled and his mouth worked. *"Corner,"* he burst out.

"Oh, look what you've done," Gail cried. Ethan's eyes moved to see her. She was a good girl: pretty, helpful, kind. A kind young woman. She would miss him; they were good friends. "He knows, and he's upset. Leave him alone; leave Tamarack alone. It would be the worst thing in the world to sell it." She looked at Charles, her eyes pleading. "You can't do it."

"I'm doing what I have to do," Charles said flatly. "William and I have the votes—"

"Not ready to sell," William rumbled.

Charles exploded. "Damn it, you're in trouble, too!"

"Please!" Nina cried. "Don't shout!" She was watching Ethan, who had closed his eyes again. "Maybe he'll go back to sleep."

"It doesn't matter," Charles said. "If he did hear us, he understood; he knows how business works better than all the rest of us put together. He'd be with me on selling Tamarack."

"Bullshit," said Leo. "He'd hold on to Tamarack till he died. What did you mean, William is in trouble, too?"

"We're all in trouble." Charles paced up and down one side of the room. "The company, Tamarack, all of us. Christ, you know what's happening around here; if we don't get out pretty soon, we won't *have* anything to sell."

Leo shook his head. "Tamarack isn't in trouble; we're doing fine here. If you mean the EPA, we can handle that. They won't find any problems. My God, those mine dumps have been here for almost a hundred years; if there's still some lead leaching out of them, we'll take care of it. Whatever it is, it isn't as bad as they're saying in Washington. The only mystery is why they picked us to test when there are old mines all over Colorado. But we'll be okay; I'm not worried about it."

"Well, I am," Charles said angrily. "How many times do I have to say it? This family is in trouble; and I'm selling everything I can to cover our losses on Deerstream—"

"That was a doomed project," William said.

Charles swung on him. "You helped put it together."

"I told you to wait for the highway."

"The money was allocated! It was a sure thing!"

"Then where is it?" asked Marian. "There's an awful lot of corn out there, and no concrete."

"It doesn't matter anymore," Charles said. "Vince said the money got reallocated in conference as part of another bill before he could catch it. I suppose it happens all the time."

"I'll write a letter to the editor of the *Times*," said William. "You can't trust a government that changes its mind in midstream."

"Just what we need: one of your letters," Charles said sarcastically. "Look, I need the money from Tamarack! Aren't any of you listening? We're going to sell it; it's the only thing left to do!"

"But Charles, dear," said Nina, "are you sure you have the votes?"

"For God's sake, we don't need votes. This isn't the Senate or the House; it's a family."

"But you're the one who mentioned William's shares."

Ethan stopped listening. He felt a deep sadness that his family was quarreling while he was dying, but he didn't know how to stop them; he couldn't make the right words come out. There was nothing more that he could do. And they'd manage; they'd figure things out. They wouldn't sell The Tamarack Company; Leo and Gail would never allow it. Everything would work out fine, and his legacy would live on. Buildings, towns, factories: they would endure. The solid structure of Chatham Development: that would endure. And Tamarack. He'd brought it back to life and it, too, would endure.

When he was a young boy, he'd made a cardboard house with so many stories it reached to the ceiling. The ceiling was the only thing that stopped it. And when he grew up, he had no ceiling to stop him: his office towers and apartments and hotels reached to the sky, and his towns touched the horizon. What great dreams he'd had, and such a long, long reach.

But not long enough to reach Anne. He had betrayed her. Oh, why did he have to remember that? It came sharply, opening a wound, and he was too tired to deal with it. It's too hard, he thought. Too terrible to think about Vince and Anne.

The words were like snakes. He tried to ignore them. Too tired, he insisted; much too tired. But the snakes grew longer and fatter and he could not step over them or run past them. He faced them. Vince and Anne. In bed, naked bodies together, faces close, skin touching. Him inside her. Vince and Anne. *No!* Ethan screamed silently.

Oh, God, he thought, and groaned. Dear God, I was jealous. And so I forced her to leave.

I didn't want her myself, he thought; not that way. I never thought of that. But I wanted her to be young and innocent and stay that way forever. I wanted her to turn to me for companionship and laughter and love. She wouldn't need other men, at least not for years and years; she was so young and I could give her everything she needed. That was what I wanted: that she look to me as if I was her god.

He groaned again. There it was again: thinking of himself as a god. And as his punishment, he had lost Anne.

But Anne was the one who suffered most, he thought. I wonder if she has ever forgiven me. I hope she understands that what I did came from my own weakness; it had nothing to do with her. She was always lovely and truthful and good. Please forgive me, Anne. I didn't understand what was happening. I swear to you, I didn't understand. Please forgive me, Anne. This is the last time I can ask you. Find peace, dearest Anne. And joy. And love.

His family's voices were growing fainter, as if they were moving away from him. No, he realized; he was moving away from them, leaving them behind. Suddenly, everything was absolutely silent. This isn't so bad, Ethan thought. No pain or struggle; just this soft fading away. It's like falling asleep in the sunshine. Warm, content, melting into the earth. I like that; it's such a good place to be. I reached so high, but this is better now: to settle down, to sink deep and deeper into the earth.

Yes. So deep. So good. A part of the earth.

It was Ethan's picture that looked up at Anne the next morning when she read the newspaper at her desk. "Ethan Chatham, one of the century's greatest builders, died yesterday at his home in Tamarack, Colorado. He was ninety-one."

Anne skimmed the story to the end. "Funeral services will be held in the chapel at Lake Forest, Illinois, on Wednesday."

She sat still for a moment. Her hand was trembling. But her voice was firm as she picked up her telephone and asked her secretary to make reservations for Tuesday night, for a round-trip flight to Chicago.

chapter 8

Gail slid past Leo and their son, Ned, to the side aisle. She walked past the people standing there, and by the time she reached Anne, her hands were outstretched. "You are Anne, aren't you? I *feel* that you're Anne. Wouldn't a sister know—?"

Their hands met, and held. "Hello, Gail," Anne said softly.

With a small cry, Gail threw her arms around Anne. "I'm so glad," she said, her words muffled. "You don't know how glad . . ."

Anne looked over her sister's shoulder at the crowded chapel. It looked like a painting: row on row of wondering faces turned to the side of the room, focused for a few seconds on the embracing women. Not a sound or breath of air broke that frozen stillness.

"Friends, we are here for Ethan," said the minister in a gentle reproach, and the room rustled again as the crowd reluctantly turned toward him. "Now that those who cared for him have spoken, I want to talk about my friendship with Ethan, going back thirty years. And then we will go from here to lay him to rest for eternity beside his beloved Alice."

Charles had not turned back to the minister. He still looked to the side of the room, and met Anne's eyes in a long look. As with Vince, she was the first to look away. Her hands on Gail's arms were trembling; her whole body was trembling. *Not yet, not yet. I know it will happen: we'll sit together, and talk, and find out what bonds still connect us, but not yet. I can't face it yet.*

"You're shaking," said Gail, drawing back.

"There's a lot going on," Anne replied with a small smile. "Like juggling emotions on a high wire. Gail, I'm getting out of here. Can you come with me?"

"You're not going to the cemetery?"

"I don't need to; I've said good-bye. I had to be here, but I don't have to drag it out. I'll wait for you, though, if you want to go with the others."

"No, I'd rather come with you. Let me just tell Leo."

"I'll be outside," said Anne. She moved quietly up the aisle and slipped through the doors, almost invisibly, just as she had come in, half an hour earlier.

"Thank God," she said, pulling off her black hat and taking a deep breath when Gail joined her outside. "It was stifling in there."

"Probably all the people," said Gail.

"And the memories." Anne looked at the lake, steel gray beneath the dark, fast-moving clouds and the flashes of sunlight that broke through, then vanished, then broke through again. "I might be able to take them one at a time, but all of them at once is too much. Where shall we go to talk?"

"We're staying at Marian's," Gail said slowly. "We could be private there."

"No, I don't want . . ." The words trailed away. Anne's hat dangled from her black-gloved hand as she walked on the path that led to the street. She had walked on that path so many times she found herself automatically skirting a curve where tall bushes had stretched out their branches to snag the unwary. But the bushes were gone; they had been replaced by a low, neatly trimmed hedge that presented no danger to anyone. No danger, she thought. And she had come this far; why not go all the way, to the house where she grew up? "Fine; let's go there. Can we walk? I'd like that."

They turned north from the chapel, walking beneath tall oaks and elms that entwined their leafy branches in a long tunnel over the street. Thin shafts of light pierced the leaves, and Anne and Gail walked through them like ghosts passing through sunlit walls. On either side, tall shrubbery and iron gates set in high brick walls allowed fleeting glimpses of brick or gray-stone mansions. Except for an occasional automobile, there was no sign of life; no one else strolled on those deserted sidewalks. Anne remembered that from her childhood: almost no one walks in the suburbs.

"Where did you go?" Gail asked.

"San Francisco." The sun had been shining, Anne remembered. It had been a beautiful April morning. "There was a neighborhood there where people went when they left home."

"Haight Ashbury." Gail nodded. "I've read about it. I can't imagine you there; it was so weird."

"No, it wasn't. It was the most loving place in the world. After a while it changed, and I went to Berkeley, to college. And then Harvard, for law school."

"Law school? You're a lawyer?"

"Yes. In Los Angeles."

"What kind of lawyer?"

"Mostly divorce."

Gail glanced at her. "Are you married?"

"No."

"Or divorced?"

"No. But you're married; you and Leo. And those lovely children sitting with you are yours?"

"Yes, Robin and Ned. Robin was just eight and Ned will be ten in September. You'll like them; they're wonderful. So is Leo. He was very close to Grandpa. He's president of The Tamarack Company. Grandpa trusted him—and me, too, I guess—to protect all his dreams."

"Tell me about Leo."

"He's very serious, very ambitious, and very protective. Here we are." She stopped walking. "But of course you know that. Isn't this the most amazing thing? Your being here? The two of us going home together?"

"Yes," Anne said. The years vanished and she crossed the

street as if she were coming home from school at the end of the day. They walked between the brick pillars and up the long driveway to Marian's house. Without thinking, Anne started for the side door, then pulled back as Gail went to the front door and opened it with her key. And once inside, Anne forced herself to walk steadily across the foyer and up the stairs and all the way to the end of the second-floor corridor. She opened the door and gazed at the room. Her room. Beyond the windows the clouds swirled, and the room was gray and somber, as it had been that dawn when she packed her duffel bag. Nothing had been changed from the day she left it. No, there was one change. There were no fresh roses on the table to match the roses that were everywhere else: in the drapes, the window seat, the wallpaper, the vanity skirt, the bed . . .

Abruptly, she turned away and pulled the door shut behind her. The sound exploded in the silent house. When Vince had closed that door, he had done it so carefully it had made no sound at all. A long breath broke from her like a sob.

"Come on," said Gail. She was standing at the top of the stairs, halfway down the hall. "Let's make some tea." She waited until Anne was beside her and they were descending the stairs. "I didn't know what you meant, when you told them that night . . . well, I was nine; I didn't know anything. I just knew it was awful, because of the way you looked, and the way everybody yelled at everybody. Marian wouldn't tell me. I kept asking her, and asking where you were, why you'd left, why nobody would talk about you—"

"They didn't?"

"Nobody talked much about anything. Daddy said it was like a tomb. It was, you know; it was terrible. I stayed after school so I'd get home as late as I could, and Marian found me a place to do arts and crafts on Saturdays, and in the summer I went to camp in Wisconsin. The whole summer. When you left, everything just fell apart. I hated it. I didn't understand anything, and nobody would tell me anything, and most of all I missed you. I can't believe you're here now;

I can't believe I'm really talking to you. I've thought about you so often, you know, and how much I missed you. I felt like I'd lost my home, and lost my family, too."

"That makes two of us."

As if there had been no break since the last time she had done it, Anne filled the teakettle and put it on the stove, turned on the gas burner, reached to the shelf above for mugs and the teapot, and set them on the counter. Every movement was exact; she did not have to think about any of it.

"Eerie," she said with a little shake of her head. "I'm caught in some kind of time warp."

"How did it happen?" Gail asked. "Did he threaten you?"

Anne's muscles tightened. She sat at the table beside the French doors that led to the backyard. It had begun to rain; there were slashes of lightning above the lake. She remembered these July thunderstorms; fierce downpours that were over within fifteen minutes, moving away on faint and then fainter rumbles of thunder, leaving behind a pall of hot, heavy air that made it hard to breathe. "I can't talk about it," she said.

"Even now? After *twenty-four years?* Couldn't you tell me anything?"

Anne shook her head.

Gail sighed. "It's just that I don't know anything about you, and I want to. All these years I've had a sister, but I haven't had a sister, and I kept wishing for you. I was too young before, but I kept thinking if you ever came back, we could be such good friends. All the time I was growing up there were things I couldn't tell my friends, and I thought if you were here, I could tell you. As if we had a head start on being close even though we never saw each other. Does that make sense? So I don't want to push you and make you miserable, but if you ever want to talk to me, I wish you would. The thing is, in some ways, I feel so far from you. Everybody said I wouldn't understand what you'd said that night, I wouldn't understand, I wouldn't understand, so finally I asked somebody at school, and she made it very clear, in a lot more detail than I wanted, but I still didn't know anything about *you.*" There was a pause. "Could you at least tell me . . . did it go on for a long time?"

Anne gripped her hands. "Two years."

"Two years? My God, you were *thirteen* when he—? And you didn't tell anyone? Why didn't you tell Marian?"

Anne closed her eyes. She felt sick, and angry. But what had she expected? That Gail wouldn't ask questions? "Marian never liked hearing about problems," she said, her voice low. "You know that. And"—she forced the words out—"he threatened to kill me."

"Oh, no. How could anyone in our family—" The teakettle burst into a shrill shriek and Gail turned off the burner. "I can't imagine anyone saying that." She poured the water into the teapot and added loose tea. Her movements were as exact and controlled as Anne's. She placed the mugs precisely in front of her place and Anne's, and the sugar and cream equidistant from the mugs. She took a plate of scones from the freezer, heated them for a minute in the microwave oven, and placed them on the table with a tub of butter, moving the sugar and cream so that the grouping was perfectly balanced.

"I do that, too," Anne said. "Are you ever sloppy?"

"Never. It would keep me up all night. Are you?"

Anne shook her head and smiled. This was better: the two of them, getting acquainted. This was what she had wanted in the chapel when they embraced: to begin with today, to ignore the past. There were almost no memories attached to Gail.

And yet they were sisters. The word was strange to Anne and it gave her a little shock each time she said it to herself. She never thought of those words—*sister, father, grandfather, aunt, uncle, cousin*—in connection with herself. But now she did. *Sister,* she thought deliberately, watching Gail butter a scone. She was not sure what that meant: what they would be to each other. Like herself and Eleanor, perhaps, but much closer. In fact, Gail already seemed closer in some ways. She's like me, Anne thought. Too neat, trying to control everything. Afraid of being sloppy because that could mean things are getting out of hand, the way they did before. And she looks like me. I like that.

"How many years did you go to camp?" she asked.

"Oh, forever. Anything was better than staying home all summer, and anyway, I liked it. I started being a counselor when I was fifteen and kept going until I went away to college. Did you ever miss us?"

"Yes. Where did you go to college?"

"Northwestern. I never got very far from home. I don't know why. Maybe I was afraid of really being on my own. I never have been, you know. I went from home to a dormitory, and I met Leo when I was eighteen, when he came to work for Grandpa, and we got married when I graduated. If you really missed us, why didn't you call?"

"I didn't think I'd ever come back." Anne sipped her tea, Marian's jasmine tea, which she had not tasted since she left, and was swept by other memories, triggered by its steaming fragrance. "I remember once, when William was writing one of his letters—does he still do that?"

"All the time. He keeps believing he can change things he doesn't approve of, and he writes to everybody—senators, congressmen, newspapers, presidents of corporations, the White House . . . he never loses faith."

Anne smiled. "Well, William was using Marian's typewriter and drinking her tea and giving me advice, all at the same time. I was about ten or eleven, and I didn't pay much attention, but it's strange, I must have been listening, because I remember so clearly how he looked up suddenly and said, 'When you grow up, young lady, you put your life together the absolute best you can, and do it all the way; don't dabble and don't hang on by your toenails to whatever's safe; plunge in, keep your eyes straight ahead, and never look back, because there's nothing there: it's all in the future.' " Anne paused. "I've never forgotten that. He was so fierce. I thought about that when I was in the Haight. I missed you—most of you—but I couldn't come back. They made me feel too alone. So I made my own life and I did what William said: I kept my eyes straight ahead and I didn't look back."

They were silent. "I'm sorry," said Gail. "I can't even imagine feeling like that. Nothing really awful has ever happened to me. Isn't that amazing? I'm thirty-three years old and I haven't had one really terrible experience. I don't remember Mother, and as for everything else . . . I've had bad things and I've been unhappy, but those times passed and didn't leave any scars. I wonder if that's true of most people."

"I think everything leaves a scar," Anne said. "We change a little bit, or a lot, every time something happens to us. Sometimes we're hardly aware of it, and other times we know nothing will ever be the same again."

Gail gazed at her sister. "Did you have other terrible things, after you left here?"

"No, I've been careful. But I deal with them in my office. My clients are usually pretty unhappy—some of them are thrilled at shedding a wife or a husband and starting again with somebody new, but most of them are having a rough time—and they all think their troubles are unique and devastating. And in a way they're right: they do feel devastated and nobody else has ever gone through their particular divorce with their particular children and parents and in-laws and property . . . the whole thing. And divorce always changes people, even though most of them are too vindictive or defensive or relieved or beat down to be aware of it at the time."

"What did you mean: you've been careful?" Gail asked.

"Oh, I don't get involved with anyone. I made a good friend in the Haight—we're still friends—but after that I was too busy. Would you like more tea?"

"Yes, thank you. You don't have any close friends? Or men?"

"I have Eleanor, my friend from the Haight. And I like some of the people in the firm." Anne poured the tea. Tendrils of steam curled upward against the rain-streaked window. The kitchen was warm and bright; it felt good to be there. "Most of us need a lot less than we think, you know. If we have work that we love, and if we're interested in a lot of things, so we're always learning, that's enough. We don't need crowds of people. We don't really need anyone."

Gail ran her finger around the rim of her mug. "You don't mean that."

"It's the way I've lived all my life."

"Not when you lived here."

"A lot of the time I did. A lot of the time I felt like a stranger. And when I needed them most, they treated me like one."

"But you came back."

"I wanted to say good-bye to Ethan. I never understood why he didn't help me that night, but I loved him and he was the one I missed the most. I wish we'd had a chance to talk before he died; I would have asked him why he let me down. And I would have told him I always loved him."

"Leo said he talked about you."

"He did? What did he say?"

"You should ask Leo."

There was a pause. "I don't think so. I'd like to meet Leo, but I don't want to see any of the others. I'll leave before they get here."

"I don't want you to leave; I just got you back," Gail said. "Oh, but you could . . . Listen, Anne, come to Tamarack with us! We're leaving tonight; Leo has to get back. Do come with us. You can get to know Leo and the kids, and we can talk all we want. You'll stay with us; we have loads of room. Oh, Anne, please say you will. It would be wonderful."

"I don't know." But already the idea had taken hold. She had not seen Tamarack for twenty-four years, and it had been her favorite place. "How many of the family live there?"

"Just Keith; you remember, Marian and Fred's son. I guess he was about five when you left. He went through a wild time, lots of booze and drugs, and then one day out of the blue he showed up and asked Leo for a job. That was about three years ago; he's assistant to the mountain manager now, and I think he's really straightened out. We hardly see him; he has his own friends."

"And that's all? No one else?"

"Well, Dora and Josh, the guy she lives with, have a house in town, and they're in and out. He's terrific; we got to be good friends. We don't see him as often as we'd like; they live in Los Angeles. If you're asking about Vince, he never comes to Tamarack. Daddy doesn't come; neither does William. Marian and Fred and Nina come once or twice a year. That's all. None of them gives a damn about the town. They were furious when Grandpa got Chatham Development to borrow money to develop Tamarack; they were always mad at him because they thought he cared about Tamarack more than the company or anything else in Chicago. We could disappear tomorrow and all they'd care about would be the money they might lose."

Anne put down her mug. "What's wrong, Gail? What are you afraid of?"

"I'm not. Did I say anything about being afraid?"

"It's what you didn't say. What's wrong at Tamarack?"

"Well. A lot. But I'm not dumping it on you, Anne. And that isn't why I asked you to come home with us. I don't even know how you figured it out."

"I spend a lot of time figuring out what people really mean when they're too worried or scared or mad to come out and say it. And I wouldn't mind if you thought I could help; I'd like it. Though I'm not sure what I could do."

"Maybe we just need somebody to listen to us. Somebody who's part of the family but not really *part* of it, if you know what I mean."

"Perfectly," said Anne, her voice cool. "You couldn't have put it better."

"Oh, no, I didn't mean . . . Oh, Anne, I'm sorry, I didn't mean you're not part of us. Of course you're part of the family; I always thought you were, even when *you* didn't seem to—" She broke off. "I'm saying all the wrong things, aren't I?"

"It's all right," Anne said quietly. "It isn't always clear what the right things are."

"Did you *ever* think of *me?*" Gail burst out.

Anne nodded. "A lot. But I didn't know you. You were so young when I left, and you had your own friends, and we hardly ever saw each other. I thought you'd barely notice that I was gone."

"Well, I did. It was as if you'd died. And the worst was not knowing, and thinking you didn't care about me enough even to call."

"I'm sorry," Anne said. "It didn't occur to me that you might be unhappy, too. I always thought you got along with all of them much better than I did; you never talked back or argued."

"I couldn't. I always got scared when people quarreled and their eyes got shiny and angry. I wish I'd rebelled a little bit, though; it might have been fun."

Anne smiled faintly. "There's not a lot of fun in rebellion; it's mostly misery. Rebellion mostly means being lost and trying desperately to find a place to belong and somebody to pay attention to you." The words lingered in the air. "I'd like to help you, if you think I can. Tell me what you'd like me to do."

"I don't know," Gail said. "I'm not sure what any of us can do. We have to find a way to keep Tamarack. Daddy's wanted to sell it for a long time but he couldn't, as long as Grandpa was alive. Last night he brought it up again—we hadn't even had the funeral!—and Leo and I absolutely refused, but if there's a vote, we could lose. This family doesn't work together. It's crazy, when you think about it, because everybody's been involved with the family company forever, but outside the office something happens to us and we don't even seem to *like* each other. I don't even know what we all want from the company, and from each other; we just don't talk much. You'd think families would talk all the time, and maybe some of them do, but we don't. So I don't see how we can sit down and work this out. I'll tell you the whole story—"

"Not now," Anne said. She looked at her watch, afraid that the family would suddenly appear, massed before her. But as much as she did not want to see them, she did want to go home with Gail. She could spend some time just with Gail's family and rediscover Tamarack and, maybe, find a way to regain some of what she had lost.

But then she pulled back. Gail's family would be the wedge; she'd end up seeing the rest of them. *Too close, too close.* She was safe where she was. She had a home and a job, she was secure in a law firm that had been her only family for a long time. It was a comfortable place to be, with rules and patterns of behavior, ritualized activities and expectations, and scrupulous care that no one stepped on anyone else's toes. A family was nothing like that; no group of people in the world was more unpredictable and potentially chaotic than a family: everybody a loose cannon primed to go off when something happened that no one could have imagined one minute earlier.

I've been careful. I don't get involved with anyone.

But if I go slowly, she thought, it might be all right. This is my family; and it might be safe to talk to some of them.

Unexpectedly, a new idea came to her. Maybe she had been wrong, to leave in such a hurry. It had never occurred to her. Maybe she hadn't lost her family; maybe she had thrown it away. *I ran off and left the rest of them intact. I let Vince have the family, and I left with nothing. I was too young; I didn't know I could fight to keep what was already mine.*

She didn't know if she could do that. But maybe it was time to try. At least to make a start and see if it was really possible, and if it was what she wanted. I could give it a try, she thought. As long as I stay in control. I have to control what happens.

"I want to hear the whole story," she said to Gail. "But not now. I have to leave. You can tell me when we're in Tamarack."

"You'll come, then? Oh, wonderful! What an incredible day this is! I didn't even think about your coming to the funeral, but here we are and it's almost as if we've hardly been apart—do you feel that, how simple everything is?—and now we'll have you in Tamarack! It really is incredible! Isn't it, for you?"

"Yes," Anne said. She put on her suit jacket. "I'll wait for you at the airport. What time is your flight?"

"Eight-fifteen, but what will you do until then? It's only two o'clock. I'll go with you."

"You stay with the others; they'll expect it. I'll meet you at the plane. Don't worry about me; I'll be fine." Anne smiled. "But thank you, anyway; it's been a long time since someone worried about me."

She took a last glance at the kitchen, and then walked back through the house. The limousine she had hired that morning had followed them and was waiting at the door. The rain had stopped and the clouds were lifting; thunder growled far away. Anne directed the driver to take the same route she had walked when she left so long ago, and she watched the village slide by. A much more stylish way to leave, she thought with a smile. But it still hurt to look at this groomed, manicured town that presented a facade of easy living and happy families, of harmony and serenity and deep comfort, and know how false a facade it was. Wealthy towns hide their agonies with ease, Anne thought, behind the work of architects and landscapers, decorators and carpenters, but the wealthiest towns beckon with such exaggerated and false promises that a young person growing up in them is trapped between wishful thinking and reality. And the only escape from that is to get out.

They passed the station where she had stood, her duffel bag beside her, waiting for the train to Chicago. The driver seemed to slow for a moment, then drove on, turning west. When they turned south onto the highway, Anne sat back in the cushioned seat. She would never go back there; Lake Forest and the houses of the Chathams held nothing for her. But she had taken the first step in rejoining her family, and she wanted this time alone, before she met Gail and Leo and the children at the airport, to think about what that meant.

It means I'll give it a try; that's all it means. If there's too much pain, or too much prying, I'll leave, and I'll be back where I was—which is fine; there's nothing wrong with it. But if I like being with them . . .

I'll wait and see. It's worth a day or two of my time, to find out.

Tamarack was a small town the first time Anne saw it, its streets snow packed and muffled, its buildings weighed down by heavy caps of glistening snow hanging low over their eaves. She was five years old and she was there with her parents and grandparents. She learned to ski that winter, and Ethan took her for a ride on a sled pulled by fourteen huskies. The following summer they hiked along a stream to a meadow where the bluebells reached their knees and the only sounds were the hum of insects, the descending trills of birds, and the rush of swift water in the stream. "It's a magic place," Anne said, her voice hushed. *"My* magic place. Someday I'm going to live right in this exact spot." "I'll build your house," Ethan said. "But you might not want to be this far from other people. You have lots of time to think about it."

She never forgot that place, though over the years, in other parts of the world, she found many others even more remote and more wildly beautiful. For ten years she went to Tamarack whenever anyone in the family decided to go, even for only a few days. She became a smooth, fast skier, and in the summers, a strong hiker through pine and aspen forests and over long stretches of rock or tundra. She always skied and hiked alone. She would have liked to make friends in Tamarack, but she never figured out how, since she was in town for such short visits.

Ethan had built a new house on sixty acres on Star Mountain that looked across the valley at the ski runs on Tamarack Mountain, to the east up Wolf Creek Pass, and to the west at some of the tallest, most rugged peaks of the San Juans. A few years later Vince bought eighty acres higher up the mountain, though he never got around to building on them. Marian and Fred Jax built a house in town with a view of Tamarack Mountain from their front windows and Star Mountain from their backyard, though they were almost never there, and Nina rented a condominium in a complex at the base of Tamarack Mountain. Charles and William never built at Tamarack. William preferred beaches and sailing, and Charles refused to put money into the town. After his father began investing heavily in it, he saw it as a rival of Chatham Development and began to dislike everything about it, even its beauty, as people do when they are eaten up with jealousy and must find flaws to justify their hatred.

But Anne loved Tamarack, and knew every inch of the town and the valley. She knew where to pick wild strawberries and raspberries; she knew the paths deer took at night; and she spent hours talking to the old people who had been in Tamarack when Ethan first arrived and who still thought of the town as theirs in spite of all the changes he had brought. Most of those old people were gone by the time she returned with Gail. And much of the old Tamarack was gone, too.

It was as beautiful as ever, but where once it had been like one large neighborhood, now it was a large town. Anne saw a few hamburger and barbecue restaurants left over from the past, one old-fashioned general store, a gas station in the middle of town, and the elementary school, but everything else was changed. Houses and town houses lined the streets, shoulder to shoulder on the narrow lots in town, and spreading beyond the town into the valley and up forested slopes. Estates and golf courses had taken over the fields where Ethan had watched horses graze. Most of the miner's cottages had been torn down and replaced with sleek homes with two-story living rooms and copper roofs. New restaurants had opened, with imported French and Italian chefs, and dozens of new shops, their display cases and racks filled with glittering necklaces and faceted rings, cashmere bathrobes and fur-trimmed ski suits, mink-lined leather jackets and designer sweaters and shoes.

"I can buy the most expensive silver in the world, but I can't always find a wastebasket for the bathroom," Gail said with a laugh as she and Anne walked on the mall.

Anne smiled but did not reply. She was trying to remember where everything had been when she roamed these streets as a child. Their plane had landed late the night before, and she had known from the lights on the ground how far the town now stretched beyond what she remembered, but it was only this morning that she understood how much had changed. She and Gail walked with crowds of tourists on either side of a small, shaded stream that wound its way down the center of the cobblestone mall past shops and outdoor cafés, and Anne recalled Ethan's tales of the days when cars bogged down as spring rains turned the streets to mud. "It does beat mud," she said with another smile. "In fact, it's charming. It's just not Tamarack."

"It is to me," Gail said. "It's the only one I know." They reached the end of the mall and walked into the park, pausing to watch the children on slides and swings. "After you left, when I came with Marian and Fred and their kids, all I cared about was skiing, and I hardly noticed the town. The first time I came in the summer was with some friends from college to go rafting and hiking. That was when I met Leo. He was Grandpa's assistant; he'd been here almost a year and was already practically running the place."

"How long ago was that?"

"Fifteen years this month. That was the most wonderful summer; I spent the days hiking and the nights in bed with Leo. Then, after I finished college we were married, and by then Leo was president of The Tamarack Company and the town was our bread and butter, so I had to start paying lots of attention to it."

At the far side of the park, Gail stopped and looked back at the crowded mall and the buildings of the town: restored office buildings and hotels from the 1890s, new brick buildings that blended with the old, and fake Victorians far fancier than the genuine ones had been. "We still own so much of this town," she said. "You have no idea what Grandpa bought when he started coming here. I guess nobody cared—or maybe they thought they'd found a sucker and they laughed behind his back—but there was a time when he owned the whole west end, half the east end, the whole mall area, most of Main Street, all the land along the base of Tamarack Mountain, and the mining claims on the mountain. That didn't include what he bought in the rest of the valley. Of course he sold a lot of it to other developers, even though he wanted to do it all himself; there just wasn't time. But we still own over fifteen percent of the town and the three biggest ranches in the valley, and it's home and we love it. I can't imagine not having it; it would have killed Grandpa if he'd known Daddy wants to sell it."

"Is he in trouble?" Anne asked. "Does he need the money?"

"That's what he says. He was supposed to build a huge development outside Chicago, and then the government canceled a highway that would have connected it to the city, so all the reasons for the development disappeared. And I guess Daddy put a lot of money up front. Too much, William says. Well, I suppose he is in a lot of trouble, but Tamarack isn't; we're doing fine. And it would be crazy to sell it; we *can't* sell it. We promised Grandpa we'd take care of it for him. And it's part of us; everything we have is here."

"But could the family lose Chatham Development?"

"I don't know. Maybe. But why trade Tamarack for a company that's been going downhill for a long time?"

"Has it?" Anne felt a sudden pang of pity for her father. How hard it must have been for him to watch that happen, and measure himself against Ethan, and know the family was doing the same.

"Leo knows more of the financial stuff than I do, but that's the gist of it," Gail said. They walked to her car. "The main thing is, we've got to stop Daddy from selling—talk to him, bargain, try to help him in Chicago, whatever it takes. He's awfully worried about building something big before he retires, and he can't do that without money, and he says he can't get money without selling Tamarack." She started the car and turned onto Main Street. "Do you want anything special for lunch? We can stop at the store."

"Whatever you have is fine."

They drove across a bridge high above a churning river, and turned onto a narrow road that climbed steadily above the valley to a broad wooded plateau with fenced grazing lands and open meadows thick with bluebells. Anne recognized landmarks and knew it was the meadow she had called her magic place. Memories swept her, far more than they had in Lake Forest the day before; it was as if, this time, she truly had come home. In the past years she had traveled to mountain resorts throughout Europe, but none of them had touched her in this way, with the ache of loss, and paradise rediscovered. She gazed at it, drinking it in; she could not look enough.

Gail drove past woods and meadows for half a mile and then through a gate to a winding drive that led to a low, rambling house of dark wood that blended into the trees. "Grandpa built it for us when we were married," she said, parking in front. "He built three others up here at the same time; we each have forty acres. I love the privacy."

Anne stepped from the car. Surrounding them, range on range of jagged peaks faded into the distance, some still streaked with snow patches in deep crevasses. Before her, the house nestled in a clearing surrounded by fields of wildflowers, and beyond them, forests and meadows of tall wild grass that rippled in the cool breeze. Bird songs floated on the stillness. No other house was visible. "Who lives in the other houses?"

"People from town." Gail looked at her across the hood of the car. "Nobody from the family, if that's what you're asking. Even if they do visit, their houses are in town. And I told you, Vince is never here; he's too busy running the world. At least that's how he talked about it to Grandpa on the phone. Grandpa told me his opinion of Colorado went down when they elected Vince. He said he had grave concerns for a country that had Vince helping run—"

"Doesn't Marian come here at all?" Anne asked.

"I'm sorry," Gail said. "I don't know why I did that; I'm not usually stupid. I won't talk about him; I can't imagine why I got started. Let's go inside."

"It's funny," Anne said after a moment, "the Chathams aren't much of a family, at least not the kind people write songs about, but there doesn't seem to be any way to talk about some of them without talking about all of them. Maybe that's what family means: everyone intertwined, even when they don't want to be. I guess I do have to know about all of them. But in small doses."

"Like medicine. Three times a day."

"Well, twice would probably be plenty."

They laughed and went into the house. It was low ceilinged, warm, and casual. Sunlight streamed through a wall of windows that framed the range of mountains running the length of the valley, with Tamarack Mountain in the center. "You've always been intertwined with us," said Gail. "I always thought so, even when I was so angry at you for leaving. I'd make family trees for school projects or sometimes for Christmas presents, and I'd put the two of us so close together it was almost one name—GailAnne, Gail Chatham Anne Chatham—and I kept thinking—what is it?"

Anne was shaking her head. "That isn't my name. I changed it a long time ago."

Gail stared at her. "To what?"

"Garnett."

"Mother's name? But why?"

"I didn't want to be a Chatham anymore. And I didn't want anyone to find me. Did they even try?"

"Grandpa hired detectives and they tried for a long time, and then they gave up. Anne Garnett. It's nice. But why didn't you say anything on the plane last night when I introduced you to Leo?"

"You said, 'This is my sister, Anne.' That was enough."

"Anne Garnett," Gail said wonderingly. "It sounds strange."

"Well, for that matter, so does Gail Calder."

Gail laughed. "Not to me; not after ten years. I don't know why I said your name sounded strange; I wouldn't have said that if you'd changed it because you'd gotten married. I guess we just don't expect women to do it on their own."

"It's the only good reason to do it," Anne said. "We

should have any name we want; so should men. Why should people be stuck with names they don't like?"

"Because it's the law. Isn't it? Isn't it illegal just to change your name whenever you feel like it?"

"You can call yourself anything you want as long as it isn't for the purpose of defrauding someone."

"Oh. Well, it sounds pretty chancy to me. I like knowing the rules so I know what to expect."

"So do I," Anne said. "But it isn't always that simple."

"I liked having a new name," Gail said as they went into the kitchen. "Did you?"

"Yes. It helped make me free." She gave a swift glance around the room. "This is wonderful; people who live in apartments dream of kitchens like this. What can I do to help?"

"We'll make sandwiches. Leo and the kids will be home soon and they'll be ravenous. Saturday-morning softball does that, it seems."

She put lettuce leaves into the sink, handed Anne a loaf of rye bread, and took sliced turkey from the refrigerator. The two women worked quietly at the center island. The kitchen was lined with pale gold pine cabinets with white enamel handles. Indian rugs were scattered on the maple floor, and along one wall was a long pine table surrounded by a collection of unmatched chairs. Next to the door was a tall mirror, and Anne glanced at it as she made the sandwiches. She and Gail looked more alike today than yesterday: each wearing Gail's jeans and checked shirts, each with her dark hair pulled back and tied with a bandanna. Gail's clothes fit Anne almost perfectly, they had discovered, but Anne had bought a few things that morning for the brief time she planned to be in Tamarack.

She kept glancing at the mirror as they worked. It felt good to see herself, twinlike, with Gail; it was comforting, like driving up here and feeling at home.

"Oh, I was telling you who comes here," Gail said. "Marian and Fred usually come for a couple of weeks in the winter. Their son, Keith, lives here, I already told you that, and their daughter, Rose—she lives in Lake Forest—she's married to Walter Holland, a poor little man who makes you want to cry, he's so afraid we're going to gobble him up—he works for the company in Chicago and he plays the poor relation until you want to shake him and tell him for God's sake go off and make a life away from all of us, but he stays, and personally I think he likes being part of the Chathams and enjoys feeling sorry for himself. Where was I?"

"Telling me who comes here," Anne said, laughing. "What about Nina?"

"Nina has had five husbands, two sons, and six dogs since you left. No, that's not right; she was married when you were at home, wasn't she? Let's see. Two husbands before you left; three since. She comes up here to recover from the disappointments of her divorces. When she's married, she and her husband, whoever he is, go to Europe. She's very sweet, you know, and I'm sorry she has so much trouble with marriages; I told her once she ought to live with a man if she likes him and not think about marriage for five years, or maybe forever, but she said that would make her seem unstable, and she still thought it was immoral to live with anyone without marriage."

"*That* would make her seem unstable?" Anne asked.

Gail laughed. "More than all her divorces, I guess. In her mind."

"Is she married now?" Anne asked.

"No, but looking. She may yet find the love of her life. She's only fifty-eight, after all, and very energetic."

"And Fred? I never paid any attention to him. What's he like?"

"Still good-looking in that odd, bony sort of way; I haven't figured out how smart he is. He's got a roving eye, especially for secretaries, which I think is dumb. Grandpa didn't like him, but he gets along with Daddy and Vince. And Marian, I guess; they've been married a long time. Let's eat on the deck; it's so lovely out." The telephone rang and Gail answered it. "Yes, Keith," she said. She frowned and glanced at Anne. "No," she said slowly, "she's not here. I don't know where she is. She left after the funeral." She was silent, listening. "Yes, we talked afterward, but then she left. Keith, if she wants to see any of us, she'll let us know."

"A little like the grand inquisitor," she said to Anne as she hung up. "He's in Chicago. Everyone wonders where you are."

"I'm sorry you had to lie for me, but thank you," Anne said. "But why Keith? He doesn't even know me. What does he care whether I'm here or not?"

"I don't know; it's peculiar. Maybe he was calling for Daddy, or Marian, or any of them."

"Is Keith their errand boy?"

"Not so far as I know. I suppose they could be uncomfortable."

"Well, we certainly don't want them to be uncomfortable," Anne said dryly.

"Hi!" The screen door slammed. "Is lunch ready?"

"Jeez, Rob, you could say hello." Ned Calder pushed past his sister and came into the kitchen. "Good morning, Aunt Anne. Did you sleep well?"

"Oh, gross," Robin groaned. "You're just showing off. You *never* talk like that, and you're the one who's always stuffing your face, not me!" She elbowed him aside. "Can I sit next to you at lunch, Aunt Anne?"

"Of course," Anne said. She was smiling. "But I'd like to be with both of you. Would it be all right if I sit in the middle?"

"You already did that on the plane," Ned said. "You have to be one-on-one with people to really get to know them."

"That's probably true," said Anne gravely.

"Ned, where in heaven's name did you get that?" Gail asked.

"From me, I guess." Leo came into the room and put his arm around Gail. "I was talking to Tim Warren about that damned cleanup the EPA wants to do, and I said if we could just get them one-on-one we might be able to make them listen to us, and Ned picked it up."

Anne watched Gail and Leo, close together, their children with them, in the solid comfort of their house, and felt a sharp pang of longing. *But I don't want this; I made that decision a long time ago. I'm happy for them, but I want a different life. I've worked so hard for what I have, and it's exactly what I want.*

"So where *are* you sitting at lunch?" Ned demanded.

"In the middle," Anne replied. "That's usually where a lawyer is."

"I thought lawyers were on somebody's side. In court with judges and everything."

"They are, but they try to bring both sides together, too." It occurred to Anne that she had no idea how to talk to children. "I like to sit between you, Ned. It's fun. And then, afterward, would you show me around? This used to be my favorite place, but I haven't been here for such a long time."

"Show you around where?" Ned asked.

"Special places. Magical places where you like to go."

"You mean places I don't tell anybody about?"

"Maybe. Do you have any?"

"Yeah, a couple. I can take you there."

"Me, too," said Robin. "Take me, too."

"They wouldn't be secret then."

"They won't be secret if you take Aunt Anne."

"Well, but . . ."

There was a brief silence. "What do you think, Ned?" Anne asked. "If you let one person share your secret, does it change very much if you share with one more?"

Ned looked confused. "It's different if it's just one person. If you told everybody, you wouldn't have anything left. I'll bet you don't tell *anybody* your secrets, Aunt Anne. I bet you'd rather die and be quartered and drawn than spill them."

A small laugh broke from Anne. "I think you mean 'drawn and quartered.' And you're right; I do have secrets that I don't tell anyone. Everybody does. It's up to you, Ned; you can have secrets with a few special people, or you can keep them absolutely to yourself. I think secrets are really important; they're a big part of who we are and what we are, and telling them to someone is like letting that person come inside us. That's a big decision."

"Yeah," Ned said uncertainly. "Well, it's okay, I guess. I

mean"—he shrugged and looked at Robin—"you can come. You're okay. Just don't tell anybody."

"Thanks," Robin said, beaming. "But what are *we* going to do?" she asked Anne. "Just us, I mean?"

The telephone rang and Gail answered it. "No, I don't. She didn't tell me. I will, if she calls. . . . No, she didn't say she would; I'm sure she will if she wants to see any of us."

Leo watched her as she hung up. "Your father?"

She smiled faintly. "You can always tell, can't you?"

"Your voice gets cool and proper and a little bit sad."

Gail looked at Anne. "You said you didn't want anyone to know."

"I don't. Thank you again."

"Know what?" Robin asked.

"That I'm not going to talk to other people this weekend. I want to spend all my time with you and your family. And you were asking me what we're going to do, just the two of us. I thought you'd choose some places for us to go, maybe in town. How would that be?"

"Are you staying?" Robin demanded. She stood before Anne, hands on her hips. "People in this family are always going away. We're the only ones who stay here; everybody else just comes for a little while and then leaves. We're always saying good-bye. And Great-grandpa just died, and I wanted him to be here forever and now he's gone. Are you going to stay forever?"

Anne shook her head. "I can't do that." She knelt beside Robin. "I have a job and people depend on me, so I can't stay away too long. But I'd like to come back. And if I keep coming back, over and over again, it would almost be like staying, wouldn't it?"

"No," Robin said flatly. "Staying means putting your suitcases in the basement and not going to the airport and you're always here to talk to."

Anne smiled. "We can always talk; you can call me up. And I'll call you."

"A very good idea," Leo said. He stood with Gail, watching Anne and his children. They made a charming group, he thought, the dark-haired boy and girl and the dark-haired woman, all of them intent on their conversation. Robin looked like Anne must have looked at eight, thin and wiry, her eyes wide and eager, her hair always seeming to need a comb. Ned was different: he had his father's stocky build and heavy brows, and his eyes were often frowning in concentration. But the most intriguing differences, to Leo, were those between Gail and Anne. He had compared them on the plane the night before, but now, when they were dressed almost identically, the differences were more pronounced. And the major difference was that, even though they resembled each other, Anne had more of everything. Her hair and eyebrows were darker than Gail's, her mouth fuller and more sensuous, her cheekbones more prominent, her eyes a darker blue. She was a shade taller and slimmer than Gail, and held her head higher. She was far more beautiful, more intense, in every way more dramatic. But somehow she was not quite real. Gail was real. Leo felt a rush of love for his wife, who gave him love and a home, who gave him a family, who was everything he had ever wanted.

And unexpectedly, he felt pity for Anne. She had great beauty, but she might have been clad in armor, so tightly controlled was she, so protected against the world that there was not even a chink through which emotions could break loose. Leo knew she had been talking about herself when she told Ned that secrets were an important part of what we are and who we are. She was afraid of letting anyone inside. She did not even know how to hold a child, he thought, watching her as she knelt beside Robin, her arms at her sides. Not once had she hugged Robin as Gail would have done with any child who talked about adults leaving and a beloved great-grandfather dying.

"It's not the same on the phone," Robin said stubbornly. "I like being *close*. You know . . . *touching*. Like reading books together and taking walks and just sitting around talking. We could read all my books if you stayed, and we could go to movies and play Scrabble. Wouldn't you like that? Unless . . . well, I guess you'd get bored with us . . ."

"No, I wouldn't," Anne said firmly. "I wouldn't be bored;

I'd like very much to do those things with you. And Ned, too. But right now I just can't." She saw Robin's face turn sullen. "Look," she said, "it's like school. You couldn't come to Los Angeles and live with me because you have school. I have a job; it's pretty much the same thing."

"I could go to school there. You could get a job here."

"Okay, Robin, that's enough," Leo said firmly. "Why don't you just enjoy Anne while she's here, instead of worrying about the future?"

The telephone rang and Gail reached past Leo to pick it up. "No," she said after a moment. She glanced quickly at the children. "I don't know where she is. She didn't say. If she wants to call you, I suppose she will. I *don't know.*" She hung up.

"Who was that?" Ned asked.

"Someone I didn't want to talk to," Gail replied. "Is anybody interested in lunch?"

"Sure. Can I have lemonade?"

Anne stood up. "What can I carry?"

They took trays to the large deck overlooking the Tamarack Valley. Aspen trees grew through openings in the deck, shading wrought-iron tables and chairs with bright cushions; below them, flower and vegetable gardens were stepped down the hill. To one side was a greenhouse and a swimming pool; on the other a badminton net was at the edge of the smooth lawn. "What a perfect place," Anne said quietly.

"It was supposed to be yours," said Gail. "Grandpa bought the land up here for all of us, and named it Riverwood, and laid it out, where we'd each have our house. He decided everything, you know; for a long time he ran Tamarack as if it was his kingdom. Anyway, he'd picked this out for you. He only gave it to us when Ned was born and we were looking for a home. He said he couldn't hold it for you any longer."

Anne remembered cross-country skiing with Ethan through the trees and across the smooth, wide meadows of the plateau. "You still think this is where you want to live?" he had asked.

"Yes," Anne had replied instantly. "It's the most beautiful place in the world. Better than everywhere else."

"Pretty far from people," Ethan said, as he had before.

"That's what I want," Anne said. "To get away." She was almost fifteen years old then. It was the last time she was in Tamarack.

"I didn't know he'd remember me," she said slowly. "I thought he was so angry and disappointed in me that he'd just push me out of his life."

"He thought about you a lot," said Leo. He helped Gail fill plates with sandwiches and potato salad. "I remember, we were having breakfast once, about a year before he died. He had his first stroke a little after that, and wasn't ever again as clear in his mind as he was that morning. He had his eyes closed and he said, 'Anne'—no, it was 'dear Anne'—and then he said, 'Sorry, sorry . . . I loved you and failed you and I'd like to ask your forgiveness. . . .' Something like that. He said you probably didn't need him because you were grown-up now, but still he'd like to make you feel safe and loved. I remember he said that: safe and loved. And he wished you'd come home so he could tell you all that, before he died."

Anne sat very still. Tears filled her eyes, but she was crying more deeply inside herself. All those years, she thought. All those years of thinking no one cared. Ethan cared. I was loved and I didn't know it.

And Gail cared. I never knew that, either. And now Gail's children. And Gail's husband.

Her tears had dried. "I wish I had come back," she said.

"*I* wish," said Gail emphatically. "But you are happy, aren't you? Your apartment sounds wonderful, and your office, and being a lawyer. It's much more exciting than Tamarack. We're awfully quiet here. You're the only one in the family who went off and did something completely separate from the company."

"Uncle Vince did," said Ned. "He's a senator in Washington. He tells the president things." He looked at Anne's closed face. "I don't like him a lot," he said shrewdly. "I don't think he likes kids. Maybe he doesn't like anybody. He did a weird thing at Grandpa's funeral. He told Keith to get rid of somebody. Like, kill her, you know. It was really weird."

"Who was he talking about?" Leo asked.

Ned shrugged. "He just said, 'Find out what she wants and get rid of her.' It was like 'Miami Vice,' but it was weird 'cause it was a funeral, you know, and it wasn't a great thing to say at a funeral."

Leo met Anne's eyes. "We can't know for sure," he said.

"He called earlier," Gail said.

"Who?" Leo asked.

"Keith," she replied, her eyes troubled.

"Can't know what?" Ned asked, looking from one of them to the other.

"What he was talking about," Gail said. "But you're right; whatever he meant, it wasn't great to say at a funeral. Why don't you tell us about your softball game? We don't even know who won."

Anne sat back and watched them talk about the game. She barely heard their voices. *Find out what she wants and get rid of her.* She could hear his voice; she had not known how well she remembered it. She felt a stab of fear, and then anger. He had already gotten rid of her once; wasn't that enough?

I was the one who left, she thought. And he stayed, tucked into the family, warm and secure. Unfair, unfair, unfair. And after all that, he wanted Keith to get rid of me— whatever that means. And Keith called earlier, asking if I was here. Why Keith? And what difference does it make to Vince? It can't be his conscience; he doesn't have one. Not fear, either, or even worry; what danger am I to him? I accused him once and no one believed me.

But of course a senator would worry; of course a senator would fear. A charge of sexual abuse would be a bomb blast. And the accusation, if there was one, would come not from a fifteen-year-old girl but from a respected lawyer, a member of an established, conservative firm.

She was a very real threat to Vince. Of course he would like to get rid of her.

Well, he wouldn't. He'd done it once; he would not do it again. She had a family now. She'd always had one, though she hadn't realized it. Ethan had cared about her, and she was sure that, in their own ways, Marian and Nina and William probably had, too, though at that terrible moment they had failed her. But now Gail and Leo were here, and Ned and Robin, and if she wanted them for her family, and maybe some of the others, too, Vince could not stop her. She would have a family again. And she wouldn't give it up as she had done before, far too easily.

This time, if anyone leaves this family, it will be Vince.

". . . Monday, Aunt Anne?" asked Robin.

Anne started. "I'm sorry, what about Monday?"

"We could go to my ceramics class together. Is that okay? Maybe you'd make something; you'd really like it. And then we could get a hot dog and eat it in the park. Is that okay?"

Anne revised her plan to leave on Monday. She would call the office early in the morning and ask her secretary to reschedule everything. "I'd like that. Where do you—"

"Hi, I heard your voices so I came through the house."

"Dora, welcome back," Gail said. "It's been a long time. This is Anna Cha—Garnett. Anne, Dora Chatham. Have you had lunch, Dora?"

"No, I've been shopping all morning. I'm starved." She turned to Anne. "I saw you at Ethan's funeral; we were all wondering who you were. Are you staying with Gail and Leo?"

Anne nodded. She could not speak. It was almost as if Vince sat before her. Dora's long blond hair waved and gleamed exactly like her father's; her brown eyes flickered over Anne exactly as her father's had; her smile was as sweet, her chin as sharp. Dora Chatham, with her angelic beauty, was a scaled-down, feminine Vince Chatham, and for just a moment, Anne cringed.

Gail looked a question to Anne. With barely a pause, Anne nodded. Dora had to know who she was; they could not keep it a secret. "You probably don't remember Anne," Gail said, "she's been gone so long, but she's my sister. She left—"

"You're *that* Anne?" Dora stared at her. "No wonder they all went crazy at the funeral. You took off when I was about five, didn't you? My mother said you didn't like us much. And you never came back until now? Where were you?"

"California," Gail said. "Anne lives in Los Angeles."

"Really? So do I. Where do you live?"

"Century City," Anne replied. Her voice was tight.

"Is that near you, Dora?" asked Gail.

"No," she said shortly.

Leo's eyebrows rose. "Problems, Dora?"

She shrugged. "I don't live there anymore. As of two months ago."

"Oh, I'm sorry," Gail said. "We had no idea. You were together such a long time."

"Three years and two months. And one week."

"And you decided it wasn't right for you?"

"He decided." She shrugged again. "Out of the blue. I thought I knew all his crazy moods, but this was a new one. He went on and on about his problems and then he just . . . invited me out."

"I'm so sorry," Gail said again. "Did you find another place in Los Angeles?"

"Not yet; I've been in Europe. I just wanted to get away. Everything was gone, you know; I didn't know what to do or who to turn to. He told me to get the hell out, so I did."

"Without even packing?" asked Ned interestedly.

Dora looked at him vaguely. "Yes, I packed. I took my clothes. I went back to LA last week," she said to Gail and Leo. "I had to fire my lawyer. He kept telling me what I *couldn't* do and *couldn't* get and *couldn't* even ask for. I think Josh got to him. That's why I came up here, to talk to Leo. You know lawyers, and you know Josh; I mean, the two of you got kind of tight, didn't you? Sometimes I thought he liked you better than me. So you have to tell me what to do. I've got to find somebody who won't be snowed by him."

"I don't know what you want from him," Leo said mildly.

"Something to show for all those years. If we'd been married for all that time and I was kicked out, I'd at least get money. So why shouldn't I get it now? Just because we weren't married doesn't mean I didn't give him everything he wanted and entertain for him and cook for him—"

"You said you hated cooking," Robin put in.

"Robin," admonished Gail.

"I tried the best I could," Dora said. "He didn't really care whether I cooked or not, you know; he was used to all that awful food on those digs of his. Anyway, what difference does it make? I did whatever he wanted, all the things a wife does, and we were together for all that time and he was happy . . . I know he was happy . . . he said *loving* things to me . . ." Tears spilled from her eyes and she pulled a handkerchief from her pants pocket. "I was happy, too, you know, and then he ruined everything, all my hopes, everything I cared about . . ."

Leo was frowning. "He didn't give you any warning at all? Or any reasons? That doesn't sound like Josh."

"You're standing up for him, just like that lawyer! He snows people, Leo, that's what I said. They think he's wonderful, but they don't have to live with him. I need somebody on my side who'll stand up to him, somebody tough, somebody who cares whether women get a rotten deal or not. You must know somebody."

"Dora, you know half of Los Angeles," Leo replied. "You must know dozens of lawyers, or people who could recommend one."

"Maybe Anne knows someone," Gail said.

Dora glanced at Anne. "Why? Are you married to one?"

"Anne is a lawyer," Gail said. "She specializes in divorce."

Dora's look fastened on Anne. "Are you any good?"

"Dora," said Gail.

"I mean, do you get big cases and do you win them?"

"Of course she does," Gail replied.

"Not unless she does her own talking."

"I'm very busy right now," Anne said coolly. "I doubt that I could take on a new client. I could recommend someone."

"What firm are you with?"

"Engle, Saxon and Joute."

"I've heard of them. They're as good as you can get. You'd recommend someone in the firm?"

"If you want. The person I was thinking of is in another firm."

Dora sipped her iced tea. "Do you think I can win?"

"I have no idea. I don't know anything about you or about the man you've been living with."

"What kinds of things?"

"Any agreements you've made, contracts you've signed, oral promises you've made to each other, statements you've made before witnesses, property you own in joint tenancy, the possessions you've accumulated."

"That's the list?"

"That's a beginning."

"This man you'd recommend; has he done cases like this?"

"Not that I know of. But he's strong and creative and he's interested in women getting a fair deal."

"Have you done cases like this?"

"Yes."

"Are you doing one now?"

"No."

"When did you do the last one?"

"Two months ago."

Dora's eyes narrowed. "Steve Hawthorne. That's right, isn't it? God, I didn't make the connection. Anne Garnett. You were the lawyer for his girlfriend. I read about you. You won."

"Yes, but I told you, I'm not taking any new clients right now."

Dora sat back. "Lawyers are always looking for interesting cases, aren't they? The kind that will help their careers? I mean, Steve Hawthorne was a big plum, but it wouldn't be bad to defend the daughter of a senator, would it?"

"I'm sorry," Anne said.

"What would it take?" Dora asked. "Anne, listen. Please listen. I'm desperate. My whole life got turned upside down, just like that. One minute I thought I had a home and I knew what the future was, the next I had no place to live and I didn't have any idea what the future would be like. I was out on the street and I was scared. I still am; I guess it takes more than a few months to believe in yourself and start over again." She saw Anne's face change. "You do understand, don't you? Anne, please do it. I want you. I don't want anybody else. I like the way you talk and the way you look and I like what you've done. Anne, I feel awfully alone and I'm so ashamed . . . I mean, to be kicked out of your own home. . . . Anne, listen, *I need you."*

Anne looked past Dora, at the peaks stepping majestically to the horizon. So much space in the world, so many people, so many ways to avoid encounters. But she sat here, at this table, and opposite her was Vince's daughter, asking for help. *Vince's daughter.* I can't, she thought. I can't get this close to him. I wanted a family, not involvement.

But what do you think a family is, if not involvement? In all of it, not just the parts that are pretty and pleasant.

If Dora weren't Vince's daughter, she would take her as a client in an instant. She was the only one in her firm who took these cases. So why let Vince, once again, determine what she would do? She had just decided she would never again let him force her from her family. Why would she let his presence determine whether or not she took a case that was exactly right for her?

He doesn't exist for me. I have a profession, I have a life, and now I have a family. I do what I want. And the past has nothing to do with it.

"All right," she said to Dora, and in that instant she felt she had taken a step in a journey whose ending she could not predict or imagine. "I'll be back in Los Angeles on Tuesday. And then we'll get to work."

chapter 9

"Very nice," said Dora with a swift approving glance at the solid English furnishings in Anne's office. "And a good view, too. I suppose they save the corner offices for people who've been here longer."

"Yes," Anne said, amused.

"Well, I bet they make an exception for you; people say wonderful things about you, really impressive." She sat in a leather chair facing Anne across her desk. "I asked a couple of people about you—you don't mind, do you? It's not that I didn't trust you, it's just that I'm so new at this I thought another opinion, well, two opinions, actually—anyway, they both said how lucky I was to get you. I didn't tell them we're related; I wanted them to think you took me because you're really interested in me and you think I have a good case, not because we're cousins . . . that is why you took me, isn't it? I mean, I'm not even sure whether I'm better or worse off with a relative. Oh, I didn't mean *worse;* what an incredibly stupid thing to say. I just meant, you might not put yourself out quite as much as you would with . . ."

Anne let the last word fade away. "I'm the best lawyer I can be for all my clients," she said evenly.

"I know, I know that," Dora said humbly. "I'm sorry I said that; I'm really so grateful . . . *really* grateful, you know; I really *need* you. Now, where should we start? What do you want me to tell you?"

Anne smiled at Dora's preoccupation with herself. She

wondered how much of her sweetness and charm was an act. Maybe all of it. Her father was an expert at that. A sudden wave of revulsion washed over her. *I can't do this. I never should have said I would.*

But Dora wasn't responsible for her father; she couldn't help it that she looked enough like him to give Anne a shock every time she smiled or turned her head a certain way; it was not her fault that, because of that resemblance, Anne found herself doubting her. She was part of the family, and most important, she needed Anne, and that was what Anne could not resist.

It was what had drawn her to the law in the first place and kept her satisfied all these years without family or close friends. Being needed. No one had ever needed her. Even Eleanor, wanting her friendship, had, in the end, needed her own family more. Anne had her clients. Many of them she did not like or admire, but that had nothing to do with it; they needed her. They sat in her office and tried to impress her with their honesty, uprightness, importance, lovableness, and how dreadfully they had been wronged. But behind their bluster and bravado, and their deliberate lies, they were reaching out for help. They wanted to be told what to do, and how and when to do it, and even when they disobeyed her, they kept coming back, asking for more instructions, more encouragement, more help. And they were almost always grateful.

"You can ask me anything," said Dora. "I couldn't have secrets from you, and I wouldn't be ashamed of telling you anything because I know you'd understand and not laugh at me. I really trust you, Anne; I don't know where I'd be without you."

Anne nodded. She was beginning to feel a lawyer's excitement as Dora spoke. Earlier, she had been so concerned with the resemblance to Vince that she had not been aware of the ingenuousness in Dora's charm, and the compelling sweetness in her smile. Now she felt the force of it, and she knew that Dora would be superb on the witness stand. She picked up her pencil. "Let's start with how you met this man. Joshua Durant."

"Well." Dora settled into the chair. "At Tamarack. Somebody introduced us at a party. He was just leaving. He doesn't like big parties, he'd only stopped by for a minute, but we started talking and then we went to dinner. And then we went to my place."

"This was a little over three years ago?"

"Three years and two months."

"So you started living together soon after you met."

"Well, not all that soon. He wanted to but I—" She stopped. A small, wistful smile trembled on her lips. "That's not true, you know. I was the one who wanted to. Josh wanted to wait. He said we should live in our own places, and see each other as much as we wanted, and then after a while decide whether we wanted more or not. I didn't want to wait; I was afraid I'd lose him. But of course we did it his way; men are always better at making rules, you know."

Anne's look sharpened. "Was that an agreement between you? That he made the rules and you followed them?"

Dora frowned. "I don't know. He never said it that way. I didn't either. I mean, we didn't have to, you know; that's just how it was."

"Tell me about him," Anne said, and saw Dora frown again. Most people frowned, in just that way, when they were asked to describe someone they had loved and now despised. They were caught in the dilemma of wanting to describe the person in a way that made the listener despise him, too, while stopping short of making him such a monster that there seemed no possible way anyone could ever have loved him.

"He's a selfish, arrogant, mean son of a bitch," Dora said. She burst into tears. "I'm sorry, I shouldn't say that." She sat straight and wiped her eyes with her fists, like a child. "He's very smart—people say he's brilliant—and he can be really sweet and loving and fun to be with, when he wants to. Women are crazy about him; he's tall and good-looking, except he's been outdoors so much that he's got lines in his face that make him look older than he is. He's always tan, from the sun, and his eyes are dark blue and his hair is sort of light brown; I guess the sun makes it lighter. He spends a lot on clothes; I liked the way he dressed. But he's not nearly as nice as he seems; he's really wrapped up in himself; he only cares about what *he* wants. He wouldn't let me bring my own furniture to his apartment, or my little animals—I collect ceramic animals; I've been written up in magazines because of my collection!—and I had to put them in storage. He wouldn't let me tell the cook what to make for dinner; he had his favorite foods and I could just eat them or go hungry. He's arrogant and cruel and a bully and a tyrant. But how could I know that until I moved in with him? He bossed me around like he bosses his workers—"

"What workers? What does he do?"

"He digs. He's an archaeologist, and of course he has workers who do most of the digging, but he says he likes to do it, too. He says he likes the feeling of unfolding the earth with his hands—I thought that was a really strange thing to say—uncovering its secrets with his hands, not with machines, so he's more a part of it, part of history, close to the people who put things in the tomb, or whatever, in the first place. Something like that. He talks that way a lot; I didn't always follow exactly what he meant, but you get the idea."

Anne repeated the phrases to herself, liking them. Unfolding the earth. Uncovering its secrets with hands, not with machines. "What else does he do?" she asked.

"Oh, everything. He hikes and skis and sails and plays tennis and swims; he even plays polo sometimes. He's a good dancer, too. And he's an archaeology professer at UCLA, and a consultant at the Museum of the Ancient World. And he buys art and antiquities, mainly when he travels."

Anne scribbled a note. "Where does he get the money to do all that? It sounds like a lot for a working archaeologist and professor."

"He inherited a lot from his grandparents; they left him a fortune. He's not like any professor you ever met, you know; he seems like a playboy. He's not; he works really hard; but he has a terrific apartment and a wine cellar, and he and a friend own a racing sailboat, and he buys Versace suits . . . he likes nice things."

"When we met," Anne said thoughtfully, "you said he didn't care about good food; he was used to the bad food he got on his digs, so it didn't matter whether you cooked or not. That doesn't fit with the fine wines and the good life."

Dora flushed. "Well, he does care about food. He knows a lot about it, he knows more than I do, and he has the best caterers in town for his parties. I just never could get into cooking. And he knew it."

"How much money does he have?" Anne asked.

"I don't know. I tried to find out, by hinting, you know, but I never did. He doesn't worry about it; I know that."

"And what about you?"

"I have enough. I have a trust fund my grandfather set up and another one from my father."

Her grandfather, Anne thought. Ethan. We have the same grandfather. And he set up a trust for her. He must have done that for all the grandchildren. All but one.

You're at work, she told herself sharply, and focused on Dora again. "And about how much do those trusts bring you?"

Dora hesitated. "I don't talk about it, except to my accountant."

Anne was silent.

"But if you have to know . . . about half a million a year."

Anne nodded. "Did he know that? Did you discuss your separate incomes?"

"No, I told you; I never really asked him. There were a lot of things we didn't talk about, you know. We went out a lot in the beginning and we talked about the people we saw and the places we went, and then, after a while—the whole last year, I guess—we didn't go out much; Josh kept saying he wanted to stay home and read. It really was the most boring time; finally I just went places by myself."

"Did he go out by himself, too?"

"A lot. Not in the beginning; we did everything together, except his work; I never knew much about that. But the last year he'd stay home and read and listen to music, or he'd go with his friends, and they were all scientists and writers, and I didn't like any of them. They talked about things I wasn't interested in and they didn't seem much interested in what I wanted to talk about, and I figured it wasn't worth the effort. So when Josh made dates with them, I'd go to parties or call a friend to go to a movie, you know, just so I wouldn't have to stay home and feel really left out."

"Did you ever talk about doing things separately, about drifting apart?"

"No, I never even thought about it. I mean, most married people do things on their own—"

"But you weren't married."

"I know, but I always forgot. I mean, we were as good as married—that's the whole point of this business, going to court, I mean—we were exactly like married people. It shouldn't matter that we didn't have a piece of paper to show—"

"Did you talk about getting married?"

"Of course! All the time."

"How? What did he say?"

"He said he wanted to marry me. He said he loved me and wanted to marry me."

Anne put down her pencil and gazed at Dora. "Listen to me. Whatever you've told other people, you're going to tell me the truth. I won't represent you if I think you're telling half-truths or fantasies or outright lies. I'll walk away from this case the minute I find that that's happening. I can't be more clear than that."

"I wasn't lying!" Dora cried. But in a minute, beneath Anne's steady gaze, she looked away. Her lower lip thrust out; tears filled her eyes. "He never said it. I waited and waited and . . . sort of . . . mentioned it, you know, once in a while . . . but he never did. It was like he got deaf every time I brought it up."

Anne picked up her pencil. "What *did* he say to you?"

"He said he liked being with me; he could relax with me. He said he hoped to live to a biblical age because he wanted to live with me for a long, long time. That was another of his odd ways of talking. He said he wanted to do a lot of traveling with me and show me the secret corners and hidden spirits of places I thought I knew. I thought that was peculiar, too, and anyway, when it came down to it, we didn't do much traveling together. He said he wanted to bring me seraphim and serpents because my world was too narrow; I never did figure out what that was all about."

Anne felt a sharp pain, unfamiliar and disconcerting. No one had ever said such things to her.

Of course not, she told herself firmly. There was no place for fantasy in her life. But she was puzzled by the picture Dora drew of Josh Durant. How odd that an arrogant tyrant, cruel and self-centered, would speak with such tenderness, in phrases a poet might use.

"That's not all he said," Dora went on. "I just can't remember the rest."

"You don't remember?" Anne asked. "You've only been apart a short time."

"Well, but he hasn't said things like that for years. He said them when we were first together. He said nice things all the time in those days. But not lately. I moved in and he started changing."

"Right away?"

"Well, not right away. In a while."

"How long?"

"Oh, I don't remember. Maybe a year."

"You were the one who wanted to move in, you said. He wanted to wait. What changed his mind?"

"Well, we were together all the time and it seemed obvious."

Anne waited.

Dora's shoulders slumped. "I kept telling him how unhappy I was. I really was, you know; I hated going home to an empty apartment, it was like being banished from his life. So I kept telling him how I wanted to do things for him and how I couldn't stand it that he didn't care enough about me to live with me and how miserable I was, and lonely. . . . I guess I made it hard for him. But we were having such a good time in those days it didn't make sense to me that we weren't really together, and I didn't have to wait to see how I felt; I wanted him all the time. So it took a while but then he said yes and we were really fine for a while, until he changed. We were fine for a year. At least a year."

There was a pause. Anne looked back through her notes. "You said you didn't talk about your incomes. Did you have any kind of agreement, financial or otherwise, when you started living together?"

"You mean like a contract? No."

"Did you have an oral agreement?"

"Like what?"

"Did you set a specific length of time you'd live together —six months, a year, two years—before talking about something more permanent? Did you agree on sharing living expenses—food, mortgage payments, and so on? Or how you'd divide your possessions if you separated? Did you agree in advance to keep separate bank accounts?"

Dora was shaking her head. "We were in love. We didn't think about money and we certainly weren't about to talk about it. I mean, we were moving in together; we weren't making rules for splitting. We weren't even *thinking* about splitting. We never thought we would."

"Did you ever talk about children?"

"No. Josh hates kids."

"And you?"

"Oh, I'd like two or three. I kind of stopped thinking about them when I was with Josh."

Anne turned her notebook to a fresh page. "Tell me about your friends."

"What about them?"

"Who they were, how often the two of you saw them, how much you talked to them about yourselves. Did you tell them you thought you'd be married someday? Did he ever mention marriage to them? Did couples compare notes about living together and talk about the future?"

"Not that I can remember. I told you, the past couple of years we didn't see a lot of other people, not together anyway, that was what Josh wanted. He wanted everything his way: his friends, his restaurants, his places to travel, his furniture, his apartment."

"And what did he say when you objected?"

"I didn't."

"You never said a word about what you wanted?"

"I told you, he made the rules."

"But you also told me you wanted to marry him and kept mentioning it. Even though he made all the rules and you didn't like them?"

"I loved him! I still do!"

"That's the first time I've heard you say that. Did you really love him? Do you still?"

"I adore him!"

"I don't believe you." Anne gave her a long look. "You'll have to tell me what you want out of this. What you truly care about and how much is just quick and dirty revenge."

Dora's eyes narrowed. *"Quick and dirty . . . ?* Who the fuck do you think you—" She caught her breath and leaned forward. "I'm sorry, I'm sorry, I'm so sorry, what a terrible way to talk to you. I can't imagine what got into me; I just don't *do* that. Maybe it was that word. Revenge. It sounds so . . . bitchy. It isn't revenge; it would never be that. I just want something out of this—" Her eyes filled with tears. "Something I can hold. If I can't have Josh, if I've really lost him forever, at least I want him to admit—in public!—that I was as good as a wife to him and I deserve the same things a wife would get. Respect, for one. I'd rather have love, I'd rather be a wife, but if I can't have those, then I want respect. And money. He would have had to pay a wife alimony; he would have rewarded her for years of being everything he wanted, and loving him and caring about him; he would have had to make sure she was taken care of before he found himself . . . somebody new . . ."

She put her hands to her face and sobbed quietly. Bravo, Anne thought. She had been right: Dora would be superb on the witness stand. It was even possible that much of what she said was the truth. Probably Dora herself did not know for sure anymore what was fact and what was imagination fueled by anger and disappointment. Neither, Anne supposed, did Josh Durant.

Thank God I don't have to go through this. It was a thought that came to her regularly as she dealt with her clients. Thank God she stayed far from intimacy, far from even contemplating living with someone or worse, marrying him, far from ever having to feel this corrosive anger and disappointment, this fury that sprang from the ashes of love, this blur of truth and falsehood that dulled reason. And it was reason, clear, hard-edged reason unsullied by emotion, that Anne had made the center of her life, in fact, her very being.

"Are you angry?" Dora asked, looking up. "I shouldn't have talked to you that way; I'll never do it again. I'm really not like that. Please forgive me, Anne. Tell me you won't . . . fire me, or whatever. You're still my lawyer, aren't you? I can't go looking for another one! The first one didn't understand me and I know you do, and in a month the trial starts and *you can't leave me now!*"

"I won't leave you," Anne said quietly. "But I meant what I said about the truth. You'll have to think about what you're saying and make sure you're not telling me what you think is true, or what you'd like to believe is true. Do you understand that?"

Dora's face was bright again. "Yes, yes, of course. I won't ever lie to you."

Anne sighed. Of course you will, she thought. But we'll do the best we can. She turned to another page of her notepad. Just four weeks to their court date. They had a lot of work to do.

Vince telephoned Dora twice a month. He liked to think she would rather talk to him than to her mother, and he always made sure he had a collection of Washington gossip with which to spice his calls. He also made sure others knew about those regular calls; they were important to his image.

"I'm about to call my daughter," he said when Ray Beloit showed up at his apartment one night at ten o'clock. "I'll be a while; we always have a lot to talk about."

"I think you'd rather hear this." Beloit walked around Vince with confident familiarity, loosening his tie as he led the way to the study. "I've been down at party headquarters. Your name came up."

Annoyed, Vince followed at his own pace. When he reached the study, Beloit was pouring himself a drink. "Want one?"

"I'll take care of it."

"It's a big night, Vince. Don't get tight-assed just 'cause I made my own drink. I've spent enough time here to feel right at home; I'll be spending a lot more. Aren't you interested in what I said?"

"My name came up. What about it? There's an election next year."

"And there's a bonzo out there in the boondocks who has a real shot at beating you."

"Is that what they're saying downtown?"

"Some of 'em. They're getting nervous. So are you."

"They're a bunch of old women." Vince poured Scotch into his glass and added ice cubes. "It might be close, but there's no way he can win."

Beloit pulled a newspaper clipping from his pocket. "The *Rocky Mountain News* took a poll yesterday—"

"I saw it. What the hell is wrong with you, Ray? This is July; the primary is next April. It's been a quiet summer; the paper's trying to sell a few copies. They may have fudged the percentages; I wouldn't put it past them. Anyway, an election poll nine months before the primary is for wrapping fish and not a damn thing else; you know that; you knew it before I did. What's got into you, anyway?"

"Uh-huh." Beloit sprawled on Vince's black leather couch, balancing his drink on the ample mound of his stomach and staring at it as if willing it to remain vertical. "Your name came up a lot. Not just for next year's race. But you gotta win that one. That's the first thing."

Vince's eyes narrowed. "And the second?"

"Well, there was all this talk about the White House. Three years downstream. Not a lot of time, with primaries and all."

A long silence fell. Vince walked to the curved wall of

windows and gazed at the fountain playing in lighted arcs in the plaza below, and the brightly lit outdoor café beyond it. Over the years, he and Beloit had talked about the presidency and had sounded out other politicians and major donors to the party. But it had always been in the future; Vince knew that a Western senator from a sparsely populated state would need an even more powerful base than candidates from the East. But if the party insiders were talking about three years from now . . .

He turned and let his gaze travel over the heavy black furniture of his study, the books on the walls, the photographs of Dora that were everywhere. He liked visitors to see them. They would help; Dora would help. It would be best if he were married. He'd have to take care of that, and soon. Not too good: three wives. But over the years the country had elected single presidents, presidents with mistresses, presidents with illegitimate kids, even a president who had been divorced and remarried. There were ways around anything in the past.

"So you gotta get reelected next year," Beloit said. "And by a landslide."

Vince glanced at him. "I told you I'm not worried."

"You said it might be close." Beloit took a long drink. "I've been watching this hick, reading up on him and so on. He's saying nasty things about you, and he's got a following. Not a big one in Denver, yet, but he's working the back roads and picking up endorsements like he's flypaper. But shit, you're not worried, right? You're not interested that we could make sure he's out of it before the primary."

"I wouldn't veto it," Vince said after a moment. "You've got enough to do it?"

"Just enough. He's almost a Boy Scout. But we found a couple things that oughta do it. If we have to, we'll use his brother; God, what a ditz. You wouldn't believe it; a few years ago he—"

"I don't want to know. Take care of it and don't talk about it."

"I don't talk, and you fucking well know it." Still lying down, Beloit held out his glass. Vince gave it a quick, cold glance and turned away to refill his own. Beloit's breathing was heavy in the silence. At last he swung his legs over the side of the couch. "I didn't finish. There's a few other things to talk about. One major one." He poured Scotch to the top of his glass and bent to sip the first mouthful. Straightening up, he groaned and held a hand to the small of his back. "Getting old. Okay, this is where we're at. I can take care of the hick, make sure you get your landslide. I can push the fellas downtown to stay behind you and not go looking for a different glamour puss for whatever crazy reason they might think up. There's a lot of work to do, but we can pull it off; my bottom line opinion is we can get you the nomination. But there's gotta be something in all this for me."

"Secretary of state?" Vince asked with a smile. "Ambassador to the Court of St. James?"

"Those aren't for me," said Beloit seriously. "I would've liked either one, but I never went to college and I don't always talk right and I look lousy in a tux. Besides, I'd never get past the background check; there's stuff that'd blow me out of the water. Stuff I've never told you about, or my wife, or nobody. Funny: you get involved in things, you don't know what's gonna come back fifteen, twenty, thirty years later, maybe more, and it's like you've been carrying this bomb around in your pocket all those years, not knowing it's there, and then all of a sudden you get this warning and you know it'll go off if you do one particular thing, and it's always the thing you fucking most *want* to do, only now there's no way you can do it. Ever. You know?"

"I suppose it's money," Vince said as if Beloit had not spoken. "How much?"

"Fuck off, Vince, I'm not talking about money. I'm talking about something classy, something like being an ambassador, but better because nobody'll give a damn about what I used to be."

Vince looked at him as if he were a child. "You can't buy class."

"Some people do. I probably couldn't. But I can *own* class. That's what I want out of all this. Listen, Vince. I want to own The Tamarack Company."

Vince stared at him. "You what?"

"Why not? It's as classy as you can get. And I need something like that. I miss Lake Forest Development; it was the glitziest thing I ever had going for me. Lorraine says I gotta find something to do, get me out of the house, make me perk up. But it's gotta be fun, Vince, and classy, and that's Tamarack. 'Course they could be having a big problem with the EPA wanting to take soil samples on the old mine dumps—the whole east end of town, right? If they decide there's dangerous minerals leaking out there, the town's got a pile of trouble. I know; I looked into it. The homeowners have to pay for the cleanup in their own backyards and they don't like that. And there's gonna be all kinds of folks who all of a sudden have shivers and shakes and they blame the pollution from the mine dumps, which means the company that owns them, and that's your family. So you'd have to move people to other parts of town and clean up the land and redevelop it . . . lots of trouble, lots of money. Who the hell sicced the EPA on your family? Somebody got a grudge against them? Or some Boy Scout in the government decided to set an example and picked a fancy resort to do it in. Well, whatever, I still want it. You say the name Tamarack just about anywhere in the world and people's ears prick up. They start thinking about movie stars, TV stars, ex-kings—what the hell, real kings, too—all that money and glamour and excitement. They think it's a hell of a place. And it is. And I want it. And your brother Charles wants to sell. He fucked up royally in Illinois and he needs the money. I'm not telling you anything you don't know."

"If my brother wants to sell, call him up and make an offer."

"No, you still don't get it. This is what you can do while I'm busy greasing your wheels for the White House. You can take care of this one little deal for me; it's all I want. Talk your family into selling; some of 'em don't want to. And talk 'em into selling low. I don't want to overpay; I've done that a few times and I don't like it, it makes me feel like people are laughing at me. This is a cinch for you, Vince; you've got influence there. The big senator, fame, influence, television; the whole bit. Families eat it up. So that's where we're at. I get to buy The Tamarack Company for a sweet price, and I do it real soon; I don't want to wait. And you get a red carpet to the White House. You got my word on that, Vince; you're gonna be president. President Vincent Chatham of the United States of America. We have got one great time ahead of us, guaranteed."

Vince poured another drink. "I'll think about it."

"No, no, I need to know you'll do it, Vince. You wanted to know about my meetings today; I told you right off the bat. Which is what I want from—"

The telephone rang. Vince picked it up from his desk and heard Dora's voice. "It's my daughter," he said to Beloit. "We'll go on with this tomorrow."

"We should settle it now."

"Seven-thirty. Breakfast. And bring whoever knows the most about where we go from here. Not a gang; just one or two people who talk sense, not campaign slogans."

"You could call her back, five minutes max."

"Damn it, I want to talk to my daughter! Nothing interferes with that!"

Beloit finally got it. "What devotion," he said with a sigh. "A good family man, a good father, a loyal, caring, *trustworthy* man. Women especially can appreciate that. I'll see you tomorrow."

"My campaign manager," Vince said into the telephone. He waited until he heard the closing of the front door. "I'll be needing a new one, though; he's not big enough for what's coming up. Listen: this should please you—"

"Daddy," said Dora, "I finally met my cousin Anne."

Vince dropped into his desk chair. "What the hell are you talking about?"

"My cousin. Come on, Daddy, I know you never talk about her, but that doesn't mean she doesn't exist. I met her last week. She calls herself Anne Garnett now; she changed it when she took off, when she was fifteen. Why didn't anybody ever talk about her? I asked her, but I can't get a straight answer."

Garnett, Vince thought. Her mother's name. That never occurred to Ethan and Charles, or those half-assed detectives they hired. "How do you know all that?"

"She told me. I met her at Gail's house in Tamarack. She was at the funeral; you saw her; remember I pointed her out and said everybody was looking at her?"

"She was at Gail's house?"

"I just said she was."

"Charles called there. So did some other people. Gail said she didn't know where she was."

"I don't know anything about that. Gail knew where she was when I got there; she was sitting on the deck, having lunch. Was there some scandal about her or something? Why else wouldn't anybody talk about her? She's an interesting woman—not your type, though; she's very strong and positive; she doesn't lean. Very sharp, too, and she doesn't bullshit. That's why I hired her."

"Hired her?"

"She's my lawyer. I told you I fired the other—"

"God damn it!" Vince leaped from his chair, pulling the telephone with him. "What the fuck is the matter with you? I told you—"

"Don't talk to me like that, Daddy. I'll hang up."

He let his breath out. "I told you to drop that suit. I thought you did."

"Of course not. Why would I?"

"When you fired that idiot lawyer, you weren't dropping it?"

"No, only him. He wasn't on my side. I need somebody who sympathizes with me. I should have had a woman from the beginning. Men don't understand these things. Look at you; you don't really care whether I get justice or not. You didn't like Josh, either. You never like the things I do."

"Don't whine; you know I hate it. Wait a minute." Vince switched the call to his portable telephone and began to pace the length of the room. The overhead light glared in his eyes and he turned it off and stood still while his eyes adjusted to the dark. A trial. And Anne.

A trial. Sex and money.

And Anne.

You got my word on that; you're gonna be president, Vince. President Vincent Chatham of the United States of America.

"Wait a minute," he said again.

Over the years the country had elected presidents with mistresses, presidents with illegitimate kids . . . There were ways around anything in the past.

He had been so sure of that.

It had to be stopped. It was bad enough when it was just Dora's lawsuit; he'd known how dangerous that could be and he'd absolutely forbidden her to go on with it. But now it was far worse. Now menace beat above him, like a great bird. Anne. Dora's lawyer. Dora's adviser. Dora's confidante. A sour, vengeful woman worming her way into his daughter's life, worming her way into the family to turn them against him. And then—*when?*—talking to the press. To turn the world against him.

She had to be stopped. She and Dora both had to be stopped. But obviously Dora knew nothing. Not yet. Vince stopped pacing and concentrated on making his voice resonant and warm. "Dora, we've talked about this. And I know you understood everything I said, and a lot that I didn't; I've never had to spell everything out for you. You can't go to court, certainly not with this kind of lawsuit; we're in the public eye—"

"You're in the public eye; I'm invisible."

"You're too smart to say things like that. You know I have enemies just waiting for something like this. *My* daughter, in court, in a palimony suit." He gave a warm, confiding chuckle. "That's quite a combination. Sex and money, and a father in politics. You know the press would eat it up. They wouldn't miss a chance to make snide innuendos about my fitness to be a senator. Dora, listen to me. *This town is full of enemies! The whole country is full of them!* They'd get the newspapers to write editorials on family environment, children's upbringing, *morals,* for Christ's sake! They'd blame me for everything you've done; they'd have a ball. And I've got an election coming up next year!"

"You're awfully excited about this," Dora said. "A lot

more than you were a couple of weeks ago. I mean, you weren't exactly happy about my suing Josh, but now you're really wild. What did I miss?"

He took a breath. "I'm worried, and I'm trying to make you understand. You're usually more concerned about me, Dora, more sensitive to what I'm up against here. I'm disappointed in you. Why is this so important to you that you'd expose me to my enemies? It can't be notoriety; you've never cared about that. Is it money? I'll give you whatever you think you'll get from him. Look, fire this lawyer, forget the whole thing. Come to Washington. I'll be entertaining nonstop, starting in September, and there's no one I'd rather have as my hostess than my lovely daughter. You'll meet some powerful men, the most powerful in the country, and I'll find the most eligible bachelors . . . it's about time you met somebody worthy of you. How about it? Will you do that for me?"

"No," said Dora flatly. "I'm sorry, Daddy, I don't like to disappoint you, but this is something I have to do. It isn't money and it isn't notoriety; it's just something I have to do." There was a silence. "I have to make him hurt," she burst out. "I can't be satisfied until I do. And Anne's going to help me. She's tough and she's smart and I don't think she likes men. And that's just what I want."

"Why is she doing this?" Vince asked after a moment.

"Why? Why not? She's a lawyer. I'm a client."

"Why did she take you as a client?"

"She probably liked the case. Or me. What difference does it make?"

Vince walked back to his desk. He sat down and pulled a pad of paper toward him. "She's using the name Garnett?"

"That's her name. Why?"

"And her firm?"

"Engle, Saxon and Joute. Daddy, what's with you? She's a *relative;* she's your *niece.* And you still haven't told me why nobody ever talked about her. What happened? Was it really scandalous? Maybe it would make my little palimony suit look like peanuts. Come on, Daddy, what was the scandal?"

"There was no scandal." He laid his pencil across Anne's name and law firm, written in his spiked handwriting. "I don't know why the others didn't talk about her; your mother and I didn't because she was nothing to us. We hardly knew she was gone. As I recall, she lied a lot. I don't even know exactly when she disappeared. I was busy with the company, and your mother and I were having problems, and I had more important things to do than pay attention to a psychotic teenager."

"Psychotic?" Dora asked.

"Well, disturbed," Vince said carelessly. "Whatever she was, she took off one day and that was that. We were all busy with other things, and she wasn't worth the time it took to wonder where she was. She wasn't anyone you'd notice; there was no sign of her being smart or tough or whatever you seem to find so impressive. I assume that's why no one talked about her. It's odd that she showed up now, out of nowhere. Did she say what she's after?"

"I didn't ask. We only talked about me."

Vince nodded to himself. Dora had always thought first of herself. Just like her mother. "If you see her again—"

"Of *course* I'm going to see her; she's my *lawyer.*"

"You're not going to give up this whim?"

"I told you, it's more than a whim; I'm serious about it. And you haven't given me any good reason to give it up."

"I have a chance to be president." The words were blurted out. "That's confidential, of course, but the party's talking about it. Three years from now. And it looks damn good. Or it would, if my daughter wasn't hell-bent on this crusade. *Make him hurt.* What about making *me* hurt? That's what you're doing here."

There was a long silence. "They really want you to be president?"

"That's what they say. And they think I can do it. Wouldn't that please you? You'd be hostess in the White House."

"Aren't you going to get married again? You've got three years to do it."

Bitch, Vince thought. But he liked it, too, that his daughter was so quick to understand what had to be done. She got that from him.

"I hadn't thought about it. I'd rather have you as my hostess; you're the most impressive woman I know. And you'd enjoy it, wouldn't you?"

"Of course. But Daddy, if they want you for president, a little lawsuit in California three years before the election isn't going to make a bit of difference. It might make a few people snicker now, but so what? You're so strong it won't touch you. It isn't you, anyway; it's me, and nobody cares about me. It wouldn't be fair for you to stop me for something that's so far off. I really want to do this suit, Daddy; it's all I care about right now. If you cared about me, you'd understand that."

Vince had always known when to give up. He retreated. "Well, of course I wish you luck. I hope you win everything you want. And next time you see your lawyer, try to find out why she came back. We're all curious."

"Sure," said Dora absently, and Vince knew she would not ask; she was too wrapped up in her lawsuit even to remember something he asked her to do.

Fucking bastard, he cursed Josh Durant. Why couldn't he keep Dora screwed and satisfied? Vince had never liked him, from the time Dora brought him to dinner one night when Vince was visiting Los Angeles; he was too sure of himself, too guarded and smooth. Tall, arrogant son of a bitch: much taller than Vince. And clever: he hadn't given anything away about himself. Vince had left the restaurant knowing little more than he had when they met. He'd told Dora that night that the bastard wasn't trustworthy; she wouldn't be able to bend him an inch. She hadn't believed him.

He remained at his desk a long time after Dora said good-bye. *President Vincent Chatham of the United States of America. We have got one great time ahead of us, guaranteed.*

He glanced down and read what he had written. *Anne Garnett.* He saw her in his mind as she had looked at Ethan's funeral: black hair, black hat, black suit, a pale, stunning face, her head high: a regal look. He remembered the girl she had been: thin, slouching, her black hair uncombed, her eyes wide and blank when she looked at him.

He had not thought about her for twenty-four years. And now she had come back, to destroy him.

Unless he destroyed her first.

He reached for the telephone, and called Ray Beloit.

chapter 10

Anne met Dora in the noisy, teeming hallway outside the courtroom at a little before ten o'clock in the morning. *"Very* good," said Dora with a swift survey of Anne's figure, her eyes calculating the price of the pale gray suit and white silk blouse, the antique silver lapel watch, the soft leather briefcase. "I like the suit; is it Valentino?"

"No," Anne said. She paused with her hand on the doorknob. "You'll stand next to me and you'll keep quiet. You won't forget?"

"I remember everything you tell me," Dora said earnestly. She flattened herself against the wall as the crowd surged against them. A huge man in an undershirt lunged past, pulling on the hand of a short woman wearing a fringed skirt. A young girl in jeans, pushing a stroller with a crying baby, rushed through the crowd. A woman adjusted a man's tie. A couple kissed in a corner. Lawyers in dark business suits stood in the midst of plaintiffs, defendants, and uniformed guards; the click of heels on the hard floor punctuated the din of shouted conversations; the August sunlight, streaming through high windows, lay in broad stripes across the gesticulating throng, raising the temperature against the laboring air-conditioning system. "This place is the pits," Dora said. "How do you look so cool? You look like ice."

"Just remember to keep quiet," Anne said, and opened the door.

"I will, unless Josh starts lying."

Anne let go of the door. "If he listens to his lawyer, he'll be quiet," she snapped. "Dora, I'll say this one more time. We're not going into a trial; the judge is hearing motions this morning. That's all. They're going to make a motion that the judge dismiss your lawsuit as unfounded; we'll tell the judge why it shouldn't be dismissed. It shouldn't take more than half an hour; probably less. And I'll do the talking; you will not open your mouth. You'll have plenty of time to talk later on. Now come with me."

She led the way into the courtroom, as noisy and jammed as the corridor, and pointed to an empty space at the end of one of the pewlike benches that filled the back half of the room. "When they call your name, come up front. I'll be there."

As she turned away, a stocky, gray-haired man came to her side. He had a sad, jowly face, large ears, and bushy eyebrows, and a broad, melancholy smile. "Hello, Anne. It hasn't been so long since the last time."

"Hello, Fritz." She returned his smile, thinking that it was too bad that, of all the lawyers in Los Angeles, Josh Durant had chosen the one she liked the best. She might have thought better of him for it, but his choosing Fritz didn't change the person he was, and what he had done to Dora.

Miller looked down at Dora, sitting at the end of the bench. "I guess Anne isn't about to introduce us. Fritz Miller, Miss Chatham." He extended his hand. Dora looked at it without moving. "Yes, I suppose so," he sighed, and lowered his hand. "Too bad," he said to Anne. "Last time we came to a nice agreement, no hostilities, everybody was happy."

"Not happy, but definitely relieved," said Anne with another smile. "Do you see a chance for that here?"

He glanced at Dora, who was watching Anne, her face rigid. He sighed again. "It won't be a picnic." They walked down the aisle to the low barrier that bisected the room, and Miller held open the small gate for Anne to walk through, joining the crowd of lawyers who sat at large rectangular tables or stood in groups talking. "She's not being reasonable, you know," Fritz said. "Josh tried; he called her a couple of times to see if they couldn't"—he caught Anne's look of surprise before she masked it—"work things out in a friendly way. He's got no ill feelings toward the lady; he'd like her to be happy; he just doesn't see why he should pay for it after he's paid so much already,"

"When a man wants out, he always thinks he's paid more than enough already," Anne said dryly. She sat at one of the tables and opened her briefcase. "We'd love to settle this, Fritz; we're not anxious for it to go to trial. If you could come up with a fair offer—"

"All rise!" cried a piercing voice, and the judge entered the courtroom.

As cases were called and groups of people came to stand before the judge, their low voices rising and falling, Anne turned to scan the crowded benches to see if she could guess which was Josh Durant. Dora had said she had burned all her photos of him. Anne's gaze passed quickly over most of them as too young or too old, or men she could not imagine Dora weeping over. She paused briefly at a few faces, then came to a stop when she met the eyes of a man sitting in the far corner, watching her with a steady, somber look.

His face had fine wrinkles at the corners of his eyes and mouth; his eyes were deep set beneath dark brows in a broad forehead, and his mouth was hard and straight. He had a square chin with a small cleft, and a prominent jawline. Not a handsome face, Anne thought, but a strong one that some women might admire. His hair was light brown, turning gray, too long in back for her taste; his shoulders were broad, and she remembered Dora listing the sports he liked. She could not see his hands but she imagined them folded loosely in his lap; he seemed relaxed, not worried, and his expression gave nothing away. Not handsome, she thought again, but he had a face that could be harsh and arrogant, and a mouth that could say savage things.

She turned away. She knew something about good-looking men who could be charming when it suited them.

When they were called, Dora and Anne stood before the judge beside Miller and Josh. Josh looked briefly at Dora, his face a mask. Dora stared at the judge or vaguely across the courtroom. Anne heard Josh sigh; she could not tell if it was impatient or regretful.

"This is a motion to dismiss *Chatham versus Durant*," said the bailiff, and the judge read the pleadings written separately by Anne and Miller. He flipped rapidly through the pages, humming in a low monotone and blinking rapidly as if amazed, though Anne knew he had seen so much in his time that it was unlikely anything dealing with divorce or separation would surprise him. More likely, he was blinking to keep awake.

The judge looked at Miller. "Counselor?"

"We ask that the pleading be stricken, Your Honor. It is without merit, false in its assumptions and conclusions. There is no cause of action; no prima facie case on the pleading."

The judge skimmed Miller's pleading again. He asked a question about one of the statements, and Miller answered it rapidly, going through an argument Anne had heard before. Nothing new, she thought. That was always one of the saddest parts of couples breaking up: they always thought they were unique because their pain was so real, but to observers, the demands and complaints, the tensions, angers, and disappointments were so similar in couple after couple that after a while it was hard to believe that people hadn't learned from friends or parents or movies how to avoid making the same mistakes, sometimes two or even three times. But somehow they never did. Two hundred years earlier, Samuel Johnson had defined a second marriage as the triumph of hope over experience. And it's hardly a joke, Anne thought, and felt satisfied again with the solitary structure of her own life, with its peaceful silences and rhythms that depended on no one but herself.

The judge turned to her. "What is Miss Chatham asking for?"

Anne stated again what was in her pleading. "We are asking that the contract between Dora Chatham and Josh Durant be fulfilled, Your Honor. It is a matter of performance: there was a verbal contract between Miss Chatham and Mr. Durant, for which she gave him consideration, and he has not performed it. Since there has been no performance of the contract, we are seeking payment for what was promised and not fulfilled."

The judge nodded. "And are there facts?"

"There are. Promises and declarations made before witnesses, as well as financial arrangements and living arrangements that implied or directly stated the intention of permanence and marriage."

The judge was leafing through the pleadings again, humming again, still blinking. Now and then he rubbed the side of his nose. "Well, counselors, I think we have a cause of action here; I think it should go to trial. Let's set it for September fifteenth, one month from now; that gives everybody a chance to do a little thinking, maybe a little talking, before the last door gets closed. If anything changes in your battle formations, I'll be pleased to hear about it."

"What did all that mean?" Dora asked as they turned away. "Was he being cute?"

"No." Anne led Dora out of the courtroom. "He was hoping we'd have the good sense to work out a settlement."

"Why should we? We can't lose. The only thing that other lawyer had to say was that I'm a liar. I'm not a liar. Josh knows that. He liked that about me. He told me once he could always count on my honesty even when he couldn't—" She broke off and looked at her watch. "What time is it? It felt like we were in there forever."

"When he couldn't what?" Anne asked.

"Nothing."

"When he couldn't *what?*" They were in the corridor outside the courtroom, almost empty now, and she had stopped walking, forcing Dora to stop with her.

Dora shrugged. "Count on me. He didn't think I was always there for him."

"What does that mean?"

"Oh, you know, listening to him go on and on about ancient cultures or digging up a tomb or something, or telling him how wonderful he was. He always wanted me to prop him up."

"Always?"

"Always. He was impossible."

"But arrogant."

"Yes. I told you."

"It doesn't sound arrogant to me to need propping up."

"Well, it was. *He* was. Are you trying to confuse me? He's arrogant and mean and he wants to be told how wonderful he is. And I did, but it never was enough for him. He likes women to make him feel important . . . well, of course all men do, but Josh is the worst. He's always had women, you know; before me there were lots of them, good-looking ones, he likes really gorgeous women. Are we going to stand here all day? I'd like to go home."

Behind them, Miller and Josh came out of the courtroom. Miller paused as they walked by. "Shall we meet in your office?" he asked Anne.

"Fine," she said. "Monday morning at nine?"

"We'll be there." He smiled. "With cool tempers and warm hearts. At least we'll try. We're all civilized people, Anne, and you're as smart as they come; couldn't you work on the whole picture, not be so hell-bent on getting blood?"

Anne looked past Miller, at Josh, who stood beside a tall window, gazing at the plaza below. His profile was harsh in the sunlight. "A whole picture means two people, Fritz, and everything they ever meant to each other. He may be able to wipe it out because of a whim, but Dora can't; she's more steadfast than that, more serious. She believed him, she believed *in* him; she put her future in his hands, and one day he opened his hands and spilled it out and told her there was no future for them together, and there never had been. He seems to have done that without a qualm, but that's impossible for Dora. You're asking her to be as callous as he is, to walk away from a tender relationship, and its hopes and dreams, without a single backward glance. She can't do that. And in all fairness, she shouldn't."

Anne was aware that Josh had turned from the window to watch her. She met his eyes, and was stunned by the deep sadness in them that seemed to alter his whole appearance. His face no longer looked harsh; he looked older than he had in the courtroom, more drawn, and almost in despair. Anne frowned, trying to understand what she saw, but Miller was talking to her and she turned back to him.

"You're terrific, Anne." He was nodding slowly, his lower lip thrust out. "That is one terrific opening statement. How could a judge hear that and not think Josh is a lousy bastard who ought to pay through the nose for what he did?"

Anne smiled at him and Miller thought he saw an impish gleam in her eye—though it must be a mistake, he thought, since no one had ever seen the cool, aloof Anne Garnett look even remotely impish. "I thought you'd like a preview," she said, "instead of waiting for the trial. It might make a difference in the discovery session on Monday."

He chuckled. "Possibly. But you know, Anne, all those golden words aren't anywhere near the whole picture; it's like a mirror in a fun house where everything's—"

"Are we going to stand here all day?" Dora asked again. "I have a lot to do."

"So do we all," said Miller promptly. "I apologize for holding you up, Miss Chatham. We'll see you Monday morning, Anne, in your office."

As Miller walked away, Anne glanced again at Josh. He was writing in a small notebook, and followed Miller, still writing. His stride was long and assured. He did not look up.

"Son of a bitch," said Dora. It was not clear whom she meant, and Anne did not ask. They walked down the corridor in silence. "What's a discovery session?" she asked a few minutes later as they got into Anne's car.

"A meeting where each side discovers what information the other side has, and how it will be used."

"You mean you give it all away before the trial?"

"I mean we go through all the facts and the evidence. It doesn't favor one side or the other; discovery helps both sides."

"And it's in your office," Dora said after a moment. "That's good. They know they have to come to us."

"It doesn't mean that at all." Anne glanced behind her, then merged with the traffic on the freeway. "The husband and his attorney almost always go to the office of the wife's attorney, and we've just gone on that way even when there isn't a husband and wife. It's some kind of archaic courtesy that doesn't have much meaning anymore, but still, it lingers."

"Probably because they know this isn't an ordinary case," Dora said, as if Anne had not spoken. "I mean, this would make the evening news if the networks ever get hold of it. Which they won't; I mean, who would tell them? Josh doesn't like publicity, and my father would die if it got on television. He's totally terrified of *anybody* getting hold of it. Do you remember him? He told me he hardly remembers you. I suppose he didn't pay much attention; Mother said he didn't like kids. I was the only one he liked. You'll have to meet him sometime; he's really very sweet when he wants to be. All wrapped up in himself, but men are like that; you just have to push the right buttons so they show you their best side. I can do that with him; we get along better than my mother and me. He likes that, you know; if you ask me, he really worked at making me like him better than her. The funny thing is, I don't, really; I like them the same; it's just easier to be with him because he doesn't tell me what to do and Mother keeps pouring out advice. I liked his second wife, but she split right after the election. I suppose he wanted her to stick around till he was elected. He's really crazy about being in the Senate; which is why he's so uptight about this lawsuit. He wanted me to drop it, you know. I felt bad in a way; poor Daddy, I never heard him try so hard to get his way. He told me to fire you and come to Washington and play hostess at his parties. I may do that anyway, after we win; it's a great place to be. He'll still want me; he really likes having me around."

Anne drove into the garage in her building. Her knuckles were white from gripping the wheel. "I'm going up to my office," she said. Her voice was perfectly steady. "I want to meet with you tomorrow; we have to talk about Monday morning."

"What *about* publicity?" Dora asked. "Will there be any?"

"Not from my office. I can't control what the other side

does, or what the press picks up; there are reporters who spend all their time checking out divorces and separations, looking for stories." They walked from the car to the elevator. "If we do go to court, we'll ask that the hearing be in the judge's chambers, instead of open court; that keeps it quiet. And after that we'll ask the judge to impound the file; that sends it to the warehouse and it can't be gotten out without a court order. The same when they prove it up—when the history of the settlement is written, describing how it was arrived at, without coercion and so on—we'll ask that that be impounded as well."

"Then no one will ever see it. I'll tell my father. It'll make him feel better."

"That isn't what I said. Anyone can get a court order to see the files, one person at a time. And there's still the trial. The judge may not agree to hold it in his chambers. Then it would be open to the public. That doesn't mean that reporters will be there, but it's a real possibility."

Dora shrugged. "Whatever. The senator is a big man these days; he'll survive."

Anne walked rapidly toward a bank of elevators. "My secretary will let you know what time tomorrow."

I should never have taken this case, she thought as the elevator doors closed. It was asking for trouble. She thought back to the conversation in Tamarack, how Dora had begged her, how her need had overcome Anne's reluctance. And she remembered being intrigued by the case; the law dealing with people living together was still being created. But she knew it was not that simple; there was a darker reason for her agreeing to do it. Somehow, in some confused way, she had seen this case as a way to triumph over Vince. She, not Vince, was the one who could help Dora. She, not Vince, was the one in whom Dora would confide, the one in whom Dora would put her trust.

But it was not a triumph. Anne had known that the minute Dora began talking about Vince. All the old feelings had come rushing back. The sound of his name could do that to her, after all these years. He could still defeat her.

But she would win for his daughter. It was more important than ever, now, that she win Dora's lawsuit. This was her turf, the neutral territory where she proved her worth to herself and others. On her own turf, she would be triumphant. Monday, she thought. We can win in discovery. We don't have to wait a month; we don't have to go to trial. We can force them to a settlement now.

She saw in her mind the sadness in Josh Durant's eyes. If he's unhappy enough, she thought coldly, he'll be glad to get it over with.

She contemplated him when he walked into her office with Fritz Miller on Monday morning. He was handsomer than she had remembered; probably the softer lighting in her office, she thought. But his face gave nothing away. "Josh Durant, Anne Garnett," said Miller. They shook hands across her desk. His palm was hard; his fingers and Anne's met with equal strength.

A court reporter sat unobtrusively in a corner. Josh greeted Dora. She nodded and sat in an armchair at a corner of Anne's desk, her chin up, looking out the window. Miller pulled out a chair for Josh at the other corner, and took a chair for himself precisely between them. Balancing his briefcase on his lap, he opened it and pulled out packets of papers, stacking them on the desk. "We have here, as you requested, Josh Durant's tax returns for the past three years, his bank statements with canceled checks for those years, stock certificates, leases, deeds, and insurance policies. His accountant and investment counselor can be made available if you wish to question them."

"We may," Anne said. Her voice was casual, in contrast to Miller's careful formality. Fritz was always as reserved and punctilious as if they had never met, and to counter it, she began with an easy air that still made him wary, even though they had been opposing attorneys on five cases. She settled back without looking at the papers Miller had put on her desk. She was wearing a white silk suit with a dark red blouse with a neckline of soft folds. "We have a lot of things to talk about, Fritz, and of course one of them is the lifestyle Miss Chatham and Mr. Durant lived while they were together, but first of all I'd like to talk about what promises were made." She turned to Josh. "Mr. Durant, you asked Dora Chatham to move into your apartment a little over three years ago, on July tenth, at nine-thirty P.M., during dinner."

"Over coffee and cognac," he said, "at La Nuit, table five, in the back." Anne looked at him steadily, but there was no mockery in his eyes or his voice; he simply recalled that night as clearly as Dora had. It was strange, Anne thought, that few people are surprised when a woman remembers precise details, especially romantic ones, but when a man does it, listeners look for hidden meanings. But he's a scientist, she reminded herself; it's his job to remember details.

"From that time on," she said, "you took a number of steps that implied a permanent relationship. You—"

"We aren't talking implications," Miller protested. "We're here to talk facts."

"I think you'll find these are facts," Anne replied. She did not look at her notes; she kept her eyes on Josh. "Shortly after Miss Chatham moved in, the two of you opened a joint bank account at First National of California." Dora turned from the window to watch Anne, nodding as Anne made each point. "You obtained credit cards with a shared account number. Miss Chatham wrote the checks to pay the monthly credit-card bills. The utility bills were in your name, but Miss Chatham wrote the checks to pay them. She wrote checks for the monthly assessment on your apartment, for the housekeeper, and for caterers for entertaining. She shopped for food. In effect, she managed your home. In September, two months after she moved in, you named her as your beneficiary on the life insurance policy you have through UCLA, where you are a professor of archaeology. That's correct, Mr. Durant?"

"Yes," he said.

"Why did you do that?"

"I had no other family," he said quietly.

"Then you thought of Dora Chatham as your family."

"No. And she didn't think of me that way. We'd just begun to live together."

"You said you had no *other* family."

He hesitated. "Yes, I did say that. As I recall, for a while after Dora moved in, we played house; we were like a couple of kids, having fun pretending we were creating a family."

"You said you didn't want a family!" Dora cried.

"Dora," Anne said sharply, stunned, as she was so often, at the ability of clients to weaken, or even ruin, their cases with a single devastating remark.

Dora shrugged and fixed her gaze again on Anne's face.

"I thought I didn't want one," Josh said to Anne. "I thought I was content without one."

"But you were willing to ask Miss Chatham to mimic a wife."

"No, I asked her to live with me. I didn't tell her how to do it; I asked for her companionship, nothing else."

"But companionship in this case included buying the groceries, being hostess at parties, paying the bills, dealing with the housekeeper, choosing the Wedgwood and the Baccarat crystal when you went shopping your first Christmas together. Those are only a few. Did she beg you to allow her to do all those things?"

"Neither one of us begged. I don't know how it happened. I did ask her to hire a new housekeeper when the one I'd had moved away, and she did, but the rest . . . just seemed to happen."

"'Just seemed to happen,'" Anne repeated. "But things usually happen when the stage has been set for them. In fact, it would appear that your relationship with Miss Chatham came about because you had a place waiting—"

"Lots of conjecture here," said Miller. "Could we get back to—"

"I'd like to hear the rest of Miss Garnett's sentence," said Josh.

"I was about to say, you had a place waiting for Miss Chatham, as if you had a comfortable pair of slippers that someone had recently stepped out of—or been forced out of—and you showed Miss Chatham how to put them on, even though—"

"That's ridiculous," he said coldly. "You didn't hear that from Dora; she couldn't have thought that up herself. Even if she could, she knows me better—"

"I don't know you at all!" Dora cried. "You threw me out—I didn't even *guess* you'd do a thing like that!"

"Now, Anne, you see?" said Miller reproachfully.

"And even if I didn't think that up, about the slippers, it's true!" Dora went on wildly. "You wanted a wife but you wouldn't make a commitment; you wanted a little home-body to make you a nest and protect you in it, but you weren't willing to fold her inside your wings and keep her close."

Josh gave Anne a curious look. "She didn't think of that by herself, either."

"It's not important. Dora, we agreed you would let me handle this."

"Good advice," Miller said to Josh. "You should answer questions, just the questions, nothing else. Let the lawyers take care of the rest."

Josh spoke to Anne. "Whatever we did, we did it together. I would have thought, if someone wanted to be protected and kept close, she would have offered the same in return. I thought the days of tough warriors and frail maidens had been over for a long time."

"What does that have to do with it?" Dora cried. "You did worse than not protecting me—you forced me to leave!"

"I did not," he said quietly.

"We'll get to that in a minute," Anne said. "First, I'd like to turn to something else. Two women shared your apartment at different times in the years before you met Miss Chatham, one for a little over a year, one for approximately two years. You got rid of both of them. Is that correct?"

"It's not relevant, Anne," said Miller.

"I think it is. One went to Europe on a job you found for her. The other moved to New York on her own. After that there was another woman you knew very well and were seen with for a couple of years. She went to Chicago a few months before you met Miss Chatham. You've left a long trail of failed relationships, and in each case you've walked away without a mark on you; you pay nothing, you give nothing, you lose nothing."

His eyes hardened. "At least I try to build relationships instead of being in the lucrative business of ending them."

"Josh, shut up," Miller said. "You're in danger of being a horse's ass here."

"Dora knows about those women," Josh said to Anne. "She knows the truth about them. Ask her to tell you the truth."

Anne was flushed. "You repeated with Miss Chatham a familiar pattern. You have a history of relationships that end within one to three years, in each case when you ask the woman to leave. We don't have to know what promises, real or implied, were made in those other relationships; intimacy breeds promises, often made carelessly from laziness or passion—"

"What a fine pair, laziness and passion," Josh said bitingly. "If that's all you know of love, you're a poor authority to tell the rest of us what we ought—"

"Josh, for Christ's sake!" Miller burst out.

"I apologize," Josh said instantly, to Anne, seeing a flash of pain in her eyes. "That was rude and entirely uncalled for. You're wrong about me, but that's still no excuse for my behavior. I do apologize. As for my past, I won't discuss it. You'll have to accept that. It has nothing to do with Dora and me. We started out with affection; I thought we were giving, not demanding; I thought we were sharing, not taking. I know now that I was wrong in believing that, but at the time that's what I thought, and I thought it for the first year, before things began to change. If I could have controlled that . . ." Abruptly, his voice changed. His gaze grew inward. "But I didn't. It took me by surprise."

He was silent. Anne, who was trying to quiet the turmoil within her, let the silence go on.

"All right," said Miller, "I want to ask a few—"

"But all through that first year," Josh went on, ignoring Miller's exasperated grunt, "the things I did probably sprang from some desire for family that I'd had for a long time and hadn't recognized—like a dream we can't recapture but that still haunts us with the mood it leaves behind. I suppose that's what happened to me. I don't know how else I'd explain the fact that, as you said, I did take a number of steps—"

Miller slammed his palm on his thigh. "We're going to slow down now." He shot a quick glance at Anne. "I've seen these sessions get a little crazy, but we're about to set a record here."

Anne did not reply; she was making notes. What was wrong with her today? She never argued with opposing clients; she asked them direct questions or spoke to them through their lawyers. But this morning she was behaving as if she were in Dora's place. Well, there's a lot going on, she thought defensively. And she found herself repeating Josh's words: *a dream that haunts us . . .*

For twenty-four years she had lived with that.

But this was not the time to think about it. This was the worst time to think about it. "I do have some other points to make, Fritz," she said firmly. "Mr. Durant, in October of the year Miss Chatham moved in, you traveled together to France; in December the two of you went to Greece; you went to England the following spring, and Egypt the next October. You paid for all of those trips, and the airline tickets and hotel registrations were in the names of Mr. and Mrs. Joshua Durant."

He nodded. "Dora wanted that. As for—"

"You wanted it!" Dora said hotly. "You said you didn't care how indifferent society was, you didn't want me to tag along as an appendage; you wanted me to belong with you wherever we went!"

Anne looked at Josh with interest. "An interesting idea," she murmured.

"But not quite accurate," he said evenly. "Dora was the one who said she didn't want to be an appendage; it never occurred to me that she would be, whatever name she used. She was my companion, my equal. I did say I wanted her to belong with me when we traveled; I did suggest that we use

Mr. and Mrs. if that would make her more comfortable. As for paying, of course I paid. I asked her to come with me to Greece and Egypt; those were business trips. France and England were vacations and I wanted her with me. So I paid."

"And nothing is proved by it," Miller said. "Where's all this leading, Anne? We've never denied they lived together. People do those things when they live together."

"A year after Miss Chatham moved in," Anne said to Josh, "you bought a house in Tamarack. The deed is in both your names."

"People do that, too," Miller said. "All it means is they liked each other. They liked living together and doing things together. They were very close. But they weren't married, they weren't planning to be, they weren't setting dates, they weren't even talking about it. Nobody promised anybody anything in any way at any time."

"As for promises," Anne said to Josh, "at a New Year's Eve party six months after Miss Chatham moved in with you, she told a friend, in your presence, that she planned to take care of you forever and keep you away from young chicks when you got too old and feeble to resist. You did not contradict her."

"Of course not," he said. "It was almost dawn when Dora said that; by then no one was taking anything very seriously. It was simpler to let it pass than to argue."

"A month later, you came into the apartment when Dora was having a fitting with her dressmaker. Dora introduced you and said to the dressmaker, 'One of these days I'll ask you to make my wedding dress, and a matching cummerbund for Josh's tux.' You did not contradict her."

"No. I was embarrassed for her—she shouldn't have said it and she knew it; her voice had that kittenish quality it gets when she knows she's wrong—and I just wanted to change the subject."

"It was simpler to let it pass than to argue."

Josh frowned slightly. "Yes."

"In July of that same year, at a barbecue in Wellfleet, Massachusetts, your hostess asked when the wedding would be; Miss Chatham said it would be soon. You did not contradict her."

Miller shot a quick frown at Josh. Slowly, Josh nodded. "I almost did. I was about to say something. But Sandra—our hostess—is one of the world's premier gossips. If I'd said anything, it would have been all over Cape Cod in an hour, and within a week it would have reached Los Angeles, embroidered with variations, all of them humiliating to Dora. I couldn't do it."

"It was simpler—"

"To let it pass," he said coldly.

"Anne." Miller was frowning. "These are all negatives, you know. He didn't contradict somebody; it was simpler not to argue . . . I don't think you want to call those facts."

"I call them facts, Fritz, and so do you. Over the years an atmosphere was created in which Miss Chatham had every reason to assume that her feelings were reciprocated and her ideas were shared. She had no reason to assume that Mr. Durant did not see the future as clearly, and in the same way, as she did."

Miller pursed his lips. "Somebody might see it that way. Somebody else could say this is a nice guy who doesn't like to hurt people or make trouble, so when a woman makes foolish statements, he keeps his mouth shut because he doesn't want to put her in a position where she looks to the world just as foolish as she is. So unless you have evidence that Josh made a direct offer or promise or suggestion or whatever, I don't see what you've got."

Anne nodded. "Mr. Durant, on Dora's birthday, three months after you began living together, you gave her a necklace, an Egyptian royal scarab on a gold chain. With it, you gave her a note." She unfolded a sheet of fine, hand-made paper and read from it. "'My dear one, the scarab is a symbol of the enduring human soul, and also of the daily rebirth of the sun—and therefore of life. This scarab, inscribed with the cartouche of the pharaoh Akhenaten, one of the few about whom we know enough to say he truly loved his wife, will be our symbol, for the life we will share together.'"

Miller's face lengthened into deep melancholy. "I want to see that note."

"So do I," said Josh. "If I may—?" He held out his hand. When Anne gave it to him, he took a long time to read it. "Only three years ago," he murmured. "I wasn't young enough to have written that."

"That's not funny!" Dora cried.

"I meant it quite seriously." He gazed at Anne, his eyes meditative. "This is a note written by a callow young man who thinks he not only sees the future, but also can control it. I was too old for that three years ago. Not because I was thirty-nine, but because I knew too much. I knew how formless the future is: how it can crack and shatter certainty; I knew how one event—a little one, an enormous one—can bend a life into a new direction and a new shape that can't be bent back. I knew all that then as well as I know it now. Of all people, an archaeologist knows first and foremost about change. If I were to try to understand why I wrote—"

"Josh, let me run with this," said Miller. "I'd like to ask Miss Chatham a few questions."

Dora looked startled. "What about? He's admitted everything."

"A little short of that," Miller said. "Miss Chatham, did Mr. Durant ever ask you to marry him?"

"You heard what he wrote! He said he wanted to share his life with me!"

"I heard it. I'll ask you again. Did he ever ask you to marry him?"

Dora's lips trembled. "No."

"Did he ever say he would marry you?"

"No."

"Did he say he wanted to marry you but some impediment prevented it?"

"No."

"In fact, Miss Chatham, did Mr. Durant ever mention marriage to you at all?"

"No."

"In three years of living together, he never brought up the idea of marriage. Why do you think he didn't?"

Tears came to Dora's eyes. "I guess . . . he didn't want to. I guess he just didn't love me enough. He never said that, though. He kept leading me on and making me feel like I was part of a . . . family, and in a little while, when he felt like it, he'd marry me. He made me think he loved me as much as I loved him and one of these days we'd get married, because that's what people do, isn't it, when they're in love and they're already like a family?"

Josh looked at Anne. She was watching Dora closely. Like a coach, Josh thought, or a director. An extraordinarily beautiful woman, but the coldest he had ever met. She was like a chiseled goddess in one of the great royal tombs of Egypt: flat, frozen, aloof from the human drama in which she played a crucial part. He wondered what had frozen Anne Garnett so that she was only a partial woman, and her beauty almost a mockery, suggesting passion but masking an icy emptiness. Empty, except for that sudden glimpse of pain in her eyes. He wondered what lay behind it. He wondered what it would take, besides pain, to wake her up.

"Well, that's very sad, Miss Chatham," Miller was saying, "but we haven't seen any real evidence that Mr. Durant was leading you on. You might have been leading him on, for that matter, convincing him you weren't interested in marriage when in fact every bone in your body was aching for it."

"*Aching*, Fritz?" asked Anne.

He nodded. "I'd say so. Everywhere she went she slipped in cute little comments about marriage, like she wanted to trip him up when he was most relaxed—parties, that sort of thing—get him to say, 'Sure, sweetie, we'll do it, just name the day.' He didn't because he didn't want to and he never pretended he did. Miss Chatham, when Mr. Durant didn't contradict you, all those times you dropped those little hints to everybody within shouting distance, from Cape Cod to your dressmaker, when he didn't contradict you, did you follow up? Did you say, 'Okay, honey lamb, let's set a date; my dressmaker's ready with the silks and satins; our friend on Cape Cod wants to give us a bash; the New Year's guests will give us a sendoff on an ocean of champagne.' Did you say that?"

"Of course not."

"Did you say anything like it? Even close?"

"No, I—"

"Why not? If you really believed he wanted to marry you, why didn't you push him on it and pin him down?"

"Because nobody pushes Josh!" she flared. "He gets mean when he's pushed. And then I'd be afraid of him."

"Afraid? What were you afraid of? That he'd beat you?"

"Well . . . maybe."

"Had he ever beat you?"

"No, but . . ."

"Had he ever threatened to beat you?"

"No, but . . ."

"In fact, had he ever touched you with anything but affection?"

"No, but you never know, do you? When men get mad, how do you know what's going to happen?"

"Have you ever seen a man beat a woman, Miss Chatham?"

"No, but my . . . I've seen men be nasty to women and that's the first step. You wouldn't say that, because you're a man, but it's true."

"My . . . what? What did you start to say, Miss Chatham? My lover? Is that it? You've had a lover, or more than one, who was nasty to you?"

Anne put out her hand. "Fritz, this has no place here."

"It has as much a place as your talking about other women Josh might have known," Miller said. "Your lover was nasty to you, Miss Chatham?"

"No," she said.

"Not a lover? Then who was it? There wasn't anyone, was there? You just wanted to make us believe you were afraid of Josh Durant, but you had no reason to be, did you? So you made up a mythical man to compare him to, but there was no man, no one who'd been nasty enough to make you afraid—"

245

"My father!" Dora cried. "Damn you, I didn't make it up! I saw how he could get cold and mean and hurt someone . . ."

"Your mother?" Miller asked. "He struck your mother?"

Dora shook her head. "Of course not. He was just unpleasant. Mean."

"And Mr. Durant reminded you of him?"

"Exactly. He's exactly like him."

"Just a minute," Anne said urgently. She wanted a minute of silence. For the first time, she was sure that Dora was lying. Until now, she had believed most of what she said. She had wanted to believe her; she had wanted to believe, even before she met Josh Durant, that a woman in the company of a charming, manipulative, arrogant man would be the victim. *That's what was wrong with me earlier. I was behaving like an angry fifteen-year-old instead of a professional.* But there was much more here than Dora was giving her. The whole picture, Fritz had said. And Dora was lying. Because Anne had seen enough of Josh Durant to know he bore no resemblance to Vince Chatham. She glanced at Josh and saw the contempt in his eyes as he looked at Dora.

"There were lots of things—" Dora said.

"Such as his being nasty?" Miller asked.

"No, not exactly—"

"Or frightening?"

"No, but—"

"Or mean?"

"He was mean, but not in exactly the same way."

"Then what *exactly* were you worried about?"

She was silent. Tears came to her eyes. They welled up and clung to her lower lashes before falling slowly, like crystal drops, to her pale cheeks. "I was afraid he'd leave me," she whispered. "I was afraid he'd get mad and impatient and go away and leave me alone after he'd promised to take care of me and be with me forever. And I couldn't stand that. I loved him so much . . ." She kept her head high and with a trembling finger, dabbed at the tears rolling down her cheeks.

A small grunt escaped Miller.

"Fritz," Anne said. It would have been time to intervene in any event, but now she wanted to get the session over with. "I'd like to review what we've got, if you'll allow me to go through it."

Miller nodded. "Let's hear it."

She stood beside the window and still without looking at her notes, gave them the closing argument she would give if they were in court. She had done this in other cases; sometimes it led to a swift settlement. "We can trace several themes in the life Mr. Durant and Miss Chatham made together for three years: each is a separate kind of promise, or contract. One is the theme of cherishing, or protection. Mr. Durant brought Miss Chatham into his apartment and, in effect, turned over to her the management of his home. She hired the new housekeeper, paid the bills, organized entertainment, chose new china and glassware, and so on. He bought a house in Tamarack, Colorado, with her, and had the deed filed in both their names. He asked her to accompany him on trips to various parts of the world, and he paid all the expenses. There was, in other words, a general pattern of caring for Miss Chatham, of enfolding her within his protective embrace."

She paused briefly. "Another theme is that of creating an atmosphere of assumptions, expectations, and assurances. Mr. Durant has told us he was the one who suggested they travel as Mr. and Mrs. Joshua Durant. He spoke of her this morning as his family—'I had no other family' were his words. In fact, he named her his beneficiary on his life insurance policy, a position almost always filled by a spouse or other close family members. And he told her he wanted her to be not an appendage but part of him."

She walked to the other side of her desk and spoke to Josh and Miller across its broad surface. "This brings us to the last theme—closely entwined with those assumptions and expectations—the theme of promises. At a New Year's party, Mr. Durant heard Miss Chatham tell a friend that she planned to take care of him forever and keep him away from other women whom he might find attractive. He did not contradict her. He did not even say, 'Well, maybe.' He let the statement stand. As far as his listeners knew, since he was silent, he might well have been deeply pleased to know that Miss Chatham would take care of him forever. Similarly, he did not contradict her when she told her dressmaker, 'One of these days I'll ask you to make my wedding dress, and a matching cummerbund for Josh's tux.' Again, he let the statement stand as if he agreed with it. And again, he was silent when, in Wellfleet, Massachusetts, she responded 'soon' to a question concerning the date of their wedding— hers and Mr. Durant's. Each time, Mr. Durant found it convenient to let Miss Chatham speak for both of them. So convenient that it's fair to wonder if he didn't like what she was saying, and agree with it. How do we know what his feelings were at the time she made those statements? He may have changed his mind later, but that would not alter the promise, the consent, he gave Miss Chatham through his silence. Mr. Durant is a scientist, a professor, a consultant to museums and to foreign governments in the preservation of their antiquities. Is it likely that such a man would let sloppy or incorrect statements slip by without correcting them? It would go completely against his character. To support this conclusion, to strongly support it, there is the birthday note that he wrote to Miss Chatham. We have only that one note, but we may suppose there were many, given the emotional nature of this one. It says, in part, referring to a birthday gift, 'This will be our symbol, for the life we will share together.' Finally, we should remember that Mr. Durant himself has said, 'The things I did probably sprang from some desire for family that I'd had for a long time and hadn't recognized.'"

Anne returned to her chair. "I would add that the lifestyle Mr. Durant led, and asked Miss Chatham to share, was a fairly opulent one in a West Los Angeles high rise filled with possessions that endure. There is nothing temporary about a dining table set with Wedgwood and Baccarat. It speaks of permanence and tradition; it speaks of generations handing treasures to succeeding generations in a line through the ages that gets its strength from the expectation and assurance of stability even in a world where much is always in flux."

She paused to sip from a glass on her desk. "Those are the themes I have identified. And to repeat something I said earlier, Dora Chatham understood what those themes meant during her three years with Mr. Durant. She gave herself to a tender relationship, with all its hopes and dreams, and thought she was sharing it with someone whose hopes and dreams matched hers. You cannot expect her to be as callous as Mr. Durant now that he has grown tired of the life he formed with her; you cannot ask her to walk away from that tender relationship without a single backward glance or the demand—the *demand*—that she be awarded something from that relationship in which she believed, since she has been barred from the relationship itself. For her to walk away with nothing would send a message that casual promises, flip asides, and unthinking silences are acceptable behavior even in one who is claiming affection and need. For her to do that would make a mockery of trust and love. She should not do it. She must not do it."

Dora gave a long sigh. Miller had made a peak of his fingers an inch from his nose and was concentrating on it with a deep scowl. Josh was watching Anne; he had watched her steadily through her long summing-up. His face was expressionless, but he knew he was in trouble. Together, these two women would defeat him in court. First, Dora would be a perfect witness. Her beauty was shallow, compared to Anne's, but, in testifying, she would come across as lovely and fragile. Her lower lip, possibly her most potent weapon, would tremble as it so often had when they lived together. He had come to detest Dora's lower lip with a fervor that amazed him. But to the judge it would be new, and as pathetic as a child's. Her large eyes would swim with tears and she would manage to force out, with new depths of choking sorrow, *He kept leading me on and making me feel like I was part of a family. I was afraid he'd leave me alone after he'd promised to take care of me and be with me forever.*

Who could resist that?

Who would feel sympathy for Josh Durant? Even if the judge found a reason to be sympathetic, how long could he hold out against the tight web of Anne Garnett's arguments? How long would anyone lean toward a man who wrote that damned birthday note and then, two years later, told the lady he wanted her gone from his apartment? Who, hearing that and a hell of a lot more, would send a tearful Dora out of the courtroom with nothing, while Josh Durant kept it all?

A brilliant summing-up, he thought. He admired it, knowing he would lose to her. He admired her mind, he enjoyed watching it work, and he would have liked to understand it better, to understand her better. Of course it was ridiculous for her to speak of something going completely against his character; she didn't know a damn thing about his character. And of course she knew it was ridiculous; she was too smart not to know it. She was smart enough to know just how low some of her other points were, too, such as his building permanence with Baccarat—a tawdry, weak, and specious argument if he'd ever heard one, but clever and telling on first hearing. And she knew, and so did he, there would be only one hearing.

The scientist in Josh saluted the fine workings of Anne Garnett's mind, even as his anger grew. Because he was stuck. He had intended to settle out of court anyway—no one in his right mind would want the kind of publicity this trial would bring—but he'd thought he could get away with a small payment, just enough to make Dora feel victorious. Now he knew it would cost him much more, because it was clear to all of them that he would not save money now by letting it go to trial. He was stuck. If he'd been as quick as Anne Garnett, if he'd thought about this as intelligently in three years as she had in one month, he would have made a reasonable financial arrangement when he asked Dora to leave, and that would have been the end of it.

"Josh," Miller said, "let's step outside for a minute."

And that's it, Josh thought as he stood up. He and Miller walked from Anne's office into a labyrinth of secretaries' cubicles divided by low partitions and green plants, and he thought, that's how the bargaining begins. Miller knew as well as Josh that they were stuck. They'd reach an agreement and he'd pay Dora a hell of a lot more than she ought to get and something less than she was asking. And Anne Garnett would oversee it, her face cool and impassive. Josh had no doubt of that. There would be no sign of triumph on her face; she would not even smile with satisfaction, at least as long as he and Miller were in the office. She might feel satisfaction or triumph—though he could not even be sure of that—but none of it would show.

I'd like to see how she looks when she feels that something wonderful is happening to her, he thought. I'd like to watch her mind work on something more joyful than dredging all she can for a client from the ruins of a relationship. But he never would; he knew that. They were enemies, of a sort, and after they reached a settlement sometime today, he would never see her again. Too bad, he thought, and then he and Miller found an empty office and went inside to plan their strategy of offers and counteroffers, to reach whatever amount he would have to pay.

Anne sat at her desk long after the three of them had left, Miller and Josh first, then Dora, who had waited, pacing and talking nervously, until she could be sure she would not run into them at the elevator or in the lobby downstairs. "It went fine," she said. "We did really fine, didn't we? It's a good thing I kept that note; some people throw things away, but I don't; you never know what's coming, so you have to keep yourself covered. God, I'm glad it's over; I couldn't stand hearing his voice another minute. You were tougher than I was; you know that? I would have taken their first offer, as soon as I knew I'd won. God, wasn't that fantastic, knowing we'd beat them into the ground? Josh looked awful, didn't he? Miserable and mad and jealous because I had a better lawyer than he did. It serves him right. I wish I could beat him again, at something else; I really had a good time. Maybe now I'll go to Washington. My father's been pretty annoyed with me, but all I have to do is say I'd rather be with him than with Mother and he'll welcome me with open arms. Oh, but he's not there; he's politicking in Colorado. Washington in August is not to be believed. Maybe I'll ask him to meet me in Tamarack. Or Europe. Or . . . something. I wish I knew what I want. Everything seems so uninteresting. I've got all this money coming from Josh; I ought to do something fantastic with it. Don't you think?" She looked at her watch. "Well, I guess I can go; they ought to be halfway to somewhere by now." She went to the door. "You'll be in Tamarack, won't you? This winter or some-time? I'll probably see you then."

Anne watched the door close behind her. That is a first-class bitch, she marveled, and was ashamed that it had taken her so long to see it; usually she saw things more quickly than other people. I would have, she thought, if she'd had any other father, or any other companion; I was blinded by that. She shook her head ruefully. It's a good thing I don't need gratitude; I'd atrophy, waiting for Dora to get around to it.

But Dora wasn't important; nothing was important except the fact that they'd won. We won, we won, she thought, exulting. Winning was what her life was about, being the victor, never the victim.

But I deserve some gratitude, she thought. Without me, those two men would have walked all over Dora. She was a full-time secretary and sexual companion, but she wasn't a wife and she never told him that's what she wanted. She never told him what she expected from that relationship. He could have argued in court that if she'd wanted more, she should have told him, instead of being coy with friends and her seamstress. Fritz had been taking that line, but I didn't give him a chance to follow it up. I got Dora Chatham a quarter of a million dollars and the house in Tamarack, worth a million and a half, and she seems to think it just happened. *It went fine.* It went fine because I made it go fine. And a simple "Thank you"—or how about a heartfelt "Thank you"?—was in order.

It's a good thing I don't need it, or even want it.

She lowered her head and rubbed the back of her neck. She was always more tense than she realized in these sessions; it was only when everyone was gone that she felt the ache in her muscles. A glass of wine, she thought, and a massage and a sauna. That's what I need. And then dinner. The thought came to her that it might be pleasant to share dinner with someone and make it more of a celebration. But there was no one special to share her triumph. Dinner at home, she decided; she would call the chef in the French restaurant in her apartment building and have her meal delivered at about nine o'clock, after the masseur had left and she had had a sauna and shower. She would open a fine bottle of wine, and afterward she would watch a movie, a comedy; she would have one delivered at the same time as her dinner. And that would be a perfect evening.

She turned on the chime on her antique clock; she always turned it off when clients were coming for a long session. Almost immediately it rang four o'clock. They had been there most of the day. Nine-thirty to four, and no lunch. Maybe some food before the wine, she thought. Otherwise, I'll pass out in the sauna. She gathered the papers on her desk, and slipping them into Dora's file, realized Josh had kept his birthday note. Maybe it will teach him to keep his feelings to himself, she thought.

She put the file in her top drawer where it would stay until his check was received. A quarter of a million dollars and a house, she reflected. What a strange double life he leads: a professor with an international reputation, and a playboy who always has a gorgeous woman and buys Baccarat and can write a check for a quarter of a million dollars.

An interesting man. It was too bad she'd never know what he was really like; how many of Dora's tales were lies. Clearly there was more to him than the picture Dora had drawn; in fact, Dora probably never really knew him. Too busy worrying about herself to try to figure out the man she was living with. Well, there was no way of knowing. It was over; she'd never see him again. The main thing was that she'd won. Such a good feeling. The best feeling she knew. She stretched again. A glass of wine, she thought. A massage. A sauna.

Her apartment was a short walk away, in another part of

the Century City complex. She walked outside and was struck by a wall of heat, humid and heavy, that turned the white buildings gray and wavery, as if viewed through a screen. Pedestrians moved sluggishly, like swimmers wading through a deep surf. Anne walked across the plaza toward her building. It was easy to forget, in the permanent coolness of her office, that it was the hottest August on record. Better off inside, she thought as the doorman held the door open and she went into the lobby. She stopped as the icy air hit her. She shivered. From the tropics to the south pole, she thought. Are those our only alternatives?

She smiled to herself as she unlocked her mailbox and stuffed the letters and magazines into her briefcase. And she was still smiling as she turned to cross the lobby to the elevator, and saw Vince standing before her.

"Hello," he said softly.

She stood still, all feeling draining from her, frozen in place in the cold air swirling around her. Her briefcase dragged on her arm, suddenly so heavy she could barely hold it.

"I have to talk to you." He turned toward the elevator. "Which floor are you on?"

He had not changed. She could not believe it. Everything in her world had changed, but Vince was the same; his voice, his arrogant assurance, were the same; he looked the same. He was a little heavier, his chin a little sharper, but his blond hair and angelic looks were exactly as they had been. He smiled at her, charm radiating from his white teeth and crinkly eyes. She could feel his hands on her, pushing her, turning her, forcing her.

She ran across the lobby, through the service door, and down the back hall to the janitors' washroom, and barely had the door closed before she was sick.

When she lifted her head, she was gasping. She knelt on the cold tile floor, resting her arms on the edge of the toilet, until her breathing slowed. Then she went to one of the washbowls and rinsed out her mouth. There were speckles of vomit on the lapel of her white silk suit; she wet her handkerchief and rubbed them until they were gone. She looked at herself in the small mirror, composing her face. Each feature was smoothed out, molded to neutrality. She could do nothing about her haunted eyes, but for the rest she looked in perfect control. She stood for a moment with her hand on the doorknob. She could take the service elevator to her floor. But he had found her once; he would again. She would have to face him, today or another day. Today, she thought. She held her head high, her shoulders back, and opened the service door to return to the lobby.

He was waiting for her a few feet from the door. "Is everything all right?"

She turned and walked to a group of chairs, and sat in the farthest one, in the corner. With a small shrug, Vince followed, and sat facing her across a small glass coffee table, his back to the lobby. Anne looked past him at the people coming in from work and stopping at the mail room on their way to the elevators. She liked knowing they were there. She held herself tightly, every muscle locked in place, and made herself look at Vince, hating him. She sat still, gazing at him steadily, hating him, saying nothing.

He was the one who looked away, but he did it smoothly, almost carelessly, glancing over his shoulder at the lobby with great interest. "Who would have thought it," he said lightly, turning back to her. "Little Anne, who never even combed her hair, living here, a lawyer, winning palimony suits. And a gorgeous woman. My congratulations; it seems running away was just what you needed."

She looked at him, her eyes blank.

"I'm sorry you left; I missed you," he said. "It's hard when a family is denied the pleasure of seeing a young girl become a woman. We would have liked to share that with you, and help you, when we could. Where did you go when you left?"

Anne was silent.

"Well." Vince sighed. "We all worried about you, you know. Every time we picked up a newspaper there was another horror story about young girls who ran away and ended up on the streets, drug addicts, prostitutes, murder victims; it kept us up nights, worrying. Especially Ethan."

He went on smoothly, about a detective, two detectives, but Anne barely heard him. He smiled and talked and gestured with his hands as if he were quite comfortable, as if there were no consequences to anything he had done in the past. And perhaps that was his experience in the twenty-four years since she had last seen him. He had come from that time to this, untouched.

"This isn't the best place for a private conversation," Vince said as people walked past them to the elevator. "Your apartment would be better."

"No," Anne said flatly.

"Well, then, coffee? There must be a restaurant in the building, or a coffee shop. Shall we go?"

"We'll stay here."

He looked around again. It was the end of the workday and a steady stream of people walked through the lobby. He inclined his head, gracefully giving in. "If you'd prefer." He settled back in his chair. "I was waiting for Dora today when she left your office; we're having dinner later. Of course she calls me regularly—I'm sure you know that—and she had told me the discovery session would be today. I thought it would be a good time for me to come in, to give encouragement, maybe comfort. But she didn't need either one; she said you did fine. I assume that means you were extremely good; Dora is very slow to give credit. A quarter of a million, she said, and the house. Not bad, considering that you didn't have to go to court for it. And you kept the media out of it. I appreciate that; it was good of you to consider my position. Dora told me she'd talked to you about it."

"What is it you want?" Anne asked.

"Yes, of course, you must be in a hurry; I'm sure your friends are waiting to celebrate your victory." He smiled at her again. "I'm curious about why you came back, after such a long time. I can understand—barely—that you wanted to come to Ethan's funeral; I'm always amused when people feel they have to pay their respects, or whatever it is they think they're doing, to someone who's dead and therefore doesn't give a damn. But you did more than that; you went to Tamarack with Gail. And you became Dora's attorney. Why?"

"For my own reasons," Anne said. "They have nothing to do with you."

"But you know they do. Anything that happens to my family has to do with me. I know how people operate; they operate politically. You're trying to make an alliance with the family, cozy up to them, and attack me from behind their protection."

"Attack you?" She shook her head. "I have no intention of attacking you."

"That's a lie," he said softly. "I know what you want; you want to destroy me. Why else would you come back? You waited a long time, until I was in a prominent position, until I was vulnerable to rumors and gossip, and then you came back. You waited until my term was almost up, until time for my reelection campaign, and then you hooked up with Gail and Dora to get at me."

When Anne was silent, he went on, in conversational, almost intimate tones. "I know you, Anne; I understand you. You were a raw little brat and I made you a woman, and you were too young to appreciate it. You've never understood what I did for you. I educated you, the same way Harvard educated you. There's no difference, you know; you had a lot to learn and you learned from experts. If I hadn't taken you in hand, you would have ended up with some pimply dolt with braces on his teeth pawing you in the backseat of a car. You were a hell of a lot better off learning from me. And you liked it; you loved it. For a long time. A long time. Then I suppose you met someone else, and you decided you'd had enough of me so you accused me in front of all of them. You didn't mention that you'd liked it. Women erase what they have no use for; they only remember what they want to. Like anger. They remember that best of all. They feed on it, like spiders. And then they want revenge. Look at you, my little spider; waiting all these years to spring at me. Waiting until you thought I was vulnerable."

He's crazy. The thought was absolutely clear in Anne's mind, but she could not hold on to it; his presence drove it away, as he had driven thought and will from her when he dominated her in her bedroom. He loomed before her like a lynx, eyes bright, poised to leap. Wherever she looked, she could not escape him. She tried to recapture the exhilaration she had felt that afternoon, at her victory, but it was gone. She saw only Vince. She could think only of Vince. Inside herself, she cringed. She would have run away again, but her legs and arms were so weak she could not move them. Even if she had been able to, there was nowhere to run: he would catch her, he would touch her.

"Of course I'm not vulnerable," he said, still smiling. His voice was soft, and grew softer as he spoke. "But you are. You're a little lawyer who's trying to make a name for herself by taking sensational cases, and you don't want to make a mistake. But it would be a very big mistake to attack a U.S. senator by accusing him of something you say he did almost a quarter of a century ago. You haven't said a word for a quarter of a century, and all of a sudden, when he's a prominent man, you come up with this fairy tale. You'd be laughed out of town. It would be obvious you were trying to blackmail me; why else would you be doing it? You'd be called a conniving, opportunistic bitch, and who'd trust you after that? It could ruin you, couldn't it, little Anne? You know it could. Look at you: terrified that your lies might backfire, and then you'd be nothing. You'd be nothing, Anne. A discredited little lawyer with no clients."

He's afraid. The thought was even clearer than her earlier one, and this time she held on to it. *He thinks I can hurt him. He thinks I can destroy his political career.* The words rang in her head and she clung to them. *He thinks I can hurt him.* Her muscles loosened just a little, and as they did, the cringing within her began to ease. *He thinks I have power over him.* She made a fist and felt strength in her arm. And she was able to remember, for the first time since Vince had appeared, that she was in her own building and she had just won a case. His looming presence began to shrink. She could see around it. She could see her own lobby, her neighbors walking past, nodding a quick greeting. Her cringing was fading away. It was easier to sit straight. *He's afraid of me.*

"I haven't been waiting to do anything to you," she said, her voice steady and very cold. "I haven't even thought of you."

He shook his head reproachfully. "Another lie. You think about me all the time. That's why you came to Ethan's funeral. An excuse to come back. That's why you went with Gail. That's why you jumped at the chance to work for Dora."

"I haven't thought of you." The cringing was gone. Her hands were in her lap and both of them were fists. "You make me sick. I never liked it, or—my God—loved it when you forced me. I hated you. You didn't make me a woman, but you destroyed my childhood, and I will never forgive you for that, or for the way you manipulated me. I was never a person to you; you treated me like a doll you could bend into any shape you wanted. I stopped thinking of you the day I left that house and I never thought of you again. I had a life to build, and if I thought of you, I was so sick, so deathly sick, I couldn't go on. I never thought of you. I try to find pleasure and satisfaction in my life, and you are such scum that thinking of you would destroy any peace I might find. Scum. I never thought of you."

His face was dark and distorted. "Bitch," he said, spitting it through his teeth. "Fucking bitch." From the corner of his eye, he saw heads turn. "No one will believe you," he said tightly, keeping his voice down. "I'll make you a laughing-stock; I'll stop you—"

"I don't want to talk about it. I don't want to publicize the past; I don't want to bring it back to life; I don't want to think about it. It's dead. I want to keep it buried where it's been, all these years."

He looked at her, his shoulders hunched. "I don't believe you," he said after a moment. "I know how you lie; you've always lied. You lied about me that night; you didn't tell them how you'd led me on and how you loved it with me; you were tired of me and you tried to destroy me. But it didn't work; you were the one who left, sneaking out like a criminal. And I stayed. I'll always stay, and you'll leave. I'm telling you: you'll leave again. I won't have you hanging around them. I won't have you showing up in magazine and newspaper stories about my family; I won't have you giving reporters something spicy to write about. Is that clear? You'll disappear the way you did before; you won't go near them again."

He's afraid, Anne told herself again. He's afraid, he's afraid. Not me; I'm not afraid anymore; he is. He's afraid. I have nothing to be afraid of. She took a long breath. "If I want my family back, I'll do what I can to be part of them again. You can't stop me. If you try, I'll beat you."

He smiled thinly. "How? By telling your lies again? I told you: they won't believe you, any more than they did the first time. So then what will you do? Tell the press? Radio? Television? I won't let you. Listen to me." He leaned forward. "Other people have tried to cross me. I've had them stopped. Do you understand? I've had them taken care of."

Anne shook her head. When he had leaned forward, coming closer to her, she had begun to feel sick again. *He's afraid, not me; he's afraid, he's afraid.* But still she felt faint. "I'm not going to tell anyone," she said, her voice almost a whisper. "Go away. Leave me alone. I just want to forget it."

Vince pulled his chair closer to the coffee table, closer to Anne, and leaned farther forward; she thought she could feel his breath. "I'm going to tell you exactly where we stand. I wasn't going to, but I think you should know. I've always been honest with you, Anne; you can believe every word of this." He paused, watching her. "Last month, when Dora told me about you, I called a friend of mine, a man who worked with me in Denver. He always took care of problems, people who got in our way, that sort of thing. We're still working together, so I called him and told him to take care of you. To get rid of you. Do you know what he said? He said he doesn't do that kind of thing anymore. He said he's almost seventy years old and he's looking for more respectable occupations. I was very disappointed in him. Ah, I see I have your attention."

Anne was sitting very still, watching him, her eyes wide, her breathing quick and shallow. Her fists had opened and her hands were lying loosely in her lap. She was very cold.

"That left me in a terrible dilemma," Vince went on. "My friend was the only one I trusted for this kind of work. I could hire someone else, of course—there are always people who'll do anything for a quick buck—but that would replace one problem with another. You would be gone, but my employee would then be the one to have an advantage over me." His voice became ruminative. "I've given this a great deal of thought. I could, of course, kill you myself, but you know, I can't do it. It isn't in me. That may surprise you—I assure you, it surprised me—but that's the way I am. I'm not a murderer."

There was a long silence. "There is nothing I hate more than being helpless," Vince said softly. "That's why I didn't come to see you weeks ago, when Dora told me about you: I had to know what my options were. This is what I've decided. If you make trouble for me, my dilemma will be resolved. If you broadcast your insane accusations to the press, I'll have nothing to lose by hiring someone to kill you. And that's what I would do. In an instant. Is that clear? I would not hesitate. If you're quiet, and disappear again, you should be quite safe. At least safe from me." He smiled. "We're in this together, Anne. Isn't that amazing, after all this time? We're together. We both have a lot at stake." He pushed back his chair and stood up. "Dora thinks you're quite clever. Sharp and tough, she called you. If she was right, I have no doubt you'll behave intelligently and circumspectly. That means, of course, staying away from my family. You're to have nothing to do with them. I said this before: I want to make sure you understand it. There's going to be a lot of publicity about me in the next few years, and I will not have you be part of it. If you go near Gail or Dora or any of the family, I'll find a way to stop you. You must take my word for that, Anne; if you go near them, I'll stop you."

He looked down at her. "I've enjoyed our chat. It's good to see you looking so well. And of course, so successful. I wish you good luck. You might do the same for me."

Anne looked at him. He stepped back from the hatred in her eyes. And then he strode away, across the lobby and out the door, too fast for the doorman to hold it for him.

Anne picked up her briefcase and went to the elevator. She looked straight ahead; she was not thinking. At her floor, she walked blindly to her door, unlocked it, and locked it behind her. The antiseptic coolness of white walls and white furniture drew her in, and she went straight to the window seat overlooking the gardens below, kicking off her shoes and curling up in the corner.

Office workers were walking across the plaza and the garden, pulling off their suit jackets as they emerged from the buildings. So hot outside, Anne thought, but so perfect in here. Not as freezing as the lobby—she stopped herself. Her thoughts veered away from anything to do with Vince. How strange, she thought, to live in two worlds at once: hot and cold, stifling and liberating, threatening and calm. Having a family and not having a family. Her thoughts raced, as if the faster they went, the more she could keep them under control. I've always had a family, she thought; I just never went after them. Vince's smile broke through her thoughts, and a sob caught in her throat. Frantically, she pushed her thoughts forward. She knew now that she would like to be part of the family again, at least some of it. She'd like to try, to see if she could. It was so hard for her to be open, to give anything of herself, to let anyone into her carefully defended life. But they seemed to like her. And she had liked being with them and making plans for future visits. She had liked the idea, when she let herself think about it, of not being alone all the time.

If you go near Gail or Dora or any of the family, I'll find a way to stop you.

She bent her head until her forehead was against the cool glass. All I want is a chance to be part of them again.

Suddenly, she was angry. She raised her head and let her anger grow. *You son of a bitch, what will you do? Find a way to kill me? You already killed me once. You killed the child in me, the youth and joy and awakening I had a right to. Do you think I care if you come after me again? Try, damn you, I'll fight you all the way. You won't crush me again. I won't let you. Never again. Never again.*

She turned from the window and leafed through her small address book for a telephone number. Pretty soon I'll know it by heart, she thought. She held the telephone in her lap and dialed. "Gail," she said, "is it all right if I come for a visit this weekend?"

you. "I'm not sure." The voice came as she spoke. "Do you have a reservation?" "Hello."

Sheridan from the window had set the fingers flashing through out the reference number. Then when all knew it by sight, right at eight flashing the telephone or touching the dials. "Oh, now." Charles put a corner for an old plush elegance.

chapter 11

On the Saturday before Labor Day, Charles showed up in Marian's backyard in the early morning, and found her cutting chrysanthemums and dahlias. "How nice," she said mildly, though Charles had expected her to be surprised; he never visited her in the daytime, or without calling ahead. "Just in time for breakfast," she said, and put her shears in the basket with the purple and white flowers. She wore a long cotton skirt and a long-sleeved blouse, pink gardening gloves, and a straw hat covering her white, perfectly waved hair. Charles thought she looked like an old-fashioned watercolor of a lady in her country estate. "I always eat late when Fred isn't here," she said.

"Where is he?" Charles asked.

"He didn't tell me. He has a girl in New York; he may be with her. Did you come to see him?"

"No." Charles took the basket and carried it into the house. "It doesn't bother you?"

"You mean about his girlfriend. Well, no, not anymore. It did, with the first one, about fifteen years ago, but it came to me after a while that what I really minded was being embarrassed because I'd married a tomcat. He is, you know; he has so many women I always imagine him prowling around dark places, looking for them. But of course you know all that; you spend a lot of time with him."

Charles watched as she filled the garden sink with water,

264

and held the stems beneath the surface to cut them. "Why do you stay with him?"

"Oh, why. Why not? I'm mostly satisfied, and I assume he is, and isn't that what you want from marriage? To be mostly satisfied? I'm not embarrassed by him anymore; I just don't pay attention, and if I don't see it, it doesn't exist as far as I'm concerned. I've made my own life—I'm quite interested in business, you know, and I've gotten myself on three boards of directors of small companies—and I have as much of Fred as I want. We do have a life together, you know; we've been a couple for such a long time. It's always easiest to live with someone you understand and can predict. Why would I want surprises at my age? I'm not interested in sex anymore—" She saw Charles' color rise. "Good heavens, Charles, we've been brother and sister for half a century; by now we ought to be able to talk about anything. I find sex incredibly boring; all those contortions and groans; they're quite incongruous when you get to a certain age. Then, one day I decided it was a waste of time and quite beneath me, and suddenly, just like that, I felt . . . *light,* as if I didn't weigh anything at all and could just . . . float. Everything seemed so much easier, nothing dragging me down, nothing making demands on me. It was so amazing. And such a relief."

There was a silence. Marian arranged the flowers in a tall crystal vase. "One of these days you'll feel it, Charles," she said serenely. "I'm sure it happens to everyone at some time or other."

"I want to talk to you about Anne," Charles said.

"Yes." Marian sighed. "It's all so strange, isn't it. Can you imagine, coming back after all these years, just appearing out of nowhere like some sort of apparition, and not greeting us, not giving us a chance to welcome her back? I was terribly disappointed. I looked for her after the funeral and she was gone. Wait a minute; I'll just put these flowers in the living room."

When she returned, Charles was standing at the French doors, gazing at the backyard sloping to the lake, his thumbs hooked in his belt. "What would you have said to her?"

"Well, I would have welcomed her and told her how much we missed her and how glad we were to have her back. I would have asked her how she is and where she lives now and what she's doing, is she married, does she have children . . . goodness, she's almost forty, you know."

Charles turned to face her. "And what would you say if she brought up that business again?"

"Well." Marian peered into the refrigerator. "I have smoked salmon and tomatoes and French bread. More like lunch than breakfast. I could toast the bread; what do you think?"

"Whatever you have. What would you say to her?"

"I don't know; I haven't thought about it." She took two plates from the cabinet and piled food on them. "I can't believe she'd bring it up. It's been so long. Twenty years. More than twenty. Why dredge it up? We've all forgotten it. Vince has made an extraordinary success of his life; it would be impossible to find fault with him. And Anne looked quite impressive at the funeral; she's obviously done well. We're all grown-up, you know—we're civilized people—and I have to assume there was some terrible mix-up that night, some confusion, and we were all so upset that we couldn't get to the bottom of it. But it's all behind us now, and I am certainly not going to be the one to bring it up; I don't even want to think about it. And I'm sure Anne feels exactly the same way."

Charles nodded heavily. He picked at some of the salmon on his plate. "She was at Gail's last week. I thought I'd go up there and ask Gail what they talked about. And whether she thinks I ought to see her."

"She's been at Gail's? Nobody told me. That's quite strange, that no one told me; I was practically her mother. How do you know she's been there?"

"Vince told me he heard it from Keith a couple of days ago."

"Keith," Marian said. "My own son. And he didn't tell me. Well, I suppose he thought I wouldn't be interested. I never talked to him about Anne, after all." She poured coffee into china cups. "If you want to see her, Charles, call her up. Why do you have to ask Gail's advice?"

"Because I don't know what to do, damn it! If I had some idea of how she feels about me—she hasn't called me, you know, not a word—if I could get a fix on how I should talk to her . . ."

"Just say whatever you want, Charles. From the heart. That's the only way to talk to a daughter. It's how I've always talked to Rose; that's why we're so close."

"So you think I should get her number from Gail and call her."

"If that's what you want. Goodness, Charles, don't be so timid. It's not like going into battle; it's just talking to your own daughter."

"What about you? Are you going to call her?"

"Well, of course I'd like her to call me. She's the one who left, and I'd expect her to make contact with us once she's back. But if she doesn't . . . well, of course I will, just as soon as I know where she is."

"I'll find out from Gail and let you know." He pushed back his chair.

"Where are you going? You haven't eaten."

"I'm going to Tamarack."

"Today? Now?"

"As soon as I can get on a plane."

"Well, that's not a bad idea. We used to go there every Labor Day, remember? I don't know why that changed. Charles, I'll go with you. I can find out about Anne for myself; I was practically her mother, you know. I'll just pack a few things; I won't be any time at all. A very good idea; why not get away for the weekend—especially with Fred gone? Give me an hour, Charles."

"Marian, I'm going now. If you really want to come, you can get a later flight and call me when you get in. I'll be at The Tamarack Hotel."

"Charles, I only asked you to wait an hour."

"Much too long. I have to go before I change my mind." He kissed Marian on the cheek. "I get awfully tired of being a coward, you know."

He wondered about that as he walked back to his house, and he was still wondering about it when he was on the plane to Denver and the smaller one to Tamarack, flying over the San Juans in the fading evening light. Why had he said that to Marian? He never admitted any weaknesses to her, or fears or troubles, for that matter; he never mentioned them to anyone in the family except Vince and lately, Fred Jax. He could not do it. Ethan never had; neither would he.

But Ethan was dead and Anne had come back. And nothing was the same.

He rented a car at the Tamarack airport and drove the two miles to Gail's house. For the second time that day, he had not called ahead. In an odd way, it made him feel more in control.

"Grandpa!" Robin cried as she pulled open the door. "We haven't seen you forever!" She held up her face for a kiss. "We're eating dinner. You can have some; we've got lots. Mommy!" she called, tugging at Charles' hand to bring him with her to the kitchen. "Grandpa's here!"

Gail and Anne turned from the table, forks suspended in air. Ned shot out of his chair. "Hi!" he said. "I just wrote you a letter; I guess you didn't get it yet." Charles was staring at Anne; it had not occurred to him that she would be there. Leo shook his hand. "What a good surprise, Charles. Would you like dinner? Come join us."

"Hello, Daddy," Gail said, standing and kissing Charles on the cheek.

Anne stood and held out her hand.

Charles started to lean past her hand, to kiss her, but Anne's frozen face stopped him. He took her hand formally. "It's so good to see you, Anne."

"We've got cake, too, Grandpa," said Ned. "Aunt Anne made it; it's chocolate with nuts and icing."

"I'd like some of that," said Charles. "I've had dinner."

"And we have coffee," Gail said, returning to her chair. "Sit down, Daddy."

Charles walked around the table to sit beside Leo. There was a silence. "I only decided to come this morning."

"You were lucky to get a flight," Leo said.

"The plane wasn't crowded," Charles said. "I guess most people are already where they want to be for the weekend."

Another silence fell. The kitchen was shadowed, except for the overlapping circles of light from two copper lamps hanging low over the table. The wide windows were deep gray, fading to black broken only by a concentration of lights, like a galaxy in the distance, that was Tamarack. The windows were open to a light breeze, and on it floated the scent of pine trees and wildflowers, and a chill that hinted at winter. Not a sound broke the stillness.

"Well, we're glad you came," Leo said. "We like it when this table has a lot of people around it. And we can talk about The Tamarack Company; talking makes more sense than all those letters we've been writing."

"Are you going to get Grandpa some cake?" Ned asked Gail. "And could you maybe cut two pieces while you're at it?"

"Have you finished your dinner?" she asked.

"Mostly. I just like to look at dessert, you know, like it's waiting for me. Like it's my future."

Smiling, Gail cut two slices. She gave a plate to Charles and set one beside Ned's dinner plate. She poured a cup of coffee for Charles and refilled the wine and water glasses on the table. Anne watched her precise movements, as soothing as a lullaby, and she began to calm down. It was up to her now, she thought.

"Would you excuse us?" she said. She stood and held out her hand to Charles. "I think we'll go into the living room."

Quickly, gratefully, Charles pushed back his chair and followed her to the door.

"I'll come, too," Robin said, leaping up.

"Not this time." Gail put her hand on Robin's arm. "Aunt Anne and Grandpa want a private conversation."

"What about your cake?" Ned asked.

"You eat it for me," Charles said. "I'll get another piece when I come back."

Ned grinned and shot a look at Gail. "He *asked* me," he said.

The living room was quiet. Anne turned on a lamp beside

a wide couch and sat at one end. Charles hesitated, then sat at the other end. For the first time, they looked directly at each other. Remembering her as a child, Charles could not believe this was his daughter. She was dressed casually, in blue jeans and a white V-neck cashmere sweater, and her hair was tied back with a white scarf, but she had an elegance and sophistication that had never even been hinted at when she was a wild, troublesome girl.

"You're looking very well," Anne said.

"Yes, I'm all right." He gestured as if it were not important. "You look wonderful, Anne. You're so beautiful . . . you look like your mother, you know, but you're even more beautiful than she was."

Anne shook her head. "I don't think so."

"I missed you," Charles said. "There were so many things I wanted to say to you. It was terrible, not being able to say them."

Anne smiled faintly. "Was it."

"I'm sorry. Of course it must have been worse for you. Where did you go when you left?"

"San Francisco. I went to college in Berkeley, and then Harvard Law. I'm with a firm in Los Angeles now."

"You're a lawyer. I would have thought you were too . . . dreamy for that sort of thing. Although you always were good at arguing." He smiled. "What kind of law?"

"Mostly divorce."

Charles shook his head slowly. "I can't get used to it. Marian said, this morning, that you're close to forty. And you're a professional woman . . . a lawyer! To me, all these years, you've been my little girl; we just celebrated your fifteenth birthday—I'm sorry," he said quickly as Anne's face tightened. "I don't want to talk about it, either. Why should we dredge it up? Tell me about yourself. You're not married?"

"But we must talk about it," Anne said evenly. "It's still between us. It won't vanish just because you look the other way. That's a trick you have, the whole family; I remember that. It's like a conspiracy of silence, denying what you don't want to see. You turn deaf and blind and smile into the silence. That was why I left."

Charles remembered Marian, that morning, saying, *I'm not embarrassed by him anymore; I just don't pay attention, and if I don't see it, it doesn't exist as far as I'm concerned.*

He looked at his hands. "I'm sorry," he said again. "You must hate us."

"Only one of you," she replied.

He briefly closed his eyes. "He still denies it, you know."

Anne looked at him, her eyes like ice.

"I shouldn't have said that. I know it's not a . . . not a . . ."

"Debate."

"Not a debate. I accept what you said—"

"Do you?"

"Yes! What can I say, Anne? I believe you. My God, it's like reliving it; the most terrible time." He hesitated. "Are you going to see him?"

"I already have. He came to Los Angeles to threaten me if I talked about the past or tried to see any of you."

Charles reared back. "Vince wouldn't do that."

"Listen to yourself!" Anne said furiously. "For God's sake, haven't you learned anything? The first thing you always say about him is that he wouldn't do it. You have no idea what he would do; you don't know anything about him. Why wouldn't he threaten me? If you believe me, you know he's already done far worse."

"Whatever he did before, he's changed," said Charles. "He's grown-up. He's a U.S. senator. He's my brother, Anne; I can't condemn him out of hand. Is that what you want me to do? Yes, I suppose it is. But I can't do that; I wouldn't do that to anyone in the family."

"You did it to me."

˙ "I didn't condemn you. I just couldn't . . . I didn't know what to do with what you were telling us, and what I thought I knew about you, and about Vince. I know I was wrong; I should have found a way to help you. But that was twenty years ago, Anne—"

"Twenty-four."

"Yes, of course, twenty-four. Isn't that enough time to get over something, to go on with your life? Why did you stay away so long? We did try to find you; your grandfather hired detectives, but they said there wasn't a trace . . ."

"I took Mother's name."

"Garnett? That's your name now? Isn't that strange, it never occurred to me to ask what your name is." There was a silence. "I always wanted to be a good father!" he burst out. "I thought, after your mother died and Marian said she'd take care of you, that you and I would be good friends; we'd go to the zoo and the Field Museum and the Museum of Science and Industry and the planetarium and the aquarium . . . I made lists of places we could go. And I thought we'd talk, sit together, you know, whenever you wanted, and talk about everything that interested you, and I'd help you understand things and deal with them. I saw us so clearly, the two of us, it was like those paintings of parents and children that always seem so bright, full of sunlight . . ." He gave a small, embarrassed laugh. "That seems foolish, I suppose, but I did see us that way. A daughter and a father, being good friends, loving each other."

"But none of that happened," Anne said.

"No. I don't know why. Maybe I didn't try hard enough. Or it took me too long to try at all. I'm sure you don't remember, but I couldn't do anything for a long time. She died so suddenly, you know. It wasn't as if she had an illness and I could get used to the idea of her being gone; it was that one minute she was calling to say she'd be home in half an hour and the next that damned car hit her, that rotten drunk, that filth, but he walked away from it and she died, in that one minute. If she hadn't called me—but she knew how I worried and she always called—or if she'd left a minute— half a minute!—later, or if she . . . But she didn't and he killed her." He shook his head. "You never get over something like that, you know; it never stops hurting."

"I know," Anne murmured.

Slowly, Charles understood what she meant. "It was a death," he said, his voice rising. "It was the end of our family as we knew it. I wouldn't ask you to forget that; it was much worse, much more devastating than anything that happened to you."

"Was it?"

"You lost your mother!"

Anne's eyes were thoughtful. "Yes. I hadn't realized . . . It seems that violation and loss and betrayal are harder to get over than even the death of a loved one."

Charles grimaced. "You think we betrayed you."

"Oh, yes."

"I didn't mean to. I told you, all I ever wanted was to be a good father. But nothing seemed to work. All those dreams I'd had of your loving me, rushing up to me when I came home and hugging me and being my little girl . . . you were nothing like that. You always seemed angry. You went off by yourself, you never asked me to do anything with you. I felt you were always turning your back on me."

"And you don't know why," Anne said.

"No. I felt so helpless. No, of course I don't know why."

"I was living in Marian's house. I was seven years old and I'd lost my mother and my home. And my father only cared about *his* loss, *his* mourning, so there was no room for me to share it. You're right. I was angry."

They were silent. Charles sighed. "I made mistakes, Anne; I know that. I'd undo them if I could. But what would you like me to do now? I could keep saying I'm sorry all night; would that help? Or we could forget the past and start from this minute and . . . get acquainted. You must want that or you wouldn't have come back." He waited. "Even if you can't forget, you could forgive. I never did anything to you from malice, you know; I always loved you; I always wanted the best for you. Please forgive me, Anne; is that so much to ask?"

"Yes," she said slowly. "It is."

"Why, for God's sake? We've lived with this pain for so long; why do you want to prolong it? You're here now;

you're a successful, lovely woman and you did it all without me. You've proved you don't need me, or any of us. It's time to forgive. I want to be your father, Anne; it's not too late. Gail and I aren't close—I suppose she told you that—she's never been warm toward me. I think she blames me for your leaving. She didn't tell me that; I just think that's how she feels. But if you forgive me, if we start again, Gail would, too; I'm sure she would. We could get back everything we lost. I'm not making any demands on you, Anne; I just want you to love me again."

Anne gave a small smile. "That's all you want?"

"My God," Charles exploded, "don't you have any feeling for me at all?"

Anne felt like weeping, but no tears came. "It's too soon. I don't forgive you. I can't love you."

Abruptly, Charles thought of Marian again. *It was as if I didn't weigh anything at all and could just . . . float.* Sexless Marian, talking of freedom. But Charles had thought of a husk—empty, dried out, weightless. And that was how Anne sounded to him. There was no pain or tension or even anger in her voice or her face. She might have been discussing a stranger.

But he was not sure. He always had trouble understanding people. Maybe she wasn't an empty husk; maybe she was a young woman who was frozen. Or asleep.

"I don't know," he said. "I just don't know."

Anne looked at him, not knowing what he meant. He was frowning at his clasped hands. He was a tall man, but now, hunched in the corner of the deep couch, he looked shrunken, and the lines in his face seemed to deepen as she watched. "Tell me about the company," she said. "I'd like to know what's happening with it. Gail and Leo said you've been having some problems."

Still looking at his hands, he smiled faintly. "Is that all they said?"

"I'd like you to tell me," she said gently.

He opened out his hands. "We had a project that didn't work out. It should have—it was exactly the kind your grandfather put together dozens of times—but it went wrong." He paused and sighed. "No, there was a difference. Your grandfather would have waited until he was sure all the pieces were in place. I didn't do that. I wanted so much to get moving, to pull this off and have one thing that would make everyone proud . . ." He shook his head and pulled himself up to sit straight. "Well, I blew it, as the young people say. And I'd borrowed all I could for it, and signed notes on my own—the banks wouldn't loan any more unless I was personally liable—so I'm not in very good shape right now."

"I'm sorry," Anne said.

"But I'll be all right, at least a hell of a lot better off, once I sell The Tamarack Company. I've already had an offer; its way off, much too low, but it's only the first; there's a lot of interest in resorts right now, including the Japanese. We ought to get a hundred million for it, maybe a hundred fifty, and that would pay our debts and leave us cash for new projects. Then we'd decide what to do with Chatham Development. I know Fred wants to be president and that's fine with me; I'm ready to retire. But first things first. I've got to get us out of this bind and the family has to help me."

"I think they'd like to, if they could," Anne said. "But you're asking them to sell a company that's their whole life. And are you sure you can get a good price? Leo says the cleanup the EPA is talking about could be a major headache; I can't imagine anyone putting down money until that's settled."

"The EPA isn't important. All they want to do is clean up a little corner of town where the soil's contaminated from old mine tailings. I don't know what Leo's excited about; once it's done, the town will be safer and the value of the company will go up."

"Isn't it more than a corner of the town? Leo says it's more like half of the east end, and most of it belongs to the company. So you'd have to pay for the cleanup, and for moving people out while it's going on, maybe as many as a hundred families. Nobody even knows how long it will take;

they don't know how far down the tainted soil goes, so they can't predict how much will have to be dug out and replaced. It could end up being enormously expensive. And the other day the EPA told Leo they're worried about poisoned dust in the atmosphere while they're digging out the old soil and carting it away. And the people there are having trouble selling their houses, and they can't get loans to fix them up because no bank will loan money in that part of town until they know what's coming."

"That's ridiculous," Charles said angrily. "All of it. I don't know what the hell got into Leo; he's blown it up all out of proportion."

"But you're being sued. Isn't that right? A couple of families living there have sued the company because their children are ill and they're blaming the mine tailings. I'd guess you'll have more of those, especially if there's dust flying around. And the publicity is already hurting the town; some lodges had cancellations after the first stories appeared nationally. If the costs go high enough, and if there's enough bad publicity, you can't predict what the value of The Tamarack Company will be."

"I told you, it's all been exaggerated. Vince checked it out with the EPA. It's a small operation; it won't cost much, and the town won't even know it's going on. If some people canceled, others will come; it isn't serious. Anne," he said abruptly. "I need your help." He smiled faintly. "I usually have trouble asking for help, you know; it's like admitting I've failed. I won't even ask directions in a strange city; I know that's ridiculous, but the words stick in my throat. I've driven around for hours rather than admit I'm lost." He shook his head. "I don't know why I'm telling you this. It's just that I'm feeling a little overwhelmed, and I'm ashamed of it. I have the feeling that if I were really grown-up, I'd be able to handle everything. That bothers me all the time. I should be wiser by now, more mature, more able to see what's coming. What the hell, I'm the age when men are called elder statesmen. But I still feel the way I did at twenty-five, that I have so much to learn, such a long way to go before I act like my father, and sound like him. . . . Well, I'm sorry; I'm really dumping on you, as they say. None of that's important, Anne; what's important is getting out of this bind so I can get back on my feet. I've got to sell The Tamarack Company. That's my only hope. Some of the family are against it, but you could talk to them about it and get them to agree; they'd listen to you; you're more objective about it than I am. Will you, Anne? I wouldn't ask you, but I haven't any choice; things are so bad——"

"Can we say good-night?" Robin asked. She stood in the doorway, poised to take the first step into the room.

"Yes, of course," Anne said. "I didn't realize it was so late."

Charles was still looking at Anne. "Help me," he said urgently, his voice almost a whisper. "Talk to them. They'd listen to you."

"Good night, Grandpa," said Robin, standing before him. She held out her arms and Charles leaned forward to hold her. "Sleep well," he said. "Maybe I'll see you tomorrow afternoon."

"Aren't you staying here tonight?" Ned asked, coming in behind Robin. "You didn't see my new bike. It's got eighteen speeds and it goes straight up the mountain."

"I'll see it in the afternoon," Charles said. "I'm going to see somebody on business in the morning, but I can be with you after that."

Ned's face froze. "Business? Like selling The Tamarack Company? You can't do that; we won't let you."

Robin poked him with her elbow. "You weren't supposed to talk about it to Grandpa."

"I wasn't talking. I was just telling him."

"Time for bed," said Leo from the doorway.

Charles stood. "I'll be going, too."

"But you're staying here," Gail protested. She stood behind Leo. "I couldn't let you go to a hotel."

"I'd rather. And I left my bag there."

"But stay for a while," Leo said. "You haven't tasted Anne's cake. And we haven't had a chance to talk."

Robin and Ned looked at him interestedly, seeing the conflict in his face. Charles turned to Anne. "Shall I?"

"Of course," she said easily. "We'll make more coffee."

She went to the kitchen and Charles followed as Gail and Leo went with the children to the other wing of the house. "You see, even the kids," he said. "They won't even consider it. But they'd listen to you."

Anne poured coffee beans into the grinder, and took the carafe to the sink to fill it. But when she turned on the tap, only a trickle came out. "Strange," she murmured. "It was fine earlier."

Charles watched her as she held the carafe under the faucet, and tried to think of something to say. But it seemed to him he had said it all—and had failed. She still did not forgive him, or love him. Suddenly, he longed desperately for her to love him. There was still time for him to be a good father.

The telephone rang, then stopped as it was answered in another room. Frowning, Anne turned off the faucet. The trickle of water had slowed to a few drops and then there was nothing. "I'd like to visit you in Los Angeles," Charles said. "Would that be all right? There's so much . . ."

Leo strode into the kitchen, his jacket slung over his shoulder. "There's a meeting at City Hall; some problem with the water. You'd better not drink it. I don't know when I'll be back."

"Should I be there?" Charles asked.

Leo paused at the door. "Why not? Either they called me because they usually do when there's a problem, or because they think the company's got something to do with it. Either way, I'd be glad to have you there."

Charles went to Anne. Once again he seemed to be leaning toward her, but again he stopped. "I'll see you tomorrow. May I?"

"Of course," Anne said. "We're taking the gondola up the mountain for a picnic in the afternoon; perhaps you'll join us."

"I'd like that."

When he and Leo were gone, Anne poured out the water that partially filled the carafe and went to the back of the house. Gail was sitting on Robin's bed. "Oh, good, you can kiss me good-night," Robin said. "And Ned, too; he'd feel awfully rejected if you kissed me and not him."

Anne met Gail's eyes in a swift, private smile. "I certainly don't want him to feel rejected," she said seriously. She bent and rested her cheek briefly on Robin's forehead. "Sleep well, Robin."

"Aunt Anne, are you psychotically anti-hugging?" Robin asked.

Anne stopped, halfway to the door, and turned a bemused look on Robin.

"Robin, what is that supposed to mean?" Gail demanded.

"I think Robin wants to know if I'm psychologically opposed to hugging," Anne said. She sat beside Robin on the bed. "I'm not opposed to it; I just don't do it very much. I'm not nearly as good at it as your mother is. I'm sorry if you feel I've let you down; I didn't mean to."

Robin knelt on the bed and threw her arms around Anne. "You could practice and get as good as Mommy."

Slowly, Anne's arms moved around Robin. They felt stiff in their reluctance, and she told herself she was being ridiculous; she was only trying to hug an eight-year-old girl. She forced herself to tighten her arms; wrapping them around Robin's thin frame. She felt the warmth of that small body through cotton pajamas, and breathed in the fragrance of soft, suntanned skin, like sunshine in a garden. Her fingers pressed against the curve of Robin's narrow ribs and the small, sharp ridges of her shoulder blades, and Robin's thin, bony arms clung tightly as she kissed Anne's cheek with loud smacks.

It was like holding herself as a child, Anne thought, before she stopped being a child. Suddenly, she felt hollow and aching with loss. And then she felt a rush of warmth toward Robin, and a longing to hold that small body forever, keeping close its innocence and purity and vitality. "I love you, Aunt Anne," Robin said. "I wish you'd stay forever."

Anne closed her eyes. "I'd like that," she said. Even though the rush of warmth still suffused her, she could not say the simple words that had come so easily from Robin. When she looked up, she met Gail's eyes; there were tears in them. Anne turned her head and brushed Robin's cheek with her lips, then carefully loosened her arms. "Time for sleep. I'll see you at breakfast."

Robin pulled the blanket to her chin. "You did that very well," she said solemnly.

"Thank you." Smiling, Anne went down the hall to Ned's room. He was reading in bed. "I came to say good-night. Would you like a hug?"

"Nah, I'm not into hugging," he said. "It's for kids."

"Okay." She bent down and lightly kissed his cheek.

"But maybe a little one," he said.

Anne gave him a quick hug. Nothing to it, she thought. I could really get into this. "Good night, Ned. Sleep well."

"Night, Aunt Anne." He had already turned back to his book.

She met Gail in the hall and they walked back to the kitchen. "You're so good with them," Gail said.

Anne shook her head. "They're good with me. It's amazing how much tougher it is to know how to behave with them than it is to handle a whole lawsuit, start to finish."

"I'd like to hear about some of those. You never told us about Dora's lawsuit. Leo said he asked you once and you didn't seem to want to talk about it."

"Not much. I told you we won; she got cash and the Tamarack house. It was more than she'd expected. She was very pleased."

"But?"

"No buts. I like to win, but I don't dwell on it; I'm more interested in the cases I'm working on now than the ones I've finished."

"I suppose you found Dora a little difficult."

Anne smiled. "That's the kind of statement lawyers make. It's called fishing with a very long rod."

Gail laughed. "Well, *I* find her difficult. I've never been able to like her, which is why I was surprised that we liked Josh so much. Most people in Tamarack like him; in fact, a lot more like him than her, and I thought maybe that was why you didn't want to talk about it. Well, I guess we don't get any more coffee until they get the water back on. Oh, wait, we've got bottles of water in the garage; there was a problem last year, not a big one, but we bought a few cases. I'll be right back."

Anne sat at the kitchen table while Gail went to the garage, propping the door open behind her. When the telephone rang, she called to Anne, "Could you grab that?"

Anne picked it up. "Hello," she said.

"Gail," said Marian. "Nina and I just got into town; we came on the spur of the moment. We're at my house and we thought you and Leo would come for a cup of tea, but there's something wrong with the water, so we'd like to come to you. I know it's late, but we do want to talk to you, and you could make us some tea, and I assume by the time we get back the water will be on again. Unless it's something really serious; there's a truck with a loudspeaker going up and down the streets saying not to drink the water, though that doesn't seem to be a problem since there isn't any. Is Charles with you? I called him at the hotel, but he's not there. Well, we'll just come up; we'll be there in a few minutes."

Anne heard an amplified voice on the Riverwood road beyond Gail's long driveway. Gail stood in the doorway, holding two jugs of water, and they listened as the voice grew louder. "Do not drink any water from the tap. Drink only bottled water and drinks in bottles and cans. Fresh water will be available at City Hall in two hours. Do not drink any water from the tap. Drink only bottled water and drinks in bottles and cans. Fresh water will be available . . ."

"Gail?" asked Marian. "Are you there?"

Anne was about to hand the telephone to Gail, but she changed her mind. She couldn't hide; she had to see them. "It's Anne," she said into the telephone.

"Well, my goodness. Anne. I had no idea you were here.

Well, we'll certainly come now; you'll wait for us, won't you? Or are you staying there? Yes, of course you must be. Oh, my dear, it will be good to see you again."

"Marian and Nina," Anne said to Gail as she hung up. "They're coming for a cup of tea."

"Nina? What's she doing in Tamarack? She isn't in the middle of a divorce." Gail poured bottled water into the carafe. "I'm getting nervous about the water. We've never had a loudspeaker with dire warnings before." She started the coffeemaker and poured bottled water into the teakettle. "Poor Anne, you're getting both barrels. First Daddy shows up, and then Marian and Nina, and now some kind of crisis with the water. You'll wish you were back in peaceful Los Angeles."

"No," Anne said. There was surprise in her voice. She thought of her all-white apartment, cool, silent, empty, all hers. No one else came there. It was her favorite place, after her office. But now, imagining it, she felt herself tighten inside. "No," she said again. "I'm glad to be right here."

"Food," Gail mused. "We have about a third of your cake left; Leo and Ned inflicted major damage on it. We'll put out some sliced meat and bread; Marian and Nina might be hungry." She took packages from the refrigerator. "Practically a family gathering. We haven't had one for a long time. What did you think of Josh, by the way?"

"Not much."

"Really? Well, I guess he was the enemy, wasn't he?"

"Opponent." Anne felt oddly uncomfortable talking about him, but there seemed no reason not to. "He seemed arrogant to me, somebody who likes his own way and isn't above manipulating people to get it."

"Oh," Gail said thoughtfully. "He is pretty sure of himself, but you know he's got an incredible reputation; he's been called as a consultant for just about every museum in the world, and governments call him to help them preserve their ancient buildings and monuments. He and Leo talk about history a lot; they're both sort of hung up on the past. Sometimes I think Josh likes the past better than the present—at least he spends an awful lot of time with it and his face lights up when he talks about it, a lot more than it ever did about Dora, I'll tell you that. I absolutely could not figure that out—why he wanted her. Grandpa used to say it was a weakness in Josh's character that he wouldn't marry Dora, but I thought the weakness was that he was with her at all. I shouldn't say that; she's my cousin after all. Our cousin. But I always thought she was also something of a bitch."

And Vince's daughter. The words hung in the air, but they were not spoken. Gail filled a platter with sliced meat, Spanish olives, and French bread. "Paper plates," she murmured, "since we can't do dishes. Paper napkins, plastic forks. We'll use mugs, though, it's the only way to drink coffee. Josh still comes to Tamarack a lot. He always came over Labor Day; if he did this time, you'll probably see him around. He comes here, too. Would you have any trouble being friendly?"

Anne was folding napkins. "Of course not. But I don't know what his feelings are."

"Well, he's very civilized."

"Then there won't be a problem."

"Sugar," Gail said. "I'm sure Nina uses sugar in her tea. And maybe lemon. I wonder what they meant about fresh water being at City Hall in two hours."

"It sounds like they're trucking it in. Which means they don't think it's going to be fixed in a hurry, whatever it is."

"Well, Anne," said Marian coming into the kitchen. "Anne, my dear. My dear Anne."

She came toward Anne, her arms outstretched. Anne stood and grasped one of her hands before it reached her, holding it in both of hers, keeping Marian at arm's length. "Hello, Marian. Hello, Nina."

"The front door was open," Nina said.

"It's always open; you know that," said Gail. "Come and sit down; I'm making tea. We're just going to stay in the kitchen."

"Oh, yes, so cozy," Nina said. "You look wonderful," she said to Anne.

"She looks altogether beautiful," Marian said. "I'm so

proud of you, Anne. You've come through, you've triumphed."

"Are you married?" Nina asked, looking around. "Is anyone with you?"

"No," Anne said. She had let go of Marian's hand and stepped back.

"Then you're divorced?" Nina asked.

"I haven't married," Anne said.

"Oh." Nina shook her head. "I'd find that difficult, not to have anyone to talk to at the end of the day and sort out what you've done and what you're thinking of doing. It seems so hard to make sense of the world when you have only your own thoughts and no one to give you alternatives. It makes me nervous, and then I can't sleep and I lie awake wondering what to believe in. There doesn't seem to be any purpose in things when I'm alone; everything seems so meaningless unless I belong to someone. But that hasn't bothered you, has it; you've managed by yourself. I do think that's admirable, Anne; it seems very mature."

"We want to know everything about you," Marian said. "Since the day you left. We worried about you, you know—"

"We're not talking about the past, Aunt Marian," Gail said decisively. "Right now we're wondering what's happened to the water. Aren't you going to sit down?"

"Yes," said Nina. "Everything looks wonderful. Is that smoked turkey? I have a weakness for smoked turkey. And what a lovely chocolate cake."

"Anne made it." Gail poured tea while Anne poured coffee. By unspoken agreement, they dragged it out, putting things away, organizing dishes on the table, waiting for their aunts to become more interested in food than talk. Anne looked up and saw their images in the full-length mirror, as she had her first time there, and had a swift moment of elation at the way she and her sister had understood each other.

"Well, when are *you* two going to sit down?" Marian asked.

"In a minute," Gail said. "As soon as I put a couple of things away." The door opened and Leo came in. "Where's Daddy? What happened?" she asked.

"He went back to the hotel." He kissed Marian and Nina as if it were perfectly natural that they were in his kitchen at ten o'clock at night, and sat at the table, smiling at Anne as she handed him a cup of coffee. "It's the damnedest thing. It looks like some bad minerals got into the water, probably from the mine tailings above the reservoir. Nobody knows how; it doesn't make sense, after a hundred years of Tamarack Creek being perfectly clean, for it to be contaminated all of a sudden, overnight, but that's what happened, and that's our water supply. They've been doing testing at the water plant once a day since the EPA got here, and late this afternoon they found the lead had shot up, way above the maximum acceptable level. So they shut off the water until they figure out what happened and find a way to clean it up."

"There was a truck with a loudspeaker," Marian said, "talking about fresh water at City Hall."

Leo nodded. "They're bringing tank trucks from Durango. We'll get water from them and take it home."

"In buckets?" Nina asked. "How quaint. Like the pioneers. And the miners."

"Not quite," Leo said dryly. "Unless you want to trade your Mercedes for a donkey."

"The land above the reservoir," Gail said quietly. "That's the company's property."

Leo met her eyes. "Right. You think the gods are mad at the Chathams and Calders?" he asked Anne. "Maybe we ought to sacrifice a goat. Or find some of the old Ute Indians who lived here and ask them to do one of their dances for us. Sorry, I'm sounding paranoid."

"I don't understand," Nina said.

"It means The Tamarack Company could be liable if the contamination starts on its property," Anne said. "That would be the second time," she added, to Leo.

He nodded. "It's hard to believe . . . all at once. Look,"

he said when Nina still looked bewildered. "The mine tunnels were dug under the east end of town and ran a couple of miles east of that, up-valley. Ethan bought all that land and dug the reservoir, and never thought about the tailings on the surface. Well, none of us thought about them. But now it looks as if rainwater, and underground water, too, washed lead from the tailings and somehow got into Tamarack Creek, which feeds into our water plant. And we have to pay to clean it up. And we're already trying to negotiate with the EPA about the cleanup in town, where people live. Between the two of them it could cost a small fortune."

"Is the water poisonous?" Marian asked.

"I don't know," Leo said. "It sure as hell isn't good for us."

"Then it has to be kept quiet," Marian declared firmly.

"Right. Tell me how to do that."

"You instruct people not to talk. That should be clear to everyone. We'll pay whatever costs there are; we're a responsible company. But our people will not be allowed to talk about it; neither will the townspeople. Good Lord, who would be hurt most by stories about poisonous water? A child could understand that."

Leo shook his head. "Somebody always talks. The big problem is that it always gets printed. And you know why. As soon as a bunch of ex-kings and television and movie stars and Arabian sheiks built their houses here, Tamarack stopped being your everyday town and turned into news. You could leak a dozen stories about Alamosa or Durango; nobody'd print them. But the first whisper about us, especially a bad whisper, and readers eat it up. And this one's very bad. When it's a question of health or safety . . . My guess is we'll get a lot of cancellations. Just in time for the ski season."

"Poor Charles," Marian said. "He'll have trouble selling the company until this is over."

"I guess that's the silver lining," said Leo. "We won't hear any more talk about selling."

"But Charles needs the money!" Nina cried.

"I don't think it's an issue anymore," Leo said, avoiding an argument.

"Unless someone's trying to pick up a bargain," Anne mused. "Someone already made a very low offer."

"I doubt he'll make another one," Leo said. "Nobody would be interested in us right now, with all the baggage we've got." He stood up. "I want to see how they're getting set up with the water tanks. I won't be long."

"May I come?" Anne asked. "I'd like to see how they do it. Gail, do you mind?"

"The great escape," Gail murmured with a smile. "Of course not: you go ahead; we'll stay here and talk."

"We'll bring water for all of us," Leo said. "Marian, we'll drop yours off at your house."

Outside, he pulled on his jacket and breathed deeply in the chill air. "End of summer. You can almost smell the snow. Were they cross-examining you?"

"Gail stopped them the first time. I wanted to avoid the second."

He opened the car door for her. "What do you want us to do if Vince shows up? Shoot him? Maybe we should make him the sacrifice to the gods; spare the poor goat."

Anne laughed. "Thank you, Leo. I couldn't ask you to do anything. If he came, I'd probably leave."

"You mean temporarily."

"Oh, yes. I won't leave for good, not again."

"I'm glad." He drove down the steep hill from Riverwood to the bottom of the valley and turned toward town. "We like having you around, Anne. I've never seen Gail so happy. And the kids are crazy about you."

"I like being here," Anne said simply. She gazed at Tamarack, glowing like a brilliant ornament nestled in the dark, encircling mountains. It was really two towns, she thought: one populated by four thousand residents who worked there, sent their children to school, voted and paid taxes, and growled about the changes taking place; the other, a town of twenty thousand tourists who came for a week or a month, demanded the finest services, complained about costs, peered around corners looking for celebrities, and left, having walked through the first town as if it were invisible. For the most part, the two towns coexisted without much rancor in an alliance fueled by the tourists' dollars.

But tourists have to trust the town, Anne thought. And if they can't trust something as basic as its air and water, they'll distrust other things, too. And go somewhere else. And a town and a company can't survive that.

Leo parked the car three blocks from City Hall. "Can't get any closer; it looks like the whole town is here." As they walked, they became part of a crowd filling the sidewalks and spilling over into the streets, flowing like a river around cars left helter-skelter by drivers who had simply walked away from them. Voices rose in the night air in a chorus of questions and attempts to find someone to blame as more and more people arrived, wedging themselves into an area in front of City Hall, in a flood of white light from temporary spotlights. On one side were two tank trucks; beside them chairs and a table had been set up with sheets of computer printouts. "Voter registration lists," Leo said, following Anne's look as they came close. "For rationing. Lodge and hotel owners will sign for their guests; tourists who're renting houses and apartments will register for the time they're here. It ought to go smoothly."

"Except for the worry," Anne said, watching the crowd. It continued to swell; the clamor of voices grew in volume and pitch. "What I want to know," someone yelled, "is how long have we been drinking poison?"

The mayor stood on the steps, waiting for workers to hook up his microphone. "What's it gonna cost, Mack?" someone shouted at him. "You expect us to pay for all this?"

The mayor shook his head. "We'll take care of it," he said, but no one heard him in the rising cacophony.

In a few minutes one of the workers nodded. "OKAY," boomed out the mayor's amplified voice. He held the microphone away from his mouth. "Okay," he said again. "We've got water for everybody; we're working to solve the problem; there isn't anything to worry—"

"What happened?" voices yelled.

"We don't know," the mayor said. "Listen, nobody wants

a quick answer more than I do, but I haven't got one. What we have got is lead and a few other undesirable minerals in the drinking water, probably from the mine tailings above the town, probably seeping into Tamarack Creek, and you all know that's where our water comes from. We don't know how it's getting there; that's the truth. When we find out, we'll stop it and clean up the water and send these trucks home. That's a promise. But until then, we'll keep bringing in fresh water and nobody'll go without. You'll just pay your regular water bill, and the city and The Tamarack Company will take care of the difference. The important thing is, there's no danger to anyone."

"How long's it been going on, Mack?"

"It's only been today. We've been testing every day since the EPA came to town, and this was caught at five o'clock this afternoon. Yesterday everything was fine. This morning everything was fine. I know that sounds peculiar, and we can't explain it, but the important thing is, we caught it right away. And there's plenty of water. We're rationing it, but we're doing it sensitively and intelligently; there's plenty for everybody. Now this is what we want you to do. When you get up to the table . . ."

"Leo," said a voice behind Anne. She and Leo turned at the same time.

"Josh, good to see you!" Leo exclaimed. "I wondered if you were in town—" He stopped as Josh's gaze fixed on Anne. "Of course you know each other," he said.

"This is an astonishing coincidence," Josh said coolly. He cast a glance around. "You're not with Dora?"

"Dora's not here," said Leo. "And I guess you don't know . . ." He raised his voice to compete with the noise of the crowd. "Josh, Anne is Gail's sister. She's staying with us for the weekend."

"Gail's sister?" Josh was still looking at Anne, a deep frown between his eyes. "I didn't know she had one."

"I've been away for a long time," Anne said.

"Dora's cousin," he said.

"Yes."

"And no one ever mentioned you."

289

"It's complicated," Leo said. He staggered a bit as the crowd surged forward. "Listen, why don't we go get a beer or a cup of coffee, and come back when things are quieter."

"Why don't you go?" Anne suggested. "I'll wait in line."

"What line?" Leo asked dryly. "This is like the opening of the Berlin Wall; everybody wants to be first. Come on, Anne, you heard our mayor. He's being sensitive and intelligent and there's plenty of water. Josh, you'll come, won't you?"

Josh and Anne exchanged a glance. His eyes were curious, filled with questions. Anne's face told him nothing at all. Someone lurched against them and Josh automatically put out his hand to help her keep her balance. "Good idea," he said to Leo. "Do we use the wedge formation?"

Leo laughed. "Okay with you, Anne?"

"Yes." She felt crushed by the crowd, and her first thought, to let the two of them go by themselves, now seemed foolish. "Which way shall we go?"

"Into battle," Leo said. "Stay close." The three of them plunged into the crowd, pushing against the flow. It was five minutes before they stood on a quiet corner, breathless and disheveled. "Like going the wrong way in a marathon," Leo said with a grin. He smoothed his hair and adjusted his jacket. "Where shall we go?"

They looked at Anne. "Timothy's," she said. "He doesn't need water; he has fifty kinds of beer."

"My favorite place," said Josh. They walked the few blocks in silence, through silent streets, and found the bar empty. Anne and Leo sat together on one side of a booth; Josh sat on the other side, his back against the unpainted brick wall, his legs stretched out on the green leather seat.

"When did you get in?" Leo asked.

"Thursday night."

"Where are you staying?"

"At the Tamarack. I bought a house a couple of weeks ago but I'm having some work done on it."

"That was quick. I wondered if you'd buy another place. Where is it?"

"Somewhere west of you."

There was a pause. "You bought the Sterns' place."

Josh nodded. "I didn't think you'd mind."

"Mind! It's terrific. You've got the other end of River-wood; walking distance. You can come for dinner anytime. I couldn't hope for a better neighbor. What are we drinking?"

"Anything in a bottle," the owner said, standing beside the booth. "Hi, Anne."

"You spend your time here?" Leo asked Anne with interest.

She smiled. "I came in last week. Timothy knew my grandfather and we had a long talk about him."

"A prince and a gentleman," Timothy said. "We miss him around here. What can I get you?"

They ordered and were silent until Timothy brought three different beers, a basket of tortilla chips, and a dish of salsa. "On the house," he said. "In memory of Ethan."

"I'm sorry I never got to know him," Josh said. "He and Dora didn't see much of each other."

"He tried to like her," mused Leo. "I think she reminded him too much of Vince." Beneath the table, Anne put a warning hand on his thigh. "You and Ethan would have liked each other," he said to Josh. "But I've told you that before, haven't I?"

"A few dozen times. By now I'm absolutely convinced you're right."

Leo smiled. The silence stretched out. "Well," Leo said at last. "Where've you been traveling? You were on your way to Greece last time we saw you; you were going to tell the government to beef up its security at some museum."

"At all its museums. There are six or eight thefts just waiting to happen there."

"So did they do it?"

"Not yet; they're studying my report. And while they do, they'll have a major theft—my guess is Corinth, because it's a superb collection guarded by one man in his late sixties—and then somebody will finally decide it's worth spending money on better security."

"And then they'll ask you to come back and give them more advice."

Josh laughed. "I hope so."

"And where've you been giving advice lately?"

"Not advice. Research. I've been in Egypt the last couple of weeks. I won't be going anywhere else for a while."

"You've got something good there?"

"Maybe. We're working on it."

"A tomb? A temple?"

"A tomb. We're not sure yet."

"A new one? A big one? As big as King Tut's?"

"Bigger, if we're right. Leo, you know I don't talk about my long shots until I know how close I am. Let me have my one small streak of superstition. Tell me what's happening here with the water. Those mine tailings are on your land, aren't they?"

Anne watched the two men as they talked. She took off her jacket and sat back, sipping her beer, listening not to their words but to the sounds of their voices. Leo's voice was compact, like his frame, his words as distinct and decisive as the steps of a soldier on the march. Josh's was deeper and more measured, the voice of a man who spent much of his time explaining things. It was strong and assured; a very good voice, Anne thought. She had thought so in her office, though it had been tense then, rougher than it was now, and arrogant.

Or had it? She wasn't sure. That had been Dora's word. She wondered how much she had seen and heard because she expected to, from Dora's descriptions.

Josh looked at her and met her eyes. "Are you planning to be here often?"

"Yes," she said. "It's a wonderful place."

"Is this your first visit? No, of course not; Gail said she's been coming here since she was five. You would have been with her."

"Yes."

After a moment, Leo said, "I'd been here exactly twice before Ethan hired me. I can't believe it now; I moved here without really knowing anything about the place. What if I'd hated it?"

"What was the first thing you did?" Anne asked.

"Hiked up Douglas Pass. I thought I'd die; weak muscles and thin air and I'd picked probably the toughest hike around. But the view knocked me out. I sat up there eating a doughnut, not another soul around, not a cloud, either, all sun and blue sky and enough breeze to cool me off, and I looked around, three hundred sixty degrees, at what I could have sworn was the whole wonderful world, peaks and valleys, forests, rivers, and Douglas Lake a couple thousand feet below, and I knew Ethan was right: it was paradise. That's still my most special place."

"Do you remember the first thing you did here?" Josh asked Anne.

"I rode in a sled pulled by a team of huskies." She smiled, remembering. "But the next summer was even better. I hiked with my grandfather, and found a magic place and said I wanted to live there forever."

"Where was it?" Leo asked.

"Riverwood. Not far from your house. Of course it didn't have a name, then; all the land up there belonged to a couple of ranchers. I called it my secret garden, which was stretching it, because the ranchers were there and their families, not to mention their cattle and horses and dogs and cats and the rabbits the kids kept in pens, but when I was there, hiding in the fir trees and sitting by the creek, it was all mine and I could absolutely believe that no one else in the world had discovered it, or ever would."

"Hiding in the fir trees?" Josh asked.

A faint flush touched her cheek. "All children have hiding places. Where were yours?"

"In museums," he said promptly. "I went once a week, whenever I didn't have baseball; my parents would drop me off after school and pick me up when they closed. I got locked in once; it scared the hell out of me. I was sitting behind a display case, drawing a statue of an Egyptian dwarf, and the guard didn't see me when he came through announcing closing time, and I didn't tell him I was there because I wanted to finish my drawing. Next thing I knew the lights went out and there wasn't a sound. Except that, after a minute, there were sounds everywhere: the place creaked and groaned and whispered at me, and it was pitch-black and I was crawling on the floor so I wouldn't crash into glass cases, and crying."

"How old were you?" Anne asked.

"Nine. I promised God everything I had in the world if I could get out of there. I even promised to practice the piano twice a day."

"But your parents were waiting for you outside," she said.

"They were shouting at the guard that he had to open the place. And he did and they found me. On hands and knees, still carrying my sketch pad, and whimpering. And I was so glad to see them I never had time to feel embarrassed."

"Did you want to go back the next week?" she asked.

His eyebrows rose. "You're the only one who's ever asked that. I wasn't sure I wanted to, but my parents thought I should, so I did. For a while, I hated the smell of the place, and the way footsteps echoed, and the angles of the shadows. It didn't last long; a couple of weeks, I think, but I've never forgotten it."

"Josh is a professor," Leo told Anne after a moment. "Archaeology, at UCLA. Well, but you know that, don't you? You probably know more about him than—" He took a drink. "Sorry," he murmured. "Lots of quicksand around here."

Josh burst out laughing. "It's all right, Leo. You don't have to tiptoe around it; it was only money and my pride, and I can deal with both of them. And Miss Garnett is a hell of a lawyer and I'd like her with me if I ever need one again."

Anne looked at him in surprise. "Thank you," she said.

Leo looked at his watch. "My guess is, it's time to go. It'll take us ten, fifteen minutes to get back and pick up our water. Is that okay? I'll be right back; I want to thank Timothy again."

Josh held the door for Anne and they waited for Leo outside. The street was empty and dark, the pale light from antique lampposts casting small circles on each side of them. "I'm busy with friends tomorrow," he said abruptly, "but I'd like to call you on Monday. May I? About noon, if that's all right."

Anne looked at him for a long moment. His eyes met hers steadily. There was not the slightest hint of arrogance in them. "I'd like that," she said.

Chapter 12

There's a place called Defiance Lake," Josh said on the telephone on Monday. "Very beautiful and not well known, so it shouldn't be crowded. I thought we'd hike up and have a late lunch, if that would please you."

"Yes," Anne said. She did not say she had not hiked for years; she would go at her own pace, and if it was too slow for him, he would either adjust his pace or go ahead. It did not matter to her; she liked the idea of hiking to a lake. I'll borrow hiking boots from Gail, she thought.

"I'll pick you up in half an hour," Josh said. "I don't suppose you have a backpack; I'll take extra gear in mine."

"No, I'll borrow one from Gail," Anne said. "I like to carry my share. What can I bring for lunch?"

"Nothing; it's all taken care of. I'll see you soon."

When he arrived, Anne was sitting on a boulder in front of the house, reading. She wore khaki hiking shorts, a blue shirt with the sleeves rolled up, and Gail's white tennis visor. "Gail and Leo took the kids to the Labor Day parade," she said, putting her backpack in his jeep. "They all say hello."

"What book were you reading?" Josh asked as he drove toward the main Riverwood road.

"The *Los Angeles Law Review.*"

"Do you always bring work when you come here?"

"Always. Don't you?"

"I'm afraid so. I can get away from my offices, but not from my briefcase."

"How many offices do you have?"

"Two. The university and the museum. Have you been to the Ancient?"

"No; I don't have much time for museums. I've heard it's wonderful."

"It is. We'll have a private tour, if you'd like, after hours one day. When do you go back?"

"Tomorrow."

"And you're here every weekend?"

"Oh, no, I can't get away that often; I'll be lucky to get here once a month. If I do manage it more often, I'll have to rent a place."

"Gail and Leo didn't say that."

Anne smiled. "Of course not. But I always prefer being in my own place; I stay with them because they insist. But even that has limits."

"But you enjoy staying with them."

"Yes."

Brief answers, Josh thought. Simple, to the point, volunteering almost nothing. A private person. *I always prefer being in my own place.* Probably without much room for anyone else, he thought. There were so many questions he wanted to ask her, especially about her place in the Chatham family, why she left them, and when—she'd said she had been gone a long time; how long was that?—and why, in all the years he'd known Dora, no one had ever mentioned her. But he kept his questions to himself. Someday they might know each other well enough that she would be open with him.

He drove across the valley and turned up a narrow road past a sign pointing to a ranch. "Friends of mine own this place; wonderful people. I hope you'll meet them one day. The trail starts on their property, which is why almost no one uses it. It's only a couple of miles to the lake, but it's steep in places; if your backpack is heavy—"

"It's fine."

The road was covered with aspen leaves sent spinning by the car into little golden tops. Anne watched them, and breathed the warm air that smelled of sun and earth, and closed her eyes briefly, remembering Ethan and their walks, and how he had taught her the names of flowers and trees along the way, and helped her clean the sticky resin of pinecones from her fingertips, and laughed at her disbelief the first time he picked up a tiny whorled shell and told her there were indeed snails in the mountains: land snails that looked just like those found in water. Everything in the world had seemed filled with wonder and beauty in those days, before her thirteenth year.

"They're out of town, so I can't introduce you," Josh said as they drove past a stone and wood house with horse corrals beyond it. "Maybe next time." The road curved and began to climb, becoming rutted and studded with half-buried rocks. They drove across a shallow stream to a small turnaround beside the road. "This is it. The trail is on the other side."

They put on their backpacks and began to walk through the forest, Josh in front. Thin, white trunks of aspen trees closed in on the trail. Sunlight cast narrow beams of light through the yellow leaves still clinging to the branches, and dappled the yellow and brown bushes along the trail, and the wine-red sumac bushes peeking through. The last purple gentians and blue mountain asters nestled beneath prickly raspberry plants with fading leaves; the dried heads of cow parsnip made faint crackling sounds in the breeze, the only sound besides the scuffling of Josh's and Anne's hiking boots in the aspen leaves on the trail. They did not speak. Anne watched Josh's back, his broad shoulders supporting his pack, his muscled calves below khaki shorts, his sure-footed steps, using jutting rocks as footholds, the easy way his arms swung in rhythm with his walk. He was an experienced hiker with a relaxed pace that Anne found almost too slow.

But in another few minutes it was not too slow. Imperceptibly, the path became steeper, and then steeper still, and as it went on and on, Anne's thighs began to ache, her legs felt too heavy to lift, her breath came in gasps, and she felt faintly dizzy. She tried to peer past Josh, to see the end of the trail, but then she decided against it. If she knew how far she still had to go, she might not take another step. And of course she would take another step, and another and another. Josh was climbing steadily—she could not hear him breathing hard at all—and she was damned if she'd give up. She'd get to the lake and she'd stay with him all the way.

"Put your shoulders back and breathe deeply," Josh said over his shoulder. "Fill your lungs. And breathe in time with your steps. Don't gasp."

She thrust out her chest, pushing her shoulders back, and took deep breaths. The dizziness vanished. She began to count as she breathed, in time with her steps, and her gasping stopped. "Thank you," she said. Now if he could just make my legs work, she thought wryly, but she did not have the energy for any more words: she just kept behind him, step for step.

Josh reached back, handing her a plastic water bottle. She drank as she walked, gulping the velvety coolness, keeping an ice cube in her mouth when she returned the bottle. The trail leveled out and they walked through a pine forest and then across high mountain meadows like bowls that trapped the burning sun. Then they were in another pine forest, dark after the golden glow of the aspen forest and the meadows; no sunlight penetrated here. The air was soft and cool, tangy with the scent of resin; the path was covered with a bed of pine needles that made it spongy and silent. Josh and Anne walked in silent harmony. Gray jays flew from branch to branch, keeping up with them; chipmunks darted alongside. Anne moved as if she were deeply a part of the earth. She felt a moment of pure happiness.

And then she glanced up, straight up, and saw the treetops swaying slightly in the breeze, their narrow trunks tapering to small points against the brightness of the sky. They creaked slightly. *Listen to that, Amy. The trees are creaking. Like in a horror movie. Close your eyes and you can believe something really awful is about to happen.*

She was crying. Walking behind Josh, doggedly forcing step after step to keep up with him, her back erect to support her pack, she felt the tears streaming down her face. The trees wavered, the road blurred, she tasted tears on her lips. She could not stop them; somewhere within her she was sobbing and the tears came of their own volition, beyond her control. She walked that way for what seemed an endless time, across a slope of rocks and boulders and into more pine trees, until Josh slowed, pointing to their left. "Defiance Lake. Named by a bunch of miners who defied a terrible winter and survived." He turned. "Anne, what is it? What's wrong?"

She shook her head. "I'll be all right." The sudden stop made her feel she was about to topple over. She knelt, pretending to tighten the laces on her boots, and took long breaths. Her tears stopped. When she stood and adjusted her pack, her voice was steady. "You were right: it's a very beautiful hike. Thank you for bringing me."

"You aren't hurt?"

"No. I'm fine."

"Was it a memory, then?"

She gave him a quick glance. "Do you have memories that can cause tears?"

He smiled faintly. "I don't know anyone who doesn't. I know you thought I was incapable of feeling deeply enough to weep over anything, but yes, I have memories that cause tears. Shall we find a place for lunch?"

"Yes."

Again he led the way. The small lake nestled like an Indian turquoise at the bottom of a bowl of pine trees. From the water's edge, the trees climbed steeply five hundred feet, then gave way to gray rock outcroppings that formed a great circle of peaks above the lake. Josh walked along a narrow strip of sand at the water's edge, then turned into the forest. Anne followed. The pain was gone. She had trained herself for many years to block out memories, to believe with all her heart that they no longer existed, and to behave as if everything were perfectly fine. She followed Josh as he turned back toward the lake, and in a minute they came out of the trees at a group of flat boulders jutting over the water. "I come up here sometimes for breakfast," he said.

"Alone?" Anne asked.

"Sometimes." He shrugged his backpack off his shoulders. "Are you hungry?"

"No. I haven't had enough energy to think about anything but my legs."

He chuckled. "They're pretty amazing legs."

Anne slipped out of the straps on her pack and set it down behind her. She flexed her shoulders. "I could use some more water."

Josh was already pulling the plastic bottle from his belt carrier. He handed it to her. "Take a lot; I have another one in my pack."

She drank deeply, then sat on the largest rock, stretching out her legs, leaning back, supporting herself on her hands. She closed her eyes, her face to the sun.

Josh sat beside her. "If you want to talk about it, I'm a good listener."

She shook her head, her eyes closed. "Thank you. There's nothing to talk about. Tell me about your work. I'd like to hear about Egypt if you wouldn't mind."

Josh contemplated her. Her nose and forehead were pink. He should have warned her about the mountain sun, he thought. He should have stopped on the trail to see how tired she was, instead of forging ahead like a caveman. He should have let her go ahead of him and set her own pace. He should have tried to help her when he saw her with tears streaming down her face, her mouth trembling with the effort to keep silent while she wept. The polished image of Anne Garnett, lawyer, came to him, sitting in the solid surroundings of her office, arguments flowing smoothly from her sensual, and cold, lips. She looked human now, and even more beautiful, he thought: sunburned, her hair windblown, her long legs scratched from twigs that had stretched across the trail, her shirt wet with perspiration. But he remembered thinking, in her office, that he would like to see her smile with pleasure, and though she looked relaxed, she still was not smiling. And now he wanted more:

he wanted to see her laugh with joy, and show warmth to another human being.

"I'll understand if you don't want to talk about it," Anne said, her eyes still closed. "I don't know much about superstitions, but I do know about keeping work confidential."

"I've been working for six years on a theory about a pharaoh named Tenkaure, who lived in the Eighteenth Dynasty," Josh said, surprising himself with the ease with which the words came out. He had not talked about this project with anyone but coworkers at the university and in Egypt. "I've found references to him, but no hard evidence; in fact, I suspect a political opponent tried his damndest to make sure he became a nonperson after he died."

"When was the Eighteenth Dynasty?" Anne asked.

"Around 1570 to 1320 B.C. The time I'm interested in was in the 1300s, around the reign of Akenaten."

"The one who truly loved his wife."

"Yes." It was not comfortable to recall that birthday note to Dora, but he was more interested in Anne's remembering such a small detail. "You remember that."

"You remember which table you sat at in a restaurant three and a half years ago." She opened her eyes, and they exchanged a smile. "And what did your pharaoh do that makes you so interested in him?"

"I don't know for sure. And I won't, until I find his tomb. It seems he was involved in some family intrigues; he'd been quarreling with his son, and possibly with the priesthood at Thebes. It wasn't any easier to maintain family harmony then than it is now. Anne, I don't know about you, but I am definitely ready for lunch."

"So am I. Once I got off my legs, the rest of me began behaving normally. Do you always hike like that?"

"When I'm alone or with friends from town. Not when I'm with someone who lives at sea level. I apologize."

"I thought it might only be with me. That you were making sure you were the one to win this time."

His eyebrows rose. "I might have been." He paused in

opening his backpack. "I know I didn't start out that way, but when you stayed on my heels, I seem to have gotten stubborn." He shook his head. "Like a teenager in a drag race. I apologize."

Anne watched him take plastic bags from his pack. She had enjoyed the honesty of that exchange. "It can't have been the first time you've lost to a woman."

Once again he paused. "It's the first time I've lost to anyone."

"That can't be true."

He set two plastic plates on the rock and filled them with thin slices of roast beef and tomatoes, lettuce, pita bread, and Calamata olives. He pulled a bottle of white wine from his pack and unwrapped two wineglasses from cloth napkins. He filled them and handed one to Anne. "You can eat quite neatly with a fork," he said, "or you can stuff everything into the pita, which is sloppy but most satisfying. And most appropriate in this setting."

Anne filled the pita bread, and when it was bulging, she opened her mouth wide and took a bite. "Oh, wonderful," she said. "What a perfect lunch."

For a few minutes they ate quietly, gazing at the blue-green lake. They watched trout jump and catch insects in the split second before slipping back into the water, to swim just below the surface until spying another prey and leaping up again. The ripples they made moved majestically in widening circles to the shore, lapping peacefully against the rock where Josh and Anne sat. Clouds were building, great towering masses of pure white billows piling up against the azure sky. Something within Anne seemed to let go and she felt a longing she had not allowed herself for as long as she could remember. She wanted more of what was before her. More beauty and serenity, more of this strange contentment that was nothing like the triumph of winning at the law but had its own rare satisfaction, more of the feeling within her of opening out to whatever lay ahead. It occurred to her that somehow she had lost touch with the small, quiet wonders of the world; everything in her life was hard-edged, high-pressured, crammed with work, brilliantly successful, absorbing and relentless. In the midst of that, the small pleasures of life had been overwhelmed.

But maybe that's how it has to be, she thought. That's the kind of life I live; I can't just change it overnight. It was something she would have to think about, not now, but later. For now, it was more important to talk to Josh. And something was nagging at her, something he had said earlier. She thought back, and recalled it. "If you've never lost," she said, "how can you have memories that cause tears?"

He grinned. "Good question, but that wasn't what I said. I said I'd never lost to anyone. I've lost to fate, or to God, or as the ancient Egyptians would say, to many gods, or to myself, but I've never been conquered by another person." He poured more wine into their glasses. "I've thought about that a lot; it sounds impossible but I don't think it is. I didn't get into fistfights when I was a kid, and I didn't compete in individual sports; I played baseball and football, and we won and lost as a team. I think that's true of most kids growing up. I was terrific at shooting marbles, and when I lost, I knew it was because I'd slipped up. Lost to myself, in other words. I think that's true of most people, too; we don't use our full potential all the time. And when my parents died, I blamed God, and every Egyptian god, and the Greek and Roman ones, too, and then fate. There wasn't any person I could blame. I think it's relatively rare that we're defeated by another person; usually that's an excuse we use to avoid facing the fact that we weren't good enough or strong enough to win; that we'd lost to ourselves."

Anne sat very still. "That's incredibly presumptuous."

"Is it? I've been told I'm too hard on myself. Why do you say it's presumptuous?"

"You can't be beaten by anyone but God. Or it takes a whole army of gods: Egyptian, Greek, Roman. But no mortal can do it; it's only when you slip up that you give some weak human being a chance to get his licks in and do better than you."

Josh looked at her curiously. "You make it sound pretty

bad. I wouldn't put it that strongly, but what if I did? What's wrong with it? Don't you think there's something inside us that could win a lot more often if we could find it; wake it up, so to speak? Isn't it possible that most of us let ourselves be conquered because it's too much trouble to fight back?"

"You don't know what you're talking about," Anne said furiously. "You don't know about the harm people can do, the destruction—"

"You're right," he said quickly. "I went too far. I do that a lot, I'm afraid; I take a perfectly good idea and keep fooling with it until it stretches like taffy to some absurd and very thin extreme." He kept talking, to give her time to calm down. He wondered if her tears today were connected with whoever had conquered her somewhere in her past. "I fight that every time I write an article. I have a great time playing with ideas, and I just keep at it until I'm way out on a limb, reaching the craziest damn conclusions. Usually, I come to my senses before I go too far. And in addition to all else I forgot to bring dessert."

"I brought dessert," Anne said. "And I'm sorry, too. I was rude. I don't know why I got so upset."

Yes, you do, Josh thought, and whatever it was, it was terrible, and you've buried it, but not deep enough to prevent its leaping out when something disturbs it, as I just did. He watched Anne reach into her pack and bring out a small gold box. "Truffles," he exclaimed. "You're wonderful. What kind?"

"Chocolate and hazelnut."

"You have impeccable taste. It's the same as mine. Thank you." He put the candy in his mouth without biting into it.

Anne did the same. Slowly, the chocolate melted on her tongue in a soft, warm, bittersweet flood that slid down her throat. She sighed, a long, luxurious breath, and looked at Josh. He grinned at her. "What every picnic needs. I can't imagine wanting anything more. Except . . . do I get another one?"

"Two more," Anne said. "I didn't think the hike was long enough to merit more than three each."

"We'll find a longer one next time." He glanced at the

clouds, larger and darker than a few minutes earlier. "We ought to leave soon if we want to beat the rain."

"I'm sorry," Anne said. "It's so lovely here." They finished the candies and the wine, and began to pack up the remains of lunch. "What upset you about Dora's suit?" she asked. "Losing to her or losing to yourself? Can you talk about it?"

"Of course. I lost to myself and to you. Money wasn't the issue. It was to Dora, but not to me, though I'd rather not have had to pay it. The important thing was my weaknesses and the fact that you used them in a way that made it almost impossible for us to build a defense. We could have shown that Dora understood from the beginning that I didn't want to marry her, and that she never had any reason to think I'd changed my mind, but once you'd established my silence when I should have spoken, any defense was weakened. Not necessarily destroyed, but seriously weakened. I've always prided myself on not letting that happen; good scholars don't let themselves get backed into corners where their positions can be torn apart and their arguments shot down."

"And your birthday note?" Anne asked.

He pulled the cords that closed his backpack with a hard jerk. "That was the poet in me run amuck. I've learned how to control it since then. The odd thing is, I'm supposed to understand the past, and know how to use it. My life revolves around the past; I'm there almost more than I'm here. But I lived with Dora in ways that had nothing to do with what I'd learned all my life; it was as if the past had no importance at all."

"Why *is* it so important?" Anne asked. "Why are you there almost more than you're here? That's such an extraordinary statement."

"And not entirely accurate. I use the past the same way I used museums when I was a kid: as a haven. Sometimes a place to get lost. When my parents died—"

"How old were you?"

"Thirteen. They were in Alaska; my father was a photographer and they were flying to the Brooks Range in a small plane, and they got caught in a blizzard and went down. For six months I wiped out the present, totally denied it, and lived in the past. I didn't go to school, I didn't see my friends, God knows I didn't play baseball. I did go to museums, and I read; I was in my grandparents' house and they had a fine library and that's where I spent my time. They were very patient with me; they worked out a deal with my high school principal so I could rejoin my class when I was ready, and make up my work after school and at night. At the time, I never thought about their feelings, but of course they were as devastated as I was; we talked about it when I was in college. They were remarkable people; they got me through that terrible year. For a long time, I thought the thirteenth year was one nobody should have to live through."

Anne was watching him, completely absorbed.

"I didn't mean to make this a life story," Josh said with a smile. "You asked about the past. I spend a lot of time there because that's what archaeologists do, and it gives me great pleasure to figure out what happened a long time ago, and why, and how it all piled up, like bricks, to build what we are today. And I spend time there because it's a retreat when I've had enough of university and museum politics, or Los Angeles traffic, or Los Angeles in general, or when I want to avoid thinking about something I've done that I know wasn't my best. The past is a good hiding place, you know; it's always there, waiting for you, and you can pick up where you left off and know that nothing's changed since the last time. And you don't have to share it to enjoy it."

He paused, looking at the lake, almost talking to himself. "That's the problem with the present: it demands to be shared. There's an emptiness in walking through each day without footsteps to match yours, and thoughts to match and challenge yours. At least, that's true for me and it's what I've always looked for. Not with Dora; she was a lovely companion, at least at first, and I was lonely and so was she, and it seemed to make sense to live together. But what I still hope for is someone to help me feel connected to the world, as if it makes a real difference that I'm here, not in a scholarly way, but in a direct and human way. I don't think any of us can do that alone, not fully. We need another person: two minds meeting, two hands touching, two hearts joining."

A heavy bank of clouds covered the sun. Shadows vanished; the lake turned steely gray. In the chill air, Anne shivered.

"Let's get out of here," Josh said. Hurriedly they took sweaters and waterproof jackets from their backpacks and pulled them on, and retraced their steps around the lake. "Do you want to go first?" he asked.

"Fine," she replied, and moved ahead, taking long steps. Going down was almost as much work as going up because she had to hold herself back on the steepest parts, but as the sky grew darker, she moved almost at a jog, keeping her knees bent, placing her feet against half-buried rocks to keep from sliding on the dirt and loose stones of the trail. She heard Josh behind her, step for step, and she thought of the words he had said. *Thoughts to match yours. Thoughts to challenge yours. Two minds meeting, two hands touching, two hearts joining.* The words beat in her mind in time with the pounding of her feet. Such amazing words, she thought; most people wouldn't think them, much less say them aloud. He's a man of ideas and lovely phrases. But how many of them are genuine? *The poet in me run amuck.* He'd said he had learned to control it, but he probably hadn't. It was pleasant to listen to him, but one shouldn't take such fanciful talk seriously.

She felt a drop on her hair, and barely had time to think of rain before she realized it was hail. In less than a minute ice pellets were striking the trees and the trail, making a tremendous roar. Anne gasped as they drummed on her head. She came to a stop. Her feet left footprints on the white trail, her hands were ice-cold.

From behind, Josh grabbed her arm and pulled her with him off the trail into the dense forest of pines and firs. The noise of the hail faded as if a window had closed; it became a harmless-sounding patter high above. He pulled a poncho from his pack and spread it on the ground beneath a

Douglas fir. "We'll wait it out," he said. "I have great respect for mountain storms."

Shivering, Anne rummaged in her pack for Gail's waterproof pants. "I didn't bring snowshoes; I hope this is the last change of weather we have for a while."

Josh chuckled. He pulled on his own rain pants and brought out a thermos. "My last offering for the day. I hope you drink coffee black."

"Yes. Do you always plan so thoroughly? I'm very impressed."

He sat back against a tree and handed her the plastic cup filled with steaming coffee. "Your grandfather must have taught you about the unpredictability of the mountains."

"He did, but I haven't hiked for years."

"Years? You're very strong; you were hiking as if you did it every week."

Anne smiled. "Lots of tennis and even more stubbornness." She held the cup in both hands, warming them. The small clearing where they sat was like a misty cave bordered by dark pines. They heard distant thunder and the steady beat of hailstones on the pine needles and branches far above. Now and then a hailstone would slip through the dense trees, and bounce near them, lying like a tiny pearl on the forest floor. Anne watched one as she sipped the coffee. She sighed and handed the cup to Josh. "That's so good. It's amazing, how cold it can get, so quickly."

Josh drank from the cup and handed it back to her. "How did you choose divorce law?" he asked.

"I found I was good at it. I had a big case in New York about a year after I passed the bar; a friend of mine sent her cousin to me and there was a lot of money involved: children, trusts, property, even a foundation. We negotiated for three months, and we got a good settlement without bloodshed or even major hostilities. There was a pretty good atmosphere for the children to grow up in, probably the best we could have hoped for. I liked making that happen."

"You were thinking of the children."

"They were the most scared. They didn't have anything to hold on to."

"And then they had you."

She shook her head. "It wasn't that dramatic. They needed someone to tell them what was happening with their parents. I was able to do that, and help them feel that people still cared about them."

Josh took the empty cup from her and refilled it. "They must have been very grateful. How old were they?"

"Nine, eleven, and twelve."

"Vulnerable ages. Do you like your work?"

"Yes." She looked at him in surprise. "Don't you?"

"Yes; we're among the lucky ones. What is it you like? Winning? Helping children? Seeing justice done?"

"All of it. If you're asking if I like being in the business of ending marriages, that has nothing to do with it."

"I apologized for that, in your office," Josh said. "I'll do it again now, if you'd like."

"No, I shouldn't have brought it up again. It made me very angry at the time."

"I was angry when I said it. That was one of those times when I went too far. I know damn well a divorce lawyer doesn't end marriages, or any relationships; they've ended long before they reach your office. All you get is the rubble. In fact, you must get very discouraged about the possibilities of any relationship. You never see the beginning, when there's hope; you only get the residue of anger and weariness and vindictiveness. I suppose that's what I was thinking of that day, destruction in general, and you seemed to be preoccupied with tearing down instead of building up."

Anne nodded. "But there isn't any life without destruction. Our job is to survive it."

He gazed at her. "Is that what you think life is all about? Surviving destruction?"

"Isn't that what you study? Cultures that prosper and then disappear because they couldn't survive one kind of destruction or another?"

He handed the cup to her, noting how smoothly she had shifted the conversation away from herself. She'd had a lot of practice in that, he thought. "I study prosperity as much as destruction," he said. "I'm interested in the strengths that make societies flourish as much as in the weaknesses that make them fail. It's the same as studying people, you know: what makes us strong and creative, how we become everything we're able to be. And also how we survive destruction. We need it all. How else can we be fully human except by building societies and relationships and ideas? Just crawling out of the ruins won't do anything but develop our defenses."

Anne was silent. She gave the cup to Josh and looked at the branches above them, listening to the silence. "Shall we try to go on? I think the storm is over."

"So do I." He drained the last of the coffee and returned the thermos to his pack. They left the protection of the clearing, Anne walking ahead, and moved down the trail. The sun was burning through the clouds, and as the air grew warmer, the trail turned to mud. It was so slippery that she kept her eyes on her feet. She looked up once, and came to an abrupt halt. "Look," she said. A silvery mist hung over the mountains, and the green and gold trees, the rock outcroppings, the jagged peaks—all shimmered in the soft sunlight, as pale and delicate as a painting on gauze. "So beautiful," Anne breathed. Her face and hands were cold from the mist, and her hair was wet, but she stood still, lost in the dreamlike scene. "I've never seen the mountains so beautiful."

Josh was close behind her, his arm touching hers. He had almost run into her when she stopped so suddenly. "It is beautiful," he agreed. "But I'd rather have sunlight and shadow. I like a more solid world."

"Do you like art that's all sunshine and shadow?" she asked over her shoulder as they walked on.

"Well, that's a good point," he said. "I collect all kinds of art. I have a good collection; I'd like to show it to you. After we do our tour of the Ancient we'll have drinks at my apartment and then go somewhere for dinner. If you'd enjoy that."

"I would," Anne said, and concentrated on the slippery trail for the rest of the walk down.

By the time they reached the car, the sun was blazing and

the clouds had settled along the horizon, like a more distant range of mountains. Anne and Josh took off their rain gear and tossed it in the back of his jeep. Anne pulled off her wet tennis visor and shook her head. Soaking wet, her hair framed her face in a wild mass of curls. Josh was watching her. "You're very beautiful," he said. "And this has been one of the best hikes I've ever had. Thank you."

"I enjoyed it," Anne said. "And thank you for lunch."

"The truffles were the high spot." He drove down the road, slowing down in the muddy ruts. "We'll explore the Ancient in a few days; I'll call you. Will you be free this weekend?"

"No, I'll be working; I have so much catching up to do. I've never taken four days off before."

"Then we'll do it at night. That really will be private; only a few guards to keep us company." He stopped the jeep at the intersection and they both gazed at the traffic on the highway into Tamarack. "It's always a shock, coming back to the world," Josh murmured. He put his hand on Anne's. "Thank you again; it's been a very special afternoon."

Quietly, she moved her hand away. "For me, too," she said.

There was a break in the traffic and Josh pulled onto the highway. They drove in silence until they reached Gail and Leo's house. "I'm looking forward to Los Angeles," he said.

Anne pulled her pack and rain gear from the back of the jeep. "So am I," she replied. "Very much." As she went into the house, she found it interesting to realize how much she really meant it.

Vince was at a Labor Day fund-raising barbecue in the mountains outside Denver when Keith Jax finally caught up with him. "I've called you three times. You ought to fire your butler; he's not giving you your messages."

"I got them. Keep your voice down." Vince steered him from the group of people to whom he had been talking, down one of the hallways of the sprawling house to a small spare bedroom. The house belonged to Sid Folker, a banker who was one of Vince's top contributors and who, just a few days earlier, had been let in on the secret that Vince was considering a run for the presidency. "We can sit here for a few minutes," Vince said.

"Hey, you could at least offer a guy a drink."

"Later. Tell me why you're here."

"Christ, Vince, I just flew in from Tamarack—"

"Why? What's going on?"

"Well, your friend's there. Anne what's-her-name. Gail's sister."

Vince's gaze fastened on him. "You saw her?"

"Right. Outside City Hall a couple nights ago; she was there with Josh. You know, Dora's guy. Former guy."

"Durant? What the hell was she doing with him?"

"You got me. Well, Leo was there, too, but she was, you know, talking to Josh when I saw her. I couldn't get close; it was a mob scene. They trucked in water, you know, well, you know all that, the reservoir zapping the water supply—"

"Is that all?" Vince asked.

"Well, what I did was, I sorta kept an eye on Gail's house today, and they took off about noon. Anne and Josh. You know, hiking. They had backpacks. He must really be hung up on that family. I always did think he was kinda weird. Anyway, you said you wanted me to find out what she wanted—"

"Did you?"

"Not yet; how did I know if you still wanted me to? I mean, that was back in July. And you know, that thing about getting rid of her; I didn't know if you still like wanted that either. Or what you meant exactly. Pay her off or what. So, anyway, I figured you'd want to know she's there so I flew in. And I oughta get a drink for that, Vince, and dinner, and I can stay at your place tonight, right? And go back tomorrow."

"There you are! Looking for you all over!" Sid Folker came to Vince, shaking his finger. "People want to see you, Senator—you sure know how to get a crowd revved up—and here you are, hiding yourself. Oh, sorry, didn't mean to interrupt."

Vince stood. "Sid, this is my nephew Keith Jax. I took the liberty of inviting him tonight; he's a kind of unofficial assistant and a damned good one; he's a big help to me."

Folker pumped Keith's hand. "Good to have you here, Keith. Anybody Vince wants is welcome here. Your uncle is an important man, Keith, a great man, but I'll bet you already knew that. You stick with him, you'll go a long way. All the way to the top, that's what we're aiming for. We're on a roll here—you sense that, Vince? You can just feel it in the air!—and there is nothing gonna stop us. Well, now, Keith, you don't have a drink! Let's take care of that. Vince, I want you to meet a couple people just moved here from California; they elected their guy president from there, and I told 'em they might have a chance to do it again, here in Colorado. 'Course I didn't say anything definite—first we take care of next November; send you back to the Senate with flying colors—but I didn't think a little hint would be out of place; these people are very big players, and they're anxious to meet you. Keith, you look like the kind of fella can find his way to the bar on his own."

Keith was looking at Vince, his eyes narrowed as he tried to take in all the information he was getting. "Sure. Thanks. I'll see you later, Uncle Vince, at your place, okay?"

"Absolutely," Vince said. "It'll be good to have you there, Keith; that apartment gets damned lonely with just me in it. It's much too big, of course," he said to Folker, "but I keep hoping I'll find some wonderful lady to share it with me."

Folker grunted. "I'm glad you brought that up, Vince. I've got somebody I think you oughta meet. A widow. Widows are good, you know; can't blame 'em for being single. She's a sweetie, sweet and simple, you'll like her. Stick around after the barbecue; we'll have a private little group for dessert."

"I will, Sid. What a friend you are. Thanks."

But it was not Sid he was thinking about as they walked back to the living room; it was Keith. He was twenty-eight years old and he had never held a job until Leo gave him one as assistant mountain manager at Tamarack. And he owed it all to Vince. It was Vince whom Keith had called from prison two years earlier; he'd stabbed a bartender in a brawl over drugs outside a Miami bar, and he didn't want his mother to know about it. So it was Vince who paid his bail, and paid off the bartender, Vince who hired a lawyer, Vince who sent Keith to a hospital outside Chicago to get clean. And it was Vince who sent him to Tamarack, and talked to Leo about giving him a job.

"I want to know what's going on there," he had told Keith. "What your grandfather is doing, how much he's expanding the place, what Leo's up to, where they're getting the money to expand . . . everything you can get. You keep an eye on things, and if I want you to do anything, you be ready to do it. I'll match whatever salary Leo pays you. But if I find you're doing drugs again or drinking more than you can handle, you're out. Marian and Fred find out about Miami and the hospital in Chicago, and so does Leo. And you can go back to Miami flophouses and fucking around with drugs and whores until you're the one who gets stabbed, probably by somebody who has better aim than you, and nobody will lift a finger. Do you need it spelled out any more than that?" Keith shook his head, and moved to Tamarack.

Not too smart, Vince thought, watching Keith make his way to Sid Folker's bar. But not quite stupid. And without a shred of a moral or ethical system to confuse him. It was actually pleasant to deal with him; he was uncomplicated, totally self-absorbed, and as loyal as a puppy. There could be no better assistant for Vince, who hated surprises, than predictable, transparent Keith Jax.

"So what was all that stuff he was making noises about?" Keith asked when Vince came home at midnight. He was sitting in the kitchen, drinking from a tall glass and eating a chocolate cake out of the box in which it had come from the bakery. "Lots of soda, a squirt of Scotch," he said as Vince shot a glance at his glass. "Check the bottle, if you don't believe me."

Vince leaned against the refrigerator. "Tell me about the crowd in Tamarack, at City Hall."

"It was a hoot. Everybody carrying jugs, signing in like good Boy Scouts, the mayor saying how things were fine, everybody talking at once, a couple reporters taking pictures . . . I mean it was a real crazy night."

"They must have blamed someone. Who was it?"

"Nobody. They never blamed anybody. All they did was worry about how long would it last, and would the tank trucks be there all day so they could get water anytime, and were they starting to fix the problem, and—"

"Who were they talking about? Who was supposed to fix the problem?"

Keith shrugged. "They. It's always 'they,' you notice that? The mayor said the town and the company were paying for the water."

"And nobody blamed the company?"

"Not that I heard. They weren't really mad; they were mostly worried. Hey, Vince, was he saying you're gonna be president? Is that true?"

"It might be."

"Wow. That'd be a hoot. Well, if I can help, you know, whatever you want . . ."

"I want you to keep an eye on things at Tamarack. Don't go running to Denver or anywhere else; I need you there. I want to know everything Leo does, how soon they figure out what happened with the reservoir, how long it takes to fix it. And that woman. I want to know when she's there and whom she sees. Whatever you can find out."

"No sweat. Is that all? I mean, you just want me to see what she does? You don't want me to pay her off or whatever? I mean, you just tell me what you want, I'll do it, but if I don't know, it's hard."

Vince felt his neck muscles tighten, as they always did when he felt frustrated. "I don't know yet. It depends on what happens. You just be there, and keep in touch."

"Right. Uh, Vince? Listen. If you get to be president, can I go with you? I'd kinda like to live in Washington."

"Why not?" Vince said as he left. "If you're careful and do as you're told."

"Wow," Keith said again. "Sure. Wow."

Vince closed the door of his study behind him and called

Beloit, who had left Sid Folker's house before dessert was served to the private group. "How much did you get tonight?"

"Six and a half million. We don't have a problem with money, Vince; you know that. We'll go into the primaries in good shape. What I want is more support from the National Committee; they can do a lot for us behind the scenes and so far they're not doing it. But we'll get there; I'm a hundred percent sure we will. You were good tonight; charmed all the ladies and made the men feel like they were in on a cabinet meeting. You're good at that. How was the widow?"

"All right."

"That's all?"

"Better than all right. I'm staying here for a few days to get acquainted."

"She's not as smart as Maisie."

"I don't need a woman as smart as Maisie. What's the problem with the National Committee? I thought you had them with us."

"I will. Sometimes it takes a little extra push. I talked to your brother; did I tell you?"

"No. When?"

"A few days ago. He turned me down; said I was too low. He wants a heap of money, Vince. He doesn't sound to me like a man in trouble."

"He is. And worse all the time. Give it a while; you'll get what you want. We've got to get the family with him."

"They're still not with him?"

"They will be. I'm working on it. We only need a couple of them and then Charles can put it to a vote. You'll get what you want. Leave it to me, Ray; don't worry about it."

"I'm not worried. I'm just waiting."

So am I, Vince thought as he slammed down the phone. He hated it. Too much was in limbo; there was too much he didn't know. What that bitch was trying to do to him; what the mealymouthed bastards at the National Committee would do for him before the primaries began; how big a margin he'd have in the Senate election in just over a year.

He was sure he would win, as he'd won before, but he had to have a huge margin. And he'd started to move events in Tamarack, but he didn't know if what he'd done was enough.

The rest seemed out of his control. In the past two months, for the first time since Ethan had kicked him out, Vince had felt, more than once, the excruciating agony of helplessness, the pricking of nerve ends forced to stay still, the tension of muscles not allowed to spring.

"Fuck it," he muttered in the silence of his study. He fingered a round glass paperweight, a gift from the Ladies Club of Pueblo. Its smoothness annoyed him; it felt slimy and untrustworthy. "Fuck it," he burst out, and hurled the paperweight across the room. It struck the paneled wall, gouging it, bounced twice on the carpet, and rolled to a stop beneath a table holding half a dozen pictures of Dora. Josh, Vince thought. That bitch was going out with him. Not only staying with Gail and Leo, but going out with Josh. What the fuck was she up to? He'd warned her . . .

Vince looked at the scar in the walnut panel across the room and he knew he would have to take control and get people doing what he wanted, and he had to do it damned soon.

Anne walked slowly along the gallery of Josh's apartment, looking at his paintings. They surprised her with their variety and brilliance, from French impressionists to minimalists. "Definitely not all sunshine and shadow," she murmured.

Josh, bringing two glasses of wine, heard her and smiled. "Not all of anything, as a matter of fact. It's not what you'd call a focused collection. My grandparents bought the impressionists when they were in Europe; my parents collected Picasso and Braque and the Eskimo sculptures in the living room; and I bought the rest. What you're looking at is a history of the Durants, especially my grandparents, as they wended their way around the world. They hadn't the faintest idea that they were buying great art; they bought because something struck their fancy, or because they liked the artists when they met them. And I think they felt sorry for them because they thought they'd never amass money or possessions or any kind of power."

"Did they think possessions were more important than art?" Anne asked.

"No, but they thought money was essential, possessions were pleasant, and power useful. They didn't see anything romantic about a starving artist. They were intensely practical Midwestern steel manufacturers who became modest patrons of the arts because they loved art and believed it was essential to a full life, and because they really thought it was their responsibility, since they had a great deal of money, to help artists survive and even prosper."

They reached the end of the gallery and walked into the living room where the fireplace mantel and a wall of shelves were filled with Eskimo sculptures: tiny birds, large dancing bears, family groups, and walruses with fishermen riding their arched backs like cowboys on bucking broncos. "It's the most spectacular collection I've ever seen," Anne said.

Josh nodded. "I've loved every one of those pieces since I was a kid. It all goes to a museum when I die. I don't want the collection broken up."

He won't leave them to his children, Anne thought. Or he intends not to have children. That was probably it; he lived like a man who was settled and entire unto himself. And Dora had said he hated kids. She wandered around the living room, looking at the dozens of objects he had collected—Egyptian scarabs, Greek vases, French cloisonné, carved German nutcrackers, Russian lacquered boxes, Chinese jade sculptures, African masks, feather necklaces from New Guinea. The apartment was enormous—two apartments he had made into one, Josh had told her—its high-ceilinged, spacious rooms furnished—overfurnished, Anne thought—with antiques, overstuffed couches and armchairs covered in slightly faded woven fabrics, and Oriental rugs with their designs softened by a hundred years of footsteps. Mixed in with the objects he had collected were photographs that ranged from a fisherman on a trawler to men and women whom Anne recognized from newspapers and magazines. His friends were as varied as his art, she thought.

"Do you want to see the rest of it?" Josh asked. She nodded, and they walked back through the gallery to the other end of the apartment. In his bedroom, on a round, leather-topped table, was a group of photographs in silver frames. Anne bent closer to look at them. They were all of the same couple, a man who might have been Josh and a tall, beautiful woman with blond curls cut short, like a cap. "Your parents," she said. "I wondered where they were."

"They belong in the private part of the house." Josh stood with her, gazing at them. "They would have liked you, Anne; they admired people who shape their own lives instead of being shaped by others."

She gave him a quick look. "You don't know that that's true of me."

"I think it is. I think something happened to you, some time ago, that was devastating. Something like the death of my parents was to me, though I wouldn't presume to compare pain; we each suffer in our own way. But you didn't let it do permanent damage to you; you shaped your life and became a remarkable woman. I admire that. And my parents would have liked you a lot. Let's go back to my study; my housekeeper made a pâté, and we have to do it justice or she'll be disappointed. And then we can go to dinner."

Without waiting, he led the way, commenting on some of the paintings they passed, telling an anecdote about an Albers drawing he had bought in an estate sale, relating a story about a Miró sketch in his study. It was as if, Anne thought, he was worried that he had said too much, gotten too close, and now was trying to erase it with a light, amusing monologue to distract her if she was upset.

But she was not upset. It was puzzling, but instead of shrinking from him, she found herself interested in what else he might have to say about her. No, not really, she thought swiftly. She didn't want analysis from him; she simply wanted pleasant companionship. And it seemed to be all Josh wanted, too. That was why she was having such a good time.

"I made a reservation at Les Plumes for eight-thirty," Josh said as they sat on a long, deep couch in his study, "but we can go later if you like." The room was small and casual, with dark green walls, polished walnut bookshelves to the ceiling, beige corduroy couches and chairs, and a green marble fireplace. And there were books everywhere, crammed into shelves, stacked in precarious piles on the floor and the windowsills, strewn on tables with magazines and professional journals. In a corner, behind more books, was a television set; nearby were record and compact-disc players. Josh had turned on some music when they came in, and the intricate ripples of a Scarlatti sonata filled the room. Anne knew that this room was where he spent most of his time.

"I'd like to hear about your practice," he said. He handed her a plate. "Do most divorce cases seem alike after a while?"

"No more than your Egyptian pharaohs do, I imagine," Anne said. She spread pâté on a piece of bread and bit into it. "Oh, this is good."

"One of Mrs. Umiko's many specialties. Wild mushrooms, about four kinds, I think. She knows every cuisine in the world; she and her husband worked in the Belgian embassy in France, and the American embassy in Switzerland, and then came here and registered with the agency I'd called just that morning. It turned out to be a perfect match."

"That's not the housekeeper Dora hired."

"No. She wasn't happy and neither were we."

"She left while Dora was here?"

"She left six months after Dora hired her. Then I hired the Umikos."

Anne gazed at him, frowning. "Why didn't you say that in my office?"

"Dora prided herself on her ability to hire people. I didn't think it was important enough to throw that up to her. It wouldn't have changed anything."

"No, it wouldn't." Still, she was amazed at his restraint. He might have used that information to weaken Dora's picture of their home life. She did not wonder if it had been Josh or Fritz Miller who had made that decision; she was sure it had been Josh. She wondered what else he had kept back. How astonishingly little Dora had known him, she thought. There was much to admire in this man.

"Well, then," he said, "tell me about your practice."

Anne described some of the cases that interested her the most, using no names but giving brief, vivid portraits that brought the people to life for Josh. He chuckled as she told him about a television actor who sued for divorce because his wife removed all fifty-four mirrors from their house and later told him he had to choose between her and his mirrors. He chose his mirrors.

"Don't you begin to wonder about people's priorities?" Josh asked. "It must be hard to deal with them every day and not pass judgment."

"Lawyers pass judgment all the time," Anne said. "I think we're the harshest critics of all because we can't walk away from all the foolishness and lying as if it were a bad play; we have to sit through every last word. We just don't broadcast our feelings; if we're really good, nobody knows what they are. You're the lucky one; your clients have all been dead for four thousand years."

"Not entirely lucky. Lots of times even a lie would be cause for rejoicing. The silence of the tomb is a definite obstacle to research."

They smiled together and were silent. Josh refilled their glasses and they sat back in the deep comfort of the couch. Beyond the windows, the lights of Santa Monica were like a mosaic against the blackness, wavering slightly in the mid-September heat; within the room, Anne felt cool air curl softly around her ankles. She sighed. On impulse, she took off her shoes and tucked her legs under her, nestling into her corner of the couch. "I'm sorry we have to go out," she murmured.

"We don't," Josh said immediately. "We could find something here. Mrs. Umiko is off tonight, but we could raid the freezer." He looked at Anne's red silk dress and paisley silk jacket, her ruby and gold earrings, her necklace of Florentine gold links. "I should be offering you elegance and French cuisine. That's what I planned for tonight. If you choose soup and salad, the best I can do is candlelight."

"I'll take candlelight as long as it's in this room," Anne said.

Josh reached to the floor and brought a telephone to the arm of the couch. "I'll call the restaurant. I like your taste; I told you that before, didn't I? This is where I eat when I'm alone. I prefer it to all the restaurants put together."

"I'm a pretty good cook," Anne said, "if there's something I can do . . ."

"Not in red silk. Maybe we'll do that sometime, but not tonight. Unless you object."

Anne shook her head. "It sounds fine."

"It sounds better than that." He was dialing the restaurant when the Scarlatti sonata ended. "Would you pick out something else?" he asked casually. In her stockinged feet, Anne went to the cabinet and opened the drawers. Hundreds of discs were arranged alphabetically. She chose Beethoven and Mozart trios, and put them on as Josh hung up the telephone. "Thanks," he said. And only then, as Anne curled up again on the couch, and the notes of the first trio wove through the room, did it strike her how completely different this was from the evening she had anticipated, or a normal evening at home, when she played her own music in her quiet apartment, and cooked a single dinner in her quiet kitchen, and read or watched a movie in her quiet study. So different, she thought; but how easily and naturally she had slipped into it, and how uncomplicated it seemed.

I'll have to think about that, she reflected. But later; not now. Right now, I really don't want to take the time.

Chapter 13

*K*eith rushed to catch up with Leo, stumbling over an office wastebasket and jabbing his thigh into a corner of a desk. "Leo!" he yelled as he ran out to the alley. "Hey! Leo!"

Leo stuck his head out of his car. "Something wrong?"

"I want to go, too. Okay?" Quickly, he circled in front of the car and got in on the passenger side. "I want to know what's going on. It's okay, isn't it, Leo? Half the time I feel like everybody around here knows things but me."

Leo shrugged as he drove off. "You can come, but it has nothing to do with you. You just take care of Tamarack Mountain, Keith; that's all you have to worry about."

"Well, yeah, but I worry about the company, too, you know. I mean, I own five percent of it that Grandpa gave me, so that makes me an interested party, right? Like if Uncle Charles ever sells it, he needs my, you know, vote. And the company's in deep shit with the water—I know that much —so I figured if they found out what happened, I oughta know about it."

Leo shot him a quick glance. His sandy hair was neatly combed, his pale, sparse beard neatly trimmed, his plaid shirt neatly pressed. A perfectly presentable, eager youth. It wasn't his fault that Leo couldn't like him. In silence, he drove rapidly through the town. The streets were quiet, now that Labor Day weekend had ended the summer season, and the people who lived in Tamarack strolled on empty sidewalks and pulled into parking places as if rediscovering

324

their town. The few tourists still there drove into the mountains for the changing colors, browsed in shops for after-season bargains, and sat in outdoor cafés in the warm, slanting sunlight of fall, letting the somnolence of the town slow them down, as it did everyone in the lull before the snows came and the bustle of thousands of skiers. It was a time of year Leo especially loved, when he could imagine the town to be once again an isolated mountain hamlet where everyone knew everyone else and they all worked together to be snug and safe in even the harshest seasons.

But that wasn't what was happening this September. In that beautiful, golden fall, people were fearful, and many were working themselves into a panic. Parents were taking children to their doctors for examinations, meeting in vociferous groups outside City Hall when they went to get water, and writing letters to the *Tamarack Times* demanding to know what the city was doing to protect them. "First the EPA tells us the whole east end isn't safe," the letters fulminated, "and now neither is our water. Who's in charge around here?"

"Who's in charge?" It was getting louder. It had started as an anxious question the night at City Hall; now, less than a week later, it was becoming a rumble through the town, building to a roar of worried, angry questions. WHAT'S GOING ON AROUND HERE? WHOSE FAULT IS IT?

And it was easy to find a villain. Leo knew that when bad things happened in a company town, the company always got blamed.

He turned onto the highway that ascended gradually toward the east and Wolf Creek Pass. "So what'd they find?" Keith asked.

"I don't know. Bill called on the car phone and told me he thought they had something to show me."

"Where?" Keith asked.

"Below the Mother Lode."

"The old mine? That's nowhere near anything."

"The drainage ditch," Leo said. He turned onto a narrow gravel road that zigzagged up a long slope, past old mines almost hidden in brush and gnarled scrub oak trees. A few minutes later they came to a pickup truck, parked in front of them. Beyond it, the road was blocked by boulders and torn-up bushes.

"Bill," Leo called, and a tall man a little distance away turned and came to him.

"Glad to see you," Bill Clausan said as they shook hands. They walked up the slope and joined two other men. "We're sure this is it, Leo. It was a slide, and a pretty good one. Cut through here, crossed the road, and slammed into the drainage ditch."

"Any idea what caused it?" Leo asked.

"Not offhand. We've been having some earthquake activity the last few weeks, minor stuff, but maybe enough to set this off. This could've been an accident waiting to happen."

"Keith, go up above and see if you can find where it started," Leo said. "Maybe you can figure out how it happened. We'll go on down, to the ditch."

He and Bill made their way down the slope, following the swath cut by earth and rocks as they picked up speed. When they reached the drainage ditch forty feet below, they stood looking at the blocks of shattered concrete. Ethan had built the ditch fifteen years earlier, as part of an expansion of the old water system he had built when he first came to Tamarack. He had built a small reservoir and dam three miles upstream of town, with a pipeline to the water treatment and pumping plant in town. The reservoir was above all the old mines in the area except the Mother Lode, the largest, that once had yielded millions of dollars worth of silver ore. When the miners dug, following the silver veins, they dumped huge volumes of rock just below the opening to each tunnel, where they formed bleak mounds of tailings: black rock and gravel spreading over the green slopes. They weren't beautiful, but the miners were thinking of silver, not beauty. What they didn't know was that they weren't safe, either. They were filled with toxic minerals.

When the miners abandoned Tamarack, water from underground springs flooded the miles of tunnels and flowed out through the tailings, picking up high concentrations of lead, selenium, arsenic, and other minerals before draining into Tamarack Creek. If it was left alone, the contaminated water would flow into the reservoir and poison the entire water supply. So Ethan had a concrete drainage ditch built to divert the polluted water to a point below the reservoir.

"It did just fine for fifteen years," Leo murmured, kneeling and running his fingers over the broken concrete. His hand was wet from water spreading through the break, heading downhill, to Tamarack Creek and the reservoir. He stood, wiping his hand on his pants. "We'll get this repaired right away. But the reservoir . . ." He and Bill exchanged a long look.

"We'll have to drain it," Bill said. "Fifty million gallons of water. And probably dig out some of the mud on the bottom, a few inches down or more; I guess that's up to the testing lab in Denver. Jesus, eight acres of mud to dig up. I can't see it taking less than a month. Maybe two or three."

Keith came scrambling down the slope, and heard the last words. "Wow!" he exclaimed. "That'll cost a pile. And we gotta keep trucking water in all that time. Wow. What a mess."

You think the gods are mad at the Chathams and Calders? Leo had said that in jest, when they'd first discovered the water problem. What the hell was going on around here? There were too many damned crises all at once. It didn't make sense that . . . *Sorry, I'm sounding paranoid.*

There aren't that many crises, he told himself. After all, Tamarack's been a resort town for forty years, always growing, and we've had two major problems in all that time: the EPA got interested in us and we had a rock slide, probably because of a minor earthquake. Hardly a reason to think the gods are angry.

"And the newspapers," said Keith, his words coming faster. "We've gotta keep them from hearing about this, right? I mean, we don't want tourists to know there's like poison all over the place . . ." He saw Leo's face and his voice trailed away.

"Did you find where it started?" Leo asked.

"Straight up, at the bottom of the cliffs. It must've been an earthquake, there's nothing else going on up there. I mean, if we'd had a blizzard, you know, or lots of rain, I guess that could've done it, but it's September and nothing's been happening."

Leo kicked a rock and sent it tumbling down the slope. "Let's get the damned thing repaired," he said to Bill. "Get a crew up here today; at least we'll stop any more of this stuff from going in. And I'll get some pumps from Durango for the reservoir. It'll be easier if we can get it done before it snows."

They knew they could not; there was always snow by the end of September. But it would melt in the warm days, and it would keep falling and melting until the warm days ended or the snows got too heavy to melt off in one day. Either way, they had to worry about time. *Maybe we ought to sacrifice a goat. Or find some of the old Ute Indians who lived here and ask them to do one of their dances for us.*

Oh, for Christ's sake, he thought impatiently; what the hell's the matter with me? It was an ordinary rock slide. Don't make a Greek tragedy out of it. He walked up the slope, taking long steps amid the rubble of the slide. One good thing about it, probably the only good thing, was that Keith was so interested. Ordinarily he didn't seem to give a damn about the company, and Leo had doubts every day that he'd last long with them. Now all of a sudden he seemed intensely interested, even excited. Maybe he'd work out after all. "Come on, Keith," Leo said, putting a friendly hand on his shoulder, "let's get back to work."

"Mr. Durant is here," Anne's doorman said on the telephone. Anne started to say she would be downstairs right away, then changed her mind. "Ask him to come up," she said. She never asked anyone to her apartment; even when Josh had brought her home a week ago, after dinner in his apartment, she had not invited him in. But now, she wanted him to see it.

"Good morning," he said as she let him in. "I'm early; if you're not ready, I'll wait."

"I just need a few minutes. There's coffee in the kitchen." Left alone, Josh found the coffeepot and a mug. Sipping coffee, he leaned against the kitchen door and gazed at the long living room, with the dining table at one end, flooded with sunlight from a wall of glass. Everything was white. There were a few startling touches of color, but the overwhelming impression was of whiteness: white wood floors painted to a high gloss, white couches and armchairs, white walls, white steel lamps, and steel tables with glass tops. After a minute, Josh was able to focus on the colors: the dining table was dark green granite; on it was a maquette of a Wolock Werner acrylic sculpture. The rugs within the two groups of furniture were Orientals in shades of rose, blue, and green. On the walls were abstract paintings, vivid swirls of color that Josh recognized, by Zorach, Putterman, O'Keeffe, Bartlett, and Rothenberg; all women, he noted.

Anne set her suitcase beside the front door. She wore narrow black jeans and a white silk shirt. "I'm about ready," she said, and began letting down the translucent, accordion-pleated shades at the living room windows. "Do you want to see the rest of it before we leave?"

"Yes," Josh said. He followed her past the all-white kitchen into a short hallway, and looked into what was clearly Anne's bedroom: an exquisite room with a pale green needlepoint carpet, a white quilt stitched with white flowers, and celadon-and-white-striped draperies and upholstered furniture. It was a cool, serene room. Josh paused in the doorway, trying to imagine a passionate moment or thought or dream occurring within it. He could not.

"This is the library," Anne said, and he followed her into the next room. White bookshelves covered all the walls, filled with neatly organized books; the furniture was upholstered in dark linen, and a modern glass and steel desk had a clean surface. Nothing was out of place.

There was no guest room. And there were no framed photographs anywhere in the apartment.

"It's stunning," Josh said as they walked back to the living room. "Brilliant and dramatic. Like a painting."

"Thank you," Anne said. "That was the way I thought of it from the beginning."

A painting, a stage set, an illustration, he thought. No

books out of place, no crooked pictures, no newspapers cluttering tables or the floor. No clutter. Superbly decorated and coldly perfect; high class, high tech, and not a loose emotion floating around anywhere. The whole apartment was as numb as if it had been anesthetized. He watched Anne as she looked around her living room and he saw her face change, become thoughtful and then slightly puzzled. He wondered if she were seeing her home through his eyes, and comparing it to his. His apartment seemed to him, as he pictured it, overfurnished, disordered, even a little lush. He wondered what she thought of it, compared to her white world, and what she thought of him. It came to him that he didn't have the faintest idea what she thought of him.

"It reminds me of Diebenkorn," he said, gesturing toward the living room. "All those clean lines of demarcation. But you wouldn't pattern your home after him, would you, since he's not a woman."

Anne looked at him with surprise. "You recognized these artists? Most people wouldn't have heard of many of them; they aren't well known at all."

He grinned. "I could try to fake it, but the truth is, I had help. I have a friend who's interested in women artists, and she gives me books to read. She's a board member at the LA County Museum and also the Ancient. I think she's hoping to find that some of the great Egyptian tombs were designed by women, but so far we haven't any evidence of it."

Anne nodded vaguely, looking around the apartment. "I'm done here; we'd better go. Isn't the plane at ten?"

"It is." He carried her suitcase and waited while she pulled on a blue leather blazer and locked the door. "Why do you collect only women artists?" he asked as they rode down the elevator.

"I'm interested in them. Like your friend at the museum. And I like their work; there's a kind of fierceness about a lot of it, and hidden meanings, layers of meanings that I like to figure out. And there are plenty of people to collect paintings by men."

"You don't find fierceness in male artists?"

"Not the same kind."

"What's the difference between them?"

"Power," she said. "Men think they have it, whether they do or not. Women mostly know they don't."

His eyebrows rose. "And you like the fierceness that comes from being powerless?"

"No. I like the fierceness that comes from the struggle to get out from under."

"We all know what that's like," Josh said. "You can't believe that all men have power, or even know how to get it."

"They have more than women, and they assume it as a right. Women see it as a glittering prize at the end of a long struggle." She gazed out the window at the Saturday traffic on the road to the airport. "For example, where are your Egyptian queens in tomb paintings? In the pictures I've seen they're always behind the pharaoh and about the height of his hand. And if they're sitting with him, they come up to his knee. Maybe not even that high."

He glanced at her. "Isis had enormous power."

"Not fair. She was a goddess. Gods and goddesses play under different rules."

He grinned. "They certainly do. Do you know the story about Isis' search for her husband, Osiris, after he was killed and cut into fourteen pieces and spread around the country-side?" Anne shook her head. "Well, she found the pieces and put them together and brought him back to life. It's the Egyptian version of resurrection. But I call it a story for our time. Without women, men wouldn't be whole."

Anne's eyebrows rose. "That's too good to be true."

He stopped at a red light and turned to her. "Do you know, I just thought of it now, for the first time. It's not bad. I may do an article on it."

"But you don't really believe it."

"Yes, I do," he said quietly. The light turned green and he drove on.

They were silent. "Have you talked to Leo about what's happening at Tamarack?" Josh asked.

"No, just Gail. Have you?"

"I called him yesterday. I'd seen the article in the *LA*

Times about the water supply in Tamarack, and a mention of the reservoir being polluted, and I wondered what was going on. Did Gail tell you?"

"She said they're draining the reservoir and everything's under control, but she sounded worried."

"There's a lot going on." He pulled into a parking spot at the airport. "Leo said they're doing some routine maintenance on the gondola this afternoon and offered me a tour. Would you like to come?"

"I can't; I promised Gail I'd go mushrooming up Hayes Creek with her and the kids."

He took their suitcases from the back of the car. "Did Gail tell you she's invited me to dinner tomorrow night?"

"Yes. I think she wants to help us along."

Josh's eyebrows rose. "Does she think we need help?"

Anne smiled faintly. "I'm sure she thinks I do."

There was a sadness to her smile that touched Josh, and he reached out to put his hand on hers. But he did not; he turned instead to lock the car, remembering that she had shown him more than once that she did not want to be touched. Even in his apartment, she had not moved beyond cool friendliness the entire evening, and had said good-night to him in the lobby of her apartment building with the same pleasant, public voice and face she had had since the night at Timothy's, when they had begun to shift from adversaries to . . . to what? Josh thought. What were they now? Acquaintances. Casual companions. Maybe on their way to being friends.

Did he want more? Oh, what the hell, he told himself; of course he wanted more. He wanted, at least, to find out what she was really like. He wanted to get past the haunting numbness of her facade to the emotions that had to be within her. He wanted to find out if they could share a moment of joy.

"Aren't we going?" Anne asked. She was looking at him quizzically as he stood by the car, his keys in his hand, gazing into the distance.

"Yes," he said briskly. They walked through the crowds to the gate and stood in line to check in. Josh glanced at Anne, beside him, absently reading over her ticket. She was so close to him he could smell the fragrance of her hair; and she was farther from him than any woman he had ever known.

She took a casual step to the side, putting space between them. Skittish, Josh thought; as if she kept a moat between herself and the world. But also very smart, very successful, good to talk to, lovely, clever, and intriguing, with an infinite sadness deep within her. You're damned right I want more than casual companionship, he said to himself. Plenty of time with her, and a hell of a lot more.

William was waiting on the deck when Anne arrived. He grabbed her hands with both of his and gripped them tightly before pulling her to him and kissing her loudly on the cheek. "You didn't come to Lake Forest so I came here," he said. "Though that's stating the obvious, isn't it? Marian says I do that all the time. She's probably right. The obvious explains so much, you know."

"I'm glad to see you," said Anne. She pulled up a chair beside his. They were alone in the house. "Are you coming mushrooming with us this afternoon?"

He shook his head. He was short, like Vince, and gently rounded, with a paunch that strained against the buttons of his vest. His face was jovial, with high color and a neat mustache that quivered when he sent words and phrases blasting with rapid fervor from his small, precise mouth. "I can't go this afternoon; I have some letters to write. About this reservoir business. Terrible thing. But what's worse is, the papers—the television—are making Tamarack out to be a dangerous place. Leo says he heard there was an article in Los Angeles; did you see it? Of course you did; you live there. Talking about tourists canceling ski vacations that are months away because they're worried about the water! Damndest thing; how'd they find out so fast? They had it in New York and Chicago before the *Tamarack Times* did! Inexcusable, these blabbing mouths. If this was a war, it could make us lose. But I'll take care of it; a few letters to the editor, explaining how simple the problem is and how fast we'll have it solved . . . that'll stop the cancellations. You're looking very pretty, Anne; I missed you, you know. I hope you know it."

Anne nodded. "I missed you, too. I kept wondering if you were happy."

He looked at her through narrowed eyes. "Why?"

"I used to think there were times when you weren't."

"Well, there were. Still are. But I don't talk about it. I never talked to you about it, did I?"

"No. You just looked unhappy sometimes."

"Did I. You were an observant little girl, weren't you? Well, those were probably the times I thought I should have gotten married. Everybody else had, you know, and there I was, still helling around like a soldier on leave. I never thought I'd be the perpetual ladies' man; I always thought Vince would be the one . . . well, where was I? Marriage. I never did, and I started feeling left out of everything—left out of *life*, more or less—but I didn't know anybody I wanted to live with for the rest of my life. Maybe I ought to find somebody now, now that I'm over sixty, and I don't have as many years left to repent a mistake or make another one, which is even worse. What do you think?"

Anne was smiling. "I think if you're ready to get married, you'll meet someone you'd like to marry."

"Is that so?" He sat back. "I hear you never got married either. Was that because you weren't ready?"

"Probably. Tell me what else you've been doing."

He waved a finger at her. "That's exactly what they told me you'd do. You don't talk about yourself, they said: you slither out of it by asking people to talk about themselves, and of course they always do because they're just waiting for somebody to ask them. I don't approve, young woman; when two people converse they answer each other's questions. Now I want to know something about you. Are you happy?"

"Yes," Anne said.

"You really are? You haven't just talked yourself into it?"

"If I have, and I feel happy, isn't that just as good?"

He glowered at her. "That sounds like a clever lawyer's

question. Are you content? There's a word! How about that? Are you content?"

Anne hesitated. "I don't know."

"Why not?"

"I don't know. I don't think about it; I'm too busy. And what good does it do? If I'm not content, worrying about it won't help, and if I am, I don't need to worry about it. People don't ask me these questions. Nobody from the family has."

"Why haven't they? They all wonder the same things I do."

"I think they're afraid to ask me too much, because then we might find ourselves talking about Vince."

There was a silence. "Do you want to talk about him?" William asked.

"I won't talk about him."

He nodded. After a minute, he said, "You know, Anne, I always thought we had a happy family. As families go, of course; everybody has troubles, but I thought we did better than most. We saw each other a lot, and there was always plenty to talk about, and we didn't have any feuds going. To me that's a good family. Marian and Nina felt the same way. Then you made us think about unpleasant things and we just weren't good at that. It wasn't that we didn't believe you, you know; I for one knew you weren't a liar. It was just that we couldn't face what you were saying. It was like you were forcing it down our throats and we were gagging, and all we could think about was that we were uncomfortable, and in an odd way we blamed that on you. I'm sorry to bring this up now, in this lovely place, but I've been wanting to tell you for a long time that I was sure you weren't lying."

"Thank you," Anne said. Her voice shook. In the warm sun, she was dizzy and shivering; he had brought it all to life again. She stared fixedly at the distant mountains, concentrating on each peak, willing the dizziness to pass. *Put your shoulders back and breathe deeply. Fill your lungs.* She sat straight, taking long breaths.

"So now you're back with us, and we're all delighted."

William was squinting at her in the sunlight, trying to make out her expression. "Of course that's stating the obvious again, isn't it? What I really want to say is, we're not so foolish as to think we can wipe out the past, but we do ask you to try to understand us and forgive us. We behaved badly, and we've regretted it all these years, and if we could have found you, we would have told you so a lot earlier. And now it's time to rebuild, and we should all work together to do it." He paused. "Isn't that why you're here?"

Anne nodded. "How sensible you are, Uncle William."

"Oh, don't 'uncle' me, my dear; nobody does that anymore. As for being sensible, well, you know, when I admitted to myself one day that my father and Vince were the smart ones in the family, and I was just ordinary—nice, mind you, and well meaning, good-hearted, friendly to people and dogs, that sort of thing, but still, just ordinary—I decided to look at everything else the same way, square in the eye, calling it the way I saw it. No dancing around to prettify things. I'll never amount to much, Anne; that's probably why I spend most of my time writing letters. I keep trying to have an effect on the world, make a difference, you know. Mostly I know that the world doesn't give a damn what I think; it's going to go its own way whether I like it or not. Wars, elections, higher taxes, lower social security, bigger toxic dumps, smaller national parks —they're all going to happen like steamrollers, and what I think won't slow any of them down or change them a damn bit. Unless . . . You see, that's the thing. Unless it does. How do I really know that it won't? Maybe one really fine letter to the newspapers or somebody in the State Department or the president's cabinet, or even the president himself, might make somebody say, 'Hey, wait a minute; here's something I never thought of before. We ought to change our policy because this William Chatham has a good idea.' Who knows that something like that might not happen someday?"

"Of course it could happen," Anne said. "I think it's wonderful that you care and that you do something about it. But that makes you very special; you shouldn't call yourself ordinary."

"Oh. Well, that's very kind of you, Anne; that's pleasant to hear. But it's not a profession, you know, or anything that takes brilliance or learning. It's just a nice little hobby. That's what Vince calls it."

"He's wrong," Anne said. "You're making a place for yourself in the world, trying to be part of it and have some influence on it. That takes a lot of thought and time and caring. I'm very proud of you."

"My goodness." William was blushing. "My goodness, what beautiful words. Thank you, Anne. Dear Anne. You've become such a lovely woman, with lovely thoughts. You should get married, though, and have a family. It's not natural, you know, just to be a lawyer."

Anne smiled. "I'll have to give that some thought."

"Now I've heard that you went hiking last week with this young man who used to live with Dora. I liked him, you know, though I didn't see much of him; he didn't spend much time with us, which made me wonder about him. But I liked him, I did indeed, and I understand he's much admired in his field. Tombs and museums and such. Have you seen him again?"

Looking past William, Anne saw Gail and Leo driving up, with the children in the backseat. One of the things about not having a family, she thought, is that no one asks any questions. "We had dinner one night in Los Angeles," she replied.

"And?" William asked.

"And we had a pleasant time."

"Pleasant. What a word; it can mean anything. What's he want with you, do you know? After all, you cost him a heap of money. So what's he doing, squiring you around?"

"I don't know," Anne said.

"But you must've asked yourself that."

She smiled. "Mostly I asked myself what *I* was doing."

"And what did you decide?"

"He's a good companion, good to talk to, good to listen to. He's interesting and I can relax with him."

"Sounds pretty bland to me. Is he bland?"

"I doubt it."

"So what's he after?"

"Friendship, I imagine. Isn't that enough?"

"With a woman who beat the pants off him in a lawsuit? Now I like him, I told you I liked him, but that does sound peculiar to me."

"He'll be here for dinner tomorrow night. Why don't you ask him?"

"He'll be here? How interesting. Has he ever been married?"

"No."

"Well, that's unfortunate. I have a deep fear that I'll make someone a poor husband because I've had no practice at it."

"You have a deep fear of marriage," Anne said. "All the other fears will disappear when that one does. Do you know what it is that frightens you?"

"Well. Well, of course you'd figure that out; after all, your specialty is marriage, isn't it, or at least the endings of them. Is that why you've never married? You hear too many war stories?"

"No. I don't think marriage is a war."

"Oh, but it is, my dear. Far too often."

Anne looked at him curiously. "Where have you seen that?"

"Everywhere. Nina and her various husbands, Vince and Rita, Marian and Fred, and too many of my friends. And your parents had their difficult times, my dear, and even *my* parents, though they were forgotten, of course, as they should have been, in the tragedy of death."

"Difficult times don't make a war," Anne said. How odd for her to be defending marriage, she thought.

"No, but marriage is a minefield, full of unpredictable emotions and violent passions. I prefer being calm. There's too much turmoil in the world; I can't bring myself to deliberately add more of it to my own life."

"But didn't you just tell me that you thought I should be married?"

"Ah, but for you it's different. You're—"

"Hi!" shouted Ned, rocketing across the deck and flinging

his arms around Anne. Robin was behind him and she nuzzled up to Anne's other side. "We won, Aunt Anne! I caught a pass and made a forty-yard run for a touchdown and only one guy was even near me, but I'm a lot faster than him. You know who it was? Phil Morton, the jerk weed who said it was my dad's fault the water's poisoned. I knocked him down for that yesterday. And today, boy, you should've seen his face when he couldn't catch me! He's an asshole anyway."

"Should you be using that word, Ned?" William asked mildly.

Anne looked up as Gail and Leo came onto the deck. "Is that what they're saying in town?"

"Some of them," Leo said.

"A lot of them," said Gail. "I wish I knew what to do about it; we can't exactly put an ad in the paper saying we had nothing to do with it."

"*I* know," Ned declared. "You tell 'em it's sabotage and we're fixing it. That's what I figure, anyway. It's like Indiana Jones. Somebody wanted something so they blew up the mountain and started the avalanche."

"Hold on," Leo said. "That's a serious accusation, Ned; I don't want you going around town with it. We have enough problems without making far-out charges that could set people against each other, wondering who did what. I'm sorry you had to fight Phil, but—"

"I'm not sorry! It was great! He apologized, too. Sort of."

"We have to talk about what we say to people," Gail said. "All we should be talking about are the things the company is saying in its ads and press releases, that nobody's in danger and we're taking care of everything and the ski season will be great. Everybody's scared, you know; all the shopkeepers and lodge owners wait all year for two months in the summer and four and a half in the winter, and now they're beginning to think nobody will come."

Leo put his arm around her. "None of that is going to happen. We'll have a rough fall, but the ski season will be fine. We'll just have to wait it out. We can do it, you know.

After all, there are four of us"—he glanced at Anne and William—"six of us, hell, a whole family, and there's nothing in the world that people can't do if they've got a family and they love each other. Right?"

"Right," Gail said, her voice low. "It's just that I hate it when things aren't calm."

Anne and William exchanged a look. "It's in the genes," William said. "None of the Chathams do well in a crisis."

"We do fine," Leo said firmly. "Hey, don't we get any lunch around here? We'd better fortify ourselves or we won't have the strength to go scrounging under trees for mushrooms."

"Let's get it ready," Gail said, "and let Anne and William go on talking."

"Well," William said when he and Anne were alone again. "That was very nice. I'm sure they have their problems, like any married couple, but they're young and flexible and they're learning to manage them. That's what I was saying about you, my dear. You're young and intelligent; you could find someone and make a good marriage, as good as could be expected—"

"Oh, how encouraging," said Anne, gently mocking.

"—but still probably better than being alone and feeling a big chunk of life has passed you by. I'm sorry I've been so afraid of it, but that's how it is, and I probably never will, now; I'll just go on giving advice. It's good advice; you should think seriously about it. What's his name again— this fella who's coming to dinner tomorrow night?"

"Josh Durant," Anne said.

"Well, you never know." William clasped his hands across his paunch and gazed contentedly at the view. "I've never been here, did you know that? It took you to get me here. I like it more than I thought I would. You say his name as if you like him."

"I do," Anne said after a moment. She wondered what exactly William had heard in her voice. She wondered about it all day, even while she was learning to identify the best of the edible mushrooms, and all the next day while she worked on papers she had brought from her office, and while she and Gail prepared dinner with the chanterelles they had picked and the trout Leo had caught that afternoon, and while she was changing for dinner into a pair of wool slacks and a cotton turtleneck sweater. Then, combing her hair in her bedroom, she found herself looking forward to the evening, to seeing Josh with the family. She stood still, with the comb in her hand, gazing at herself in the mirror. This was not normal for her. She had friends in Los Angeles, both women and men, but she didn't think her voice changed when she talked about them, and she couldn't ever remember thinking it would be nice to see them within a family.

What's he want with you? You cost him a heap of money. I like him, but that does sound peculiar to me.

"Damn it," Anne muttered. She finished combing her hair and pinned it back with silver clips, and slipped on a silver and turquoise bracelet. I don't want to analyze anything; I just want to have a nice time.

But I won't talk much tonight; this will be a time for listening. Whatever William heard in my voice, it would be better if no one else heard it, at least until I know what it was.

It turned out to be easy to be quiet because there were eight people for dinner. Not only was William there; at the last minute Gail had invited Keith.

"Boy, am I glad to meet you," he said, pumping Anne's hand. "You're a real celebrity, you know? Everybody's talking about you."

Anne's eyebrows rose. "Who?"

"Oh, like people in town. You know."

"No, I don't."

"Well, you know, people. Like Timothy. I was in there having a beer the other day and he said he, you know, saw you."

"He just happened to say that?"

"Well, not exactly. I said like I'm your cousin and did he know you and he said like sure. I've been really wanting to meet you, Anne; it's great that Gail, you know, invited me.

So how long are you here for? Are you gonna like move here? There's a lot of lawyers in town, but I guess there's always room for, you know, one more. Specially divorce; there's a lot of divorce around here; you could really clean up."

"I'm not moving here; I live in Los Angeles," Anne said. "If you'll excuse me, I'm going to help with dinner." She fled to the kitchen. "Is he the local CIA?" she asked Gail.

"Who?" Robin asked, coming in from setting the table.

"Keith," Anne said. "He doesn't talk; he just asks questions."

"I'm really surprised," said Gail. "He's never paid attention to us before, even when he's here for dinner, which isn't often. Maybe he's between girls; he really wanted to come tonight—in fact, he was the one who called, for a change."

Anne looked through the doorway and watched Keith talking with great animation to Josh, Leo, and William. "Does it strike you that there's something a little off-key about him?"

"Off-key? Like what?"

"It looks to me more like rampant curiosity than paying attention."

"Oh. Well, that could be true. Maybe he's realized he doesn't know too much about any of us and he's beginning to care about having a family. Poor Keith, he's not too smart but he does his job, and it means a lot to Marian to know he's settled down; he had a bad time with drugs a while back."

They worked in silence. "Robin can do this," Gail said. "You haven't had a chance to talk to Josh."

"We have the whole evening," Anne replied. "I'll talk to everybody."

"Even Keith?" Robin asked.

"Robin, you keep all this to yourself," said Gail. "He's our cousin and our guest."

"I still don't like him," Robin said.

"Why?" asked Anne.

Robin shrugged. "I don't know. He's always looking past

you. Like he's thinking about something else when you're talking to him."

"Poor Keith," Gail said again. "He tries so hard but nobody seems to like him. I hope he does have some girlfriends who make him feel good about himself." There was a pause. "You're very quiet tonight," she said to Anne. "Is everything all right?"

"Yes." She put her arm around Gail. "I'm glad to be here. Shall we start taking things to the table?"

"Sure."

Robin and Anne carried food to the dining room while Gail cooked the trout, and then everyone was seated around the large round table. Beneath a wrought-iron chandelier, candles flickered over a centerpiece of red grapes and golden aspen leaves, and the flames were reflected in the broad windows that framed the last streaks of umber and tangerine from a brilliant sunset. "Well, this is very good," said William, pulling his chair closer. "Very good indeed, all of us together like this. I drink to your health. I'm sorry Charles didn't come with me; we talked about it, but he's doing some kind of negotiating and couldn't get away. He would have enjoyed this gathering."

"What kind of negotiating?" Gail demanded.

"Well, you know it's about Tamarack, my dear; there's no sense pretending. Your father is terribly worried; well, we all are. We may not survive, you know. You tend to ignore that, Gail, but you have to face it: if we lose Chatham Development, we all suffer. Not as much as Charles, it's true, because he's the only one who put his personal fortune on the line, but just in general, you know, it would be a black day for all the Chathams to lose the company Ethan Chatham founded. You wouldn't want that to happen."

"Tamarack was Grandpa's company, too," Gail said stubbornly. "And he loved it more than Chatham Development, at least for the last years of his life. I feel bad about Daddy, but he shouldn't ask us to let him sell The Tamarack Company. It was Grandpa's dream and now it's ours, and up until the last couple of months it was doing wonderfully, and I want to get it back there again, not sell it to somebody who doesn't give a damn about it the way we do."

"Nobody's about to buy the company right now," Leo said. "Not with all its problems. Whatever Charles is negotiating, it isn't us."

"When do you think you'll get all this stuff fixed?" Keith asked.

"Early November, probably. In plenty of time for the ski season. We've got a lot of help; it's wonderful the way people are offering to do whatever we need. They're distributing water at City Hall, and delivering it to people who can't get there themselves, and almost fifty people have volunteered to help dig out the reservoir. I'll tell you, this is a terrific town; I'm proud to be a part of it."

"Yeah, but what about all the, you know, lawsuits?" Keith asked. "I mean, there's people around here who are like crazy. They got like a sick kid, they sue the company. How much is all this costing us, anyway?"

"We're insured against suits," Leo said shortly. "And it's only a few people who are suing; most of the town is behind us."

"Gail," said Anne, "dinner is wonderful."

"It is," Josh agreed. "Leo, next time you go fishing, I'd like to tag along. If you don't mind giving lessons to someone who's never held a fishing rod."

"I heard there were like fifteen lawsuits already," Keith said. "Are we insured for that much? I mean, you know, that could be like hundreds of millions of dollars. You're a lawyer, right?" he said to Anne. "It could be a hell of a lot of money, couldn't it? More than the insurance? Then what do we do? I mean, we could all be out of work like tomorrow!"

"Not tomorrow," Leo said dryly. "Or the day after. If you're worried about your job——"

"And what's it costing to fix the reservoir?" Keith's voice rose in excitement. "I mean, yeah, I'm worried, Leo. Aren't you? Really? I mean, shouldn't we all be like worried?"

"Keith, for heaven's sake," Gail said with a glance at Robin and Ned, who sat without eating, their mouths open, their heads swiveling from their father to Keith. "Everything is being taken care of. You'll be taken care of. Don't be so dramatic."

"How much is it costing?" Keith asked Leo. "The reservoir and, you know, trucking in the water and like the whole thing. And all those ads we have to, you know, buy. I mean, how much, not including the lawsuits?"

"A couple of million dollars," Leo said flatly. "And that's not good. Look, we're not crazy enough to think these problems aren't serious, but we'll get past them. If we don't have a good winter, we'll hang on until summer; and if summer isn't as good as we hope, next winter will be. I don't think we'll have to wait that long, but even if we do, we'll survive. There are a lot of places we can save money. We won't compromise on maintenance, but we can put off new projects, and we can cut staff, too, as a last resort. I can't predict how the lawsuits will go, but we can't assume we'll lose them; that's being defeated before we even start. Josh, what did you think of your tour yesterday? Did I manage to impress you?"

"You did," Josh said, ready to help Leo shift the conversation. "William, you should ask Leo to show you the gondola. It is impressive."

"What gondola?" William asked.

There was a stunned silence at the table. "It's been open for three years," Gail said. "But then, you haven't been here, have you?"

"Don't you *read* about us?" Robin demanded. "It's been in all the papers; it's the longest gondola in the country."

"I can tell you anything you want to know," Ned declared grandly. "There's these cars, they're round, and six people sit in them, and you go to the top of Tamarack Mountain, then you ski down and ride up again. It goes in the summer, too, but now it's September so it only goes on weekends. Come back at Thanksgiving; I'll take you up and show you around. You don't have to ski," he added kindly. "All kinds of people go up just wearing shoes."

"It's a fascinating system," Josh said. "The bull wheel

alone is bigger than this room, and the gears look like a paleontologist's dream: some newly discovered dinosaur's teeth."

"You really had a good time," Gail said. "You sound like Ned every time Leo takes him up there."

Josh chuckled. "Exactly how I felt. It's so massive, and at the same time it's so simple anyone can understand it. That's enough to bring out the kid in all of us."

Leo launched into a description of the building of the gondola, and then they talked of other things, and no one returned to the problems in Tamarack. As they all got up after dessert and coffee, Josh said to Anne, "You're very quiet tonight; is everything all right?"

"Yes. Thanks. Sometimes I just like to listen."

"I'm hiking tomorrow morning, just a short one; would you like to come?"

"I can't; I'm sorry. I brought a lot of work with me."

"I'm sorry, too; I'm leaving for Egypt and I'd hoped we could spend some time together first."

"Josh," Leo said, putting a hand on his shoulder. "Thanks for helping out. I don't know what's wrong with Keith; he been following me around ever since this mess began over Labor Day, and he can't seem to stop talking about it. Sorry, did I interrupt something?"

"Yes," Josh said with a smile, "but we're always glad to talk to you."

"I just wanted to say thanks. And to tell you how much it means to me, and to Gail, to have you around. Listen, all this talk about selling The Tamarack Company . . . do you know about that?"

Josh nodded. "Anne told me last week."

"Last week? You weren't here then."

"In Los Angeles."

"Oh." A slow grin appeared on Leo's face. "Well, good. So you know about it. I don't have to ask you to keep it to yourself."

"I don't spread stories, Leo."

"I know it. I'm just feeling nervous. We're trying to figure out what to do. Anne thinks we ought to find out how the rest of the family feels and line up support before Charles gets a serious offer. But maybe we'd be better off just sitting tight, not getting everybody upset and forming battle lines. Maybe Charles will scare up the money somewhere else; I really can't see anybody looking twice at us right now. We're in worse shape than I let on earlier."

"I agree with Anne," Josh said. "You ought to know where you stand. It doesn't have to be a feud; families can deal with anything if they care more about staying together than scoring points."

Leo shrugged. "The Chathams run away from trouble; they never want to face—oh, shit," he muttered with a sidelong glance at Anne. "I didn't mean that the way it sounded. Look, I interrupted you two; I'll go see what everybody's doing in the kitchen."

Josh contemplated Anne's stony face. "Do you want to tell me what that was all about?"

She turned to look at him. His eyes were steady and warm, and for the briefest of moments, she thought she could tell him about her running away, and why she had done it. But of course she could not; she had never told anyone; she never would. "A misunderstanding," she said. She paused, trying to find some other words. But she could not. "You said you were leaving? For Egypt?"

"On Monday. I hadn't planned on going for another few weeks, but I had a call this morning that my crew wants me there now."

Anne looked away from him, dismayed at the disappointment that shot through her. What was wrong with her? She barely knew this man; he took up such a small part of her life, what difference did it make whether he went or stayed? In fact, it was probably good that he was going; it would put a stop to Gail and Leo's attempt to manufacture something between them. "How long will you be gone?" she asked.

"I don't know. It depends on what I find there. A couple of weeks; maybe longer. I'm sorry you don't have an Egyptian client; I could show you some of my favorite tombs. An offer you probably haven't had from too many people."

She smiled. "You're the first. I hope you have a successful trip; I'll be glad to hear about it when you get back."

"I'll call from Luxor when I have an idea of my schedule."

They were silent. It was amazing, Josh thought, how awkward they had become.

"I think I'll look for the others," Anne said at last. "I ought to do my share of cleaning up." She turned toward the kitchen. Josh walked beside her. "Have a good trip," she said, knowing she had already said it. She was annoyed with herself for not being able to find a simple way to end the conversation. "I hope you find what you're looking for." She had said that, too, she thought, and plunged into the crowded kitchen where everyone was helping with the dishes, and nibbling on what was left of dessert. If you can't talk like a grown-up, she grumbled to herself, don't talk at all. She picked up a towel and began to dry the glasses draining on the sink.

She had so much work to do; she should be thinking about that. She should stay in Los Angeles, and get back to working the way she always had, sixteen hours a day, seven days a week. And she had to decide whether to take two new clients who had come to her the past week: one famous in television and the other a fashion designer known around the world. Both of them would help her career enormously. Spending time in Tamarack wouldn't do a thing for it.

She stopped drying and stared unseeing at the crowded kitchen. She couldn't ever remember a time when she had let anything come before her career; as recently as July she couldn't even have imagined a debate on whether to take the cases of two such highly visible clients. But Tamarack kept pulling at her. Gail and Leo loved her, and Marian and Nina said they wanted to come back, to spend time with her, and she'd promised Ned and Robin that next time she came they would go on a hike, just the three of them, and she was looking forward to that. In fact, every time she left Tamarack, she found herself already looking forward to being back.

Suddenly, she had more things to balance in her life than ever before. More than enough without thinking about a man who took off for Egypt just when they were becoming friends. She began to dry the glasses again, and take in the activity in the room. Gail was at the sink with Robin and Ned. Josh and Leo and William were talking together as they carried clean plates and cups to the hutch in the dining room, going back and forth through the swinging door. And Keith . . . Keith was looking at her.

Anne felt a jolt of wariness. He had such an intense curiosity about her; what could she possibly be to him?

William came through the swinging door, and she thought of Charles. They had not spoken since Labor Day when he had been in Tamarack. My father, she thought, and she did not know what meaning the words had for her. She had tried to think about him, but her thoughts kept veering away.

I'll have to do it, though, she told herself: think about him and everyone else in the family. My family. And my work. And my friends in Los Angeles; I've hardly seen them lately. I haven't even had time to read a book. It was a nice feeling, to have such a crowded life. It's quite enough for anyone, she thought, hanging up the damp towels she had used.

The dishes were done; the others were going into the living room. Aware of the sudden silence, Anne looked around. Josh was standing in the doorway, talking to Gail. He looked up and met her eyes, and smiled. Oh, all right, she thought, a little crossly. I can think about Josh Durant, too. And I would like to hear about his trip when he gets back; especially his favorite tombs. I'll probably never see them, so it will be nice to hear him talk about them.

Something else to look forward to, she thought, and went to join the others in the living room.

chapter 14

J osh sat on the aisle of the plane filled with Arab business-men and groups of tourists. He had made the trip so many times he could imagine the scene below without ever looking up from his book: an endless expanse of dun-colored desert slashed with black rock outcroppings. And bisecting it, the long line of the Nile, bordered by green, cultivated land that stretched as much as five miles on each side or as little as a few feet. The Nile was Egypt. Whatever the maps showed as the country's boundaries, the people lived along the sinuous line snaking through the desert, and in the fan-shaped delta at the north where the river flowed into the Mediterranean. The rest was sand, and silence.

The plane, from Cairo to Aswan, made one stop at Luxor, and Josh and many of the businessmen got off, descending the metal steps into the dense heat of the October evening. He took off his jacket and slung it over his shoulder. He wore khaki pants and a short-sleeved shirt and carried a bulging canvas suitcase, a scuffed leather briefcase, and a canvas camera bag over his shoulder. "Mr. Durant, hello," said the young woman who glanced at his passport as he went through the terminal. "Mr. Durant, welcome back," said the taxi driver who always seemed to be waiting for him when he arrived. "Mr. Durant, how pleasant to see you again," said the manager of the Winter Palace Hotel, who personally escorted him to his room on the sixth floor looking across the Nile toward the Valley of the Kings, the center of Josh's world.

He stood at the window. Below, along the entire length of Luxor's riverfront, brightly lit tour boats were docked two and three deep; on their upper decks, tourists were having cocktails before dinner. Beside the Nile ran the wide, newly paved corniche, its lampposts barely illuminating the dim roadway next to it where cars sped by without headlights, their drivers playing their car horns like fervent performers in an orchestra. There were no stoplights. By now, Josh was used to Egyptian traffic and was as adept as a resident at darting nimbly across the street between cars and horse-drawn buggies, and ignoring the buggy drivers' offers to take him anywhere, for a price so low it was hardly worth mentioning.

Josh loved Luxor. It was an ancient village trying to be a modern city; it was dirty, shabby, and poor, but it was wonderfully full of life. And it sat astride the ancient capital of Thebes like a gateway to the wonders of another age, a town where Josh felt at home with pharaohs and courtiers dead four thousand years, and with modern friends who invited him to their homes for dinner. Luxor, and all of Egypt, and his work, were clear-cut to Josh; they had none of the sloppiness that had embarrassed him in his relationship with Dora, none of the fuzziness that seemed to define his relationships with women so that he never found one that would last. Absorbed in his work, walking the streets of Luxor, he had a focus and a purpose and the rigor of a scientist. It seemed to be the only permanence in his life. And now, in Luxor, he hoped to make the greatest coup in exploration since the discovery of King Tut's tomb in 1922.

"The most wonderful thing in the world," said Carol Marston as she and Josh sat at dinner his first night in Luxor. Tall and dark haired, with a lively face and almond-shaped brown eyes that darted everywhere so she would miss nothing that went on around her, she was the newest and youngest member of the board of the Museum of the Ancient World. "The most wonderful in the world, and for me, too," she said as she finished her dessert and sat back with a deep sigh. "I have to tell you, Josh, I'm having more fun than I've had since Whit died. It's the first time I've been anywhere that people aren't feeling sorry for me, and I like that; I like not being surrounded by people who're making sure I'm not alone. That sounds ungenerous, and I don't mean to be, but it's nice to be part of something huge and historically magnificent for a change. I have to thank you for that, for letting me come along."

"I'm glad you're here," Josh said, liking her. "But this may not be a historically magnificent week. We've been working on this project for six years, and we've dug in a dozen places without finding anything."

"You'll find it; I'm betting on it. You have a very confident look. Tell me what we're going to do tomorrow."

"Check out a possible site for Tenkaure's tomb. You know about him."

"Only what you told the board; you think he was a real pharaoh but you're not sure."

"Sure enough to keep looking for six years. There are enough references in the histories of the pharaohs who came after him to make it look like a good bet. There seems to have been a family split, and an attempted coup, and then it looks like his successors conspired to make him a nonperson after he died. And they almost succeeded. But if I'm right, he's got a tomb somewhere, and that's what we're looking for."

Carol sighed. "I like the way your voice sounds when you talk about it. I wish all of us had some kind of project tucked away in a closet or a drawer, something we really, really care about, so when we're left alone, we can pull it out and get so involved that's all we think about. And when we talk about it, we'd sound like you, excited and wound up in something a lot bigger than us and our problems. That's what I meant. Historically magnificent."

"You still miss Whit so much," Josh said.

"I do. That's surprising, isn't it? I thought four years would make everything more tolerable, but I still want him back all the time, and I'm still furious at him for dying and leaving me. And I still talk to him when I'm alone, especially at night. I guess, in a way, I'm still holding on to him because it's unbearable to think of letting him go completely."

I've never known anything like that, Josh thought, or a woman who would inspire that kind of mourning and clinging if she should suddenly be gone. And then, thinking that, he thought of Anne.

He had been thinking about her since the beginning of his trip, when they were flying over Europe and he glanced out the window at the long expanse of Lake Geneva nestled in a landscape of farms and towns so neat they looked chiseled. There had been a storm; now the clouds were dissolving, casting shadows on the surface of the lake. Between the shadows, the sun glinted in thousands of sparkling lights. *Anne would like this.* The thought came to him without warning, and once it lodged with him, it did not leave.

And then, in Luxor, he discovered that he was seeing the town, and the dig, as if for the first time, through Anne's eyes. It was as if she walked with him up and down the narrow streets, and stood with him when he and Carol took the ferry across the Nile early the next morning. Standing with commuting workers, he looked at the western bank of the river, where a solid line of hills six hundred feet high hid the Valley of the Kings. The hills looked like hammered gold in the low morning sun, and the clear, dry air that made every object stand out, sharp and distinct. "My God, it's gorgeous," said Carol. "I had no idea it would look like this."

"The desert sun," Josh said. "It's magic. These hills turn purple and bronze at sunset; wait and see."

But it was not only Carol to whom he spoke; it was also Anne. He was storing up things to tell her; he was memorizing the landscape. For the first time in twenty years he thought of using his camera not to document the area where they would dig, but as if he were a tourist, to bring back images of that ancient place. He looked beyond the golden cliffs ahead. Later, as the sun moved higher, ripples of heat rising from the desert would make the sand dunes and distant hills shimmer and almost disappear into the softly blurred sky. It was an effect no camera could truly catch. She'll have to see it for herself, he thought.

He could not remember a woman who had engaged his curiosity as Anne had done—even more, it seemed, since he had left America. Being more distant by several thousand miles, she seemed elusive in yet another way.

He wondered if it was her elusiveness that so interested him. That was part of it. But there was also her beauty and her sharp mind, and the mysteries about her, and also, perhaps most intriguing of all, that air about her, as if part of her had yet to be awakened. To Josh, the scientist who had never been able to pass up a puzzle or a riddle, Anne had everything that would stop him in his tracks. What else would have made him put aside his determination to be alone for a while and figure out where he was, and how he'd managed to be such an ass about Dora?

He'd decided he needed six months alone, maybe even a year. But since he'd met Anne at the City Hall in Tamarack, he hadn't been able to get her out of his thoughts.

He and Carol stepped off the ferry with his crew of diggers, and walked to the cars waiting for them, and drove into the Valley of the Kings. In an instant, they had left the Nile and its boats and Luxor behind, and were dwarfed by limestone cliffs, towering dunes of sand, and rock etched with deep gulleys. In that moment, it seemed that four thousand years dropped away, and once again ancient Egypt was alive.

They drove deeper into the isolation, leaving the main road and jouncing along the gravel bed of a long gully that started high above them in the hills. "Here we are," Josh said at last, and they came to a stop. The two cars looked as tiny as a child's toys at the base of hills of sand and rock that rose steeply to rough-edged ridges starkly etched against the cloudless sky. Not a single plant could be seen in any direction, nor an animal, nor another person. The sun's heat radiated in the bowl-shaped valley as if it were trapped in an oven. "Not too bad," said Josh, rolling up his shirtsleeves. "It's about thirty or forty degrees cooler than in July." He glanced at his watch. "Hosni ought to be here in a few minutes. We'll wait up above."

The workers had moved up the gulley and disappeared behind a hill. When Josh and Carol reached them, they were sitting on the ground, knees to their chins, their pickaxes beside them. Nearby was a deep hole, and piles of gravel. The two guards who had been there all night spoke to Josh in Arabic, then left.

Carol looked at him, eyebrows raised in question. "Everything's fine," Josh said. "Nobody tried to grab our hole in the ground. The government pays these guys; we don't work without official support. It's not like a hundred years ago when archaeologists and hobbyists dug up the valley on their own and hired guards to fight off everybody else—the government, other diggers, tomb robbers, whoever was around. It's hard to imagine how crowded this place was in those days. There were diggers everywhere, looking for the shafts that led to the tombs, and then there were hundreds of workers hauling treasures out and taking them to boats on the Nile."

"Why did you pick this place?" Carol asked. "There's nothing special about it."

"Not on the surface. But a friend in Washington sent me satellite photographs that show disturbances in the contours of the land, and some of my graduate students made three-dimensional surveys with them on the computer. It's a tool we never had before, and it's not infallible, but it's better than poking around blindly. We've had six failures without it, so I've put a lot of faith in this one." He looked up as a short, dark man in white pants and yellow shirt joined them. "This is Hosni."

The two men shook hands and Josh introduced Carol. "Hosni is an archaeologist from the University of Cairo; he's in charge of this dig. When we find our tomb, he and I are going to tour on television together. We're working on our act. So what do we have?" he asked Hosni.

"Look here." Hosni knelt at the edge of the hole behind the workers, and Josh knelt beside him. There was a depression along one side of the hole, as if the stones and gravel had sunk in. Josh leaned forward to study it, and for the first time since he had begun his trip, he forgot everything else.

"Irregularities underneath," he murmured.

Hosni nodded. "We got to this part yesterday afternoon. I decided to wait for you."

Josh stood up. "Let's see what happens." His voice was calm, but excitement was stirring inside him. He tried to ignore it. Six failures before this, he reminded himself. He moved away from the workers and sat on his heels. Carol joined him, sitting cross-legged on the sand. They put on hats, and they waited.

Hosni spoke to the workers, who began digging at the side of the hole with the depression. The sound of their shovels crunching into gravel was loud in the silence. When they pried up rocks and broke them apart with pickaxes, the clanging sound of iron on stone rang through the silent valley, echoing off nearby hills like receding church bells. Josh watched, as if mesmerized. All his research in libraries and museums, the books he read, the articles he scanned, the satellite photographs, his calculations late into the night—in the end, it all came down to this: a group of men in the heat of the desert, digging with shovels, and lifting pickaxes high above their heads and bringing them down onto rock.

An hour went by, and then two. Josh photographed the hole as it deepened and widened, and the surrounding hills and gullies. He and Carol drank from water bottles. The sun blazed, making the sand glare until it, too, seemed to be a sun, burning upward, into the sky. There was no breeze. Carol took a large parasol from her canvas bag and opened it and held it over her and Josh. The workers hummed and grunted, their bodies and hair gray with powdery dust that was streaked with perspiration, while Hosni stood with them, directing where he wanted them to dig, occasionally grabbing a shovel himself. Miraculously, his white pants stayed clean. "Did we bring anything to eat?" Carol asked.

Josh looked at her as if she had disturbed a dream. They

had been digging for three hours, and he had barely moved except to photograph the site. "Food," he said. "I'm sorry; I never think of it until someone reminds me." He pulled two apples from his canvas bag, and boxes of crackers. "A feast. We'll go back to Luxor for lunch. It's too early now; it's only ten o'clock."

"Oh, no, it must be noon." She looked at her watch. "I can't believe it; it feels like afternoon. But then we started at the crack of dawn, didn't we? Four-thirty in the morning . . ."

"We'll stop about one and come back at three. I did warn you."

"You did. I didn't think you were serious about four-thirty."

"Josh." Hosni's voice was high with excitement. In an instant, Josh was beside him, Carol right behind. They looked into the hole, following Hosni's pointing finger.

A corner of a rough stairway was sticking out of the rubble.

Josh slid to the bottom of the hole and dropped to his knees. He touched the top step with his fingertips. He ran his hand over it, pushing away gravel and rocks. Elation filled him like a burst of light. He imagined the stairway descending into the earth, becoming a rough-floored passage pushing its way at a steep angle deeper and deeper into blackness, the air becoming hot and close, until it ended at a stone door. . . .

Carol had followed him; now her fingers brushed his as she, too, touched the steps. Josh barely noticed her. He had never had a moment like this. Most archaeologists never had a moment like this. He had prepared for it, dreamed of it, planned and schemed to raise the money for it, but there was no way to be fully ready for this moment, when his fingers touched a stairway that had been built and buried and forgotten thirty-five hundred years ago. He imagined the workers hacking the steps from solid rock, and then the corridor and then the many chambers, the wall paintings. the riches— "Of course we don't know if we're the first," Hosni said.

Slowly, Josh stood up. The spell was broken. "But we are," Carol protested. "They just dug it out. Nobody got here before us."

"They might have, three thousand years ago," said Josh. "Robbers found a lot of tombs soon after they were hidden, sometimes within a few years. There's a village near here where all the houses are built over tomb shafts. The robbers built them there so they wouldn't have to commute to clean out the treasures, and their descendants still live in them, very proud of their heritage. There was no way to guard the whole valley, of course, and too many people worked on the tombs for them to be kept secret. Anyway, it was part of the culture that pharaohs were buried with enough possessions and wealth and even food to get them through the next life. And it was part of the robbers' culture that they'd go after it."

"And smash their way in," said Hosni. "Of course this is a great find, a magnificent find, even if it's empty; we'll still have the writing and paintings on the walls. But we won't know what we have until we get to the tomb. So we dig."

Josh nodded. He had had his great moment; now there was nothing to do but dig. And wait. He photographed the steps and stood to the side, holding his camera. Carol stood beside him. The workers were more careful now, using their shovels to remove loose gravel, then sweeping the steps clean with brooms and brushes. Josh and Hosni examined the large pieces of rock to make sure they were not part of the steps; those that were not, the workers hauled out of the hole with a hand winch.

Josh photographed the workers in the swirling clouds of dust that turned their lean bodies to ghostlike figures swaying in the sunlight. He photographed Hosni, in his amazingly white pants. He photographed the long line of the gully in which they worked and high above, the dunes and jagged rock ridges that surrounded them. He had never taken so many photographs that had nothing to do with his work. For Anne, he said silently. So she can see it all.

In his mind, he saw his hand spread out on the ancient

stone of the stairway. Once in a lifetime, he thought, one of the great moments of a lifetime. She should have been part of it; it should have been her fingers that brushed his as they touched the stone. He wanted her to share all that he did, the small triumphs as well as the large ones, and the disappointments as well.

He shook his head and put his camera back in its case. It was too soon to say that, too soon even to think it. He didn't know anything about her.

He knew that she haunted his thoughts.

For a long time he stood still, transfixed by the heat and the rhythmic lifting and falling of the workers' arms and the hum of their voices in the still air. Then it all stopped. The workers moved down the gully toward the cars. "Lunch and a beer," Hosni said to Josh. "Will you be at the hotel?"

"Yes." Josh turned to Carol, feeling guilty for ignoring her. "You must be hungry."

"And a trifle warm," she said cheerfully. "But I loved it. I wandered around; you were too busy taking pictures to notice. It's the most amazing thing: fifty feet from here there's nothing to see but sand and sky, as if the world just emptied out. It's the scariest thing I've ever seen; you feel so small. Are we going back for lunch?"

"Right now. Hosni, you'll join us?"

"Yes, thanks." They walked back to the cars. "Josh, we could use more workers."

"To speed it up? There isn't room for them at the stairway."

"I could use them to keep the opening clear when we get deeper. This is going to take a hell of a long time if we keep this pace."

"We don't have enough money," Josh said.

There was a pause. Hosni shrugged. "So be it, then."

That was the Egyptian way, Josh thought. *So be it, then.* How many Americans would accept an obstacle so readily, as if it were fate? "We'll get the money," he said firmly. "I'll go to Cairo tomorrow instead of next week. There are people I can talk to in the government."

"The government is tightfisted these days," Hosni said. "Hard times around here." He got in his car. "I'll see you at the ferry."

"What will you do if the government doesn't give you the money?" Carol asked as they drove back to the riverbank.

"Talk to private investors. There's money in Egypt; it just isn't visible. We'll find it. Do you want to come to Cairo tomorrow?"

"I think I'd like to stay here for a while. When will you be back?"

"Not right away; it would make more sense to go straight home. There really isn't anything to do, until they dig out more of the stairway and corridor. Would it change your plans if I didn't come back?"

"Not as long as Hosni lets me watch the dig and take my own pictures."

"That's no problem. He likes an audience." Josh parked near the dock and they walked onto the ferry. He'd talk to the government officials day after tomorrow; if they couldn't provide the money he needed, he'd see the private investors the day after that. And then he'd fly home.

That had not been in his mind when he told Hosni he would go to Cairo; he had meant he would go for a couple of days and then return to Luxor. But when he talked to Carol, he knew he had already changed his mind. Because he wanted most of all to go home.

Charles took the train from Chicago to Washington. He thought it would be a peaceful interlude, a chance to think calmly about the past year and what he could do to save himself. Instead, it turned out to be an agonizing trip.

He was suffering. He was not in the habit of complaining to his family or his friends, so he endured in silence a prickling nervousness and burning stomach pains that had begun about the time Ethan died, and had gotten steadily worse since then. He had trouble eating and sleeping, too, and he had hoped the train would lull him so he could eat in a leisurely way, and then sleep to the rhythm of the wheels.

But as he sat in the lounge car before dinner, sipping Scotch and soda, hearing Anne say Vince had threatened her, worrying about Ray Beloit's low offer for Tamarack, haunted by the calendar, with the date coming up for the next interest payments on his loans, his thoughts began to come faster, and grow louder and more insistent, and the wheels of the train forced them to rhythms that seemed to mock him with a jolly drumbeat. When he went to dinner, no one sat at his table and so he ate alone, his thoughts hammering inside his head like desperate prisoners pounding on a padlocked door. The train was Charles' prison. He left his dinner untouched and paced the length of the train. Then he turned and retraced his steps. His dinner plate was gone but his table was still empty, so he sat down and asked for coffee. His head hurt; he drank a brandy. His stomach hurt; he sucked on a handful of tablets. He began to yawn and could not stop. And when he went to bed in his room, he did not sleep.

He walked into Vince's office feeling as if he had fought a war. "I'm grabbing an early lunch; you can come if you'd like," Vince said. He was signing letters and had not looked up. "I have a meeting at one."

Charles sat down and yawned. "I'll have coffee with you; I'm not hungry. Vince, I have to talk to you."

Vince signed the last two letters. "Good. Did you hear from Ray about buying Tamarack?"

"Yes, but he's crazy. Where the hell's he getting his numbers? Any damn fool would know the company's worth twice what he's offering, maybe more."

"Ask him; I don't know anything about it. You think you can do better somewhere else?"

"Damn it, I know what it's worth! You didn't tell him I was anxious to sell, did you?"

"Of course not; it's not something anybody should know." He set the signed letters to one side. "I've been thinking about this, though, since you haven't had any other offers. I'm worried about you, Charles; we have to do something to get you off the hook."

361

His head tilted back in a massive yawn, Charles heard one word echo in his mind. *We.* Vince was worried about him; Vince would help him. "How?" he asked.

"Well, we have to talk about that. But one way might be for me to work on the family. You haven't any leverage until you can deliver enough of them to make a bona fide sale; maybe Beloit hasn't raised his offer because he's not sure you're serious."

"He doesn't know anything about the family. How would he know?"

Vince scowled. "You didn't tell him?"

"For Christ's sake, Vince!"

"Well, it sounds to me as if he may have heard about it. He learns a lot by hanging around and being invisible, and God knows what he knows about the family. You haven't changed anybody's mind?" Charles shook his head. "Then I'd better try to get things moving." He drummed his fingers on his desk. "One thing I might do is talk to some people here, at the EPA. They're pretty busy these days; they'd probably be just as happy to call off that cleanup, especially if we found other towns that were just as bad. If I do that, I imagine we could round up a few grateful votes in the family; there's more than one way to get what you want."

Something stirred within Charles, the reminder that he had had something important to ask Vince. "Vince, there's something else we have to talk about."

"This minute? We're talking about saving your ass; that's usually all you want to talk about these days. Isn't that why you're here?"

Another yawn held Charles in its grip for a long minute.

"What the hell is wrong with you?" Vince demanded.

"Nothing. I didn't sleep last night. Vince, listen to me. Did you threaten Anne? Did you say you'd kill her if she came back to the family?"

Vince reared up. "For God's sake! That's a hell of a thing to ask your brother!"

"I'd rather not ask it. But I've got to know. Did you?"

"You couldn't make it up; where the hell did you get it? Have you seen her? *Have you?*"

"Yes."

"Where?"

"Tamarack. Damn it, Vince—"

"What did you do? Ask her forgiveness for sticking with your brother? And she told you I'd threatened her? She told you that? The little bitch hasn't changed, has she? The first thing she does is start accusing me."

"Damn it, Vince, *did you say it?*"

"For Christ's sake, of course not. I don't go around killing anybody. You ought to be the first to know that—and *defend* me, damn it, when anybody says anything like that! Did you? Did you tell her your brother isn't a murderer? *Did you?*"

Charles looked at him helplessly.

"You didn't. My own brother didn't say a fucking thing in my defense. What did you say?" He raised his voice to a falsetto. "'I'll ask him, sweetheart. I'll ask my brother if he threatened to kill my daughter.' What the hell is wrong with you? What's wrong with *her?* Does she think she's Joan of Arc, hearing voices? Why would I want to kill her? I forgave her a long time ago; she was a mixed-up kid and she did a terrible thing, but it's past, she's outgrown it—well, shit, I thought she'd outgrown it, but it looks like she hasn't. But that doesn't mean I'd threaten to kill her; it wouldn't occur to me, for Christ's sake. Well? Is there anything else you want to know?"

Charles shook his head. Vince had gone on talking too long, but he didn't know whether that was because of guilt or justifiable outrage because he was innocent. *Listen to yourself.* Anne had flung that at him when his first instinct had been to defend Vince. *Listen to yourself. You have no idea what he would do; you don't know anything about him.*

That's true, Charles thought with a deep and terrible sadness. I don't. But I don't know anything about my daughter, either.

In fact, he thought despairingly, I don't know anything about anything. What happened in the past, what's happening now, what will happen tomorrow. He yawned again and suddenly felt panic-stricken. He could not explain it; he only knew that he was terrified. I can't! he cried silently. Can't what? he wondered. He looked around wildly; the room was closing in on him, locking him in as the train had locked him in the night before. He could not stay, but he could not leave; he could not move from his chair. No, no, no! he screamed inside his head.

He yawned again, and was stabbed by a sudden, fierce burning in his stomach. It spread until he felt he was being consumed by fire. It clutched his chest as he yawned, and he began to tremble. Heart, he thought. Heart attack. His hands shook and the heels of his shoes drummed on the floor. A long moan tore from him; he squeezed shut his eyes.

"What the hell—!" Vince came around the desk. "What is it?"

Charles clawed at his chest with shaky fingers. "Heart," he gasped.

Vince shouted to his secretary and his assistants, who ran in, bending over Charles, surrounding him, making comforting sounds. And that was all Charles remembered until he awoke in an ambulance and looked up and saw Vince. On his other side was a medic, but the most important person was Vince. Charles was so grateful for his presence that he forgot everything else. "Thanks," he said.

"You're okay," Vince said. "Your heartbeat is fine, not defibrillating; they don't think it was a heart attack."

"Terrible pain," Charles said.

"They found these in your pockets." He held up two boxes of antacid tablets. "Do you use them a lot?"

"My main food these days," Charles replied with a weak smile. "I thought about going to a doctor; I guess now I will."

"They said it could be an ulcer; sometimes the pain feels like a heart attack. Or a panic attack with an ulcer, though I told them nobody in our family ever panicked that I know of. Do you know of anybody?" Charles shook his head and closed his eyes. "Fine, you should sleep. I can't stay anyway; I'm going back as soon as I make sure you're settled. I'll call later and find out how you're doing."

Eyes closed, Charles nodded. Panic attack. Ulcer. Not his

heart. He wouldn't die. Modern medicine knew how to take care of ulcers. And panic, too, probably. Why had he panicked? *No, no, no.* He could still hear the scream inside his head. What was wrong with him that he'd gone off the deep end like that? Weak, Charles thought. He'd always been weak—Vince had told him often enough—and now the smallest thing could knock him over. What had he been thinking about when it started? He couldn't remember. What difference does it make? he thought. Whatever it was, I couldn't handle it. Vince could have handled it. So could Dad. But not me. I panic and pass out.

"We're here," Vince said. The ambulance stopped and the medics opened the back doors. "I'll call you later." He looked down at Charles' closed eyes. "You'll be fine." He jumped out of the ambulance and strode away. A goddamned coffin, that's what it had felt like, careening through the streets smelling of medicines, smelling of death. He never went to hospitals; he hated them. Even when Ethan was in one, he had gone only once, when he couldn't avoid it. Not again, he had vowed then, and remembered it as he took a taxi to his office. Not again. His secretary would call. And visit if necessary.

In his office, he called Keith, in Tamarack. "Nothing new," Keith said. "They're about done with the reservoir, another week, maybe. The ditch was fixed a long time ago; you knew that. The EPA's holding hearings in January. We've got two weeks to go till Thanksgiving, and it's been snowing for a week so everybody's happy. That's it."

"That's all? It's been over a month since we talked."

"Listen, this town is dead. It's between seasons, remember? The most exciting thing that's happened in a couple months is that I had dinner at Gail and Leo's a while back."

"You didn't tell me that."

"I didn't learn anything you didn't already know. I had a little chat with your niece. Great bod, but what a cold fish. She didn't seem to like me much."

"Why not?"

"How do I know? I told you: she's an iceberg."

"Did she say why she's there?"

"I didn't ask. I was trying to find out about the company."

"And?"

"I didn't get much. There was this little act going on between Leo and Josh to keep changing the subject."

"He was there?"

"He's around a lot. He was in Egypt in October; since he came back he's in Tamarack every couple weeks. Usually with your, you know, niece. Let's see, what did I find out. Anne says she isn't moving to Tamarack, in case you wondered. Gail feels bad about her daddy; she knows things are terrible for him and she'd like to help, but she's not about to help him sell The Tamarack Company. Ethan's dream, she called it, and now theirs. She gave a good speech. Something between a sob and a raised fist."

"What?"

"I said—"

"I heard you." Vince's eyes were thoughtful. Since when was Keith a sharp observer with a clever tongue? He'd been hiding behind that stupid-asshole act—and Vince hadn't caught on. Watch him, he thought suddenly. "What else?" he asked.

"Leo thinks nobody'll buy the company because it's in a mess. That was maybe sounding brave in front of his kids; he's a lot more worried than he says. But he's talking big. The reservoir'll be open in a week or two; the skiing'll be good—the mountain's got a twenty-inch base already—and the EPA's keeping quiet until January and maybe for good; who knows? Your niece got the newspaper publisher to write an editorial about getting every fucking survey done on Tamarack starting with the dinosaurs, and she's got a local lawyer going to a judge to get an injunction so nobody can do a cleanup until the town's had time to, you know, study all of it. She's a first-class agitator, you know that? Vince? You still with me?"

"Go on."

"Well, so they're yelling for all the surveys and the EPA's waffling, like it takes time to get everything together, you know. Maybe it's too much trouble; you could probably like find out; you're right there. So maybe they'll drop it. Which means Gail and Leo could like tell the family to wait for spring, see what kind of a season they have. They've spent over a million bucks so far, on the reservoir and trucking in water and running extra ads saying everything's hunky-dory, and there's a pile of lawsuits against them, but they probably could, you know, ride it out if the season is good. Leo already said they'd put off improvements and expansions, and cut the staff."

There's more, Vince thought; he's holding something back. "What else?"

Keith's voice became casual. "Oh, just something Leo said. He said he wouldn't compromise on maintenance. And he means it. But when things are tight, who knows?"

The son of a bitch, Vince thought. He found himself reluctantly admiring Keith. He kept an eye on everything, looked everywhere for possibilities, did what he was told, and didn't ask questions. But beside his admiration, the clang of warning he'd heard in his head a few minutes earlier sounded again. Watch him. Much too smart for his own good.

"Nothing else," Keith said. "I'll let you know if anything else comes up. You'll be there, right?"

"I'll be out of the country for a couple of weeks after Thanksgiving. Then I'll be here."

"Keeping our allies in line?"

"Something like that." He hung up, annoyed at Keith's prying. It was all right at Gail and Leo's when he was doing it for Vince, but it was not all right when he did it with Vince. He was a nosy kid with a sharp eye, and he wouldn't know a damn thing about Vince except what Vince wanted him to know. He certainly would not know that Vince was going to Europe on his honeymoon.

"Senator," said his secretary, standing in the doorway, "you told me to get you out of here by two o'clock so you could catch your plane."

Vince stood up. "Thanks." He pulled on his coat. "I'll see you in Denver in three days. I can't get married, you know, unless my staff is there."

"We'll be there, Senator. We're looking forward to it. It's

so good of you to include us, and to pay our way . . . we want you to know we're very grateful."

Vince nodded. "If Ray Beloit calls, tell him I'll meet him at the airport. If Sid Folker calls, tell him I'm expecting him to meet my plane. The wedding will be in his house, so you can reach me there if I'm not home."

"Yes, sir," the secretary said, and Vince realized he had told her all this before. Why was he acting like a nervous kid, about to get married for the first time?

He wasn't nervous; he was filled with exhilaration. This was the real beginning of the presidential race. He still had the Senate race ahead of him, but he had no doubt he would win it. He was already looking past that, and that was why he was getting married to the perfect woman, the perfect partner: sweet tempered, pretty enough, wealthy, well connected, and busy with good works. Every American's dream of a perfect first lady. And when she looked at Vince with adoring eyes, she became his dream of a perfect wife.

Why not? Vince thought, settling into his limousine. If you wait long enough, everything comes to you.

Bianca's corridor or somebody else's, we won't know for a
month, maybe. You'll see that I get home to dig out the carvings.
...while...
"The banks—let first those—they'll follow me. You when
we get under... something... the inner chambers are inside
I have slides, the... the...
"You have them with you."
"Yes, I packed them up on the way here, but they can
wait.
"No. I'd—to see them now. How wonderful! I didn't
think you'd have them so soon. Would you mind?"
"Of course not."
...in minutes. She turned on and said...

chapter 15

*H*e called for her at eight, and when she opened the door to the white cocoon of her apartment and smiled at him, saying, "Welcome back," he was so glad to see her he instinctively took her hands in his. She pulled back, of course; had he taken a moment to think about it, he would have been able to predict that she would. Angry with himself, and with her, he followed her into the living room where wine and hors d'oeuvres were on the glass coffee table.

But she was glad to see him. He sat on a white couch while Anne stood before him, pouring the wine. She wore a short dark-blue silk dress that fit closely and showed off her long, elegant legs; her dark hair was loosely brushed back, framing her face. She seemed quite content to let the silence linger, so Josh thought about her, and the look in her eyes as she had greeted him. Warm, welcoming, glad to see him, a little bit surprised. Surprised, he thought; she hadn't expected to be glad. Or to be as glad as she was. But then she pulled away.

We'll have to talk about that, he thought. Sometime soon. And of course she knows it.

"Does coming back early mean success or failure?" Anne asked as they sat on the couch.

"Success." He raised his glass in a silent toast. "At least, possible success. We found the entrance to a corridor leading, we hope, to somebody's tomb. Whether it's our pharaoh's corridor or somebody else's we won't know for a month, maybe two; it'll take that long to dig out the debris."

"From what?"

"Earthquakes or flash floods We'll know that, too, when we get farther in and see the damage to the pillars and walls. I have slides; they'll give you an idea of the setting."

"You have them with you?"

"Yes, I picked them up on the way here, but they can wait."

"No, I'd like to see them now. How wonderful; I didn't think you'd have them so soon. Would you mind?"

"No, of course not."

"I'll get the projector." She jumped up and went to the other room, returning almost immediately with the projector and tray. She was nervous, or perhaps, Josh thought, she had become nervous since that look of surprise flashed in her eyes. "If you want to put the slides in . . ." She handed him the tray. Josh felt her discomfort, and wondered at it. Silently, he filled the circular tray and gave it back to her, watching as she fit it into the projector. She reached behind her and switched off the lamp, and they were in darkness barely relieved by the faint glow of a small lamp across the room. Anne pushed a button, the slide fell into place, and a large scene sprang to life on the wall at the end of the room: the vast expanse of barren rock cliffs and shadowed sand dunes of the Valley of the Kings. Anne drew in a sharp breath, leaning forward. "How magnificent," she breathed.

Josh contemplated her rapt profile. "Why?"

"The scale, the sheer overwhelming size of it. It's the reason I love the mountains: that special kind of beauty that's so massive and elemental, and enduring. It makes it possible to believe in eternity."

"It's why I keep going back," Josh said. "If I didn't have work there, I'd have to invent some."

"But you have the mountains, too."

"They're a little more human; there's life in them. You'll have to see the desert; it's wonderful and terrifying at the same time. It's as unforgiving a landscape as you'll find anywhere, but it draws people back again and again. It's a little like the dark side of our selves; harsh and cruel, but perversely attractive."

Anne's eyes were fixed on him. After a minute, she shook her head. "That's a long way from the beauty I was talking about." She pushed a button to advance the next slide.

For a few minutes, the cool, white living room was transformed to a brown and gold landscape of rough textures and blinding light. Anne could feel the waves of heat that rippled over the dusty bodies of the workers hacking at the rock; she could almost feel the gritty sand between her teeth, and hear the clang of steel on stone. She was still leaning forward, drawn into the exotic scene that almost surrounded her. I'd like to be there, she thought. I wish I'd been there when these pictures were taken.

Josh described each slide, his deep voice relaxed, but with a kind of passion that made it seem he was actually leading Anne through this world she had never seen. He told her about Hosni—"the best supervisor anyone could ask; a self-taught Egyptologist who knows more than a lot of the experts; and the only man who excavates in white pants and never gets them dirty"—and named the workers, whom he had known all the years they had been searching for Tenkaure's tomb. At that his voice became more charged with the excitement of what would come next. "They'll dig out the corridor—fairly quickly, unless they find paintings on the ceiling and side walls; then they slow down to a crawl, doing hand work—and Hosni will call me when they get to the first door. That usually leads to a large, square room with another door in the far wall; beyond that is a passage with other rooms leading off it. The air is heavy, and hot; it feels old, as if nothing could live in it. But we've seen tombs with wheat placed beside the pharaoh, to help feed him on his journey to the next life, and it sprouted, in that dark, sealed place, before dying for lack of water. It's a wondrous thing, that tenacity of life; more elemental than any emotion. Except love, I suppose, because that's a synonym for life." He paused. "We don't have any idea how many rooms there might be, or how big they are; we do know that the last room always holds the sarcophagus, with the mummy in its coffin, inside. If we're among the truly blessed, it's there now, waiting for us; the stone lid of the sarcophagus, waiting to be lifted . . ."

Anne was caught in the spell of his words and the intensity of his voice. "I'd like to see it. And touch it. And feel the air . . ."

"We can arrange that," said Josh. "You really should be there; a camera only hints at it. There's one last slide."

Anne pushed the button. The stone steps filled the lighted area, with a woman's fingers spread out on one corner. "Carol's hand," Josh said. "The friend who loans me art books; I mentioned her to you. She's still over there; she was more excited about the dig than I thought she'd be. That's the last of them."

I wish it had been my hand. I wish I'd stood there, next to him, and looked at those steps and imagined what lay at the bottom of them.

"They're wonderful slides," she said. "For a while it felt very warm in here." She turned on the lamp behind her. They blinked in the light and smiled at each other. Anne's nervousness returned, and she turned her attention to removing the slides from the tray and returning them to their small yellow boxes. The memory of her pulling from him so abruptly when he arrived gnawed at her. She had turned a simple greeting into a complicated maneuver, and that was not like her. It should have been quite casual; he had only been gone a little more than a week. But it had felt longer, and she had been so glad to see him, and that had taken her by surprise. How had she let Josh become such a part of her life that eight days seemed a long time? *I'll have to think about it. And we'll have to talk about it if I want to keep seeing him. Not tonight, but sometime soon.*

But they did not. They saw each other only occasionally. Anne had taken two new clients early in October and had even stopped going to Tamarack. Josh took two brief trips that fall, and his days and nights were taken up with his classes and meetings with students, committee meetings at the museum, writing, and talking by telephone to Hosni, who, so far, had nothing to report. Then, at the beginning of

December, he invited Anne to a dinner to benefit the Museum of the Ancient World.

The dinner was in the museum, with cocktails in the interior courtyard, with its gardens of herbs and flowers from ancient times, sculptures from Rome and Greece, a blue-glazed faience hippopotamus from Egypt, and small, squat pre-Columbian figures in glass cases along the walls. It was the first time Josh and Anne had been seen together in Los Angeles society.

The guests crowded around, friends and colleagues who had not seen Josh in some time, and they eyed Anne as if to try to figure out from her appearance whether she had whatever it took to hold on to Josh Durant. This was Josh's world, the world of the wealthy and the well connected; he knew most of the guests, and he moved easily among them, exchanging news of travels and shared friends. And now, in an instant, it seemed that he and Anne had become a couple. Society did that, Anne knew: it needed to think of itself as structured and harmonious, stable, purposeful, and enduring, and so, as quickly as possible, it settled people into niches so there would be as few surprises as possible. She heard someone ask a question about Dora; someone behind them was talking about Josh and the work he had done in Sardinia and Turkey and, lately, Egypt; and someone else said what a great couple she and Josh made.

She knew it was true. He wore his tuxedo as easily as he wore jeans and hiking shorts, and she was in strapless black satin that clung to her figure, with a long slit up the side of the skirt. She wore gold earrings with a sapphire and gold necklace. Her head came to his shoulder and they moved the same way, their heads high, their eyes taking in everything around them. And as they walked through the room, everyone turned, to watch them pass.

Anne found herself enjoying it. Usually she hated being the center of attention, except in the courtroom, but sharing it with Josh was almost like a game, a secret they held together. And she liked being at his side as he commented on the people she met in a voice meant only for her.

"He's waiting to be sentenced for pocketing ten million

dollars from an S and L that went under," Josh murmured as a couple approached them. "It's been a boon for a couple of churches in town; he's been showering them with some percentage of his ill-gotten millions in a kind of yellow brick road to heaven or a light sentence, whichever comes first."

A small laugh broke from Anne, and Josh gave her a swift, pleased look before the couple was before them, the man in a funereal black shirt and dark purple tie beneath his tuxedo, the woman carrying a glittering Judith Leiber bag like a talisman to ward off the darkness.

A few minutes later a tall, angular woman approached them. She wore a turban and a red cape over what looked like a long white nightgown. "She's giving all her money to museums, a million or so a year," Josh said. "She wants the money to run out when she dies, but not a minute before, so her accountants and doctors compare notes four or five times a week on how she's doing."

Anne laughed again. "Why museums?"

"Because she says they're the only institutions besides herself that celebrate and preserve the exotic. She says she wishes she'd lived in Rome under the Caesars."

"Does she know how women were treated there?" Anne asked.

"I tried to tell her once; she wouldn't listen, so I let it go. Why would I try to chip away at someone's dream?"

Anne looked at him in surprise. "Isn't that what scientists do? Force the truth on us whether it's pleasant or not?"

"We point it out, and we live with it. But we don't force—" He stopped as the woman in the turban reached them. "Lillian, how good to see you. May I introduce Anne Garnett."

They did not talk long before others came up to them. "Oh, this one I know," Anne murmured as a rotund, bearded man came toward them. "Colin Riley. He produces the 'Rosie' show on television and his wife divorced him because she said he preferred Rosie to her."

"Rosie is a dachshund," Josh protested.

Anne nodded. "She said if he'd chosen a classy sporting

374

dog like a weimaraner or a wirehaired pointing griffon, she might have tried to see his point, but to be more interested in a dachshund than in her meant he'd sunk to a level she couldn't tolerate."

Josh chuckled. "Was she your client?"

"Yes. It was an easy one, they both really wanted out. The toughest part was the yacht; they both really wanted that, too."

"But she got it."

Anne gave him a quick look. "Yes."

"How many cases have you lost?"

"None. Colin, how nice to see you. May I introduce Josh Durant."

A few minutes later the crowd moved to the Great Egyptian Hall for dinner. Josh had given Anne a tour of the museum weeks earlier, but she paused at the double doors to admire once again the brilliant panels of tomb paintings and carvings that lined the walls. The guests, finding their places at round tables with silver cloths, seemed to blend into the panels. Their bright gowns and sleek tuxedos bore no resemblance to the short skirts of the men in those paintings, and the long, filmy dresses of the women, but Anne could imagine everyone, regardless of the thousands of years separating them, having the same hopes and dreams, and the same worries about families and jobs and friends. The idea pleased her and she turned to tell Josh. "Oh, here's Carol," he said just then. "I want you to meet her. Carol Marston, Anne Garnett."

"I'm glad to meet you," Carol said as they shook hands. "I've heard good things about you; I know a couple of women you worked miracles for."

"Not quite miracles," Anne said. "I have to be able to do repeat performances or I'm out of work. I think the definition of a miracle is that it only happens once."

"I was lucky enough to be in on a miracle a couple of months ago," Carol said. "Josh probably told you all about it."

"Hard work and luck," Josh said.

"And wonderfully exciting. I'm going back as soon as I can; I want to see a lot more than I did. Aren't you going back, too, Josh? How can you bear to stay away when they're working on your tomb?"

"I'll be there soon. And Hosni won't open the first door without me. Where are you sitting tonight?"

"Table Eight. Oh, you're at One. What a shame. Maybe we'll talk later," she said to Anne, and went to another part of the hall.

Josh held Anne's chair and said something, but she did not hear it. She was in turmoil about something she could not name. Carol, she thought. And of course, Josh. Carol Marston—tall, young, with striking almond-shaped brown eyes that seemed to take in everything and everyone around her—had been in Egypt with Josh.

Until a few minutes earlier, Carol had been a faceless museum board member who had been in Egypt with the rest of Josh's crew. If Anne had thought about her at all, it was as an older woman, vaguely sixty or more, a little drab, lonely or bored, who filled her time by working as a director of the Museum of the Ancient World. But to meet Carol Marston, and to imagine her in Luxor with Josh, walking with him in the magnificence of the Valley of the Kings, sitting with him in restaurants, spreading her hand on those stone steps for him to photograph . . . that was enough to make Anne tighten up inside and feel a strange, unfocused sense of being left out.

The president of the museum welcomed the dinner guests and introduced Josh. Anne watched his tall, lean figure as he took the few steps to the podium and stood easily in the spotlight. He was extraordinarily handsome, she thought. His face had strength and determination; his mouth had a suggestion of stubbornness, even when he smiled, but it also gave promise, perhaps only for those who knew him, of warmth and tenderness. And then she knew why she was in turmoil. She was caught by an emotion she had never had before. She was jealous.

"I'm glad to join in welcoming you here," Josh said, his

voice amplified by the microphone. "This is your museum; your support literally keeps the doors open and makes it possible to plan for the future."

Anne stared at him. It was as if she were looking at a stranger. She was trembling. What she had thought was a friendship, one she was beginning to treasure, had turned into something terrifying. Jealous, she thought, and felt ill. Jealousy afflicted lovers; jealousy meant involvements, closeness, attachments, demands. No, she cried silently. I can't. I can't.

". . . show you some of what your support has meant to the projects the museum has organized in the past year," Josh was saying. The lights dimmed. Behind him, a screen came down. For a few minutes a rapid succession of slides showed the foundations of an ancient palace in Mexico, the remains of Roman shops unearthed on the Corso in the old city of Jerusalem, the columns of a Greek temple on the coast in Turkey, primitive workers' tools found in northern Iraq.

Anne could not concentrate on the slides or on Josh's voice. How had she so completely lost control of herself? She was always careful. No one could be more than a casual friend. Well, except for Eleanor, of course, and Gail and Leo, but they were different. What had happened to her that she had let slip the perfect control she had worked so hard to build? It was as if she had left a door unlocked and someone had walked in and now she was threatened. She gripped her hands to stop their trembling. I didn't want anything like this. Everything was fine; I won't have it destroyed.

"And finally," Josh said, "the one that fits most properly in this great hall." Once again, Anne was looking at the Valley of the Kings, with workers hacking at rock, and Hosni standing nearby. "We're digging on the far side of a low ridge—here in the background—that runs along the known part of the Valley of the Kings. What we found a few weeks ago was this." The slide of the steps appeared, with Carol's hand. A murmur went through the room. "Stone steps in the Valley of the Kings," Josh said, letting the moment stretch out. "We'll know in the next few weeks where they will lead us. And you'll know, almost as soon as we do. We'll keep you informed about everything we discover." The lights came up. "The hand in that picture, by the way, belongs to Carol Marston, a member of our board of directors. No museum can function without an active, involved, caring board, any more than it can without the financial support you, and others with you, give each year. And with their continued help, and yours, we'll make the Ancient the best museum of its kind in the world."

The guests applauded as Josh returned to his chair and the president returned to introduce the auctioneer. "Who will whip them to a happy frenzy," Josh murmured to Anne as he sat down, "so they'll bid huge amounts for items people have donated and we won't have to go through this hat-in-the-hand routine for another year. Is something wrong?"

Anne started to speak, but the noise around them had risen as the auctioneer chanted into the microphone, and bids were called out by spotters around the room. "We can talk about it later," she said, raising her voice just enough for Josh to hear.

Immediately, he stood up. "I've done my part. Unless you're anxious to hear this, let's go."

They made their way through the noisy throng to a small door at the other end of the room. "The quick escape route," Josh said. "Used only by insiders. We can cut through my office."

He led the way down a short corridor, into a large room lined with bookshelves. There was no desk; only a long table covered with books, slides, journals, and notepads. Anne had been there before, and she remembered now how Josh had talked about his work, the same way he talked about his dig.

Everything she knew about him showed him to be a man absorbed in his work, fascinated by the challenges around him and wanting to cram as many as he could into each day. An archaeologist, a professor, a museum consultant. A man who moved comfortably in society, who lived well, who had good friends, who liked women. Regret filled her. She admired him; she enjoyed their times together. She had looked forward to more.

Josh held the door for her and locked it behind them. They walked in silence to his car in the parking lot, and they were silent as he drove to Anne's apartment and pulled to a stop near the entrance. "Do you want to talk about what's bothering you?" he asked.

"Yes." She met his eyes. "I can't see you anymore, Josh. I'm sorry. I like you and I enjoy being with you, but there are reasons why we have to stop."

"No," he said. He felt a sense of loss, almost of bereavement, that was made worse by his admiration for the way she said what she had to say without looking away. She met things head-on and did not flinch, and that was one of the things he always looked for in people. But then he felt angry. She was taking herself away from him as if he had nothing to say about it. "I'd like to know the reasons."

"I can't talk about them. They have nothing to do with you."

"Nothing? But I'm the one you don't want to see again."

She flushed. "Yes, that was foolish of me. I meant, it was nothing you did or didn't do. It's entirely within me."

She did not look for excuses, Josh thought; another reason to admire her. "You know I would help you with it if I could."

"I know. Thank you. No one can; I told you, it's within me."

"And unchangeable?"

"Yes."

"In all circumstances? Forever? As eternal as the desert?"

Again, she flushed. "It may sound as if I'm exaggerating or being overemotional or irrational, but this is something I have to deal with, and it's very strong, and no one else can pass judgment on it."

"That's true," Josh said quickly, "that was presumptuous of me. But you know you're making me deal with it, too."

"It's not a part of you. You'll deal with it the same way you would if someone withdrew funding for your dig. You'd find another donor."

The cruelty of it stunned him. Did she really think he was so shallow that he could segue from one woman to another with no more involvement than if he were fund-raising? But then he thought, let's look at it as unsparingly and precisely as Anne does. And he knew she was right. He would find someone else. Whatever they had been building together hadn't gone deep enough to change his life, much less turn him into a monk.

She might have changed his life, given enough time, but she would not allow that to happen. And then he thought of her, and knew that the cruelty of her words were turned more on herself than on him. She would be alone because something within her was so strong she could not do anything else, while Josh would find a new companion. And because they had been together so little, they would leave barely a ripple in each other's lives, no more substantial than the ripples on Defiance Lake caused by the jumping of the trout.

He walked around to Anne's side of the car and opened the door for her. When she stood before him, he took her hand before she could stop him and kissed her cheek. "You're a remarkable woman, Anne. I wish we could have had much more time together. I wish you well."

She stood on the walk as he drove off, watching his car until it turned the corner. She felt empty inside. The air around her seemed to darken. The evening had been clear and calm, but now it looked cloudy, and the wind had come up. It's going to rain, she thought. She went into her building, absently greeting the doorman, and took the elevator to her floor. I'm sorry, she said silently as she unlocked her door. I'm so sorry. She walked into her living room and curled up in the window seat without turning on the light. She was in her own home, she was alone, she was safe.

Safe, she thought. Safe. And then she realized she was weeping.

Keith stood in the crowd gathered around the towering spruce tree, snow sifting lightly under his collar, his hand firmly gripping the back of Eve's lovely neck. "When is this damn thing going to take off?" he asked.

"They said five o'clock," Eve replied. "Are you cold?"

"I'm bored. Out of my mind."

"Oh, I'm not, it's too exciting. I guess it's because I'm new here. It's so nice, all these people, thousands of them—"

"Two, three hundred," Keith said.

"And the snow, and the wreaths on the lampposts, and all the lights on in the Forstmann House, with those darling lace curtains at the windows . . . it's like a Christmas card. I guess it's too romantic for you. You're not a very romantic person, Keith."

"I feel romantic about you," he said automatically. "I'll prove it to you later."

"I didn't mean romantic that way." Eve's mouth tightened. She had definite ideas about the world. She worked two jobs, as a waitress at breakfast and lunch time, and a bartender at night, and she dreamed of big cities, limousines, silks, furs, and penthouses. And love. "Romantic is sitting and talking about things and making plans, and kissing and cuddling. All you want to do is go to bed."

"Merry Christmas, everybody," the mayor said, "and a very Happy New Year to one and all!" He pushed a button and the spruce tree burst into light. The crowd applauded; a group of schoolchildren began singing, "Hark, the herald angels sing"; and Keith turned to go.

"Isn't it perfect?" Eve asked wistfully. "So beautiful . . . like a painting. Keith, *look* at it!"

Keith turned back and contemplated the tree. He drove past it every day; it was part of the town. But he had to admit it was a terrific tree, sixty feet tall, perfectly shaped, shading Gideon Forstmann's front yard since he had planted it in 1889 at the corner of his handsome brick house. Keith gazed at the hundreds of colored lights and ornaments hung by schoolchildren, and thought of all the years he and his sister, Rose, and their parents had decorated Christmas trees. They'd had a good time. Everything was more fun in those days, he thought. But that was a long time ago.

"Don't you love it?" asked Eve. "This is such a nice town, everybody doing things together, sort of like a song, you know, with Christmas spirit and things . . ."

"It's the most fucking boring place in the world," Keith said. "Tourists come here and have a good time, but if you live here, what the hell is there to do? I mean, there's nothing going on. No deals, no nothing. I'm getting out of here as soon as I can and get to a decent city."

"Oh!" Eve cried. "I didn't know! Take me with you! Would you, Keith? Please?"

"I thought you loved it here. A great town, like a song, Christmas spirit, all that crap."

"Well, but I thought . . . I mean, I didn't know you didn't like it."

Keith grinned. "I do. I love it here. I'll never leave."

"You're just saying that to confuse me. You'll take me, won't you, Keith? I'd love to live in New York; I've dreamed about it forever."

"Not New York. Washington, D.C., capital of our country. That's where I'm going."

"Oh. I don't know anything about Washington. But I'm sure it's wonderful; it's a very important city. When are you . . . I mean, were you thinking of any special time to go?"

"As soon as I can." That was the trouble; setting a date. He always got to this point and then got stuck. It wasn't that he was scared of leaving the valley; he wasn't scared of anything. It was more that he wasn't going to dangle out there alone anymore. He was going to latch onto somebody; that's the way people got what they wanted. Being part of deals, and people doing what you told them to, and everybody envying you. The point was, there was no way you could stay a kid forever, but you could make sure there was always somebody out there who'd take care of you. That was the thing; it was really shitty to have to grow up, but there were ways to make it more fun. That's what he was working on.

And maybe he'd take Eve with him. She was really pretty in a sort of china doll way, and she'd be good to him; he could bend her around his little finger. He caressed the back of her neck. "I'll let you know when I'm ready to take off. And I'll think about taking you with me. I promise. Isn't that a pretty tree? And isn't the town pretty?"

Eve nodded, trying to keep up with the shifts in his mood. "I like it, the way everybody keeps the lights on all the way to June."

Asinine, Keith thought, but it made people like Eve happy, and the tourists, too, and everybody else who thought it was romantic.

"Very pretty," he said again. "Like you. Are you ready to go?"

"Where?" she asked.

Not bed, he thought, though that was where he had planned to spend the evening. Bed was out of the question until later; her tight mouth had told him that. "Drinks at Timothy's," he said, "and dinner at Larch's."

"Oh, Keith." Her eyes were shining. "Sometimes you say exactly the right thing. But . . . Larch's! It's awfully expensive, you know."

"We're celebrating. Twenty days to Christmas, the Forstmann House tree is lit, and we're having a good time. Why shouldn't we celebrate?"

Eve put her hand through his arm and squeezed it. "And we have all night to do it."

Keith glanced at her as they walked on the snow-packed sidewalk with the crowds of people bundled up in sheepskin and furs and colorful down ski jackets. She wore a red and black puffy jacket and her mouth was full and glossy, not tight at all. Keith grinned. You don't get anywhere by being romantic, he thought, but you can get a long way by using romance. He decided that was a hell of a profound thought, and he was exceedingly pleased with himself.

Everything pleased him that night, and he awoke the next morning feeling invincible, with his future stretching brilliantly before him. He eased Eve out of his apartment as soon as he could, and called Vince. "Listen, I've been thinking; there are things— Oh, are you busy?"

"I'm about to go into a meeting. What things?"

"I can call back if you don't have time."

Vince was silent. There was an odd jubilance in Keith's voice; what the hell was he up to? He sat back, his voice casual. "I have a few minutes. What's up?"

"Well, I'm like wondering how much longer you're going to need me here. I mean, there's rumors all over town that The Tamarack Company's about to be sold, so if everything changes, you know, I'd be like out of a job. Two jobs. You know, assistant mountain manager and also with you."

"I haven't heard that rumor."

"Well, it's around. I mean, there's this guy, Ray Beloit, from Denver; he's been up here telling everybody how he's gonna fix up the place when he buys the company. Like the stores need neon signs because that's what tourists are used to, and we need a real hotel, you know, a Ritz or a Sheraton to get lots of conventions, and we oughta have high-rise apartments like in Vail 'cause that's where the real money is, and four-lane the highway and then like put a parking lot where Grover Park is . . . he runs off at the mouth like a goddam faucet. People're going nuts; there was even an editorial in the paper. He's a total ass; if he's for real, he'll never make it around here even if he does end up buying the company."

Vince drummed his fingers on the desk. Beloit had never mentioned a visit to Tamarack. "He said *when* he buys the company?"

"Right. That's what got the rumors going. So what I thought—"

"What does William say? And Marian and Fred? You could have called them, and asked; you're part of the family and you live there, and it would have made sense for you to call."

"They'll be here for Christmas. I can ask them then."

"Christmas? All of them? They never come for Christmas. Most of them never come at all."

"Well, they've all been here; I told you that. To see Anne. And they're coming for Christmas."

"What about her?"

"Anne? She's sort of in and out. I see her every day when she's here; she always goes up the gondola with Leo when he does his morning inspection. It's like a ritual; nine o'clock sharp, up they go. And I saw her last night at the, you know, tree lighting, with Gail and Leo and the kids. She looked sort of out of it, she didn't look, you know, happy." He waited, but Vince said nothing. "Anyway, I thought you could talk to Uncle Charles and find out if he's sold the company or what. It'd be kinda weird if he had; I mean, I don't see why the rest of them would want to, with things going better now. I mean, there's lots of skiers in town for this early and we've got tons of snow, and people who like canceled when the water was bad are coming back, or maybe there's other people coming, whatever, business is pretty good and the locals are all of a sudden happy as clams. So why would they sell now, when they wouldn't last September, when the water was zapped? I mean, they don't talk to me so I don't know, but I thought maybe they're in lots of trouble and nobody knows it but them. Like, they spent a pile on cleaning up the reservoir, and they're still running jillions of ads to convince everybody Tamarack's safe, and it must be working 'cause there's all these people here already, and we've still got February and March when it's always busy, so unless they're really out of money and like desperate, I don't get it. Anyway, what I was thinking was, with all this going on, I've got to figure what I do next—"

"I think I'll come up for a couple of days," Vince said. "I haven't been there for a long time; I'll wish everyone a happy New Year in person."

There was a dismayed silence. "I thought I'd come to Washington," Keith said. "I mean, I thought you trusted me to like keep you up to date. I mean, that's what you told me you wanted, and I thought I'd, you know, go to Washington so we could talk about you and me, 'cause when this guy, or anybody, buys the company, I'm out of here. I've got a couple ideas but I definitely think we shouldn't, you know, talk about them on the phone. . . ."

"I'll be there"—Vince flipped through his calendar—

"December eighteenth, Wednesday, with my wife. Get us a room at The Tamarack for that night. We'll be in town as much of Thursday as I need; then we'll fly to Denver. Make sure there's a car waiting for me at the airport. I'll take the family, whoever's in town, to dinner in the hotel dining room. It's still good?"

"Great. It and Larch's are the best—"

"Find out who'll be in town and make a reservation for Wednesday night. Thursday morning you'll have breakfast with me there, at seven. If I want to talk privately to anybody in the family, I'll do it on Thursday and fly to Denver on Friday. If there's anything urgent for me to know before the eighteenth, call me; otherwise let it wait until I get there. Anything else?"

"No." The jubilance was gone from Keith's voice. "It's okay, I can do all that. It . . . it'll be good to see you."

When Vince hung up, he immediately called Beloit. "When were you in Tamarack?"

"Last? Thanksgiving. I've been there half a dozen times in the past year, Vince; you know I wouldn't buy a place without checking it out. Your brother turned me down again, you know. You think the third time'll be a charm? I'm getting kinda antsy about this, Vince. If it took me this long to get your campaign together, you'd be in real trouble."

Vince took a sharp breath. "I'm going up there in a couple of weeks; I should be able to wrap it up then. In the meantime, stay out of there; you've got people crazy with all your talk about neon and conventions and whatever the fuck else you've been babbling about."

"I thought they'd be grateful. They oughta be grateful; that place needs waking up. *Shaking up* is what it needs. I'm all for charm and small-town atmosphere, but what good is it if it cuts into profits? You gotta be practical, and believe me, those people are light-years away from practical."

"Don't go up there again until you hear from me, around Christmas." Vince hung up and stood beside the desk, drumming his fingers on its polished surface. *I'm getting kinda antsy about this, Vince. If it took me this long to get your campaign together, you'd be in real trouble.* The son of a bitch, threatening him with a slowdown on his campaign. He wouldn't threaten him much longer, though. The day after the primary, Beloit was out. He'd lasted too long already, hanging on, throwing his weight around, because he was too strong in the party to ignore. But after the primary, when Vince was on his way to reelection with no serious opposition, and on his way to the White House, it would be easy to find other powerful figures in the party who knew where the money was, and how to get attention at the right time, in the right place. And Beloit, who'd been clinging to him for twenty-five years, would finally be gone.

He pulled on his suit jacket, tightened his tie, and stuffed papers and books into his briefcase for his committee hearing. It was the first of what would be months of hearings on acid rain, stretched out to run into the November election; it was a perfect subject for a reelection campaign. No matter what the testimony, it would make the network evening newscasts and the morning papers, and Vince, who was now committee chairman, would be in the center: handsome, experienced, concerned, every voter's humble servant. A man in charge in the Senate. A man to take charge of the country.

If it took me this long to get your campaign together, you'd be in real trouble.

Head down, he walked to the door. Four months to the primary. He could talk about getting rid of Beloit, but right now Beloit was running his campaign, and Vince could not do without him. Already he'd lined up bankers and insurance men who'd never supported Vince before; he'd convinced local governments all over the state to hold a "Senator Vince Chatham Day" with parades and voter registration when Vince visited them in the month before the primary; he had newspapers and television stations running stories on Vince three or four times a week in a blizzard of free publicity; and most important, he'd eliminated one opponent, the most threatening one, using information Vince didn't know about, and had no intention of knowing about. Beloit was creative, tireless, unprincipled, and discreet: the absolutely essential ingredients of a good campaign manager.

Vince took his briefcase and left the office. Four months to the primary. Four months of keeping Beloit happy. And that meant getting The Tamarack Company into Beloit's hands at a bargain price. It was past time it was done, Vince thought, whether Beloit was involved or not.

I should have done it myself, from the first, he thought. Charles can't be trusted with a damn thing, even though he's the one who's desperate to sell. Once I'm there, it won't take long; a family dinner will do it. And then I'll get the hell out of there. *We'll* get out of there. It was amazing, how hard it was for him to remember he was a married man.

But his family remembered, and when he got to Tamarack, it was clear that they were pleased about it. "Clara Chatham," Nina said, coming up to them in the restaurant. She kissed Clara on both cheeks. "I like the sound of it, like a lady in an old-fashioned novel. I'm so glad to meet you, Clara; it's nice to see that Vince hasn't lost his faith in marriage." She smiled at Vince and patted his arm. "We're optimistic in this family, Clara; you'll find that out. We do believe that good things will happen if we wait long enough."

Vince put an arm around Nina's shoulders and kissed her cheek. "Nina believes in love. She's the best sister in the world, because she loves all of us, so of course we're optimistic. A universe that has Nina in it has to be a good place."

Nina's color rose. She looked at Vince with wide eyes, flattered and grateful, but also puzzled. Vince smiled at her, pretending not to see the puzzlement. He knew none of them really trusted him, but he was about to change that.

The maître d' led them to a private room. William and Marian, and Gail and Leo, were already there; Vince had kept them waiting exactly eight and half minutes, the perfect length of time, he had found, to heighten anticipation without causing annoyance. "You're late," William rumbled as they walked in. Vince did not reply. He introduced them to Clara and, as they talked to her, watched with amusement the approval in their eyes. Everyone approved of Clara; it was astonishing that a small woman with pale brown eyes, a small, pretty mouth, and brown hair streaked with gray, worn simply, to her shoulders, could get as much attention and affection as Clara got. It was the reason he had married her, of course, but even after a month of marriage he did not understand it.

"Hello, Uncle Vince," said Gail coolly. They were standing at one end of the small room that was furnished with a mahogany dining table set with crystal and china for eight. Nearby was a small bar. Gail let Vince kiss her cheek. "I hope everything is all right; Keith made it sound like this dinner was terribly important."

"The most important thing is seeing you," said Vince. "You're a lovely woman, Gail. I stay away too long and I forget how beautiful you are." He smiled wistfully. "I lose track of everything, in fact. Marian tells me Robin and Ned are great kids. I'm ashamed to say it, but I've forgotten how old they are."

"Eight and ten," Gail said briefly.

"That's about what I thought. I have some things for them in my room upstairs; I'll bring them down before you go. It's terrible, how little I see of all of you; it makes me angry sometimes. Washington's a long way away, and I'm too busy to take much time off, and then I've got this damn campaigning—and there's no end to it, Gail; there's always someplace else they tell me I have to be, as if I'm some kind of puppet they're pulling around the country. You have no idea how I hate politics sometimes—of course I love it, too; that's the problem. And then the older I get the faster time slips away from me. I don't know if you feel that, too; you're so young . . ."

"Sometimes," Gail said. She could not take her eyes off him; he was so handsome, and his smile embraced her and made her feel very special, the focus of his attention.

"I feel it all the time, that I'm losing too many important things, that I can't get everything organized so I can find what I've lost. I admire what you and Leo are building together—I have to tell you, I envy it, too—and it's terrible, to me, that I haven't managed to share in it. I feel I've wasted a lot of good years. I'd like to make up for it, if you'll let me. Maybe you'll all come to Washington and stay with us. Would you? It would give us all a chance to get acquainted."

"We might, sometimes." Gail frowned as she heard her words. She shook her head as if to clear it. This is *Vince,* she thought. "Why did Keith say we absolutely had to be here tonight?"

"Did he say that? Well, Keith tends to go a little overboard; he's an enthusiastic young man. I certainly wanted you here; I couldn't imagine coming to Tamarack and not seeing you. Gail, you're being very hard on me. Couldn't we talk and be friends without other people getting in the way?"

"You mean Anne," Gail said coldly. "No, we can't. I wouldn't be here at all if Leo hadn't wanted me to come. I'm sorry I'm not nicer; I'm usually a nice person. Excuse me."

Vince was left standing alone, a small, sad smile on his lips, until Marian and Fred came to him. "How pleasant and unusual to see you here," Marian said with a small peck on his cheek. "I didn't think there were enough votes in Tamarack to make it worth your while to visit it."

Vince chuckled and put his arms around her, forcing her into a quick, tight hug. "Dear Marian," he said, letting her go. He reached out and shook Fred's hand, still looking at Marian. "I've missed you. You used to have such a vague look about you, but now you're as sharp as they come, aren't you? Who would have guessed it? I could use you on my campaign staff. In fact, you could *run* my campaign staff; you're smarter and quicker than anybody I've seen in politics." He tilted his head. "It's a good idea, you know. Would Fred let you go for a few months? You and I would make a good team. We could go straight to the White House."

"Arm in arm," said Marian dryly, but her eyes were curious. "Is this talk about the White House for real? We've heard it from a few people. Are you serious about it?"

"Dead serious. There's so much I want to do, and I can't

do it from the Senate. I want this, Marian, and I know I can do it."

"You can, too," Fred said. Usually he let Marian speak for both of them, since families bored him, but now he felt he had to let Vince know he was there. "We'd be with you, all the way. Raising money, making speeches, whatever you need."

"Wouldn't that be something," Marian said. "President Vince Chatham. It has a nice ring. Aren't you amazing, Vince, to pick yourself up and go so far. Well, I must say, I thank you for the compliment, but we both know I couldn't run your campaign. I don't know the first thing about politics; I'd be a chicken that the experts would pluck right and left. But it's nice to hear kind words. I've missed you, too, you know. You're the most interesting of the five of us—"

"You and I are the most interesting," he said.

"That might be true, but you're more devious. And when you behave, you're quite a pleasure to have around. And of course I admire what you've done with your life. A lot of times I've wished we could go back and do a few things over in our family; we'd all be a lot happier."

"Nobody wishes that more than I do," Vince said mournfully. "I owe you an apology, Marian; I never gave you my side of—"

"I don't want to hear it. This is today; the past is gone. Let's not churn things up, Vince; let's move ahead. You're my brother and I'd never turn my back on you; I've always believed you had the capacity to be a good man. Whatever mistakes you made are done with. I'm proud of you for being in Washington; God knows we need good men there. Now I'm going to talk to your wife; if anything makes me sure you've grown up, it's your marrying Clara."

With a smile, Vince watched her tuck her hand under Fred's arm and walk away. He was still smiling as William came up to him. "Old home week," William said. "I must say, it's good to see us all together. Well, most of us." He took the vodka and tonic the bartender handed him. "Too bad Charles couldn't make it; was he too busy?"

"I didn't ask him," Vince replied. "I'm going to talk about him tonight, and I thought it would be best if he wasn't here."

William's left eyebrow rose. "You might have let him be the one to decide that."

"I couldn't. I'm too worried about him. I really thought this would be best, William."

William's eyebrow stayed up. "Kind of you," he said at last. It was clear he was having difficulty with the idea of Vince being thoughtful of others. "He'll be here for Christmas, you know. So will just about everybody else. Dinner at Gail and Leo's."

"All of you?" Vince looked surprised. He would not let any of them know that Keith kept him informed. "The family never came here at Christmas; we were always in Lake Forest and then everyone went off somewhere. *You* always went to some beach."

"Well, but here I am. And everyone else is coming in the next few days. We'll be about eighteen for dinner. It's a pleasant prospect; we haven't had that many around the table for a long time. You know, I haven't given it a lot of thought, but I think it has to do with Anne." He paused a moment, scrutinizing Vince's expressionless face. "Everyone's curious about her, but there's more to it: they like her, and they like to be near her. There's a kind of *surge* when she comes in, if you know what I mean. She doesn't like anybody to get too close, but you can see how they're drawn to her. It's damned fascinating: she's got a look about her of knowing things, as if she has some secret that the others are hoping to find out. Anyway, she's made things more interesting, and I'd bet that's why we'll all be here instead of on some beach or in Europe. What about you and Clara? I'm sure Gail would find room at the table."

"No." Vince finished his Scotch and soda and impatiently gestured to the bartender to fix him another. He bent his head in thought as he waited for the drink. *As if she has some secret.* What was going on here? William knew what her secret was; what kind of game was he playing? *She's made things more interesting.* She was up to something. And

William was fishing, to get Vince's reaction. Well, William would get nothing; Vince was a master at not giving anything away.

But something was going on. Until now, he had begun to think that she'd meant what she said about not wanting to bring up the past; that she was ready to forget her crazy idea of vengeance. But now he knew otherwise. That would have been too simple for somebody as sly as she was. *As if she has some secret.* The bitch was letting everyone know she had a secret, hinting, dangling little suggestions, priming them for the day she would throw her bomb. A bitch never forgets. He knew that. He wouldn't forget either.

He took the drink from the bartender and turned back to William. "No, we can't come up here, I'm sorry; we have to be in Florida with some friends. It's too bad; I'm just discovering how much I've missed all of you, and the idea of a family Christmas is wonderful. Maybe next year we'll do it; it's been too long since we drank a toast to the New Year together. She's not here this weekend?"

"You mean Anne? No, she wouldn't be; she's coming for five days at Christmas, and that's the most she can get away. She's enormously successful, you know, the top of her field—well, you know what she did for Dora—and she did it all on her own. I think she works too hard, buries herself in the law and hasn't room for any social life, especially the past few weeks, but she's an amazing young woman, and I'm very fond of her. We all are. Well, I wanted to ask you about Washington, but it seems I've done all the talking, and now I'm starved. When are they going to get around to serving dinner?"

"Right away. We can talk about Washington after dinner, if you want; I've got some stories that'd curl your hair. Of course you can't quote me on anything I say, but you'll have a good time listening."

William chuckled. "Sometimes I'm very good at listening."

They sat around the table, and Vince, standing at his place, proposed a toast. "To the Chathams, and the memory of Ethan. He was a great man and he cared deeply about all of us. What I'm really proposing is a toast to that spirit of love and caring that I didn't take seriously enough when I was young—" He stopped for a moment, and cleared his throat several times. "Sorry, I didn't mean to be teary. I threw away a lot that made the Chathams a wonderful family, and I've regretted it ever since, and I ask your forgiveness. I hope Clara and I will become as deeply a part of the Chathams as any of us ever dreamed of when we thought about the best that a family could be."

There was a long silence. Nina wiped tears from her eyes. Marian looked at Vince with amazement and admiration. "Well, well," William rumbled. Leo looked at Gail, who stared stonily at her plate.

Clara smiled at Vince with love and pleasure. He had told her the whole story shortly after they met: how he had rebelled against his father's authority at home and in the business, and finally, in a fit of temper, had sold his shares in the family company and left home and deliberately lost touch with everyone but Charles. When he was planning this dinner, she had gently insisted that he apologize to them. Clara understood Vince. What he needed was someone who would tell him what he had to do to get along with people. Because, as brilliant and politically astute as he was, and terribly concerned about the welfare of his country, Vince did not understand people. Clara knew that. It was a strange flaw in an otherwise perfect man. But he had found her, and she knew she could guide him to say and do those things that would smooth his path wherever he went. She would be Vince's Seeing Eye dog, leading him through the thickets of human relationships. It was her mission.

"What I really want to talk about is Charles," Vince said after the waiter had served their soup and left the room. "I'm terribly worried about him. He comes to see me in Washington fairly often, and he's as honest with me as any brother could be. I've come to think of him as one of the bravest men I've ever known. But he also has serious limitations, and that's why he's in such trouble. And I want to help him."

He paused and pushed his soup bowl a little away from

him. "I've *got* to help him. It haunts me that one of us should have such terrible problems. And I love him. He's much older than I, but we've always been close. We're the best of friends. But I'm going to be very honest about this—I've thought about it for months and we can't help him by closing our eyes to the truth—Charles is a weak man. And a frightened one. He can't take decisive action—sometimes he can't take *any* action—because he's sure the consequences will be bad. And he's been right often enough to make him even surer of it. Just this year, to take the latest example, when he made a major decision and moved on it, it was a disaster. That was the Deerstream development in the northwest suburbs of Chicago that depended on a highway that was never built. You all know that story."

He looked around the table. No one was eating; they were listening. "The problems really started when Dad lost interest in Chatham Development and put all his energies into Tamarack. Poor Charles was left behind, and let's be honest, none of us helped him. We'd let Dad built up the company, and we weren't willing to go in and bail Charles out when he was letting it go to hell. William liked to work a few hours a day and spend the rest of his time writing letters; Nina was trying to find someone she could love, who would love her as much as she needs and deserves; Marian and Fred wanted a big company and knew how to run one, but they weren't willing to move in and take it over—"

"Fred wanted to," Marian put in.

"In the right circumstances," Fred added quickly. "Not by myself, of course; Walter's been wanting to move up, too . . . my daughter Rose's husband," he said to Clara. "We haven't been happy, watching the company go downhill, but I couldn't exactly elbow Charles out of the way; after all, he's the eldest son and Walter and I only married into the family."

"Whatever the reasons," Vince said easily, sidestepping the fact that Ethan had disliked Fred and kept him away from the top even though Fred had been angling for Vince's place long before Ethan kicked him out, "we all let Charles down. I wouldn't blame anybody—we're all busy and we have our own problems—but the fact is, we abandoned him. And I have to tell you, I weep for him. A couple of weeks ago, when he came to Washington, he brought me Chatham Development's latest financial statement. I know you've all seen it, but let me run through it, so we'll all be talking about the same thing. The banks are pushing for a ten-million-dollar interest payment on the company's loans; they won't make any more loans until they get it; and there's no cash in the company to pay it. Maybe even more important, there's no cash to start new projects that would get the company moving again. And Charles himself—poor Charles, trying to keep things from crashing down—has personally borrowed forty million dollars, putting up everything he has as collateral. He's absolutely on the ropes, and we all know it."

Vince took a sip of water. "Now. If The Tamarack Company is sold, Chatham Development could end up with thirty to forty million in cash after Tamarack's debts are paid. Charles could pay the banks their interest and get them off his back; he could repay part of his own loans; and he'd still have ten or twenty million to begin some of the projects he and Fred have thought up. They're ready to go. They haven't been sitting around on this; they're dead sure they can turn everything around. All they need is the tools. They need money."

He looked at each of them. "So that's where we are. Charles is in Chicago trying his damndest to make us proud of him, but the company keeps shrinking under him, and every time I see him it's obvious that he's more and more a broken man. I couldn't stand it anymore, so I came out here to see if I couldn't get us together to help him. He's our brother! And your father, Gail! How much longer will we let him suffer? He's asked the family for one thing: to sell The Tamarack Company so he can use the money to pay his debts and put Chatham Development back on its feet. I've told him I'll help him all I can, that I won't let him down, and I'm sure—*I am absolutely sure*—the rest of you won't let him down, either. There are lots of things we can do to help, even after we get him the money. Maybe we ought to think about some changes in the company. Maybe it's time Fred took over; he'd make a fine president. And of course Walter would work closely with him, and they'd continue Dad's legacy better than anyone could. I'll bet Charles would be delighted; he'd be chairman of the board, and he'd know he wasn't a failure."

The waiter came in to take the soup plates. Vince waved him away. "I know how you feel about Tamarack," he said to Gail and Leo. "But the rest of us grew up with Chatham Development; that was Dad's first dream, and it was the one we all had a part in. If I'd been a better person, I'd still have a part in it. But that's why I'm doing what I can, now, for Charles and also for Dad. I threw away my part in it because I was young and a damn fool, but I never lost my love for it, and I never stopped feeling that I had a responsibility toward it. Well, look, that's my problem, not yours; you don't have to help me try to make amends for my mistakes. But I think we all love Dad's company and we all feel a sense of responsibility toward it. I don't think I'm wrong about that."

He leaned forward, his eyes warm and intimate, his voice soft but urgent. "We must do this! All of us together can save Charles and Dad's company; we can give them both a new life. What better Christmas present for Charles, and for all of us, than to know we've done this good thing?"

His voice died softly away. There was a brief silence. "Oh, my," Nina said. "Poor Charles. How could we say no? He needs us."

Marian nodded slowly. "I love Tamarack," she said. "I wouldn't want it changed."

"Why would it be changed?" Vince asked. "It's been successful for a long time; why would anyone fool with it?"

"There's a man going around town, telling us how he'd fool with it," Gail said angrily. "He's talking as if the company's already his and he's ready to remake the town. His name is Ray Beloit and he's your campaign manager, and you probably know all about what he wants to do."

There was an almost imperceptible pause. "Ray wants to buy The Tamarack Company? He never told me. He was probably afraid I'd try to talk him out of it because he's so involved with my campaign." Vince looked thoughtful. "I can talk to him and find out what's going on; maybe that's what I'd better do. If he's got enough backers to buy The Tamarack Company, that could be the best thing that ever happened to us. He and I've known each other for almost twenty-five years; he'd listen to me, to all of us, for that matter, if we had concerns about what happens to the town. But he might not be the one to buy it, you know. If we put it on the market, we'd have serious interest from a number of sources. Leo? What do you think about all this?"

"We'd be damn fools to sell," Leo said bluntly. "We're coming out of a difficult position right now; we've had problems that have weakened us, and even if I supported a sale, which I don't, I know we couldn't get the price we could get in six months or a year, when we've recovered. But the point is, we shouldn't sell at all. This is still a healthy company, and it doesn't make any sense, business or otherwise, to sell a healthy company in the faint hope of saving a failing one." He took a long breath. "Listen, I worry about Charles, too. It's not easy to see Gail's father in this mess, but selling The Tamarack Company won't save him. How do we know that Chatham Development will ever be strong again? It needs more than money; it needs a driving energy and a purpose and a goal and imagination, and it hasn't had any of those since Ethan left it. We all know that. And that's what we ought to be thinking about: helping Charles and the company put together a good plan to be profitable on their own, not going off half-cocked and selling The Tamarack Company when that could be throwing more money down the drain. And throwing away Tamarack, too. It doesn't make sense."

"Oh, dear," Nina sighed.

"But you don't know how much we might get for Tamarack," Marian said. "If it's higher than you're supposing it will be—and I do think you're making too much of these little problems you've had, Leo, the water and so on; you're just too close to it to be objective—it might be enough to pull Charles out and make the company healthy, and we'd all be better off. We really have no idea what would happen if we put it on the market."

"You'd get low offers," Leo said. "And then it would be hard as hell to pull back; you'd have money dangling in front of you and you'd want it. Charles would want it."

"Leo, really, he's not foolish," Marian said chidingly. "Charles knows what he needs. He wouldn't want us to sell if it wouldn't help him."

"He'd want what he could get," Leo insisted. "He'd begin to think he could work miracles with whatever he could get."

"No, we could control that," William said. "That's not the problem. The problem is Charles and what we owe him, and I don't like it, but I think Marian's right. We owe it to him at least to find out what we could get."

"But we haven't talked about anything else!" Gail cried. "Other ways to help him, other things we can do . . ."

"We'll do that, too," said William. "But we have to start with The Tamarack Company; it's a bird in the hand. We don't have any other good ideas, do we?"

Gail bit her lip. Leo put his hand on hers. "Then we've got to set a good price, and not sell below that."

"That's a little rigid," Vince said gently. "We're talking about Charles; not cold real estate."

"Well, of course, it's all Charles," said Nina. "We're doing it for him. We don't have to hold out for the absolute highest price; that might discourage buyers. Whatever we get would help him, don't you think?"

"We'll get a good price," Marian said. "We don't have to hold out for the moon, but we'll do fine; this is a prestigious company."

"Let's see what offers we get," William growled. "Then we'll make a decision."

No one looked at Leo and Gail. They all knew the lineup of the shares in Chatham Development that Ethan had distributed: that Charles, with Marian and her family, controlled 42 percent; and Gail and her family 13 percent. Either William or Nina could join Charles and Marian in a vote to sell, and that would be the end of it.

The waiter looked into the room again. This time Vince gestured to him to clear the soup plates and serve the next course. It was time for them to enjoy a family dinner.

Chapter 16

Keith watched Leo and Anne step into the gondola car for
the ride up the mountain. He checked his watch. One
minute to nine, on the dot. He looked up and met their eyes,
and smiled brightly. "You never miss a morning," he said to
Leo as he walked beside their slow-moving car. "Even
Christmas day."

"What about you?" Leo asked. "Didn't I say you could
take the day off?"

"I just wanted to make sure everything was okay. I'm out
of here in a couple minutes." The car reached the end of the
gondola building and the door automatically slid shut.
"Have a good time," Keith said, waving, and turned away as
the car rapidly picked up speed and moved up and away
from him.

"How about that," Leo said. "Showing up on Christmas
morning to make sure everything's okay. Keith always
manages to surprise me." He settled back on the cushioned
seat. The car was made to hold six people, three facing up
the mountain and three down, toward the town. Anne and
Leo sat facing the town. The streets below were quiet so
early on Christmas morning, the rooftops heavy with snow,
the parks a jumble of sled tracks and footprints in the snow,
guarded by snowmen. The peaks encircling Tamarack were
pink-gold in the sunlight, but in the valley, the town was still
in shadow, and the Christmas lights were like necklaces

draped over trees and buildings, and outlining the roofs and front porches of houses.

Anne forgot Keith and the discomfort she always felt when he was around. She liked sitting in the small, enclosed car with Leo, watching the mountain slide past beneath them. He was a good friend, easygoing and undemanding, as close to a brother as she could have. Fleetingly, she thought of Josh, and she knew that she would have liked him to be the one sitting beside her as they swung above the earth in sunlight and silence. Well, he won't be, she thought. It won't happen. She took a long breath, gazing through the clear plastic window that encircled the upper half of the car, and thought instead about Tamarack.

After so many years, it felt like home again, a place where she belonged even though she only came for short visits. It was still, in many ways, the town she remembered, and many of the people were the same, too: as eccentric a bunch as any she had met in California—stubborn, fiercely independent, warm and welcoming to those who loved the mountains and wanted to protect them, coldly contemptuous of those who came to use Tamarack for their own exhibitionism, hoping for some of its glitter to rub off on them. Many towns in one, Anne thought, and all, somehow, coexisting so that most of those who lived there found a niche and felt, as she did, at home.

"Peace on earth," Leo said a little bitterly as he and Anne watched the town recede below them. "Who'd believe that people are fighting over that little bit of real estate, and some of us just lost?"

Anne shook her head. "I can't believe that. There must be something you can do."

"We can't think of anything. They just rode over us, and they have the votes. The damndest thing is, a couple of weeks ago Josh came up with an idea that isn't too bad—we're not crazy about it, but it would be better than selling the company—but there's not enough money in it to satisfy Charles and Fred, anyway. God, can you imagine how much money they've gone through in Chicago? They're like a vacuum cleaner; they suck it up and it's never seen again."

"What was Josh's idea?" Anne asked.

"To sell part of The Tamarack Company. Last time he was in Egypt he talked to private investors and government officials, and it turned out that the government didn't want to share his dig with anybody else in Egypt. I guess it could be the greatest thing since Tut's tomb, and they want the royalties and film rights and the rest of it. So the private investors were looking for something else, and Josh suggested Tamarack. I couldn't believe it when he told me; what would Egyptians want with an American ski resort? But what the hell, the Japanese do it, and the Dutch and the British own pieces of this country wherever you look, so why not the Egyptians? I was impressed that Josh thought of it; there he was, trying to line up money for this dig that's the most important thing in his life, but he had time to think of us."

"What happened next?"

"We sent them a bunch of literature and financial statements. Not that we were about to say yes, but I didn't want to throw away any alternatives. I called Fred and asked him what he'd say if that kind of offer was ever made—I didn't tell him we had anybody interested—and he said forget it; it wouldn't give them what they wanted. Damn it, there ought to be compromise here, but how do you compromise with greed?"

"Is it really greed?" Anne asked.

"No, I suppose not. I suppose it's Charles being desperate to make up for his failures, and Fred's anger that he hasn't been able to run the place the way he wants, and everybody trying to do things right."

Anne frowned. "Why doesn't anyone talk about selling Chatham Development?"

"My God, that would be like selling the Queen Mother. That company's been their whole life; they've never known anything else. And the truth is, it really wouldn't help. They've mortgaged almost everything they own, so they'd end up with enough to pay the interest on the loans that are due next month, and that's about all. They need a hell of a lot more, especially to pay off Charles' personal loan. It's a

403

terrible thing, the way they've run that company down, and there aren't any options that everybody likes. I wanted to talk about it at dinner tonight, but Gail says I shouldn't even bring it up; it'll ruin Christmas for everybody. As if ours isn't ruined already." He brooded at the last corner of the town before it disappeared behind the mountain. In the distance, the airport runway was a dark slash in the center of white fields; far beyond it, a bright red barn glowed like a beacon in the sun; and farther yet, snow-covered hills and ranges of jagged peaks marched to the horizon.

"It's not just my job, you know," Leo said slowly. "It's not even just the company. It's our home, a place we're helping to make, and make better. How many people can say that about what they do every day of their lives? It's damned hard, you know, to make a resort be a real town for its people, but we're working at it, and I want to keep doing it. We have a lot of influence around here"—he laughed—"as much as anyone can have in this town. We own enough property to have a say in what happens, and we get along with the city council, and there's a lot we can do for the schools and the hospital and library and art museum, and the teen center . . . well, what the hell, I keep talking, but it's all fantasy by now. Somebody like that bastard Beloit will buy it and turn it into Coney Island, and we'll be long gone, and we'll lose Ethan's dream, and ours, too. This has been a good home for us."

"The whole thing sounds wrong to me," Anne said. "I think it needs a lot more talk, and I think it ought to be tonight. It happened too fast, didn't it? You said it was all settled before you'd even finished your soup. How could any of them have really thought it through?"

"They didn't. Vince didn't give them time. I have to say, he was very good. Smooth, warm, playing on people's weaknesses, unbelievably persuasive—" He stopped. Anne was sitting stiffly, her hands gripped in her lap. "He talked them into it," Leo finished lamely.

They were silent, gazing at the groomed ski runs below them, snaking between long, undulating groves of snow-covered pines and firs as the gondola moved higher, to the terminal at the top of the mountain. The door slid open, and Anne and Leo stepped out, lifting their skis from the rack on the outside of the car. "Let's go over to number ten," Leo said as they stepped into their bindings. They were standing in the sunlight, with mountains looming all around them, gold and white peaks rising above slopes of silvery green trees and gray-blue shadows on the snow. Anne turned in place, gazing in all directions as if she were breathing in the pristine beauty. She felt at peace. "You go first," said Leo.

She pushed off, skating to gain speed until the ground began to slope and she could let the skis run. Leo followed, admiring the fluid line of her body. She wore black stretch pants and an emerald-green jacket, and her black hair was held in place by a gold headband. She was a superb skier, Leo thought, skiing hard and fast, staying close to the fall line, moving with the same grace and concentration with which she hiked and worked around the house, and he was sure, practiced law. She chose the straightest route to get where she was going, and she took off in a way that made it clear she would not brook interference or let herself doubt the choice she had made.

Leo stopped at the side of the run and watched Anne reach the bottom and turn to see where he was. A smooth, controlled skier, he thought; one of the most beautiful he had seen on a mountain that attracted the best. He pushed off to join her.

Anne saw him moving, and waved before she skied off, staying at the side, along the trees, where the snow was soft and untracked. She flew down the slope, the forest beside her a blur of green pines, the snow spraying from beneath her skis in sparkling showers that hovered in the air before falling slowly back to earth.

This was when she felt the most free, when she was barely connected with the earth, when she could revel in the youth and strength of her body, her energy that exploded in speed and power, and nothing else in her thoughts. There was no past or future, there were no fears or pressures or regrets.

There was only the exhilaration of speed, the beauty of a sparkling world, the cold, clear air filling her lungs, and the rhythm of her body.

The smooth slope gave way to moguls, large bumps formed by skiers pushing snow to the side as they skidded their skis to slow down. Anne made short, rapid turns, following a straight line between them, until she reached the bottom, where the snow was smooth again, the slope leveling off. She stopped, breathing hard, smiling. It was the closest she ever came to feeling joy. She looked up the slope and her smile grew as she watched Leo following her down. He was very fast, his knees deeply bent, skiing powerfully, looking, Anne thought, like a compact tank hurtling through the moguls.

He came to a stop beside her. "Good run," he grinned. "You're a lot prettier to watch than I am. Great to ski with." He looked at her bright face. Her beauty took his breath away. It was like the perfect control of her skiing: nothing out of place or out of harmony with the rest of her. Perfect control, he thought, and as in the past, he felt a quick rush of pity. It was great for skiing, but what the hell did it do to her emotional life?

"What happened between you and Josh?" he asked as they skied slowly up to lift ten.

"We aren't seeing each other anymore."

"That much I know. Gail asked him. I'm sorry; I thought you liked each other."

"We did. We still do. It just seemed better to stop it. He called me when Gail asked him to dinner for tonight. He wanted to know if I'd mind his being there."

"And you said no."

"Of course. How could I tell him not to come?"

Leo listened to her calm voice; he studied her perfectly controlled face. He dropped the subject. "I won't be long," he said, and went to talk to the lift attendant. "Everything's fine. Let's go up."

They rode the chair lift to the top, where he checked with the attendant sitting in the lifthouse at the controls for starting and stopping the lift. Then they stood for a moment, watching the crowds of Christmas skiers who were appearing all around them. Their ski suits were of every color and design, from sleek black to riotous swirls and lightning bolts of fluorescent dyes that transformed the green and white mountain into a turning, flowing kaleidoscope. Near them, a skier fell, leaving a trail of skis, ski poles, hat, dark glasses, and goggles. "Garage-sale fall," someone said, and other skiers stopped to help. Leo smiled. "I still do that once in a while. Humbling experience."

They skied down to another chair lift and then another, Leo talking briefly at each stop with the attendants and the ski patrol he met on the way. "Keith doesn't like it that I check the mountain every day," he said when he and Anne skied to the bottom and were once again at the gondola where they had begun. "He says it's his job, and of course it is, but I don't see a way around it. I can't let him be assistant mountain manager on his own until I'm convinced he can really do it."

"Why did you hire him?" Anne asked. Carrying their skis, they walked to Leo's car.

"Vince asked me to, and Keith really pushed for it; he said he wanted to straighten out his life. How do you turn down somebody who says that? I figured he'd grow into it. And in some ways he has. Like showing up today; who would've figured that? But there's something wrong about Keith; I don't know what it is, but it bothers me."

"He's unformed," Anne said. "It's as if he hasn't finished growing up, and maybe never will. He has that look of a little boy who's always on the verge of getting angry because he's sure he won't get what he wants, or get taken care of the way he thinks he deserves."

Leo thought about it. "Pretty harsh, but you're probably right. I wonder how long he'll stay in this job."

"As long as it gives him whatever it is he wants." She and Leo locked their skis in the rack on top of the car and walked toward town. "Do you know what that is?"

"I only know what he said: that he wants to straighten out his life. It seems to me he's done that; I'd lay bets that he isn't on drugs and I've never seen him drink. He's got a girl, very pretty, and she seems crazy about him. And he could make a good career here, assuming the new owners keep him. That ought to be enough."

"I don't know," Anne said thoughtfully. "He looks hungry to me."

"For what? Money?"

She hesitated. "I think he likes the kind of power that comes from hurting people."

Leo swung a sharp look at her. "Then he's dangerous."

"He might be."

They found themselves amid the crowds in the streets. "Merry Christmas, Leo," someone said, and Leo stopped briefly to chat. Many tourists had stayed in town for the day, window-shopping or sitting on the benches on the mall, heads back and eyes closed in the warm sun. In the shade the air was cold, but in the sunlight people unzipped their jackets, took off their gloves, and smiled in the warmth. "Hi, Leo; happy holidays," a tall, burly man said. Leo stopped, and introduced him to Anne. "So how's the water?" the man asked. "No more trouble?"

"Everything's under control," Leo said.

"Take care it doesn't happen again," said the man as they separated.

"Was that a warning?" Anne asked.

"Pretty close to it," Leo replied. "He flies in and out of here every couple of weeks in his own plane, and he likes us all to stand at attention, the way his companies do. He doesn't bother me; he's mostly harmless."

They reached the end of the mall, where carolers sang beside a spruce tree. Children came up to finger their old-fashioned costumes and try on the men's top hats. Later, the carolers would walk through town, stopping to serenade sick people in their homes, and in the hospital. A block away, a lone trumpeter played "Noel," his dog curled up at his feet. Through restaurant windows, waiters and waitresses could be seen putting flowers on the tables for dinner; at George's Mountain T-Shirt Company, customers were having shirts custom printed as last-minute gifts; and on the hill to their right crews were smoothing the snow for that afternoon's children's sled races.

"Leo, Anne, having a good Christmas?" Timothy asked. "Could be a lot more crowded, if you ask me."

"You're not busy in the tavern?" Leo said.

"Oh, busy. But not *busy,* if you know what I mean. I think people are still scared to come here."

Leo shook his head. "Look around you; nobody's worried."

"Yeah, but these are the ones who *came.* What about the ones who canceled and went to Vail or Aspen? They read the papers, you know. And they think twice about us."

"Tim, are you really hurting?" Anne asked.

"I didn't say that. But business is down; nobody can deny it. And houses aren't selling like they used to, and we've had a few shops close."

"How much worse is it than last year?" she asked.

He shrugged. "Maybe ten percent. It's not so bad now, but I guess I'm scared it could get worse. I don't think people trust us anymore, you know? They get worried once, they don't forget in a hurry."

"Well, don't broadcast it," Leo said. "You never know which of these happy tourists is a reporter from 'Good Morning America' or the *New York Times.*"

When they walked on, Leo was frowning. "The worst publicity for a town is its own people. But how do you make them understand that when they're scared? They put all their eggs into this crazy basket of a resort town, and then they pray for the right weather and word getting out that this is a glorious place to be. Which it is, God knows, but that won't get people here if they think it's not safe."

In Carver's Pharmacy, Leo bought his regular newspapers, and the soft drinks Gail had asked him to bring, and they turned to walk back to the car. "Are you going to bring it up at dinner?" he asked Anne.

She nodded. "I'll tell Gail in advance; I think we have to talk about it."

"It could be awkward, with Charles here."

"Then I guess it's going to be awkward."

Leo glanced at her. She was looking straight ahead, her face showing no emotion. All that hurt, he thought, still deep inside her. And so she chose his and Gail's feelings, and their future, over those of her father.

He watched her that evening as she and Gail worked in the kitchen while the family was gathering. The two sisters had put on long, plaid skirts with deep fringes at the bottom; Gail wore a dark green turtleneck sweater and Anne a wine-red one, with a silver Indian necklace and long silver earrings. Once again Leo realized how much more beautiful she was than Gail, and how much more dramatic. He knew everyone would turn to Anne first, and then notice Gail, and the familiar sense of protectiveness of his wife rose in him. But he knew Gail did not need it; she felt no envy of Anne, only pity, and love.

Anne looked up and smiled at him. Their morning trips around the mountain had drawn them close, and sometimes Leo thought he might be the one to help her break free of her rigid control. But of course it would not be him. It had to be someone who was able to take her a step beyond that, and give her a chance to love. He knew he was right the moment Josh came into the house, and Anne looked across the room, and their eyes met. That isn't over, Leo thought. I wish I could do something to help them. But he could not do that either. All he could do, he and Gail, was hang around, ready to lend a hand if either Josh or Anne, or both of them, needed it.

"Merry Christmas," Josh said, coming up to Anne. "You look very lovely, and very festive."

"Thank you." She felt relieved. What an odd emotion, she thought, to feel relieved to see Josh. And very glad. "I'm glad to see you." She smiled as she took in his dark red sweater, almost the same color as hers, over a white shirt, open at the collar. "We all dressed for the season."

"Life and growth," Josh said. "The colors of the plants that thrive despite winter. It makes hope seem quite reasonable. Have you been well?"

"Yes, thank you. And you?"

"Very well. I've missed you."

She looked at him steadily. "I've missed you," she said quietly, because she could not lie to him. "Has your crew reached the tomb yet?"

"No, but Hosni thinks we're close." He wanted to talk about the fact that they both had missed each other but still stayed apart, but it was not the time, with family members gathering around them. "I'm going back in a few days. They're very far along, almost three hundred feet; it would be remarkable if it was much farther than that."

"And then they'll reach the door." Anne tried to picture it in her mind: the long, dark corridor illuminated fitfully by lamps, ending at a sealed door that waited for someone to break it open. "I envy you," she said. "To step into a whole new world, so completely different from ours . . ."

"Not completely. It's amazing how characters and plots repeat themselves. The pharaohs behaved like every king in history, and the workers were like all workers; they even went on strike. Part of the fun of studying the past is finding how much of it is still here. We're not unique, though we'd like to believe we are."

"We're all unique," Anne said. "Our pain and our pleasure are our own; no one else can feel them or even completely understand them."

Josh gazed at her somberly. "You mean we're alone in the universe, with no chance, ever, to share, or to touch another person."

Startled, Anne gazed at him. She had never thought of it in such absolute terms. She saw sadness in his eyes and for the first time understood how lonely her world must seem to others. But I'm not lonely, she thought; I'm much too busy to be lonely. And I don't need to lean on anyone for sympathy; I'm fine on my own. Josh's words echoed behind her own: *No chance, ever, to share.* Well, that's the way it has to be, she thought defensively. That's the way my life is and there's nothing I can do about it. *No chance, ever, to touch another person.* The force of his words swept against her.

No! It burst inside her. *That isn't what I want.*

She was looking at Josh, her eyes wide. "I don't know,"

she said, and there was bewilderment in her voice. "I don't know if we're alone or not."

"Anne dear," said Charles, his hands outstretched as he came up to them, "how wonderful to see you." He leaned forward, then stopped, and a little awkwardly, held her hand in both of his. "I'm so glad we're having Christmas together. Hello, Josh, we haven't seen you in a long time. Leo tells me you've bought a place up here. Lucky man; it's a beautiful spot. I never had time to do anything like that myself—this was Dad's place and mine was Chicago—but I might think about it, one of these days. It seems that all of a sudden we're all turning up here; quite a change, you know."

He was nervous, Anne thought, talking too much and too fast, his eyes flickering over the family in the living room, then back to her and Josh. It occurred to her that he had already sold The Tamarack Company and was steeling himself to tell the rest of them. No, it's too soon, she thought. But he may be close, and feeling guilty. She watched him as he and Josh talked about mutual friends in Chicago. He looked more uneasy than he had in September, with pouches under his eyes and lines deeply etched on each side of his mouth. There was a tremor in his hands. For the first time, she felt sorry for him.

"—ulcer," he was saying to Josh. "Nobody in our family ever had one, as far as I know, but it really knocked me out for a while. Of course they know what to do about those things, now, without any special diets or that sort of thing; the biggest problem is figuring out how to stop being so tense—"

Fred Jax put his hand on Charles' shoulder. "Did Beloit call back? Anne, Josh; merry Christmas. It really could be a great one for Chatham Development, couldn't it? Have you heard from him, Charles?"

Charles looked haunted. "I told you he said he'd get back to me after the first of the year."

"Right, but he's been so hot for it, I figured he'd talk to his accountant and be back the next day. You could ask Vince what's happening; he'd be up on it."

"Vince isn't involved in this," Charles said shortly.

"Why would he be?" Josh asked curiously.

"Well, they're together all the time," Fred said. "And you know they've got to be talking about a lot of things besides politics."

"Beloit is Vince's campaign manager," Charles said when Josh still looked puzzled. "They were business partners in Denver. But it has nothing to do with us. Nothing's settled," he added angrily.

"Yet," Fred said. "Well, we can wait; we know he wants it. Marian and I feel very comfortable about it, you know, and Walter, too. There's a great future at Chatham Development; you watch: we'll put the name right back on the map where it belongs."

"How?" Anne asked interestedly.

Fred smiled. "You wouldn't be interested, Anne; nothing near as glamorous as the law and the glitzy people who line up outside your office. Great projects, though, for a developer; just what we need. That and a little capital, and we'll be surefire."

"Merry Christmas, my dear," said Nina, inching herself into the cluster they formed near the dining-room door. "What a lovely evening, isn't it? All of us together like this. It's too bad about Vince, but senators do have such demands on them. Is that what you were saying, Fred, about being comfortable? That we're finally all together?"

"That we're selling The Tamarack Company," said William, just behind her. "That makes Fred and Marian comfortable."

"Well, not exactly," Marian said. She slid around the group to insert herself between Charles and Anne. Keith was behind her, listening. "We're not comfortable—what an odd word, Fred—we're very sorry and not happy at all."

"I'm going to help Gail," Charles said. "Pour the wine or whatever she needs . . ."

Gail, coming from the kitchen, heard his last words. "Thanks," she said. "We're about ready to eat." She was holding a stack of butter plates, and Anne took them from her. "I forgot my job," she said, and began to put the plates around the table. Robin joined her, laying a butter knife on each one, and Ned came in with the water pitcher. Leo put more logs in the large fireplace open to the dining room and the living room. "More drinks for anybody?" he asked.

When they finally were seated, there was a silence. Leo held his hands to each side, and around the table, everyone took a neighbor's hand. Josh, who had found his way to Anne's side though it had been planned that he would sit at the other end of the table, held her hand lightly; her other hand was in Leo's firm grasp. Gail lit the candles that ran down the center of the table amid arrangements of holly, spruce, pinecones, grapes, and red and yellow pears, and took her place at the other end.

"Dear God," said Leo quietly, "we're grateful for the many good things of the year that's ending, for the good fortune that gives us a comfortable life, for our health and energy that help us live fully, for our curiosity that makes the world full of interest and excitement, and for our work and the sense of fulfillment it gives us. But most of all, we're grateful for our family. It protects us and nourishes us, it makes it possible for us to give as well as take, and this year, it finally became complete. That's the greatest gift we could have asked, and we'll hold it close, whatever else happens to us and the dreams we have."

"Amen," rumbled William. "Very good, Leo. Very good."

Anne's eyes were fixed on the bright berries in the center of the table. My family, she thought. *To share . . . to touch another person.* She joined Gail at the sideboard, to fill soup bowls and carry them around the table, to Josh, who sat beside her empty chair on Leo's right, then Robin and Ned, Fred, Marian, and Nina. On the other side of the table, on Gail's right, were Charles, Keith and his friend Eve, William, three-year-old Gretchen Holland, and her parents Walter and Rose. I don't like all of them, Anne thought as she set a bowl of clam chowder at each place; a few of them I don't want to know any better than I already do. But except for Josh, they're my family— Her thoughts stopped. *Except for Josh.* But he sat there talking to Robin and Ned, so much a part of the group it was hard to imagine the table without him. And in the past weeks she had missed him. She had missed his voice and his smile and the easy way they shared ideas and understood each other, often without completing a sentence. Oh, enough, she told herself angrily; I was thinking about the family. She looked around the table again. They had betrayed and wounded her, but now she found herself leaning toward them, wanting to have a place among them. I want to do something for them, she thought; help them if they need it. But mostly she wanted to help Gail and Leo, who had not been part of that long-ago betrayal, and who had been the first to welcome her back.

She returned to her chair and Josh stood to help her. "Of all the good people in the world," he said, "Leo is the best. Does he ever get angry, do you think? Or hold a grudge?"

"Not since I've known him." Anne tasted the chowder and glanced around the table to see how the others liked it.

"It's perfect," Josh said. "You made it?"

She nodded. "A friend of mine in New York gave me the recipe, years ago; she always spent summers in New England and this is supposed to be authentic."

"Anne—" he began.

"That's a lie!" Ned yelled.

Conversation stopped. "Ned?" Leo asked.

Ned's face turned red. "Well, it is. It is a lie. Uncle Fred says we're selling the company."

"Ned, we're not talking about that tonight," Gail said quickly.

"Talking about what?" Ned glared at Leo. "Dad, you said you wouldn't sell it! You *said!*"

"Your mother's right," Charles murmured. "We shouldn't be talking about—"

"We should too! Dad, did you say you would?"

"No, he didn't," Marian said firmly. "But it wasn't up to him. We all own shares in the company, and we decided to find out how good a price we could get for it. That's all we did."

"And to sell if we got a decent price," said Walter. "We aren't fooling around, are we? We're looking for a price that sounds okay, aren't we? And then we'll take it?"

"It has to be significantly better than okay," Marian said.

"How much is significant?" Walter's voice rose. It was bad enough that he always felt smothered by the family; he couldn't stand it when they made their pronouncements as if he'd hardly spoken. Fred had told him they were going to run Chatham Development together, and they'd have to pay attention to what he said. "I thought we had a deal, here! I thought we were all set in Chicago and you'd be getting us a hunk of money and we could get going again!"

"It's all right," Fred said shortly. "It's under control. We decided. It's fine."

"It's not fine," Gail shot back. "It's terrible and you all know it. It doesn't make any sense to try to prop up a company that's going under—"

"Gail, dear, you're talking about your father's company," said Nina in dismay.

"Not the time for squabbles," said William firmly. "It's Christmas, and Leo gave a prayer about families and nourishing and all that, and that's what we ought to be thinking about. There's plenty to talk about besides things we don't agree on." He looked around the table as if waiting for someone to start.

"William," Anne said, "would you mind if I asked a few questions?"

"Why should I mind?" he asked. "What about?"

"Selling The Tamarack Company. I don't understand it."

"Don't understand?" Fred asked, leaning forward to look past Marian.

"I must be very slow about these things," she said to him apologetically.

"For Christ's sake, it's so simple an infant could—"

"Careful," Marian murmured to him, "Anne isn't slow about anything."

"It's settled," Walter said, "and it'll be all done with after the first of the year. Why do we have to go over it again?"

"All done?" Ned cried. "You said you were *finding out*—"

"It isn't done," Marian said, "it's being explored."

"That isn't what he said! He said—"

"We have someone interested," Walter said impatiently. "Why do we have to keep chewing on it?"

"I'd like to hear Anne's questions," said Rose. Everyone looked at her in surprise; she so seldom spoke at family gatherings, and never against Walter.

"Well, all right, then," William pronounced. "What's wrong with a few questions, a little discussion, maybe some fresh air on the subject? Anne wasn't at our dinner a week ago when we made the decision to sell; why shouldn't she have as much information as we have? Go ahead, Anne; what can we tell you?"

Gail and Robin cleared the soup plates and listened as they filled dinner plates at the sideboard.

"I'm sorry if I seem confused about this," Anne said, looking around the table. Charles met her eyes briefly, then looked at his hands. His mouth was tight with anger and dismay. Keith's head was tilted as if he were memorizing everything. The others met her eyes with puzzlement or interest. Only Leo watched her with anticipation. "But I just don't understand what's going on. Why are you selling The Tamarack Company?"

"To save Chatham Development," Marian said before Fred's impatience could explode. "And your father. I thought you knew the finances, Anne; Charles is in a terrible mess and he needs at least forty million dollars to pull out of it. Then he and Fred and Walter will build the company up again. They're planning new projects; they've trimmed the payroll; all they need is the capital. It isn't a happy time, my dear; we're all unhappy about losing Tamarack. But losing Chatham Development would be worse."

"Why?" Anne asked.

"Because it was the work of Dad's life," Charles burst out. "It's a monument to him. It was his creation, his dream."

"He got tired of it," Gail said. "He came here and made this his creation. He chose to die here; he wanted his ashes scattered here. If he knew you'd had him buried in Lake Forest, he would have told you what he thought of you. If he'd known you wanted to sell this company, he would have hated you."

"That's too much, Gail," Marian said. "But I must say, it's true that he came to love Tamarack more than Chicago or Lake Forest. We all felt a little abandoned when he came here, and when Charles got himself in this pickle, he didn't seem to care what happened, as long as he had Tamarack. That hurt me; it hurt all of us."

"Then why is Chatham Development more important?" Anne asked.

"Because we're there," Fred said furiously. "Your father, your aunt and uncle, your cousin Walter and his family. Leo likes to yammer on about family so much; well, this is your family and we need money, and you're sitting on it!"

Anne nodded thoughtfully. "So, if I understand you, you'll build up Chatham Development to its former strength and reputation, is that right?"

"Where've you been?" Walter asked. "That's just what Marian said a couple minutes ago."

"Yes, I heard her." There was a frown between Anne's eyes. Josh was watching her, a faint smile on his lips. He had seen that frown before, in her office, and heard her seemingly simple questions. What a pleasure it was to be on her side this time as she went to work. "But, from what I've been told," Anne said, "Chatham Development, including its subsidiary, The Tamarack Company, used to be worth about three hundred fifty million dollars, and it had an international reputation for brilliant, innovative projects. And now its net worth is ten million, with a reputation for losing money." Out of the corner of her eye, she saw Charles wince, and felt a stab of pity for him. But she went on. "And the three of you are planning to build the company back to its original position?"

"Damn it," Fred snapped, "how many times do we have to tell you—"

"Gail, the pheasant is absolutely delicious," said Nina. "And I don't know what you did to the wild rice, but it's the best—"

"Just a minute, Fred," said Marian. She was looking at Anne. "I remember you used to do this when you were a little girl. You kept asking questions that seemed foolish, but then, suddenly, they didn't seem foolish at all. What are you getting at, Anne?"

"I'm trying to understand what happened," Anne replied. "When did Chatham Development slide from three hundred fifty million in assets to ten million?"

"Mostly in the last ten, twelve years," William said, his voice deep and slow. "When Dad was really gone. Charles found it a lot tougher than he'd thought it would be. And we didn't help, you know; Vince was right about that. We hardly paid any attention; we just went on the way we always had, as if Dad was still there. Only it wasn't Dad, of course; it was Charles."

"But some of you were with him," Anne said. "Weren't you a vice president, Fred? You didn't ignore him, did you?"

"You're damn right I didn't."

"And Walter? You were there, too?"

"Right. All the time."

"But then . . ." Anne paused and looked around the table. "You were all involved with Deerstream?"

There was a silence. Marian let out her breath in a long sigh. "Charles put Deerstream together," Fred said hastily.

"We all did," said Charles. "You know damn well we did, Fred. In fact, you were the one who heard about the highway first; that was why we went after the land."

"I told you about the highway? I couldn't have; I heard it from you. But even if I did—"

"You were there," said William. "You and Walter were with Charles all the way. You bought the land and hired the architects and drew up the plans and then found out the highway'd been canceled. But we all have to share the blame; we didn't even ask any questions. We're all at fault for letting you do it."

"*We* didn't *do*—"

"And the Barrington Mall," Anne said, her clear voice cutting across his. "Wasn't that yours, Fred?"

"What?"

"The Barrington Mall. Am I correct that you were in charge of that?"

"Where are you getting all this?" Fred demanded. "Who the hell is giving you all this crap?"

"I never get to say those words," Ned complained.

"Hell," said three-year-old Gretchen, beating the table rhythmically with her spoon. "Hell, crap, hell, crap."

"Stop it, Gretchen, those are terrible words," wailed Rose. "Oh, Daddy, look what you've done."

"Well, take her away from the table!" shouted Fred. "She doesn't belong with adults anyway."

"She's part of the family!" Rose exclaimed.

"Maybe Robin could take her to play," said Nina.

"That's not fair; I want to listen!" Robin cried.

"Of course you'll stay," said Leo. "So will Gretchen. This is a family dinner."

There was a brief silence. "My family always fights at holidays," said Eve helpfully. "But we always get over it."

"Thank you, my dear," said William solemnly.

"Could I have more wine?" asked Keith.

"What was the Barrington Mall?" Leo asked as he went around the table refilling wineglasses.

"A vertical shopping center we built in Barrington, outside Chicago," Charles said. "It was a mistake; vertical malls don't belong in the suburbs. Fred thought we'd save on the land, and we did, because we needed so much less, but people didn't like the idea, and then the design was bad; you couldn't see all the shops from the atrium so nobody ever shopped in them, and we had a high vacancy rate. Everything about it was wrong."

"What did you lose on it?" Anne asked.

There was a pause. "Twenty-five million," Charles replied.

Nina gasped. "No one ever told me that."

"It was in the year-end statement," Charles said.

"Well, I just don't read those," Nina said sadly. "I don't understand them."

"And the Chatham O'Hare Tower?" Anne asked. "Wasn't that yours, Walter?"

"Jesus—!" Fred said furiously.

"It's filling up," Walter said defensively. "The market's slow now."

"How full is it?" Anne asked.

"About fifty percent."

"And when was it built?"

"Five years ago," he snapped. "The market's been slow."

"It's been the biggest market in history," said William. "You didn't tell us it was only fifty percent full."

"How much has to be rented for you to make a profit?" Anne asked.

"Seventy percent," Marian said. "I looked into it. That would be a marginal profit, but I thought we were there. Fifty percent? What went wrong, Walter?"

He shrugged angrily. "It got overbuilt out there. We came in about the time everybody else was building—"

"A year late," said Charles. He still had his faintly puzzled look, but he also seemed relieved at being able to talk openly; it was almost as if he were relishing exposing the darkest corners of the business after having pretended for so long that everything was fine. "We were arguing over how much to spend on it and how big it should be, and by the time we broke ground, everybody was ahead of us."

"I moved as fast as I could," Walter shot at him. "You kept fiddling with it; every time I turned around, you had something new you wanted. I couldn't get you to make one lousy decision! I could have made that building work if people'd just left me alone!"

"Is there more pheasant?" asked Nina. "It's so good, dear . . ."

"The best I've ever had," William said. "Thank you, Gail. I'd like more, too."

"Me, too," Keith said. "This is a great dinner."

Gail met Leo's eyes. "Yes, I think maybe it is," she said.

"Do you have any more questions, Anne?" William asked.

Walter pushed his chair back. "Listen, could we just for Christ's sake stop talking? Could we just *sell* the goddam company and be done with it? Damn it, sell it and give us the money! We're the ones that need it!"

"Just a few more questions," Anne said. "Leo, what kind of shape is The Tamarack Company in?" She glanced at Walter, who hovered uncertainly between standing and sitting, and at last sat down.

"That's on last year's end-of-year report," Leo said easily. "We've gone up steadily for the last six years."

"Since you took over," said Gail.

"Ethan was a big part of that," Leo said. "We worked together up to the time of his stroke. And I'm still working with his plans. We've bought new properties in town and in the valley, and sold others; we've made improvements to the mountain, the major one being the gondola, and increased our share of the state's skiers; we built The Tamarack Hotel, and we've had full occupancy in the high seasons and higher than average the rest of the year. We had problems with the EPA and the water supply this year, and they hurt us, so we're down for this quarter, and maybe the next two quarters, but there's no reason to think we won't come back; we're very strong."

"How many Chatham Development enterprises show a six-year growth?" Anne asked, looking from Fred to Charles to Walter.

"None," Charles said shortly.

"So Tamarack is the only subsidiary that's profitable?" Charles nodded.

"And you're going to sell it?"

"We have to!" shouted Walter.

"For what?" Anne asked. Her voice was crisp. "To put the money in the hands of the same people who failed with Deerstream and the Barrington Mall and the Chatham O'Hare Tower? To get rid of the one profitable subsidiary left after all the other Chatham subsidiaries have been sold or shut down? To add money to the sums poured into Chatham Development by mortgaging its properties so there's nothing left to pay the interest on your bank loan? To try to lift up a company that's sunk to the bottom, with the same management and staff it's had all along, and nothing new to offer its shareholders?"

"Oh, dear, oh, dear," sighed Nina. "It sounded just fine last week, when Vince was talking, but now it sounds terrible; it really does, you know."

Charles was hunched in his chair, his eyes closed. Anne felt a wave of shame for what she was doing to him. She felt his agony and his own shame, and for the first time in all the years since she had left home, she thought of him as a person in pain who needed help. But she was helping Gail and Leo; they came first, at least for now. And after them came the others, who were watching her with frowns of concentration and dismay. She had wanted to help all of them; it turned out she could help only some. But saving Tamarack would help everyone in the long run, she thought; no one would be happy if they lost it.

"Does it make sense to stake everything on one company?" Anne asked. "Why would you, unless you're absolutely sure of it? How much confidence do you have right now in Chatham Development? You know its track record, and you know Tamarack's performance under Leo; where does the future seem more certain? Wouldn't it be smart to concentrate on alternative plans, ways to raise money to do part of what you want, even if you can't do everything? Shouldn't you be concentrating on your strengths when you're in trouble, and not your weakest point?"

"Right," William said heavily. "Absolutely right; we can't pretend it's not. But then what? We're nowhere."

Fred slammed his fist on the arm of his chair. "God damn it, we're where we've been from the beginning; we're selling this damned company and going ahead in Chicago! There's nothing here worth all this talk; it's no paradise; it's a little company in a little cow town that nobody gives a damn about except when they come for a week to ski their brains out and then go home. Nobody cares about this place; it's not real; it's a fantasy. We've got jobs on the line in Chicago, and a company that's been around for a long time, and you voted last week to keep it going. Nothing's changed since then; you all voted to sell—"

"No, we didn't," Marian said. "We decided to look into selling. We didn't even have a real vote."

"The *intent* was there. We all knew what we were talking about. Vince knew what we were talking about; we were talking about *selling* as soon as we got a decent price. And nothing's changed since then."

"Well, but you know, Fred, it must be different because it

sounds so different," said Nina gently. "Of course you know much more about business than I do, but it seems to me Vince gave us just part of the picture. And Anne, who speaks so well, I'm very impressed with Anne, gave us the rest of it, and the background, and the little details, and details are so important, aren't they? It seems to me Vince left them out—politicians don't like details; they keep avoiding them, have you noticed?—and I think we should take a real vote now, I really do. I'm terribly sorry, Charles, I do love you and it's very sad that you're in such trouble, but I can't imagine selling The Tamarack Company right now and giving you all that money. Good heavens, what if you lost it, the way you lost everything else? What would we have left?"

There was a profound silence. That Nina, who did not even read the financial reports of Chatham Development, had so neatly skewered Vince, and so precisely summed up the argument against selling, was enough to silence everyone.

"Well, what's next?" Marian asked after a moment. "Anne, what do you think? You've pulled all the rugs out from under us; do you have any suggestions? I know you've been talking about business, I understand that, but what about Charles?"

Anne looked at Josh. "Leo told me about your idea. I think this is a good time to talk about it."

"I do, too," Leo said quickly.

"Josh?" demanded Walter. "First Anne and then Josh? You're letting a couple of *outsiders* tell us what to do?"

"Anne is part of this family," Gail said icily. "And Josh is our friend. And he cares about us."

"I suggest you sell part of The Tamarack Company," Josh said. "You could sell as much as forty-nine percent and still retain control. If you get a good price for the shares, it could cover the ten-million-dollar interest payment that's due next month, and Charles could pay back some of his personal loan. You'd still control two companies, and you'd have bought time to come up with the money to pay off the rest of Charles' loan and get a new project started. Maybe if you brought in a new president from outside the company, you could take some new directions."

"Outside?" Fred shouted. "Who the hell do you think—"

"Fred, cut it out," Marian said wearily. "I like Josh's idea. I move we find somebody to buy up to forty-nine percent of The Tamarack Company. I'm not sure about bringing in a stranger as president; maybe vice president under Fred. We'll have to talk about that. I'm sorry, Charles, but I think you'll have to step aside. We've never had a separate chairman of the board; you might want to do that. Gail, as soon as we've voted, I'll help clear the dishes. I'm stiff from listening to all this talk. Maybe now we can enjoy dessert."

There was another silence, this time, it seemed to Anne, from exhaustion. "I second Marian's motion," said William after a moment.

"I vote yes," said Rose, not looking at Walter.

"A very good idea," said Nina, and put up her hand to be counted, as if she were in a classroom.

"I vote yes," Gail said quietly.

Everyone turned to Charles. He shook his head. "It won't bring in enough to do what we planned. You shouldn't have done that," he said to Anne. "You should have been on my side. We could have made it work this time. We know what to do."

"Are you sure?" she said softly. "Or do you only know what not to do, because it did such damage the first time?"

Their eyes met in a long look, and both of them knew that Charles had more to learn than making a reorganized company a success; he had to learn to be a father to his daughter.

He was the first to look away. His shoulders were slumped. "Go on with your vote; I won't fight it."

"We don't need a vote," said William. "It looks unanimous to me. Oh, Keith, what about you?"

"I'll go along with everybody," Keith said. "No problem as far as I'm concerned."

"Unanimous, then," said William.

Leo went to Gail, at the other end of the table, and sat on

the arm of her chair, his arm around her shoulders. "Thank you," he said to the others. "I take that as a vote of confidence, and I want you to know we'll do everything we can to make you proud of us."

"That's it?" Ned cried. "We get to stay?"

"We get to stay?" Robin echoed.

"So *now* it's done!" Ned finished triumphantly. "It wasn't before, but now it's *done!*"

"That's enough, Ned," Gail said sharply. "When you're in the majority, you ought to be gracious about it."

"It's all right," William said. "He can cheer a little bit; it's all right. Now, as long as we're unanimous, we should think about—"

"Anne didn't vote," Gail said abruptly.

"It's all right, Gail," Anne said sharply. Josh was looking at her; it was the first he had realized she owned no shares in her family's company. "It's all right," she said again. "I'm satisfied. Leave it alone. Please."

"It's not all right," Gail said stubbornly. "Just because you weren't around when Grandpa divided up his shares—" She met Anne's eyes. "Okay, I won't push it. But you did so much today—"

"More than enough for one day," Anne said firmly. "William, what did you start to say?"

"What did I start to say? Oh. Well, since it's unanimous, I was going to ask how about this fellow Ray Beloit. Charles, will he buy forty-nine percent of The Tamarack Company?"

"No," Charles said. "He wants it all."

"Then we'll have to dig up someone else," William said. "It shouldn't be hard. I must say, I'm glad we've gotten where we've gotten; I feel fine. I wasn't happy about that dinner last week; it made me nervous whenever I thought about it. I'll feel even better when we find a buyer."

"I've already talked to someone," Josh said. "Let me tell you about a meeting I had in Cairo a few weeks ago." Anne sat back and watched as the conversation drew in everyone around the table, except Fred and Walter. And Keith, Anne noted; he had not participated at all, but had stared intently at each person who spoke. His eyes were eager, his sparse beard quivered as he smiled, and he seemed the most excited of all as Josh described the Egyptian investors. The others hardly noticed him; they were absorbed in what Josh was saying. And they were pleased, Anne thought, as if, once again, they could avoid unpleasantness. She felt a moment of exasperation. When would they learn that they had to come to terms with their problems themselves, instead of letting others solve them or sweep them away? I made it too easy for them, she thought with a touch of bitterness; I ran away. I wonder what they would have done if I'd stayed around and forced them to confront me. Maybe they would have learned how to do it.

It was too late to think of that. Take them as they are, she thought; that goes with being in a family. She relaxed in her chair. She had eaten none of her dinner and she was hungry, but she could take care of that in the kitchen when they were cleaning up. While Gail and Robin and Marian cleared the table, she let herself enjoy the pleasure she always felt when her arguments swayed a jury. Of course this had not been a trial, but she thought it had been her real entry into the family. There had been one bad moment, when Gail talked about her owning no shares in Chatham Development and a remembered surge of anger and resentment had struck her, at what she had lost: her childhood, her family, a simple growing up with love and trust . . . and her heritage.

But it was done; it was over. Too late, she thought again. Some things can never be retrieved.

Josh turned to her and his shoulder brushed hers. "Will you have dinner with me tomorrow night? I want to show you my new house; it's almost finished. And there's so much I want to talk to you about before I leave for Egypt."

Yes, Anne thought. Yes, I'll have dinner with you and visit your new house and talk to you before you leave the country. She met his eyes, close to hers, and warm; he was smiling at her. She liked sitting next to him that way, as part of the family. She had liked it that he was there, watching her change the family's decision, sharing it with her instead of being her opponent. Yes, she thought; yes, I'd love to see you tomorrow night.

She imagined herself in his new house, walking through the empty rooms in the silence of the winter night; she saw them standing before a window, looking across the valley at Tamarack Mountain, its slopes gleaming in the moonlight like white rivers between the black pine forests, and then she felt his body touching hers, his arms around her, his mouth close to hers . . .

Her stomach knotted up; her throat tightened in terror. "No," she blurted. "I can't. I'm sorry. I just can't. I'm sorry."

His face changed; he pulled back. "I'm sorry, too," he said coolly, and then it was as if he dismissed her. "You were very fine tonight; I admire your skill. I'm sure it's a good thing for all of them; I'll be interested in seeing how it plays out. If you'll excuse me . . ." He turned away as Robin brought him a cup of coffee, and he began talking to William, across the table.

Anne sat very still. That was cruel, she thought. But then, what should I expect? I keep turning him away; what can he do but turn away from me? He deserves better. He deserves at least an explanation. But she knew she could not do that. If she either had to talk about the past or close the door on a friendship with Josh Durant, then she would close the door.

But it doesn't matter, she thought. I have so much that it doesn't matter. I have tonight. Around her, everyone looked friendly. Even Walter and Fred were calmly drinking coffee and talking to the others as if everything would still work out. Charles was leaning toward Gail; he was not smiling, but his defensive look was gone. The conflict was over.

I did it, Anne thought. I won, I won. She held it to herself as she held all her victories, all the work that filled her life and gave her satisfaction. I won. That was all she needed. Marian put a plate in front of her with a wedge of pumpkin pie sprinkled with candied ginger. "Thank you, my dear Anne," she said in a low voice. "You were wonderful and you saved us from doing a terrible thing."

Anne looked at the pie. She and Gail had made it together; it was a symbol of her place in her family. What difference did it make that she had no shares to vote when they made their decisions, or that Josh had turned from her and was talking across the table to William? Everything was fine. There was nothing to regret.

Anne looked at the ple, who and Carl had made it—
together. It was a symbol of the place in her family. With
a flush, she told herself that she had no choice but to think
Lucy McKendrith, the phone, so that she had missed Lisa's...
and was calling to apologize. "Come in," she said...
the. There was nothing...

Chapter 17

*I*t was wild," Keith said. The telephone was propped
between his ear and his shoulder, his feet were on his desk,
and he was cleaning his nails with a small file. "She just, you
know, ran away with it, and everybody just flip-flopped and
changed their mind; it was fucking unbelievable; you could
like see it happening."

"What the hell did she say?" Vince asked.

"Not much; that's what was wild. I mean she just asked a
lot of questions. And they sort of squirmed and fudged and
did a little yelling and then like changed their vote. Well,
they didn't really vote, they just said what they, you know,
thought, like they really didn't want to sell, except, you
know, like I said, they'd sell part of the company to these
guys from Egypt. She asked questions and they talked and
Nina kept saying 'Oh, dear,' you know how she is, and then
all of a sudden she got tough—I mean, have you ever seen
Nina tough?—and sort of zeroed in on everything, and then
everybody, you know, did the same and then it was all over.
Unanimous. It was a blast. And it was all her. Anne. She's
fucking unbelievable, you know?"

There was a long silence. Keith finished the nails on his
left hand and began on his right. He was alone in the office;
seven-thirty in the morning, the day after Christmas, only a
damn fool would even be out of bed. But it was two hours
later in Florida, where Vince was spending the holiday with

some politicians, and Vince always told him to call early. "You still there?" he asked.

"Yes," Vince said. He was stretched out on a chaise by the pool, the sun beating on his bare legs and chest, and he tried to picture Tamarack in the snow. Hatred filled him. He hated that town. He hated the people who lived there, and the tourists, and his family who had homes there. And more than any of them, he hated that bitch.

He'd been right about her from the day he'd seen her in the chapel, last July. His instincts were always right about people who were out to hurt him. And why else would she have come back? Women did that: once they got an idea they'd been hurt, they tucked it away and kept it inside them and fed it so it grew until, years later, they took it out and got angry all over again, and then went to work. Men weren't like that; they wrote off the past and forgot it. Women were vultures with clawing, clutching memories.

So she was in Tamarack, poisoning his family against him. In one evening, if Keith was right, she'd trashed everything he'd done the week before. But she'd done more. She'd latched onto Josh Durant, the son of a bitch who'd almost derailed Vince's political future by forcing a sordid lawsuit that could have ended up on every front page in the country. And then she egged him on to find investors to buy into the company . . . the one scenario that hadn't occurred to Vince.

When he thought of her, he no longer saw a young girl with wide blank eyes and small breasts bending over him in bed; he saw instead a dark hulk of a woman, her mouth twisted with vicious hatred, hunkered down to block his path. He gazed at the tray of drinks floating in the pool— champagne and orange juice, to speed the recovery from Christmas—and his wife and their hosts slipping into the water to swim to it. Everything in his life should have been as smooth as their long, easy strokes. His reelection was assured, and money was coming in from people who were talking about bigger money when the race for the White House began. He'd made a name as an environmentalist who also was on the side of big business, and in the past few months he'd begun to make himself an expert in foreign policy and finance. His wife charmed everyone. She liked politics, too, and she loved Vince. She was, in fact, perfect. She was the dullest woman Vince had ever met, but the best thing he had ever done was to marry her.

And the worst thing was to let that bitch wander around, getting in his way. A long time ago she'd gotten him kicked out of his family; now she was hell-bent on getting him kicked out of his future. He should have gotten rid of her the day she came to Ethan's funeral.

"I told you once to get rid of her," he said to Keith.

"Yeah, but I didn't know what you meant. Anyway, that was July; this is, you know, December, and I keep telling you like everything about her and you haven't said anything—"

"Get rid of her. It's a damn shame you can't get rid of Leo, too; he's a fucking nuisance. But he's small potatoes; you take care of her and that'll be fine."

There was a pause. "Did you have anything particular in mind?"

The swimmers were treading water, chatting and drinking; they waved to Vince, motioning for him to join them. He wondered if they were talking about him. You couldn't really trust anyone, he thought; you never knew what they might do an hour or a day after they'd told you they were on your side. But he had to trust Keith, at least for now; there didn't seem to be any choice. He hated him—he hated his smart-ass voice and the way he saw more than people realized—but he was Vince's boy and he was there, in Tamarack. He'd do what he had to do, and Vince could take care of him later. First things first, he thought, waving back at the swimmers.

"I thought *you* had something in mind," he said casually. "Didn't you tell me once that Leo might cut back on maintenance if money got tight?"

Keith grunted. He hated it when people remembered things he'd said and quoted him to himself.

"I didn't quite get that," Vince said. "Did you hear me?"

"Yeah," Keith said, thinking. "Sure. I'll think about it."

"Not too long; I want this taken care of. Call me as soon as you've done something about it. No details on the telephone; just whether you're on top of it. I'll be here for another week." He hung up. He took off his dark glasses and left the chaise and dove into the pool. The water closed around him, cooling his hot skin like the embrace of an anonymous woman. Nearby were the slowly-moving legs of his wife and their hosts treading water; he could hear their voices. He felt a leap of exultation. *Done.* There was nothing in his way anymore. He was as close to everything he wanted as he was to these three people who were on his side, and who would do anything to help him. With a powerful kick he broke the surface of the water, pushed his gleaming blond hair out of his eyes, and smiled boyishly at them. "I feel so good," he said, and smiled even more broadly at the admiring warmth that sprang to their eyes.

Anne and Leo stepped into the gondola, behind Robin and Ned, at one minute to nine. It was four days after Christmas, a cold, clear morning with the sun just touching the peaks of the mountains beneath a brilliantly blue sky. Outside the gondola building, hundreds of skiers waited for it to open, at nine o'clock, their upright skis jutting above their heads like the staves of a medieval army. "Good crowd," Leo said. "In fact, it's been good all week. We've definitely turned around; it's going to be a great winter." The car moved slowly on the curved track inside the building. "No Keith this morning," Leo said. "I've gotten so used to seeing him it's like I'm missing a piece of a puzzle."

"How come Josh isn't here?" Ned asked. He and Robin sat on the seat facing the town. "He's gone up with us every day this week."

"Packing, I guess," Leo replied, watching the gondola operators open the building to the waiting skiers. "He'll be leaving for Egypt in about half an hour."

"I wish he'd take me," Ned said wistfully. "I've done Tamarack Mountain a gazillion times; I'd rather see the mummies."

"I'd rather be here," Robin said. "I like it when school's out and we get to go up early. I like going ahead of all the people."

"Yeah, that's okay," Ned conceded. "I like not standing in line."

"What do you like, Aunt Anne?" Robin asked.

"Being with you," said Anne. She turned from the seat where she and Leo sat, facing up the mountain, and smiled at Robin. "In our own little car that's taking us to mysterious places."

"Just to the top of Tamarack Mountain," Ned protested.

"Are you absolutely, definitely sure? How do you know we won't take off like a flying saucer and end up on another planet?"

"Because we're hooked onto the cable," Ned said practically. "We can't go anywhere but up the mountain."

"Probably not," Anne sighed. "But wouldn't it be fun if we could?"

Leo smiled. He liked watching Anne with the children; it was the only time she allowed herself to relax and become fanciful. With the rest of them, even now, after the months they had known her, she still kept her control, and her distance. He and Gail often talked about it at night, in bed, wondering what they could do to help her feel safe enough, loved enough, to let go and just have a good time without monitoring every word and gesture. And then there was Josh. Something had happened between him and Anne at Christmas, but there was no way they could ask what it was. Whatever they did, however close they thought they were to Anne, there came a moment when it was as if a door came down, shutting them out.

They reached the end of the gondola building, the doors slid shut, and the car was switched from the slow speed track to the cable. Immediately it shot forward, picking up speed as it began its ascent. The cars behind them were filled with skiers, their skis standing upright in racks on the outside; so many skiers had been waiting in line that there were six people in each of the round, bright red cars that moved up the mountain like beads carefully spaced along a string.

Leo watched Anne talk to Robin and Ned. If only she'd treat Josh and the rest of us like children, she'd be a lot happier, he thought wryly. I'll have to suggest it to her; she might find it amusing enough to give it a—

The car jerked.

"What was that?" Robin asked, her eyes widening.

Leo grabbed his CB radio. He could have sworn the car had slipped, though he didn't see how the hell—"I don't know, sweetheart. Maybe a gust of wind."

Anne met Leo's eyes. There was no wind.

"Patrol," Leo said into the radio, trying to reach the ski patrol communications center.

"We slipped, I felt it," Ned said hoarsely. He and Robin were gripping the center post, their ski mittens pulled into taut wrinkles by the force of their grasp.

"Patrol," Leo shouted. There was no response. "This is Leo; shut the gondola down! Patrol!"

They passed Tower Number Four and began to climb sharply, seventy-five feet above a long, moderate slope that Leo had named Ethan's Run. And then the car stopped moving. They hovered in space. "Daddy!" Robin screamed. A deafening screech filled the air, from the cable still sliding up the mountain. "We broke off!" Ned yelled.

"*Patrol!*" Leo shouted into the CB radio. "Kill the gondola! We're loose on the cable—"

"Dad!" Ned yelled. "They're gonna hit us!" Leo and Anne turned and saw the car behind rapidly closing in on them. The skiers in the car were gesturing wildly, their mouths open in shouts that could not be heard over the screeching of the cable.

Anne scrambled to her knees on the seat and flung her arms around Robin and Ned, who were staring wide-eyed at the approaching car. "Turn around," she commanded. Terrified, Robin and Ned turned on their seat to face her. She pulled them against her as tightly as she could over the back of the seat that was between them and pulled their heads down, trying to protect them in the circle of her arms.

There was a thunderous crash. Robin's and Ned's screams were muffled against Anne's shoulders as the other car smashed into them, crushing steel and plastic. The force of the collision was too much for the second car; it tore from the cable and fell seventy-five feet to the ground. It crashed on the soft snow and slid thirty feet down the slope before coming to rest against a cluster of pine trees. The impact shook a glistening shower of snowflakes onto the bright red car, which lay very still and very quiet as the sounds of the crash died away.

The gondola came to an abrupt stop. The cars swung wildly back and forth in the silence. Then, distantly, the muffled shouts of the skiers inside the fallen car could be heard, and their hammering on the gondola doors as they tried to force them open. "Anne!" Leo called. "Robin! Ned!" He was on the floor, where he had been thrown by the impact, wedged between the seat and the front of the car. His voice was hoarse.

"We're here," Anne replied. She was kneeling on the seat, afraid to move, her back to him, her arms gripping Robin and Ned. She was trembling, stunned by the raw terror of the crash, of watching the other car fall, and of feeling their own car swing wildly in the minutes after the crash. The car steadied, but then she realized it was tilted forward, and she clung to the sobbing children to keep them from falling out. "Hey, I think we're okay," she said, forcing her voice to be calm.

"Wait—" Leo grunted. He tried to move.

"Don't!" Anne said sharply. "Don't move, Leo!"

"Why?" he said. "What's—"

"I'm afraid we might fall."

"Fall?" Leo tried to grasp it. Fall. The car might fall. He opened his eyes, but the sunlight blinded him and he closed them again. The pain in his head hammered into him; he felt he was dissolving into it. "Why?" he asked.

"We're . . . dangling," Anne said. Her voice was tight with the attempt not to let the others hear her fear. She tried to turn around to see Leo, but she was afraid to let go of Ned and Robin. "Are you hurt, Leo?"

"No." He lied automatically, listening to his children's sobs. "Wait," he said, and forced himself to crane his neck and look up. The car was dangling from the cable, swaying as they made the slightest movement. "My God," he whispered. He closed his eyes, trying to think.

Robin's crying slowed, and Anne loosened her embrace. "Don't," Robin cried, clutching her. "Don't let go, Aunt Anne! I hurt, my leg hurts, don't let go!"

"Me, too," Ned gulped. "My leg hurts, too." His voice rose. "It won't move! I can't move it! What're we gonna do? Dad?"

"It's okay, I'm here," Leo muttered. "Wait . . . I'll try to—" He tightened his muscles and inched himself up. The car shuddered. He moved slowly, fighting the pain in his head, pulling himself up until he was on his knees, his head resting on the seat.

Ned looked over Anne's shoulder. "Dad!" he shouted. "Your head's all bloody!"

Robin let out a screech and buried her head in Anne's arm.

"Leo?" Anne cried.

Leo raised his hand to his head. He felt the warm, sticky blood matting his hairs. "Not too bad," he said, trying to grin at Ned. He felt his face twist and wondered how he looked to his son. "Takes more than that to knock out a Calder." He paused, breathing hard, getting up the strength to go on talking. "What was that crash, Ned? Can you see anything?"

Ned turned to look back down the mountain, and gave a yell, gripping Anne's arm. "We're all open!"

Leo forced himself higher to look past Anne. The entire back of their car was gone. "My God," he groaned. His eyes closed. He was drowning in pain.

"I can't move," Robin whimpered. "Aunt Anne, I can't move!"

"They got here!" Ned cried excitedly.

Again Leo looked through the open back of the car. Farther down the cable, skiers in another car were pointing at the gaping hole in Leo's car. Their mouths were open in shouts that could not be heard. "They got here!" Ned cried again, and Leo looked down, at the slope, and saw the fallen gondola car. No! he thought; it can't be . . . we have so many protections . . . it couldn't fall. . . . But it lay on the snow like a bright red Christmas ornament, and then Leo saw the ski patrol moving around it, prying open the doors. In the clear air, their voices carried to Leo and Anne.

"Get it open at the top!" "Okay, but the bottom . . ." "Careful; she's lying against the door!" "Hold her away from it!" "Got it open, but this guy's wedged against it . . ." A patroller in a snowmobile drove up, his small car like a beetle on the white snow; others were behind him, the roar of their engines filling the air.

"Leo!" The patroller in the first snowmobile was standing below them, his head back, shouting. "Anybody hurt in there?"

"Not bad," Leo said, but the words came feebly.

"Leo's hurt," Anne called down. "And we have two children who may have broken legs. How soon can you get to us?"

"We're working on it," the patroller shouted. "It might be a while. Use Leo's radio while you're waiting; you can talk to the patrol or the gondola office; they've got a doctor there."

"Leo," Anne said over her shoulder, "can you hand me your radio?"

There was no answer.

"Your radio, Leo!" Anne said.

He opened his eyes. "What?" he asked.

"Your radio! I need it."

He nodded, and gasped as the pain tore through him. "Have to find it." He looked around but could not see it, then reached down to feel on the floor. In a moment his hand touched it, jammed beneath the seat, crushed by the steel that had folded back on itself in the impact. "God damn it," he whispered. "No good," he said to Anne. "Smashed. Damn it," he added, sick with helplessness.

"We gotta have a doc check these people," a patroller said, standing beside the fallen car. "Can't move 'em until we know—"

"He's on his way. We radioed."

There was a long silence, then voices came again. "Okay, this one can be moved. Take it easy! Lift her out this way!"

"Ted," another voice said. "Can you check out this guy?"

"In a minute; hold on . . ."

Leo heard the voices and pictured the dazed or unconscious passengers being taken from the fallen car. Not dead, he thought; please God, not dead. He tried to raise his head. I hurt, I hurt, he thought. He felt like a child and wished he were being held by Anne, as Ned and Robin were. He was sleepy. He was so hot he felt he was burning up, and wanted to take off his ski jacket, but it was too hard; it was too hard to do anything. It was almost too hard to breathe. "Anne," he whispered. She did not hear him. He forced his head up and pushed his voice through the throbbing in his head. "Anne."

"Yes," she said. She turned as much as she could while still holding the children, but she could not turn far enough to see him.

"We'll be okay."

"I know," she said. Leo marveled at the coolness of her voice. "Stay quiet, Leo; I wish I could help you."

"No. The kids. More important. I'll just wait. They'll come."

"I know," Anne said again. "We'll be fine. Just don't move, and don't worry about us; we're all right." Leo let out a long breath. Anne would take care of everything; she was strong enough for all of them. He heard the voices of the doctor and the ski patrollers on the slope below, confident, terse, working together. They knew what to do. He knew them all, he'd hired the best team in the world for Tamarack Mountain. Everybody was helping; they didn't need him. His head fell forward and his breathing slowed.

"Dad?" Ned called. "They're getting the people out of that car. One guy looks dead."

"Or knocked out," Anne said firmly. "That's all we can tell from up here."

"I guess," Ned said doubtfully. "Dad? Doesn't he look dead?" He looked over the seat. "Dad! Dad!"

"I think he's asleep," Anne said. "Let's not wake him up; I'll bet his head hurts and he's a lot better off sleeping until we're rescued."

"Hey, up there!" the patroller called. "What's with the radio?"

"Ned, why don't you talk to him?" Anne asked. "You've got a great pair of lungs."

"Yeah." Ned leaned forward. "Ouch!" he cried. "Oh, damn, it hurts, Aunt Anne—"

"It's all right, Ned, I'll talk to him—"

"No! I want to do it!" With Anne's arm around him, and his hand reaching back to grip the center pole, he took a deep breath and hung over the edge. He looked through the ripped wall, seventy-five feet down, and felt a moment of absolute joy in the danger of it. Wow, he thought, this is unreal. The sun was warm on his head; the air on his face was cold. Below, patrollers were skiing down to the fallen car, pulling long sleds with supporting sides. They laid people in them and strapped them in, and skied down the mountain, their skis in a V-shape to slow them down, pulling the sleds behind them while other patrollers skied alongside to keep an eye on the injured skiers. Other patrollers were bringing ropes and pulleys up the mountain on snowmobiles, getting ready to evacuate the gondola. It was the most exciting thing in Ned's whole life, and he drank in the scene, forgetting his leg and his father and the swaying tilt of their car as it dangled from its cable, high above the world.

"Me, too," said Robin, and gripping the center pole, she leaned forward with him. Their weight pulled against Anne's arms, and she loosened them slightly, flexing her wrists and forearms and breathing deeply, trying to relax. Her terror was gone; in its place was a steady fear—for Leo, for their safety in the car until they could be rescued, for the people in the fallen car and those in all the other cars, for Tamarack, for her family. She flexed her arms again; they were sore after keeping a grip on the children for . . . how long? she wondered. She stretched her arm to see her watch, and peered at it in disbelief. It had to be wrong. It had been only twenty minutes since they stepped into the gondola, only fifteen minutes since the car first slipped on the cable. Surely it had been at least an hour; everything seemed so agonizingly slow.

"Hey, guys!" the patroller called from below. "You okay?"

"I think my leg's broke," Ned shouted cheerfully. He'd be telling people about this forever. "My sister's, too, maybe. And my Dad's asleep." He remembered the blood, and his voice began to shake. "His head's all bloody; he looks awful."

"Who else is with you?" the patroller asked.

"My aunt. She's okay."

"Where's your radio?"

"It's broke."

"Damn. Well, we'll get there as fast as we can; we just can't talk to you while we're doing it. You know the drill, though, right?"

"Sure, my dad told me. But we're kinda loose up here; do they know that?"

"Loose? What do you mean?"

"*Loose.* Like we could *fall.* The gripper thing—you know, the J-grip? That hooks us onto the cable?—it's hardly doing anything, it's not holding like it ought to, or whatever . . . anyway, it's real shaky up here."

"I'll tell them," the patroller said. "They know what to do. Take it easy, Ned, you'll be out of there in no time."

"Yeah. Hey, who's going to get us?"

"I don't know. Pete, maybe. That okay?"

"Oh, yeah; he's great; he taught me to ski."

"Ned, I've gotta go. You guys hang in there. It won't be too long."

"Sure," Ned muttered. He hung over the edge for another minute, his exhilaration fading. Most of the patrollers were gone, and most of the snowmobiles. In all directions, the long runs winding through the forests were empty, glistening in the sun or dark in the shadows, silent and waiting, like an empty house or an abandoned, ghostly mountain.

"No one came up on the Number One Lift," Anne said.

"They probably closed the mountain," Ned said knowledgeably. "They don't want a bunch of people all over the place when there's an accident. They're a real pain in the butt. Especially if somebody . . . dies." As if he could not stop himself, he glanced at Leo. His eyes filled with tears. It was awfully quiet, he thought; it was like everybody'd gone home and they were left hanging there and nobody cared.

"Everybody still okay up there?" a patroller called from below. He was sitting on the slope, the only one left behind to make sure they were not alone.

"Great!" Ned yelled angrily. "When are they coming for us?"

"Anytime, Ned; hold your horses; it takes a while to get set up."

"Sure, sure," he muttered. Even with that guy down there, they were really alone. He and Robin and Aunt Anne and their dad were up here alone, and nobody knew for how long, and they could fall any minute. . . . He felt the tears sting his eyes and he fought them back. He couldn't cry; his dad was out if it and that left him the only man awake in the car. He settled back into the circle of Anne's arms. "I guess we're okay," he said, trying to be casual. "I mean, we haven't fallen or anything."

"And it isn't snowing," Robin said. "It'd be awful if it was snowing."

"And anyway they'll be here pretty soon. Like five or ten minutes."

"Or an hour," Robin said.

Anne heard the hollowness in their voices that came with fear and a sense of loss and the effort to pretend that everything would be all right. She knew that feeling. She knew what it was to be a child, and to feel that everything familiar and trusted was in jeopardy. "Well," she said thoughtfully in a story-telling kind of voice that Ned and Robin recognized, "if they held a big net below us, I could drop you down to them. You'd bounce a few times, you might even do a somersault or two, but then you'd bounce right out and somebody would give you a ride on a snowmobile, and I'll bet your mother is in the gondola building right now, waiting for you."

"That's pretty dumb," Ned muttered. "They don't even have a net."

"Well, maybe your friends at school would help us out," Anne said, her voice very quiet and soothing. "How about your football team, Ned? They could throw a rope ladder up to us and we could use it to climb down."

"It'd be too big," Ned said. "It'd be huge, and it'd weigh a ton, all folded up; nobody could throw that, not even somebody from the Broncos."

"We could tie our clothes together," Robin said, "like when people escape from jail, and slide down."

"That's stupider than the net," Ned grumbled, but the fear had left his voice. Anne led them on, talking about rescue techniques, weaving stories in a steady, soothing murmur, while she kept her eyes on the slope below. The car swayed gently beneath the intense blue sky. Birds flew from tree to tree below them, yellow mountain canaries, gray jays, iridescent blue jays, brown and white chickadees. Far above, a hawk wheeled in great circles, its huge, outstretched wings motionless except for a slight quiver now and then as it adjusted its position. Tamarack, snow covered and sunlit, lay nestled in its valley. Leo slept; Anne heard his slow breathing. Robin and Ned lay heavily against her arms, staring blankly into space, waiting. She sat quietly in the little car listening to the silence. How strange, she thought, that we can be sitting in the midst of such beauty, and such danger, and perhaps, death. That's probably true all the time, whatever we're doing: danger and even death may be close by. But we can't see them or even sense them until something happens and we look up. . . .

She saw herself lying in the forest, struggling. *You want it. You want to. Don't lie to me. I know what you want!*

She shrank into herself, her arms tightening fiercely in defense. "That hurts!" cried Robin, and Ned said, "Hey!"

Oh, God, oh God, it never ends. Anne relaxed her arms. "I'm sorry; I didn't mean to do that."

"What were you *doing?*" Ned demanded.

"I was thinking about somebody I don't like, and I guess I got carried away."

"Boy, I wouldn't like to be him," said Ned.

"You must really hate him," Robin said, looking at Anne as if seeing her in a new light. "I didn't know you had people you hated."

Ned looked below, at the patroller sitting stoically on the slope. He had found a piece of wood lying on the snow and was tapping out a jazz beat with it on his ski boot. "Nothing's happening," he said. "Nobody's coming." His hand brushed his leg and he gave a yelp and jerked his hand back. "It's all swelled up." He looked wide-eyed at Anne. "Maybe I'll be a cripple. I won't ever ski again, or ride my bike or play baseball—"

"You'll do everything," Anne said briskly. "So will Robin. I'm absolutely sure of it."

"Hey, Ned, they're on their way!" the patroller called.

"Where?" Ned swung around, craning to see up the mountain. The car shook wildly. "Aunt Anne!" He clung to her. "I didn't mean to! I didn't mean to make us fall!"

"We won't," Anne said, but fear clutched her as the car shook. Robin was whimpering softly. Anne held them to her. Don't let them be hurt, she prayed. Don't let Leo be hurt; take care of them; let them be fine and on the ground and at home. And let no one be dead; let everything be all right; please let everything be all right.

"Hey, Ned, it's Pete. You waiting for me?"

Ned's head shot up. "Pete!"

A redhead with a broad grin was looking through the window on the uphill side of the car. He saw Leo and his grin faded. "Jesus. Is he . . . I mean, is he asleep, or what?"

"Asleep," Anne said over her shoulder. "Tell us what you want us to do."

"Well, we've gotta start with Leo, but I'm putting a rope on the car first, otherwise we could all end up crashing down when I put my weight on it. So sit tight, folks; one thing at a time."

They watched through the window as Pete tied a rope

between the roof of the car and the gondola cable. Then, slowly, he stepped onto the roof. The car shuddered beneath the added weight, and, with a sharp retort, broke away from the cable. Robin screamed as they dropped about a foot, and jerked to a stop, hanging from the rope Pete had fastened.

"Wow-ee, fun and games," Pete said. They heard him but could not see him; he lay on the roof, holding on, until the car stopped swinging. "Okay, next step. Ned, I can't get in the car until you guys move, so how about crawling over the seat?"

Ned looked up. "You sure the rope's gonna hold? Every time we move in here . . ."

"It's fine. I guarantee, this car's going nowhere. Go on, crawl over."

Anne loosened her hold and Ned wriggled over the seat, headfirst, biting his lips against the pain in his leg. He squeezed into the corner of the seat and gently touched Leo's head as it lay on his folded arms. "Hi, Dad," he said. "Pete's here; we're gonna take care of you."

Pete swung into the car beside Anne and Robin. "Okay, Ned, you're my helper."

"Right," Ned said proudly.

"Here's the harness. You know how it works; we get it on your dad; fasten it around him . . ."

Anne turned to see if she could help. She let go of Robin for the first time and turned in the seat to face uphill, the way she had begun the trip. Her legs were completely numb from having been folded under her for so long, and she gasped with pain as the blood rushed into them.

"You have to pick him up," Ned said. "It goes over his head."

Anne raised Leo's head, and Pete and Ned slipped the harness over it and around his body, fastening it tightly. "Thanks, buddy," Pete said to Ned. He took the rope that was attached to the harness and crawled back to the roof of the car where he hooked it to a steel ring with a carabiner. By now, Anne saw, there were a dozen patrollers on the slope below, shading their eyes as they looked up at Pete. "Here it comes!" Pete called. He waved to the patrollers and tossed the rope out and away from the car. It uncoiled in a graceful spiral as it fell.

Pete had swung back into the car. "We've got to lift him out," he said to Anne. "You kids squeeze over to give us room." Robin and Ned flattened themselves against the side of the car. Anne took a long breath. Her legs were tingling and so painful she could barely move, but she bent down and lifted Leo's legs and slowly pushed the heavy, limp body as Pete pulled it toward the jagged opening.

"What?" blurted Leo. His eyes were open and unfocused. "Christ, my head. Can't see . . . Gail? What is it?"

"Dad!" Ned cried. "We're right here."

"Hey, Leo," said Pete. "We've got a little problem here; you just let us take care of it, okay?"

"Pete?" asked Leo.

"That's me. Everything's under control; just don't fight us. Okay?"

"Accident," Leo muttered.

"You got it. But we're okay. We're gonna get you to the ground, you know how; you've done it with us in drills. We're gonna swing you out—" As he spoke, Leo's eyes closed. His body lay across the seatback. "Hold on," Pete gasped. Anne stopped, breathing hard. "Ned, hold your dad like this, okay?" Pete said.

"I want to help!" Robin exclaimed.

"Sure thing." Pete shifted Leo's body to lie across the outstretched arms of both children; then he leaned forward, through the opening, and waved to the patrollers. "All set!"

On the ground, two patrollers began to pull slowly on the rope. Pete and Anne, with Ned and Robin helping, held Leo above the seatback and kept him steady as the rope on his harness tightened until he was free of the car. "Good-bye, Daddy," Robin whispered. She was crying. Leo hung in the air for a moment; then the patrollers began to let out the rope, controlling his descent by playing it slowly through the ring on the top of the car.

Anne watched Leo's still form, turning slowly in midair as it was lowered from the car. He looked so small and helpless, and she held her breath, waiting for him to be grabbed by the patrollers on the slope who stood in a circle, waiting, shading their eyes. We're all helpless at different times in our lives, she thought, but if we know there's someone waiting to catch us . . .

She thought of Josh. She saw his somber eyes and heard his deep voice on Christmas night. *You mean we're alone in the universe, with no chance, ever, to share, or to touch another person.* And she remembered the cry that had burst within her. *No, that isn't what I want!*

"Got him!" Pete breathed, and Anne realized the patrollers were cradling Leo in their arms while one of them unfastened the harness. As soon as it was loose, the patroller shouted, "Okay!" and Pete hauled it in while the others laid Leo on the waiting sled and began to strap him in.

Anne let out a long sigh. They'll take care of him, she thought. They'll take him to the hospital; he'll be all right. The fear of the past hour was gone; it had vanished as soon as the work of lowering everyone from the car had begun. Now it seemed quite reasonable to believe that everything was going to be all right. "How about that," she said to Ned and Robin with a wide smile. She put her arms around them in a quick hug. "He's going to be all right. And so are we."

Pete brought the rope and harness through the opening into the car. "Next," he said.

"Aunt Anne," Ned announced.

Anne shook her head. "Take Robin first, then Ned."

"No!" Ned shouted. "Men go last!"

"Unless they're injured," Anne said quietly. "I'm not hurt, and you are, and the sooner a doctor gets to your leg, and Robin's, too, the better. That's the right way to do it, and you know it."

"She's right, Ned," said Pete. He brought the harness to Robin and slipped it over her head. "I need you to help me lift Robin out of here, okay?"

"Yeah," Ned muttered. He was very quiet, but he worked with Pete to steady Robin as she swung out from the car and descended to the waiting patrollers. A few minutes later, it was his turn to look down and see the slope rising to meet him, and the patrollers waiting to grab him, and he felt excitement bubble up inside him. He had done this once before, in a drill with his father, but never for real. "Aunt Anne!" he called up to her; he could see her watching from the jagged hole in the gondola car. "Wait'll you do it! It's great!" But mostly he was thinking about telling this to the guys at school.

Pete returned to the roof, to check on the rope he had tied there, and Anne waited in the empty car. She heard the patrollers below, talking to each other, and to Ned and Robin, as they strapped them securely into separate sleds. Two of the patrollers, pulling the sleds, skied down; others followed them. *I don't know if we're alone.* She had said that to Josh, at Christmas. And for a moment he had smiled at her with such warmth that she had wanted to reach out to him, to tell him . . .

To tell him what? She gazed at the hawk, still wheeling smoothly, tirelessly, in the vast expanse of blue sky, alone, strong and independent. It blurred, and she realized her eyes had filled with tears. I don't know how to stop being alone! she cried silently.

"Okay, Anne, your turn," Pete said, swinging into the car for the last time. He pulled in the rope with the harness at the end, and together, they fastened it around her. They shook hands. "Pleasure to do business with you," he said solemnly.

"Thank you, Pete. For all of us. I hope I'll see you in town. ˜'d like to do something for you."

˜'Buy me a drink at Timothy's," he said with a grin, and pushed her free of the car.

They lowered her as smoothly as they could, but there were still little bumps and jerks as the rope fed through the ring. Still, Anne thought it was a delightful way to return to earth. She could not keep herself from revolving, but that gave her a view in all directions, and when she looked down and saw that she was descending into a circle of strong arms, she felt a leap of joy. Not alone, she thought as the arms grasped her and brought her to the solid, snow-covered slope. Not alone. Not alone.

"You okay?" a patroller asked as he unfastened her harness.

"Fine. Thanks," she said. "Thank you, all of you, so much. Were Robin and Ned all right?"

"Great. They're great kids."

"And Leo?"

"Sure. By now he's at the hospital. Your turn. You want the sled?"

"Ned told me to ask for a snowmobile."

"Smart kid. Okay, hop on and hang on tight."

Not alone, Anne thought as they followed the road down the mountain. Her arms were around the patroller's waist. Snow blew past them in a fine spray, the sun shone, and the town waited below, bustling with people, serene and welcoming. *Not alone.*

When she was back, when she knew that Leo and the children were fine, when things were normal again, she had to find out exactly what that meant.

Chapter 18

The corridor, three hundred feet long, plunged sixty feet into the earth from the glaring heat of the desert, stepping down on rough-hewn stairs, pausing on stone landings, then going on, down and down, into darkness. Josh and Hosni, holding powerful lights, followed the workers as they filed through the narrow space, passing false doors and corridors built by the pharaoh's crews to fool tomb robbers, until they came to a stone door fitted tightly into its opening. Two spitting snakes, painted upon it in bright colors, swayed upright, prepared to strike any intruder. "Fair warning," Hosni said with a smile. "But I think we'll go in anyway. We've loosened the door, Josh, but it hasn't been opened."

Josh laid his hand upon it. The stone was warm. "Let's do it," he said. His voice was tight with anticipation. So many years lay behind this moment, and now that they were here, they might find that the tomb had been plundered once, or many times, over the past centuries, leaving them nothing but fragments, and perhaps, the stripped and mutilated mummy of Tenkaure. Josh stood before the door and said a silent prayer.

Before he had arrived, the workers had carefully chiseled along the plaster camouflaging the door and exposed the edges of it. Now, with Hosni giving directions, they began to pry it loose, sliding pieces of wood into the cracks they made along the sides and the top and the bottom. When they could feel it move beneath their fingers, they concentrated on one edge, prying it open, pulling on it. Slowly, almost begrudgingly, the door began to swivel outward. Their voices echoing in the corridor with the scraping of stone against stone, the workers pushed at the door, widening the opening until a man could get through. Josh, with Hosni just behind him, stood at the entrance, and played his light through the doorway. It illuminated a room so large he could not see its corners. But he was not looking at the room. On the wall just inside the doorway was a chiseled cartouche, the seal of the pharaoh. He held his light on it and read the hieroglyphics filling the oval outline. "Tenkaure," he murmured. He looked at Hosni. "Tenkaure!" he shouted, and they threw their arms around each other in a hug of jubilation.

"Now we start!" Hosni exclaimed, and they walked into the room, their powerful lights playing on the walls and ceiling and square pillars, wondrously painted. A fierce, excited murmuring broke out among the workers. "We're the first," Hosni whispered. *"We're the first!"* Hidden beneath continuous rock slides, like the tomb of Tutankhamen, Tenkaure's tomb had escaped the robbers who had combed the Valley of the Kings through the ages; it had waited, untouched, for twentieth-century scientists to bring it into the modern world.

They walked into the center of the room, the workers behind them. Stepping on piles of rubble that had fallen in the same earthquakes that had caused the rock slides above, they held high their powerful lanterns. And in an instant, everything that had slept for centuries sprang to life. "My God," breathed Hosni, and behind him, the workers drew in their breath in a long hissing that echoed off the stone. All around them was the gleam of gold. Furniture, statues, bowls, jewelry—all of gold, poking through the rubble, and piled on shelves on the walls. And with the gold were alabaster jars so delicate they were nearly transparent, brilliant jewels, wooden bowls containing grains and herbs, game boards that looked like checkers and Parcheesi, models of funerary boats, a head of a cow goddess covered with gold leaf, and tiny, gaily painted wooden figures called *shabti* who were meant to serve the pharaoh in the afterlife.

And surrounding all of it, where the limestone had not flaked away, every inch of the ceilings, walls, and pillars were covered with brilliant paintings of daily life of thirty-five hundred years ago. Protected in that total darkness from the relentless, bleaching desert sun, the paints shimmered with the same brightness as the day the artists had used them, and the people almost seemed to move: men hunting rhinoceros, fishermen standing in papyrus boats to cast their nets, teams harvesting grapes and making wine, women weaving, workers slaughtering cattle, chariots leaping to war behind teams of horses, slaves in chains. Josh and Hosni moved from room to room, through doors beneath the widespread protective wings of great painted birds. They gazed at funeral scenes, life-size portraits of Tenkaure and his wife greeting gods and goddesses, and entire walls covered with the text and illustrations from the Book of Life and the Book of the Dead.

"Can you believe this?" Hosni murmured. "God damn, can you *believe* this?"

And then, at last, they reached the burial chamber, a square room with walls covered with paintings of the life of Tenkaure, and in the center of the room, a stone sarcophagus with Tenkaure's cartouche and gold-leaf paintings of the goddess Isis. Josh let out a long breath. The lid was intact. The mummy would be inside.

"You *did* it!" Hosni exploded. "You did it! God damn, you are one hell of a guy!"

Josh stood as if in a dream. He felt as he did when he reached the peak of a towering mountain, out of breath, a little dizzy. His whole life had led to this moment; nothing else had driven him as had this quest. He stood in the midst of the splendor of these rooms, the thousands of objects brought there with reverent hands; so much wealth, so much variety, so much brilliance in the paintings. In the seven rooms of Tenkaure's tomb were stored more pieces of the past than most scholars handled in a lifetime. Josh turned slowly in place and stretched out his hands as if to embrace it all. Every scholar dreamed of a moment like this. Only a handful of them ever reached it.

Hosni was already kneeling, clipboard in hand, making a map of the tomb and sketching the location of the major objects. Later the decisions would be made which treasures would be allowed to go to Josh's museum in Los Angeles; the majority of them would stay at the Egyptian Museum in Cairo. "We'll need a whole section just for this," Hosni muttered happily. "Like King Tut. He has his own rooms in the museum; we'll have ours for Tenkaure. And a separate room for the mummy. . . . My God, Josh, can you imagine when we get the mummy?"

In many ways, it would look like the mummies of other pharaohs, they knew that. The embalmers followed formulas that remained the same for thousands of years. They would lift the stone lid—it would take a whole crew to do it, with scaffolding and a hoist—and look inside at the gold and jeweled coffin shaped like a human figure, and the one inside that, and the one inside that, each lavishly inlaid with lapis lazuli and precious stones set in thick gold leaf, and within the final coffin they would come to the mummy itself, wrapped in strips of hundreds of yards of fine linen. And when they x-rayed and scanned it, they would see Tenkaure, his head back, chin high, arms folded over his chest, his skin and hair still intact, his features recognizable after these thousands of years.

For many, it would be the most dramatic find of the tomb. For Josh, the inscriptions that would tell the true story of Tenkaure and his son were more exciting, and so were the kitchen utensils, game boards, and furniture, for they led him back and back, into the everyday lives of those ancient times, and they gave him the art and artifacts with which to build life-size exhibits in his museum for the people of his own time. That was the work of his life: to bridge the centuries and weave the past into the present so that each was illuminated by the other.

He breathed deeply of the musty air. It was the most glorious moment of his life. It should have been perfect. But perversely, it was not. Because he wanted Anne to be with him. We ought to be sharing this, he thought; I'll never have anything like it again.

He knew well enough that she shied away from any efforts to probe the past, but there had to be ways for her to understand what the past meant to him. She could avoid confronting her own, if she liked, though he thought that was a mistake, but surely she could see how a man could spend his time and energy deciphering other ages, for what they could tell us about our own, for locating ourselves in the long line of peoples who are part of us because we are all part of the human race, and also for the pure joy of learning. Anne loved to learn; she could understand his passion, and share it. Then, perhaps, she could break the shell within which something in her seemed to sleep. Or perhaps she would let him be the one to break it. And wake her up.

He shook his head, smiling ruefully to himself. The tomb was getting to him; he was weaving fantasies like a school-boy. He looked through the doorway, back the way they had come. "A year, at a guess, to get everything catalogued and out of here. What do you think?"

"At least," Hosni agreed. "Why rush it and take a chance on messing things up?"

"We'll need extra guards. How many have you had here until now?"

"Three. We'll need an army. I'll talk to the Luxor police; they'll get us started until Cairo sends more. Do you want to work on the schedule now?"

"Not alone; we've got to call your boss at Antiquities and Tourism. If we don't keep him happy, and everybody else in your government, I have a feeling my museum could be very politely shut out in the cold. This thing is so big Egypt is going to want all of it, and I understand that, but I intend to get a chunk of it for us."

"You should, you should, you did the work, you raised the money—"

"But it's Egypt's heritage, so most of it stays here. I don't

454

have any problem with that; I just don't want to be left out. Okay, why don't you go back to Luxor and find us three shifts of guards? I'll call Cairo; they'll have people here tonight. It shouldn't take more than a week or two to get crews and equipment; then we'll start taking things out of here."

When Hosni had left, and the workers had gone to the surface to eat their lunch in the shade of the cars, Josh walked through the rooms alone. Excitement and jubilation buoyed him, but his movements were careful and precise as he photographed each room to illustrate the articles he would write describing his find. His was the only light now, and as he carried it, or set it down, fantastic shadows were flung across the walls and ceilings, making the scenes shift and seem alive. He propped the light on mounds of rubble and used his flash to photograph each room from all angles. The silence was absolute: calm, peaceful, indifferent to the world above. A curious juxtaposition, Josh thought: in this place of death, beauty and serenity seemed supreme.

As he photographed the jumbled objects and took close-ups of individual pieces, he realized he was photographing as much for Anne as for his future writings. He was already planning his description of each slide as it burst into life on the wall in his apartment, telling Anne the stories that made up the whole of Egyptian mythology.

If we ever do that again, he thought, or do anything at all together. But that did not stop him from thinking about her as he moved from room to room, and soon it was as if she walked beside him, wide-eyed at the splendors he was photographing, her voice echoing his excitement, her hands touching the gold statues and alabaster vases with gentle fingertips, leaving everything exactly as it was until the teams of experts would come to remove it. And when Josh had finally worked his way back to the rough staircase, and was climbing to the world above, Anne's presence was so real, her place beside him so natural, that he knew that, somehow, he would find a way to bring her here.

* * *

In his hotel in Luxor that night, he called her in Los Angeles. Ten hours earlier, he calculated, and began to give the operator her office number before remembering that it was Sunday. But when he gave her number at home, there was no answer. He sprawled in his armchair, staring through the window at the boats on the Nile. It was four days after Christmas; she might still be in Tamarack. But now, suddenly, he was reluctant to call her. What would he say? *I want you here; it's the most amazing time in my life and I want you to be part of it.*

There would be a silence at her end; he could feel her pulling away from him even over the telephone, even at a distance of ten thousand miles. *Why, Josh? Why do you want me there?*

He gazed absently at the people on the upper decks of the tour boats. They wore evening dress and the light sweaters they brought out as soon as the sun went down, and were being served appetizers by waiters in gleaming white coats and white gloves. He could hear their voices, and the ripples of their laughter. He sat alone in his hotel room, watching them, and thought of how much of the world he had seen, without sharing it. *Because, incredible as this experience is, it isn't enough: I want you to be part of it. Because whatever I do from now on, I want to share with you. Because I love you.*

He had loved her for a long time, he thought, perhaps from the day they had hiked to Defiance Lake. Before then he had been impressed with her toughness and her formidable skills. Hiking with her, he had seen, beneath the cool face she presented to the world, the passionate spirit that pushed her on and responded to splendor. That was what he loved. Whatever was in her past that acted as a terrible brake on her emotions, she had survived and in many ways, been victorious, her fine mind and her wit intact, even if it seemed she could not, at least not yet, love.

He wanted to tell her. But he could not do it. It was not the kind of conversation he could have on the telephone.

He watched the decks of the tourist boats empty as everyone went below for dinner. The trouble was, he had to tell someone, someone who knew what he was doing, a friend. He reached for the telephone again, and called Gail and Leo.

It rang for a long time before a strange voice answered. "Hello, Calders'."

"Who is this?" Josh asked in surprise.

"Lena; I clean house for the Calders. They're not here; they're in Albuquerque. I could take a message."

Let down, so full of his story he was spilling over with the need to talk about it, Josh picked up a pencil. "Can you tell me how to reach them there?"

"Uh, the hospital. I can get the number—"

"Hospital! Why?"

"Well, the accident, you know. Everybody knows about—"

Josh's heart seemed to stop. "What? What accident?"

"The gondola. Gosh, how'd you miss it? It been on the TV and everything. It fell. Not the whole thing, you know, just one of the cars, but another one was smashed and that's the one Leo was in. Nobody got killed; it was first thing in the morning so nobody'd gone up the mountain yet."

First thing in the morning. *"Josh, Anne and I are going up tomorrow morning; you want to go along?" "I can't; I'm leaving early for Egypt. We'll do it next time."*

"Who else was hurt?" he asked tightly.

"The kids, Robin and Ned, they broke their legs. Gail's sister was there, but she's okay. They say she saved the kids, she held on to them so they wouldn't fall out. There's lots of stuff going on around here; it's kind of a mess—"

She's fine. She's fine. She's fine. His hand was shaking and he forced himself to unclench his fingers from the telephone. I've got to be with her, he thought. And then he knew he wanted to be with all of them: Anne, Leo and Gail and the children, William, Nina, Marian . . .

"—found the number in Albuquerque," Lena was saying. She read it to him. "They're in room fifteen. You can call them there."

"Thanks," he said, and immediately called the number.

When he finally reached Gail, she sounded weary. "Oh, Josh, how wonderful to hear your voice. We don't know very much yet; he has a skull fracture and maybe an epidural hematoma; that's why we're here, in case he needs surgery. Anne is with Robin and Ned at the hospital in Tamarack; they each have a broken leg, but they're doing fine. Why don't you call them?"

Again, he called the hospital in Tamarack, and then he heard Anne's cool voice, so close he felt they could be touching. "Are you really all right?" he asked. "I want to be there, but I can't get away for a few days."

"We're fine; we're mostly worried about Leo. It's very good of you, Josh, but you shouldn't hurry; we don't need anything."

"It isn't your need; it's mine," he said. "I want to be there with you. With all of you."

"Thank you." Her voice was low and now he heard the stress in it. "This isn't a good time, Josh; all those people injured—no one killed, thank God, but one of them has a broken back, and the others have broken bones and of course they're all banged up and angry and still scared—and there's a lot of anger in town, too; people are talking about sloppy maintenance, even negligence. And the tourists are leaving. You'd think we're in a war zone; they're just going to the airport and sitting there until they can get on a plane."

"Why? What are they afraid of?"

"The devil, I suppose." Her voice was wry, but Josh heard a note of desolation in it, and he knew he was the first person she had been able to talk to without having to put on a show of confidence and reassurance. "It's as if they think we've been possessed by something evil. The newspapers and television keep going over the other problems we've had, and the EPA investigation just hangs there because they won't send us the documents we want so we can't do anything to end it. So people leave. And the ones who live here are hurting and blaming the company."

"What happened to the gondola?"

"No one knows. The investigators are already here, from the State Tramway Board, and they found a bolt missing, but it wasn't part of the grip that held us to the cable. No one knows why our car slipped on the cable."

"What did the missing bolt do?"

"It was part of a safety mechanism. If the grip failed on a car, a device was supposed to sense it and stop the gondola. It didn't work on our car because the bolt was missing, so we started up the mountain, and when we got to the steep part, the cable kept moving but we didn't, and the car behind us, which was gripped just fine to the cable, crashed into us. I can't believe two things went wrong at once—something happening to the grip and a bolt falling out—but right now that's what they've found."

"And Robin and Ned?"

"They're fine. I'm in Robin's room now; she's watching television. Ned is across the hall, talking on the phone. They're both so excited about the accident they can't stop talking about it. I think the whole school will be here tomorrow; the phones haven't stopped ringing. I envy their resilience; they've turned the whole thing into a movie. Ned calls it *The Gruesome Gondola*, which won't make his parents happy, and Robin's named it *Blood on the Snow*, which isn't any better, and they're the producers and of course, the stars. I think it's good for about fifty years of retelling."

"And what about you?" Josh asked.

"I wasn't hurt. I can't believe it, really; I'm the only one out of ten people who doesn't even have a scratch."

"That isn't what I meant."

"I know." There was a pause. "No one else has asked me that."

Her voice had changed; suddenly she was not guarding it. And in that instant their voices seemed to touch as if there were no telephone, no distance between them, no Egyptian hotel or Colorado hospital, just their voices, touching without constraint. They had never been so close.

"Tell me," he said.

"I've hardly thought about it. I don't really know how I feel. Relieved, of course, but still scared, in an odd way; I keep feeling us swaying up there, not knowing if we'd fall. I didn't know how badly Leo was hurt, and I didn't know if anyone in the other car was dead, and I knew I couldn't protect Ned and Robin if we broke loose. . . . I guess I stored up a fair bit of anxiety, and it doesn't all go away at once."

"No," Josh said. "Terrors always linger, don't they?" Anne was silent. "But it's easier if you have friends. I hope to be there by Wednesday, Anne."

"I'll be—we'll all be glad to see you," she said. She wanted to tell him how welcome his voice was, how grateful she was for his call, how her breath had caught when he said he would be there in three days. She wanted to tell him she had thought of him while waiting for help in the gondola. But all that came out were those formal words. "Very glad," she added, trying to make up for it. "Tell me about your dig. Did you get to the tomb? Is it all there?"

"Yes, and yes." Anne heard the smile in his voice. "You don't want to hear about it now, though—"

"Oh, I do. All of it. How wonderful for you, Josh. You've waited for this for so long. Was it Tenkaure's?"

"Yes, his seal was just inside the door."

"So it was the first thing you saw. What an incredible feeling that must have been. Were you the first?"

"We were. Nothing's been touched. Tumbled around by earthquakes, but it's amazing how little is broken; even most of the alabaster seems intact. Anne, you've got to see it. You can't believe the beauty, and the incredible mass; everything from soup ladles to gold thrones."

"And Tenkaure?"

"He's there. We won't get to him for a while; we have to clear the other rooms and the corridor first. But he's waited a long time; he can wait a little longer."

She gave a low laugh. "It's like a fairy tale. How many people in a lifetime ever have anything like this? I'm so glad for you. How can you be so calm?"

"I'm not, really. I feel like a kid. It's been the most incredible day, from the minute we got to the door." His words came faster, pouring out, as if, Anne thought, he had been storing them up until he could talk to her. "You remember the steps, the way they looked at the top, if you can picture them going all the way in . . ."

She listened, seeing the rooms through his vivid descriptions, feeling the cool alabaster and warm gold; breathing the hot, still air. He had been walking through those rooms, in the midst of discovery, while she sat in the hospital, waiting for Robin and Ned to have their legs set, waiting for Gail to call with news from Albuquerque, waiting to hear what the Tramway Board had found.

She thought of those two places: a pharaoh's tomb and Tamarack. And she recalled one of the doctors saying, that morning, that the town was as quiet as a tomb. We weren't so far apart after all, Josh and I, she thought wryly.

"I'll have slides a few days after I get back," Josh said. "If you'd like, we'll have another show; it's not as good as being here, but it's the best we can do for now."

"I'd like that," Anne said simply. There was a pause, and she knew he had been prepared for her to refuse, as she had refused just a few days before, on Christmas. "And I'd like to talk to you about the accident," she went on. "There were so many things happening, and then too much to do when we got down. . . . I haven't sorted it out in my mind, yet."

"We'll have plenty of time to talk," Josh said, and there was a note of buoyancy in his voice. "I'll call you from New York, as soon as I get through customs; by then I ought to know when I'll get to Tamarack. You *will* be there, won't you? When are you going back to LA?"

"Not until Gail gets back; I can't leave Robin and Ned. I'll be working here, in Leo's office; my secretary can send me most of what I need."

"And you don't think Gail will be back in the next three days?"

"I doubt it. But even if she is, I'll wait for you."

The words sang on the wires that spanned the miles

between them. Anne listened to their resonance and waited for Josh to reply, afraid he would try to push her further. "I'll see you Wednesday," he said at last, very quietly, "as early as I can make it."

When they hung up, Anne sat still, curled up on the sofa bed in Robin's hospital room where she had slept the night before. Robin was in bed, watching a movie, her headphones tight to her ears. Anne gazed out the window. A dense cloud filled the valley, blotting out the mountains on each side; snowflakes skittered in the gray air, the beginning of what was predicted to be a blizzard. A cloud lay on Tamarack, too, Anne thought; the exhilaration of a good beginning to the season had vanished with the fall of the gondola. She had felt it ever since they were brought down from the mountain the day before, and the clouds had closed in. There were whispered conversations in the corridors of the hospital, and in town; everyone speculating on what had happened—and what would happen next.

But for now Anne sat in Robin's room, the telephone beside her, and realized she was feeling warm and relaxed.

I'll see you Wednesday, as early as I can make it.

"Aunt Anne!" Ned called from across the hall.

"Coming." Anne stood up to go to him. She did not know what would happen next, she did not even know precisely what she wanted to happen next, but her step was light as she crossed the hospital corridor.

We'll have plenty of time to talk.

I'll wait for you.

Vince heard about the gondola accident on the evening news as he was dressing for dinner. He stood in the center of the room, his shirt open, his tie dangling from his fingers, and watched the pictures, from that morning, of the fallen car on the slope, the car above still dangling from the cable, and the empty mountain. "Fear walks the streets of Tamarack tonight," the reporter proclaimed. "Fear that the people who run this posh, glamorous resort may have gotten careless with success; fear that the problems of the past few months may be more than they can handle." He was standing in front of Timothy's, frowning solemnly and gesturing toward the people walking on the mall. "Visitors are leaving; cancellations are coming in. As one skier said to me today, 'I can control my skiing; I can't control the guys who're supposed to keep the gondola running.' He left this afternoon. For Aspen."

Vince used the remote control to flip to another channel.

"—no deaths, which officials say is a miracle. The people in the fallen car suffered major injuries, but all are expected to recover. Leo Calder, president of The Tamarack Company, was in the car above; he was flown to a hospital in Albuquerque with a fractured skull. His two children, who were with him, suffered broken legs. The fourth person in the car, Anne Garnett, the noted Los Angeles divorce lawyer, escaped injury. The ski patrol says she saved the lives of the two children by holding them when the cars collided and the back of their car was torn—"

Savagely, Vince switched channels.

"—tried to interview Miss Garnett, but she has stayed out of sight. As for the injured, in both cars, they're in hospitals in Tamarack and Durango, and we haven't been able to talk to them, either. I did talk today to Keith Jax, the assistant manager of Tamarack Mountain." Keith appeared on the screen, smiling self-consciously into the camera. "We never had any problems with the gondola; it's got safety built in, like, all over the place. I mean, we take, like, thousands of people up the mountain every day, and nobody's ever been, you know, hurt. Somebody coulda got to it I guess, but I don't know who or why they'd want to; this is an awful thing to do to this town, scaring people, you know, and then they talk about the water, how it was, you know, poisoned last fall, but that's all over, and I don't think it's fair to, you know, like, blame the town because we've had some problems. I mean they could like happen anywhere."

Vince turned off the set. A little too clever, he thought. But not clever enough to get rid of her. He clenched the remote control. Still here, still here, still here. What the hell was he going to do about her?

She hung over him like a sword. She had not spilled her story to the press, showed no sign of spilling it, but it was still coiled inside her, ready to spring when she unleashed it . . . when he was close to the top, almost touching it. . . .

She'd been teasing him with it for months by moving in on the family and manipulating them, showing him she could attack him piecemeal and from a distance, before she used the weapon that would finally destroy him. And he'd been so busy he'd relied on a small-time, incompetent henchman. He should have taken care of her himself. That's what it came down to. And he had to do it right away. He could be in Tamarack in a few days, as soon as he could cut short his visit to Florida; he'd spend a day or so there, and then Denver, checking in with his people there, and be back in his office before Congress reconvened at the end of January. He was known for his record of attendance; he didn't want to spoil that.

But as he thought about it, it began to seem less urgent. She was out of sight for now; she'd probably be kept busy, with Leo and the kids in the hospital. And the truth was, Keith hadn't done such a bad job with the gondola. The more Vince thought about it over the next two days, the more pleased he became. He could do a lot with it; he'd know better when he was in Tamarack, and could talk to Keith.

"How did you do it?" he asked when the two of them were sitting in his suite at the Tamarack Hotel. He poured Scotch into two glasses, added ice, and sat back, looking past Keith at the ski mountain. A few skiers were coming down, stopping short at the road above the closed gondola building to ski to the other side of the mountain where the chair lift was operating. The empty gondola cable stretched up and out of sight; the cars had been taken off and stored in a shed at the top of the mountain until the investigation was completed, and repairs were made.

Looking at the cable, Vince thought of the town as it had

looked from his taxi window on the ride from the airport that afternoon. Wide, silent streets, houses and lawns hushed beneath a foot of new snow, sidewalks plowed and swept, waiting for the crowds that did not come. The town was eerily quiet. It was New Year's Day and in a normal year the streets and malls would have been crowded with visitors shopping or coming down from skiing for drinks and snacks and the last hot tub of their holiday. But not this year. This year, most of them had left early; the few who had stayed were doggedly trying to look cheerful, so they could get their money's worth. A ghost town, Vince thought, and grinned. It's a goddam ghost town.

"Well?" he asked. "How did you do it?"

"Maybe it's better if you, like, don't know," Keith said. "I mean, if they ask you anything, you could say . . . you know."

It occurred to Vince that Keith strongly resembled a weasel. Sandy-haired, his face a thin triangle above his sparse beard, his eyes narrowing when he spoke, he looked sly and shifty, and Vince remembered that he had only trusted him because there was no one else. "I asked you a question."

Keith shrugged. "It's a little hard to, like, explain if you don't know how the gondola works, but basically what I did was like block the J-grip so it wouldn't hold—"

"What did you use?"

"To block it? A piece of wood; you know, a two-by-four."

"What happened to it?"

"It fell out somewhere. What difference does it make? I mean, it wasn't there when the investigators, you know, checked, so the grip looked fine to them. You want me to go on?" Vince nodded. "Well there's this safety backup; it's like a switch that stops the gondola if the J-grip isn't grabbing right. So I fixed that, too; there's a bolt that holds part of the switch in place, and I just, like, took it out."

"The bolt?"

"Right. So the J-grip was jammed but the switch wasn't getting signals from it, so it couldn't shut the gondola down.

So the whole thing kept going instead of, you know, stopping, and when they got moving up the steep part, the J-grip couldn't hold against, you know, gravity, so the car stopped. I mean, the cable kept going and the next car like rammed into them. You shoulda heard it. The whole thing was like pretty simple, you know?"

"Where's the bolt?" Vince asked.

Keith grinned. "I hid it."

Vince waited.

Keith drained his glass and poured from the bottle of Scotch. He refilled Vince's without asking. "See, Vince, this is the thing. I've gotta get out of this place. I mean, I've had it up to here with Leo and the company and the whole resort bit; I'm like bored up to my kazoo. There's lots of things I can do; I mean, I've got lots of talents, only there's no way I can do anything creative in this hole. And I promised a little lady I'd take her with me when I go."

"Nobody's stopping you," Vince said. "You want Denver? Chicago? New York? I can call a few people if that's what you want. You were telling me where you hid the bolt."

"No, I wasn't. Not yet. See, those are all nice cities and it's nice of you to say you'll, you know, help me and all, but this little lady wants to go to Washington, and I think that's a great idea. I mean, I said something about this before, you remember? I asked if you'd take me with you."

"I don't remember. Everybody wants to go to Washington; they all want a free ride."

"Not me," Keith said quickly. "No way. I'm ready to work. I'm good, you said so yourself, and there's lots of things I can do. I mean, I have all these talents, you know, and I'd never get to use them if it wasn't for you. So I thought we'd make a deal now, and pretty soon, when things, like, settle down here—it wouldn't be smart for me to leave right away—but later, maybe in a few months, I'd come to Washington and we'd be, like, partners. I mean, you'd be president and I'd be your assistant. Chief assistant. You said that, remember? I said could I go with you when you're president and you said why not?"

"I don't remember. But I'm a long way from president. When it happens, you can remind me about all this. If you can't wait until then to get out of Tamarack, my friends in New York or Chicago can find a way for you to use your talents. If you're trying to impress me, Keith, you're doing a lousy job. I asked you for a report and you haven't finished it."

"The other thing is, there was a call in the office this morning. Those guys from, you know, Egypt backed out. I mean, they read about the gondola and they figured it's not such a good deal. I keep my eyes and ears open, Vince; I mean you really, like, need me. What I wanted was, you know, a promise."

The light was fading, and Vince reached behind him to turn on the table lamp. It threw Keith's thin face into relief, making his cheeks seem more hollow, his Adam's apple more pointed. His legs were stretched out on a hassock, crossed at the ankles, and he looked relaxed and cheerful, but he was watching Vince so intently he was almost squinting, and there was a small twitch at the corner of his mouth that gave away how important this was to him. Important enough to try to hold Vince up for it.

Fuck it, Vince thought, he's right; I do need him. And I will for a while. Then he can be bought off or sent somewhere. It won't be hard; he'll collapse like a balloon the first time somebody punctures his tough act. Me or somebody else. There's always somebody to do these things.

"Of course I promise," Vince said easily. "I didn't know it meant so much to you. You're a valuable part of my team, Keith; I wouldn't want to lose you." He shook his head slowly. "People in government don't have many real friends, you know; people they can truly trust. That's what I meant by people wanting a free ride. But you're not one of them; you know how to do a job, you don't mind getting your hands dirty, and you take pride in your work. We're a lot alike, you and I. You're right: we make a good team."

Keith squinted in the lamplight. "Thanks," he said, giving nothing away. "I'll tell my lady friend we're moving. Like,

April? That's, you know, four months. Plenty of time for things to calm down here."

Vince felt himself being squeezed, and fury swept through him. He smiled gently. "That may be a little soon for me. April is a hellish month in the Senate; you'll know all about that when you're working there. Let's think about June, when we're in recess. I'll have time to show you and your lady around, help you find a place to live, make you feel at home. Keith, I hate to break this up, but I've got a lot to do and it would help if you finish your report. You did a fine job with the gondola—of course I never doubted that you would—and you were very good on television. You said 'somebody coulda got to it.' Did anybody ask you what you meant?"

"They couldn't; I got out of here right afterward. I mean, I went to Durango to, like, do some errands; I figured I ought to talk to you first."

He hadn't missed a trick, Vince thought. It was too bad he was such a weasel; he really was a sharp kid. "Good for you," Vince said, and waited.

"Oh, yeah, the bolt," Keith said. "I hid it in front of somebody's garage." He grinned at Vince. "There's workmen finishing this remodeling job and there's a lot of crap in Dumpsters, construction stuff, you know, and I tossed it in there. I mean, it's different from all the other junk in there; anybody looking couldn't miss it. If they were told where to look."

"Whose garage?" Vince asked.

"Josh Durant's," Keith replied, and his grin widened until his thin face was shiny with stretching.

Vince erupted from his chair and began to pace around the room, a wonderful excitement stirring in him. "That's what you meant when you said someone could have gotten to the gondola."

"Could be. I mean, I can't remember exactly what I was thinking."

"They'll ask you that. You'll have to say something better than that."

468

Keith shrugged. "That's all I know. Like somebody coulda. It's not, you know, guarded or anything; it's just there and people go through it. I mean Josh went through it, Leo took him and like, you know, explained the whole fucking thing. And he hung around—"

"Who?"

"I'm telling you. Josh. Whenever he was in town, he went up in the morning with Leo and Anne. Only that day he didn't. I heard he left town."

Vince shot forward, pacing again, suddenly filled with energy, his muscles coiled with power, his thoughts racing. He knew what he would do and how he would do it; the scenario played out in his mind without a hitch. Keith had done far better than he knew. "Who's in charge of the investigation?" he asked. He was standing near Keith's chair; the only way he could tower over him.

"Something Halloran." Keith looked up at him. "Irving or Ervin, something odd like that. He's staying here, in the hotel. You want me to get him for you?"

"I'll take care of it." Vince moved to the door and opened it. "I'll call you tomorrow or the next day, before I leave. And we'll be in touch when I'm back in Washington."

Reluctantly, Keith lifted himself from his chair. "I better call you. Tomorrow. I mean, we've got a lot to, you know, talk about, and I'm, like, in the middle here, people asking me questions and Leo coming back one of these days, and I don't like being left hanging out there. . . ."

"Keith, I have complete confidence in you," Vince said warmly. He hung a heavy arm around Keith's narrow shoulders. "You can handle anything. You've been a real help to me, a real friend. I'm not worried about you being here, Keith; there's nobody I trust more to take care of things the right way." He edged him toward the door. "You can call me anytime, you know that. And I'll call you before I leave town. That's a promise."

When he was gone, Vince stood beside the desk and called Beloit in Denver. "It's all yours. Call Charles tomorrow morning; they may pay you to take it off their hands."

"There's those Egyptians," Beloit said.

"Not anymore. They changed their mind. I'm telling you, Ray, it's yours. At just about any price you name."

"God damn. You're a hell of a friend, Vince. And we're going to run one hell of a campaign. When're you coming to Denver so we can celebrate?"

"Tomorrow. I'll call when I get in."

Then, still standing, he called the front desk and asked for the room number for Irving or Ervin Halloran.

"Arvin Halloran, yes, sir," said the operator, and rang the room. An hour later, Halloran was in Vince's suite, and drinks had been sent up.

"This is very good of you," Vince said as they sat in the armchairs beside the window. Tamarack Mountain was lost to the darkness now, but here and there on its broad face, gleaming like the brightest planets in the sky, were the Sno-Cats, working in pairs, smoothing the slopes for the next day's skiing. Vince filled two glasses and put the cheese board and baskets of crackers and walnuts in the center of the table between them. "I appreciate your making time for me."

"We never turn down information, Senator," said Halloran, taking a fistful of walnuts. He was a huge man with shaggy hair and wire-rimmed glasses that magnified sharp brown eyes. "Anyway, it's an honor to meet you. You've got a lot of fans around here; I want you to know we're real proud of you, Senator."

"Thanks," Vince said. "I need to hear that. Those of us in government need to know people understand what we're trying to do. It's pretty discouraging, otherwise." He sipped his drink. "I'm discouraged about Tamarack, too. It's not good, what's happening to this town. And to my family, of course. I think you've met a lot of them by now."

"I have. Good people, Senator; you're a lucky man to have such a close family. It's too bad they've had such rotten luck."

"Is it really luck? I don't know where you are in your investigation."

"Well, we don't talk about it, you know. But I don't have any trouble telling you, Senator; you're not about to broadcast it to anybody. We've talked to everybody who can talk to us who was in those two cars, and it's pretty clear that the J-grip failed. You probably don't know what that is—" Vince let him describe it without interruption. "It seems to be working now, and there's no evidence of poor maintenance or tampering, but we'll have to wait for lab tests to be sure of that; it was damaged in the collision. We do know why the gondola didn't shut down when it should have; there's a bolt missing from the support bracket of the safety mechanism, so it slipped out of its operating position."

Vince frowned deeply. " 'Missing.' It fell out?"

"We don't know. It might have loosened due to vibrations, and been swept up by the cleaning crew, though they say they didn't notice it—it's big, you know, and odd shaped; you'd think they would have seen it. There was a full test of the gripping mechanism five days before the accident; the bolt could have been missing for some or all of those days; you'd never know it until the J-grip didn't clamp right. Anyway, we've searched for it and I'd bet my job it's not there now. Either the cleaning crew swept it up and tossed it out with the other trash, or . . . somebody removed it from its bracket and took it away."

Vince looked up sharply. "Why do you say that?"

"Well, the assistant mountain manager, Keith Jax, hinted that's what happened. Weird kid—oh, I'm sorry, he's a relative of yours, isn't he?"

"My nephew. A little strange, I agree, but generally reliable. What did he say?"

"That somebody could have done it. We're looking into that, but that's really up to the sheriff; we're just supposed to pass on the maintenance of the system. And that looks okay. Leo Calder—he's married to your niece, right? We talked to him in the hospital in Albuquerque, by the way; he's doing pretty well; it looks like he won't need surgery. Anyway, he and his crew have always been absolute tops in my book; they've got a perfect record of testing and inspection, and their maintenance is as good as you can get. But then you have this mess, so it looks like they slipped up somewhere. Or they didn't, and somebody did tamper with the system, though I don't know why the hell anybody'd do that. But the point is, even if we never know exactly what happened, we'll have to recommend that all the safety bolts be secured by locking devices so they can't jiggle loose, and that the whole system be tested daily for a couple weeks before they start up again. That's what I think'll happen. I wish we could give 'em a clean bill of health, Senator—I know this could cut like hell into their business—but I just can't do it. Not as of now, anyway."

"My God, Arvin, you're not talking about cutting into their business; this could ruin them." Vince stood, his thumbs in his belt, looking down at the floor, his face troubled. "They work so hard to make this place a success . . ." He pondered it, slowly shaking his head. "Well, I have to do it; I don't have any choice," he said at last. "I'd rather not, but . . . Arvin, what if you found the bolt?"

"Well, we'd have a shot at knowing what happened. Defective bolt, sabotage, whatever." He took another fistful of walnuts and gave Vince a long look. "Is that why I'm here tonight, Senator?"

Sadly, Vince nodded. "I'm afraid so." He sat again and refilled their glasses. "It's an ugly story. The only good part of it is that I'm absolutely sure my family has nothing to do with it."

Halloran sat back, his glass almost hidden in his broad hand. "I'm listening, Senator."

Vince let a brief silence hang between them. High up the mountain, the Sno-Cats were working their way down Ethan's Run, under the gondola cable, their headlights illuminating the slope where the car had fallen. "There's a man named Josh Durant," he said. "Lives in Los Angeles, an archaeologist and I think a professor at UCLA. He and my daughter had a thing going for a while, so I've known him, though not well; he's a cold bastard, hard to get friendly with. He spends a fair bit of time here; I heard he bought a new house in Riverwood. He's been coming here for years and never paid any more attention to the town or the company than any other tourist. Then, a few months ago, he was all over the place, talking to people about the company and the problems it's had—you know about the pollution in the reservoir, of course; unfortunately the media had a field day with it—and he started spending a lot of time with Leo Calder and his family; he even got himself invited to family dinners. And then he asked Leo to show him around the gondola, take him to the upper level and show him how it works, the safety features, the whole bit."

Halloran leaned forward.

"You'll understand how odd it seemed," Vince went on, his voice troubled and confiding. "Some of us began to wonder if he might be thinking about buying The Tamarack Company. God knows why; maybe he decided he was tired of mummies and wanted some action." He and Halloran exchanged a smile. "Anyway, that's what it began to look like to us. Of course the family hasn't had any intention of selling, and in fact, as far as I know, he's never said anything directly. But then, at Christmas—I couldn't be here; my damn politicking kept me in the East—this Durant got himself invited to dinner, and my nephew Keith told me that out of the blue he said he'd lined up a bunch of Egyptian investors to buy into the company. *Lined up,* mind you. What the hell was he doing? Running around the desert asking every sheik who went by if he wanted to buy The Tamarack Company? Let me tell you, it struck a false note with a lot of us, and it worried the hell out of me. You're a family man, aren't you, Arvin?"

Halloran nodded. "Four kids, two grandchildren, another on the way."

"Then you know what I mean. Family. Christ, what else is there that really means anything to a man? And I'll bet you've got your family around you, in Denver."

"Aurora. Same thing. Yeah, we're lucky; they all stayed close."

"You're more than lucky; you're blessed. I'm stuck in Washington; how much can I do to help these people? Not that I don't love the Senate; it's become a real passion with me, working for my state and my country. But I see this son of a bitch trying to take advantage of my family, and I'll tell you, it damn near drives me crazy. Well, anyway, I gather he said his so-called friends, these foreigners, didn't want a controlling interest in the company. But who knows what he really had in mind? By this time he probably thought the family could use some help. Maybe he even thought they'd be anxious to sell. But Leo and his wife didn't want to, and said so. I gather there was quite a debate at Christmas, and the most Durant could get from them was a willingness to talk to the Egyptians if they came over here. In the past couple of days, it's occurred to some of us"—Vince paused—"that Durant might have thought there were ways to convince them to sell, and at a price he and his Egyptian friends could afford."

"'Convince them to sell,'" Halloran repeated. "By causing an accident that could make the company less attractive?"

Vince held his hands up, the fingers spread wide. "I'm not accusing him. Let me just tell you what else I've put together. It seemed to all of us that Durant never forgave my daughter for breaking off with him; we think he's had it in for the family ever since. But here he is, sucking up to them and buying a house in their neighborhood. And one of the ways he tried to get close to them, and maybe to the gondola, too, was to go along on Leo's inspection trips up the mountain. Leo went every morning at one minute to nine; you could set your watch by it. And Durant went along whenever he was in town. They'd ride up in the gondola, ski around the mountain to check in with the lift operators, talk to some tourists, and ski down. The only day Durant missed was the morning of the accident. That morning, he got out of town. A long way; all the way to Egypt. He'd had a crew digging there for months, looking for a tomb, as I understand it, but all of a sudden it became urgent that he go that very morning."

They drank thoughtfully, and Vince refilled their glasses. "You say he bought a house here," Halloran said.

"In Riverwood," Vince replied. "Just down the road from the Calders. He's having extensive remodeling done."

"He'd be a fool to throw away the bolt at home," Halloran mused.

Vince shrugged. "He has no reason to think anyone would look for it. Or maybe he thinks a bolt is a bolt and the Dumpsters at his house are full of materials torn out in the remodeling, and what better place to hide another piece of hardware?"

"It doesn't look like any other bolt in the world."

"So you said. An archaeologist probably wouldn't know that."

Halloran revolved the glass in his fingers. "He's still in Egypt?"

"I don't keep track of him, but I think so."

Halloran drained the glass and stood up. "Can I use your phone? I'm going to call the sheriff."

"Of course. I'll leave the room."

"I don't have any secrets from you, Senator. In fact, you've got a better right than anybody to hear this, especially if it leads to something."

Vince walked to the windows and looked up at the bright planets moving slowly down Tamarack Mountain, smoothing the slopes. Not planets, he thought. Stars. My very lucky stars. Making things smooth. Beloit is happy; Leo and the family will be out in the cold; we're taking care of Durant. And then we'll get to Anne.

If you wait long enough, he thought cheerfully, everything comes to pass the way you want it.

The Tamarack County sheriff, with two of his men, spent the next day patiently sifting through the construction debris in the Dumpster outside Josh Durant's garage. About halfway down, shoved beneath torn pieces of drywall and old flooring, they found the bolt, winking at them in the sunlight.

And on Wednesday evening, when Josh stepped off the plane at the Tamarack Airport and was raising his hand to greet Anne, the sheriff blocked his way, and told him he was under arrest.

chapter 19

It was done very quietly; no one around them knew what was happening. But Anne saw Tyler Schofield's hand on Josh's arm, and the sudden anger in Josh's face. They were standing at the foot of the steps that had been wheeled to the plane's door, and as other passengers walked the short distance to the terminal, Anne slipped through the door and went to Josh. She had never seen him so angry.

"—what the hell you're talking about—" he was saying.

"I can't tell you now, Josh," Tyler said, almost whispering. "You've just got to come with—"

"Can't tell me? You'll damn well tell me; I'm not going anywhere until I know what the hell is going on."

"Damn it, Josh, you've got everybody and his aunt looking at—"

"What difference does it make? I'm not hiding anything; you're the one who's playing games."

"Not me, by God. Listen, mister, you're in big trouble here and you'd better watch—"

"Hello, Tyler," Anne said. "Welcome back," she said to Josh.

Their hands gripped. And she did not pull away. "Did I interrupt something?" she asked.

"Yes," Tyler snapped.

"I'm glad to see you," said Josh. He heard the anger and bewilderment in his voice and wondered if he looked as adrift as he felt. "I don't know what's going on here, but Tyler tells me I'm under arrest for the gondola accident."

Anne looked at Tyler in disbelief. *"Josh?* You're not serious. Why? Tyler, this is crazy. He doesn't know anything about it. He wasn't even in Tamarack that day."

"Listen here," Tyler said in exasperation. He looked around the tarmac and into the terminal. They were not crowded, since most tourists had canceled their trips, but there were enough people to make him nervous, and a few of them were casting glances at him and Josh. "We can't talk here. Let me get this part over with—"

"Anyway, why arrest him?" she asked. "Ordinarily, you'd just take someone in for questioning."

"There's too much at stake! Oh, Christ." Tyler lowered his voice. "Listen, Anne, you don't have anything to do with this, okay? I shouldn't even be talking to you. Now you just go on home—"

"She has everything to do with it," said Josh firmly. "She's my lawyer."

Anne's eyes met his in a quick look, bright and pleased. She took her hand from his and stepped back, cool and professional. She could have been wearing a pin-striped suit, Josh thought, instead of black stretch pants and a sleek blue-and-black ski jacket. "So there's no question of my going home," she said to Tyler. "You don't want to be in the position of denying Mr. Durant legal representation at his booking."

"Oh, hey," said Tyler. "Listen, we're all friends here, Anne. We've got a hell of a mess is all; the newspapers and TV are shafting us every day; and we've got to do something to show that we're on the ball . . . well, shit, I shouldn't even be saying that."

So they'd panicked, Anne thought, and made a quick arrest. But of all people, why Josh?

"Tell us about it on the way into town," she said.

From then on, she and Josh listened, and she did not let him talk until he had been charged and fingerprinted and was out on bail with the money he had had wired from his bank in Los Angeles. "You'll be around here for a while?" the judge asked.

"I have a class to teach in two weeks, in Los Angeles," Josh said.

The judge contemplated him. "We all know each other around here; it'd be hard for me to make a case that you're a threat to anybody or that you'd skip bail. You can go where you want, Josh, but let me know in advance. I don't want any surprises; the last few months we've had too damn many of those."

Outside, in the quiet of Main Street, snow had begun to fall, a steady curtain of flakes that seemed to encircle them as they walked to the car.

"It looks like Gail's," Josh said.

"It is." Anne walked around to the driver's side. "I'm using it while they're away."

"How is Leo? I haven't had a chance to ask about him."

"He'll be fine; he doesn't need surgery. We were very lucky. They'll be back tomorrow morning. Have you had dinner?"

"No. I'd forgotten about it. As I recall, we planned to go out tonight, after you met my plane."

She smiled. "Yes. Would you like a restaurant, or Leo and Gail's?"

"I'd rather not go out."

"Neither would I." She drove down Main Street, through the falling snow. The flakes rushed toward them in the headlights, as if the car were plunging into an illuminated cone. The street was almost empty and they drove in silence to the turn that led out of town. "The bolt couldn't have gotten into the Dumpster unless someone put it there," Anne said, letting her thoughts flow into words.

"Someone who went there for that reason." Their thoughts merged, and so did their voices. "No one strolls around Riverwood in the middle of the winter."

"It may not have been that deliberate. What if one of the carpenters or plumbers or electricians brought it with him?"

"Why would a carpenter or plumber or electrician sabotage the gondola?"

"Why would you?"

There was a pause. "There's no reason for anyone to do it," Josh said. "It's insane. To risk all those lives . . . No reason is compelling enough to do that."

"Hatred," Anne said. "Greed, envy, fear. Maybe all of them at once. I've never stopped being astonished at the cruelty they bring out in people." She turned onto the road that climbed to Riverwood. "I was impressed with the way you controlled your anger tonight."

He gave a wry smile. "I was thinking about that when I told the judge I had classes in a couple of weeks. The infinite flexibility of the human spirit. I'd already learned to live with this craziness and I was making plans around it. I guess we can do that with almost anything; it just requires constant adjustments."

"Yes," Anne said quietly. In a few minutes they reached the house and she drove into the garage. When they stood together in the brightly lit silence beside the two cars with Leo's cluttered worktable and Gail's gardening tools along the back, skis lined up in racks, and four bicycles hanging on the walls, there was something so domestic and intimate about the scene that they hesitated, caught in its spell. "We have a lot to talk about," Anne said at last, without looking at Josh, and they went into the house. "And the first thing," she added as she hung her ski jacket in the closet and used a bootjack to pull off her high boots, "is the fact that I'm not licensed to practice law in the state of Colorado."

Josh paused in hanging up the sports jacket he had worn from Egypt. "I didn't think of that. You're only licensed in California?"

"And New York. You'll have to retain someone here. I've met a couple of people I could recommend; one in particular, Kevin Yarborough, seems very good."

"But you'd work with him."

"If you want me to. And as much as I can. I'm going back to Los Angeles tomorrow, Josh; I have a lot of catching up to do."

He smiled ruefully as they went into the kitchen. "Do all

your clients behave as if you have nothing to do but think about them?"

"All of them. I would, too." She opened the refrigerator, and then the freezer, rummaging through them. "I think I'll call Kevin and ask him to come over tonight; you should get to know him as soon as possible. And we can talk about what we're going to do. I wish I didn't have to leave. I may be able to get back in a week or two, at least for a day; I'll let you know."

She set a carton and two packages on the counter and turned back to him. Josh took her hands in his: cold, slender fingers that lay within his warm ones. In her stockinged feet she seemed smaller than he remembered. "Anne, listen to me for a minute. There were a lot of things I planned to tell you tonight, starting with how much I thought about you in the past few days, and how that whole miraculous time wasn't complete for me because you weren't there." He watched her eyes, wide and startled, a little stunned. But not frightened, he saw. *Not frightened.* He felt a wild elation. But beneath it was the current of his anger and bewilderment, and the beginnings of alarm at what might be ahead for him. "I'm sorry; I'm trying to juggle everything. I want to concentrate on you, but other things get in the way."

"That's what we have to talk about. What we're going to do next." She turned away, becoming busy at the counter. Josh worked with her, easing open a foil wrapping and putting a cake on a glass plate. He unwrapped bread and put it in the oven to thaw. Anne was aware of him looking in cabinets for plates and glasses, opening drawers to find silverware. She had thought about him so vividly on the gondola, and pictured him so clearly when he called from Egypt, that now, as they worked together in silent harmony, it seemed like a continuation of her thoughts; as if, somehow, they had become a part of each other.

Outside, snow was falling heavily, whirled around by gusts of wind. The kitchen was warm and hushed, its pine cabinets and table and chairs glowing golden in the light. Anne felt at peace. The anxiety of the past few days had dimmed for the moment; her fears about Josh's closeness, though they had flickered for a moment in the garage, had faded; her tension over his inexplicable arrest was held in abeyance. As they moved about, coming close and parting, she felt neither wariness nor excitement; what she felt was a sense of rightness. How amazing, she thought. She had never felt it before, except in her work.

She looked up and met his eyes, and they exchanged a smile. She did not probe how she felt, or even wonder about it; she just let it settle within her. She trusted him; it felt right that they were together, in this safe haven, while the storm built outside.

"This is a good place to be," Josh said casually. He was organizing place mats, plates, and wineglasses on a tray. "It wouldn't be hard to forget that, as our friend Tyler said, we've got a hell of a mess here." He paused, contemplating the silverware in his hand, then laid it on the plates. "Except that we can't forget it. And you're right; I have to figure out what comes next." He took napkins from a drawer and folded them. "And there's the rest of it. What we can do for Leo and Gail. And the whole town. I don't see anybody having an easy time in the next few days or weeks. Unless we find out that one of my trusted workmen had a grudge against Leo or the company—I don't believe it, but—"

"No, I don't believe it, either." Anne stirred the pasta sauce with a long wooden spoon. Tendrils of steam wound upward, curling around her white sweater and flushed face. She was more relaxed than Josh had ever seen her. She was stunningly beautiful, and there was a new serenity in her face that drew him toward her and made him ache to take her in his arms. "Something is terribly wrong here, Josh. It's not logical for a workman, or anyone, to put that bolt in your Dumpster. There are trash cans all over town between the gondola and Riverwood; there's no reason to choose someone's home unless—"

"It was supposed to be found," Josh finished quietly.

"Which means someone had to find it." They carried the tray and bowls of food to the living room and arranged them on the glass coffee table. "There's only one way that could happen. There wasn't any search for it; it would take an army to go through every Dumpster and garbage can in Tamarack, and it would be weeks before they got to River-wood."

"So someone told them where to look."

"Yes."

Josh was at the fireplace, lighting the kindling. He knelt there, staring at the thin flames as the wood caught. "I don't know anyone who hates me enough to do that."

"It may be someone who thinks you're convenient because you left town that day. Something like that."

He shook his head. "It still wouldn't make sense. I haven't the remotest reason to damage the gondola."

"Or Tamarack?"

He turned to her sharply. "You know I haven't."

"Pretend you're Tyler. Someone calls you and tells you the missing bolt from the gondola is at Josh Durant's house, and sure enough you find it there. What do you know about Josh Durant? It's pretty certain you know about the tour of the gondola; you told me you talked to a few people when you were there. And anyway, you weren't trying to keep it secret. And a lot of people know you left town the morning of the accident. And then there were the Egyptian investors."

"Tyler doesn't know about them."

"He might. That wasn't a secret, either, and anybody who was at dinner on Christmas might have told other people."

Josh sat beside her on the couch, watching the fire. "So what? I only found them; I don't have anything to do with their buying into the company." He paused. "Unless Tyler thinks I do. That I'm using them. That I'm the one who really wants to buy into it. But that's crazy, too. He has no evidence for that; no reason even to think it."

"No. Unless . . . Unless someone suggested it to him."

"Why would—? Well, I suppose if we believe someone led Tyler to my house to find the bolt, we can believe someone would suggest almost anything to him. But what would he do with it? Why would I sabotage the gondola and send all the tourists scurrying home? Nobody's lining up to buy a business in trouble—" He stopped. "But of course the price would be lower."

"Yes." There was a silence. "I don't believe it," Anne said decisively. "It's too weak. No prosecutor would go to court with it."

"If that's all they've got," Josh said.

"Can you think of anything else?"

"No, but I wouldn't have thought of stringing those things together and coming up with that conclusion, either."

"I'm going to call Kevin," Anne said. "I don't think they have any kind of case against you, but he may see things I don't. Anyway, he has to be part of this. He can join us for coffee."

But when she returned to the living room, she told Josh he had an appointment for the next morning, in Kevin's office. "He doesn't want to go out; he says we've had six inches of snow already and they're predicting fourteen to twenty."

Josh was opening the bottle of wine he had brought from the wine cellar. "I'll have to borrow Leo's snowshoes to get home," he murmured absently.

Anne went to the front door and opened it. A blast of wind blew snow across her stockinged feet. The snow was falling steadily, a heavy curtain of flakes shining in white streaks in the light from the lanterns flanking the door. "I don't think you should go anywhere, with or without snowshoes," she said. "Kevin's right; it's a night to stay home." She slammed the door against the wind, and locked it.

Josh looked up. "I'd like that, if you don't mind. As I recall, this house is full of guest rooms."

Anne felt a rush of gratitude and warmth at his casual matter-of-factness. They would have a night straight out of a nineteenth-century novel. She wondered if that was easier for Josh than for most men because he spent so much time in the past. She smiled to herself. I'll have to ask him sometime, she thought.

"Three," she said, as casually as he. "One is mine; you have your choice of the other two. Gail keeps them ready; they're always having unexpected guests."

"Good. I'll tell Kevin whatever you and I decide tonight."

Anne smiled faintly. "This isn't my specialty, Josh; I don't want you to think I can do the same kind of work I do in divorces."

"I like the way you work." He poured some of the deep red Barolo into his glass and tasted it. "And I admire Leo's cellar. I keep finding more reasons for cherishing him as a neighbor."

"If he stays here. I don't know what's going to happen with the company."

Josh filled their glasses. "Dinner," he said, and handed her a plate.

"Thank you. I can't believe it, with everything that's going on, but I'm starved."

Josh raised his glass. They were sitting close to each other; when Anne touched her glass to his, their hands brushed. "To my lawyer," he said.

"To my client," she responded easily.

They filled their plates and ate quietly for a few minutes, watching the fire curl and leap around the piñon logs. "This might become a habit," Josh said thoughtfully. "The first time we planned to go out to dinner, we changed our minds and cooked together in my apartment."

"Last September," Anne murmured.

"The eighteenth," Josh added. "We raided the freezer that night, too. You wore red silk. And we listened to Beethoven and Mozart."

Anne remembered. The evening had been warm and uncomplicated; more pleasant than she had anticipated. But still, all during it, and in all their times together after that, there had been her wariness, her instinctive withdrawals, her fears. She watched the leaping flames and wondered what had happened in the months from that night to this to make everything feel so right. Time, she thought. Weeks and months when Josh was becoming part of her life, slowly, gradually, without planning or pressure. And something else. Tonight he was in trouble and she was helping him. Tonight, for the first time, she did not feel he stood on an indestructible platform of triumphs while she balanced on a fragile base patched together by her defenses. She had always been able to help strangers; now she could help someone close to her, and that gave her a new feeling of strength, and ease.

She put her plate aside. "We have to talk about strategy."

Josh nodded. "Yes. But I have a favor to ask. We have all tonight, and early tomorrow, for strategy, and I'm in no hurry to get to it. If someone's trying to frame me, it won't change in the next few hours, and at the moment it seems a lot more manageable than it did earlier tonight. Wine and the fire, I suppose, and being with you; I just can't work up a strong sense of urgency right now. What I really want is to tell you about Egypt. I've been wanting to since we took the first step into the tomb." He shook his head. "It seems like years ago. It's the damndest thing; I was flying so high; I'd found everything I'd dreamed of and I knew you'd be waiting for me . . . And then Tyler was there and it all blew up."

Anne was watching him somberly, offering no soothing words, waiting for him to work out his feelings by himself. "But that's for tomorrow," he said. "For tonight I want to get back to the wonder and beauty of what I found, and I want to do it with you. One of these days, when we get through this damn business, I want to take you there, but for now I want to tell you about the tomb and try to make you see it. Is that all right with you?"

"Yes," Anne said. "I'd like that very much."

He refilled their wineglasses and reached behind him, turning off the lamp, leaving the room in darkness except for the bright, dancing light of the flames. Anne's face glowed in the firelight and he wondered if his face looked the same: warm, rosy, peaceful. They could sit here all night, he thought, with the storm outside and the fire within; this was their time, separate from the rest of the world. They would be inundated with everything else quickly enough, the next day. "I don't have photographs or slides," he said. "I haven't had them developed. All I have are words—"

"And passion," Anne said softly. "And I'd like to share

that with you, and everything you saw. Through your words, and your voice."

Josh felt a rush of joy. Instinctively, he put out his hand to take hers. But he stopped before he touched her. Not yet, he thought, not tonight; one step at a time.

"The door had been plastered over," he began. And his voice filled the quiet room, and Anne's imagination.

"THE NEW KING TUT!" trumpeted newspapers and television commentators the next day, as soon as the Egyptian government and the Los Angeles Museum of the Ancient World jointly announced the finding of Tenkaure's tomb. "UCLA PROFESSOR DISCOVERS TOMB OF KING TENK!" "TOMB INTACT, FILLED WITH FABULOUS RICHES!" "TOMB'S TREASURES TOP TUT'S!"

Like homing pigeons, the reporters swooped down on Los Angeles. When they learned that Josh was not there, they wheeled about and flew straight to Tamarack. For some of them, it was the second time in a week; they had been there to cover the gondola crash. For the science reporters, it was the first time, and they used the flight to read hastily purchased histories of Egypt, especially the tumultuous times in the middle of the Eighteenth Dynasty.

And then, when they got to Tamarack and were renting cars and buying maps of the town, some of them picked up a local paper and read that Josh Durant, the famous archaeologist, had been charged with causing the gondola accident, and was out on bond.

It was a reporter's dream: two major stories in one place with one villain who was also a hero, or the other way around. "FIRST A TOMB, THEN A CELL?" headlined *USA Today,* and the New York *Daily News* shouted, "PHARAOH-FINDING PROF NABBED FOR GONDOLA CRASH." The headlines were picked up by papers around the country and reported with flourishes on television's morning shows and evening news. Only the *Los Angeles Times* was restrained, since Josh was one of theirs. The reporters camped at his house, their cars parked along the narrow road in a scraggly line that stretched almost the full mile to Gail and Leo's house. On the day they came home from Albuquerque, the cars were the first thing they saw. Leo looked at them in bewilderment as Gail turned into the road to their house, driving between the high banks made by the snowplow early that morning, when the storm ended. They had gone straight to the Tamarack hospital from the airport, to spend the afternoon with Robin and Ned. Now it was almost dark, and the clouds were low again; more snow was predicted. Leo strained to see how far the cars stretched. "What's going on? Nobody has a party at four in the afternoon."

"It has to be reporters, because of Josh," Gail said. "Damn them, why can't they leave him alone? Why didn't the storm hang on so none of them could get there? How did they even know he was here? Someone in Los Angeles must have told them. Why couldn't they keep it to themselves?"

"It's too good a story," Leo said. He got out of the car, carrying himself carefully so he would not jar any bones and send tremors through his aching head. "I guess that's why we couldn't get him on the phone this morning; he's probably not answering it. Let's go over there; he's practically under siege."

"You can try to call him again, but you're not going there," Gail said firmly. "You know what the doctor—"

"Right, I know. But I have to get to the office tomorrow, Gail. You're going to drive me and I'll be fine."

"I know you will," Gail said. She walked beside him into the house. "I'm not so sure about Tamarack. Or us."

"They're all coming over tonight, aren't they?" Leo asked abruptly.

"All of them but Vince; he told William he had to stay in Denver. I tried to make them wait a few days, but they're scared. They want to sell, right away, to anybody who comes up with a decent offer."

"They promised to wait for those Egyptians. What's got into them?"

Gail shook her head. "I didn't tell you in the hospital; the Egyptians changed their mind."

Leo swore softly. "It's a good thing Robin and Ned aren't home yet; I wouldn't want them here tonight." He walked carefully to his study off the living room.

"Dinner in an hour, so we'll be done before they get here," Gail called, and went to the kitchen. It was as neat as if Anne had never been there, except for an apple pie on the counter, with a note beside it. "Apples and cinnamon have been known since ancient times to heal skull fractures, so this is my contribution to Leo's recovery. I'm sorry I won't see you; I really have to catch an early plane. I'll call from LA, and I'll try to get back in a week or two. Welcome home!"

Gail walked through the house. Not a trace, she thought. The sheets from the guest room had been washed and the bed neatly made; the cushions in the living room were plumped. But there had been a fire in the fireplace the night before, she saw; the ashes were still warm. She felt a stab of sadness at the thought of Anne sitting alone before a fire on a snowy night.

She raked the ashes and laid kindling and logs on the andirons. Another fire tonight; maybe it would make everyone feel more pleasant, and not in such a panic. And they'd have Anne's pie, warmed up. Warm fire, warm pie, warm hearts. Maybe.

But when the family sat in the living room that night, they were tense and jumpy, not interested in pie, barely aware of the huge fire Gail had lit, wanting only to get through, and leave.

"I'm sorry, Gail, I'm so sorry," Nina kept saying. "I'm so *sorry*. But what else can we do?"

"We can wait," Leo said angrily. He and Gail sat close together on the couch facing the fireplace. "Listen, you know that gondola didn't fall by itself; Gail called all of you and told you what they've found so far: somebody wrecked it!"

"*Josh* wrecked it!" Fred shouted. "What difference does that—"

"He didn't!" Gail cried. "Nobody in his right mind could ever believe—"

"Most likely not," Marian said. "But they must have something, or they wouldn't have charged him—"

"Poor Josh," Nina said. "I did like him. What could have gotten into him—"

"Nobody knows what happened," Leo said loudly. "Look, I'd rather not shout; it hurts like hell when I do. Could we have a conversation here instead of a yelling match? There's something we have to be clear on. *Nobody's blaming us.* This guy Halloran came to Albuquerque and told Gail our maintenance was terrific—"

"Who cares about Halloran?" Fred cut in. "He doesn't buy lift tickets; tourists do. And the tourists, the newspapers, TV, *everybody* is blaming us. Look around, for Christ's sake, this town is dead."

"It's like a, you know, albatross," Keith said to the room at large. "I mean what can you do with it, it's a, you know, white elephant."

Marian ignored her son. He had turned into a foolish version of Fred. "I don't see what good it would do to wait," she said to Leo.

He leaned forward, too quickly, and winced from the pain in his head. "When we're cleared of negligence, we can get people back, Marian, I know we can! It's not as if we're some remote little village; we're one of the top ski areas in the world! People come here from all over, they come year after year—"

"Leo, you don't have to sell it to us," Marian said sadly.

"It looks like I do. As far as I can tell, you've forgotten everything you ever knew about this place. This isn't an ordinary town; it's got a history and a life of its own, and tourists like that. And we've got a mountain that skiers in every country talk about. And none of that has changed—"

"It's all changed," William said. "I'll tell you why. Precisely because of what you said, Leo. It isn't an ordinary town: it lives or dies on the goodwill of visitors who come here to have a good time. And they won't have a good time if they don't feel safe. And they won't feel safe if they don't think we can keep our house in order. It's as simple as that.

It won't matter to them whether we didn't do proper maintenance or we were sabotaged; what matters is that the gondola crashed and people were hurt. That's what gets remembered. And that's what's killing us."

"It won't be remembered if they believe it won't happen again," Leo said desperately.

"No one can ever be sure of that," Marian said firmly. "Every time something goes wrong here—and it's odd, but we've had a lot of things wrong lately—it gets harder to sell."

"We don't have to sell it! Listen, Vail had a gondola accident, years ago, and they went on to be bigger than ever! There's no reason why we can't, too!"

Fred shrugged. "Vail's a lot different. And it didn't have all these other things going wrong."

"That doesn't—"

"Leo," said Marian, "we went along with you the last time this came up, but we can't keep doing it forever. Too much has happened. I don't see any other way than to sell as soon as we can, while we can."

William grunted. "You'll get your money, Charles. That should make you happy."

"It will help," Charles said. He was looking at Gail, who was crying. Leo's arm was around her. "Marian's right," he said to her. "We can't hold on to it."

"Did you talk to Beloit?" Fred asked.

Charles nodded. "Sixty million, cash, if we make the deal tonight."

"For Christ's sake!" Fred exploded, and at the same time Marian cried, "It's worth twice that!"

"What do you want me to do?" Charles asked tightly. "Call the Egyptians back? Call Matsushita? Or Sony? What the hell do you want me to do?"

"Sell," Walter said. He and Rose were on a hassock near the fireplace; he was the only one who had eaten his pie. "Take the sixty million and get out. I've had it with all these debates; I'm tired of worrying about it. Let somebody else do it for a change."

"I'm so sorry," Nina said to Gail and Leo.

"Nobody's happy about it," William rumbled.

"It's very sad," Marian said. "But I really don't see any other way—"

"Yes," Fred said emphatically. "I vote yes."

There was a pause. "Yes," whispered Nina. One by one, the others echoed it. Gail and Leo were silent. The fire burned brightly.

The faint whisper of the flames was the only sound in the room.

"I'll call Beloit," said Charles at last. "He'll want a letter of intent."

"Write it up," said William. "You and I can sign it as officers of Chatham Development."

Charles took a folded sheet, and a pen, from the inside pocket of his sports jacket and held them out to William.

"I'll be damned," Fred said admiringly.

William leaned over the coffee table and read the letter. Charles' signature was already on it. William signed his name and handed it back.

"We have to get back to the hotel," said Rose, standing up. "We're catching the first plane tomorrow."

"Yes," William said. "We'd better go."

"It's snowing again," said Nina. "It's going to be hard, driving down the Riverwood road. Oh, dear," she burst out, "there are so many things to worry about!"

Marian put her arm around her. "We'll drive slowly."

"I meant there are *other* things—"

"I know," Marian said. "Come on, we'll get our coats."

They all bent over Gail and Leo, kissing them good-bye, and then they left. Flakes of snow drifted in each time the door opened. When it closed for the last time, Leo took Gail in his arms and held her to him. They were both crying. They sat there for a long time, while the fire burned down, and then went out.

Josh went to see them early the next morning, wearing snowshoes to walk the mile from his house because the plow had not yet reached Riverwood. The unplowed roads kept the reporters away and he had the walk to himself. The sun was breaking through the clouds in flashes of light on the unbroken expanse of snow that had been smoothed and rounded into high dunes by the wind; when the clouds closed in again, he moved through a landscape of black pines and white aspens against the pure white snow. The only color came from his blue ski pants and jacket, and his face, reddened in the bitter cold. By the time he reached Gail and Leo's house, he was almost jogging, his face icy, his body sweating.

"Just in time for breakfast," Gail said as she opened wide the door of the mud room. He burst in, breathing hard. "We'll be waiting for you in the kitchen."

"Thanks," he gasped. He pulled off his snowshoes and boots, and by the time he hung his jacket on the crowded coat tree, his breathing had returned to normal. He went into the kitchen in his stockinged feet, thinking of Anne. They had been there only two nights before.

"You look too damn healthy," Leo growled.

"And you look like you'll give me a run for it in a couple of weeks," Josh said. Leo stood and they hugged each other. "I'm glad to see you whole."

"I was lucky. And I had Anne. She kept the kids from falling out of that damn car, kept them busy until the patrol came, and she's been with them at the hospital every day while we were in Albuquerque. I love that lady. Sit down, Josh; have some breakfast. We have to talk about you."

Gail brought orange juice and pancakes to the table while Leo poured coffee. She moved back and forth between the table and the stove, talking as she made more pancakes. "It's absolutely crazy, thinking you had anything to do with it, even *thinking* that you could do anything criminal—"

Josh heard the tension in her voice, the high note that was like a muted scream. "What's happened here?" he asked. "Something's wrong. Something more about the gondola? About the company? Come on, we're not going to talk about me until I know what's going on with you two."

"They voted to sell the company," Leo said. "They were here last night; it took about ten minutes. This guy Beloit came in with an offer that no good businessman would look at twice, and they grabbed it. They were scared and they didn't know what to do, so they took it, and it was done. Just like that."

Josh shook his head. "I'm sorry. They should have waited. The town will come back; it's just a question of time."

"I told them that. They didn't want to hear it."

"So I don't know how much we can help you, Josh," Gail said in that tight, high voice. "I don't suppose we're going to have much clout around here from now on."

"You don't have to worry about me," Josh said. "I've got a terrific lawyer. Which reminds me: that's an incredible Barolo you've got in your cellar, Leo. We held ourselves to one bottle, which, believe me, wasn't easy."

They looked at him in bewilderment. "Who did?"

"Anne and I. She didn't tell you? I thought she would have, before she left."

"We didn't see her; she just left a note. You had dinner here? When?"

"Two nights ago. She met my plane."

"Oh." For a moment, Gail forgot the family meeting. "You made a fire."

"We ate dinner in front of the fire. And I stayed in your other guest room, because of the storm."

"I'm so glad. I was feeling sad about Anne being alone in front of the fire, with a storm outside. I'm glad she wasn't. I'm glad she was with you."

"Who's your lawyer?" Leo asked.

"Anne."

"Oh. Well, good, except, how can she—"

"She's working with Kevin Yarborough, here in town. I saw him yesterday morning, and he agreed to work with her any way she wants. He thinks she's terrific, too."

"You got past all those reporters?" Gail asked.

"I promised them an interview when I got back."

"And?"

"And I gave them one. Nothing about me; everything

494

about the tomb—well, I haven't had a chance to tell you about that—"

"We heard it yesterday, at the hospital; Ned had the TV on," Leo said. "The trouble was, it was two stories—Egypt and the gondola—and neither of them was very clear."

"You tell us, Josh," said Gail. "All of it, starting with the gondola. Tyler doesn't really have anything, does he? What *can* he have?"

Josh sat back, his mug between his hands. The sun was fully out, now, flooding the kitchen, and he sat in its warmth, feeling as much at home as he had with Anne. This had become his family, and his place. It was partly because of Anne, he thought; as she became more deeply involved with Leo and Gail and the children, he had wanted to share that with her. But also it was because of Leo and Gail themselves. He enjoyed their love for each other, their reliance on each other, their solid marriage, the stability of their life with their children. The contrast with his own personal life, with Dora and with the others before her, was so great that Josh was drawn to them as a man in the shadows is drawn to the light.

They talked for a long time that morning, until Gail and Leo had to leave for the hospital, to bring Ned and Robin home. "What will you do now?" Gail asked. "Are you going back to Egypt?"

"Not until this business is cleared up. I wouldn't go back right away, anyway; I'm teaching a class this semester. And I have enough here to keep me busy; I have all of Tenkaure's walls to read."

"You mean your photographs," said Leo. "You really can read them? The drawings and the hieroglyphics?"

"Like a book. In fact, it is a book only it's on the walls. It's a history of Tenkaure's reign and his time, the way the people lived, and traded with other countries, and fought wars and revolutions . . . the whole story. And we don't have it yet; all we know about Tenkaure so far is a few pieces I put together from tombs of the pharaohs who came after him. His son and the attempted coup. That's about it."

"What about his son?" Gail asked.

"He was the heir to the throne, and evidently he got involved with one of his father's wives and his father banished him. We don't know any more about it; I hope the whole story is in the tomb. We do know that, afterwards, Raneb, the son, went to the delta and hired mercenaries and plotted a coup to overthrow his father. Somehow, Tenkaure found out about it and stopped it, and probably sent Raneb out of the kingdom. We don't know for sure, but he never shows up again, and he didn't become the next pharaoh, so I'm assuming he never came back, or at least became part of the family again. The world doesn't change much, does it? Family quarrels sound pretty much alike when they're reduced to their basics."

"They sure do," Leo said. He looked at Gail. "It could almost be the story of the Chathams."

Gail shook her head quickly. "Not really."

Josh's eyebrows went up. "How?"

"Well, it's not really that close," Leo said. "Ethan, Gail's grandfather, kicked Vince out of the family a long time ago. You wouldn't have known that; I doubt that Dora knows it, she was a baby when it happened, and she's the only one who might have told you. No one's talked about it, as far as I know, since it happened. Anyway, Vince was out, and he sold his shares in the family company, so he was out there, too. He didn't plot a coup or anything like that, but he left and he never really came back. Ethan never spoke to him again."

"Why did he kick him out?" Josh asked. In the silence, he looked from Leo to Gail. "Come on; it's the obvious question. And you said it was a long time ago."

"But it's not our story," Gail said. "Not ours to tell."

Frowning, Josh gazed past them, at the distant peaks. The scientist in him always looked for connections; that was his life work. Now he made the connection between three facts: something had so wounded Anne that it was as if part of her was frozen, or asleep, and had been that way for a long time. Vince had been kicked out by her grandfather a long time ago. Anne had left home a long time ago, and had only recently come back. He felt cold inside, as if, like Anne, he were frozen. My God, he thought. My God, it can't be. He looked at Gail and Leo. "Did it have anything to do with Anne?" he asked.

Gail sighed. "We just can't talk about it, Josh; there's nothing we can tell you. Anyway, we were talking about people who lived thousands of years ago; they don't have anything to do with us. All we care about is that you found the tomb; we're excited and happy for you." She carried their mugs to the sink. "We're picking up Ned and Robin at the hospital; do you want us to drive you home so you don't have to run that gauntlet of reporters? They probably came back the minute the road was plowed."

Josh shook his head. "I like the walk, and I can handle the gauntlet; I just talk about Tenkaure. It's the best publicity in the world for what we're doing there."

"They don't want Tenkaure; they want to know about you," Leo said.

"They'll take what they can get; I don't talk about me." He helped Gail finish clearing the table. "Thanks for breakfast; I'll do the same for you when my house is finished. Right now I'm camping out in one room and half a kitchen. Give my love to your kids; tell them I'll take them to the Chocolate Factory as soon as you say they can go."

When he left, he took long strides on his snowshoes, breathing deeply in the clear air, warm in the sunlight, cold in the shade. He moved steadily through the trees and across the open meadows, staying away from the cars parked on the road. He would meet them outside his house and give as long an interview on Egypt as they wanted. And afterward, when he was settled in the finished living room where he lived and slept, he would call Anne. Not to ask her questions; that would come when they were together. He would call as her friend, and of course as her client. And later, when she returned to Tamarack, or he was in Los Angeles, he would ask her about the years of her growing up. It was time they talked about all of that.

* * *

Most of the guests had left the ballroom of the Brown Palace Hotel in Denver; only a few friends of the organizers remained, sitting close to Vince like camp followers huddled around a fire for warmth and reflected light. "I figure a couple million, and that's net," said Ray Beloit. "People love a winner, Vince; they'll put money on you way past the time you'll need it."

"Ain't no such thing," said Sid Folker. "In politics or out, ain't no such thing as too much money or a time you don't need as much as you can get."

"Senator," said a young woman behind Vince, "could you give me a few minutes? I'm with the *Rocky Mountain News.*"

Vince turned, already smiling. His smile broadened when he saw her: tall and slim, with short blond hair swinging about her heart-shaped face, and green eyes meeting his with almost worshipful intensity. "You missed the press conference?" he asked.

"Oh, no, I was there; I'd never miss hearing you. But I thought, if we could talk a little bit, if you could be a little more personal . . ."

"Ah, you're one of those who truly cares about her calling. How could I resist?" Vince took her arm and led her to one of the round dinner tables that had been cleared by the waiters. "First of all, I'd like to know your name."

She flushed. "I'm sorry. Sara Benedict."

"Sara. A lovely name. Well, Sara, what would you like to know?"

"I'm interested in your family. I've been reading about them, of course; the bad luck they've been having in Tamarack—such an awful story, the gondola crash, and that somebody deliberately caused it!"

"A stranger," Vince said. "An intruder trying to wreck the family by wrecking the gondola. He'll be taken care of."

"Yes, but that's only one of their problems. They've had others, and they're in trouble in Chicago, too. And the thing is, Senator, I can't help but contrast that with your great success."

Vince waited for the question. Sara waited, too, as if she had asked one. "Well, yes," Vince said at last, "you could say there's a gap between us, but if you leave business out of it, if you just talk about them as people who are good and decent and honorable, you'd have to say my family is ahead of everybody else, me included, I suppose."

Sara scribbled briefly in the notebook folded back on her knees. "That's very generous of you, Senator, but I wasn't thinking about whether they're nice or not—I'm sure they are—I was just wondering how it is that there's a whole family who can't seem to make it, and you stand so tall above them, even running for president—"

"No, no, Sara, my dear Sara, you mustn't say that, and you certainly must not write it, because it isn't true."

"Everybody says you're going to run for president."

"Well, whoever 'everybody' is, they can say what they like, but in this case they're wrong. What I am running for is a second term to the Senate of the United States, and I expect to be elected this November, and I expect to serve a full term and do the best I can for the people of Colorado." He smiled as if he were a little embarrassed. "That sounds like a campaign speech, but it's from the heart, Sara. I want to serve this state; these people have confidence in me. Do you know how it makes me feel when they go into voting booths by the thousands and *choose me?* It makes me feel loved and trusted, admired, needed, relied upon. Of course everybody wants that; maybe politicians want it more than anyone else and that's why we go into government—I don't know; I'm not a psychologist—but I know that it makes me feel like a king, and I wouldn't let those people down for all the power and glory in the world."

Sara's eyes were shining. With a little start, she looked down and wrote for a furious minute. "But you succeed," she said. "Your family fails."

"Oh, no, my dear," Vince said very gently. "They love each other, they help each other, they love me and help me. They're rich and triumphant in affection."

"But in business they fail."

"Well, yes, but we can't use that as the only measure of a life."

"Yes, Senator, but it's all part of the same thing, isn't it? What I'm really interested in is the *human* element. How could you all come from the same roots—Ethan Chatham was one of the most brilliant, powerful men in the country —how could you all come from him and only one of you be like him?"

Vince nodded thoughtfully. "There is usually one true heir in a family, Sara. But that has nothing to do with how good that family is. My family's troubles are my troubles. They're as fine a family as a man could want, and I lie awake nights trying to think of how I can help them. There's only so much I can do, of course; they're proud and stubborn— and I'm not criticizing them for that; I respect them for it—and so little of my time is my own; but I do care, deeply, and I'll always do as much as I can. We'll pull them out of these troubles—these sloughs of despond—"

"These what?" asked Sara, writing.

"S-l-o-u-g-h-s. It's from *Pilgrim's Progress.* You know, I keep that book by my bed and read it over and over; it's like a map of our own time."

Sara nodded. "So how will you be helping your family?"

"I don't know yet. I'll know better when we talk everything over, probably before I return to Washington at the end of the month. Shall I call you when I have something to report on that?"

Sara looked up quickly from her notebook. "Would you?"

"It would be a pleasure. I like talking to you, Sara." He glanced behind him at the others, looking his way, ready to leave. "Do you have enough, or are there other things you'd like to ask me?"

"Oh, millions, but this is wonderful, Senator. You've been so generous. And if you're going to call me sometime—"

"I'll call you often. Why shouldn't you have a little edge on the others? *They* didn't go after a personal interview; you did." Vince put a warm hand on her shoulder and felt her body lean slightly toward him. "I've enjoyed this very much;

500

more than any other interview I can remember. You'll be hearing from me." He turned to go.

"Oh, Senator!" Sara was fumbling in her purse. "My card." She held it out to him. "You'll need it. And wait"—she wrote on the back—"my home number, too. You can call anytime."

"I'm sure you'll be out on dates at night; you're too lovely to stay home alone," said Vince with a smile. "I'll call you at work; I'll be sure to find you there."

He slipped her card in his jacket pocket as he returned to the group. But even as he talked to them, she lingered in his memory. There was a freshness to Sara, almost as if she were still unformed. She was a woman, of course, and a professional at that, with a major Western newspaper, but there was that look in her eyes, of wonder and undisguised response, that one saw only in a woman who had not yet been with an experienced man. A delightful child, Vince thought that night as he was getting ready for bed, so young and pliable; and he added her card to a small packet he kept in his wallet. She could be a pleasant diversion in the busy months ahead.

And she could be more than that. One never knew when a friendly reporter could mean the difference between smooth sailing and slogging. Through the slough of despond, he thought, amused. Good touch; he'd give it to the speech writers tomorrow. And tell them to read *Pilgrim's Progress* so they could remind him what was in it—he'd last looked at it in high school, nearly forty-five years ago—and whether it really could work as a map for our times. He hoped it could; it was a memorable phrase and it had just jumped out, as if his mind were always working, always planning, never asleep.

On a roll, he thought happily, and went to join his wife in bed.

Josh returned to Los Angeles a week after his arrest and called Anne from his office at the university. "I want to take you to dinner," he said. "I've missed you. I've reserved a table at L'Ermitage, for eight o'clock. Is that all right?"

"Yes," Anne said, and he heard the smile in her voice. He thought about that all afternoon; she was smiling. And when he pulled up in front of her building, she was waiting for him. She wore a short black silk dress with a silk jacket of black and white stripes, and as always when he saw her after an absence, she took his breath away with her beauty. And she was smiling. "Hello," she said, holding out her hand, and their fingers met in a brief clasp. She sat beside him in the car. "Were you glad to get out of Tamarack?"

He smiled. "I gather Gail told you about the reporters."

"She said they were a nuisance for everyone and a burden for you. Why are they still hanging around?"

"I guess they like Tamarack," he said lightly. "Maybe they like skiing."

Anne was silent. In a few minutes Josh pulled up at the restaurant, and the valet opened the door on Anne's side of the car. "Okay, you're not worried," she said as they walked inside. "It's just a minor disturbance in your schedule. Do you expect me to believe that?"

"No," he said. Their table was in a quiet corner near the fireplace and they sat together along one side. "It's more than a minor disturbance; I guess it could be very serious. I suppose the reporters are hanging around because they think something new will break any minute. There's no sign of it; I haven't heard a word from Tyler or anyone else. I assume he doesn't think he has enough against me; he's still talking to people. He's talked to both gondola attendants, and Keith Jax, about my tour of the gondola. They all heard the questions I was asking. The scientific method," he added wryly. "Leave no stone unturned or question unasked. I even asked what could fail on it. I don't remember that we talked about the J-grip, but Keith told Tyler we did. Then Tyler questioned the workmen at my house, but I gather they didn't have anything to tell him. And he asked for the name of my Egyptian investors, and I gave them to him, but I don't think he's called them yet."

Anne shook her head. "How depressing to think of Tyler scraping the bottoms of all those barrels, looking for dregs."

"Well, Tamarack has its share of depressing days. Anne,

502

it's wonderful being able to talk to you; I haven't wanted to bother Leo and Gail; they have enough—"

The wine steward came to their table. Absorbed, Josh gave him only a brief glance. "Bring us your favorite burgundy."

"Truly? My favorite, monsieur?"

"Yes, of course." He had already turned back to Anne. "They have their own problems to deal with. But it's hard to be in Tamarack these days. It looks the same, as beautiful as ever, but people are frightened, and they can't stop talking about it. They're closer than ever, which is good, but it's an embattled closeness: them against the world. They stand on the mall in little clusters, or sit in the cafés, huddled together, no one laughing, looking for someone to blame. So far nobody's been throwing rocks at me—"

"What?" Anne asked.

"They're not; they've been defending me and calling Tyler an ass. It's made me feel more a part of Tamarack than anything else that's happened. But they haven't anyone else to hold responsible. Oh, Leo and the company for not having a twenty-four-hour guard on the gondola, but that's just talk. They want a villain, and there isn't one available, except for me, and some people are beginning to point a finger because that's the only way they can tell the world they're cleaning house. Of course they don't know the family voted to sell. You know about that?"

Anne nodded. "Gail told me. But I can't worry about it right now; we have to worry about you."

The wine steward held a bottle so Josh could read the label. "Fine," Josh said.

"Monsieur, this is more than fine; this is a miracle!"

At that, Josh gave him his attention. This man's pride in his wines was no different from his in Tenkaure's tomb. "Then we should savor it," he said, and watched closely the steward's reverent ritual of opening and decanting the wine. He tasted it. His eyebrows rose. "Excellent," he said. "Thank you."

Mollified, the wine steward nodded solemnly, and filled their glasses.

When he was gone, Josh and Anne raised their glasses. "To the time when this is over," she said.

Josh was about to add something about all the things they would talk about when that time came, but he did not. They might be sitting amid the floral displays and Persian rugs of L'Ermitage, but this had turned into a business dinner, not a romantic one, and he would stick to that. Until it was over.

Anne sat back, holding her glass, a small pad of paper and a mechanical pencil beside her. "Let's go over the background again. I want to fix some times. Leo said the bolt could have been taken anytime in the five days between the last inspection and the accident, but I want to be able to show you couldn't have done anything the morning of the accident itself. So let's start there. I know we've done this, but let's do it again. What time was your plane that morning?"

"Nine-fifty. I was at the airport about nine twenty-five."

"So you left your house about nine?"

"A little after."

"And you saw no one before that?"

"No, I was packing."

"What about the workers on your house?"

"They weren't there; it was Sunday."

"And your maintenance man?"

"I'd talked to him on Saturday. We always get together the day before I leave."

"You didn't get any mail because it was Sunday. You must have gotten telephone calls."

"No, it was quiet."

"Did you call anyone?"

"No."

"When did your people in Egypt know you were coming there?"

"On Friday. Hosni called and asked me to get there as soon as possible."

"So we can prove you didn't decide at the last minute to leave town. The trouble is, you had plenty of time to get to the gondola and get back home before eight o'clock when the ski patrol arrives."

"How did I get in?" Josh asked suddenly.

Anne frowned. "I don't know. Of course the building is locked; I've seen Leo open it. Who else would have a key? Keith, probably; he's the assistant mountain manager. Maybe one of the ski patrol or one of the attendants, but I doubt it; they change schedules. I guess it's Keith and Leo or someone we haven't thought of. And you didn't have access to their keys."

"I was at Leo's for dinner on Christmas and I stopped in a couple of times after that. If I'd been looking for it . . ."

"But Leo would have noticed it was gone."

"Would he? He wouldn't need it unless he was scheduled to open the building. And he usually didn't get there until nine, after Keith or someone else had opened up."

"It's awfully thin," Anne said.

"They're building a very thick file on awfully thin material," Josh said dryly. He looked up as the waiter stood beside them, and they gave him their order.

"We have to find out who did it," Anne said. "It's not that Kevin and I can't defend you, and probably get an acquittal because there's really so little here, but it would be by exposing the holes in their case, not by unequivocally clearing you. I'm not saying that's not a lot better than being found guilty, but I'd rather prove your innocence. So we need a villain. Just like everybody else in Tamarack."

"Where do we begin?" Josh asked. "We don't even know what the motive was. If it was what Tyler seems to be accusing me of, trying to lower the price, then blame it on what's-his-name, the guy from Denver who's been dickering to buy The Tamarack Company for months. Beloit."

"Ray Beloit," Anne murmured. "No, wait, not Denver. Josh, somebody was talking about him, not so long ago. You were there; do you remember—?"

"Christmas," Josh said. "It was Charles; he said something about . . . no, it was Fred. Asking Charles if he'd talked to Vince."

"About Beloit!" Anne exclaimed. "Because he's his campaign manager. And they were business partners in Denver. They go back a long way."

"Amazing," Josh said dryly. "Out of the whole world of people who might want to invest in a ski resort, the one we get is Vince's campaign manager."

They were silent. "I don't know what it gives us," Josh said slowly. "He'd want a lower price, but he couldn't gain by destroying the very company he's trying to buy. And how could he be involved in anything that's been going on up there?"

"Maybe he hired it done," Anne mused.

"How could he find anyone he trusted enough? And suppose he did. Why hide the bolt in my house? Why not just throw it in the nearest trash can? You were wondering that, before."

"He probably wanted a villain, too. Everybody does; it makes everything seem so simple."

"But we can't have a villain until we know the motive. It's probably something so obvious we just don't see it. Like your list a couple of weeks ago: hatred, greed, envy, fear. Pick one."

The waiter served their soup; they were so absorbed, they barely noticed. "Fear causes all of them," Anne said. "I think anyone who is greedy or envious or full of hate must be terribly afraid, of many things. Fearful people who don't admit they're afraid are the most dangerous people in the world, I think. Which do you find most often on the walls of your tombs?"

"All of them," Josh said thoughtfully. "It's almost like reading today's newspaper. People play out the same dramas over and over, through the centuries; they use the same words; even the expressions on their faces are the same. I told Gail and Leo the story of Tenkaure and his son, and they said it sounded like your family."

Anne went very still. "What story is that?"

Josh hesitated, angry at himself. He had been so absorbed he had not realized where he was heading. But he could not back away from it now without making it worse. Briefly he outlined the story. "They wouldn't tell me why Ethan sent Vince away; they said it wasn't theirs to tell."

Anne was looking across the room without seeing any of its activity. *Tell him, tell him. Gail and Leo opened the door for you. You can trust him. See what you can build with honesty and trust.*

But she could not say the words. A feeling of shame she thought she had buried welled up in her the minute she thought of talking about it. She felt anguished and helpless. She remembered that moment on the gondola, holding Robin and Ned. *Oh God, oh God, it never ends.*

Josh was silent. Slowly Anne let out her breath. She didn't have to explain anything. She was afraid he might have drawn some conclusions from knowing that Ethan had banished Vince, but why would he? Why would it even occur to him that anything about her might have something to do with Vince's quarrel with Ethan? Someone would have to look very closely to imagine any connection. She picked up her soup spoon. Her hand was steady. "I suppose there are endless reasons for family quarrels, but after a while they do begin to sound the same."

"Probably." His voice was low and sad, as if she had disappointed him, Anne thought. They ate in silence. "But the stories aren't really alike," Josh said at last. "Vince didn't organize a coup against his father."

"No, he went his own way. Anyway, what would he have fought for? The Chathams hardly had a kingdom for him to grab."

"They had a thriving company."

"But he didn't pay any attention to it. He made his fortune in Denver and then was elected to the Senate."

"People hoard their anger, though," Josh said thoughtfully. "Don't you find that in divorces? Anger, resentment, whatever it is, simmers for a long time until one day it boils over."

"Yes, of course." Anne watched the waiter refill their wineglasses. "Sometimes—in fact, a lot of the time—people hug their anger to themselves, almost enjoying it. It becomes important to them to be angry, not to enjoy life too much, because they think if they did, they'd lose some kind

507

of advantage. And their anger becomes so much a part of them, so deep inside them, that no one sees it except at very close quarters."

"You're describing Dora," Josh said. "And her father, as far as I could tell. But even if he did hang on to his anger all these years, and let it grow, what did he do with it? He didn't try a coup like Tenkaure's son after he was banished; he didn't raise an army to destroy his father . . ."

"He didn't have to," Anne said suddenly. "That's the whole point. He did try a coup, only a much more modern one. He didn't need an army, he didn't need to destroy his father, he didn't even need to attack the family. All he had to do was harm the family's company. Maybe even ruin it."

Their soup plates were removed, their bread replenished, fresh silverware was brought. Anne and Josh were looking at each other. "That highway that never happened," Josh said.

"It just seemed to vanish," Anne said. "One day it was going to be built and the next no one knew anything about it. And Vince was on the committee."

"And maybe gave them reasons to cancel it."

"Gail says he apologized to all of them; he told them he'd done his best to keep it."

"And maybe he did." Josh toyed with his spoon. "After all, he had nothing against the family; it was his father who kicked him out."

"But he was dead," Anne mused. "And if Vince's anger was still there, would it go away because my grandfather was gone?"

"It might not. Then he'd kill the highway because it would do serious harm to Ethan's company, and Ethan's eldest son, and the whole family." Josh smiled. "Somebody could accuse us of making a case as thin as Tyler's, about me."

"Josh," Anne said. "If he wanted to hurt Chatham Development, he might have wanted to hurt The Tamarack Company, too."

The waiter brought their dinner plates and placed them carefully on the table. "The ditch that broke," Josh said. "The reservoir being polluted."

"And the EPA all of a sudden telling them the entire east end of town was poisoned."

"And the gondola."

Anne shook her head. "No, wait, it's just too much. I can't believe . . ."

They thought about it. "You're probably right," Josh said. "It would make a great story, but it would mean he's a monster."

There was a long silence. Anne stared at her plate. Josh looked at his, admiring the artistry of the arrangement, the balance of color, texture, and shape. You need the right pieces and then you put them together, he thought. Like finding a tomb beneath centuries of earthquakes. And identifying a villain. He picked up his fork. "Of course there could be explanations we haven't even thought of, that have nothing to do with causing harm to the family or lowering the price of the company. Maybe someone was out to get the company that manufactured the gondola. Or it was random vandalism. Or it really was an accident, pure and simple, start to finish. Of course the bolt is a problem, but we could probably find an explanation for that, too."

But he is a monster. "He would have needed people there," Anne said, having heard nothing of what Josh said. "He's been in Washington. Anyway, he wouldn't go crawling around a reservoir to contaminate it."

"That's not how it happened." Josh let his speculations go; he did not believe any of them. "Leo said the polluted water got into the reservoir because a ditch that diverted it was broken. By a slide, he thought; he said they happen all the time. Of course . . . I suppose one could help that along."

"By some kind of explosion? Dynamite, maybe, somewhere above the ditch. I don't know if that could do it; I don't know anything about drainage ditches. Or dynamite either. I wonder if that could be checked. Oh, probably not in the winter; there would be three or four feet of snow up there."

"That may not stop them. We'll ask Leo. If there was a

dynamite charge, the rock above the ditch would show signs of it. If Vince hired someone, all he had to do—"

"But who would that be? Whom could he trust enough? It's like putting your life in someone's hands."

"I don't know. I don't think that matters now. If they find evidence of dynamite, we'd concentrate on that. I'm going to call Leo; I'd like to *do* something instead of sitting around waiting for Tyler to make a move. Is that all right with you?"

Anne hesitated. Up to now, it had been an exercise in reasoning; suddenly, it was becoming a hunt. And Vince was the quarry. She shrank from it. She wanted nothing at all to do with him; she could not bear the idea of being connected to him even through something as tenuous as asking others about events that might revolve around him. Leave it alone, she thought; it's safer to stay away. Don't get involved.

But she was involved. This was not six months ago; she had a family now, and perhaps someone was deliberately trying to ruin them. And she had the friendship of Josh Durant, and he was in trouble and had come to her for help.

It was past the time when she could retreat to the cocoon of her apartment. Whatever happened from now on, she was part of her family, and somehow, part of Josh's life, and she would have to take what came with having found a place among them.

"I can call now, if you don't mind," Josh said.

She nodded. "Call him."

He signaled to the waiter and asked him to bring a telephone. "What else can we do?" he asked while they waited. "How about the EPA? Can we call someone there? We could find out how that cleanup idea got started."

"It would be better in person," Anne said. "Could you get away for a couple of days, to go to Washington?"

"Not now; I've got to get ready for my classes. What about you? Could you go?"

"I don't think . . . Well, I will; I'll find the time. And while I'm there, I'll try to talk to somebody on the Public Works Committee."

"A good idea. I'm sorry I can't go with you."

"So am I." I really am sorry, she thought. It's much better to work with someone than to work alone.

The maître d' brought them the telephone. Josh took a small address book from his pocket and opened it to Leo and Gail's listing. He dialed the number and looked at Anne as the telephone rang in Tamarack. "Here we go," he said.

"So am I," I told her, remembering the moment. It's much better
present with documentation than to work alone.

The outline of my notebook in the briefcase. Jean took a
small address book from his pocket and opened it to the
and Clark Estate, Inc., 612, ... I dialed and looked at Anne
as the telephone rang ... [the edge of my past in it, said

chapter 20

Senator Zeke Ruddle of Utah, short and cherubic, long-
time member of the Senate Environment and Public Works
Committee, walked around his desk to greet Anne as she
came toward him across the expanse of his office. "Delighted," he said, shaking her hand and holding it a moment
too long. "I've read about your exploits, Miss Garnett; you
have your opponents quaking in their shoes. We politicians
could learn from you."

"It may be that we learn from you," Anne said with a
smile.

"Ah." His tiny mouth stretched wide in appreciation. His
eyes, hard as agate, and unblinking, did not change.
"Please," he said, gesturing toward a leather chair, and they
both sat down. "What can I do for you?"

"I have a client—you understand, I won't be able to give
you too many details—"

Ruddle nodded sagely. "I do understand. But you know,
we in government know better than anyone else how to keep
a secret."

"True," Anne said thoughtfully. "Perhaps, after all, I
could give you some of the background."

Ruddle leaned forward, his arms folded on his desk. "I
assume your client is well known."

"He's one of those men whom reporters follow around;
they camp outside his house; it becomes quite difficult for
him. That's why I've come here in his place."

"Reporters. Turds. But a necessary nuisance; those of us who work for our country have learned to live with them. Movies or television? Your client, I mean."

"I can't tell you that. I can tell you that he deals on an international scale with enormously valuable materials and properties, some with a value almost beyond calculation."

"Most interesting," Ruddle murmured.

"Now, we have a conflict in this case that is extremely sensitive," Anne said. "What is at issue is a large segment of land northwest of Chicago that is owned by Chatham Development, a Chicago corporation. As I understand it, at one time the intention of Charles Chatham, the president of the corporation, was to develop it, to build an entire town there, called Deerstream Village."

Ruddle frowned. "That's Vince Chatham's brother. I've met him a couple times. Deerstream? Never heard of it."

"I believe this goes back a couple of years. What is at issue here, Senator, is that opposing sides are interested in that land, and its potential for development seems to be in doubt." Anne took a sheaf of papers from her briefcase. "This morning I read the proceedings of the Environment and Public Works Committee in its discussion of a proposed highway from northwest Illinois into Chicago. The chairman was absent that day; you were acting chairman. The committee voted to recommend to the Appropriations Committee that the Illinois highway be postponed indefinitely and the funds go instead for a new highway across Colorado and Utah along the edge of Mesa Rosa National Park."

"Oh, that one," Ruddle said. "Hard to remember all the hearings we have, you know. Well, what can I tell you? You read the proceedings; that should give you the whole shebang."

"I'm curious about the way the funds were shifted from one project to another. I didn't find anything in the printed proceedings that tells me where the idea came from in the first place."

"Oh." He looked at her blankly. "I don't know. It's been a while you know."

"Yes," Anne said. She had heard that answer, truthful or not, too many times on the witness stand to let it give her pause. "I assume, if it had been your idea, you certainly would remember it."

"Well, I don't remember all my great ideas, but most of 'em I do, and that one I don't. It most likely wasn't me, anyway; I don't pay much attention to what's happening with highways in other states once we recommend funding."

"Do you mean that something was happening in Illinois that made it impossible to fund the highway? And that was why this person, whoever it was, had the idea to switch the funds?"

Ruddle gazed past her, his tiny mouth pursed in concentration. "Seems to me somebody said something about they couldn't figure out where to put it, you know, the best route for it. Squabbling over it, somebody said. So we figured, if they didn't want it enough to get it laid out, and they'd already had a long time, years, now that I think of it, then we'd put the money where the people really wanted it and were ready to use it."

"Yes, that was in the hearings," Anne murmured.

Ruddle's gaze swung back to her. "Well, if you already knew that, why'd you ask me?"

"I was hoping it would help you remember what went before that. You said 'we figured, if they didn't want it enough.' Who was 'we'?"

"The committee," Ruddle said.

"But who suggested it to the committee?"

Ruddle shook his head. "You got me."

Anne let a silence go by. "You were acting chairman that day, Senator. Why was that?"

"Right, I was. Let's see. Well, I don't know. Vince—that's Vince Chatham, the chairman—was sick or out of town or whatever, and I took over."

"Had he left instructions for you about questions to ask or how to handle the discussion?"

"*Instructions?* Vince doesn't give me *instructions;* we understand each other. We're on opposite sides a lot of the time, but we have the greatest respect for each other; the

514

greatest respect. He's told me more than once that he trusts my instincts and relies on me . . . oh, now I've got it. Vince thought of it. We had a meeting, breakfast, I think, and we talked about Mesa Rosa and the problems of building a highway through a national park, lots of opposition, you know; people don't understand the real value of highways; they're the veins and arteries of our country and without them we'd die, and the more we have the healthier we are; it's as simple as that. Vince understands that. He said he'd be just as happy with a highway straight through the middle of the park, but he knew we'd have all these folks chaining themselves to trees, things like that, to stop it, so he got the idea of running it along the edge of the park so everybody'd be happy. But that meant more money, you've got to figure a million dollars a mile for a highway these days, and when I said there was no way we could get it out of Appropriations, he remembered Illinois and said they were still messed up there and going nowhere. He said he'd been working with them for years, trying to help them decide on routing the highway; he said he'd kept demanding new drawings, but they couldn't get their act together. But around here you know, if there's anything Vince Chatham is really a champion at, it's finding ways to get things moving when they're stuck in dead center. So we got it going. Damned good solution; I told him so at the time."

There was a pause. Slowly, Ruddle frowned. "Did you say his brother owned land up there?"

"Yes," Anne said. She was sitting very still, stunned by the enormity of it. When she and Josh had been speculating, it was like a puzzle, some pieces fitting, others not. But now this part of it was whole. Vince had manipulated events so that Deerstream would fail. So that Charles would fail.

"Along the highway route?" Ruddle asked. "And he was going to build a town there?"

"Yes," Anne said. "Called Deerstream."

"Deerstream. The name never came up. All we were talking about was a highway from northwest Illinois into Chicago. But Charles Chatham had a thing going there? How about that. *How about that.* You know, I remember telling Vince at the time that I was damned impressed that a senator would give up a highway in his family's state for the good of another state. But you're telling me he even gave up a highway that would have helped his brother! And never told me he was doing it! By God, can you believe it? Now that does take the cake!"

"It certainly does," Anne said. She returned the photocopied pages to her briefcase. "Thank you, Senator; that gives me a much clearer picture of what happened. I gather there's still a chance the highway could be built."

"Always a chance. The committee's always looking at highways, past, present, and future. 'Course money's tight, but then it's always tight, isn't it? But if your client wants to put a high figure on that land because it could have a highway going smack through the middle of it, feel free. If it comes up again, we'll look at it objectively, the way we do all of them, and we'll do the best thing for the state and the country."

Anne stood up and he walked with her to the door, nodding and smiling. But she felt sick and angry as she pictured Vince having breakfast with Zeke Ruddle, and cheerfully doing his best to ruin his brother.

It's monstrous. It would mean Vince is a monster.

But he is a monster.

I have to call Josh, she thought. But she had no time; she had another appointment. And a few minutes later she was walking into Bud Kantor's office at the EPA, holding out her hand, preparing her questions.

"I'm glad to see you," Kantor said. He was young and earnest, with a round, rosy-cheeked face that was his despair because he thought he looked like an eighth grader. He had a small mustache, and short hair, like a Marine, to look older, and he always wore dark suits and blue-striped ties, to look like a diplomat. He shook Anne's hand, admiring her unabashedly. She wore a houndstooth suit and an ivory blouse with lace on the collar, and it was obvious that she was not what Kantor had expected when she had called for an appointment and said she was an attorney from California. "We don't see the public very often here," he said as they sat down in his small, spare office. "I mean, we work behind the scenes, you know; we don't talk to the public like the senators and representatives do."

"You do research for legislation?" Anne asked.

"That's it. Whatever they want us to check out. But it starts a long time before there's legislation; months, sometimes years. You can't ask Congress to spend money until you're truly sure you know what the downside is, you know, risks to the environment."

Anne watched him intently, amused at his attempts to look older. "You have a tremendous responsibility," she said.

"I do," he replied solemnly. "We all do."

"That's why I knew you'd be able to help me." She opened her briefcase and removed some papers. "As I told you on the telephone, I've been trying to find the history of the proposed cleanup in Tamarack. I found your name on several of the later reports, but I can't find any studies that go back to the beginning, when the soil was first analyzed."

There was a pause. "That goes back a ways," Kantor said slowly.

"It seems to be ongoing," Anne said gently.

He nodded. "True. These cleanups do tend to go on and on. The fact is, Miss Garnett, a lot of that file's still in my office. Those people in Tamarack—are you representing them, is that it?"

"No, but I'm working on behalf of some of them in another case, and the cleanup might have a strong bearing on it. I need all the information I can find; as a professional, you know how essential that is."

"Right. But we haven't even started a cleanup there, you know; they got an injunction . . . Were you involved in that?"

"Yes."

"Well. Well, I don't know . . ."

"Mr. Kantor, you and I aren't necessarily on opposite sides here. Right now I'm just looking for information. That shouldn't give you any trouble, should it?"

"Well, no, I always believe the more information the

better. An informed electorate can't do anything without information. Well, you know what's happening in Tamarack; they've stopped us for the time being. They've had a lot of other problems, and they haven't wanted us digging up part of their town while they're dealing with everything else. And I'm not blaming them; I can understand how they're worried about their town, and now on top of everything else they've got this gondola thing; that could really be bad for them. Anyway, Miss Garnett, they stopped us—I guess I should say *you* stopped us, shouldn't I?—and we're deciding what files we can make available to them, and until we do, I'm keeping them here."

"Well." Ann smiled. "I won't ask you to let me see them because I know you wouldn't break the rules. But it would help me a great deal if you could give me some background."

"I might could do that. I'd be glad to."

"Well, then, how did all this start? All the mountain states have old mines under them, and I suppose most of them are leaching chemicals into the soil from underground water." She waited until Kantor nodded. "Well, then, why Tamarack? It wasn't the biggest of the mining towns, so I don't see how it could have been the worst."

"Well, we never claimed that, Miss Garnett. We just looked at it, you know, and decided—"

"You did that simultaneously in several towns?" Anne asked.

"Absolutely. That's how we do it."

"And they all needed a cleanup?"

"Well, there were different time scales. Some were so bad we were real worried. You know, like Love Canal or Times Beach? You find things that bad, you don't wait."

"But Tamarack wasn't in that category."

"No, no, nothing like that. Tamarack didn't have sick people or a history of higher rates of cancer or anything like that."

"Then what did it have?"

"Well, there was a possible danger from the lead buildup in the soil. We can't ignore that, Miss Garnett; that's what the superfund is for, to give us the tools to do our job and keep the planet clean."

"Possible danger," Anne repeated. "Didn't the initial report sent to Tamarack say something about 'imminent danger'? Am I wrong about that?"

"Well, I'd have to check—"

"I don't think you have to check," she said evenly. "I'm sure you remember every part of every report that goes out of this office, because you're conscientious and you care deeply about what you're doing. I think that report was exaggerated, and I think the time schedule was speeded up. I'd like to talk about that, since you won't let me see the file."

There was a pause. "We don't do things like that," Kantor said. "We're straight with people. But in this case, I was worried that the people in Tamarack might be complacent; you know how mountain towns are, they don't think anybody can tell them how to do things."

"You know that for a fact? You've been to a number of mountain towns?"

"Well, no, unfortunately, I never have been. But Senator Chatham told me about them; he knows a great deal about them. So we felt it was important to make the problem sound a little more urgent than it really was. I didn't lie—I'd never lie to people—it's just that these things might could get terribly dangerous if they're ignored. So I thought it was essential to get people moving."

"Senator Chatham told you about mountain towns," Anne said.

"He was worried about Tamarack. Of course the decision was made by the whole department, but Senator Chatham was the one who first brought it to my attention. It's his state, and he was afraid for the safety of the people, so he asked me to look into it."

"And to exaggerate the danger."

"To alert the people. I explained that. We didn't exaggerate; we used language that would get their attention. That's our job, Miss Garnett. Of course you understand that we take senators' requests very seriously—they certainly know the needs and the dangers in their own states—and when Senator Chatham suggested we emphasize the danger, we were quite satisfied to convey that urgency to the people of Tamarack."

"And the time scale?" Anne asked.

"Well, we might could've waited, that's true, but the senator was very worried that if we put it off, it'd get put on the back burner and nothing would happen, maybe for years—that does happen, you know—and then people might could start getting sick or dying and then the clean-up'd cost a lot more."

"So he insisted on its being done right away?"

"He urged me to consider it very seriously for the well-being of everyone. I agreed it was the good, cautious thing to do, and I sent the recommendation to the department."

And he is a monster.

"Did he press you on it?"

"Oh, no," Kantor said swiftly. "Nobody *presses* the EPA. He made known his concerns to me, and I did what I thought was necessary to avoid a dangerous situation developing."

"What would you have done if you thought you had more time?"

"Well, like I say, we would've done a full study—"

"More complete than the one you did?"

"Well, longer, but not necessarily more complete. And we would've had more meetings with the people in the neighborhoods; we do try our best to accommodate them. Now you people went and got that injunction, and I must say, Miss Garnett, if they'd had a life-threatening situation there, what you did would have been downright irresponsible."

"But if you had convinced the judge that it was life-threatening, there would have been no injunction."

Kantor gave a short nod.

"It seems it was not life-threatening, so you really had no reason to be in such a hurry. And you had no reason to exaggerate the danger to alert them, since their well-being was not threatened, at least in the near future."

"Well, now, that's too strong—"

Anne returned the papers to her briefcase. "You did this because Senator Chatham was worried about the health of the people."

Kantor's worried frown smoothed out. "He was and I was. That's exactly it. We respond to danger, Miss Garnett, and Senator Chatham was concerned that his constituents might be in danger. He wasn't worried about his own self; he doesn't live there. He was worried about families up there in the mountains. He's an amazing man, the senator; he never stops thinking, looking ahead, making plans; you wouldn't think he'd have the time for a small town with a problem that hasn't even got near the crisis stage, but he always makes time; he's never too busy to pay attention to details. And I was grateful for his pointing out the problem, because we rely on that kind of information, and we believe in the cautious approach. Ignoring danger signals is the worst thing we could do."

"I agree with you," Anne said, standing up. "You should never ignore danger signals. Thank you for your time."

He frowned again. "I don't know how I've done you any good."

"You've given me information. I'm grateful for that." She went out into Washington's pale, wintry sunshine, her anger a hard knot within her. Whatever her father and her family had done, to her or to anyone else, they did not deserve this.

She took a taxi to the airport. Josh was in Tamarack; she was to meet him there. They had to decide what to do next.

"Keith checked it out," Leo said. He and Josh were sitting on a bench on the mall, watching a few skiers walk toward the lift a few blocks from the silent gondola. The mall was almost silent. Local people shopped for bargains in the sales at all the stores, but it was a halfhearted kind of browsing, because the empty town, and closeout sales in January, meant a disastrous season. "As soon as we saw the drainage ditch was broken, we figured it had to have been a slide somewhere up above, so Keith climbed up and checked it out. He said it was an ordinary rock slide. They happen all the time, and there wasn't any way we could have predicted it. Pieces of the mountains are always breaking off, you know, and the ground shifts all the time; we have a few earthquakes a year, minor ones, but they loosen a lot of rock. After you called the other night I talked to Bill Clausan about going up there. He said he'd do it sometime this week."

Josh tapped a rolled-up newspaper on his knee. "One of the problems of being a scientist is you can't rest until you see for yourself. And I'm only here for a couple of days. Where do I find Bill Clausan?"

Leo gave him the telephone number. "I'd like to go along."

"But you won't. You've done your three hours at the office today. You've got a tough head, friend, but it still needs time to recover. I'll see you later." Josh left him there, brooding at the sky and the too-quiet town, and that afternoon he and Bill Clausan drove into the hills east of town, above the reservoir, to the road that climbed close to the drainage ditch.

"The ditch is that way," Bill said, gesturing to the right. "We figured the slide came from up there"—he pointed to the cliffs above them—"and Keith said he found the slide area just above the base of the cliffs. It's not too steep, but walking through this stuff is like treading molasses. You sure you want to try it?"

"Sure." Josh tightened his snowshoes, pulled on his gloves, and took up his ski poles. "Lead the way."

It took them forty minutes to hike through the brush and snow. They took long strides, then short ones, shoved snow aside or walked on top of it, lost their balance on the rocks and wavered before getting their footing and moving on. The only sound was their heavy breathing. "Damned hot," Bill grunted once; that was all. They reached the base of the rock cliffs at the top of the hill and turned, traversing along them, until Bill stopped. "Probably right about here," he said. "The ditch is straight down the hill."

He took a shovel with a telescoping handle from his backpack and began to shovel and push the snow to both sides of the rock face, clearing a wide area and exposing a layer of autumn leaves, some of them still showing traces of bronze and russet. Beneath them were long blades of crushed grasses and dried flowerheads amid tumbled rocks. "Nothing here," Bill muttered, and moved to sweep a larger area. Josh dug with his own shovel, and the two of them moved the snow outward, their breath rasping in their throats. Josh's dark glasses kept sliding down his nose, wet with perspiration; his hands were clammy inside his gloves. Bill took off his hat and unzipped his jacket. And they kept enlarging the cleared space.

The sun was lower in the sky; Bill zipped up his jacket and put on his hat. Josh took off his dark glasses. "About half an hour more?" he asked.

Bill nodded. "You sure you know what you're looking for?"

"Yes." Furiously, Josh pushed the snow away, and in another five minutes he stopped. He was looking at an area free of autumn leaves and grass. Just above it, at the base of the cliff, a section of rocks looked pale against the dark gray rock around it, as if it had been newly washed.

"Bill," he said, "I want you to be part of this."

Bill looked at the pale rock. "It broke off, not so long ago. It's not weathered like the rest of the cliff."

Josh nodded. "Look here." His finger traced a star pattern of fractures radiating from the pale rock. "That's from a blast."

"Some damn fool playing around up here; why the hell won't people learn to leave things alone?"

Josh ran his fingers lightly over the area at the base of the star pattern, and found a few pieces of broken wire. "Fuse wire," he said, and put them in his pocket. He took his camera from his backpack and photographed the pale rock, focusing on the star pattern. He had seen that pattern all over the world, in archaeological sites where workers were blasting. He stood and photographed the area of the drainage ditch below, and then their location, from several angles. "We've almost lost our light," he said. The sun was just touching the ridge of mountains on the other side of the valley.

"Got enough?" Bill asked. "Let's get out of here."

Josh stowed his camera and shovel. As they walked back along the trail they had made at the base of the cliffs, he spoke over his shoulder to Bill. "This should be kept quiet for a while."

"Why? I'd like to print it in the paper, that people are fooling around up there, around the drainage ditch, and they oughta—" He stopped. "The drainage ditch. That's what you're saying? Somebody set off a blast to break the ditch?" He thought for a minute. "Shit. Somebody fouled up the reservoir? Nobody'd do that." He shook his head. "Nobody'd do that."

"Will you keep it quiet for now?" Josh asked.

"Sure," Bill said. His voice was subdued. But when they reached the jeep, he said, "Listen, why not just blow up the reservoir if that's what they wanted to do? It doesn't make sense to go through all that rigmarole, dynamiting some rocks so they slide into the drainage ditch so the reservoir gets poisoned."

Josh tossed his backpack into the back of the jeep. "You all thought it was an accident, didn't you? An act of nature that couldn't have been predicted or avoided. But if the reservoir had been blown up . . ." He looked at Bill as he got in the jeep.

"We would've had a manhunt," Bill said slowly. "We would've torn this place apart to find the son of a bitch that did it." He backed the jeep out onto the highway. "You got any idea who did it?"

"No. I hope to find out. That's why it has to be kept quiet."

"Gotcha." They drove toward town. The air had turned cold, and Bill turned on the heater. At the outskirts of town, he stopped at an intersection and turned to Josh. "Why the hell would anybody do that? It hurt all of us, the whole town, is what it did. Why would somebody want to do that?"

"Whoever did it never thought about the people," Josh said. "Or if he did, he didn't give a damn about them. I'd guess that all he thought about was himself and whatever he wanted." He glanced out the window. "My car is in Leo's parking place at his office; would you let me off there? I have to get to the airport."

"Leaving town?"

"No." He looked at the clock on the dashboard. In less than an hour, he would be with her. "I'm meeting a plane."

They sat around the long pine kitchen table, finishing dinner, waiting for Robin and Ned to go to their rooms so they could talk. "You've been very quiet tonight, Ned," Leo observed. "Something bothering you?"

"Nah," Ned muttered. "Do I get an extra piece of pumpkin pie 'cause I cleaned my room, even being lame?"

"I did, too," Robin said. "And I'm lame, too. Ned tried to beat up Simon McGill," she said to Leo.

"We weren't gonna say anything!" Ned shouted.

"Well, I thought you were brave."

"What was it about?" Gail asked.

"Nothing!" Ned shouted more loudly.

"What was it about, Ned?" Leo asked.

Ned shook his head stubbornly.

"Robin," Leo said.

Robin looked away from Ned. "He said we'd be moving away 'cause you were fired and the company was sold, and we didn't even have a right to be in school 'cause"—her eyes filled with tears—"we didn't belong here anymore."

"Oh, no," Gail said. "Why didn't you tell me when I picked you up?"

Ned gave an exaggerated shrug. "We figured it was true," he muttered.

"Christ," Leo muttered. "Listen," he said, putting his arms around the two of them. "I haven't been fired. We're not about to move away."

"But the family did decide to sell the company," Gail said. She sat on the arm of Robin's chair, her arm around Robin's shoulders. "We can't pretend they didn't. And they have a buyer. And that means, maybe, sometime, we don't know when, we will have to leave."

"But it hasn't been sold, has it?" Anne asked. She and Josh were sitting on the other side of the table. "I didn't know anything was final."

"Not yet, but—" Gail looked at Leo.

"Your grandfather signed a letter saying he was accepting an offer for it," Leo said to Ned and Robin. "And when it becomes final, the new owners probably will bring in their own people to run it. So then we'll have to think about going somewhere else, where I can get a job. But we don't know when it's going to happen, and until it does, you two belong here as much as anybody. You don't have to beat up Simon or anybody else to prove it, Ned; just keep going to school the way you always have. They'll get the point."

"No, they won't." Ned forced the words through clenched teeth. "They're staying and I'm not. They're *home,* and I'm not!"

Robin looked at Anne through her tears. "You just got here and everything was so nice and now it's all changing."

"It won't change with us," Anne said. She came around the table and knelt in front of Robin and Ned. She put out her hands and the children took them. Her heart ached for them. They had never had to wonder about where they belonged. "It's hard, I know it's hard; it feels so empty when you're not sure where home is anymore. But the important things aren't going to change; we won't let them. And it's important to me that I'm part of this family and I always will be. And I'll be with you, wherever you live. I couldn't let you go."

She had never said those words before.

"Oh, Anne," Gail said softly. Her eyes were shining. Anne looked up and they exchanged a long look. "It would be awful if you weren't here. Ned, wherever we are, as long as it's all of us together, that's home. You can't ever get fired or kicked out of that; it's all ours. Forever. And Anne will be part of us."

"Josh, too?" Robin asked.

There was a pause. "Josh, too," Josh said easily.

"Yeah, but—" Ned began.

"We have plenty of time to talk about it," Anne said. She stood and began to stack their plates. "And I wouldn't be so sure we know what's going to happen to the company. I'd hang in there, Ned, and not make any quick judgments or try to beat anybody up. Just tell them a lot of things are happening and nobody knows anything yet."

"Is that really true?" Ned asked.

"Word of honor."

"I'm going to cut the pie," Gail said. "Two pieces for Ned and Robin because they cleaned their rooms, casts and all. Two for Josh, because he did a lot of work today, in the snow. Two for Leo because he's getting better. And one for Anne and one for me. There goes the pie."

She bustled about while Anne poured coffee, and as soon as possible Gail and Leo shepherded the children to their rooms to do their homework. "Okay," Leo said, "where are we?"

"You first," Josh said to Anne. He sat back, enjoying the feeling in the room, a kind of electricity that had begun when he said, so casually, *Josh, too*. It was as if events were settling around him and Anne, giving them a calm place to find each other in the midst of the stormy happenings surrounding Tamarack. So now the four of them sat around the table in a circle of light—friends, partners, family. "Should I take notes?"

Anne smiled. "I already did." In a level voice, she described her meetings with Zeke Ruddle and Bud Kantor.

"Vince did that?" Gail cried as Anne told them about Ruddle. "To his own *brother?"* And when Anne talked about Kantor, Leo shook his head. "It had to be something like that; there wasn't any reason to start here. . . ." When she had finished, Leo burst out, "God damn son of a bitch! How could he do that to Charles? And to us? What did we ever do to him?" He saw Gail and Anne look at each other. "For Christ's sake, *we* weren't the ones who kicked him out!"

Anne shrank back, thinking they had told Josh everything

about her. In an instant, the warmth and closeness of the room collapsed; she felt trapped. She pushed back her chair, wanting to flee.

"I remember, we talked about that," Josh said casually. "One of these days I'd like to hear that story. But most families quarrel, you know, without one of them trying to ruin the others. It sounds to me as if there's a lot more going on. You haven't heard about what I did today."

"Oh, yes, tell us," Gail cried.

"You and Bill went up there?" Leo asked.

"This afternoon." Josh could feel Anne slowly relaxing beside him. As he spoke, she quietly slid her chair back to the table and leaned forward, watching him. When he finished, he took a small rock he had pocketed that afternoon and showed it to Leo. "Of course it could be a fresh break from a natural slide, but if you put this together with the blast fractures we found, there's no doubt in my mind that it was dynamite. Whoever it was probably found a section of the rock that had already separated from the cliff, and set a few dynamite charges in the crack, fused to go off together." He reached into his pocket. "Leftover fuse wire," he said, laying it on the table. "It wouldn't have had to be a big blast, certainly not big enough to be heard in town. Hikers might have heard it, but there aren't any well-known trails around there, and even if someone did hear it, there's always blasting of some kind around here, in the winter for avalanche control and in the summer for construction. Anyway, it only had to be big enough to start a small slide; they pick up speed and force as they go, and the drainage ditch probably was weak to begin with. He might have checked that first."

"He," Leo repeated.

"I'm assuming it was the person who went to check out the area after it happened and said he didn't find anything unusual."

"He might have thought it was a natural slide," said Leo.

"He might," Josh said.

"Who checked it out?" Gail asked.

"Keith." Leo was turning the rock around in his hand.

"But I don't see Keith doing anything like that. He's involved here, he knows how tourists are, how they'll go somewhere else if they read about things going wrong here."

Anne was looking across the room, remembering isolated events of the past few months, particularly Keith's piercing interest in her at dinner months before, and his too-bright smile and close looks at her and Leo the morning he met them at the gondola. She had never understood that peculiar interest in her; she remembered thinking he looked like a schoolboy memorizing her for a report he had to make. *A report he had to make* . . . "Is Keith close to Vince?" she asked abruptly.

"I don't think so," Gail replied. "Why?"

"I wondered if there might be a connection. If Vince was trying to damage Tamarack by getting the EPA here, and someone started the rock slide to hurt Tamarack—"

"Oh, no," Gail breathed. "You mean Keith might have done it on orders . . . oh, no, oh, no, he couldn't. Anyway, where would he get dynamite?"

"The ski patrol uses it for trail clearing and avalanche control," Josh said. "As assistant mountain manager he'd have easy access to it."

"Vince never comes up here," Leo said. "So if they spend any time together, it's somewhere else."

"Denver," Josh said. "Or Washington."

"With Ray Beloit," Leo said. "Vince's campaign manager."

"Who wants to buy The Tamarack Company," Anne said quietly.

They looked at each other. "Christ," Leo swore softly, "you could go crazy with all these guesses. We don't know who set off the dynamite and if it really was Keith, we don't know if he ever talked to Vince, or that Beloit was part of anything they talked about. . . ."

"We might be able to prove whether Vince and Keith were in touch," Anne said thoughtfully. "They wouldn't have had to meet in person; they would have used the telephone most of the time. And if Keith called from the office, you'd have records of that."

"You mean phone bills." Leo grinned. "It takes a divorce lawyer to think of that." His grin faded. "My God, what we're talking about . . . Well, sure we have a list of every long-distance call we make, and the length of the call. But damn it . . ." He was shaking his head. "Damn it, have you thought about what we're saying? All of them together—the highway, the EPA, the rock slide . . . If he really did all of them, what kind of man is he?"

"Oh!" Gail cried. Her eyes were wide and fearful. "The gondola!"

"We can't say that," Josh said. "We don't know enough about it."

"We know someone tried to frame you," Leo responded. "Someone who knows the gondola, who could have taken out that bolt, and planted it at your house. And maybe he did it on somebody's orders."

"He wouldn't," Gail said. It was almost a moan.

"If he did, he would have had to do more than take out the bolt," Josh said. "He would have had to disable the J-grip."

"Right," Leo said. "And we don't know what happened there. They've done a week of testing and they can't find any reason for the grip to fail."

"But something happened and it had to be deliberate," Anne said. "Someone wanted a gondola accident. Someone tried to make one of the cars fall. I don't suppose it was planned that two cars would collide, but we can't be sure of that either."

Gail poured more coffee. Her mouth was tight and her hand shook. "What kind of man is he?" she murmured.

"Suppose you wanted to make a car fall," Josh said thoughtfully. "How would you do it?"

Leo shook his head. "I don't know enough about the mechanics of it. The real expert on that is probably the tramway inspector who's been testing all week. Jim something. We could call him, I guess, but I don't know where he's staying in town. And I can't remember his last name."

"Matheny," Gail said quietly. "And he's staying at the Red Lion Inn; he called here once and left a message for you."

"I'll call him," Leo said, and reached for the telephone. They sat in silence. The enormity of it, which had struck Anne again and again in Washington, seemed to fill the room, dimming the lamplight. When Leo turned back to them, he found them sitting exactly as he had left them. "He says, hypothetically, that the simplest way would be to jam something into the J-grip so, literally, it couldn't grip."

"You'd have to be up there, then, on the second floor," Josh said, "waiting for a car to pass, and then jam something in."

"What would you use?" Anne asked.

"Could be anything," Leo replied. "A hunk of wood, a piece of pipe, anything hard that would wedge it open. Jim said it would have been knocked out in the crash, but nobody's found anything that looked out of the ordinary."

"Leo," Anne said. She was frowning, trying to remember. She was sitting in the gondola, holding Robin and Ned, looking out at the peaceful scene, wondering at its beauty. Below, a single patroller had remained behind to let them know they were not forgotten until they could be rescued. He was sitting in the sunlight on the bright snow, looking up at them or out across the valley, and there was a rhythmic noise. . . . "Jazz," she said. "The patroller who stayed below when we were in the gondola was tapping a jazz beat on his ski boot. He'd picked up a piece of wood, maybe a two-by-four, and was using it to beat out a rhythm."

Josh got it first. "He picked up a piece of wood *in the middle of the slope?*"

"Yes," Anne said.

"No way," Leo said. "We don't allow junk on the slope. How long was it?"

"Oh, maybe a foot."

"No way," Leo said again. "The ski patrol would have seen it before any skiers came up. I'd bet anything it wasn't there before the gondola opened."

"Maybe it's still there," Gail said. "Oh, you couldn't tell; we had all that snow the other night."

"I'll call the head of the patrol," Leo said. "He may have heard something about it." He reached again for the telephone, and again they waited until Leo turned back to them. "He'll call whoever it was and get back to me."

"But what do we do with it if we find it?" Gail asked. "You can't prove anything with a piece of wood."

"Jim said there probably would be gouges in it from the J-grip mechanism if it had been jammed in. Theoretically, we could match the marks and prove it was that piece of wood in that particular grip."

"And then what?" Josh asked.

"I don't know. Anne, what do you think?"

"We have to make a list of what we know and what we're guessing," she said. She went to the desk in the corner of the kitchen, piled with cookbooks, recipes, grocery lists, and a basket of Christmas cards. She found a spiral notebook and brought it to the table. "We know Vince was the one who suggested taking the highway away from Illinois; I don't see how it fits in with everything else, except that it hurts a Chatham. Maybe that's enough; I don't know."

She wrote as she spoke. "We know that Vince put the EPA onto Tamarack and tried to hurry up the cleanup. We know that the rock slide was started by a small dynamite blast above the drainage ditch and that Keith went up to check it and said he found no evidence of any problem, and he deals with dynamite in his job and ought to recognize blast marks. That's all we know for sure.

"We think that a bolt was removed from the gondola checking mechanism. It could have been removed at any time, since it didn't cause the accident; it only kept the gondola from shutting down. It may have fallen out and been found by someone who took it to Josh's house, but that seems highly unlikely. We think someone called the sheriff and told him where to look for it. We think a piece of wood was used to jam the J-grip and cause the gondola accident. It had to be done by someone who was familiar with the gondola and could be there without arousing suspicion, and Keith fits that description, but possibly others do, too. We think Keith may have been in touch with Vince, perhaps even working with him; we'll know more about that when we check the telephone records."

She put down her pencil and looked at Josh, and Gail and Leo across the table. "We don't know for sure why one J-grip was jammed and not another."

Leo sucked in his breath sharply.

"What does that mean?" Gail asked. "If you want to cause an accident, what difference does it make—"

Leo put his hand on her arm; he was looking at Anne. "You mean we have another coincidence. That out of one hundred sixty-eight gondola cars, the one that was jammed was the one you and I were in."

Gail stared at him, and then at Anne.

Josh grasped Anne's hand and held it tightly, and her hand curved around his. She felt the strength of his long fingers, and his hard palm locked to hers, and for the first time that she could remember she warmed to the supporting warmth of another person. His strength became part of her strength, his closeness was not a threat but a protection. They sat that way for what seemed like a long time, and then the telephone rang.

"Yes," Leo said, answering it, and after a few minutes, "Thanks. Yes, tomorrow morning. Let me know." He hung up and turned to the others. "The patroller tossed the piece of wood over to the base of the gondola tower, to get it out of the way. They'll go find it tomorrow; he knows exactly where it is."

"Anne," Gail said, her voice almost a whisper, "he wouldn't try to *kill* you . . . Or Leo. He *wouldn't!*" But she was remembering that Anne had said, months earlier, that Vince had threatened to kill her. "I don't believe it," she said, and there was desperation in her voice. "This is our family and some of us may do things that aren't nice, but we don't *kill*—" She choked on the word.

"We don't know," Josh said tightly, clamping down on the agitation in his voice. He was gripping Anne's hand. "There's too much we don't know. It could be that he picked on the first car to go up that morning and didn't know or care who was in it. That's possible. But we can't rule it out that it was deliberate. Anne, if it was aimed at you, he'll try again. We've got to make sure you're protected."

Anne looked swiftly at Leo and Gail. "Not only me." A shiver swept through her. *I'll never be free of him; he'll never let me go.*

She shook her head. "Wait. We have to think about this. If Vince was behind it—and we have to remember that we're not sure of anything—if he was, I'm sure he wouldn't try again, not for a long time. Nobody could miss the point if Leo or I had two . . . accidents in a row. I think we're all right for now; in fact, if we really were in danger, this is probably the safest time of all." She looked at the three of them. "I am not going to hire bodyguards. I am not going to let him, or anyone else, put me under siege. I'm going to do everything I can to find out what really happened and make sure it doesn't happen again."

Josh nodded. "Well said. But you'll still be careful crossing streets."

"Oh. Well, yes, I suppose . . ." The chill swept her again. "You, too," she said to Leo and Gail. "I guess we don't have to worry about Robin and Ned as long as they're in casts and stick close to you."

"Listen to us," Gail said. "How can we be talking this way?"

"Let's stop," Anne said. "I think we're saturated. Anyway, we can't do any more until we have more information." She paused and looked at each of them. "I want to tell you," she said slowly, "as awful as all this is, in another way it's been very special for me. The way the four of us have been together, working together and *being* together . . . it's meant so much to me. And I want to thank you, for being so close."

Quick tears sprang to Gail's eyes. "You don't have to thank us; it's wonderful for us, too, Anne. We love being close to you; we love you. I can't imagine all those years without you."

"We should be thanking *you,"* Leo said. "You've brought so much to us. Do you know how much our lives have changed because of you? I've been grateful for a long time. We do love you, Anne, and we all like it a lot that you're part of us."

"You're part of all of us," Josh said quietly. He had felt the pain of what lay behind her words, the emptiness in so much of her life before now, and he had had to force himself to sit still and not hold her close. Dearest Anne, I love you, he told her silently. Only Gail and Leo could say that aloud, at least for now. *I love you. And there won't be any emptiness for you, ever again, if I can help it.*

"But we can't stop yet," Leo said. "We aren't any closer to getting Josh off the hook. Even if they find that piece of wood and it fits, then what?"

"I don't know," Josh said. "But scientists collect facts for a living. Lawyers do, too. So we've made a start." He pushed back his chair. "Anne's right; we can't do any more right now, and we've had plenty of this for one night. And I have to go; I still have a lot of work to do tonight."

"I'll walk you partway back," Anne said. "I'd like some fresh air."

"And walk back alone?" Gail asked.

"I'll be fine," Anne said. "Gail, this is Riverwood and it's late and no one knows I'm going to be taking a walk."

"It's damned cold," Leo said.

"I won't go far and I'll dress warmly. I just want to think about something else for a while. I'll be back soon."

They walked on the narrow road, their breaths making white puffs in the crystalline air. The black sky was thick with stars on either side of the wide, white ribbon of the Milky Way. Near the horizon was a crescent moon, with a star hanging from its tip. The only sound in the clear silence was the soft padding of their boots on the hard-packed snow. The warm lights of Gail and Leo's house vanished as the road curved, but the snowfields surrounding them shimmered in a faint glow from the starlight so that they could just make out each other's face.

They walked together, not speaking, letting the ugliness of what they had been talking about fade away in the splendor of the night. When the road curved again, and they both slipped and caught themselves on a patch of ice, Josh casually took Anne's hand, and held it. Hardly romantic, he thought dryly, since they were wearing heavy ski mittens and the difference between holding hands and not holding hands could barely be felt, but he knew they were linked, and that was enough for him.

Anne glanced down, and smiled. In that icy, silent world, with their two figures moving in rhythm like shadows in the starlight, she felt even closer to him than in the warmth of the kitchen they had left behind.

"I'd like to hear about your teaching," she said, and he told her about his graduate students who helped with his research, and about the discussions they had in class and in the campus coffee shop that often gave him new ways to think about his work. Anne heard the affection in his voice, and knew it was not only for students, but for people in general. He was open to them for what all of them could share, and he seemed to have no hostility, even for those he found he could not like; he had understanding, if not always sympathy.

A remarkable man, Anne thought, and then she wondered if no one had ever made him angry or jealous, or had caused him the kind of pain that one could not forget or even forgive. And she realized what a long way she was from really knowing him.

And what a long way he was from knowing her. But that could not be changed. She would not tell him about herself. Even thinking of saying the words made her colder than she was, and a long shiver ran through her body.

At once Josh stopped, midsentence. "You'd better get back," he said. They stood in the middle of the road. He took her other hand and they looked at each other in the faint light.

"Good night," Anne said. "I'll see you tomorrow."

"When are you leaving?" he asked.

"Tomorrow afternoon. Shall we meet in Leo's office first thing in the morning? That way we'll be there when the patroller brings in that piece of wood."

"Yes. What time tomorrow afternoon? I'm on the four o'clock."

Anne smiled. "Then we'll travel together. Good night, Josh."

Through the heavy mittens, their hands clung for another moment. "Good night, Anne," Josh said, and they turned in opposite directions.

Anne walked in long strides, suddenly very cold. Her face was icy and stiff, her fingertips felt frozen, and she curled her hands into fists inside her mittens. When she reached the house and opened the kitchen door, the shock of the warm room made her dizzy, and she leaned against the wall, blinking against the tears that had come into her eyes the last few minutes.

"The coffee's hot," Leo said.

They were sitting as they had been when she and Josh left, Leo's arm around Gail, her head on his shoulder. Anne pulled off her heavy clothes and poured a mug of coffee, and sat opposite them. "It's freezing out there, but it's beautiful. Grandpa was right; Riverwood is the most perfect place in the valley. He must have loved this house."

Gail nodded. "He did. But he never felt it was completely right, because you weren't here. You haven't told Josh anything, have you?"

"No. And you haven't either?"

"No!" Gail exclaimed. "But he's very smart, you know; he asked us if Vince's getting kicked out had anything to do with you."

"What did you tell him?"

"That it wasn't our story to tell. But you should tell him, Anne; you can't build a wall around it forever—"

"Sweetheart," Leo said quietly, "she'll tell him when she can." He looked at Anne and smiled, loving her, aching for her. He felt that all of them, at that moment, were precarious, but she was the only one with a wound so long lasting, and so devastatingly deep, it might never be healed. "Gail and I were wondering, while you were gone, whether, out of all these terrible things, one truly wonderful thing might come."

Anne met his eyes with a startled look. "I don't know." She took a sip of the hot coffee, then another, feeling it warm her body. "I don't know," she said again.

* * *

The patroller brought the wet piece of wood to Leo's office and laid it on his desk. "Just where I left it; we just had to dig it out from under."

"Thanks," Leo said, and gave it to Josh, who turned it around in his fingers, looking at the gouges in it. "We'll check it against the J-grip; I called Matheny last night, and he said he'd be here at seven-thirty."

Josh gave the piece of wood to Anne. "It's the damndest thing," he said, his voice bemused. "Like visiting a country you've read about in a book. Or finding a tomb. We talk about things and imagine them and speculate about them, and then, suddenly, we're touching them."

"Here's something else," Leo said, and slid a small packet of papers across the desk. "Copies of the telephone bills from our office for the past six months." He watched Anne and Josh leaf through them together. "I marked the ones to Vince's office and home; the area code 305 is Miami. I traced that one; it's some big-time Florida politician."

"He must not have worried about being overheard," Anne said after a few minutes. "He kept using the office phone."

"Cheaper than calling from home," Leo said dryly. "One of our small overhead problems."

"Once a week or more, beginning last July," Josh murmured. "I don't see anything before that. What happened last July?"

"I went to Ethan's funeral," Anne said. "May I?" Josh gave her the stapled pages. She riffled through them. "Most of the calls seem to be in September and October, and then again in December."

"September," Josh said. "The reservoir. The drainage ditch."

Leo nodded. "And December the gondola crashed."

"What about October?" Josh asked.

"Nothing," Leo mused. "Except . . . I think Beloit was in town that month—remember, Anne?—talking as if the company was already his."

Jim Matheny knocked on the office door. "No secretary, so I came in."

"Jim, look at this," Leo said. He took the piece of wood and the two men walked to the outer office. He returned in less than a minute. "He'll check it right away; they've got the J-grip in their trailer. What do we do with these phone bills?"

"Hold on to them," Anne said. "They don't prove anything except communication, but if they fit into a pattern, we still could use them." She paced around Leo's office, standing at the window that looked up Tamarack Mountain. "There really is a pattern, but I don't know what we can do with it."

"Maybe we can't do anything," said Josh.

"Well, we have to do enough to get you out of it," Anne said, still looking at the mountain. She turned to him. "And we won't get enough from Jim Matheny to help us with that. Even if it turns out that someone did jam the grip with that piece of wood, you could have been the one who did it. There's so much loose time that we can't account for. Josh, can we go over that morning again, when you were packing? Wasn't there anything you did that involved someone else? We've gone over this so many times, but let's do it again. It takes twenty minutes to drive to the gondola from Riverwood; you would have had to get to the second level and jam the wood in the grip; then get out without being seen, and drive twenty minutes back to . . . oh, wait a minute." Her thoughts raced ahead. "This could change everything. Leo, if you wanted to disable a particular car, you'd have to wait until it moved directly below you, is that right? And jam that particular J-grip as it went by?"

Leo nodded. "That's it."

"Why would I pick your car?" Josh demanded.

"I don't know, but that may not be important. Nothing else may be important but this. Josh, we've got to be sure of the times. You'd need at least an hour, and that would be pushing it, to drive to town, park, somehow get into the gondola building and upstairs without attracting attention, wait until one minute to nine when Leo and I got into the car, jam the mechanism, get out of there in the confusion of the crash, and drive twenty minutes to your house."

"He could have done all that," Leo said. "If no one saw him between eight and nine that morning . . ."

"No," Josh said suddenly. "I couldn't have."

He met Anne's eyes. She was smiling, her eyes bright. "You couldn't have done it because you left the house at a little after nine for the airport."

"In a taxi," he said.

"And the company will have a record of the trip from Riverwood to the airport. But even if we stretch it, if you'd left for the airport at nine-fifteen, or as late as nine-twenty, you couldn't have been on the second floor of the gondola building at one minute to nine and gotten back to Riverwood to call a taxi and then take it to the airport."

"God damn!" Leo was grinning. "There's no goddam way you could have done it!"

"It doesn't even matter if our car was the target or not," Anne said. "The grip would have had to be jammed sometime in the minute it takes to travel at slow speed until it clears the gondola building and gains speed."

There was a silence. "Is that enough?" Josh asked Anne after a moment. "If they have the time nailed down, will Tyler drop the charges?"

"I don't know what else he can do. If Jim tells us that's what was used on our gondola car, there's absolutely no way you could have been in the building at the time it was done. We'll call Kevin this morning, and as soon as we get the taxi company's time sheet, we'll go to Tyler's office. It could be over that soon."

"Except for knowing who tried to frame Josh," Leo said. "Unless it's part of the pattern you were talking about."

Anne nodded. *A monster. A monster.* She had no proof, but the pattern was there. *And he is a monster.*

The three of them sat in silence, until Jim Matheny returned. He laid the piece of wood on Leo's desk. "How'd you know it wasn't an accident?" he demanded.

Leo looked at Anne. She was very pale. "It fits?" she asked.

"Like a charm. How'd you know? You know who did it?"

"No," Leo said sharply. "And nobody else does, either." He picked up the piece of wood and ran his fingers over the gouges.

"Nice clean gouges, easy to check," Matheny said. "One thing, it sure lets you off the hook, Leo. Somebody got it in for you? I'd watch out for dark corners, if I was you. Well, I'll give it to Arvin; he'll be happy; he hates to close an investigation without any idea what happened. He'll give it to Tyler, I guess; let him run with it from now on."

There was another silence when he left. "Dark corners," Leo murmured. "Everybody's beginning to sound like a crime novel."

"We have to call Kevin," Anne said.

"Thank God," Leo said. "At least, thank God for this part of it. Your part, Anne. From now on, you don't have to worry about what happens. You didn't even have to do as much as you've already done; you're Josh's lawyer, not ours. If someone is sabotaging us, it's our problem, not yours and not Josh's."

"Someone was looking for me, or for you, when we were in that car," Anne said quietly. "That doesn't tell me I have nothing to worry about. But that isn't the only thing. Even if it wasn't aimed at me, I'm part of this. As long as you're in trouble, it's my problem, too." She picked up her coat. "I think, if it's all right with you, after we see Kevin and Tyler, we'd better have a talk with Keith."

"You've gotta be kidding," Keith said, shaking his head in slow amazement. *"Dynamite?* God, you sure coulda fooled me. Like, who woulda thought of dynamite? I mean, you know, I wasn't exactly looking for it. God, Leo, I'm sorry if I missed that; I mean I really, like, let you down. Jesus," he said abruptly, "you mean like somebody really did it on purpose? Jesus, what a shitty thing to do. Why'd they do that? And how'd you find it? I mean, there's a lot of snow up there now; it's, you know, like amazing that you could even find it. You sure it's the right place? I mean, all this snow and it's hard to know exactly where we were, so how do you know it's like the right rocks and all that? I mean, it's kinda dangerous, isn't it, to go blaming somebody for blowing up a, you know, mountain when you're not even sure you know what you've got."

"We know what we've got," Leo said evenly. His gaze was intent on Keith, who sat at his desk in the corner of his office. The room was so small that Josh and Anne had to stand in the doorway, and Leo at the edge of the desk beside the single chair and file cabinet that took up the rest of the space. Keith sat straight in his chair, his chin thrust forward, his eyes wide with interest. But his hands constantly fidgeted with a pencil and an eraser, and Anne heard a nervous tapping of his shoe.

"Well, I wish I could, you know, help you, Leo. If I really like fucked up on that, I feel lousy about it, but it was, you know, a long time ago. I mean I don't see what I can do about it now."

Anne nodded. "We're trying to find people who saw anything unusual on the morning of the gondola crash. Could you think back and tell us if you saw anything?"

"Hey, what is this, an inquisition? I mean, you all barge in here and start in with all these questions, and I already told Halloran everything I know, so what's with this? How come you're not asking him?" He pointed his thumb at Josh. "I mean, he did the, you know, whole thing; so like who else do you need?"

Anne and Josh exchanged a quick glance with Leo. Less than an hour ago, Tyler had agreed to drop the charges against Josh. But there was no reason to tell Keith that.

"Anyway," Keith went on, the heel of his shoe tapping even faster, "I wasn't there. I got in late, just after the car fell. I'm sorry, Leo, I let you down there, too. I'm really sorry, but, you know, Eve and I were, like we had this thing going in bed, and I lost track of the, you know, time. I mean, if I'd known . . . but how could I? I mean, I couldn't know, could I? And I'm there every morning early, you know, I mean I was even there Christmas morning, remember? I'm always there. You know. I mean I missed this one morning, but I didn't think it would be such a, you know, big deal, but how was I to know—"

"You were in bed with your girlfriend?" Anne asked.

"Right, that's what I said."

"And she was awake the whole time."

"Oh, boy, was she," said Keith, and winked at Leo.

Leo glanced at Anne. "Okay, Keith," he said. "I didn't realize you weren't there the morning of the crash; we'll have to talk about that. I'll see you this afternoon."

His face a mask, Keith watched them leave. His hand was already reaching for the telephone. But then he pulled it back. He didn't know what they knew, but he knew what they suspected, and the worst of it was he couldn't figure out how they'd gotten there. Until he knew what was going on, and where he'd slipped up, there was no way he was going to call Vince. Right now Vince thought Keith Jax was God's gift to the world, and you could bet your ass that Keith wasn't about to tell him those assholes were sniffing around, and it was maybe because of some mistake he'd made, somewhere along the way. He stood up and pulled on his ski jacket. Leo wanted to see him that afternoon. That was okay, he could handle Leo. But he didn't see why he had to sit around waiting for him. He'd go skiing for a couple hours, clear his head, do some serious thinking. His future might be speeding up, and he sure as hell planned on being ready for it.

"Vince killed the highway to Charles' development," Leo said as the three of them walked toward the café on Main Street for lunch. "He sicked the EPA on us. He could have arranged with his nephew to foul our reservoir. He could have arranged with the same nephew to knock out the gondola; that perfect alibi doesn't mean a damn thing since his girl will back him up. So he could have done it, maybe aimed at Anne or me or both of us, and framed Josh, though I don't get that part at all. In fact, I don't get any of it. No sane person would do all that."

"You could put it another way," said Anne. She was

putting on her dark glasses against the bright sun. "He talked once or twice a week by phone to his nephew, who was always around when things happened in Tamarack that looked like accidents but in fact were carefully planned, and who had easy access day or night to the places where those things happened. The problem is, there's no trail. There's a pattern but no proof, and no arrows pointing anywhere for us to look next."

They sat outside the café, looking over the low wall at businesspeople coming for lunch, mothers pushing babies in strollers toward the Town Market, and a group of tourists coming out of a rental shop carrying skis and poles. "Nice to see a few of those," Leo said. "You know, Ethan and I used to sit here a lot, in happier times. It was his favorite place; he liked watching the town go by. We were here that day he said your name, Anne. I'm glad he's not here now; I'm glad he hasn't seen the things that have happened, and heard us trying to work it out and ending up every time with Vince. I'm glad he won't see Tamarack go to that swaggering son of a bitch who's buying it."

"Beloit," Anne said. "He's probably the biggest part of the pattern, if we could put it all together. What if Vince, for whatever reason, wants Beloit to have Tamarack? He could have done all these things to make the family sell to Beloit. Of course Vince may not even be involved, but let's assume that he is. He'd want the family to vote to sell at a low price. And they did. But it took a fairly long time, and maybe that was why the level of danger in what was happening kept going up. It started with a highway and the EPA, and got to the gondola and maybe"—she stopped a minute, choking on the word—"murder. But we can't prove any of that; we can't even find evidence that points to a deliberate attempt to lower the value of the company." She paused, frowning. "Or maybe not."

"Not what?" Leo asked.

"Maybe we don't need to have all the evidence after all. We might not be able to prove everything, but at least we might be able to stop the sale of The Tamarack Company.

Maybe it's enough to have a little evidence and a lot of logical suspicion." She turned the glass salt shaker around in her fingers, watching the sun's rays glance off it. "How likely do you think it is that anyone in the family would want to sell the company if it seemed that the sale price, and probably the vote to sell, had been manipulated by behind-the-scenes maneuvering and sabotage and attempted murder?"

"Charles," Josh said instantly. "If he knew about all this, what we're sure of and what we're guessing—"

"He'd call it off!" Leo exclaimed. "Especially if he knew we think it was Anne who was almost—oh, Christ, I have trouble every time I try to say this—murdered."

"And you," Anne said. "And his grandchildren."

"All of it. The whole lousy mess. He'd be as sick as we are. Of course he wouldn't sell to Beloit. At least he'd wait while we try to find out the truth. Why wouldn't he?"

"He needs the money," said Josh.

"Well, we'll have to find the money some other way," Leo said impatiently. "We have to tell him. This afternoon. Tomorrow. Before they sign anything. I know they haven't because Marian told us, but it can't be far off. Tomorrow? We could all fly to Chicago."

Josh and Anne exchanged a glance. "I don't belong there," Josh said. "You two go."

"I'm not sure," Leo said slowly. "I think it may be for Anne to go."

"It's your company," Anne said.

"And your father. What do you think?"

She gazed across the valley. She had not talked to Charles in almost three weeks, since Christmas. Before that, they had talked a few times by telephone, without ever mentioning Vince. It could not be seen as personal vengeance now, she thought; she was doing what she had to do for Leo and Gail. And Charles should know what his brother had done, and might have done. He should know that it was possible that his brother had tried to have his daughter killed. Not proven, but possible.

She would rather go to Chicago with Josh. Or with Leo. But this was something that had been waiting since she came back: for the two of them to face the shadow of Vince at last, and deal with it, together.

"All right," she said. "I'll call my office and push everything back a couple of days. And tomorrow I'll go to Chicago. And talk to Charles."

chapter 21

*F*rom his desk on the sixty-fifth floor of the Sears Tower, Charles could look through walls of glass in one direction at the sprawl of Chicago fading into the hazy distance, and in the other, across Lake Michigan to the Indiana shore. It was a view he savored each morning as he walked in, striding across the blue carpet Marian had chosen for Ethan when he had signed a lease for Chatham Development, soon after the building opened. The carpet, and everything else in Ethan's office, was now Charles', and no matter how bad his days had become, the view always gave him a feeling of satisfaction. He was still there, still president of his company, riding high above Chicago, and he might still come back in a way that would make his family, and the whole city, admire him just as they had admired his father.

But the day Anne arrived, there was no view. While Charles waited for ten o'clock, when she had said she would be there, he gazed at a layer of heavy white clouds below him, stretching to the horizon. The only evidence of the city below were the antennas of the Hancock Building thrusting through the clouds. There were clouds above, as well, and between those two white layers, Charles' office seemed bleached and ghostly, floating in a colorless world.

Anne wore a red suit and black sweater, with a Florentine necklace and earrings of gold and silver links. She was like a bright beacon in the unearthly light of his office, and Charles watched her walk toward him with a sense of wonder that this stunning woman, who seemed to bring light with her, was his daughter.

He stood indecisively behind his curved desk that Ethan had designed, then walked around it to meet her, holding out his hand. "This is very nice. You've never been here."

Anne took his hand and leaned forward and kissed his cheek. "Can we sit here?" she asked, and led the way to a gray suede couch near the windows. A silver tea service stood on the walnut coffee table in front of it. Charles, flushed with pleasure, followed her. "I remember the furniture from Grandpa's old office," she said as she sat down. "He gave me blueprints to play with and I watched him work. You haven't changed anything."

"No, he'd brought it all with him when he moved here, and I couldn't think of anything I wanted to be different. I didn't remember that he brought you to his office. How old were you?"

"About seven, the first time."

"Right after your mother died. I was traveling a lot in those days, on business."

"Yes."

There was a pause. "I'm sorry," Charles said. "I know I didn't spend enough time with you. I wish I had; I wish I'd known how to be what you wanted. I didn't plan it that way, you know; a lot of the time I didn't even know what was happening."

When Anne was silent, he spread his hands, then let them drop. "The saddest thing, for me, is that I didn't make myself part of your growing up. I look at my friends who have scrapbooks and stories to tell going back through the years, and even though they may have had some bad times with their children, they have their memories and they know they were part of something that was as important as anything else in their life. And now they have friendships, the kind that grow, because they've been growing, too, right along with their children. It doesn't always end so happily, I know that, but I look at my friends who've made it with their children, and they seem so much more complete than I am. They have love, and a place to belong, and a feeling of the generations blending into each other that I've never had. And I envy them."

He paused, frowning slightly. It seemed to Anne that her coming to him had freed something in him so that the words spilled out; it was as if he had been waiting for that kiss on his cheek.

"I've never been friends with either of my daughters," Charles said, his voice low. "I'd like to learn how." He glanced at Anne, then, quickly, away. "You said once, last September when I was in Tamarack, that you didn't forgive me and couldn't love me. I keep hearing you say that. I don't know what I can do to change it. I've lost all those years of your growing up, but if we could find a way now . . ."

He sat up straight, changing the subject as if afraid of what she might say. "I'm sorry, I'm not being a good host. Would you like tea? Or coffee?" He touched the silver teapot. "This is cold, but we have plenty in the kitchen, keeping hot. What would you like? Croissants? Or toast? I bought éclairs, too; I remember you used to love them— what is it? Is something wrong?"

"No." Anne shook her head sharply. *There is nothing in the world as good as chocolate éclairs. They're wonderfully messy to eat. Definitely my favorite.* "I don't eat them anymore; I haven't for a long time. Just tea would be fine."

Charles went to the door and opened it and spoke to his secretary, who followed him almost immediately with another silver teapot, this one steaming, and a covered basket. "I haven't had breakfast; I hope you won't mind if I eat."

"Of course not." Anne watched him spread jam on a piece of toast. His hand was shaking.

"Would you pour the tea?" he asked, and began to talk again. "I really don't know anything about you, that's the terrible thing; I don't know what I can talk about and what I should stay away from. You know"—he paused to swallow a bite of toast—"Christmas dinner, when you were asking all those questions about Chatham Development and Tamarack, I wanted to tell you to stop; I couldn't stand it that you weren't on my side. I knew you weren't because you hadn't forgiven me, but I kept thinking of how wonderful it would be if we were together, you and I, maybe even working together; that seemed so wonderful to me." He reached with a nervous hand to take another piece of toast from the basket. "You see, I really don't know what to talk about."

"You could start with me," Anne said quietly.

Startled, he looked at her, his hand suspended above the toast basket. "What does that mean?"

"That so far I've only heard about you." Anne gazed at her teacup. She remembered the pattern; Marian had bought it at the same time she bought the carpeting, a Villeroy & Boch flowered china, too delicate for an office, but Ethan had liked it for just that reason, and Anne had always felt grown-up and festive when the secretary brought the tray for just the two of them and Ethan took a few minutes from his desk to join her on the couch. "There's always been something missing in our family," she said, looking up at Charles. "A kind of caring that connects people to each other. You've always been so wrapped up inside yourselves, all of you, except Gail, you haven't had room for anyone else. You just told me all the things that you wished you'd done differently so you'd feel happier and more complete, and I'm sorry you have so much sadness, but I can't see that it's even occurred to you that if you'd done those things differently, your daughter might have benefited; she might have been happier; she might have had a father to trust when her uncle was"—her throat locked and she began to gag, but she pushed the words out— "forcing himself on her week after week and destroying what was left of her childhood."

Charles had drawn back into the corner of the couch. The toast had fallen to the floor, but he had not noticed it; his eyes were fastened on Anne, and he seemed to shrink as she spoke.

"And then you talked about Christmas dinner," Anne said. "That I wasn't on your side because I hadn't forgiven you. You might have thought, if you were thinking about something beside yourself, that I was worried about Gail and Leo, and trying to help them keep their home and their company, that I was being part of their family, that I wanted to be connected to them in a way that nobody in my family ever tried to connect with me."

She stopped. Her voice had grown intense, almost heated, and she had promised herself, before she arrived, that she would stay calm. She had been feeling closer to Charles with each discovery they had made about Vince, and her kiss when she arrived had been genuine and spontaneous, but then, as he spoke, her anger had returned, and within her there had come a familiar bleak emptiness, the same sense of loss that had welled up in her as she sat at the dinner table on her fifteenth birthday.

But this time she was not alone. This time Gail and Leo and the children were with her. This time there was Josh.

"I didn't mean to jump on you," she said with a small smile. "I hoped we could begin to find out what we could build together; I didn't mean to get carried away and talk like a prosecutor."

Charles was still hunched in the corner of the couch. His face was drawn. "Is that really us?" There was bewilderment in his voice. His head lowered, his breath came out in a long sigh. "A daughter shouldn't have to teach her father how to be a father. I never realized . . ."

He rubbed his forehead with the knuckle of his first finger and suddenly Anne felt like crying. She remembered that gesture from when she was very young; her father, sitting alone, rubbing his forehead and weeping after her mother died. "You're right; you're right about us," he said. "We're not reflective about ourselves. You're different, Anne; you think about what goes on inside people and how their relationships work, and we just never seem to. I don't know why we don't; we aren't bad people, you know."

In a minute Charles sat up. He took his cup from the coffee table and sat back, more relaxed, as if, once again, Anne had freed him to talk, this time by making him look at himself in a new way. "It might be because of Dad. I think about him all the time these days; it's as if, when he died, he got even bigger, though that's hard to believe because he was the biggest man I ever knew. Maybe he dominated us so much that we all closed up, to get away from him. Or maybe we were jealous of him, or in awe of him and spending all our time trying to please him, or impress him, and that didn't make us very generous to each other." He sighed. "I don't know; I'm no good at figuring out why people do what they do."

Anne smiled. "I don't think we should blame our parents for everything that goes wrong."

Charles, too, smiled. "But it's so handy. And so comforting."

They laughed together. And then they stopped, and exchanged a long look. They could not remember ever laughing together.

The sound of their laughter lingered, warming Anne, and for a moment it seemed to her that she could be a daughter with a father, sharing the things of the world in a way different from any other sharing a man and a woman found. But she knew it would not happen. It was too late. She thought they would find friendship, and even companionship, but that was all. Too late, she thought, and regret filled her. Too late. Too late.

"Maybe there were just too many men," Charles said, still looking for explanations. "After my mother died and Dad was in such a bad way over it, and then *your* mother died, and it took me so long to give a damn about anything after that, everything was so different, so out of balance. I never thought of this before, but I don't think we had enough women in our family. Only Marian and Nina were left, and they were always so . . . vague, I guess you'd say. Marian's much sharper now, much more aggressive—when you left, she seemed to be in shock, and after that she began to change—but when you were young, she just sort of floated around. You probably remember that. So for years there were just men running our family, almost like a business. Not enough women. Not enough gentleness."

Anne nodded. "Maybe. There's hardly ever one neat explanation for everything that happens. My clients are always looking for one; some tidy way to explain the failure of a marriage or of living together. But it's always so much more complicated and there's usually plenty of blame to go around."

"But that wasn't true when you were young. What happened to you was—"

"I can't talk about that."

"But I thought—"

"We can talk around it. I've been doing that for twenty-five years."

"You've never talked to anyone about it? Not one person who could help you?"

"I've never needed anyone. I managed by myself."

"My God," Charles said softly. "You made yourself what you are without anyone to lean on, anyone to take your hand. . . . My God." He thought for a minute. "I've always needed other people. I've always looked for someone to smooth the way, or at least point it out to me, help me get to it. . . . Whoever it was, my father, or Vince, whoever seemed to have some secret about getting through life in triumph, instead of failure. I was always so afraid of failing, of seeing people point their fingers at me because they'd known all along I wasn't good enough. Where did you get such strength?" he burst out.

"Desperation," Anne said. She tried to say it lightly, but it came out with absolute seriousness. "I was ashamed of myself; I think I hated myself. I had to find a way to like myself again, and be proud of what I was, and I couldn't talk about the past because it made me sick and ashamed, all over again. And maybe I got some of my strength from my grandfather. The biggest man you ever knew."

Slowly, Charles nodded. "He told me once the worst thing he ever did was what he did to you that day. He wouldn't blame the rest of us; he only blamed himself and he never forgave himself for it. He never stopped hoping you'd come home so he could ask you to forgive him. For a long time, he refused to lock his front door, because he wanted you to be able to walk right in."

They were silent for a long time. Thank you, Grandpa, Anne said silently. Thank you for understanding what happened that day, and for loving me, and for wanting me home. "Thank you," she said aloud, to Charles. "I'm so glad to know that."

Charles began to say that he'd been afraid of failing as a father, too; that he'd wanted someone to show him how to be one, to point the way. But he did not. There had been enough excuses; he owed his daughter more than that. He moved closer to her and took her hand. "I've always loved you, Anne. That was one of the things I never said often enough, or in the right way. I know I said it when I kissed you good-night or left for business trips, but I'm not sure it ever came out as if I really meant it. I did, though; I always loved you, and I admired your spirit and your marvelous mind. Do you remember, I went to some of your spelling bees, and you always won? I was so damned proud. I'd sit in that auditorium and watch you stand so straight and spell those incredibly long words that I'd never heard of—and I didn't have the faintest idea what they meant—and I'd tell myself I'd always take care of you and keep you happy. But I didn't know what you needed; you seemed to be doing fine by yourself, and I was proud of you for that, too. I'm so sorry; I don't even know how to begin telling you I'm sorry. I don't know how much I could have done for you, because I'm not exactly a hotshot at anything, but I could have tried; I could have tried my damndest, and then maybe you would have had a father and I would have had my daughter Anne for all the years of your growing up. Instead of that I failed you in just about every way one person can fail another. I wish I could make it up to you: it's so damned . . . *feeble* just to say I'm sorry."

Anne leaned toward him and laid her cheek against his, and they sat still, their hands clasped. "Thank you," she said again.

An enormous love for his daughter filled Charles; the force of it astonished him. He drew back and smiled at her. "And that business of not forgiving me, and not loving me . . ."

"I do forgive you," Anne said.

Charles waited. But that was all she said. He felt as if a

light had dimmed. Well, then, later, he thought. Next month, next year, someday. Someday she'll say it. Someday she'll mean it. It will all work out. It has to. Whatever we all did, we can get along; we can all love each other. We're not bad people, after all.

"We're not bad people," he murmured.

"One of us is," Anne said. She tested the teapot and finding it still warm, poured more tea for both of them.

Charles looked surprised. "I thought you said you didn't want to talk about——"

"I don't. This is something else." She walked to the window, looking out at the flat, white landscape below her, with the two antennas thrusting through it. "Do you know why the highway to Deerstream was never built?"

"The highway to——? No, no one knows why. Some committee changed its priorities, I suppose. We never did find out what happened."

Anne turned to face him. "Vince killed it."

Charles stared at her. "What are you talking about? He didn't kill it; he tried to save it."

"He killed it. He told Zeke Ruddle, the senator from Utah, that the people in Illinois couldn't decide how to route it, so you didn't deserve it and the money ought to go to Colorado and Utah. Which it did. Senator Ruddle told me all about it a week ago; I have his telephone number if you want to call him."

Charles was still staring at her. "Why?"

"I don't know. If I were to guess, I'd say he wanted to hurt you, perhaps destroy Chatham Development. I think he's wanted to harm the family for a very long time."

"I don't believe it." He was shaking his head. "I don't believe it; Vince was worried about me; he'd never——" He jumped up and began to walk about the room. "Ruddle told you? He said it, just the way you told me?"

"Close. He thinks Vince is a hero for doing it. Giving up a highway his brother was interested in, for the good of the country. Something like that."

Charles bumped into a corner of the desk, and cursed, rubbing his thigh. "We talked it over and over; he knew how everything depended on that; how desperate I was . . ." There was a silence. "Ruddle *told* you."

"Yes," Anne said.

"I want his phone number."

She went to Charles' desk and copied it from the address book in her purse.

When she moved back to the window, Charles leaned over and read the number. "He said he was trying to help me. But then we lost it. And he was right there, right in the middle of things. Son of a bitch," he muttered. He straightened up. "What did you mean, he's wanted to hurt the whole family?"

Anne told him. Beginning with Bud Kantor at the EPA—and writing his telephone number below Zeke Ruddle's—she went through all that she and Leo and Josh had discovered about the dynamite blast, what had caused the gondola accident, and what they knew about Keith.

"Wait," Charles said. He was leaning against his desk, frowning. "The EPA . . . that's Vince's job, part of it, anyway. His committee is responsible for the environment, for hazards. . . ." He paused. "This guy. Kantor. He said Vince pushed it, wanted them to exaggerate the danger and speed up the whole thing?"

"Yes," Anne said.

"Well, there could have been reasons . . . you'd have to know everything that's gone on. Anyway, that's all you know. The rest—the dynamite, the gondola—that's just guesswork."

"It's not guesswork that someone deliberately caused them. We have no proof of who it was. But there are a few other points. One is a pattern that begins with the highway, which hurt you and Chatham Development and the whole family; and goes on to the EPA, which is hurting Tamarack and The Tamarack Company and the whole family; and goes on to the drainage ditch and the gondola accident, which badly hurt Tamarack and The Tamarack Company and the whole family. Then there's the fact that Ethan kicked Vince out after I left, the sort of thing that might lead someone who is capable of monstrous acts to plan others, in revenge. And finally, there's the strange coincidence of the connection between Vince and the buyer of The Tamarack Company."

"Ray Beloit," Charles said.

"It never bothered you that he was so close to Vince?"

"Why should it? Vince told me Beloit wanted to buy a glamorous company, and he knew I had one I wanted to sell. He made the contact with Beloit; he was helping me out. What was there to be suspicious about?"

"Even after everything that happened to Tamarack? One thing after another that made the family panic and agree to sell at a terrible price. You know it's terrible; you know you could get more than twice what *Vince's friend and campaign manager* has offered if the value of the company hadn't been lowered by all those so-called accidents. And we know now they were not accidents. They were deliberately caused by someone who calculated the effect they would have on the town, and the company, and the family."

The office was very quiet. "You think we were manipulated into selling," Charles said at last.

"Yes," Anne said.

Slowly, heavily, he shook his head. "It's too filled with hate, too . . . evil."

"Yes," Anne said again. "And there's something else. The gondola accident. We have no proof of this, either, and it's possible we never will. And it may simply be another coincidence. But we don't think so. There are one hundred sixty-eight cars on the gondola, and the one that was jammed was the one Leo and I had just stepped into."

Charles slumped against his desk, his eyes closed. "No," he groaned. He lifted his head. "What are you saying? He wouldn't. It was a terrible coincidence, an accident, a random . . ."

"We found the piece of wood," Anne said. "It wasn't an accident; it was planned."

"Well, yes, I understand, that part was planned, but not with a particular car. Whatever else he's done, he wouldn't . . . for God's sake, he's not a murderer!" His gaze moved from Anne; he was remembering that she had told him

557

Vince had threatened her before. "Why?" he burst out. "You and Leo? What would he . . . my God, my God, I can't believe it; there's no reason . . ."

"I don't know why. Except that Leo's always been against selling The Tamarack Company, and I have a story about the past that could end his political career."

"That's not a reason to kill two people!"

"I wouldn't think so. But if you were planning to cause an accident anyway, and you had a chance at the same time to get rid of some people you thought were in your way, and you were the kind of person who could make such plans in the first place, it might seem quite reasonable."

"Reasonable!"

"To someone capable of monstrous acts," Anne said evenly.

"My God!" Charles cried. The horror of it all, the accumulation of facts and guesses, struck him, and he felt he could not bear it. His daughter had been raped; his daughter had almost been murdered. And so many people had been hurt in between those two crimes—himself, the family, the entire town of Tamarack—how could anyone fathom that in someone he thought he had known, and admired, and loved? Too much, too much, Charles thought; too much to comprehend, too much to accept. But he had no choice in that; he had to accept it. Even if it were not all exactly as it seemed, what they knew for sure was damning enough.

"Even the possibility," Charles muttered, "the chance that he might have . . ." He shook his head, talking to himself as if he were alone. "But even if he didn't . . . even if he had nothing to do with the gondola—or maybe he did but he didn't mean to hurt anyone—even then, the other things he's done that were aimed at all of us . . . and he lied to me. About everything. For *years* . . . Playing with me, with all of us, as if we were his puppets. And my God, we were. We almost were. Ruddle. Kantor. Everyone he knows. I can call them . . . I will call them . . . but I know it won't change anything, because I believe Anne. Because she's telling the truth; she always has. The goddam son of a bitch, he knew how I felt about him, he knew I depended on him, and he let me trust him, and he lied, played his games with me, almost ruined me. Left me hanging out there with everybody thinking I was the ass who blew the company. . . . *Son of a bitch."*

He moved around his desk. He pushed his chair out of the way and still standing, reached down to take a folder from the bottom drawer. He laid it on the desk and opened it. On the top was a letter with his signature. He picked it up, read it, and held it for a moment, wavering. It meant sixty million dollars that he needed so badly he could taste it. "But I can't do it," he murmured. "I can't be part of this. *I won't let him do it."* And with one sharp motion, perhaps the most decisive he had made in his life, he tore it in half. "I have to talk to him," he went on, still to himself. "I have to hear it from him."

He took the ripped letter to his secretary, and Anne watched through the open door as he placed it on her desk. "Write a letter to Ray Beloit at this address, telling him I'm canceling the sale of The Tamarack Company. Send it by fax; tell him I'm returning his earnest money by wire this afternoon, with interest for the few days we've held it. If he has any questions, tell him to talk to my lawyer; as far as he's concerned, I'm out of the office indefinitely."

He returned to the office, shutting the door behind him, and looked at Anne with a little start, acknowledging her presence. "I don't know what happens next," he said. He walked back to his desk, as if that was where he felt most secure, and attempted a smile. "I keep botching things. Now I've even failed at selling a company to help keep this one alive."

"This was a victory, not a failure," Anne said. "We'll find a way to help you here; we'll all do it together. It won't be a battle anymore."

Charles smiled at the confidence in her voice. Once again, a great love for her swept through him, and he wondered how he had survived for so many years without it; his life before this day seemed dreary and meaningless. "I wish that was enough," he said ruefully. "I wish I could walk away from here, with you and the family on my side, and say I had everything I wanted. But I can't do it; I can't let this company die, even though I've done more than my share to kill it. I still think I could bring it back, you know. Not to what Dad made it; I can't fool myself any longer about that. But if I had time, and money, I could make it solid and respected again. Money!" he exploded. He kicked shut the file drawer he had left open; the sound reverberated through the room. "Money! Money! Christ, I'm buried under so many goddamned debts, I can't move! I'm behind ten million dollars in overdue interest and the banks will foreclose if I don't pay it this week: I can't put them off any longer. I've been all over town looking for that money. All over the country. I haven't got any credit left. All I had was The Tamarack Company, and I just tore that up, and I haven't anywhere else to go. I'm sorry, Anne; you deserve a father you can look up to. What you've got is a failure who hasn't got any options left. Unless you believe in fairy tales: the good prince who writes one check and says, 'It's all yours.' I haven't believed in fairy tales for a long time."

Anne walked across the office to Charles' desk. She picked up a glass paperweight and gazed at it thoughtfully, tilting it. An elf stood in the center, hands on his hips, a sly grin on his face. "How about an evil prince?" she asked.

"What?"

"You said you wanted to talk to him anyway," Anne said softly. "To ask him about the highway, about the EPA, about the gondola . . ."

Their eyes met across the desk for a long minute. The thought of confronting Vince clanged within Charles like a terrifying alarm. No one confronted Vince; he confronted others. He confronted the world, and always won. Charles could not imagine facing him, accusing him, demanding from him a check for . . . good God, Charles thought, this is insane.

But Anne was there, her eyes steady on his. And he knew he owed this to her, even more than to himself. It was time he chose his daughter over his brother; it was twenty-five years overdue. I can do it, he thought. For Anne, for myself, for the family. Maybe I couldn't do it before, but I'm not alone now. I have Anne, and the rest of them are behind me; they'll be with me from now on. Whatever happened to me before, everything is different now. . . . *Now.*

The word was like a starting gun in a race. Briskly, making sure he had no time to change his mind, Charles walked to a closet in the corner and took out his overcoat. He pulled it on, and buttoned it, and took his hat and gloves from the shelf. "We'll catch the next plane for Washington." He held out his hand. "I want you to see it happen," he said.

Vince had just returned from Denver for the opening session of Congress. He was alone; Clara had stayed behind for another week. His butler had unpacked and put everything away; he had showered and had had a Scotch and soda, and he was in his bedroom, dressing for dinner, a second drink near at hand, when the doorman called to say Charles Chatham was in the lobby.

"Well, Charles," he said, striding into the living room as the butler opened the front door. But it was not Charles who came in; it was Anne. Vince stopped short, his eyebrows drawn together, his thoughts racing from possibility to possibility as Charles followed her into the room.

"Vince," said Charles. He did not hold out his hand. He eyed Vince's tuxedo, his shirt open at the top, his tie dangling around the collar, and he felt, as he frequently did with Vince, that he had intruded in his busy life. "I'm sorry for the short notice; we just came in from Chicago. I don't think . . . I hope this won't take too long."

"I hope not," Vince said shortly, but he did not say he was going out and they could see him tomorrow. He had to know what they wanted, why Anne was here, why Charles was nervous. "Well?" he said. "What is it you want?"

"May we sit down?" Anne asked quietly, and Vince felt a muscle in his throat begin to throb at the ease with which she had exposed him in his rudeness instead of standing awkwardly in the middle of the room, as he had intended.

He led the way past deep chairs and couches to a game

table near the curved windows overlooking the harbor. "A drink?" he asked briefly, gesturing toward a stocked sideboard.

"No, thank you," said Anne. Charles shook his head. Vince poured a Scotch and soda and sat down, one ankle resting on his knee, his chair away from the table and tilted back, balancing on two legs. He looked at Charles, and waited.

"We've been talking to Keith," Charles said.

Vince's head jerked up. His eyes were hooded, but his voice was smooth and only faintly curious. "Keith?"

"Your nephew. Who the hell else would I mean?" Charles took a breath. He was feeling stronger. There was something in Vince he had never seen before that made him think of an animal about to be cornered: not really worried, yet, but alert and prepared to retreat. "I'll tell you, Vince, too much has been going on lately. It's hard to believe that one family could be in the middle of so many catastrophes. There was that business with the highway to Deerstream. We had a senator on our side and he was on the right committee at the right time, but with all that, we lost it. And there's the EPA investigation in Tamarack, bad for the town and the company and the family, especially the incredible publicity it's had, and it just hit like a ton of bricks even though we had a senator on our side. And there was the pollution of the reservoir in Tamarack, bad for the town and the company and the family. And there was the gondola accident in Tamarack, terrible for the town and the company and the family. And then there was the offer to buy The Tamarack Company, when no one had been trying to sell. There was just too much going on, and after a while it got too hard to believe it was all coincidence. So we've been talking to people to try to track down what happened, and when and how. We talked to Keith. And to Zeke Ruddle, you know him, of course, the senator from Utah. And to Bud Kantor, I'm sure you know him; he's with the EPA."

Charles drew back at the flare of rage in Vince's eyes. He looked down at his hands, white knuckled, hidden in his lap, because he was confused whenever he looked at Vince. Vince's blond beauty was as pure and angelic as it had been when they were boys, his figure as trim, his hair as thick. Nothing seemed to touch him. Invulnerable Vince, Charles thought, and recalled that he had heard he was going to run for the presidency.

Vince smiled, so sweetly that Charles thought he must have been wrong about rage. "You've been so busy," Vince said softly. "I thought you were concentrating on saving Dad's company, and instead you've been running around, interviewing people in Washington and Tamarack. Or maybe you're not the one who's been doing it. Who's this 'we' you're talking about?"

"I didn't believe it at first," Charles said somberly. "We've been so close, and I've admired and trusted you— God, there's never been a time when I didn't admire you and trust you—and I couldn't believe you'd do anything to hurt me. All those times you told me you were doing everything you could to help me, help the company, help all of us—"

"And I was," Vince said. "How could you think anything else? I worked on that highway for months, but I couldn't get it moving; every damned farmer up there and his uncle had a different idea on where it should go. When Zeke came to me, what could I say? I'd tried everything I knew. And Bud Kantor came to me, even though he's pretty low on the totem pole around there and should have gone through channels, but he was worried about Tamarack and he knew my family was running it and he thought I'd be sympathetic. And I was. You know damn well there isn't anything I care about as much as the health of that town, in fact anything this family does—"

"That's a lie. All of it." Charles was pale, and he was squeezing his words out through clenched teeth. If he had stopped to think that he was calling Vince a liar, he might have fled. But he kept pushing out the words, glancing at Vince and then away and then back again. "I told you, I didn't believe it at first. But after a while I kept remembering one thing. It's probably a little thing to you; you may not even remember it. It was a walk we took one night after dinner, along the C and O canal. There was a little kid who came up—sprang at us, I guess you could say—wanting money. Not a lot; five dollars, I think; maybe ten. And you started to beat the hell out of him. It was the damndest thing; I couldn't believe it was you. That was the night Dad had his stroke. I flew to Tamarack and forgot what had happened. But now I can't stop thinking about it. Because there's that side of you that can beat up a little kid. And beat up your family."

"Charles, Charles," Vince chided gently. "You don't mean any of that." He brought his chair down and leaned forward. "This isn't the Charles I know, making such wild accusations. Someone's turned you against me; you're hardly even looking at me! Charles, we've had some rough times in our family, but we've never let outsiders poison our feelings toward each other. My God, what would Dad say if he could hear you? Accusing me as if I'm some kind of monster out to ruin you. He couldn't stand it if he knew—"

"Leave Dad out of this! Christ, Vince, you've betrayed everything he ever cared about; he would have kicked you out ten times over if he'd known about all this. And who the hell is the outsider? This is our family I'm talking about; everything we've done has been inside the family. You wanted to know who 'we' are? *All of us who belong in this family.* If anybody's an outsider, it's you."

For a split second, the room was silent. Then Vince flung himself around, facing Anne. "You fucking bitch," he rasped. "You put him up to this."

"Shut up!" Charles shot to his feet and towered over Vince. "You don't talk that way to my daughter! You did enough to her when she was a baby! If you want to go after anybody, go after me! I'm telling you what *I* think, not what anybody else thinks or says. Look at me, damn you; I'm talking to you! I want to talk about the deals you cut with Zeke Ruddle. And Bud Kantor. And the dynamite that started the slide above the drainage ditch in Tamarack. And the gondola accident. The piece of wood Keith jammed into the grip *on the car Anne and Leo were riding in,* and the bolt he took out and planted at Josh Durant's house. I want to talk about—"

"I don't know what the fuck you're talking about!" Vince's voice had risen to match Charles'. He stood up, facing him, his fury increasing because he was not tall enough to have his eyes level with Charles'. "You didn't get any of that from Keith! He didn't tell you a goddam thing because there isn't anything—"

"You don't know what he told us. Do you really trust him? Do you think you know what he'd say, how much he'd say, no matter who's asking the questions?"

"You son of a bitch—!"

"Is there anything you need, Senator?" the butler asked. He stood in the doorway, his face perfectly bland.

"No," snapped Vince. "And don't bother us again." He waited until the butler had withdrawn, as silently as he had come, then he turned to Charles, calmer, a small, puzzled frown between his eyes. "If Keith told you any of that, what does it have to do with me? It sounds like a kid trying to be James Bond. I didn't think Keith was like that. Dynamite? Why would Keith talk about dynamite? And wood jammed in a—what? A grip, you said? And a missing bolt? And something else; the car Anne and Leo were in. That's a little sly, isn't it, Charles? Are you implying Anne and Leo were targeted? You've gotten quite dramatic. But I can't help you; I don't have any idea what you're talking about. And I can't believe Keith has such flights of fantasy. I hardly ever talk to him, but when I do, he seems to me to be a fine young man, not the kind to make up stories that could hurt other people. In fact, you don't know a damn thing." He took a few steps away from Charles, and turned back, almost carelessly. "You've been making up a bunch of fairy tales that don't have a goddam thing to do with me, and I'm tired of listening to you. We don't have anything to talk about, Charles. I'm terribly disappointed in you; I thought we were as close as brothers could be, but—"

"This is a list of the days Keith called you in the past six months in Denver and Washington and Miami, with the length of each telephone call," Charles said, taking a slip of paper from his pocket and laying it on the table. "If you've been close to anyone lately, it's been him."

There was a pause. Vince glanced at the paper but did not move to pick it up. "That's a lawyer's trick, isn't it? To spy on people and keep track of their phone calls. I suppose I shouldn't be surprised, should I, Charles? You never did have a mind of your own. You used to bend every which way, depending on whatever I said; now you've switched to somebody new to tell you what to think."

Charles drew in his breath. It had been true for too long. He glanced at Anne. She had not moved the whole time; she had kept her eyes on him. Now she smiled at him, very calmly, very softly, just for him. She would not let him or Vince know how Vince's voice made her cringe within herself, the bile rising in her throat, her head so tight with remnants of fear and shame she thought it would burst. But this time she was not helpless; this time she had a life of her own, and she burned with a pure flame of anger and contempt. Vince would not dominate her, ever again, and if she had anything to do with it, he would not dominate Charles, either.

"As a matter of fact, it *was* my idea," she reminded Charles. "But everything else we've done has involved all of us at different times. Nobody can get far without teamwork. And respect."

"Keep out of this," Vince spat, but he saw that Charles was smiling, no longer wavering, and he turned back to him, to try to get him off-balance again. "Look, Charles, what are you accusing me of? Keeping in touch with my nephew? What about all the times I called you, or you called me, so we could keep in touch?" He waited, but Charles said nothing. Vince let out his breath in an angry burst. He walked the length of the room and stood beside the foyer leading to the front door. "Get out, both of you. We don't have anything to talk about. I don't know what the hell you expected me to say; I don't give a damn. I want you out of here. Now."

"I want sixty million dollars from you," Charles said loudly, to cover the uncertainty that kept welling up in him. They had no proof of anything; Keith had not told them anything. But he had gone too far to stop. "I've canceled the sale of The Tamarack Company and I need the money at Chatham Development."

Stunned, Vince stared at him. "You canceled the sale? You couldn't have."

"I'm the president of the parent company. I signed the letter of intent. And I tore it up this morning. Beloit already knows about it. I've returned his earnest money. It's over."

"No." Still stunned, Vince shook his head. "It was a deal. It was set."

"Not anymore. I need that money, Vince. I'm serious. I need it and I need it right away."

"You're out of your mind. You killed that sale . . . no, you didn't; I'm going to see that it goes through. You made a deal and you'll goddam well stick to it. But you tried to kill it, and now you're crying for money and you think I'll give it to you. *Sixty million dollars?* You're out of your mind. I wouldn't give you a penny! You invade my house and throw a bunch of accusations at me as if I'm some kind of criminal; you scream at me like a fishwife; you accuse me of attempted murder, for Christ's sake, and tell me I'm an *outsider* in my own family, and then you want money from me! Sixty million dollars! For Christ's sake, you're insane. You're both insane; she thought of this, didn't she? Lawyers are used to blackmail; they do it all the time. Well, not me! You don't blackmail me, you bastard; you aren't getting a fucking thing from me, *ever!* Is that clear? Don't you ever come whining to me again about your problems because we are through! You and your little bitch; you're—"

"God damn you—!" Charles shouted, starting for him.

"Wait," Anne said. "Let me answer that." She stood up. Her back was to the window and Vince could see only her silhouette, not her face. "It doesn't do any good," she said to him, her low, clear voice carrying the length of the room. "All your foul words can't touch me, or my father, either. Everything you've done to this family has been as foul as your tongue, but when it doesn't get you what you want, all you can think of is more foulness. Do you really think we don't know what you've done? You've left a trail of evil; it was there for us to follow. You've connived and manipulated, you've lied, you've used people and tried to frighten and divide them, *and kill them;* you've made a mockery of the idea of family . . . all for yourself, to get whatever it was you wanted when you wanted it. You don't have the right to call yourself Ethan Chatham's son. He built towns; all you can do is try to destroy one. But Tamarack is still there, and the family is still there, and it's gotten stronger. People learn to live with evil because there's so much of it in the world; they learn to deal with it, and sometimes even ignore it. There are always scars left when evil has been done, but we survive, and a lot of the time we become stronger because we have to, in order to go on. And because there's a satisfaction in knowing we've faced the worst in people, and triumphed."

"Get out," Vince rasped. "I don't have to listen to this. You're in my home. Get out."

"The amazing thing about evil people like you," Anne went on evenly, "is how much you're like babies. All you really think about is what you want. You want, you want, you want, and you think no one has a right to stand between you and what you want, because the most important thing in the world to you is satisfying your appetites. Not family, not friends, not work, certainly not the welfare of the country, just your own appetites, that seem to grow larger the more you satisfy them. So you lash out with your fists, and have tantrums, like a baby, but you do far more dangerous things, too, up to murder, or attempted murder. That's another way you're like a baby: you foul yourself. Only you foul others at the same time—"

"You goddam bitch, I should have—"

"What?" Anne flung at him. "Should have what? Hired

someone more efficient to make the gondola crash? You always do hire other people to do your dirty work, don't you? Like Ray Beloit and Keith Jax. You don't do any of it yourself; you talk a lot and make threats, but you don't *do* anything. You're a little man, and a coward, and you hide behind people who are even littler than yourself."

Vince gave a strangled cry. His face was taut with rage, and he stood in a half crouch, prepared to leap. His breathing was loud and fast, with a faint whistle, as if his throat were too tight to let it through. Then, slowly, he straightened up, and his face twisted in what Anne knew he meant to be a smile.

At that moment, she thought he was probably at his most dangerous, and she knew Charles thought so, too, because he came to stand beside her. But she could not stop talking. Her own anger and pain were pouring out as she had never allowed anything to break out of the frozen depths within her, and as they did, her feelings began to awaken and break free. With her father beside her, with her family and Josh waiting for her, with the strength she had built within herself for so many years, she took her longest steps to being free.

"Except for one time," she said with icy contempt, "when you did your own dirty work. You were so brave, overwhelming a *child*, humiliating a *child*, vanquishing a *child*. You must be very proud to have that memory. It's amazing, the memories some people hold close; evil people treasure memories that would give most people nightmares and send them into hiding in shame and self-loathing. But not you; you have no shame; you love yourself for what you do. And you think no one can stop you, or even slow you down, because you're smarter than everyone else. But you're not smart, you're only sly. And that's why this family will beat you."

Vince was walking toward her. "Bitch," he said. "Bitch." It was as automatic as a chant. *"Bitch."* He walked stiffly, rigid with the effort not to leap at her and feel her throat between his hands. "All that talk, but there's no audience to hear your lies. You've been waiting for that, waiting for an audience, putting it off to make me worry when you'd start babbling to anybody who'd listen. All this other crap—murder, dynamite, the gondola—it doesn't mean a fucking thing; you just used it to get a hold on Charles. You're out to ruin me the way you tried before; that's all you care about. But who'd believe a cheap little lawyer against a U.S. senator? So you're lining up the family to be on your side, with this other shit. Listen, you bitch, what I did to you you had coming—"

Charles closed his eyes, cold and sick. He had believed Anne; he knew Vince had lied. But now it was Vince who was saying it, and Charles could hear Vince's voice threatening Anne, he could see Vince forcing her . . . He bent over; he thought he was going to throw up. I can't, he thought, can't look weak, can't let Anne down. He straightened up.

Vince was still talking. "—smart-ass kid. You weren't a *child*, for Christ's sake, you *went after me*, you *wanted* it. But you decided you didn't like it—cold bitch, Jesus were you cold—and you've been waiting to use it against me ever since, keeping track of me so you could choose your own time to try to destroy me."

Anne shook her head.

"Well, when?" The word tore from him. "When, you bitch? *When?*"

She shook her head again. "I told you I would not do that."

"But I would," Charles said abruptly.

Anne looked at him, alarm in her eyes.

Vince wheeled about to face him, his mouth working. "What the hell are you talking about?"

"I'd tell the world," Charles said. There was a sour taste in his mouth, but his voice was steady. "Whatever reasons Anne has for keeping quiet, they're hers, not mine, and they have nothing to do with me. And I think it's about time we stopped hiding it."

Anne was staring at him. He would not do that to her; she knew he wouldn't. But she could not tell for sure, from his face or his voice. She thought he must be bluffing, but if she could not be absolutely sure, neither could Vince. He was so good, she thought with pride. As good as Vince. Perhaps better.

Charles did not look at her, his eyes were steady on Vince.

"Bullshit," Vince said, but his voice was thin. "If she doesn't want it talked about, you wouldn't do it."

"I'd do it for me," Charles said. "My God, how could I sit back and see you elected president? How could I even let you have a shot at it?"

Vince felt as if the ground had shifted and something was sliding out from under him. He had never thought of this. "What the hell does politics have to do with this?" he shouted. "This family scores a lot of points because of me; you've got more status and clout than you ever had, because of me. The higher I go the better off you are. You'd be a damn fool to throw that away."

"I've been a damn fool about a lot of things, mainly you," Charles said. "I don't want your status and clout, Vince; so far all they've done is make trouble for me and my family. I don't want to score points because of you. What I do want is to keep you out of the White House. It's as simple as that. And I have ways of doing it. I'll go public with Anne's story; she can't stop me, and she'll learn to live with it. And I'll give the reporters the story of what you did to the highway and how you manipulated a decent little guy in the EPA so he'd hit Tamarack a lot harder than he had to. And I'll tell them everything we've put together about the contamination of the reservoir, and the gondola, including which car was targeted. Even the best newspapers never turn down sensational guesswork, you know; the best thing that ever happened to them was the word *alleged*. They don't even have to put it all together; their readers will do that, and put your name on it. You've been screwing this family for a long time, Vince; why shouldn't I make sure the world knows it?"

Everything was sliding away. Vince shook his head, trying to steady it.

Charles still had not looked at Anne, but he knew her eyes were steady on him, and he felt her strength. Never in his life had he done anything like this, or even thought of trying anything like this, and as he saw Vince weaken, he was astonished and exhilarated. We should never see anyone as a god, he thought; we give them far more power than they would ever have if we treated them like human beings.

He knew that what he was doing was flawed—it would be far better if he could get Vince out of the senate and out of public life entirely—but he thought it was the best he could do for now. He had no idea what Vince might do if everything was taken from him at once, leaving him no reason to be cautious. And Charles knew he could go only so far with his bluff. He would not force Anne to deal with her pain in public; he would do nothing to upset the balance she had created for herself. This is the best I can do, he thought. And then another thought came to him, a more cheering one. *He could lose the election this fall. And have nothing.*

"You wouldn't do it," Vince said shrewdly. He was studying Charles through narrowed eyes. "She just said she wasn't going to do it. She *just said* it. You haven't talked to her about it; you don't know what she wants. You wouldn't force her into it if she doesn't want it."

"I told you I would," Charles replied. He was very calm, but his exhilaration was growing. He knew he had won. "Anne will understand. And she'll find ways to deal with it. After all, she isn't the one who has something to be ashamed of."

"It's been twenty-five years," Vince said. "Nobody gives a damn."

"Then it won't matter. We'll find out."

Their eyes met, and for the first time in their lives, Vince was the one who looked away. His shoulders were slumped. He went to a nearby armchair and dropped into it. There was no sound in the room.

He sat in a slouch, his arms outstretched on the arms of the chair. The ground had stopped sliding away; everything seemed frozen in place. He knew he should be thinking of the future, of the steps he had to take in the days to come, but he could not. He could not focus on anything. But then he became aware of the silence in the room. It was as heavy as a blanket. He felt smothered by it. He had to cut it away; he couldn't breathe. He was about to be destroyed. Charles was about to destroy him. And Vince knew he would do it. He knew Charles better than anyone in the world, he had always seen through him, and he knew without a shadow of a doubt that Charles was not bluffing. Charles would do it.

Without warning, Vince thought of Beloit, admitting he would never be secretary of state or ambassador to Great Britain. *You get involved in things, you don't know what's gonna come back fifteen, twenty, thirty years later, and it's like you've been carrying this bomb around in your pocket all those years, and then all of a sudden you know it'll go off if you do one particular thing, and it's always the thing you fucking most want to do, only now there's no way you can do it. Ever. You know?*

So Vince had no choice.

"Those were only rumors, about the White House," he said. His voice was a monotone. "They kept asking me, but I never promised. I always felt I owed it to the people of Colorado to work for them. I told a reporter that, just the other day, that the voters need me, and I wouldn't let them down." His voice slowed, then dragged out. "It's a question —of—priorities."

No one spoke. Not enough, Vince thought. The son of a bitch wants more. His thoughts twisted this way and that, looking for a way out, but he could not see one. Money. For Christ's sake he'd be damned if he'd bail Charles out; if Charles wanted money, he could damn well go crawling to Beloit and try to put that deal together again.

Even the best newspapers never turn down sensational guesswork, you know . . . they don't even have to put it all together; their readers will do that, and put your name on it.

No place to hide. No place to hide. It beat within him. After a moment, he shrugged. Fuck it. Ethan had always said Vince knew better than anyone when to cut his losses. He'd find a way to get everything back; it would just take a while.

"The most important thing," he said at last, "is Chatham Development." He was looking past Charles and Anne, at the black expanse of his windows, with the bright lights of the harbor like small, scattered stars filling his vision. "We mustn't ever forget that. Dad's company." His voice dropped. "Sixty million dollars," he murmured. "I'm sure I could manage that."

The top portion shows faded, partially legible text bleeding through from another page.

chapter 22

This is truly the man of the decade!" exclaimed the host of the Sunday-night news show. "Folks, Senator Vince Chatham has made just about the greatest sacrifice a man ever made for his family, and believe you me, for those of us who believe in the sanctity of the family, nothing could be more thrilling!"

"I'm glad you think so," Vince said with a smile of such sweetness that the director told the cameraman to move in for a tight close-up. "It's thrilling for me that I'm able to do it."

"And we're grateful to you for coming in like this at a minute's notice," the host went on. "Let's tell our audience exactly what you've done, in case there's one or two people who haven't heard yet. This is it, folks: Senator Vince Chatham is giving his entire fortune to save his family! *Sixty million dollars* to keep one of his family's companies from going bankrupt, and to keep the other one out of the clutches of people who would have ruined it. We're going to talk about all of that tonight. Senator, first of all, that's quite a fortune. Where did the money come from?"

In his bedroom, dressing for his news conference, Vince watched himself on the program, which had been taped that afternoon, and smiled thinly. Not many people would have been so crude as to ask that, but if it hadn't been asked, he would have brought it up himself. People were always suspicious of anyone with $60 million and this had given him the chance to take care of that.

On the television screen, he lowered his eyes briefly. "I've been very fortunate. My father was one of the greatest builders this country has ever seen. He gave me my start. I wouldn't be here without his help and his confidence in me, and his love. He died last year, and not a day goes by that I don't thank him, and miss him. I had some money from him and I used it to start a company of my own in Denver, building shopping malls and office buildings. Denver is one of the greatest cities in the country—healthy, spacious, rich in resources, and even richer in its people, real achievers, like their pioneer ancestors—and I got there at what you'd call a boom time, and Denver was very good to me. I made a lot of money and invested it, mostly in Colorado, and now a lot of it is going to stay there."

"In Tamarack," the host said eagerly. "Now this part you folks out there may not know," he said to the camera. "Tamarack means glamour and glitter and celebrities to a lot of people, but lately it's been in a little trouble, and it looked like it might have to be sold. So the senator . . . well, Senator, you take it from here."

"There's not much to add, except that my family owns The Tamarack Company, and all of us love that town more than we can say. It's our true home; our spiritual home you might say. My father discovered it when it was a little ghost town hidden in the mountains, and he built it up to a place known all over the world. And The Tamarack Company, which my father founded, is deeply rooted in the life of the town and its people. But all companies have their ups and downs, and for a while now the company's had a series of problems that worried the family to the point that they thought they had no other choice than to sell."

"And then we know what would have happened," the host said, "but let's remind our audience. Folks, what the senator did was save that mountain town from the kind of development that environmentalists are fighting every day on our behalf. You tell 'em, Senator."

"Development of itself is not a bad thing," Vince corrected gently. "But it has to be controlled, because it's like a child whose eyes are bigger than its stomach. We should never pave over the land, or build on it, without the most careful study and for the best reasons. I opposed the sale of The Tamarack Company, and I gave the money to keep it in our family, because the people who wanted to buy it had no respect for the land or the history of the town. They wanted to cram it with high rises and parking structures; they wanted to build a four-lane highway the length of the valley, with overpasses and underpasses that would have increased pollution and destroyed the natural beauty that brought all of us there in the first place. They had no plan for protecting the elk and the birds and the purity of the streams; they had no concern for the children who live there, the families who thrive there, the values we all hold dear—"

"Senator," the butler said, standing in the doorway, "the reporters are downstairs."

Vince turned off the television set and walked through the living room, tightening his tie. Clara was still in Denver. He had told her to stay there; everything was under control. She might have stood at his side for the press conference, but it was not necessary. Not yet. The man of the decade. Well, why not? There would be many ways to use that. And that was when he would want Clara at his side.

He paused at the door to the conference room on the lower level of his building, counting the reporters sitting on folding chairs, waiting for him. He had expected a hundred; he'd gotten about thirty. Someone hadn't done his job. Mentally Vince reviewed the members of his staff to think of who it might have been. He'd told them how he wanted this pushed, blown up far beyond what would otherwise have been a nice little story no bigger than the stories about someone's donation of a private art collection or the funding of a new hospital. It had been easy with television talk shows; this was the kind of human interest story they hungered for, and a few phone calls and letters had put him on screens all over the country. But the press was tougher; he'd have to work on making sure the press gave him the kind of coverage he wanted.

He stood behind a podium on a small raised platform at one end of the room and glowed like a benevolent preacher as camera flashes burst around him like fireworks. "What can I tell you that you don't already know?"

"What are you going to live on now?" someone called.

There was laughter, but Vince answered seriously, "I have a little of my own money left."

"How much?"

"What's your salary?" Vince shot back. The room filled with laughter again; he saw them all smile at him, admiring him, and he knew that most of them envied him. It was a lie; he had millions still hidden in real estate and land trusts, but no one would know that. "A little," he repeated firmly, "and my salary as a senator. And if my family wants to take care of me in my old age"—he chuckled—"I may not be in a position to say no. But we're a family. We'll always help each other; we'll always be part of each other. That's what this is all about."

At the back of the room, Vince saw a rapt face, heart shaped, framed by short blond hair. Sara, he thought. Her green eyes watched him worshipfully. Little Sara—what was her last name?—from the *Rocky Mountain News*. Come all the way from Denver, to see him.

"Senator," a reporter said, "there's a problem with taxes here that nobody's talked about yet. Your office said you were *giving* your family this sixty million dollars. You're not really doing that, are you?"

"Not literally," Vince said with a smile. "You're absolutely right; if I handed that money to my brother, who's president of Chatham Development, he'd have to pay gift tax; if I gave it to the company, they'd owe corporate tax. In either case it would run about fifty percent. Now you know I'm not in the business of taking revenue away from my government, but if I clean out my bank account to help my family, I want them to be able to use every penny of it. So it won't be an outright gift. My brother and the company lawyers have worked it out that they're creating a special category of preferred stock in Chatham Development Corporation, and selling it to me for sixty million dollars. The stock has no voting rights, it doesn't pay dividends, it won't appreciate in value, and I can't sell or transfer it without the approval of the Chatham Development Board. In my vocabulary, that's a gift."

"Not bad," a reporter said approvingly. "Must have been hard to give all that up, though. No rights at all in sixty million dollars' worth of stock?"

"We don't ask for rights when we give gifts, unless they come with strings," Vince said softly. "I don't attach strings where my family is concerned."

"Hearts and flowers," muttered a reporter to her neighbor. "Do you really believe all this?"

"Senator, what happened to Chatham Development?" someone asked. "Your father started it, right? And it was one of the Fortune 500—"

"Yes, and it will be again. All companies have their ups and downs; Chatham Development will be up there at the top again, where it belongs."

"Right, you said the same thing about The Tamarack Company, but what *happened?*"

"Well, I'm afraid I'm going to have to disappoint you on that question; I'm just not going into it. When companies run into trouble, a lot of factors are at work: management, customers, supplies, the economy, even the United States government, with all its regulations. It's not helpful to single out any one of those; it's all in the past, and now that they've got the money, they're going to come back and be a fine, strong company again. They've promised me that and I believe them."

"A little too nice," a reporter murmured to the cameraman next to him. "What do you want to bet we're hearing about a tenth of the real story?"

"But what do you think about the management up there?" someone else asked. "Isn't it true that when a company gets in trouble, the first thing you do is look at management? Could you talk about that a little more?"

"Absolutely not," Vince said firmly.

"Well, could you tell us something about the buyer? Who was it? In an article in yesterday's *New York Times* you were quoted on all the things that would have happened to the town if the company'd been sold, but you didn't say who was going to buy it. Who was it?"

"Various investors were interested, from as far away as Egypt," Vince said, "but since nothing came of any of those offers, I don't think it would be appropriate for me to name them. After all," he chuckled, "I've been a little harsh in my criticism of them."

"Was it anybody you knew?"

Vince hesitated. "Some of them." He smiled. "I won't be spending much time with them anymore."

"Senator, can't you give us some names?"

"Not if I can help it." He was still smiling. "The curse of the politician is he has to keep his mouth shut. Especially around you people."

He watched them laugh again. "How about the White House?" someone asked. "Anything to tell us about that, Senator?"

"Well, yes." Vince watched them lean forward on a collective breath. He gave them a boyish smile, but behind the podium rage was locked inside him, the rage he woke with each day and went to bed with each night so that it was becoming a permanent part of him. But the only one who caught a glimpse of it was Sara, who looked puzzled. "I've been honored by the number of people—top-notch, patriotic people—who've urged me to run for president. And because they've been people I admire and respect, I've given the idea serious thought. As you know, we even commissioned a couple of polls that turned out to be very favorable. But I've decided I am not going to run."

The room burst into activity. Cameras began flashing again, reporters sat straight. "How come, Senator?" "What happened?" "Are you going to—" "What will you—" "Just a week ago you—" "Did the president have anything to do with—"

"If you'll let me," Vince said, his voice riding over the uproar. His hand was raised, and the questions died away. "The people of Colorado, the best people in the world when you come right down to it, sent me here to do a job for them and I promised them I'd do it as completely as I could. I like doing it, and I think they like what I'm doing. So I'm staying right here, in the Senate. That is, if they tell me I can, in November. If they don't, I'll go back to being a builder, nothing to be ashamed of, but not as satisfying as working for the good of one's state and one's country. So, if it's all right with the voters of that great state, you'll see me here for a long time. That's all I'm going to say about it. Are there any more questions about the gift to my family?"

"Senator, have you talked to the president? Did he have anything to do with——"

"I said I wouldn't talk about that."

"But Senator, that last poll, candidates would give their eye teeth for a poll like——"

Vince shook his head. His rage pulsed inside him.

"Senator, couldn't you tell us what changed your mind? You knew you were representing the people of Colorado last week, too, but there was still a lot of talk about the White House from some of your staff."

"They hadn't cleared that with me," Vince said. "Sara," he said as her hand went up.

Her voice was small but clear. "Did your family ask you to give up the idea?"

"*What?* Sara, I'll say it once more: I won't talk about my decision. I will say that no one in my family would ask such a thing; they trust me at least as much as the voters of Colorado do." A low ripple of laughter met his chuckle. "And I trust them, which is why I'm making a gift of sixty million dollars to get them back on their feet."

"Well, okay, let's go back to that," another reporter said. "How do you feel about being without that money? You'll have to change your whole lifestyle, won't you?"

Vince answered with a humorous anecdote about his father teaching him to be self-reliant when he was a boy by taking him hunting in Tamarack. He had never hunted, and neither had Ethan, but the reporters wrote it down; it was good human interest. He answered their questions for exactly thirty minutes, then turned toward the door. "Come on, now, that's enough. I can't talk about myself anymore.

Unless you want to ask me about my committee work, or the bills I'm sponsoring."

"But this is a tough act for anybody else to follow, Senator. If you change your mind about the White House, you'd have a head start it'd be tough to beat."

"I didn't do it to have a head start on anything. I did it because my family needed help and thank God I was able to give it. That's what makes me feel good right now. Though I confess I never object to a friendly press." He smiled as they laughed appreciatively, and then he stood on the platform as if in a halo of sunlight, watching them leave. It was his greatest triumph, and he wore it like a crown while rage gnawed inside him and the glittering image of the White House mocked him from a distance, like the lights of the harbor he had seen through his window and mistakenly thought of as stars.

Some of the reporters came to him on their way out of the room, and he stepped down from the platform and shook their hands. "Good to see you," he said to them. "I look forward to seeing a lot of you between now and November."

"I hope you change your mind about the White House," said the last reporter, a columnist for the *Denver Post*. "We need men like you. One thing: you're a sure thing for reelection this fall; everybody knows it."

Then they were all gone. All except Sara. She stood at the back of the room, clasping her notebook, her eyes fastened on Vince.

"Hello," Vince said warmly. "I'm glad to see you again. Did the *Rocky Mountain News* transfer you to Washington?"

"No, I wish they would. I came on my own, Senator. I couldn't believe anybody would do such a wonderful thing; you know how everybody talks about greed and selfishness, and then I read about you, and you remember, you talked to me in Denver a couple of weeks ago—"

"I remember. I said I enjoyed our interview."

She flushed. "I'm sorry about that question I asked; I didn't know it would upset you."

"It didn't upset me," Vince said gently. "I was just surprised. What made you ask it?"

"Well, all these things about your family; I was just wondering . . . Could I ask you a couple of things?"

"Of course you can," Vince said, and they sat together on folding chairs.

Sara turned to a fresh page of her notebook. "If your family asks for help, would you be giving them advice or even going back, someday, and working with them again?"

"No," Vince said sharply. Then he softened it. "Senators don't get involved in business, Sara; not even with their own family."

"Well, yes, I know, but someday you might want to go back to them, mightn't you? I mean, after you sold your interest in Chatham Development before you went to Denver—"

Vince frowned. "How did you know that?"

"It was in one of the old *Rocky Mountain News* issues, from when you started Lake Forest Development and built your first shopping mall. I went back and read them all. Your partner told a reporter that you'd gotten your start in Chicago and then sold your shares back to your family because you wanted to build your own company. I thought it was wonderful that you'd make it on your own, and I just thought, now that you'd done this incredible thing for your family, they'd want you back, and maybe they asked you not to run for president."

Vince shook his head gently. "First of all, Sara, I never really left them. And when I gave them the money, I told them it was theirs, just as the companies were theirs, and that my place was here, in the Senate."

"And you weren't angry about that?"

"Angry?" Vince looked at her closely. "Why would you think I was angry?"

"Well, I could be wrong; but you were making a fist and . . . I'm sorry, it sounds silly; forget I said anything."

"No, I want to hear it," Vince said. "I was making a fist and what else?"

"Your face was . . . tight. Like you were gritting your teeth."

"Well." Vince smiled. "You're an observant young lady. You'll be a great reporter if you keep that up. You're right, Sara, I was gritting my teeth, but it wasn't anger. I still get nervous in front of a crowd—talk about being silly, that beats yours any day—and it was worse than usual tonight because I don't like people to treat me like some kind of saint. Most people help their families, but with smaller amounts of money, so no one pays much attention. I was uncomfortable, being singled out as somebody special; that's what you saw. I thought I was hiding it pretty well; I'm going to have to be careful around you."

Sara flushed again. "Thank you," she said. "I appreciate your honesty."

"And I appreciate yours." Vince gazed into Sara's ardent eyes and felt a surge of desire. Such a sweet child, lovely and worshipful. Her skin had a purity that matched the softness of her lips; her breasts were small and her shoulders were slightly rounded, as if she were leaning toward him. She could be much more than the pleasant diversion he had imagined when they first met; she could be his little friend, his pupil, his playmate. His. Always waiting for him, waiting to please him. Sara would be his relaxation, the only thing he could be sure of in a world that suddenly was full of snares.

And she was a reporter. She could be his mouthpiece; she could help him build up the foundation of the family he had begun tonight. *I hope you change your mind about the White House, Senator; we need men like you.* With Sara, he might find his way back to that path; with a loving Sara poised to do whatever he wanted, anxious to do what would make him happiest, he could do almost anything.

Vince looked at his watch. "You know," he said thoughtfully, "I'm supposed to go to some fancy dinner party tonight, but I need some quiet time after all this hoopla. Would you have dinner with me, Sara?"

"Oh. Yes, I'd love . . . But your wife . . ."

"She's in Denver. She spends a fair bit of time there; her

family likes it. And we all know that families come first." He stood and held out his hand, smiling into her bright eyes, smiling past his rage. "I'll take you to one of my favorite little places where nobody will pay any attention to—"

"Hi, Vince, they told me you were here," said Keith, and gave a little salute as he walked in. His gaze settled on Sara. He held out his hand. "Keith Jax. I hope I didn't interrupt anything. I'm Uncle Vince's nephew."

"Oh," said Sara. Her face showed her confusion as she shook hands with him, wanting to interview him to find out more about Vince, but wanting even more to have dinner with Vince, just the two of them, in one of his favorite little places. She hoped Vince would not invite Keith to join them, and she glanced at him to see what he was going to do.

Vince's face was impassive. "I've been calling you for the last five days."

"I wasn't there." Keith grinned. "But I guess you already know that. I thought it would be fun to drive here, you know, like see America first. God, it's a hell of a lot of driving, though. I mean, I didn't know it was so goddam far from Tamarack to here."

"You're from Tamarack?" Sara asked.

"Sara," Vince said. He put his hand under her elbow and walked her a few feet away, his voice low. "Would you wait for me upstairs in the lobby? I should talk to Keith for a few minutes; then we'll have our dinner. I'm sorry for this, but he's driven all this way and I can't ignore him."

"Of course," Sara said. She looked at Vince's face, hoping to learn more. "He seems very happy to be here. He must like you very much."

"I hope so." Vince gave her the tiniest nudge toward the door. "I'll meet you upstairs in a few minutes."

He watched her leave, then turned back to Keith. "What the hell do you mean, taking off without telling me? When I call you, I expect to find you there."

"Well, I'm sorry about that, Uncle Vince. I mean I got the idea, you know, in a hurry and I just like took off."

"Well, you'll turn around and go back in a hurry. Tomorrow." Vince took out his keys. "I'll call my doorman and tell him to let you in. I'll see you at breakfast; I want to talk to you before you leave."

"It's okay if I stay there? I mean, you don't want the place to yourself for the, you know, little lady? No, you wouldn't; you're too smart for that. I mean, it's a lot like safer to go to her place."

"Keep your mouth shut," Vince snapped. "And make sure you're up early tomorrow; we'll have breakfast at six-thirty. You'll leave right after that."

"No, see, you don't get it, Uncle Vince. I'm not going back. I mean I'm like *here*. I've got Eve in the car, and all our, you know, luggage. Everything. I'm going to work for you, you know, do everything you need me to do, like your, you know, chief assistant, the way we talked about, remember? I'm the one who does a lot of the work, but the newspapers don't know anything about me. I mean I'm not trying to be, you know, famous or anything, you're the one who's into that, you're like terrific at it; I just want to be, you know, part of everything, helping the people of Colorado, and kind of like . . . indispensable."

Once again, Vince felt as if the ground were sliding out from under him. The terrible feeling that he was losing control, the worst feeling he knew, settled over him. "What did you tell them?" he asked harshly.

Keith looked surprised. "Who?"

"Leo. Charles. Anne."

"Charles? When? I mean, I haven't seen him since Christmas. Anne and Leo came to my office with a lot of bullshit questions about, you know, dynamite above the drainage ditch, and the gondola crash, but I just like listened; I didn't say a thing. Oh, yeah, I did; I said I was in bed with Eve the morning of the, you know, crash, and we were like having a good time and she'd, you know, remember it."

"That's all you said?"

"Well, sure. I mean, I'm not *dumb*, Vince. If I was, you wouldn't want me for your assistant. See, I know what you need, Vince. You need people like me. I mean, you talk a lot about who's in your way and what you'll do about it, who you'll get rid of, you know, but you never do. You know? I mean, you don't have the guts, Vince. You talk big, but that's all it is. So it's a good thing I'm around, right? And I'm going to be around forever, so you don't have to worry; you won't ever lose me." He jingled the keys in his hand. "We won't stay in your place long; I mean, we don't want to be any trouble; we'll find a place of our own like right away. Oh, we might need a, you know, down payment to buy something, you know, just a loan, but that's all. I'll be earning a good salary, so I can like pay you back and we won't be a, you know, burden or anything on you. More like partners. You know."

Vince was silent, his thoughts racing. He'd known he would have to deal with Keith; he'd just been too busy to think about it. And now he was here, and he thought he'd be staying forever. The stupid ass; of course he wouldn't stay forever. Vince would get rid of him when it suited him. I'll use him for a while, Vince thought; but if he thinks he's going to stick to me for the rest of my life, he's a fool. Nobody blackmails me; it's just a matter of choosing the best time to act. Stupid ass; he doesn't know what I can do. No one knows yet what I can do.

He looked past Keith as if he did not exist. I'll take care of him when it's the right time. I'll take care of anyone who gets in my way. And Sara will be on my side. Sara will help me get everything back.

"Well," Keith said when Vince was silent, "I'll go tell Eve we're all set; she was like worried that everything wouldn't be okay. I told her it would, but you know how women worry. I told her we didn't have anything to worry about, ever again. I mean, this is going to be great, Vince, you know? You and me. Whatever you need, I'll do it. You can count on me. You've got me, Vince. Forever."

Just outside the room, Sara heard Vince walking toward the door, and scurried upstairs. She was very excited, and sad, too. She felt a deep sense of loss that Vince Chatham wasn't what she had thought he was. Of course that could be because he didn't like his nephew, but Sara thought it was more than that; she thought she'd heard more about the real

Vince Chatham in the last twenty minutes than in all of his press conferences, and their interview in Denver, and the hundreds of newspaper articles she'd read. That was what excited her: everything was more than it seemed.

How fascinating, thought the reporter within Sara, alert, puzzled, intensely curious. She was so excited she had to order herself to calm down before Vince came to fetch her for dinner. She didn't know exactly what she had in all the fascinating tidbits and hints she'd heard, but it looked as if there might be a story here a lot more complicated than a senator's giving $60 million to his family because he was generous and loved them.

Or maybe it's more than one story, Sara thought; maybe there's a whole series of stories. Maybe even one of those investigative books reporters are always writing. It could take months, maybe even years, to track down everything about the senator and his family. She didn't even know what she was looking for, but that was all right; one thing always led to another in these investigations. And it didn't matter how long it took, either; she had lots of time. And one thing her boss had always complimented her on: she had lots and lots of patience.

She took a small mirror from her purse and put on fresh lipstick and combed her hair. This could be my future, she thought, and folded her hands neatly in her lap, to wait for Vince.

chapter 23

Josh was waiting at the Luxor Airport when Anne's plane landed. "I'm so glad you're here," he said, holding both her hands. "It's been a long three weeks."

"Very long," Anne said. As busy as she had been in Los Angeles, catching up on her work and trying to get ahead so she could make this trip, she had found herself looking up from her desk, gazing out the window, wanting to be with him. And there had been a leap of gladness within her when she saw him waiting for her as she walked toward him from the plane. It might partly have been the strangeness of the place, she thought, looking about her at the dingy airport. It was a small, one-story building with everything squeezed into one room: tourists milling about their guides, businessmen in suits and ties, some wearing turbans, soldiers in rumpled uniforms, security guards, languid airport workers, and foreign visitors who knew their way around and walked briskly to the exit. Anne looked at Josh, tall, confident, with strong features that no longer, ever, seemed harsh to her, and knew it was not just the strangeness of the place. "I'm glad to be here," she said.

Josh took her carry-on bag and the garment bag she carried over one shoulder. "How much more luggage do you have?"

"None." She smiled at his raised eyebrows. "You told me it would be casual."

589

"So I did." He smiled. "I like the way you travel. It's the same way I do; it simplifies everything."

They walked past the crowds impatiently waiting for baggage to be unloaded, and walked to Josh's car. "Not much to see this late at night," he said. "We'll have a daytime tour whenever you want."

"After we go to the tomb," Anne said. "I brought your letters and pictures; it's hard to believe I'm really going to walk through it. It's hard to believe I'm here at all." She gazed through the window at the scattered lights, feeling a strange kind of calm excitement. Until now, she had always traveled alone, entering each new city with her own eagerness and her own agenda, and she had been filled with doubts as she flew to meet Josh. But his letters were in her shoulder bag, and she had reread them as she changed planes in London, and then Cairo, and finally reached Luxor. He had been called back to Egypt the day after she went to Chicago to see Charles, and since then he had written every day, warm, friendly, noncommittal letters spilling over with enthusiasm for what the tomb was revealing as it was slowly being cleared. And each time he had urged her to come to Luxor and be a part of his adventure, she found fewer reasons to say no.

And now that she was here, driving down the dimly lit street lined with hotels on one side and docked tour boats on the other, she felt the excitement of being in a place unlike any she had visited in Europe, and of sharing Josh's great find, still being written about in newspapers all over the world. Sitting beside him, she felt calm and unafraid, and filled with anticipation.

"The Winter Palace," Josh said, pulling up at a square building flush with the sidewalk. "We can get dinner in one of the cafés around here if you're hungry."

"I'm not, thank you. The steward on the plane from London recommended a restaurant in Cairo, and I had so much time between planes I had dinner there."

"Which restaurant?"

"Mahfoud."

"One of my favorites." He smiled ruefully. "I imagined

myself leading you by the hand through the strange, murky streets of Egyptian cities. You seem to do very well on your own."

"I've done it for a long time," she said, her voice suddenly cool. She stepped out of the car and waited while Josh took her bags from the backseat. They walked into the lobby of the hotel, and Anne filled out the registration form the manager gave her. "Do we leave early in the morning?"

"Seven, if that's all right. Breakfast at six-thirty."

"Fine." She handed the form back to the manager with her passport and credit card.

"We're delighted to have you with us, Madame," he said in flawless English, showing none of his curiosity, and handed her a key. "Your room overlooks the Nile. I trust you'll be comfortable."

"Thank you." She turned to Josh. "Could we have coffee? I'm really not hungry, and I haven't slept since yesterday sometime, but I can't bear to shut myself into a hotel room, at least not yet."

"Good idea," he said. He asked the manager to take Anne's luggage to her room, and they went out again into the soft night air.

"Oh, is this all right?" Anne asked, looking down at her light wool pants. "I brought a skirt, if I need it."

"You're fine," Josh said. She wore, with her dark gray pants, a pale gray silk blouse, open at the neck to reveal a silver necklace, and a red leather blazer. After fourteen hours in three airplanes, her clothes were unwrinkled, and she had none of the pasty look of fatigue so many travelers have when flying halfway around the world. "In fact, you're perfect. Sometimes there's a problem here if women wear very short skirts or very low necklines, or shorts, but even that's fading away; they need tourist dollars too much to alienate anyone who comes. You'd be amused at how many of their concerns sound like Tamarack's."

They walked away from the hotel, past men drinking coffee in tiny outdoor cafés of three or four tables, and groups of men sitting cross-legged on the sidewalk, talking animatedly and smoking water pipes. A child came up to them, her hand out, fingers rubbing together. "Baksheesh," she said. She was very pretty, with a colorful scarf over her head, a long flowered skirt, and Nike running shoes. She kept pace with Josh and Anne, bumping into them, her hand out. Nearby, her mother, swathed in black, watched somberly. "Baksheesh," said the little girl. "Baksheesh."

"No," Josh said.

"Baksheesh," the child said as if he had not spoken. Her eyes were blank, looking at them but not seeing them.

Josh looked down. *"No,"* he said. It was the voice a parent uses to a child. The little girl turned away without a sign of disappointment, and crossed the street, looking for someone else to accost. Her mother followed.

"I could have given her something," Anne said.

"So could I," Josh replied. "And then fifty of them would have been all over us. And tomorrow another fifty and then another and another. They're bright and funny, with a lot of charm, and they do pretty well with the tourists. The first time I came here I emptied my wallet the first day. After that I learned how to say no. Let's walk through the market."

They walked up a short alley and suddenly were plunged into the noises and smells of the market, just closing for the night. Vendors on both sides of the narrow street were moving their wares into minuscule sheds that could be locked up: barrels of spices, bolts of fabric, blouses and *gebalas* hanging from racks, tightly rolled carpets, displays of scarab paperweights and small carved pharaohs to sell to tourists. Others were preparing to push huge carts out of the market area with what was left of the day's fruits and vegetables, while the bakers were putting out the fires in their ovens and closing up their small shops. Children in the uniforms of their schools walked hand in hand, whispering and giggling; women swathed in black or dark purple did the last of their shopping, balancing on their heads high woven baskets or plastic laundry baskets; tourists took pictures, posing beside a donkey or a table of cone-shaped piles of herbs that had not yet been put away.

Anne looked from side to side, enjoying the color, the lyrical rhythms of Arabic, the high voices of the children, the smells of spices and coffee, breads and ripe fruit, wool and dust, and woven through it all, the clip-clop of horses pulling open buggies along nearby streets and the incessant punctuation of horn-blowing from drivers who enjoyed the din and would feel inferior without contributing to it.

"Let's cross here," Josh said. He took her hand. "Stay close; crossing streets is an art around here." They waited until a break came in the stream of cars with headlights off and horns blowing, and dodged between two of them and an aggressive horse-drawn buggy, to the corniche on the other side. "Nimble feet and a casual attitude toward a long life will get you across any street in Egypt," Josh said. "Though Luxor is a breeze compared to Cairo."

"And Rome," Anne said, and they smiled together.

It was quieter now; they were on the broad corniche that ran the length of town beside the Nile. Anne contemplated the dozens of boats docked stem to stern beside them. "Are there always so many?" she asked.

"Not in the summer when it gets too hot for most tourists, but in the winter they're all out, almost two hundred of them up and down the Nile. I can remember when there were only four, just a few years ago."

Voices in several languages carried in the still air from the top decks of the boats where men in dark suits and women in silk dresses sat at tables with drinks and coffee. From some of the boats, music came: a French chanteuse, a German band, an Italian tenor, an American folk singer, blending with the Arabic of the town. It seemed to Anne that she and Josh were completely alone: two Americans in Luxor, Egypt, in mid-February, separate from the tourists on their boats, separate from the market, separate from the culture through which they walked. It was as if the two of them were in a small magic circle that kept them apart from everything else.

"Down here," Josh said as they came to a stone stairway. The steps led to the riverbank and the tour boats, but on a broad landing halfway down was an outdoor café with blaring Arabic music and the pungent smell of Turkish coffee. "I took you at your word," he said. "This is a *gahwah;* they only serve coffee. If you change your mind, there's a good place farther down where we can get dinner, but no coffee. We'd come back here for that."

"No, this is fine; I like it," Anne said. She sat on one side of the café, at a small round table with a checkered cloth, and studied the lively groups of men at other tables gesticulating as they talked, while Josh went for their coffees. He brought the cups to the table and sat beside Anne, pulling his chair close to hers so they could hear each other beneath the wail of the singer.

"This is a new feeling," he said. "Usually when I wander around Luxor, I'm with locals and they're like camouflage. But here we are, two people so obviously American we couldn't be missed by anyone, and wherever we go, we're separate; not even part of the Americans on that boat next to us. They've got their boat and their guide and their group; we've got our feet, a car, and each other. I've felt close to you for a long time, but this is different, as if we're on our own island, and no one can really touch us. Do you feel that?"

Anne felt a rush of pure happiness. She wanted to touch Josh, to put her hand on his and thank him for being with her and seeing the world as she did. But she could not do it; her hand stayed in her lap. "I was thinking the same thing on the corniche," she said. "A magic circle."

He smiled. "I like that better than an island."

The smells of strong coffee, tobacco, and sweet fumes from water pipes curled around them; music pounded over them. It wove in and out of the waves of sleepiness that swept over Anne, then receded, then returned. She sipped her coffee. "Shall I tell you what's been happening since my last letter? It seems so far away it's like trying to remember a book I read a long time ago, but I could try."

"Yes, tell me," Josh said. "Then we'll forget it, at least for as long as we're here."

"I'd like that," she said. "I'd like to forget a lot that's happened since Christmas." She paused. "You know about the newspaper stories on Vince."

"Only the one you sent me from the *LA Times*. I assume it was all over the country."

She nodded. "And on television." She shook her head. "It never occurred to us that he'd turn it into one of his greatest triumphs."

"But it doesn't make any difference to the family, does it?" Josh asked. "If he was responsible for even half of what we think he did, it might have been satisfying to see him grovel, but we don't have enough to convict him of anything, so isn't the most important thing that Charles has the money, and the family still has Tamarack?"

There was a pause. "Yes," Anne said. "I'd rather he wasn't in the Senate, but—"

"But that isn't what you were thinking of," Josh said.

"No. He's evil. And it's terrible to see an evil person always come out on top, always finding ways to turn whatever he does to his own advantage, no matter how awful it was."

Josh did not ask her why she said "always." He thought he could guess, but he could not tell her that, or comfort her for the anguish in her voice; he could not say anything until she confided in him. Instead he asked casually, "But he didn't come out on top, did he? He's lost his fortune and any chance at being president, and I thought those were the two things he cared about the most."

Anne nodded. "Of course," she said quietly. Her voice was almost drowned out by the music. She sipped some of her coffee. "Let's see, what else has been happening? Charles has interviewed a few people for vice president of Chatham Development; he won't try to get rid of Fred, but he says he wants a powerful counterweight to him. I think if he can have one successful project, he'll retire. And then I think he'll move to Tamarack. Not because he wants to be Ethan Chatham, but because he has a family there and he really doesn't have anything left in Chicago. What else? I wrote you that the Tramway Board closed its investigation with a finding of sabotage, but no finding of guilt. Nobody liked that, but there wasn't anything else they could do. Tyler is keeping the investigation open, but no one has much hope of finding the person who caused it. The best part was that Halloran wrote a separate report commending the company for what he said was a thorough, highly professional maintenance program that wouldn't have failed if it hadn't been sabotaged. Leo is using that in a series of new ads; he's hoping to salvage the rest of the season. I think he will; Gail said a couple of days ago that the resort association was already getting calls for reservations."

"And Robin and Ned aren't worried about leaving Tamarack," Josh said.

"No." Anne smiled. "They're planning a celebration for whenever we come back. They're very excited; it seems that the town thinks it's because of Leo that they won't have high rises and neon signs, so all the Calders are heroes, and at school that means Ned and Robin. So, no more fights to prove they belong there." She paused, remembering Robin clinging to her the last night she was there. "Robin told me that ever since I came back, her family's gotten bigger. They all used to be visitors, she said, and now they come more often and stay longer. As if"—Anne's voice dropped and Josh leaned closer to hear her—"everybody belongs."

"She's right," Josh said. "They used to avoid each other. They didn't know how to be a family; they needed someone to hold them together. Ethan did that, when he was alive. And now it's you."

"And Tamarack," Anne said. "I think they feel now, after we almost lost it, that it's home, and a place to be at peace."

They sat quietly for a moment. Nothing seemed farther from the dust of ancient Egypt than Tamarack, nestled beneath glistening snow and a crisp blue sky, but they both could envision it. A place to be at peace. Their eyes met. There were many places to be at peace.

"More coffee?" Josh asked casually. His heart was pounding. He felt everything he cared for and wanted was in this crowded, vibrant town, and everything he had ever longed for was coming together in a way he could not have dreamed only a short time ago. Seven months, he thought. From August, when I first sat in Anne's office, to this night, when we sit here, in a magic circle.

"Yes, please," Anne said. She sat very still, as if afraid to break a spell.

He brought two more cups to the table and sat beside her, his arm just touching hers. "Have we finished with the news, or did anything else happen?"

"Keith is gone," Anne replied. "He left a note on Leo's desk about two weeks ago, saying he wanted to see more of the world, and he thought Leo had lost faith in him. I don't believe a word of it; I'd guess he's gone to Vince, to ask for a job in Washington, and I'll bet he gets it; they probably have something on each other. Leo is glad he's gone, though he felt guilty when he told Marian; she liked the idea of his working there."

"Marian sees Keith about as clearly as she sees Fred," Josh mused. "It seems she's come to terms with both of them, and with staying where she is. It's like William with his letter writing that never gets results, and Nina with her various husbands; people make patterns for themselves and get comfortable in them, and it takes a lot to make them move. Charles was the one who changed course; from what you told me, I've never heard of anyone breaking free of a way of life the way he did, with Vince."

Anne was silent. She felt Josh's arm against hers. My father and I, she thought, breaking free of a way of life. But she knew she would not really be free until she told Josh about her past. If she had ever seriously thought she could avoid it and still discover what they might be together, she knew now that she could not. I have to let him share it with me, she thought, the same way he wants me to share his work. To share it all. The bad and the good. But immediately a wave of sleepiness swept over her, and she felt her eyes closing. *Tomorrow. Or the next day. There's plenty of time.*

"That's enough; you've got to get some sleep," said Josh decisively. "We can put off the tomb for a day if you don't want to get up early."

"No, I want to do it tomorrow. Starting with breakfast at six-thirty. I've enjoyed this, Josh. What a good way to feel like part of a strange town, sitting in a café and drinking coffee with the locals."

"And their music," Josh said. And they laughed as a clash of cymbals split the air around them.

That was what Anne was thinking about when she slipped into bed in her hotel room: their shared laughter. Good night, Josh, she said silently, as she had said to him in the elevator. *Sleep well,* said his voice in her thoughts, as he had said as she went to her room. *We'll have a wonderful day tomorrow.*

I had a wonderful day tonight, she thought, and smiled.

Around the tomb, it seemed as if a small town had sprung to life. The barren valley, stretching narrowly between brown hills, was crowded with trucks and cars, folding tables and chairs, packing crates, piles of tools, flashlights and high-powered torches, sections of scaffolding, boxes of food and bottled water, armed Egyptian soldiers, workers, journalists and photographers, archaeologists, apprentices, government officials, and a small group of privileged visitors. They all moved about in a haze of dust beneath a blinding sun. Anne remembered the slides Josh had shown her of the valley, silent and still, as desolate as if it were at the end of the world, and she could not believe it was the same place.

"I would have liked you to see it when we first came here," Josh said, watching her take in the crowded scene. "But to tell you the truth, I have a feeling this is how the place looked when the pharaohs lived and died. There were always workers digging new tombs, and artists painting and chiseling them, and other workers loading them with the treasures and everyday things the pharaoh would need in the afterlife. And they worked two or three shifts, so there were always people coming and going. I don't know if the valley ever was empty for more than short periods of time until the pharaohs were gone. And by then, even before that, in fact, the tomb robbers were at work. Shall we go inside?"

They began the long descent down the rough stone steps. Workers had built a crude handrail along one side, but Anne wanted to go into the tomb as Josh had the first time and she did not use it. Lights had been strung above, casting blunt shadows on the stone, making it look to Anne as if she were burrowing into the center of the earth. So, when Josh stood aside at the entrance to the first room and she went in before him, she stopped abruptly in pure astonishment.

The room was a blaze of color: huge lights illuminating brilliant, pristine colors that had been preserved by dry air and total darkness. Surrounded by that riot of color and design, Anne no longer heard the chatter of people in the other rooms. It was as if she and Josh were alone, and suspended in time. Rolling up their shirtsleeves in the oppressive heat, drinking the bottled water Josh had brought, they walked slowly along the walls and into adjoining rooms, their heads tipped back, gazing at the life-size and miniature figures. As they strolled and stopped and strolled again, Josh told Anne the stories behind the scenes, and the stories of the treasures stacked along the walls and others still tumbled about as they had been found. His was the only voice she heard; the grandeur of the tomb seemed to belong to him. He had found it and opened it to the world, and he talked about it as if it were a book of family photographs.

"We photograph each item," Josh said, "write a description of it, give it a catalog number, wrap it and put it in a packing crate, and then haul it out of here and truck it to boats on the Nile that take it to the Egyptian Museum in Cairo. Each one of them is priceless, of course, which is why you see part of the Egyptian army patrolling the valley."

"Have you any idea how many objects there are?" Anne asked.

"Not yet. At a guess, close to ten thousand."

Anne tried to imagine documenting and moving out that many objects, from tiny carved figures to full-size thrones heavy with jewels and gold leaf. Josh had said it would take months, perhaps a year. She wondered how much of that time he would be in Egypt.

They came to the last room, with the enormous stone sarcophagus in the center still awaiting the scaffolding and hoist that were necessary to lift its stone lid so workers could remove the pharaoh's mummy. Suddenly, Anne felt dizzy from the heat. "Just a minute," she said, and leaned against the wall, her eyes closed.

"My God, I'm sorry," Josh said contritely. He took her arm and led her to a stone ledge along one wall. "Sit here; drink a lot more water. We'll leave as soon as you're ready. I am sorry; I get carried away and I forget that other people aren't used to this." He was angry with himself, and Anne heard it in his voice.

"I could have asked you to slow down," she said, smiling at him. "But I didn't want to. I've never seen anything so magnificent."

Josh sat beside her. "There really is nothing like it, anywhere. But we could have divided it up into two or three days."

"No, this was the best way." Anne looked about the square room. There were fewer pictures here; the ceiling was filled with gold stars on a blue background, and the walls were covered with hieroglyphics: column after column of prayers from *The Book of the Dead*. "I wanted to feel swallowed up by it," she said. "I wanted to be lost in it."

"Why?" Josh asked.

It was the first time he had asked her directly about her feelings, and instinctively Anne drew back. She met his eyes and she was the one who looked away, because she was ashamed. "To be part of it," she said after a moment, "so I could feel the way you feel about it. I think you let it consume you the way I let the law consume me, and I thought if I could be as completely swept up by this as you are, I could understand that part of you, and I'd know that you understood that part of me. Also," she added hastily, giving Josh no time to comment on what she had said, far more revealing than anything she had said to him, or anyone else, "when I travel I like to become part of the country, and in Egypt that means the chaos of Cairo's streets or a Luxor café or the incredible splendor of a tomb. And today was the tomb."

Josh nodded. "And you're feeling better now."

"Much, thank you. Sitting helped. I'd like to hear about this room."

He walked along the walls, translating some of the hieroglyphics, and then he knelt beside the sarcophagus, running his fingers along the carvings of Isis and the paintings of sacred animals while narrating their legends. Anne felt like a child hearing a bedtime fairy tale: as warm and protected as if she were wrapped in blankets, and soothed by his voice re-creating an ancient, wondrous world.

"Lunch," Josh said abruptly. Anne started, as if she were waking up. "We'll go back to Luxor." He looked at her searchingly as she stood with him. "We can come back this afternoon, if you'd like, or tomorrow and every day after that; there are dozens of other tombs, some quite different from this one, and temples and monuments, depending on what you want to see."

"Or?" Anne asked.

"Or we could get out," he said bluntly. "No matter where else we go around here we'll have hordes of tourists; the Valley of the Kings is not the place for privacy. Neither is Luxor."

Anne nodded. "Where would you like to go?"

"On the river. A friend offered me his boat while he's out of town. We could see a part of Egypt you can't see any other way."

"And be more private?" Anne asked with a smile. "With two hundred other boats?"

He grinned. "They keep their distance and we don't allow boarding parties."

There was only the briefest pause. "I'd like that very much," Anne said.

"Good." Josh led the way back to the rough stairway and into the blazing, relentless sun. "Lunch on the boat, then. As soon as you pack, we'll be ready to leave."

The boat was named the *Hapy,* for the god of the Nile. It was a small yacht gleaming white and green in the sunlight, with a lounge and two staterooms above, and quarters below for a crew of three. Josh stowed Anne's bags in one of the staterooms, and they went to the polished deck and stood beneath a broad green-and-white-striped awning, watching the town of Luxor recede as the boat moved almost sideways to the middle of the river.

The Nile was brown along its banks and blue-green up the middle where the *Hapy* sailed, heading south. The steward served a cold vegetable salad and white wine at a table beside the railing covered with a green linen cloth and set with white china and heavy antique silver. From the shore, young boys shouted and waved, and music drifted to them from small villages, but otherwise there was no sound but the hum of the *Hapy*'s engines and occasionally, the horn of a passing tourist boat. The afternoon slipped by as softly and quietly as the ripples on the Nile. Josh and Anne sat in wicker armchairs deeply cushioned in bright cotton, gazing past the railing at the life on the river and its banks. A table stood between them with glasses of iced tea beaded with moisture, and replenished at intervals by the steward. A cool breeze whispered past them as the boat picked up speed. They talked or were silent, lulled by the rhythm of the river. On the banks, women in black washed clothes, pounding them on large flat stones, gossiping together, stopping now and then to call to naked toddlers who were exploring too close to the water. Older children swam nearby, shouting exuberantly to each other. Farther off shore, young men stood in tiny fishing boats, flailing the water with long sticks to frighten the fish into fleeing, so the older man at the other end of the boat could sweep them into his net. Wiry young boys skimmed the surface of the water in small feluccas that were identical to the boats used in the times of the pharaohs, their white sails billowing like a dancer's body curved in flight. On green terraced fields stepping up from the river, one farmer tilled the soil with his hand plow as he walked behind a plodding ox; another rode a bright red tractor. And just beyond the fields, and the ancient cities with minarets, and the small clusters of factories whose chimneys sent streams of black smoke into the sky, was the desert, stretching empty and unbroken all the way to neighboring countries.

Except for the red tractor and the few factories, it was as if they had gone back thousands of years, and Anne watched it all in a fascinated reverie. She sat on the cool deck of a modern yacht on the Nile, watching men, women, and children move in timeless patterns that seemed to make them part of the earth and its rhythms, and were as far from modern Los Angeles and a hushed white apartment as if they were on different planets.

"I couldn't imagine living that way," she murmured, watching a woman gather her laundry from the stones where she had spread it to dry, "but it would be nice to bring some of it to today."

Josh nodded. "Enough to slow down and think about how much we're still part of our past, or ought to be. I think about that a lot when I'm here. Of course the Egyptians have their own problems, trying to be a modern country, but this is a good place to be reminded that we should come to terms with our past and make it part of our present."

The sun slid below the crest of a bank of high sand dunes. It reappeared through a deep notch, and was reflected in a blazing swath of burnt orange across the Nile. In another minute, it was gone for good. The river turned dark blue, then black. The air grew cool. There was no long, slow twilight here; there was only sunlight, and soon after, a blackness that swallowed up the land, leaving only scattered lights on shore to mark the boundaries of the Nile.

"I'm going to change for dinner," Anne said. She stood up, stretching; she had sat unmoving for the whole afternoon. "Is that all right? I'd like to."

"Of course," Josh said. He stood with her. "Eight o'clock? We can eat out here or in the lounge."

"Here, please. And eight o'clock is fine." She went through the lounge to the stateroom where Josh had put her things. It was a small room with a double bed covered with a white eyelet quilt, an olive-wood desk and armoire, and a blue chintz armchair. The window was the width of the room, and was slightly open; Anne could hear the quiet slap of waves against the boat. A door led to a tiny bathroom tiled in pink marble, with a tub just large enough for a child, or an adult with knees steeply bent. Anne smiled. She liked everything she saw. She liked everything that was happening.

But her smile wavered. *This is a good place to be reminded that it's best if we remember our past and come to terms with it.* Yes, she thought. I know. Just give me a few more minutes.

The bath water was steaming, and she sat with water to her chin, washing off the dust of the morning, feeling exhilarated by cleanliness. She dried her hair and left it loose, a little wild, and slipped on a gold silk caftan as fine as tissue. When she returned to the deck, Josh was waiting for her, dressed in slacks and a dress shirt, open at the neck, and a dark blue blazer. His eyes admired her as she came to him. "You look wonderful."

"So do you. But this boat deserves our dressing up, Josh; it's so fine."

He smiled. "I think so, too. A number of my friends have boats, but this is my favorite. And it had to be the best, for you." He contemplated her. "I bought you something in Luxor, before you arrived." He took a slim box from his jacket pocket and watched Anne open it. Nestled on a bed of velvet was a necklace of oval cabochons of lapis lazuli joined by thin gold rods. Anne drew in her breath. "Lapis and gold," Josh said. "The colors of the pharaohs. If I could have chosen something for you to wear tonight, I would have chosen gold silk."

"It's so beautiful," Anne said, and handed it to him so he could fasten it behind her neck.

He stood back, studying her. "A pharaoh's queen," he said softly, "though far more beautiful. And very much alive, not mummified, and therefore, I would guess, ready for dinner."

He took her hand and they crossed the deck to the dinner table, moved since that afternoon to a spot sheltered from the breeze that now and then gusted to a wind. Josh filled their wineglasses and raised his. "I'm glad you're here; I'm glad we're here. I like seeing Egypt through your eyes. It's good to be reminded how it looked when it was brand-new; we forget too quickly. So, thank you for helping me look with fresh eyes at a place I love."

"Thank you for getting me here." Anne touched her glass to his. "I'm having a wonderful time."

They ate slowly, sitting close together, their voices low, while the steward brought each course, beginning with *tahini* and soup, and then a spicy stew of rice and beef served with large circles of flat bread. "I always liked to experiment with food," Josh said as he helped himself to more stew. "Dora never did."

Anne gave him a swift, startled glance. He had not talked about Dora for months.

"She had a fine palate and she was never willing to chance a less than excellent meal." His voice was casually reminiscent. "I think what gave her a reason to leave me was her discovery that I was a less than excellent man."

Anne's eyebrows rose. *"She* wanted to leave?"

"She forced it. She told me with amazing regularity that she'd stay if I would change and become what she wanted. I wouldn't do it, and she wouldn't stop demanding it, so finally I said she had to leave." He leaned forward and refilled their wineglasses. "It sounds dreary and trite, even to me; I can imagine how often you hear variations of it in your office. But it seemed important to me. I'd lived with two other women, and both times it hadn't worked out; they were sorry and so was I, and we're still friends. I'd known I didn't want to marry Dora, but for a while we'd enjoyed each other, so it was another failure. I knew there were ways I could have changed to satisfy her if I'd wanted to, but I didn't want to. That told me more about my feelings for her, or lack of them, than anything else."

"What did she want you to do?" Anne asked.

He smiled wryly. "There was a long list. In Dora's self-centered world nothing was ever enough." He paused, his mouth somber. "What I thought I saw in Dora at first, and for some months after she moved in with me, was an insatiable desire to experience everything. But that turned out to be an insatiable desire to possess everything. No, it was more than that. It was a compulsion to possess and manipulate, to bend everything and everyone to her will."

He paused. "It seems she takes after her father in that. Anyway, after a while, in spite of her sweetness and charm, all I saw was that drive to manipulate, and her endless fascination with herself, and that was when I went back to working my regular schedule, fourteen hours a day, six or seven days a week. Dora wanted me to stay home more. It doesn't seem like a lot to ask, and of course I could have done it. But by then I didn't want to. I'd always worked those crazy hours before we began living together, and I couldn't see any reason to stay home." He contemplated his wineglass. "To be accurate, I hadn't always worked like a madman. I started cramming my days when my parents were killed and it became a way of life. First the past was an escape and then it was where I was most content. I always knew how it would come out; there were no surprises. That seems extraordinarily weak now, but for years it satisfied me and I didn't question it."

He leaned back, stretching his legs along the side of the table. The candles in the hurricane lamps had burned low and there were deep shadows on his face. "For all those years, I never was in love with anyone. I'm not sure if that was because I was involved in the past, or if I was involved in the past because I couldn't fall in love. What I do know is that the past isn't enough for me anymore, and that means my work isn't enough. There was a time when finding Tenkaure's tomb would have been the greatest event of my life; it would have been the measure of my success as a human being and the purpose of my days. But right now it isn't any of those things. It's important to me, but nowhere near as important as you are."

He was silent for a moment, his eyes holding Anne's. She did not move. Except for the faint vibration of the boat beneath them, it seemed to her that the whole world was still.

"I love you, Anne," he said quietly. "I think I must have made that clear in a dozen ways by now, but I haven't let myself say it; there seemed to be too much going on in your life, and God knows there was plenty going on around us. But I want you to know that once I knew I was in love with you and that I wanted to bring you into my life, and make myself a part of yours and your family's, the past slipped away to the background. Where it belongs."

The steward brought coffee and cognac and a tiered plate of cookies. "Over there, please," Josh said, gesturing toward a low wicker coffee table, and when the steward had left, he and Anne moved to a cushioned love seat and pulled the low table to them. Anne poured coffee. She could not speak. She was in turmoil. *Sweet little Anne. People should love you.* No man had spoken to her of love since she had left home. But in Josh's voice, it had not sounded anything like the word in her memory. It was as if she had never heard it before; it resonated like a foreign word with new layers of meaning. And even as she had felt herself tighten and shrink back, she had felt a small spark of excitement, a sense of possibilities, and she wanted to hear him say it again.

But she did not know how to talk about love. I wish, I wish, I wish. She ached with wanting to be able to talk to him. But she was silent.

Josh had leaned back, holding his cup. He looked relaxed, but Anne felt the pressure of his waiting for her to speak, and she felt a flash of resentment. He had no trouble speaking of love; he'd had plenty of practice, and no memories crushed him, leaving him breathless and sick, whenever he thought of all the things that love could mean.

"We're docking," he said, and at that moment the boat's engines cut back to an idle.

Startled at the sudden drop in the steady hum she had heard all afternoon, Anne looked at the lights of the bustling trading town on the shore, and the familiar lights of tour boats docked along its corniche.

"Edfu," Josh said. "We'll dock here tonight, a little farther up, away from the tour boats. We can go ashore tomorrow, if you want—if we go early, we can avoid most of the crowds—or we can sail before breakfast. The only schedule for this trip is what we want to do."

The *Hapy* glided silently along the dock, away from the other boats and the center of town, until they came to an empty section of shore. A group of men, waiting for them, grabbed the rope flung by the crew and fastened it to an iron stake embedded in the ground. Music drifted from the cafés, as it had in Luxor; voices and the heavy scents of coffee and spices, baking bread, and smoke from water pipes floated on the breeze as they had in Luxor. Anne had the feeling that time and space had blurred. She was in one place and many places; she was in an ancient land and her own modern world; she was in Egypt, or she was on a river without beginning or end, flowing or standing still.

She and Josh were the stable center. Once again, she felt alone with him, separate from everything else. Whatever happened beyond this boat, in the past or the future, this was her stable center. It seemed to her that she had never before known this feeling of coming to the center of her life.

She did not know what to do with that, yet. When she thought of saying it to him, simply and straight out, the words would not come; she was afraid of opening the door to something she could not control.

But even if she could have told him, it was not the time. She knew that. There was something else she had to tell him first.

He had helped her, by talking about Dora. He had done it casually, but he had had a reason. *The past slipped away to the background. Where it belongs.* That was what he wanted her to do. Force it to the background. And it was time that she did.

She put her cup on the coffee table and turned to him. "I want to tell you about something that happened to me a long time ago. I haven't ever talked about it; I haven't been able to. I was thirteen. My mother had died when I was seven, and Gail and I were living with Marian and Fred. Everyone in the family had houses within a few blocks of each other, and we almost always had Sunday dinner at my grandfather's. It was a command performance, but I think everyone liked it. Except Vince. He hated rules, anyone's rules, and I'm sure he wouldn't have shown up at all except that he was afraid of confronting my grandfather. I think Ethan Chatham was the only man Vince was ever in awe of."

She gazed into space, at the lights of Edfu some distance away, and the blackness of the river all around them, but what she was seeing was Marian's house, the dining room with the flowered wallpaper, the long yard beyond the French doors, stretching smooth as green velvet to the lake, and the forest where she had talked to her made-up friend. What was her name? She had forgotten. She'd been talking to her, she remembered, and writing in her notebook, when Vince—

"What happened when you were thirteen?" Josh asked, bringing her back.

"Vince raped me," she said. She gasped with pain and shame, and with the shock of hearing herself say the words aloud for the first time.

Josh sucked in his breath. "My God, my God," he breathed. He had guessed, but there was no way to be prepared for the impact of hearing her say it, nor for the agony in her voice, nor for the murderous rage that swept through him. He saw Anne with Vince—he tried not to picture it, but it was there, driving into him—Anne's head falling back, Vince making her bend and yield, forcing her . . . He could not stand it. "My God," he burst out in fury, and reached for Anne, to snatch her from that image in his mind.

Anne jumped. She leaped to her feet and moved away from him, and stood beside the railing, nervously running her hand along the smooth brass. "I have to tell all of it," she said. Her voice was low but clear across the space between them. She had made up her mind, and with the same steely drive that had taken her from Lake Forest to Haight Ashbury, and then to Berkeley and Harvard and the law, she would see it through. "He raped me for a long time. He came to my room. At first he was always there, and then he had a schedule and I had to be ready for him. And act a part, and say words that meant nothing to me. That, ever since then, have meant . . . nothing to me."

She closed her eyes briefly. She could feel his hands on her in the prison of her bedroom, she could hear him giving orders, commanding her to respond, hissing furiously when she did not. *God damn it, feel something when I play with you!*

I can't do this, Anne thought, I can't, I can't. Her breathing was sharp and painful, as if she had been running for too long. Her hand clenched the railing.

Josh held himself in, torn by anger and pity. "And you didn't tell your family," he said quietly.

Anne's eyes flew open in surprise at the sound of his voice in her recollecting. There had never been another voice when she fought with her memories; it had always been hers alone. *But I'm not alone now.* She looked for a long moment at Josh. His eyes were on hers, dark with anger and pain, and she knew it was her anger and pain as well as his own that he was feeling. *I'm not alone anymore.* She began to understand how that could mean a sharing of horrors, and pain.

"I couldn't tell anyone," she said. "I let him do it!" And then the words rushed out, like cord unwinding from a tightly wound ball that had been embedded inside her, its coarseness chafing a sore that never healed. "I was so ashamed, and angry at myself for being weak and . . . bad. He told me I'd led him on and I believed him because why else would he have started it? I felt dirty and sick and ashamed, but I let him do it. Over and over and over. I've tried to understand that—whenever I let myself think about it or I can't avoid it—how I could let him do it, week after week, while I went on with the rest of my life and no one guessed. He came and went and did what he wanted, and I did what he wanted . . . except for responding; I never did that. He hated it; he hated me for not feeling anything. I thought it was like a marriage, what I thought a marriage was like, with one person belonging to another. No, that's not right. I never felt that I belonged to him. It was as if my body wasn't mine, it was his, and the more he used it the more it became his and the less I had any control over what happened to it. He had the control. I had my thoughts and my feelings, they were never his, but he decided what would be done to my body. He told me he'd kill me if I told anyone. He said they wouldn't believe me anyway, and I believed him. He was a grown man, married, he had a child, he worked with my grandfather in our family company, and my grandfather trusted him. And people admired him. He seemed to walk through life with everybody clearing a path for him, and if there were things or people in the way, they got knocked down and nobody paid much attention. I thought he was invulnerable. I was thirteen and not especially well behaved and my family was always telling me what I was doing wrong."

Anne paused and slowly loosened her clenched fingers from the rail. "It went on for two years." She heard Josh draw in a sharp breath. "And then one day I told them. It was my fifteenth birthday; we were at dinner, and I told my grandfather, with all of them listening. I can't remember why I finally did it; I just remember the words coming out and the looks on their faces. Poor Nina and William tried to pretend I hadn't said anything, and Marian tried to put everything off until another day, and Vince and Rita called me a liar. And my father . . . chose . . . Vince. He didn't believe me. My grandfather kept asking me to tell them more, to tell the truth. He wasn't willing to believe he'd heard it the first time. I think he was willing to believe me if I pushed it, but at the time all I saw was that he seemed to be hoping I wouldn't force him to. No one wanted to believe it; it made them too uncomfortable. I left home that night."

Josh could not hold back any longer. He jumped up and took Anne in his arms. Reflexively, she stiffened. "Wait—" she began. But then something inside her let go, and her body seemed to melt against his. She began to cry. In Josh's arms, her forehead against his shoulder, she sobbed with the despair of the child she had been, and the frozen pain of the woman she had become.

Josh held her, his cheek resting on her hair, one hand cradling her face as if sheltering her from a storm. They stood that way for a long time. Anne's sobs subsided. She drew a few shuddering breaths and then breathed quietly, leaning against Josh, thinking nothing at all. "Oh," she said at last, and pulled back. "Your jacket . . ."

They both gazed at the soaked lapel of his blazer. "A deluge," Josh said lightly. "Not serious; in fact, beneficial."

He took off the jacket and draped it over the railing, then put his arms around Anne again. And as he held her close, she brought her arms up, slowly, and held them around his waist. He had imagined the feel of her slender bones beneath his hands so many times that it was almost familiar, but still, he felt as if he had walked into a dream and was not sure what was substance and what was hope.

"You knew," Anne said, her voice muffled. "Gail and Leo told you."

"No," he said quickly. He held her away so he could look at her. "They did not tell me; I told you that. But Anne, the information was there, especially for someone who spends his life putting pieces of information together. I guessed, and didn't want to believe it, but then I did. I knew Vince; not well, but well enough."

"So did my family. But they were willing to turn away and leave me with the shame of—" Her eyes filled with tears again. "Oh, God, it never stops. I thought when I told you—"

"Listen to me," Josh said. He put his hands on her arms and his eyes held hers. "Whose shame is it?"

She frowned. "What?"

"You keep saying you were ashamed, you are ashamed, you live with the shame of it. But why should it be yours? He's the one who did it. The ugliness is his, the monstrousness is his—you knew that; you called him a monster—the shame is his. You have none; you've never had any. Vince has, but not you. Anne, you have nothing to be ashamed of. You've never had anything to be ashamed of."

Anne was still frowning. Why had she never said that to herself? It sounded so simple . . . and if it were true . . . But why wouldn't it be true? In Josh's deep, matter-of-fact voice, it sounded obvious, something she should have recognized years ago. "I don't know," she said slowly.

"You do. You do know. You were too young to see it when you left home; you'd been terrorized for too long. You believed what he told you, that it was your fault, and you thought you'd been tainted by being with him so that you weren't a good girl anymore; you weren't lovable. None of that was true, but somehow, even under all your professionalism, you never stopped being frightened, so distance didn't help you see what had happened to you. You let shame become a part of you, like a splinter that never worked its way out. But it isn't part of you, Anne; it was put in you by others, and by your own fears and helplessness, and you can pull it out."

Anne smiled faintly. "So simple."

"It may not be. But you can do it. You've done a lot that was harder."

"Maybe." She felt the strength of Josh's hands on her arms, and after a few minutes she began to feel something else, a kind of lightness within her that she did not recognize. It made everything seem new, as if she stood on a mountain trail and the sun, shining at a different angle, showed the landscape as she had not seen it before. She felt she was waiting for something, without fear. And she knew she was beginning to believe him.

The lights of Edfu had gone out; the tour boats were dark. It was almost midnight. The steward returned with a fresh pot of coffee and left, pushing the dinner table before him as he went out. The door swung shut behind him.

Josh held Anne to him again, his cheek resting on her hair. Oh, she thought, surprised because nothing in her shrank from his touch. She rested against him, her lips feeling his heartbeat through the fine cotton of his shirt. It was a good place to be, and she let lightness fill her, and buoyancy, and in a minute she recognized that what she felt was hope.

She raised her head to look at him. And when he saw her eyes, he bent to kiss her, his mouth meeting hers with an easy naturalness that took him by surprise. He had not known how it would happen that she would be able to accept him without being trapped in the past. If she had passed that hurdle, they could—

But Anne's muscles had tightened and a silent scream rose in her throat. A mouth covering hers, smothering her, robbing her of herself. . . . She twisted away, yanking free of

Josh, and stepped backward, her teeth clenched to hold back the scream. She was trembling so violently she could barely stand. She looked at the deck; she could not look at Josh.

"It's too late." The words were wrenched from her. "I'm sorry, Josh; I'm sorry; it's too late." He put his arm around her and she shied away, feeling she was crumbling inside. "Oh, God, why can't I be free of this?"

"You will," Josh said firmly. He was filled with doubts, and for the first time felt the beginnings of despair, but he did not let Anne see it. He kept his voice firm, and his hand was firmly around her arm as he ignored the sag of her body and led her back to the love seat. "You will because we're going to make it happen. There's a lot more involved than our making love; there's a life at stake; the life we're going to make together. I want us to get married and have children and build something a lot more solid than anything either of us has ever had. And that's worth fighting for."

"We should have met when we were ten," she said seriously. "We could have grown up together and nothing would have stood between us."

"Nothing stands between us now that we can't deal with," Josh said quietly. "Listen to me. Stop being a lawyer who always analyzes, and a woman who relies on her wits and her intelligence; trust your emotions for a change, and just listen. I love you, Anne. I love you for what you are and what you were, the things you do now and the things that happened to you a long time ago. I love all of you, not just the prettiest parts or the easiest parts." He laid his hand along her cheek. "Dearest, lovely Anne. There's so much I want to do for you. But I want you to do for me, too. I want us to be to each other everything we've always thought we could be alone. We've been alone long enough; you've been busy running away from the past and I've been hanging out in it, and now we're done with that. We're going to make a life together, and a life isn't a place or a time—it's not a law firm or an apartment guarded by a doorman or thousands of years of history—it's someone, or more than someone, a whole family if we're lucky, to welcome us and make a space for us to nest. It's having someone who will always greet us with open arms. It's a door that will always be open to us. I want that from you. And I want to give that to you, so you'll never have to shut doors inside yourself again."

Anne was concentrating on his voice, deep and very close. At first she had hung on each word; then the words had blended together and wrapped themselves around her like the music of an orchestra that soars until it seems to come from within each listener. They became part of her; they flowed through her. She was buoyed by the warmth and rhythm of his voice, and by the steady touch of his hand along her face. She closed her eyes and listened.

"There are so many things I want us to do together," he said. "Places to see together, even if we've seen them separately, books to read together, plays to see, people to meet. We'll finish the Tamarack house together and spend a lot of time there. We'll hike our favorite trails and we'll discover new ones together; we'll go skiing and bicycling and sailing, and I've never gone fishing, but maybe we'll do that, too. We have to start right away; there's so much to do." He went on, his voice a murmur, talking about the home they would make together in Los Angeles, the gardens and the home they would make together in Tamarack, the hours they would spend together. He talked about their separate work, which would always fill a big part of their lives, and the curiosities and wonders and beauties of the world. "And we'll share them. I haven't wanted to share most of them with anyone until now, but at this minute I can't think of anything I want to experience alone."

Casually, he slipped his arm around her. It was like an extension of his voice, warm and embracing, and without thinking about it, without even opening her eyes, Anne settled herself into it, resting easily against him.

"There's a trip I want us to take very soon, from Geneva to Paris," Josh said. His voice was like a reverie now, and Anne felt herself become part of his dream. "Just outside Geneva, we drive through a spectacular series of canyons at the edge of the Jura Mountains. We can do it on a fine day or we can wait until there's a snowstorm. It's like a dream, then: clouds swirl from the depths of the canyons to high above us, and all around, the rock formations are a magical silver and black that seem to float in the mist."

He paused. There was no sound. Their boat was like a softly lit room in the vast blackness of the desert and the Nile. Clusters of pale stars winked in a hazy sky; the moon hovered over the town as if caught by a minaret. Anne nestled in the strong clasp of Josh's arm. And then she felt his long fingers stroking her hair and the side of her face, at first very softly, then more firmly. She opened her eyes, but then she closed them again and gave herself up to those slow, rhythmic strokes, like the caress of warm rain. "Then the road levels out," Josh said in that even murmur that seemed to flow from the warmth of his fingers, "and we drive through wine country, low rolling hills, dark green fading to pale green and then blue-gray at the horizon, with small houses clustered like flocks of white birds that came to rest in the middle of the fields."

Anne saw it in her mind. She felt the timeless serenity of it as she felt the peacefulness of the place where they sat, the small, private boat, the quiet Nile so still beneath them, the slumbering town on the shore. And Josh, steady and protective, holding her close, his hand slowly caressing her forehead, the smooth skin beside her eye, her high cheekbone and the faint hollow below it, and the long line of her neck. From his fingertips, warmth spread through her body like wine and honey; she felt languorous and content.

He was talking about other places, and Anne saw the scenes he described. She could feel the rough stone of ancient monuments beneath her palms, she breathed the fragrance of wild thyme and mint and oregano, and she felt the heat of the sun beat upon them as they walked together through fields of wildflowers that bowed before them as they passed. They were so close in that vision, and the world pressed in upon them with such blazing splendor, that Anne felt herself open to it. The sights and sounds and scents of Egypt that had swept her up combined now with those visions of other places, and she felt a surge of wanting. She remembered wanting like this on their hike to the lake, but this was more, so much more. She felt open to everything there was to discover. And she felt herself open to Josh, wanting more of him than she had ever known.

Her eyes still closed, she lifted her face to his. The low murmur of his voice stopped. His lips touched hers, lightly, as a breeze might at evening. Anne's mouth opened. And then Josh's mouth softly, slowly joined him to her, breathing with her, his touch, like his voice, flowing through her and gathering her to the one enclosed place within his arms. He tightened his arms around her, and slowly, his tongue met hers.

Anne felt the shock of it; her tongue fluttered briefly, looking for escape. But Josh stayed where he was. He did not force her but neither did he move away, and in a moment Anne met him. Suddenly, she wanted to feel his body tight against hers, and tighter still; she strained against him, knowing that, for the first time, she was feeling passion. She freed an arm from the tightness of their embrace and held him, her fingers in his hair. Her tongue twined with his. She felt a freedom that filled her with exultation.

A small sound escaped her, and Josh raised his head. "I love you," she said. The words hovered in the air. It was the first time she had said them freely since she was a child.

"Dear God," Josh murmured. It was like a prayer. He shook his head slowly, in wonder. "All the times I dreamed of hearing you say that, and that you would come to me freely . . . and I was never sure it would happen."

"I thought it wouldn't," Anne said. A quick shudder went through her. "I couldn't imagine that it could be different."

"It has nothing to do with anything else," Josh said, the words driven by the anger still within him, slow to leave. "We'll make our own way and our own discoveries; we'll make our own love." He smiled. "We have to come to terms with our pasts, but we don't have to bring them into the bedroom."

Anne returned his smile. "We won't have any of your ghosts either? None of your old shadows?"

"Not even a fragment of a memory. There's just now, this moment, and the two of us alone, and one of the world's eternal rivers beneath us." He stood, bringing her with him, and they held each other close. Anne's face lay against his shoulder; her eyes were closed again. The silence settled around them.

We'll make our own discoveries. Our own love.

The quick shudder ran through her body again. *No! I won't be afraid.* She had felt the exultation of freedom; she had wanted his touch. It's time, she thought. She raised her chin, as if steeling herself, and took Josh's hand. They turned and walked across the deck and through the lounge, to his stateroom.

A wall sconce cast a fan of pale ivory light toward the ceiling; the rest of the room was in shadows. Josh closed the door behind them and locked it. He turned to Anne and took her hands, studying her. In the dim light, he saw a glint of determination in her eyes and a tilt of her head that was not what he would have called romantic. His heart ached with pity for her. There was no way he could know exactly what she was going through; he could guess, he could love her and try to help her, but he could not share it. It was her battle, and she would have to fight much of it alone. She had fought a lot of them, and always completely alone. But she wasn't alone now; at least that much had changed. And now they both knew that there were fires in her that were waiting to leap to life. It would take a while; they had been banked for too long. But they would burn again, and consume them both.

"My dear love," Josh said softly, giving her time. "I want you to be part of me; I want us to be part of each other."

A sigh broke from Anne. She wanted his touch, she wanted to be in his arms. Josh kissed her, a long, gentle kiss, and then he turned her and unfastened the button at the back of her gold caftan.

Take off your pajamas, I want to see you.

No! Anne cried silently. No, no, no!

And then the memory was gone, and she was standing in the soft light of Josh's stateroom, her hands at her sides, feeling the warmth of his palms pushing the silk from her shoulders, down her arms, past her waist and hips. "My God, you are so wonderfully beautiful," he murmured.

Once again Anne let his voice soothe her. The cool air from the open window curled over her skin as Josh slipped off her silk underclothes, and she felt no shame, only a swift pleasure in her strong, lithe body that she had cared for so well for twenty-five years.

But then she was staring at Josh's jacket and white shirt. *I have too many clothes on. For Christ's sake, take off my clothes.*

No! she cried again. Stop, please, please stop.

And then, again, it was gone. Josh was taking off his clothes, swiftly and easily, and Anne watched him with wonder. He made it seem so simple; there were no demands on her at all. And when he put his arms around her and for the first time in her life she felt the long line of a man's naked body against hers without force, she nestled against him in gratitude. The passion she had felt earlier had disappeared in those moments of panic; her openness and wanting were gone, and so was that brief moment of exultation in her freedom. But she had gratitude, and she clung to that: Josh would not force her to do anything.

They stood without moving for a long time, their bodies close and warm, the cool breeze touching them lightly. Then Josh took Anne's hand and led her to the wide bed covered with a finely woven throw. He pulled it back and drew her with him to the smooth sheets, and lay beside her, leaning on his elbow. Anne felt him watching her. She saw the angle of his arm and the pulse in his throat, and suddenly the room seemed to darken. Her thoughts stopped; her body moved of its own volition. She sat up and bent over Josh, and with cold precision her skillful mouth closed on his penis.

Appalled, Josh wrenched away. And Anne jerked back as if she had been stung. She was crying bitterly, and she pulled herself into a fetal ball in the corner of the bed, shaking her head over and over, cold and alone.

"No," Josh said. "You're not alone." He sat beside her and tried to make her look at him. Her eyes slid past him. "Anne, listen to me." She was still shaking her head, and he took her hand, gripping it when she tried to pull away. "I'm going to talk and I hope you'll listen. There are two of us here, and whatever we do, we do together. And we do what we want, there's no *should* or *ought* or *have to* between us. Do you understand that? There aren't any rules; there is nothing here but our own desire. And love. I love you, Anne, and you love me, and we are going to love each other. We're not acting out another life in another time; we're not following anyone else's script. And you're not walking in the footsteps you made when you were a girl. You're a different person now, and you're with me, and the two of us are creating something that never existed before. No one, no memory, can stop that from happening. There isn't any monster in the shadows or inside you; he's gone. He can't touch you, ever again."

"He's never gone," Anne said almost inaudibly. "The things that happen to us don't disappear. They're always part of us."

"Yes, they are. But once you face them down, they lose their power. Anne, my love, there is nothing to be afraid of; you've faced the worst that was inside you and you've moved beyond it. Of course it's still there; it's too much to hope it could vanish, but it's not powerful enough anymore to dominate you. Or us. It can't hurt us. It can't even take up any room between us. What we're building together is far more powerful, and it's alive and part of us and nothing can harm it. We won't let it. Listen to me: *we* won't let it, Anne. Together. You don't have to fight anything alone anymore."

There was a long silence. Anne was unmoving, her eyes closed. Then, slowly, she relaxed the locked grip of her arm around her knees. She uncurled her body, stretching out her legs, and lay back, half-sitting against the headboard, letting Josh's voice echo in her thoughts. "I believe that," she said at last. In another minute, she opened her eyes and raised her head as if she were just waking up. The room seemed brighter than before against the blackness at the windows. Nothing could be seen there; the stars had faded; the moon had set. How wonderful, Anne thought, to be in a small world of light, with Josh.

Then she was in his arms, their lips together, and they lay together that way, still kissing, their arms around each other, stretched out on the bed. "I love you," Anne said against Josh's lips. "I love you."

At last she was able to gaze at him. His body was lean and muscled; his skin darker than hers, the center of his chest covered with fine brown curls. In the soft light his eyes were deep set, dark blue and intent, as if he were memorizing the lines of her body and the small, barely perceptible quiver at the corners of her mouth.

"Dearest Anne, my dearest love," he murmured, and he bent over her and began caressing her, slowly, in long, gentle strokes, following the curves of her shoulder and her slender waist and her long thighs. His palms were hard, but his touch was so light Anne found herself straining to feel it. She reached out and laid her hand on his chest, touching his skin as if she had not touched skin before. And with her, Josh felt the newness as his hand moved along her body. *Thank you for helping me look with fresh eyes.* He caressed as if for the first time, as if his body and hers had just sprung to life in a world where everything was fresh.

The sheet beneath Anne was warm now; it cradled her as her breathing grew faster and she began to move beneath Josh's hand. He bent lower until his lips touched her breast and rested briefly there. His hand stroked her body as he took her nipple into his mouth and ran his tongue slowly across it. And when it puckered like a small tight rose he moved his lips to her other breast. A small moan escaped Anne; she felt herself drawing up, as if his fingertips were tracing fine lines of flame upon her and gathering them into his hands.

She looked up at the planes and shadows of his face. It was all she saw; there was only Josh, filling her vision. Nothing else could intrude. Her body moved to the movement of his hand. And then, as if a door had been flung open, a world of sensation flooded in; the passion she had felt earlier returned. Naked, she felt free; she was all feeling. And she was open, opening wider, wanting, already forgetting what it had been like to be frozen shut. The joy of letting herself feel desire built within her until she thought she could not contain it. And she felt Josh's desire, in the fluid tension of his body and the intensity of his eyes. *Whatever we do, we do together.* She laid her hand on the taut line of his thigh, and then they were a circle, their hands holding each other, the line of flame flowing between them. Josh's eyes met hers, and he lay upon her.

The feel of him covering her, the weight of him stretched upon her, was so good that Anne's eyes widened. A rush of exhilaration swept her up and a laugh broke from her. Josh smiled, in relief as much as joy. Anne brought his face to hers and kissed him. "I love you," she said; she could not seem to say it enough. Her body felt powerful with rejoicing, exultation, and the heat that ran through her was like a river spilling over its banks. She became the river, coursing tumultuously, taking into its depths the sun and the sky. She raised her hips and parted her legs, spreading them wide to embrace Josh, and brought him to her.

He barely moved, but he was inside her. Anne gasped with the quick, sharp pain, but he lay still and then it was gone. She felt the hardness of him within her and she felt herself clasp him and cling to him, tight and hot, making him merge with her. She felt tears in her eyes at the rightness of it. He was not an invader. He came into her and filled a place welcoming him, where he belonged. He was part of her. She had been waiting for him. "My love," Anne said, and raised her hips to pull him in more deeply. And they were joined, not in battle, but in desire and love. And in a cherishing she had never known.

They moved together, finding their own rhythm. Josh would have gone slowly but Anne led him, moving with freedom and abandon. She was lifted up by sensations, by the heat pouring through her and the joy of being open and taking in. Their breaths and murmuring voices mingled. "My love, my love, my love," Anne said, and then, for the first time in her life, she came to a climax.

Her head dropped back to the pillow. Small shudders

rippled through her. She heard Josh's hard breathing and then a cry burst from him, and he lay on her, holding her, not moving. She turned her head to let her lips rest against his. A warm languor spread over her, and then she felt the breeze, much cooler than before. Without moving, Josh reached down for the throw he had pulled back earlier, and covered them with it. "Oh, lovely," Anne murmured, her lips moving against his.

She felt his smile. "I hope so," he said.

"I never knew," she said simply. "I never knew."

Josh raised his head and met her eyes. "Everything I ever hoped for, everything I ever dreamed of, is in you," he said. "Whatever I can give you, for the rest of my life . . ."

"We'll find it together, and share it," Anne said. Her voice was slow and lazy. She smiled up at him. "I am so extraordinarily happy."

Josh drew in a breath of wonder, and bent to kiss her. He had not realized how desperately he had longed to hear her say that, to see that smile on her lips and in her eyes, to hear the contentment in her voice. There's nothing we can't do now, he thought; we've gotten past the hardest part.

They lay on their sides, facing each other, touching each other. Anne ran her fingers slowly over Josh's face, tracing his eyebrows, the straight line of his nose, the smile on his lips. "There's so much I don't know about you," she said.

His eyebrows rose. "After that tour through Tenkaure's tomb? After saving me from the sheriff in Tamarack? After having dinner in my apartment and hearing me go on about my parents? After tonight?"

"I don't know what you want to do tomorrow," she said.

"Sail further up the Nile," he responded promptly. "And after we get to Aswan, I'd like to turn around and sail back to the Mediterranean and keep going. How about it? Shall we sail for three or four months and forget the rest of the world? We have books and music and food, people to wait on us, and so much still to discover about each other. A few months is only a start, but it would be a good one. Is it all right with you?"

"I'd love it," Anne said easily.

"Good. I'll call the university tomorrow, and the museum, and tell them to hold everything until May or June."

"And I'll call my secretary. She'll take care of everything. We'll have to call Gail and Leo, too; they'll be wondering."

There was a pause. "You're calling my bluff," Josh said a little accusingly.

"Was it a bluff?" Anne's eyes were wide and innocent.

He burst out laughing. "Half wish, half bluff, and you know it. You're going to be tough to live with. We'll do it, though, someday—maybe we'll do it right and sail around the world—when we get our lives organized. Anne, I said earlier I want us to get married. Have you thought about that?"

"I want it, too. But I haven't lived with anyone for a long time, Josh; I might be very hard to get along with."

"I'm not worried about it. We'll have a wonderful time getting used to each other. Where shall we live?"

"I'd like to find a new place that we can make together."

"Yes, but if we don't find one right away, then what?"

"We'll live in yours; I don't want to go back to mine."

"No, you don't belong there anymore." He brushed her hair back from her face. Her skin was flushed, her eyes were shining; her beauty had a depth and softness he had not seen before. Her body was like ivory silk against the white sheet, with small shadowed curves and hollows that rose and fell as she breathed. "You need bright colors," he said, "and the most lavish, sensual fabrics we can find. I want to wrap you in velvet and silk and cashmere and angora, everything soft and rich that will make you feel luxurious, all the luxury of feeling you kept buried for so long; I want you to *feel*—"

"Yes." It was a cry of gladness. Anne kissed him. She stretched her body against his; she wanted to melt into him. She pressed her hands along his back and down his thighs, pulling him more tightly to her even though they could not be any tighter than they were. She stretched one leg over his hips, clasping him, and moved against him. Her lips had opened to an O of surprise. She wanted—*again, again, always*—and the desire that surged through her body as it pressed against Josh's was so overwhelming it made her dizzy. "I didn't know," she murmured again. There was so much she had never known.

Josh kissed the long line of her neck as her head fell back; his lips lingered along her breasts, the firm skin of her stomach and the soft hollows where it met her thighs. Anne listened to her rapid breathing in the quiet room; she looked down, at her fingers deep in Josh's hair, and when she felt his tongue, quick and slow, probing and sure, waves of pleasure washed over her. She felt she was drowning in heat as enveloping as that in the desert, and the room spun around her like a whirlwind. She fought it, trying to steady it, but then she let herself sink into it and kept her eyes open, watching Josh. He seemed to waver, and she knew that once again there were tears in her eyes. "Josh," she said, but it was only a breath, and then she felt herself come together and burst beneath the insistent touch of his tongue, and she cried out and a tear fell on her pillow.

He lay beside her again, and cradled her, kissing her wet eyes. Anne's breathing slowed; her body quieted. "Why were you crying?" he asked.

"Because it was so beautiful." She looked at Josh. "It's a terrible thing when something beautiful is fouled. And even though I knew what had been done to me, I never knew that that was happening, too: that something beautiful and good was being fouled."

"And now you've found it, as it ought to be," he said.

"We found it. I had to have you with me." She gazed about the room through half-closed eyes. Suddenly a chill touched her, and she sat up. *A flowered bedroom that was their whole world; they sat in it and lay in it and talked in it. It was just like a married couple's house, only smaller.* "Josh, I want to go outside, to the deck."

"A good idea." He cast a swift glance at her troubled face. "It does get stuffy in here. Hold on; I'll get our robes." He took a white terry-cloth robe from the closet and pulled it on, and went to the other stateroom to bring one for Anne. He held it for her and she slipped her arms into it and tied it around her. With those simple actions, the flowered bedroom faded from her memory. And as she turned with Josh to walk back through the lounge, Anne knew, somehow, that it would not come back.

In a sheltered corner of the deck, Josh spread large green and flowered cushions and they lay back on them, looking up at the hazy stars. "Much better," Josh murmured. He held Anne to him and pointed at a wide-flung group of stars with a row of three stars in the center. "Orion," he said. "The three stars are his belt. When I was a kid, I made up stories about him, that he ruled the sky and watched over the earth and reached out to whoever needed help on any of the planets. Sort of a father and school principal and god all rolled into one. We got to be good friends. Every kid needs somebody like that, more visible than God, more accessible than the school principal, and so far away you can confide all your fears, and dump all your anger, and know they won't come back to haunt you."

"I had a friend named Amy," Anne said, this time remembering the name. "I invented her when I was about eight or nine, and she was with me until Vince came. Then she disappeared. Maybe if she'd been up there, in the sky, I could have kept her with me. But when she went, there wasn't anyone else. Josh, you said you wanted children."

"Yes. I've wanted them for a long time, off and on. It always worried me, though—it's such a presumptuous thing to do, to create human beings and decide how they ought to be formed—and I couldn't find anyone I wanted with me in tackling it, so I always said I traveled too much to be a good father. I don't feel that way now. I'd risk being presumptuous as long as I'm with you."

"I may be too old," Anne said.

"Then we'd better get started right away."

She sat up, looking at him gravely. "I'm almost forty, Josh."

"And I'm forty-two." He crossed his arms behind his head and smiled up at her. "You think we'll be doddering and nodding off when they want to stay up late and talk about life? Or our memory will be so bad we won't be able to give them a full briefing on sex when the time comes?"

"That's probably the last thing people forget," Anne said with a smile. "And it wouldn't be fair if I forget it; I got to it so late I don't have enough years as it is."

"You won't forget and you're not too old," Josh said quietly.

"And maybe I can't have children. Maybe I've been closed up for too long. I know that's not scientific, but it's a worry I have."

"Then we won't have any. We'll have each other and a life together; we don't need children to make us feel complete." He gazed at her. "Would you feel bereft if we didn't have them?"

"Yes," Anne said simply. "It hurts, sometimes, when I'm with Robin and Ned, and I think about what it would be like to have my own children and give them a real childhood. There's so much I want to give . . . but it was fantasy; I didn't let myself really think about it. Until now."

"We'll both think about it," Josh said. "And we'll do our damndest to make it happen. But however it turns out, my love, we'll be fine. It doesn't matter whether we have half a dozen kids or spend four months on a boat or live in one apartment or another. The wonder is that we found each other."

"And that you woke me up."

"You woke yourself," Josh said. "I helped, but it came from within you. You must know that."

"Yes, but I couldn't have done it alone, or with anyone else."

Josh reached toward her and she took his hand. She kissed his palm, and then his fingers, one by one. "I never knew it would be so simple," she said. "To do, and be, and feel so much. And that it would feel right. And good."

She looked down at his lean body stretched out beside her. One arm was still beneath his head; he was smiling at her. Anne felt the shock of desire burst within her once again. It was becoming familiar now and she embraced it, stretching like a cat in sunlight as it spread through her. Her skin was so sensitive the breeze seemed to leave small traces along it; she heard clearly each tiny slap of the waves below them; she saw with brilliant clarity the pale outline of the boat and the pillows nestled beneath them. How wonderful that everything was so clear, and that she was part of all of it.

"Greedy," she murmured, bending over Josh with a smile. "I never knew I was so greedy."

He slipped his hand inside her robe, holding her breast, caressing her breast. "I love that in you."

She untied Josh's robe and opened it, and bent over him as she had earlier. But now there was no cold precision in her movements, no shadow from another time. There was only her desire. And her love. And Josh. She curved above him, moving slowly, dreamlike, feeling her way, letting it be as new as the touch of her fingers on his skin.

She kissed the dark hairs on his chest. His heart pounded beneath her lips and he moved restlessly as she slid the tip of her tongue along his smooth, hard skin. "Dearest Anne." The words stretched out, long and low.

Her hands held his hips, her breasts brushed his thighs, and smoothly, easily, she took him into her mouth. She filled herself with him, with the solid living warmth of him; she pulled him deep into herself and lost herself in the feelings that swept her and lifted her and opened her to everything they would discover together. *I never knew it would be so simple. And it would feel right.* There were no more closed doors, no more frozen days. She was free, and alive, and awake. A laugh of pure joy trembled in her throat.

Josh lifted her up and pulled her astride him, spreading open her robe. Anne bent low to kiss him. There was a wildness in them they had not known earlier, a passion and urgency that drove them. Josh's fingers dug into Anne, fiercely pulling her onto him, and Anne took the skin of his neck between her teeth as if she could not find enough ways to make him part of her. They looked down, just able to make out in the shadows his shaft disappearing into her, then emerging, glistening in the faint light only to plunge into her again, faster and more fevered, until they cried out together. Slowly, as if coming down from a mountain they had scaled together, they relaxed, and stretched, and at last were still. They lay without speaking for a long time. Anne was stretched full length on Josh, her legs covering his, her lips resting against a slow pulse in his neck. Her body grew cool, and her blood coursed more slowly but still with the richness that filled her, all of her, for the first time. *I want to wrap you in velvet and silk . . . all the luxury of feeling you kept buried for so long. . . .*

"I feel so luxurious," she said with a long sigh. "Like coming home on a bitter night into a room with a fire, and a long, soft robe, and something hot to drink, and knowing it was waiting for me and that's where I belong."

She slid from his body to lie on the tumbled cushions beside him, curled within his arm, her hand on his chest. She closed her eyes, wrapped in a deep darkness that held them both as if in a sheltered nook. Then she heard voices, and sprang up.

"They're raising the anchor," Josh said. He sat beside her and closed her robe and tied it, then tied his own.

"Oh, Josh, the sky," Anne said in wonder. It was pale gray, with bands of rose and peach and violet that changed before them to orange and then the white-gold of the desert sun. The Nile shimmered in wavy glints reflected in the windows of the lounge, sending lights dancing across their white robes. From the town, the call of the *muzzein* rang out, high-pitched, like a creature of the night that had just awakened and was gazing in delight at the world at sunrise.

"So much beauty," Anne said softly. "So many ways to be alive." She stood at the rail, watching the people beginning their day amid the small stucco buildings and dusty streets of the town. "Josh, I'm not at all sleepy; can we go ashore somewhere today and do some exploring?"

He laughed, standing with her, his arm around her. "Anywhere you want. For this little time, there's nothing to stop us from anything we want to do. We'll deal with the rest of the world next week."

Anne put her arm around his waist and rested her head against his shoulder. In bare feet and white robes, beneath the blue and gold sky, they watched the shore as the *Hapy* glided to the deeper waters of the Nile and exuberantly picked up speed. A breeze came up. On both sides of the

river, tall banana plants with huge glossy leaves lined the
shore; behind them, farmers were arriving to till their
terraced fields, lush and fertile, holding back the barren,
hostile desert. The boat sailed smoothly and steadily between those long fields that were a celebration of life. Josh
and Anne held each other. He smiled at the light in her eyes.
"Good morning, my love," he said.